THE
PUSHCART PRIZE, XIX:
BEST OF THE
SMALL PRESSES

THE PUSHCART PRIZE XIX

1994 1995

BEST OF THE SMALL PRESSES

*Edited by
Bill Henderson
with the
Pushcart Prize
editors.
Poetry Editors:
Lynn Emanuel
David St. John
Essays Editor:
Anthony Brandt*

PUSHCART PRESS
WAINSCOTT • NEW YORK 11975

Note: nominations for this series are invited from any small, independent, literary book press or magazine in the world. Up to six nominations—tear sheets or copies, selected from work published, or about to be published, in the calendar year—are accepted by our December 1 deadline each year. Write to Pushcart Press, P.O. Box 380, Wainscott, N.Y. 11975 for more information.

Distributed by W. W. Norton & Co.
500 Fifth Ave., New York, N.Y. 10110

Library of Congress Card number: 76–58675
ISBN: 0–916366–92 -8
    0–916366–98–7 (paperback)
ISSN: 0149–7863
First printing, August 1994

This book was produced in
The United States of America
by RAY FREIMAN & COMPANY
Stamford, Connecticut 06903

Acknowledgments

Selections for The Pushcart Prize are reprinted with the permission of the authors and the following presses:

Introduction © 1994 Bill Henderson
Honey In the Carcase © 1993 Threepenny Review
A Thousand Buddhas © 1993 The Georgia Review
Suite For Emily © 1993 Kenyon Review
The Big Ear © 1993 Willow Springs
Theng © 1993 TriQuarterly
Exodus © 1993 Paris Review
Bowen © 1993 Threepenny Review
Marabou © 1993 Paris Review
My Mother's Shoes © 1993 The Southern Review
Island of the Raped Women © 1993 Volt
Yarn Wig © 1993 Michigan Quarterly Review
The Chamber © 1993 Colorado Review
Riders to The Sea © 1993 Bomb
My Father, Dancing © 1993 Grand Street
My Students © 1993 Agni
Imhotep © 1993 Harvard Review
The Crying House © 1993 Missouri Review
Who Do You Love © 1993 American Short Fiction
Skunk Dreams © 1993 Georgia Review
Over All © 1993 Ploughshares
A Portrait of the Self As A Nation, 1990–1991 © 1993 ZYZZYVA
Twice Removed © 1993 Volt
Age of Reason © 1993 Ontario Review
In Broad Daylight © 1993 Kenyon Review
My Father's Place © 1993 Hungry Mind Review
Song © 1993 The Southern Review
Practicing Death Songs © 1993 Antioch Review
Watermelon Tales © 1993 Kenyon Review
'Orita On The Road to Chimayó © 1993 Shenandoah
The Line © 1993 Alaska Quarterly Review
Fiction and The Inner Life of Objects © 1993 Gettysburg Review
Inventing the Filipino © 1993 Kenyon Review
Journal of the Thousand Choices © 1993 o•Blēk
The Way It Felt to Be Falling © 1993 Threepenny Review
Between The Pool and The Gardenias © 1993 Caribbean Writer
Eating the Angel, Conceiving The Sun . . . © 1993 American Poetry Review
Nash © 1993 Georgia Review
The Triumph of the Prague Workers' Councils © 1993 Iowa Review
Against Sincerity © 1993 American Poetry Review
Capitalism © 1993 Colorado Review
Lost Brilliance © 1993 Black Warrior Review

7

In Memoriam:
RALPH ELLISON (1914–1994),
A Founding Editor of
The Pushcart Prize series

INTRODUCTION
by BILL HENDERSON

RALPH ELLISON died on April 16, 1994. This book is dedicated to him because he touched many lives and ours, also. When Ellison signed on as a Founding Editor of *The Pushcart Prize* series in 1975, he did so with enthusiasm, and an apology; "I'm afraid I can't do too much real work. I'm too busy with my writing."

Pushcart said that was fine. We'd appreciate whatever support he could give us, and for almost two decades he continued his support, as have hundreds of other distinguished founding and contributing editors such as the late William Stafford, Lynda Hull and Sonia Raiziss. Because of their editorial assistance, this series, driven only by volunteer effort, has thrived while the commercial establishment seems to have lost its moral roots entirely and become a mere cash machine (oh yes, there are exceptions: Knopf, FSG, Norton—Pushcart's distributor—and one or two others).

It's taken the publishing industry a mere two decades to get lost. Back in the 70's ABC television and the Mattel toy company (makers of Barbie Dolls) slugged it out for control of Macmillan. Pundits pondered: what would become of the thoughtful book if either ABC or Barbie triumphed?

In the 80's Simon and Schuster's Dick Snyder predicted that soon the many American commercial houses would be reduced to the few ("Seven Sisters" he dubbed them) as the larger publishers devoured the smaller. He was correct, except he had the numbers, geography, and animal wrong and he failed to see that he too would be devoured. We will end up with fewer than seven bloated Sisters; their geographical influence will be Global not merely American; and the animal more closely resembles a shark not a sister. Indeed, why not call them Global Shark One and Global Shark Two.

We small press people have watched all this feeding frenzy with bemusement. Recently we have also noted a growing panic among the global book investors: today's pundits have proclaimed the era of the Information Superhighway, an electronic, paperless, speed-crazed, gizmo gaga giant that will render The Book an instant road kill. Wannabe investors in Global Publishing One and Two worry they might lose their funds because The Book is doomed. Their money—and we're talking billions here—was bet on the wrong lifestyle artifact. (Has anybody noted that life is now merely a matter of style?) Wouldn't it be best to jettison The Book and concentrate on CD Rom and Audio? Perhaps multimedia is the cash path to follow?

Pushcart's publisher observed the same anxiety when he was employed at a firm known as Doubleday in 1971. Doubleday, now a mere subsidiary, was a colossus in those times, pumping out 800 titles a year and dominating the industry. Yet when Marshall McLuhan foresaw the death of the book, overnight Doubleday reprinted all its stationery with the line "A Multi-Media Company." No way were Doubleday's investors going to be caught dead in the water with mere *books* for sale. Of course Doubleday's future was to be quite different. Nelson Doubleday abandoned publishing and purchased the Mets baseball team; his family company was eventually gobbled up by Germany's Bertelsmann, one of the Global publishing contenders. It turned out the Germans knew The Book had a future after all, even though Nelson Doubleday discovered that the Mets, from time to time, seemed rather shaky.

Recently Pushcart was telephoned by a columnist for the *New York Times* and asked to comment on The Future of the Book. The reporter noted that Pushcart has recently started a club— The Lead Pencil Club—a pothole on the information highway, with the motto "Not So Fast". The members of our club honor the old and perfectly adequate technology of the pencil whenever possible and eschew various whizzbang gadgets that seem to come and go making a fortune for the electronic industry. We think the pencil has a promising future.

Yes, but what of the future of the quaint printed and bound object that you hold in your hand and that has been around in its present form for a mere 500 years? Is it curtains for The Book? *The New York Times* reporter wanted to know. Book investors were about to jump ship.

Pushcart opined that the true horror was not that we'd lose The Book but that we'd lose our very souls to the superhighway and its news, data and facts masquerading as knowledge; or the 500 TV channels shilling various products at the speed of light and reducing us to consuming cyphers.

As long as souls are in reasonable shape, The Book will do just fine, Pushcart prophesied. We may surrender a few encyclopedias to CD Rom but most books will stick around. Nobody will sprawl in a hammock and read a novel on a flickering plastic screen. Never. Books are nifty things—portable, light, durable. You can hurl them across the room when you disagree with the author, or you can toss them in the air in joy when the author finds your heart. Books are sensuous—you can feel them, smell them, turn down the page corners as reminders of great passages, scribble comments in the margins with a pencil, use them for pillows, sleep with them.

In his introduction to *Pushcart Prize X*, George Plimpton recalled Ray Carver taking a copy of *Best American Short Stories* to bed with him because he was so pleased at having one of his early stories in it. In her Introduction to *Pushcart Prize XIV*, Tess Gallagher remembered "Ray was in the habit of turning down corners of the pages where a poem, story or essay had risen above the others to recommend itself further. I relied heavily on these cues and would browse his enthusiasms, calling out to him when something really hit me. . .".

Ray Carver knew the various uses of The Book. As does E. Annie Proulx, author of *The Shipping News*, winner of many literary prizes recently. In her 1994 address at the Pen/Faulkner Awards, Proulx noted that books are a tactile pleasure; and they can be works of art, from the dust jackets to the binding, paper and text design: and a social indicator too—to appreciate a person, you notice the books on the shelves, not electronic apparatus.

Proulx continued: "It is possible that the premature obituaries for the book merely cover our confusion about the clouded direction of change in the culture. As the big publishers try for best sellers at the expense of serious books, it is increasingly the small publishers and university presses that are finding and publishing interesting new writers."

We are certain that you will discover many of these new writers in *Pushcart Prize XIX*—the largest volume in our history: more presses, more selections, more pages than ever before. And we could have produced a book twice this size—there is that much terrific work out there. Far from the cash machine crowd, our writers are keeping the faith and small presses are too.

Pushcart was helped this year by 181 Contributing Editors and hundreds of small press editors who made nominations. These nominations were read for this edition by Lynn Emanuel and David St. John (poetry), Rick Moody, Lee Smith and myself (fiction) and Anthony Brandt (essays).

Lynn Emanuel and David St. John have both contributed poetry to these pages in the past. Lynn teaches at the University of Pittsburgh and is the author of *The Dig* (University of Illinois Press, 1992), a National Poetry Series winner. David St. John teaches at the University of California at Los Angeles, and is Poetry Editor of *Antioch Review*. He is the author of *Hush* (Johns Hopkins) and his work has appeared in *Antaeus* and other journals. Both editors have selected poets that, for the most part, have never appeared in the *Pushcart Prize* series.

Rick Moody is the author of *Garden State*, winner of Pushcart's Editors' Book Award, and most recently the novel *The Ice Storm* (Little, Brown). Lee Smith is a free-lance editor and writer. Anthony Brandt, the editor of the-soon-to-be-published *The Craft of The Essay: Two Decades of the Best Pushcart Prize Essays*, was a columnist for *Esquire* and is a frequent book reviewer, critic and author of *The People Along the Sand* (Canio's Editions, 1992).

Last year, I asked the poetry editors to make statements about their selection process. This year, the prose readers were invited to respond. Their statements follow:

ANTHONY BRANDT

Every year for the last nine I have read between 200 and 300 essays for the *Pushcart Prize*, out of which I can choose no more than nine or ten for inclusion in the volume. Yet some years it's been easy. The essay is a deceptively loose, inviting form that will embrace just about any topic, from the memoir to criticism to political opinion, and a lot of writers get lost in its commodious folds. There have been years when a mere seven or eight essays among all those submitted stood out, and the choices were obvious.

But not this year. This was a wonderful year for essays; my right-hand pile, the "not right for us", pile grew only slightly more quickly than the left-hand, which is where I place the pieces I must re-read, the pieces for possible inclusion, and when it came time to winnow this pile down the choices were hard. Any one of the top 20 or so deserve to be in the volume.

Why one year should embarrass us with riches this way I do not know. It would be comforting to think that it's a sign of progress, that the essay that does nothing more than express entirely predictable, boringly correct attitudes about this or that issue, the I-never-sang-for-my-father essay, the disease-of-the-week essay, have so saturated the small press scene that editors have finally gagged on them and we shall see no more for awhile. It would be comforting.

But as it happens one of the best essays in this collection is one by Robert Love Taylor that might be said to fit the I-never-sang-for-my-father type. I didn't think anyone could be original on this subject again, it has been done so many times; but one must always be ready, as an editor, to abandon one's prejudices. Taylor not only comes at the subject in a totally unexpected way, his tone is unexpected, too, and the result is stunning and brilliant, a work of art. So with Brenda Miller, whose account of her experience with massage somehow, without your quite knowing how, becomes so much more, an account of profound emotional change, and whose last line, so precise and yet so enigmatic, rings all the bells in your heart; yes, it has that authority and that resonance.

Rejoice, then. It's a happy occasion when we can only praise these essays plus terrific work by Charles Baxter, Louise Erdrich, Sherod Santos, Kim Stafford, Vicki Hearne, Edward Field, Louise Glück and Andre Dubus III.

These are works of art, moving, amazing, overwhelming. We are lucky to have them.

I admit a preference for "experimental" writing. I sought it out.

How could it be otherwise when, as Bill Henderson wrote in last year's introduction, Moody and I were both in grade school when the first Pushcart was published? In our subsequent schooling, I was taught that only fiction serious about the postmodernist adventure and its excursions, its philosophies, theories, histories (all co-spirited by the premise that language is not a representation of experience but experience itself) could render accurately, and entertainingly, what I took to be our particular place and time in history.

Unfortunately for "experimental" fiction, when it aims to satisfy those very requirements, its nomenclature is typically academic, as is the source of its poverty.

In fact, the majority of the fiction submitted is in a more naturalistic vein, and of course some of it too is bad. However, the reason those stories fall short is due less to some loss of nerve than to the inability to articulate a self, or selves, that is the same reason for much of life's failures and sadnesses.

Let it be of some consolation to writers that in our experience reading for this volume many well-known authors do not always write well; and it should serve as a source of great inspiration to those same writers that many unknown authors are writing extremely well. If your efforts have been overlooked here, embarrass us further with your renewed efforts next year. For an editor the only pleasure that approaches the satisfaction of being right is the self-knowledge that issues from the recognition of being wrong.

And, about the noise surrounding the closings and firings at large trade publishing houses here in New York: All three fiction editors—Henderson, Moody and myself—have worked as trade editors, and yet we know that it's not editors, but writers who read who make American literature. Editors, the best ones, bless them, also know this to be the case: their role is to avail us of American literature. This formidable and still youthful institution is in no danger so long as the writers and readers whose informal and devoted membership compose this body exist. Moody in fact is characteristically optimistic that, like the independent music scene in the early '80s, this period may figure as a renaissance of

American publishing. Think of it! All across the United States: One person, a publisher, editor, publicist, marketing director and salesman combined, one person crazy about book publishing and selling them out of his garage, like Bill Henderson.

RICK MOODY

We work alone as writers. We wrestle with our personal demons up in the garret or after work, untutored by the academies, and then we bring our genius, fired by solitude, to the masses. That's the romanticized version, and sometimes I like to flatter myself with it. I like to imagine I'm really not processing a whole range of influences and histories and thirty second spots in my work. Then, while I'm worrying about this stuff, March rolls around and Bill Henderson sends along *the box of manuscripts*. And any ideas I had about what's going on in American literature are flooded out all over again.

What is dissimilar about American writing—when you look at a log of it all at once—is a lot easier to pin down than what is similar about it. There is no preeminent style; there is no prevailing esthetic; neither gender has the upper hand; no ethnicity reveals itself to have a stranglehold on the language; there is no particular politics to this work. I didn't see much rugged individualism this year. Or Yankee ingenuity. Or special interest fiction. And there's not a convincing melting pot in the whole stew. On the other hand, all of these observations are only partly valid. There are no rules in this terrain, only good hunches. What you learn, reading for Bill Henderson, in fact, is that the small presses, are publishing *everything*. That's what they should be doing. That democracy is what separates small press publishing from the engulfers and devourers.

Still, I get a little terrified when *the box* arrives. This year, based on last year's experience, I had an idea what to expect. And that's the scary thing. *It's just hard to take in all these feelings*, to remember that, good writers and bad, we are all creative people and that we are all trying to capture the slipperiness of human emotions. This effort commands respect. It's the basis for what is happening in these pages. *We all have something to say.*

17

I see it this way: the anthology you have in your hands, in preserving the heterodoxy and sprawl of American fiction (and poetry, and essays), coast to coast, border to border, is a sort of revolutionary act. Really. Its project, theme, and narrative concern finally the *enormity* of American literary civilization. The polyphony of the music of these territories. Most name-brand editors (and I used to be one) are as scared of this enormity as I am in March when the box first arrives. Democracy confers responsibility upon you. It requires pluck. So if the gods didn't put Bill Henderson in Wainscott, we'd have to make him up. When I read what Bill has done in this anthology for almost twenty years, I remember that, as a writer, I'm not at all alone in a garret. I'm part of a community. Surrounded by voices.

THE PEOPLE
WHO HELPED

FOUNDING EDITORS—*Anaïs Nin (1903–1977) Buckminster Fuller (1895–1983), Charles Newman, Daniel Halpern, Gordon Lish, Harry Smith, Hugh Fox, Ishmael Reed, Joyce Carol Oates, Len Fulton, Leonard Randolph, Leslie Fiedler, Nona Balakian (1918–1991), Paul Bowles, Paul Engle (1908–1991), Ralph Ellison (1914–1994) Reynolds Price, Rhoda Schwartz, Richard Morris, Ted Wilentz, Tom Montag, William Phillips, Poetry editor: H. L. Van Brunt.*

EDITORS—*Walter Abish, Ai, Elliott Anderson, John Ashbery, Ed Sanders, Teo Savory, Grace Schulman, Harvey Shapiro, Leslie Silko, Charles Simic, Dave Smith, Elizabeth Spencer, William Stafford, Gerald Stern, David St. John, Bill and Pat Strachan, Ron Sukenick, Anne Tyler, John Updike, Sam Vaughan, David Wagoner, Derek Walcott, Ellen Wilbur, David Wilk, David Wojahn, Jack Gilbert, Louise Glück, David Godine, Jorie Graham, Linda Gregg, Barbara Grossman, Donald Hall, Helen Handley, Michael Harper, Robert Hass, DeWitt Henry, J. R. Humphreys, David Ignatow, John Irving, June Jordan, Edmund Keeley, Karen Kennerly, Galway Kinnell, Carolyn Kizer, Maxine Kumin, James Laughlin, Seymour Lawrence, Naomi Lazard, Herb Leibowitz, Denise Levertov, Philip Levine, Stanley Lindberg, Thomas Lux, Mary MacArthur, Jay Meek, Daniel Menaker, Frederick Morgan, Cynthia Ozick, Jayne Anne Phillips, Robert Phillips, George Plimpton, Stanley Plumly, Eugene Redmond, Russell Banks, Joe David Bellamy, Robert Bly, Philip Booth, Robert Boyers, Harold*

19

Brodkey, Joseph Brodsky, Wesley Brown, Hayden Carruth, Frank Conroy, Paula Deitz, Steve Dixon, Rita Dove, Andre Dubus, M. D. Elevitch, Louise Erdrich, Loris Essary, Ellen Ferber, Carolyn Forché, Stuart Freibert, Jon Galassi, Tess Gallagher, Louis Gallo, George Garrett, Reginald Gibbons, Bill Zavatsky.

CONTRIBUTING EDITORS FOR THIS EDITION—*Robert Pinsky, Sharon Olds, Frankie Paino, Ed Ochester, Joyce Carol Oates, Naomi Shihab Nye, Sigrid Nunez, Josip Novakovich, Susan Neville, Kent Nelson, Carol Muske, Henry Carlile, Richard Burgin, Christopher Buckley, Rosellen Brown, Scott Bradfield, Michael Bowden, Marianne Boruch, Philip Booth, Linda Bierds, Andre Bernard, Susan Bergman, Michael Bendzela, Timothy Geiger, Suzanne Gardinier, Kenneth Gangemi, Lynda Hull, Tony Quagliano, Richard Kostelanetz, Kathy Callaway, Marie Sheppard Williams, Diane Williams, Theodore Wilentz, Ellen Wilbur, Sam Vaughan, Dennis Vannatta, Lloyd Van Brunt, Gerry Locklin, Paul Zimmer, Christina Zawadiwsky, Gary Young, Lois Ann Yamanaka, Robert Wrigley, David Wojahn, Karen Bender, Joe David Bellamy, Robin Behn, Charles Baxter, Rick Bass, Steven Barthelme, Will Baker, David Baker, Jennifer Atkinson, Tony Ardizzone, Alice Fulton, H. E. Francis, M. D. Elevitch, Barbara Einzig, Stuart Dybek, John Drury, Rita Dove, Carl Dennis, Philip Appleman, Antler, John Allman, Jack Marshall, Clarence Major, Joseph Maiolo, D. R. MacDonald, Barry Lopez, Gordon Lish, James Linville, Stanley Lindberg, Reginald Gibbons, Ehud Havazelet, James Harms, Marilyn Hacker, Patrick Worth Gray, Louise Glück, William Kennedy, George Keithley, Dennis Loy Johnson, Ha Jin, David Jauss, Mark Jarman, Josephine Jacobsen, Richard Jackson, Elizabeth Inness-Brown, Colette Inez, Edmund Keeley, Laura Kasischke, Mary Karr, Joan Murray, Lisel Mueller, Susan Moon, Susan Mitchell, Leonard Michaels, Jay Meek, Sandra McPherson, Kristina McGrath, Campbell McGrath, Lynne McFall, Rebecca McClanahan, Robert McBrearty, Donald Revell, C. E. Poverman, Joe Ashby Porter, Eileen Pollack, George Plimpton, Robert Phillips, Mary Peterson, Janet Peery, James Solheim, Arthur Smith, Jim Simmerman, Laurie Sheck, Joanna Scott, Lloyd Schwartz, Dennis Schmitz, Ruth Sasaki, Alison Deming, Lydia Davis, John Daniel, Philip Dacey, Mark Cox, Stephen Corey, Jane Cooper, Elizabeth Spires, Roger Weingar-*

ten, Eliot Weinberger, Bruce Weigl, Hayden Carruth, Jean Valentine, Lee Upton, Ron Tanner, Pat Strachan, Pamela Stewart, Maura Stanton, Dan Stern, Gordon Weaver, Michael Collier, Henri Cole, Judith Ortiz Cofer, Kelly Cherry, Steve Watkins, Michael Waters, David Foster Wallace, Andrew Hudgins, Christopher Howell, Tony Hoagland, Edward Hoagland, Jane Hirshfield, Edward Hirsch, Walter Pavlich, Barbara Selfridge, Sherod Santos, Vern Rutsala, Sharman Apt Russell, Gibbons Ruark, Ken Rosen, David Romtvedt, Pattiann Rogers, Brenda Hillman, DeWitt Henry, Patricia Henley, Robin Hemley, Norman Lavers, Dorianne Laux, Wally Lamb, Thomas Kennedy, JoEllen Kwiatek, Maxine Kumin, Carolyn Kizer, Len Roberts, David Rivard, Alberto Alvaro Rios, Molly Giles, Gary Gildner, William Matthews, Cleopatra Mathis, Lou Mathews, Philip Levine, Melissa Lentricchia, David Lehman, Dan Masterson, Michael Martone.

ROVING EDITORS—*Lily Frances Henderson, Genie Chipps*

EUROPEAN EDITORS—*Liz and Kirby Williams*

MANAGING EDITOR—*Hannah Turner*

AT LARGE—*Marvin Bell*

FICTION EDITORS—*Bill Henderson with Rick Moody, Lee Smith*

POETRY EDITORS—*Lynn Emanuel, David St. John*

ESSAYS EDITOR—*Anthony Brandt*

EDITOR AND PUBLISHER—*Bill Henderson*

CONTENTS

23

THE
PUSHCART PRIZE, XIX:
BEST OF THE
SMALL PRESSES

HONEY IN THE CARCASE

fiction by JOSIP NOVAKOVICH

from THE THREEPENNY REVIEW

IVAN MEDVEDICH was washing his silvery mustache after eating a slice of dark bread with honey when a whistle cut through the air, deepened in frequency, and sank into an explosion that shook the house so that a bar of soap slid from the mirror ledge into the sink.

"Lord have mercy!" his wife Estera said. "What was that?"

"The *chetniks*, what else."

Soon, another whistle, and another explosion.

"Run for cover!" Estera shouted.

"What cover? This is the safest place in the house." Ivan had built the house alone—actually, with a little help from his oldest flat-footed son, Daniel, who had groaned more than he had worked. It took Ivan twenty years of careful labor to finish the house, but one thing he had skipped, a cellar, perhaps because snakes had nested and floods crept in the cellar of his childhood home. *God is my fortress and my strength* was his motto. But now, in addition to God, a cellar would help.

He turned off the lights and prayed, and after his last Amen, no bombs fell for the rest of the night.

Next morning Estera walked to the bakery, early, because after six o'clock, the dark whole-wheat disappeared, and only milky white, soft, cake-like, as expensive as sin, remained. The old baker's wife said nothing, handing her a two-kilo loaf as usual. When Estera exited, she heard a dog howl and then a high-pitched whistle. A bomb fell in a ditch ten yards away from her, exploding with a terrible blast. Shrapnel flew over her head, shattered the bakery attic windows and riddled the tops of the faces of the nearby houses, which now looked like lepers' foreheads. She walked home hurriedly.

If the bomb had fallen outside the ditch, the shrapnel would have flown low and struck her. She and Ivan concluded that God had saved her. Still, as Estera peeled onions that day, her neck twitched, jerking her head to one side. Estera had borne Ivan five sons. The youngest, whom she'd had at the age of forty-six, died several years before because the wall between the chambers of his heart had collapsed. Since his death silver streaked her hair.

Ivan played the violin by heart. Estera still chopped onions. Tears, from the onion fumes, glazed their eyes. They grieved so that salty water flowed, as though their swollen eyes, like balloons, needed to drop sand to gain in altitude; tears slid down their cheeks like little eyes, mirroring knives and violins.

Ivan walked out to the rabbit cages. Rabbits' split lips quickly drew grass into their mouths. He took a white rabbit by its long ears and held it in the air. He had often petted the rabbit, so the rabbit was not scared, not even as his fist went down and hit the neck. The rabbit twitched several times and went limp. He shuddered and walked into the house and lay the rabbit on the table to cool. "You skin it this time," he said.

That day he could not eat rabbit, his favorite meat, for the first time in his life; he ate more bread with honey, old honey that had crystallized into white grains.

At dusk, more whistles, and about a dozen blasts, all in the near neighborhood. It went on like that for a week—blasts at dusk and at twilight. A large crater loomed in their street between two shattered houses.

When he cautioned Estera not to go early in the morning to buy bread, she said, "I am used to explosions."

He said nothing to that, but hummed a tune, sounding like a buzz of bees, and bees it was that he was thinking about. It was the time to collect honey in his apiary, ten miles east, on a meadow of wild flowers near an acacia grove. He drove his old pick-up, put on a bee-keeper's hat and gloves, and opened the hives. His bees were so ardent that they had made honeycombs even outside of the frames; Ivan carved these additions out, and without draining honey, stored them. He placed framed honey-combs in a circular barrel, a separator. Turning the wheel, he listened to honey fall out of their hexagonal wax trenches and hit the metal wall, sticking to it and dripping. He did not mind bee stings—he'd got more than a dozen that day—because he believed they benefited his heart.

He harvested alone. His sons used to help him, dancing around the honey separator like Joseph's brothers around the grains of Egypt. But now, one of his sons was in Australia, another, Daniel, his first-born, worked as a doctor, the third one, Jakov, worked as a carpenter in Germany, and the youngest, Branko, stayed at home, studying for his entrance exams at the school of agricultural engineering.

When Ivan returned home with three barrels of honey and saw his son Daniel, he rolled up his sleeve because Daniel always took his blood pressure—especially after Ivan's heart-attack. (Ivan still suffered from angina pectoris but could not get a retirement settlement because his Communist boss hated him and, he suspected, wanted him to die at the factory.)

Daniel talked about how in the village where he doctored, chetniks went door to door, beating up old Croatian men, as though these men had been *ustashas*. "The chetniks with skulls and crossed bones painted on their caps drove people out of their homes, stole TV sets, burned haystacks. They cut off three old men's testicles and forced them to eat them. One bled to death, the others I stitched up as best I could."

"You should leave the village," said Ivan, "because of your young wife and child."

"That's right. A colleague of mine has invited me to work in the Osijek hospital."

"Are they going to have enough work for you there?"

"More than enough! Thousands will be wounded." He waved his hand as though to chase away a slow and fat fly.

Before his parents and brother could react, he was out, in his wobbly Citroen. This was the first time in five years that Daniel had visited without taking his father's blood pressure. Ivan rolled down his sleeve and turned on the radio.

The announcer said that Vinkovci was eerily quiet. Eerily quiet was a cliché in a newscaster's voice, but not so through the window when Estera opened it. No machine-gun fire, no cars, not even birds singing; only a woman's wailing far away.

"Estie," Ivan said, "We must take care of the honey. You know how the Montenegrin poet says, *A glass of honey asks for a glass of spleen, together they are easiest to drink.*"

"What kind of poetry is it if it doesn't even rhyme? Besides, give me no Montenegrin junk when you know that Montenegrin chetniks are bombing us."

Ivan let the honey sit in the barrels for several days, and then he scooped the creamy top—foamy, white, and exceedingly sweet. He was certain that this was ambrosia, the drink of Greek gods. He and Estera poured honey all evening long into glass bottles. Ivan looked back at the filled larder shelves and said, "It's good, isn't it?"

Just then a bomb fell at the edge of their garden so that the floor-boards shook and squeaked and the tiles on the roof quivered and slid, like teeth grinding. But the honey stayed calm in the bottles. Soon another bomb fell to the same spot. Ivan and Estera stayed in the larder, the safest room in the house because it had no windows.

Next day a couple of Federal MiG jets flew low, sharding people's windows, but no window burst on Medvedich's house. At night light from houses on fire flickered through the shades that could not be quite shut; red light on the wall seemed to be painting a message. The following morning, despite continuous mortar explosions, Estera wrapped a scarf under her chin and walked out.

"Where are you going, old woman?" Ivan asked.

"To buy bread."

"I think you shouldn't."

She walked out, proud of her courage.

Half an hour later, when she was not back, he stood on the threshold, and chewed a honeycomb with fresh honey. Chewing the wax calmed him better than chewing tobacco could. The phone rang; it was the baker. On the bakery steps, mortar shrapnel had struck and wounded Estera.

Ivan picked up Estera—unconscious, her abdomen torn—and drove to the hospital. A doctor took a quick X-ray and found that shrapnel had penetrated her liver. He dug in with his scalpel and gloved fingers, saying, "Too bad that we're out of anesthetics." As he fished for the metal Estera came to and swooned again. Just as the doctor tossed the bit of iron in the garbage bin, mortar hit the hospital, setting the roof on fire. Electricity went out. The doctor sewed up the wound with Ivan holding up a flashlight. They carried Estera to the basement, where the stench of crap and vomit hung about mustily.

For several days Estera lay half-dead, half-alive, green in the face, unable to sleep, too weak to be awake.

Ivan spent many hours with her but more at home lest brigands should break in, steal, and burn the house. He prayed but lost the meanings of his words in reveries and forgot to say his Amens. *Words without thoughts to heaven do not go.*

He missed his bees, abandoned behind the enemy lines. As he drank his ambrosia, he decided that next morning he'd drive into the eastern fields—no matter what, even through the hail of bullets—to his apiary. But next dawn a bomb fell in front of his house, shattering the windows and digging holes in the stuccoed bricks. The gate collapsed. Another bomb fell in the backyard, and demolished his pick-up. The shrapnel pierced through the house windows. Luckily, his son, trembling on the floor, was not injured.

A pharaoh did not weep when Persians slew his sons and raped his daughters because his sorrow was too deep for tears, but he did weep when after it all his ex-minister came by in rags and begged him for silver. Just so, Ivan had not wept when his wife bled in dirty hospitals, when his house had been nearly demolished, and when the truck he had saved for, for fifteen years, burst into pieces and shriveled in fire. But that he could not go out into the fields and take care of his bees, that made the cup— not of honey—overflow. He wept in his armchair, in his wooden shoes, will-less, nearly motionless, and daydreamed.

And reminisced. As a child he saw on the outskirts of his village Croatian peasants, dead, their eyes plucked out. His father had forbidden him to talk about it since this part of history was politically incorrect—*am strengstens verboten*—to recount.

One noon four Croatian soldiers walked in and asked for Branko. He was in the bathroom, but Ivan said he'd gone to the university library. He was surprised to hear himself lie, but then he remembered that Abraham lied that his sister was his wife so he would save her from a marriage in a foreign land. That Branko should be a soldier struck him as absurd. Ivan had raised him on "Turn the other cheek." For years boys beat him, broke his nose, yet he would not fight back even when Ivan told him to. Ivan had complained to the school president, who asked, "Is your son gay?" That was all he offered in the way of help, so Ivan had to protect Branko, giving him a beekeeper's mask to save his face, and walking him home while boys threw stones and shouted, "Baptists, Claptists." Branko, who had grown up as a theological experiment, without a malice in his head, spent his days developing landscape photographs in the darkroom, a shed, so that his eyes stayed watery and bloodshot.

Estera began to improve and her son Daniel took her to Osijek, together with Branko (to hide him from the draft), but Ivan would not leave his house, as though it was his skin. Now, on his block there were fewer than a dozen people left, and in the city, out of forty thousand, perhaps three thousand had remained. Neither phone or electricity worked anymore. He lived on water from a hand-pump in his yard and on honey.

He had been a corpulent, double-chinned man, but in a month in which it was all the same to him whether he was alive or dead, he became a thin man with sharp pentagonal jaws, overgrown in a Mosaic beard. Perhaps he would not have eaten honey either if it had not reminded him of his bees; he ate it in their remembrance, a sacrament to the little striped and winged tigresses.

One crisp morning Ivan felt tremendously alert. He wondered whether he was about to die, since before death one could get a moment of lucidity, to summon one's family and deliver blessings—that lucidity was a *sine qua non* in a Biblical death, and he, a father of several sons, would of course have a Biblical death. Or had his diet cleared his coronary arteries? The following day, since he still felt lucid, he concluded that honey had healed his heart and saved his life.

He biked to his brother David, the carpenter, in Andriasevci, in their father's house, ten miles away. On the way he saw starved shaggy cattle roaming, masterless. Horses rotted in dried-up sunflower fields. Blind dogs stumbled into trees. Cats with red eyes purred so loudly that he could hear them even as he rode over cracking branches. Heads of wheat bent in the fields like contrite sinners; nobody harvested them.

David and Ivan hugged and kissed as brothers. After they had slurped rosehip tea, David said, "I have presents for you: one coffin for Estera and one for you. Come, take a look!"

"What? But Estera is alive. And I am all right."

"Of course. But in case you get killed, you won't be dumped in a mass grave if you have a coffin with your name."

Next morning Ivan decided to go back to Vinkovci. Not that he had not thought about death enough, or seen it enough—but that his young brother, who used to spend most of his time making tambourines and singing, should see the world as a plantation of coffins, incensed him against the invading armies. He rode through the groaning countryside.

From the edge of the village a black German shepherd followed him all the way to Ivan's home. There he wagged his tail, licked Ivan's shoe, and did all he could to endear himself to Ivan. Ivan gave him an old slice of bread and honey. The dog loved that.

Ivan stood on his threshold and stared at the cloudy horizon, with dark blue clouds. The stink of putrid animals, borne on an unusually warm wind, continued to hit his nostrils. Smoke and gangrene.

And when the rains began, a ghost crept along the surface of the earth, not as an image, white and gray, but as a stench of wet smoke and pus. The muddy soul of the Panonian valley sought fire to solidify into bricks of a tower of Babel, in which all languages would merge into one, Serbian. *Govori Srpski da te ceo svet razume.* Speak Serbian so the whole world could understand you, the Serb folk saying went.

He rode his bike to a foundry converted into a bomb factory and volunteered to make bombs for the under-armed Croatian soldiers. At the end of his shift, he always found the German shepherd, waiting for him.

One dawn MiG jets bombed the factory, mostly missing and hitting people's houses nearby, but they did damage it enough to shut it.

Ivan could finally take it no more, so he dragged a cart east, through Mirkovci. Now and then he stopped and scratched his dog's fur. He ran into a checkpoint made of stacked beer cases in the middle of the road. A chetnik asked him, "Where the hell are you going?"

"I need to take back my bees from the fields."

"Bees?" The chetnik pulled out a knife. "Your ID?"

"I have none."

"I'm gonna tattoo you so we can recognize you next time." He pushed his knife against Ivan's face. The dog growled, ready to pounce. A chetnik grabbed his comrade's arm. "Don't be crazy. Don't you see *he's* crazy. Let him get his bees." And turning to Ivan, he winked, and said, "God protects the crazy ones. I like that, bees. Bees!" When Ivan was at a fair distance, they shot at the German shepherd but missed.

That he had managed to pass surprised him. Perhaps the brigands had understood his beard as an emblem of Serbdom.

Ivan waxed entrances to ten beehives and stacked them on his cart. When he passed by the chetniks, they again shot at his dog, and this time they killed him. Ivan turned soil on the side of the road with a shovel and buried his friend.

It took him five trips—and a dozen kilos of honey as the "road tax" to the brigands—to take back all his bee-hives.

Ivan built a brick wall around the hives. He melted sugar for his friends so they would survive the winter. Since he had seen a sign that the winter would be a long one, Polish geese migrating south, he thoroughly filled the cracks in the hives with frame-wax.

For hours he listened to the congregation of bees. They were his revelation. *For the invisible things of him from the creation of the world are clearly seen, being understood by the things that are made, even his eternal power and Godhead . . .* Yes, the invisible Godhead and his plan are revealed in bees. Bees fulfill the Old Testament through the perfection of their laws and the New Testament through the perfection of their love for the Queen bee, for whom every bee is willing to die. Ivan thought that even if he had never read the Bible, from studying his bees, he'd conclude that a rational God existed.

After thinking so, he'd bring the bees several pounds of honey, apologizing for having taken it in the summer. He admired the heaven on earth, the earth in heaven.

His son Daniel visited and told him that Estera, although anemic, had nearly fully recovered. When asked to join her in Osijek, Ivan said, "Somebody has to stay here and protect the church and the bees."

The shack where his son had developed photographs had served as a chapel ever since Ivan had excommunicated himself from the Baptist church. Like-minded Baptists and Pentecostals, for whom their churches had not been pious enough, used to worship in the shack with Ivan and his family, until they discovered that they were not like-minded. Nobody came now, but still, it used to be—and it would continue to be—God's space.

Ivan played the violin in his chapel and studied scripture. He was disappointed that scripture mentioned bees only a few times and lions many times. It consoled him that in one verse bees got the better of the lion: *There was a swarm of bees and honey in the carcase of the lion.*

One passage intrigued Ivan: *And it shall come to pass in that day, that the Lord shall hiss for the fly that is in the uttermost part of the river of Egypt, and for the bee that is on the land of Assyria.*

He whistled and hissed to call out his bees, and none came out. Then he made a flute from a wet willow branch, with a low note, and found a hiss that indeed excited the bees so that they came out and criss-crossed the sky into a mighty net. When they came back, they tossed out their drones, and they kept tossing them for days. A peculiar fratricide—that aspect of bees theologically troubled Ivan. Some kind of wrath of God built in the natural order of things? In front of the beehives fat drones with stunted wings curled atop each other and shrank; the ditch filled up with drones. On a sunny day so many crows flew over Ivan's head, to feast on the drones, that it grew dark.

After a prolonged bombardment, a band of chetniks came to Ivan's street. He was now the only person living on his block. When he saw them coming, he unplugged the bee-hive entrances and hissed on his flute. At the same time a bomb flew, with a low whistle, fell in the street, and did not go off. Bees from several beehives grew agitated and flew out into the street where several sweaty chetniks, having loaded his neighbor's furniture on a truck, turned their eyes to Ivan's house.

37

Thousands of bees covered each brigand, giving him the appearance of an armored medieval knight. The brigands ran, helter-skelter, dropping their weapons. One of them staggered in circles and fell dead in front of Ivan's house; he kept swelling even after the rigor mortis gripped him.

Nominated by Robin Hemley, Susan Moon

A THOUSAND BUDDHAS

by BRENDA MILLER

from THE GEORGIA REVIEW

My hand's the universe,
it can do anything. —Shinkichi Takahashi

I

I HAVE NEVER been touched by someone blind, but I can imagine what it would be like. She would read me like Braille, her fingertips hovering on the raised points of my flesh, then peel back the sheets of my skin, lay one finger on my quivering heart. We could beat like that, two hummingbirds, and become very still. Her hands might move across my abdomen, flick the scar below my belly button. My eyelids would flutter at her touch, and my skin dissolve into hot streams of tears.

I have never been touched by a blind person, but I have given whole massages with my eyes halfway closed, and the bodies I touched became something else. Their boundaries disappeared, and they spread out on the table—masses of flesh, all the borders gone. I touched them in tender places: between the toes, under the cheekbones, along the high-arching curves of their feet. When I opened my eyes they coalesced into something human, but I walked outside and slipped into the pool, feeling like a primordial fish, all my substance gone. I'd see them afterward, and they leaned toward me, their mouths open, but they hardly spoke. My arms opened and they fell against me; I held my hands on the middle of their backs, holding their hearts in place.

Sometimes they cried. I was too professional, then, to cry, knew that I had to keep some distance in order to make this re-

39

lationship work. If I had cried, then we might have been lovers, and that would make it wrong somehow when they handed me the check for thirty dollars. Sometimes they pressed the payment into my hands and looked away, and said *I can't even tell you.* I nudged them in the direction of the baths, and they went like obedient children, their naked bodies swaying under their towels as they shuffled across the old, wooden bridge.

II

I have a picture from that time—of myself in the hot tub at Orr Hot Springs. At least, some people claim it is me, pointing out the slope of my breasts, the flare of my hips, the unique circumference of my thighs. Positive identification is impossible since the woman in the picture cradles her face in her hands.

Light streams through a low doorway into the gazebo, and this young woman leans her back against the deck. The sunlight zeroes into a circle on her belly. Jasmine bush and bamboo are reflected in the glass. The woman bends her head and covers her eyes as if she were about to weep. Steam rises and beads on the glass, obscuring detail and memory.

The woman is not weeping. She is scooping up the water from the tub and splashing it to her face. If this woman is me, she is mumbling some kind of grateful prayer, alchemizing the water into a potion that will heal.

It's easy to know what we're doing, once we're not doing it anymore.

III

Before I lived at Orr Hot Springs, I spent a summer baking bread for fifty children on a farm outside Willits. I didn't know I was in practice for becoming a massage therapist, but I knew I mended wounds buried deep inside me as I handled the huge mounds of dough. ("Talking things out" carves paths around and in-between the issues, but the body knows things the mind could never face.) The repetitive motions of grasping and pushing, the bend of my waist, the slow ache in my shoulder—before long, I

40

became automatic and blank. I kept my hands covered in flour and thought continually of food, of what is nourishing. I dreamed of my mouth always open and filled.

Children clustered around me, tugged at my apron, took little balls of dough and rolled them lightly between their teeth. The bread rose and came out of the oven, broke into tender crumbs, tasted good. I watched the children and gave them small lumps of dough to press. I touched their miniature shoulders and smiled, but I said very little. At the midsummer dance, they braided flowers into my hair and held my hands, as if I were an old person convalescing from a long, wasting illness.

IV

Today I look at my hands. I remember the bodies I've touched, the lives that came through them. Sometimes I trace the edges of my fingers, as children in kindergarten do on newsprint with green tempera paint. Hands become what they have held; our hands shape themselves around what they hold most dear, or what has made an impression, or what we press on others.

My friend Dana once grabbed my hand off the stick shift as I drove through L.A. "These," he said running a fingertip around my palm, "are healing hands."

I drove with my left hand on the wheel, while he examined every finger of my right. I swerved to avoid a dog.

"They're like a sculptor's hands," he said dreamily, dropping my hand and gripping his own.

Dana is a sculptor with a propensity for twisted nude forms, estranged limbs, fingers in a bowl. Once, before he left for Peru, he painted all his walls, the appliances, even his books, a startling white: a "blank canvas," he said, for his friends to spill upon. And we did, troweling up purples and reds, oranges and blues, a cacophony of personalities rolling across his walls.

I pressed my hands in blue paint and hand-walked an awkward bridge along the wall above his couch.

V

What follows may, or may not, be true:

"It's been too long," the man said.

41

My old lover Jon stepped inside, closed the door, and settled himself carefully on the edge of my massage table. "I just came to soak in the baths, decided to get a massage on the spur of the moment," he said. "I didn't know it was you."

We stared at each other. I don't know what he saw in my face—a barrier, perhaps, a careful retreat—but in his face I saw a deep sorrow. My eyes involuntarily shifted into professional gear, scanning his body and making notes: a slump in the left shoulder, a grim tightness in the left arm and fist, chest slightly concave, breathing shallow.

In massage school, before we were lovers, Jon and I had been partners. The teacher insisted on partner rotation, but somehow Jon and I ended up together more times than not. We learned well on each other. We breathed freely; we allowed each other's hands to cup the muscles and slide, so slowly, down the length of connecting fibers and tissue; we allowed thumbs to probe deep into unyielding spots. It was like a dance—the way our teacher said it always should be: an effortless give and take, back and forth, with the breath as well as the body. Communication— transcendent and absolute.

"Listen," Jon was saying. "I understand if you don't want to do this." His body leaned toward me, and my spine tipped forward in response. A massage room is a very close environment. Intimacy is immediate; truth prevails.

I glanced away and gazed at the far wall, at the painting called *A Thousand Buddhas* he had given me as a graduation present. For the last year, I had looked at that picture every day, and every day it reminded me of Jon less and less. A process of pain, moving ahead on its own momentum. The primary Buddha sat in the center, immovable, surrounded by a helix of buddhas that spun around and around.

My palms relaxed—a good sign. "It might be awkward," I said, "but I'll try." I took a deep breath, and whatever had been prickling at my throat subsided.

What did my body feel when I placed my hands on Jon's back? My palms curved instinctively to the crook of his shoulders; my own shoulders softened when I asked Jon to breathe, and I inhaled with him, stretching my lungs, and on the exhale my hands slid down his back, kneading the muscles on the downward slide, pulling up along the lats, crossing over his spine, and again and again, until he seemed to flatten and there was no distinction between the flesh of his back or the bones in his arms or the curve of his buttocks—no distinction, in fact, between his breath and mine. I felt a small opening in my heart, a valve releasing, and an old love—a love aged and smooth as wine—flowed down my arms and sparked on Jon's skin. I knew, then, that sometime in the night I would remember this gushing, and I would be shattered by a sense of tremendous loss, a grasping ache in my palms, and I would cry, but even this certainty could not stop my hands in their circular route through Jon's familiar and beautiful body. He inhaled and began to sob. The tears shuddered through his back, his arms, his legs, and I felt them empty from him in one bountiful wave. My right hand floated to rest on his sacrum. My left hand brushed the air above his head in long, sweeping arcs.

There is a powder that covers the heart, a sifting of particles fine as talc. It is protection—gauzy and insubstantial, but protection nonetheless. Occasionally, a hand rubs against you and wipes a patch clear. That's when the heart bulges, beating with a raw and healthy ferocity.

VI

I keep another picture hidden in a drawer: me before I moved to Orr Springs—before I even knew such places existed. I am young, young, young.

I am standing barefoot on the porch of a cabin within Prairie Creek State Park on the north coast of California. It is late summer. I am wearing a purple tank top, tight Levis, and a forest ranger's hat. The morning sun is full in my face, and I am smiling a goofy, lopsided grin, my hands at my sides, my feet planted solidly on the wooden planks.

I am pregnant—about three weeks along—and the embryo is curled tightly in a fallopian tube. The pregnancy will end one week later in a long, terrifying miscarriage, but in the picture I do not know this. I don't even know I am pregnant. I am twenty-one years old and healthy from a long summer in Wyoming. It is a beautiful morning, and I am happy to be back in California. My world has not yet shifted to include the indifferent hands of nurses, the blind lights of an operating dome, the smell of bandages steeped in antiseptics and blood.

If you look carefully at the belly for some sign of the child, at the face for some indication of motherhood, there is none. The snapshot is flat and ordinary: a young woman on vacation, nothing more. But I look at this photo and sense a swelling in my pelvis, a fullness in my breasts. I feel my skin inviolate and smooth, the substance of everything I've lost and meant to regain.

VII

Someone called them midwife's hands. A midwife's hands cradle and protect, hold a life between them. Recall the classic posture for the hands in photographs: one hand cupped under the baby's emerging head, the other lightly curled on the baby's crown.

There is a polarity position like this: at the client's head, cradling, not pulling but imparting the sense of emergence just the same. If you stay long enough—motionless, breathing little sips out of the air—the head appears to become larger, grows and trembles. The eyelids flutter. Sometimes I have touched the top of my head to the top of my client's head, and we were plugged in; we took deep breaths, heaved long important signs.

VIII

Sean was born. Not from my body. From Rhea's. I held the mirror at an angle so she could see the crown of his head as it split her body in two.

The midwife placed one hand on the skull and rotated it so the face pointed toward heaven. The eyes were open, glazed with an unearthly shine.

Rhea screamed. The world paused and listened. The body followed, sheathed in cream and wax.

IX

What does the body contain? And how do the hands release it? In the late seventies, "hug clinics" opened on college campuses

44

in California. Distraught people were invited to drop in if they needed to be secured for a moment by a pair of strong, encircling arms.

One of the most powerful massage holds I've used has the client on his side, curled into a fetal position. I cupped one hand to the base of the spine, laid the other on the back between the shoulder blades. These are the two places our mother's hands fell when holding us as babies.

Some people cried with little shoulder-shaking sobs. Others fell promptly asleep. Most of them believed my hands were still on them long after I'd walk away.

X

In the hospital, the nurse stuck an IV needle into the back of my hand, over and over. I squinted and clenched my teeth.

"Does that hurt?" the nurse said, looking up, scowling.

I nodded.

"It's not supposed to hurt," she said, setting the needle aside and trying again.

When she was done, I lay on top of the covers, shivering, my eyes halfway closed, my palm flat on the bed. The IV fluid ticked into my blood. Already, I could feel myself forgetting everything.

My body was a container of pain. And then it contained nothing—an absence so absolute I couldn't even cry.

XI

The hand is shaped to touch the different parts of the world. We hurt, and the hand reaches to the chest. A newborn's head fits snugly into the center of a palm. Fertile soil runs through our fingers, or we mold our hands into a cup sealed for a drink of water. We can use our hands like primeval jaws to pluck whatever is ripe.

The midwife had fingers so long I almost asked her if she played the piano. The words were nearly out of my mouth, but then she handed Sean to me, and I forgot about pianos, about that kind of music.

I held him while the midwife and Rhea struggled with the afterbirth. I held him against my shoulder. His eyes were open; he blinked slowly and rarely, like a baby owl. The light in the room was gold, the color of honey. I thought I saw something in his eyes, but I can't be sure. I thought I saw a nod of acceptance, a little man bowing to me, his hands pressed together in an attitude of prayer.

XII

They came to me hot and pink from the baths, most of my work already done. They came naked and slick and gorgeous.

What did I give them? Nothing but myself—and not even that, but rather the benefit of my whole attention, the focus of my hands on them, the focus of my heart. I don't know how long the change lasted. They left the room and lingered in the baths, got out, got dressed, and drove home. I waved goodbye and walked up the steps to my cabin, looked out my window to the luscious woods, and thought about these people more than I probably should have. When the time approached for me to leave Orr Springs, I thought about them with a frantic longing for a life that could be balanced and whole.

I wanted to massage myself before I left. I wanted to send myself off with a stroke of my fingers and a hand along my spine: an affirmation for abundance, a momentary release from every memory that weighed me down. I thought it might help, if only for the drive out on the rutted and dusty road.

XIII

Years after I left Orr Springs, I worked for the Human Resource Council in Missoula, Montana. I didn't massage people anymore. I tried, but I zipped through the parts of the body as if I were taking inventory. I chattered like a barber giving a haircut. I thought about dinner, gas mileage, bills to be paid.

In my job, I interviewed clients and determined their eligibility for a heating-assistance program. Many of the people I saw were elderly and disabled; all of them had stories to tell, stories

46

that could take a lifetime. I had only twenty minutes to spend with each one. I found that when I gave them my whole and complete attention for even five minutes, that was enough. I looked them in the eyes and smiled, laughed with them, murmured consolations. They looked back and told me what they knew. My hands kept very still on my desk.

One seventy-six-year-old woman spoke to me in short, disjointed sentences, her head nodding emphatically with each word, spittle forming at the corners of her mouth. She smelled of cigarettes and bitter lemons. As I walked her to the door of my office, she swirled about and grabbed me around the waist. She was only as tall as my chest, and I settled my arms onto her shoulders. We stood like that for a few seconds under the fluorescent lights, the computers humming around us. Then I slid one hand down her back and held her there; my hand quivered, near as it was to her old and fragile heart.

XIV

I'm lying on my massage table. It's for sale. I'm lying on it, and I feel utterly relaxed. My breath swirls through my body in a contented daze.

I'm lying on my back. I open my eyes, and I see my face. I see me leaning over the table. My right hand comes to rest on my womb; my left hand hovers over my throat.

Forgive Me. Those are the words that pass between us.

Nominated by Rebecca McClanahan, Joan Murray, Ellen Wilbur

SUITE FOR EMILY

by LYNDA HULL

from THE KENYON REVIEW

1. The Letter

Everywhere the windows give up nothing
but frost's intricate veined foliage.
Just engines shrilling pocked and frozen streets
wailing towards some new disaster.
No *bright* angel's ladders going to split
heaven this Chicago instant where the pier's
an iced fantastic: spiked, the glacial floes
seize it greedy like a careless treasure—

marquise diamonds, these round clear globes, the psychic's
crystal world spinning in her corner shop
when I passed, a globe boundaried with turning
silent winds and demons. Out here the pavement's
a slick graffitied strip: *There's more to life
than violence.* Someone's added *Yes, Sex and Drugs.*
Hello, Plague Angel. I just heard your wings
hiss off the letter on my table—Emily's

in prison again, her child's lost to the State,
Massachusetts. Fatigue, pneumonia,
the wasting away. In the secret hungering,
the emptiness when we were young would come
the drug's good sweep like nothing else,

godly almost the way we'd float immune
and couldn't nothing touch us, nothing.
Somehow I'd thought you'd pass her over—

positive yes—but never really sick,
that flayed above her door there'd be some sign
of mercy. But there's only January's
rough ministry peeling my face away.
Light like the cruel light of another century
and I'm thinking of Dickinson's letter
"Many who were in their bloom have gone
to their last account and the mourners go about

the streets." The primer pages yellowing
on her shelf beneath an album of pressed gentian:
"Do most people live to be old? No, one half die
before they are eight years old. But one in four lives
to see twenty-one." She'd known the bitter sponge
pressed to the fevered forehead, the Death Angel's
dark familiar company, how she'd rustle her veils,
how she'd lean over the ewer and basin

blackening the water. This arctic water, this
seething rustle—lamé, sequins, a glitter wrap
trailing from a girl's shoulders so the shadow pimps
go *hey princess, why you so sad tonight,*
let me make you happy, when she's only tired,
up all night and needing a hit to let her sleep.
We know that story, the crest and billow
and foam and fleeting fullness

before the disappearing. Discs of hissing ice,
doors you (I?) might fall through to the underworld
of bars and bus stations, private rooms of
dancing girls numb-sick and cursing the wilderness
of men's round blank faces. Spinning demons.
Round spoon of powder hissing over the flame.
Worlds within worlds, beneath worlds, worlds that flare
and consume so they become the only world.

2. Holy City, City of Night

What is that general rule which tells
    how long a thing will live? The primer answers,
Whatever grows quick decays quick: soon ripe,
    soon rotten. The rust-blown calla gracing
my table, those Boston girls twenty years gone,
    young men in lace and glitter washed alien
        by gasoline sunsets, the burning sphere
lapsing below night's black rim. *Live fast, die . . .*
we know the rest. Reckless anthem.
    The pier cable's ice-sleeved beneath
my hands—miraculous, yes, to be here
    januaried by this lake's barbaric winterscape
Dickinson might read as savage text
and emblem of a deity indifferent. Her embassy lay
    beyond the city of jasper and gold, the beaten
wrought towers scripture promised the saved

would enter. What heaven she found she made.
    And so did we, worlds that sear, consume—earthly,
delirious. *Ignis fatuus.* Strike the match,
    the fizzing cap. But oh Reader, the wild beauty
of it, the whirring rush, blond hiss of aerial
miles, worn stairways in every burning school
    of nodding classrooms, the buzz-snap of
talk blurring hallucinatory fraught

avenues. Illusive inner city, drugged
    majestic residence spiraled with staircases,
balustrades rococoed, lapidary. Invisible empires
    dreamt beneath the witchery of birds
circling the Commons with twilight, their caw
and settle, the patterns as they wheel
    over the pond's reflective mirror bruised
roseate, violet, deeper, the swanboats

darkening into night's charged dazzle,
    Park Square joints gone radiant, the bus station
burnished before the zap, the charge the edge.

It was the life wasn't it? Compatriots you'd
just love to die for, who'd jump you
in a New York minute. But the glory
    as the lights went up, torching the air chartreuse,
lipsticked pink, casting embers, seraphic fires

fallen earthward. Fallen, the furious emblems.
    We were so young we'd spend and spend
ourselves as if there'd be no reckoning, then grew
    past caring. All the darkening chapters.
Dream time, the inner time
where towers and battlements erect
    their coruscating glamour and how we'd glide,
celebrities among them, the crowds falling back,

dream deeper, gone and wake to daylight's assault
    knocking another bare room, the alley, the bathroom
you inhabit like the thief you are. *Ignis fatuus.*
    I can follow you there, Emily, we girls
setting out a thousand ruined nights in the splendor
of the torched and reckless hour.
    Who wouldn't trade heaven for that fleet city
when winter beaks the shattered pane,

when summer's a nauseous shimmer
    of sexual heat, though sex is a numb machine
you float above. When the place you walk into
    is a scream in the shape of yourself.
When it makes perfect sense to blow someone away
for twenty bucks beyond even your bleak human universe.
    When the only laughter that falls down
is iron and godless. Here, I—the one who left—

must falter where persists
    this chrome traffic shrill, where the cable's
bitter alloy comes away in my hand,
    this metaled pungence of hair and skin
in wind persists riven as the taste of myself,
the blood blooming healthy

real in my mouth, a future's lavish venues
spread stunned before me. These hands.

3. Combat Zone/War Stories

The district's been demolished, sown with salt.
The dazzling girls, girls, girls in platinum wigs
have been lifted away by some infernal agency,
the queens, exotic Amazons and rough-trade gay boys.

Sometimes I go back to walk the streets all shops
and swank hotels, the office blocks and occasional
burnt out shell. So American, this destruction
and renewal, cities amnesiac where evening's

genesis falls through vast deserted silences,
towers grown otherworldly with light
thrown starlike from some alien world. Gone the Show Bar,
the Mousetrap, the whole gaudy necklace

of lacquer-dark underground lounges, halls
of mirrors, music billowing dancers
clean out of themselves beyond the dead-faced tricks,
the sick voyeurs. The Combat Zone. I can map it

in my mind, some parallel world, the ghost city
beneath the city. Parallel lives, the ones
I didn't choose, the one that kept her.
In all that dangerous cobalt luster

where was safety? home? when we were delirium
on rooftops, the sudden thrill of wind dervishing
cellophane, the shredded cigarettes. We were
the dust the Haitians spit on to commemorate

the dead, the click and slurried fall of beads
across a doorway. In the torn and watered silk
of night, the Zone exploded its shoddy neon orchid
to swallow us in the scent of fear, emergency,

that oily street perfume and weeping brick.
Gossamer clothes, summertime and leaning
against the long dusty cars, cruising siren songs.
Summer? My memory flutters—had I—was there summer?

Dancer, and floor, and cadence
quite gathered away, and I a phantom, to you
a phantom, rehearse the story.
And now it's autumn turning hard to winter,

Thanksgiving, 1990, and all she wants is sweets
so it's apple pie barehanded and Emily's
spinning war stories, how bad she is: *So, I say,*
go ahead and shoot me, put me out of my misery.

Cut me motherfucker—my blood's gonna kill you.
Then she's too tired to sit and in the blue
kaleidoscopic TV shift I stroke
her hair, the ruined hands *I didn't know*

how sick I was—if the heroin wanted the AIDS,
or the disease wanted the heroin. She asks me
to line up her collection of matchbox houses
so we can make a street, so we can make a neighborhood.

4. Jail, Flames—Jersey, 1971

The psychic's globe whirls its winds: demons,
   countless futures, the pasts. Only
      thirteen the first time
   I saw you in jail, just a kid looking
up at me, the usual gray detective clamor,

inkpads and sodium flash. Hauled out by the officials,
   exemplary bad-news girl, they shoved
      a lyric sheet at me. Command
   recitation to sway you from straying.
"King Heroin," James Brown pompadoured like nobody's

business and here's Death cartoonishly aloft on a white
    winged horse, grim reaper lording it
        over the shivering denizens
    of a city, exaggerated as any Holy City,
going down, down, down. Just a kid, you, peering out

the jungle of your dark hair, greasy jeans a tangle
    of beads at your throat. Ludicrous,
        I know, me declaiming within
    the jail gleam that never sleeps all over us,
that effluvium of backed-up plumbing. On my palm,

the bar's iron taint lingered for hours after.
    It didn't mean that much to me, seventeen,
        my practiced sangfroid
    chilling the terror, that long drop
inside, the way you collapse to fall in flames.

I might have said you'll pay for the wild and reckless hour,
    pay in the currency of sweat and shiver,
        the future squandered, the course
    of years reconfigured, a relinquishment so
complete it's more utter than any falling in love. Falling

instead in flames, burning tiles spiraling to litter
    the courtyards of countless places that will
        never be yours, the fingerprints,
    tossed gloves and glittering costumes, flared
cornices and parapets, shattering panes, smoked out

or streaked with embers, the tinder of spools, such
    a savage conflagration, stupid edge-game,
        the way junkies tempt death,
    over and over again, toy with it. I might have
told you that. Everything you ever meant to be, *pfft*,

out the window in sulfured match-light, slow tinder
    and strike, possession purely ardent as worship
        and the scream working its way out

of your bones, demolition of wall and strut
within until you're stark animal need. That *is*

love, isn't it? Everything you meant to be falls
    away so you dwell within a perfect
      singularity, a kind of saint,
   Pearl of great price. Majestic, searing,
the crystal globe spins futures unimaginable, that

crucible you know so well, Emily, viral fever refining
    you to some essence of pain more furious
      than these winter trees
    stripped to black nerves above
the El's streaked girders, a harsh equation, some

god's iron laughter combing down time's blind
    and hush. *Hush child, forgive me.*
      Twenty years later, you say
    that night in jail you looked up
at me and wanted to be me. And I didn't care.

5. Address

Hello Death Angel, old familiar, old nemesis.
    In the deepest hours, I have recognized
your floating shape. I've seen your breath
    seduce the torn curtain
masking the empty window, have crouched with you
    in the doorway, curled in the alley
hooded in your essence and shadow, have
    been left blue, heart-stopped
for yours, for yours. Death,
    you are the bead in the raptor's eye,
Death you dwell in the funneling depths
    of the heavens beyond each
star's keening shrill, Death you are the potion
    that fills the vial, the night
the monuments have swallowed. You live
    in the maimed child wrapped in a wreckage

of headlines. Death you center
    in the fanged oval
of the prison dog's howl. Death you dwell within
    the necropolis we wake to in nightmare's
hot electric wind. You glint
    the edge of the boy's razor,
patient in the blasted stairwell. Everywhere
    you walk deep lawns, TVs pollinating air
with animals wired up to dance
    for their food, with executions
and quiz shows. You're in the column
    of subway wind roaring before each
train's arrival. I've seen you drape thoughtlessly
    a woman's hair over her face
as the shot carried her forward into stop-time
    and beyond anything she'd lain
her money down for. Death your sliver works
    swiftly through the bloodstream.
Hello Death Angel, Plague is your sister.
    I've seen her handiwork, heard
the tortured breath, watched her loosen the hands
    of the dazzling boys one from each other.
For love, love. I've seen the AIDS hotels
    and sick ones begging homeless
in the tunnels, the whispered conspiracies.
    Shameless emissaries with your powders
and wands, your lunar carnivorous flowers.
    Tricks, legerdemain. I've seen you draw
veined wings over the faces of sleepers,
    the abandoned, the black feather that sweeps
so tenderly. I've seen the stain you scribe
    on the pavement, the glossy canopy of leaves
you weave. I've seen waste and ruin, know
    your kingdom for delirium, the furious thumbprints
you've scored on the flesh of those you choose.
    I've seen you slow-dance in a velvet mask, dip
and swirl across dissolving parquet.
    I've seen you swing open the iron gate—
a garden spired in valerian, scullcap, blue vervain.
    Seen you stir the neat halfmoons, fingernails

56

left absently in a glazed dish.

    Felons, I've cursed you in your greed, have spat
and wept then acquiesced in your wake. Without rue
    or pity, you have marked the lintels and blackened
the water. Your guises multiply, bewildering
    as the firmament's careless jewelry.
Death I have welcomed you to the rooms
    where Plague has lain when the struggle is passed
and lit the candles and blessed the ash.
    Death you have taken my friends and dwell
with my friends. You are the human wage.
    Death I am tired of you.

6. Dartmouth Women's Prison, 1992

Emily, delirium's your province.
You dwell feverish in prison
voiceless to plead
your need before the agencies
of government who *cannot hear the buildings*
falling and oil exploding, only people walking
and talking, cannon soft as velvet from parishes
that do not know you are burning up,
that seasons have rippled
like a beast the grasses beyond
the prison.

        They cannot hear the strummed harp
of the nerves, black trees swaying winter,
cannot know your child is lost to you.

The human wage that's paid and paid?

Once, we were two girls
setting out towards that city
of endless searing night, the route taking on
the intricacy, the fumes and bafflements
of a life a woman might dream turning
feverish in her prison bunk. Probation violation,

when broke and sick, no way home
from the clinic the detective going
ride with me, just talk, that's all
I want. Twenty bucks and him crowing
we just love to run you little sluts in.
Em, if I could reach you through the dust notes'
spinning, infernoed dreams, I would dwell
in the moon's cool glistering
your cell, the rough cloth, the reflection
of your face given back in the steel basin's
water, in the smooth moan of women loving women,
a cacophony of needs. I am there with you lost
in the chaos of numbers, that nattering PA buzz,
in the guards' trolling clank and threat echoing
walls so eloquent
with all the high-frequency sizzle
of anguish they've absorbed.
Emily, I will bless your child, will
hold for you the bitter sponge,
would give you staff and orb, a firmament
radiant and free.

                    But these are phantoms, lies—
I cannot follow where you are. On my street,
the psychic's crystal globe whirls pasts, futures
but where you are is timeless.
"Pain—has an Element of Blank—It cannot recollect
when it Began—or if there were
a time when it was not—
It has no Future—but itself. . ."

Off the lake a toothed wind keens
and it's just me here, the one who's left.
Just me helpless to change anything caught
in this ellipsis between traffic, this
fleet human delay, all around
the wind singing like a mechanical ballerina
a girl might hold in her hand, the one
that watched your childhood bed, porcelain
upturned gaze, stiff tutu, dust in the folds

of that spindly piercing music sounding
of voices winged over water, becoming
water, and gone.

7. A Style of Prayer

There is a prayer that goes Lord I am powerless
  over these carnivorous streets, the fabulous
    breakage, the world's ceaseless *perpetuum mobile,*

like some renaissance design, lovely and useless
  to harness the forces of weather, the planet's
    dizzy spin, this plague. A prayer that asks

where in the hour's dark moil is mercy?
  Ain't no ladders tumbling down from heaven
    for what heaven we had we made. An embassy

of ashes and dust. Where was safety? Home?
  Is this love, staff, orb and firmament?
    Parallel worlds, worlds within worlds—chutes

and trapdoors in the mind. Sisters and brothers,
  the same thing's going down all over town, town
    after town. There is a prayer that goes Lord,

we are responsible. Harrow us through the waves,
  the runnels and lace that pound, comb, reduce us so
    we may be vessels for these stories.

Oh, the dazzling men torn one from the other,
  these women taken, these motherless children.
    Perhaps there's no one to fashion such new grace,

the world hurtling its blind proposition
  through space and prayer's merely a style of waiting
    beyond *the Hour of Lead*—

Remembered, if outlived,
  As Freezing persons, recollect the Snow—
    First-Chill—then Stupor—then the letting go . . .

But oh, let Emily become anything
  but the harp she is, too human, to shiver
    grievous such wracked and torn discord. Let her be

the foam driven before the wind over the lakes,
  over the seas, the powdery glow floating
    the street with evening—saffron, rose, sienna

bricks, matte gold, to be the good steam
  clanking pipes, that warm music glazing the panes,
    each fugitive moment the heaven we choose to make.

Nominated by David Baker, Suzanne Gardinier, Marilyn Hacker, James Harms, David Jauss, Lou Mathews, Lisel Mueller, David Wojahn, Paul Zimmer

THE BIG EAR

fiction by ROBIN HEMLEY

from WILLOW SPRINGS

THE BIG EAR, nearly as large as Peter, and brightly colored, stands out wherever he takes it, but no one really knows what it is, unless they ask. Peter practices withering looks on the people who ask, especially if they're kids. With the seriousness of purpose and steadiness of a Civil War photographer, he stands beside his Big Ear on its black tripod. He pretends to make fine calibrations on the plastic orange cone, bending into it and tapping it with a finger. Most people never get close enough to bother him with questions. That is one of the wonderful things about The Big Ear; it is a powerful device. You can set it up almost as far away from people as you like, 200 yards, and it still picks up what they're doing. It can listen through windows. It can penetrate plaster walls.

A golf course surrounds the lake; the groundskeepers supposedly use mercury to treat the greens. The mercury leaks down the hill to the lake where the fish ingest it, so you're not supposed to eat fish anymore from here. Before he found out about the mercury poisoning, fishing was Peter's favorite activity. A few weeks ago, he caught 15 catfish off the dock, and gave them to a girl he'd just met who he had a crush on. He hasn't seen her since, but that, probably, is just coincidence.

A couple lie by an inlet on the water's edge. They're positioned behind a nearly rotten log. Peter stands on a hill overlooking them. He feels like a general observing a sleeping enemy camp. He swivels the cone towards the couple. From the distance, he can't make out their features. In fact, he has not seen the woman at all. The man's face bobs above the log, and sometimes he reaches out and grabs at a slender branch rising from the top of the log. Dry rattle, then a crumbling sound as he strips the branch of its dead leaves.

"You've got to call Catherine," the man says.

A duck calls, the water laps steadily, there is a smacking noise like chewing gum. From somewhere Peter picks up the sounds of Magic 98. "Back to back good-time oldies," a cheerful man says, then drowns. Something metal-sounding snaps.

"Her dog's dying," says a woman's voice.

The couple burst out laughing. There's a scrabbling sound, twigs breaking, bodies repositioning themselves. "Oh God," says the woman, breathless. "That's not what I meant."

"What did you mean?" says the man.

A match flares up and then a long in-suck of breath.

"Now come here. I didn't mean that."

"No, wait. Later."

"What later?"

"Are you going to salad control tonight?" That's what it sounds like. Salad control. Sometimes, Peter can't make out words too clearly. Maybe the man meant salad control. Maybe he didn't. If there's one thing Peter's learned since his mother bought him the Big Ear for his birthday, it's that people speak in code. You could have all the Big Ears in the world lined up, and still you wouldn't be able to make sense of what people tell each other. He figures there's something people aren't telling *him*, the clue to the code. Not his teachers, not his mother, not his friends. Whatever it is, he needs to find out soon, before he's too old. It just seems so strange to him, life, the whole nine yards. That's his Mom's favorite phrase. She uses it most often on the phone when she talks to Guido. At two in the morning, three, when she thinks Peter's asleep. But he always listens. He thinks she calls Guido so late not only because she wants privacy, but because she wants to wake Guido up. She wants to aggravate him the way he aggravates her. That's love.

She's not hard to hear. Her voice bounces through the whole house. "What do I want, Guido? I'll tell you what. The whole nine yards!"

"Hey, look at that kid up there," the man says, startling Peter.

62

"What?" The woman sits up, arms folded across her chest. "Where?"

"Up there." The man points at Peter.

Peter pretends he hasn't heard them. If the man starts towards him, he can run off with his Big Ear before the man's halfway up the hill. Peter goes to the front of the cone, leans inside, and makes a fine calibration. Then he swivels the cone straight up towards the sun as though this were his intended target all along. An experiment: sunspots and their means of communication. When he looks next, the couple is gone, or maybe hiding behind the fallen log.

"Did you catch anything?" his mother asks, coming around to the trunk of her Taurus so Peter can stash his gear. Obviously, he's not carrying a fishing pole. Clearly, he's not carrying fish. But his mother seems to see conversation as useful even when it makes no sense. The obvious can never be overstated. Fishing poles, Big Ears, they're all the same to her. What matters is that she's talking. He heard the word for it last year in sixth grade when he was studying government. Filibuster. His mother filibusters life. She filibusters words the way Peter's father used to filibuster beer—to fill up the silence in the pit of his stomach.

"No, I didn't catch anything, Mom."

"Oh well. Maybe next time. We've got to hustle. My class is coming over in two hours, and I haven't even bought the booze. How do I look?"

Over the last couple of months she's started dressing stranger and stranger, and it's a little embarrassing bringing friends over. Today she's wearing too-tight black jeans and a white tee-shirt that reads, BUTTON YOUR FLY in bold black letters. Over that, she's got a thousand tons of Mexican silver bangles.

"Shouldn't you wear something a little more conservative to teach in?" Peter says.

His mother smiles as though Peter's given her a compliment and says, "They hate me here anyway. So just answer the question. Do I look all right? By the way, I've got to go to Atlanta next week."

Peter doesn't say anything, but gets into the car beside her. She gives him a fleeting look of guilt, tears at a fingernail. "Oh damn," she says when she sees it's bleeding. "I've got to," she says. "This is the last time, I promise. We're going to try to figure out a way to patch things up. If not, that's it. Finis. A bientot."

His mom is always trying to patch things up with her boyfriend, if you want to call him that, Guido. Eunuch, is how she refers to him when things aren't working between them—which is always.

"You're going to need a pretty big patch, Mom," Peter tells her.

She laughs and shakes her head. "Don't I know it, kiddo."

"Who's the lucky gal this time, Mom?" Every time she goes she leaves him with a different student.

"Oh, you mean the baby-sitter?" Peter cringes at the word. "You'll meet her tonight. Just your type."

That evening twelve women sit in the living room, nodding like dashboard figurines to the choppy rhythms of each other's poetry. Peter's Mom likes him to sit in on her classes so "you won't grow up to be another prick." She doesn't say it, but she could just as well add "like your father." She says her classes are political with a small "p," never a large "P." Usually, Peter reads X-men or Spiderman during his Mom's classes, but she never seems to notice. Just as long as he "absorbs the ambience." She says the word "ambience" with a slight French accent.

Instead of a comic book, Peter flips through his mail-order gag catalogue tonight. This is where he purchased the Big Ear. While he half-listens to the student poetry, he checks off the items he'd like to own: joy buzzers, itching powder, fake vomit. There's also a large group of things that squirt—Peter already owns a squirting toilet seat, but would like to add to his repertoire. Of course, the famous squirting flower is in the catalogue, but who wants something as obvious as a fake flower? There are plenty of other squirting things: a transistor radio, a diamond ring, a chocolate bar. The squirting products all have the same type of illustration. They show someone innocently bending down to take a peek at a friend's diamond ring, or a bite of a generously-offered chocolate bar, or to listen to the latest song on a top forty station. The results are similar. A jet of water from the diamond ring blows out the offending eye. A flood shoots through the ears of the rock fan. A geyser chokes the chocolate lover. And in each picture, at a safe distance from the mayhem, stands a little cartoon guy with a big head and electrocuted hair, grasping himself around the waist, bent over with his knees locked together. "HA HA HA!" is written in bold black letters all around the ad, and in smaller letters are the words, "Thousands of gags for incredibly low prices!" To own all those gags—that would be the whole nine yards.

Tonight, one woman reads a poem about shopping for boyfriends at the Winn-Dixie. Some of her boyfriends she describes as canned vegetables, condensed green giants who give her botulism. Her old boyfriends are stretched out in the frozen food case, lewd smiles on their faces. The guy she's dating now is in the fresh meat section, a butt steak. Everyone laughs at this part except for Peter. How did they get in the frozen foods section in the first place? he wants to know. Were they murdered?

The next woman speaks so softly everyone has to bend close to hear her poem. She has a lilt to her voice and an accent, like Georgia or some place like that.

Strikebreaker

Your body,
tied to routine like a turbine,
your private Industrial Age
a cotton gin rakes seed.
Blind workers strive
for a world the bosses would never
know or approve of, a new light, lighter
than air machine,
engineering nearly bloodless revolutions.
Still, I'm lucky knowing,
at least, the factory in which I work.
I agitate, pass out
leaflets, never knowing the real conditions
or understanding your demands.

Peter listens quietly throughout the poem, and looks around to see the others' reactions. Almost everyone looks bewildered, except for his mother. She has her hands in front of her face as though she's praying. The rest of the class looks down at their laps or up at the ceiling. A woman next to Peter picks the shag carpet. He glares at her until she looks up and stops.

Peter looks at the woman who read the poem. She has her head tilted slightly. She looks like she cares a lot what's going to be said.

No one speaks for a second when the poem is finished, but then there's a yelp from the bathroom.

Peter looks around to see if anyone else has noticed, but they're still thinking about the poem. The bathroom door opens and the woman who was in there sits down on the living room floor again. She looks a little pale, but other than that, acts like nothing unusual has happened to her.

As everyone starts talking about the poem, Peter gets up quietly and goes to the bathroom to check on his gag. When he lifts the toilet seat, the little red bulb with an eye-dropper attached isn't there anymore. He checks around and finds it at the bottom of the wastebasket. Peter picks up the bulb and dries it off with some toilet paper. He unscrews the eye dropper from the bulb and runs some water. When the water gets cold enough, he places the bulb under the tap. Then he screws the top on again and places it under the toilet seat with the eye dropper pointing up.

Peter has nothing against his mother's students. In fact, he likes most of them. He would like to talk to them but he's shy.

He presses the toilet seat gently and a thin stream of water shoots up. Good. Hair-trigger action. The illustration in the catalogue for this device shows a man with his pants around his knees tumbling through the air on top of a fountain that shoots up from the toilet. The little insane man laughs in the background, but not so much as in the other illustrations. This time he's just snickering. He looks a little shy, too. After all, he's in the bathroom watching someone on the toilet.

The next poem is about cutting off some guy's dick and wearing it around the poet's neck. The woman reading this poem is the woman who got squirted with Peter's gag toilet seat. The woman whispers the poem and her hands shake as she reads. She glares at Peter. She fingers her collar as though the dick is dangling there. She looks like a nun working rosaries. She looks like

66

she's praying. She looks like someone about to be sacrificed to some ancient God.

Peter's mother is staring down at the carpet, shaking her head, rolling her eyes. Peter wants to cover his ears because the poem is so stupid. He sits in a corner against the wall, hugging his knees.

The poet mentions God, sort of. The poem ends with her stamping a foot three times like a horse, slowly, and saying the word, "Goddess."

When it's over, half the students clap, and Peter's mother exhales. "Whew," she says after a moment's silence, "I need a cigarette."

At break, they all go out on the porch. This is where his mother has set up a pony keg for her students and a mountain of Dixie cups. Peter joins his mother out there. He could have a beer if he wanted. His mother doesn't want him to think drinking's a big deal. But he doesn't want to drink tonight. He wants to watch his mother smoke. His mother always steps out on the porch for her smoke. Even though it's her house, she's considerate of other people's feelings about smoking—and so she smokes outside when people visit. "Consideration," she's told Peter, "means that you want what's best for other people, not only yourself." Peter wonders why then she doesn't quit smoking, knowing that he hates it.

She's talking to the student who read the poem about the Strikebreaker, and Peter stands around listening as though he's interested, but he's really waiting for her to light up.

They start talking and giggling about the poem with the dangling dick. Their voices are low, and they stomp their feet. Peter's mother is almost breathless with laughter. "Oh no, not circumcision!" she yells in a stage whisper, clutching her side and holding on to her student for balance.

Peter doesn't understand everything they're talking about. He never does when his mother talks in this language. This is the language she uses with her favorite students. It is a language of raised eyebrows and short laughter, of people and places that Peter doesn't know. It is a language she speaks with confidence. It is the language of absorbing the ambience. Then there is the language of Guido, full of sighs and complaints and accusations.

67

Peter understands neither language; they seem spoken by two completely different people. Sometimes, he thinks his mother *is* two people—and that neither would like the other if they ever met.

"Don't you want a cigarette, Mom?" Peter says, interrupting them. "Break's almost over."

The student and his mother turn to him at the same time. His mother smiles and says, "Is it? Well, we can take a few extra minutes. This is Nan, Peter. She's going to be baby-sitting for you when I go to Atlanta."

"I wouldn't call him a baby," Nan says.

"He'll always be *my* baby," says his Mom, trying to give him a squeeze, but he squirms out of her reach.

"Cool poem," Peter tells Nan, bobbing his head and not looking at her.

"You liked it?"

Peter has exhausted his literature discussion capabilities. He *said* it was cool, but she seems to want him to say more.

"I raised him to be sensitive," says his mother, brushing back some hair from his eyes, too late for him to duck.

"Mom, break's almost up," Peter says.

Nan looks at him and then at his mother. "Is he always this conscientious?"

"Always," says his mother, smiling.

Nan shakes her head wistfully. "I wish you were ten years older," she tells Peter. "If I believed in marriage, I'd wait till you were about thirty. I can't wait to see what you'll be like then."

He wonders if she's kidding. She looks serious.

"I'm too fickle," he says. His mother uses that word when she talks about Guido. Now she loves it and so does Nan. They both crack up, then Nan says, "Me too. We were made for each other." But he thinks she's just kidding.

His mother finally takes out her pack of cigarettes and withdraws one. Peter's not sure if it contains the load, but he made sure that one was sticking up farther than the rest when he replaced it in the pack.

"Mind if I mooch one from you?" Nan asks.

"It's not good for you," Peter says.

"What?" his mother says. "It's not good for her, but it's fine for me?"

"You're hopeless," Peter says.

"Thanks," says his Mom.

"Me, too," says Nan, reaching for a cigarette. "I'm hopeless and I'm fickle. I sure am learning a lot about myself tonight. I can't wait to house sit. This should be an enlightening experience. And you're out in the country, too. I love the country." Nan blows out smoke from her nose and then inhales fresh air.

"I wouldn't call it country," says Peter's mom. "It used to be country, back when Joel and I first moved here. All that's left from those days is the well out back."

She launches into an extended history of the subdivision, gesturing over the rail into the dark. Peter listens to everything else around him—the trickle and murmur of conversation from the dozen people crowding the porch. The slopping of drinks. The clean sound of the glass door as it slides open. The pumping of the keg which seems to pump sounds from the night as well: crickets and a breeze and the rush of the highway a mile off.

The pop seems to come from Nan's finger, and all three of them startle. Nan's sleeve is on fire. He just stares at it. This wasn't supposed to happen. Nan stares at her burning sleeve, too, as though it's something she's imagined. One of his mother's other students stumbles over from the keg and douses Nan's sleeve with beer. Then, without a word, she works her way back to the keg and stands in line for more.

"I'm sorry," Peter says, and he is. He meant to blow up his mother, not Nan.

"I'm so embarrassed," his mother says.

"That's all right, really," says Nan, but he can tell she's upset. This has probably ruined his chances with her.

"Why can't I can't keep violence out of the picture. Where does he get this from? TV? His genes?" She seems not to be talking to Nan, or anyone else in particular. She's gesturing over the railing, as though filibustering the entire subdivision or a multitude, like the Pope in St. Peter's Square.

Peter's mother has been gone nearly all week, and she's only called him once, to tell him she arrived safely. She must be having fun, but Peter doesn't care. He's having fun, too. Nan hasn't held a grudge against him. Not like some of the students his mother's left him with before. They all held grudges against him, or seemed to, not for anything he actually did or didn't do. He never set any of *them* on fire. Still, they held a general grudge, like he was some ailing houseplant or ancient cat, beyond concern or repair. Most of them couldn't even keep the houseplants alive. He stayed away from these students, skulking in the background, blowing up plastic soldiers with Black Cat firecrackers in the back yard. Nan's different. For one thing, she's funny. She's taught him the word, "indubitably." He has no idea what it means, but he loves the sound of it. "Indubitably," she says in a British accent and he cracks up.

With Nan, he listens to sounds closer to home.

One night, Peter sets up the Big Ear outside her bedroom and listens to her breathe. The phone rings and Peter freezes.

Nan emerges from the bedroom, rubbing her eyes. She jumps when she sees the big orange cone in front of the door. "My God," she says, hand over her heart. "What the hell is that?"

"My Big Ear."

"Your *what?*"

"Sometimes I can pick up radio stations late at night," Peter says, looking at the floor.

"Kind of like a satellite dish?" she says.

Peter runs for the phone so he won't have to explain any more.

"Peter," his mother says, breathless. "I'm in love. I met someone in the airport. His name is Antoine."

"What about Guido?"

"Look, I'm staying another week. Antoine has got to go back to France, and I just can't bear the thought of being separated from him before then."

What about me? he wants to say, but instead says, "What about Guido?"

"Look, are you getting along with Nan? Do you like each other?"

"A lot. She says she's going to marry me when I'm thirty."

"See, I told you she was your type."

"What about Guido?"

"Why this sudden interest in Guido? I thought you hated Guido. Anyway, Guido's not giving me what I need, you know, the whole nine yards. With Antoine, at least I get nine yards for two weeks."

70

"I don't get it," he says, It's true, he hates Guido, but his mother can be awfully tricky. He wants to be sure she's finally gotten over him this time.

"You'll get it when you're older. I know it doesn't make sense, honey, but one thing you've got to understand sooner or later is that no one knows anyone else's expectations. If we knew each other's expectations, there would be no need for secrets. There'd be nothing to hide, and people always have something to hide. Guido had his expectations and I had mine, and that's why I've been messed up for so long. That's over. I promise, honey. No more traveling. I have no idea at all what I want now and I don't expect anything from anyone and I've never been happier. It's crazy, but the world's crazy. It's harmless, so don't worry about me."

Peter hasn't thought about worrying until that moment, but he *is* worried about her. When she gets in a mood like this, she can convince herself to do anything. When she returns, he knows, she'll be so down he'll have to scrape her off the floor. She's met this Antoine before, though his name was Robert last time and Clark before that. She'll come back to Guido, and she'll laugh and cry at the same time and say, "God, how could I be so stupid? How could I fall for Antoine's tricks?"

Most afternoons, Peter sets up his Big Ear in the front yard of his house and points the device down the road. Peter doesn't always know what he wants to listen for. Sometimes it reassures him when he doesn't hear anything.

Nan spends half her days out back, practicing her Tae Kwan Do, the house between them.

At night they sit up in his mother's room, where Nan is sleeping. They sit cross-legged on the bed, and she sings for him, ancient folk songs about lonesome murderers. For someone who's so small, her voice is deep and rich, and suited to songs of backwood hollows and the hangings of innocent and guilty men. He never asked Nan to sing, and she didn't really offer. It just happened the first night after dinner. After that first night, they were friends. She doesn't only sing, but she talks to him, too. She tells him things about her life that no stranger has ever told him. Not even his mother. She tells him about a trip last year to Europe

71

with a man named Phil, and how they argued, and how he left her in the middle of this bridge with no money and no way to get home.

"What did you do?"

"I managed."

"How could he do that?" Peter asks. He imagines a giant white bridge with pillars topped by lions' heads, Nan standing in the middle of the deserted bridge, and a bent figure in a trenchcoat hurrying away.

Peter remembers the day his father left them. They were in the kitchen. Peter's mother said he was threatened by women, and his father laughed.

"You know it goes both ways," he said.

"Yes it does," she answered calmly. "I'm not denying that. It's natural to feel threatened. Why shouldn't we feel threatened? That's the only thing we're experts at, inspiring fear and weathering it."

"I'm not afraid of you," he'd said.

"You're not listening," she said calmly, her arms folded, but Peter could see she was trembling.

"The fuck," he said.

Peter takes out a pack of Wrigley's gum from his pocket, but if you look closely at the wrapping, you notice that it doesn't really say Wrigley's but Wriggles. So Peter always feels justified when he offers people this gum. If they're paying attention they'll notice the fake name and won't fall for the trick, a mouse trap that snaps on your finger when you pull the stick of gum from the pack.

He thinks of the last person he offered the gum to, a girl named Susan Macnamara. Susan wanted to go steady with him a few months back, and he agreed, but he didn't know what he was getting into. One day, she led him down to a gully near her house, to a hollowed-out log where she said she used to sit and think. She told him she had a surprise for him and then kissed him.

"Ow," Peter said.

Susan pulled back. "Ow? Why'd you say ow?"

"I don't know," he said, feeling ashamed. "I thought you were going to do something to me."

72

"Peter Costello. You're not supposed to say 'ow' when a woman kisses you."

"Okay," he said and closed his eyes and puckered his lips. But she didn't feel like kissing him now. That's when he offered her the gum.

"Phil sounds mean," Peter tells Nan.

Nan looks up at the ceiling and says, "I never thought of Phil as mean when I was with him. He didn't do anything outwardly cruel. But it was inside of him all the time. To this day, he probably gets a kick out of it, thinks it proved something that he was able to abandon me like that. If I ever see him again. . . . All my life I've been involved with murderers. Part of the attraction of the relationship was the pain, but I really think that's the last time I'm going to let that happen. That's why I'm taking Tae Kwan Do, not so much for the self-defense, but for the confidence. I *was* taking Judo. Judo teaches you to use the attacker's own force against him, but you know what? It doesn't work. We've been going that route much too long. I'm never going to put myself in that position again. You know that Billie Holliday song, 'God Bless the Child That's Got His Own?' "

Peter shakes his head no, entranced.

"Do you want to hear it?" She starts to sing, but she stops and looks at him seriously. "You're not going to be that way, are you? You wouldn't leave anyone stranded in the middle of a bridge."

"Not you," Peter answers.

She narrows her eyes and says, "Not anyone."

"Okay," Peter says.

"Promise?"

Peter nods.

Nan bends over and kisses Peter's forehead, strands of her hair tickling his face. He doesn't understand how someone could hate her as much as Phil must have. He imagines himself and Nan together when he's thirty, watching TV, picking up nonsense on the Big Ear.

"I like this," Nan says.

"Me too."

"Men should stay twelve, don't you think?"

"Indubitably," Peter says.

73

"Come to think of it," she says, but doesn't finish the thought. "Oh you have gum?" she says, reaching for it.

"It's my last piece," he says. "I'm saving it." Peter puts the gum back in his pocket. He knows how selfish that sounds. He'd like Nan to read his mind, to know she doesn't really want this fake gum. She smiles and touches his leg and says, miraculously, "That's fine. I don't need it."

Peter hears the telephone ringing. It's his mother. He knows her ring, and he knows what she's going to say before she says it, that things with Antoine didn't work out, that she misses Guido, that she's returning home early. Peter looks at Nan and she looks at him, and for some reason, they both burst out laughing. He wishes that it could always be like this, that he could relay and receive telepathic messages, speak different languages, that distance didn't matter, that every nerve in his body was attuned to the slightest sounds.

Nominated by Josip Novakovich, Willow Springs

THENG

fiction by SUSAN ONTHANK MATES

from TRIQUARTERLY

THE NIGHT Theng Khavang, once a student of literature, arrived in Providence, the moon split in half and ate itself behind a passing veil of clouds. His younger brother, Luon, who had lobbied and bribed unremittingly for five years to get Theng out of Cambodia, then Thailand, then the Philippines, went to bed, finally, at two in the morning, because he had to work at six. Luon lay quietly on top of the blankets, next to his wife Sokunthea, and passed abruptly into sleep. He dreamt of empty sky, of Theng's gaunt middle-aged face, of their dead parents, their dead sisters, and of his own life, as irrevocably changed as if he had died himself. It was his first dream in months.

Theng sat on the bare floor of the children's room, smoking a cigarette. The floor was hardwood, the house a solid tenement built for the Irish, but lived in, mostly, by Italians. Savoun, the four-year-old, and six-year-old Chan stared at Theng as he whispered answers to their questions. "I am your father's older brother," he told them. "I lived for five years in Khao I Dang camp. I was born in Battambang, like your father." He talked to the children in matter-of-fact Khmer but his words flew by them like pelicans lifting off the great lake Tonle Sap.

"What is starving?" asked Savoun. "What is escape? Why aren't you married?"

"Shut up," said nine-year-old Mok. But he listened like the others when Theng ignored him and explained.

And so the names Sisophon, Aranyaprathet, Piopet, and the idea of bachelorhood seeped into the house with the smell of cigarette smoke. Where there had been no photos, no mementos, no heirlooms, no people attached to the words "grandfather," "aunt," "cousin," now there was Theng.

Not that there weren't signals before, omens of memory spelled out in the children's stomachaches at school, in the way Sokunthea, home drunk from the factory in the late afternoons, would curl like a baby on the living-room floor, in Luon's sudden pain when, supervising plastic-tubing operators and surreptitiously studying for his night class in accounting, he glanced out the dusty windows to see a plane overhead, because he had been about to make fighter-pilot, all those years ago. But now there was Theng, come like a premonition into their lives.

At the Refugee Resettlement Office, the worker was unimpressed when Luon pushed Theng forward. "This is my brother," Luon said. "He speaks five languages. He taught university in Cambodia. A good translator."

Outside, Theng said, "No, I can't."

But Luon, the younger son, the one who hadn't been sent to college and had paid ten thousand dollars and promised to keep Theng off of welfare said, "You will remember."

They went to Indo-Chinese Social Services, where Luon was known, because he worked in the Khmer Community Council, and his wife, too, with her problem, but still there was no job. They went to all the hospitals, the courts, the welfare offices. Once, Luon's old Toyota stopped without warning and they had to walk home through a snow squall, the first Theng had ever seen. That weekend, Luon took Theng to his church and found an overcoat for him in the box of clothes downstairs in the Sunday school. "I've become Christian," he said, and when Theng shrugged his shoulders, Luon added, "You go by yourself now. I can't take any more time from work."

By spring, Theng was translating for the psychiatric social workers who worked outreach for state mental health. He was hired by Refugee Health, but funding was short, so one of them would say, "Hey, Theng, you do French?" and there would be a Haitian family, a woman from Cameroon, French-Canadians from Woonsocket, just north of Providence. The first time Theng tried French, the words stalled and faded in his mouth and even the aide asked if there was something wrong. Theng shook his head.

But when he got home, he told the boy, Mok, about the wide and gracious boulevards of Phnom Penh, and the sudden rains that stirred the dust of the sidewalks into clouds.

Most of the time, though, Theng translated for Southeast Asian refugees. Usually, there was a swift and resonant exchange in Khmer, but with the more recent Cambodian immigrants, he spoke slowly, repeating sentences and raising his voice. "Peasants," he told the staff, "look at them, let their kids do anything. Mountain garbage. Khmer Rouge." He pointed out their darker skin, their bare feet, the girls' teased hair. But he made passes at the women, and sometimes when he drove the van from the community center to the clinic, he would arrive a half-hour late, with only one giggling passenger.

The staff ignored it because he was a good translator, even with the Vietnamese and the Hmong, a mountain tribe so stubborn and far from western medicine that they still died of treatable diseases and demon curses, even in Providence. Their language was difficult and, though Theng pretended to translate, he really spoke to them in signs. The social workers laughed, because they could do better themselves.

One day the district supervisor stormed in, shut himself in a room with Theng and shouted so the whole clinic could hear: "Don't ever date patients. Don't ever take women in the van by themselves. Don't ever fool around on clinic time." And the outreach workers said to each other, we should have said something, we should have stopped it sooner.

Through all of this, there was the unrelenting work, the stories, four clients an hour, all day. They shot my parents in front of me, my children starved, I was tortured here, and here, look at the scar on my shoulder, my son is blind from a land mine in the forest near the border, oh my husband, he's been that way since he came out of the army, no, I can't have babies, they took out that part, an operation in the Thailand camp, I would have died otherwise. Sometimes Theng would say, this one really has trouble, or, this one just trying for welfare. The clinic staff rushed, complained, joked, drank coffee and always felt guilty that they didn't stop and weep. But Theng never faltered.

When the police found the apartment empty, one August afternoon after Chan rode his bike into a car and broke an arm, the

77

children said, "Uncle Theng," so they called the clinic. The Department of Children and Families caseworker came that weekend and Sokunthea made tea. Luon pulled a chair out from the kitchen so the woman sat like a queen over them as they squatted on the mat on the floor. They held a cup of sweetened tea up to her and didn't tell her how Sokunthea had been fired for not coming to work, how she was gone for hours from the house and no one knew where, how she began setting an extra place at the table for the baby, when the only baby in the family was the one who died before Luon went back over the border to get her.

"I am president of the Community Council and deacon in the church," said Luon. "My brother is translator for mental health. He used to be a teacher in Cambodia." The caseworker, a fair-skinned young woman, third-generation Irish, told them severely that someone had to be home to care for the children or they would be taken away. After she left, Luon told Theng he'd seen him on Broad Street hiring a girl, and if he wouldn't stop, to get out of his house. Theng laughed and lit a cigarette.

In September Mok was put in the highest track at school while a note came home concerning Chan, that he was dreaming in first grade. Savoun went to scholarship kindergarten in a private school on the East Side, where she made Play-Doh flowers and beasts in fantastic shapes and colors. After school the children walked a mile from where the bus let them off, to the clinic, because Sokunthea was working again, a jewelry factory out in Pawtucket, three to eleven.

Theng put the children in a back room behind the interview cubicles and told them to do their homework. The clinic knew about his sister-in-law from Community Services, and, besides, the children were always well-behaved. Sometimes, when it was raining and no one came, Theng would stand over Mok and touch his books, fingering the paper, slowly reading the text. Once, Mok was reading an English assignment, and said suddenly, "Listen, uncle. Isn't it beautiful?" Theng laughed. The boy turned to look at Theng and saw himself reflected in the pool of his uncle's eyes, in the groove of his cheeks, in the sliver of straight black hair that fell across his forehead.

Luon grew busier and busier with the Community Council and the church. He drove the elderly to hospital appointments, he sued a landlord on behalf of Cambodian tenants, and still he

78

worked and went to school. Get on with your lives, he told his people, live for the next generation, try to do good. And, because the past had welled up in him like a tidal wave, he told his own story, over and over. Look what I overcame, he would say, no one had it worse than me, tortured by the Communists, escaped to Thailand, all my friends shot, then arrested by the Thai soldiers, *me*, they thought I was Khmer Rouge, blindfolded, thrown off the truck into the prison yard like a sack of rice, escaped out of prison, back across the border for my wife and baby, how could it be worse? To his wife he said, "You must get over this, pull yourself together." But in the middle of the night, he awoke and watched the moon over the neighbor's roof change from full, to half, to crescent, to fingernail-thin, and wept.

In October, Sokunthea drove the Toyota into a side rail on the Newport Bridge and killed herself.

A brittle sheet of ice lay across all of Providence that winter. It was a kind of cold that never seized Cambodia: words froze coming out of Theng's mouth, and Luon, although he'd been in the U.S. longer, stopped moving entirely. Sitting across the kitchen table from each other, each brother knew, without looking, the way the veins stood out on the other's hands, the way the other's legs crossed narrowly together, the way the eyelashes of each passed, slatted, across their wide-set eyes.

At the clinic, patients slipped and fell coming in the door. The secretary posted a sign, "Watch your step," and so they watched, helplessly, as they fell anyway. The staff had come to Sokunthea's funeral out of respect for Theng. On the way out of the church, one young woman bundled her coat close and said to Theng, her breath clouding her glasses: what can we do, we aren't sure in your culture. . . .

And Theng, standing outside in his shirtsleeves, unaware of the cold, had turned to her, bewildered. "No," he said, "we are no different."

Luon gave up night classes and church, and stayed home with Chan and Savoun, who would have no one else. He fed them sweetened tea and rice, coconut soup and spoke to them only in Khmer. "Come on my sweetlings, my little snakes, my fish," he sang to them, until they fell into the bottomless sleep of childhood.

79

But it was Theng who visited the school on behalf of Mok, in whom grief had taken the form of insatiable studiousness. Look, the boy said. The heart is a muscle that moves blood through the body like a pump. It is divided into four chambers called auricles and ventricles. Archaeologists are people who dig for things from the past. They found tablets about ancient kingdoms in the upper Mesopotamia area, which is today northeastern Syria. Maybe a psychiatrist, said the teacher. Maybe if he could talk about his loss. Maybe, said Theng, and left. To Mok, he said, tell me what blood is made of. Tell me where is Syria.

At the clinic, there wasn't time for mourning. A Guatemalan threatened to kill his family, a Liberian woman saw flashing messages in the sky, some swamp Yankees from southeastern Rhode Island brought in their sister who set the house on fire and through all of this Theng talked and translated and explained Cambodians: the Khmer Rouge came, I starved, my children died, my parents, we escaped across the border, which camp? Khao I Dang, Aranyaprathet, when did they transfer you to the Philippines? How do you pay the rent, go to Indo-Chinese Social Services?

Sometimes Theng left in the middle of an interview and stood outside, smoking a cigarette. By November, he would come to work late smelling of sweat and cheap perfume. When they asked him at work what was wrong, he said "nothing," but once he tried to explain, anyhow: too many words.

He came home late, sometimes not at all. "If you want to go out, why don't you go to night school," said Luon. "Instead of whoring." Then the brothers stopped talking to each other.

One night after midnight, Theng rang the doorbell and leaned against the porch, bruised, his clothes ripped, his wallet and keys gone. When Luon answered the door, the two men stood staring at each other until, finally, Theng looked down.

The children rubbed their eyes in the kitchen doorway, watching Luon wash Theng's face and arms. "Go back to bed," said Luon, and they did, unspoken questions gathering like dust in the corners of their room. The next Sunday, Luon started taking the children to church again.

"Our Father," they prayed, "who art in heaven, please give us back our mother."

When Christmas came, Theng went to the Salvation Army and bought a couch and chairs for the living room. He carried them up the stairs himself so it would be a surprise. Savoun jumped on the cushions until Luon stopped her, but even he laughed and thanked his brother. "Theng," he started, and suddenly he remembered Theng's apartment in Phnom Penh with its elegant European furniture and rows of books. Luon had been there only once, because it was a long trip, and he had been a very junior pilot.

"Come," said Theng, "let's take a walk." So they walked down Smith Street together, past the pink and yellow double-deckers, past the 7-Eleven, past the fluorescent glow of the laundromat.

"Do you remember," said Luon, "the smell of our father's pipe?"

"Yes," said Theng.

"And do you remember the new rice, how green it is?"

"Yes," said Theng, looking down at the sidewalk where the ice had melted during the day and frozen again when the sun went down.

"Theng," cried Luon suddenly, "why don't I die, too? Why me?"

"I don't know," said Theng. After that, they walked in silence.

The next day, when Theng got home from work, Mok was waiting. "Uncle," he said, as they walked into the apartment. "What is the cerebellum? What makes metal rust? Can I become an archaeologist?"

Theng put water on the stove for tea. "You ask too many questions," he said.

"But you're a teacher," said Mok.

"No," said Theng, putting out the cups. "I am not the person who was a teacher. That person is dead."

"My mother is dead," said Mok.

Theng took tea bags from the cabinet over the sink and arranged them carefully in the cups. "Yes," he said, then paused for a moment, because he was remembering something he had forgotten. *À la recherche*, he remembered, the silent wingspread of cormorants. Wild ducks flash brilliant orange, green and red, in and out of the water's edge, snapping at beetles on the surface of the lake. Egrets pick their way through a bristle of water grass, the rattle of cranes in warm evening air. Houses rise up from the water on wooden pilings. A young boy, lying on the floor of a house, drops rice through the cracks and watches the fish swarm up like jewels. The boy, grown to a young man, wears leather sandals in the university library. The smell of books.

Du temps perdu, he thought, and the memory of thinking in that way rushed through him. His hand shook as he picked up the kettle, and he recognized the prominent knuckles, the fingers, thin and jointed like stalks of bamboo, the faint crescents rising at the base of the nails. It was the hand of that younger man. "Yes," he repeated. And then he poured the tea.

Nominated by TriQuarterly and Norman Lavers

EXODUS

by ROBYN SELMAN

from THE PARIS REVIEW

> *Open your eyes, O beloved homeland, and behold your son, Sancho Panza, returning to you. If he does not come back very rich, he comes well flogged. Open your arms and receive also your other son, Don Quixote, who returns vanquished by the arm of another but a victor over himself and this, so I have been told, is the greatest victory that could be desired.*
>
> *—Cervantes*

I

And so I went forth, exhilarated
in uniform: worn-through jeans, muscle tees,
stripped of bras and ancestral history.
Since I had nothing real to take along,

I took along a fig-shaped stone,
a bag of gold buds, a resin-stained bong,
hash oil, in which papers were coated,
and two tabs of four-way blotter acid;

lactose-laced cocaine, cut to average,
a fifth of scotch, which was a parting gift,
a poncho, a guitar, feminist sheet music
and *Court and Spark*, which I'd tape-recorded.

With all this I'd find someone of my own.
An ill-equipped bride-to-be, I left home.

II

The old man waves to me through iron bars
on his window, and I wave back at him.
Ten years back, at a spring semester end,
I went to Greece with three other women.

Joanne, whom I called Joey, my lover then,
was the only woman I knew who'd speak
the word proudly. She worked and was older
and didn't do drugs like I did, or bars.

She even looked what I thought was the part:
hair close-cropped, the top in a boyish mop.
We met in a club called The Other Side,
then fell in side by side later that night

on a futon with psychedelic sheets
that lay in an attic under beamed eaves.

III

An ill-equipped bride-to-be, I left home.
The coke I'd flown with in my underwear
had melted into a yellowish loam.
Cheryl, who'd once caused a fire somewhere

drying her wet shirt in a microwave,
suggested that we lay the gluey high
on the warm radiator to try to save
what stash we could, and I agreed to try.

Moments later, the flakes began to fly
down to the floor like mocking stalactites.
My new roommate looked on, removed, dry-eyed.
She was a grad architecture student

with pre-fab plans for life in blueprints.
I befriended Mike with the good hash pipe.

IV

We lay in an attic under beamed eaves,
then headed to New York from Washington.
My new lover, whom I didn't discover
for weeks was depressed and addicted,

for real, to caffeine and cigarettes,
piloted a Buick big as a hearse.
And when the speed she was sipping kicked in
the car did ninety. I waited for sirens.

We were rushing to a conference on women:
Millet, Morgan, Griffin, Rich, and Steinem.
I asked a woman who wasn't Millet
for her autograph. Mistaken, somewhat

humbler, I returned to Joey in the stands.
They called the next panel, "New Lesbians."

V

I befriended Mike with the good hash pipe
and a constant yen for bourbon on ice.
I stayed straight. A consequence of having
no clue how I'd get that other kind of date.

I wore lavender tops, ankhs, stopped shaving,
carried code books face out though my arms ached,
hoped *she'd* recognize *Lesbian Nation,*
Millet's *Flying,* poems by Susan Griffin.

As I grew needy, the book chimney grew.
Finally, I turned back to what I knew:
the last of the coke, the dope, me and Mike,
moved in together with the good hash pipe.

He was pretty, but he wasn't a girl.
Next came Bob, but before him I had Phil.

VI

They called the next panel, "New Lesbians."
I spent the day in the bleachers transfixed.
Joey had to walk off her nicotine fit.
We went to the ladies' (women's) room and kissed.

We were in love, we weren't saying we were.
I wasn't saying that the words I'd heard
were having a drug-like effect: *gay pride*
shot through me, some other blood mixed with mine.

The women I'd known didn't call themselves
lesbians, but winked across tennis courts
in short shorts, and gave slaps in locker rooms
that took the place (psychically) of bedrooms.

Was that sex or athletics? One panelist
asked, "Is sex as much fun with politics?"

VII

Next came Bob, but before him I had Phil
who wore overalls with an unlatched bib
and an army sweater worn at the wrists.
He liked Schumann, Mao, Marx and Joplin's *Pearl*.

He rarely shaved, he washed infrequently
and spoke with a strong uncorrected lisp
which made him seem younger than twenty-six.
I didn't move in. He broke up with me.

Bob was a prize my mom couldn't resist:
six foot, an accountant-to-be, Jewish,
a hard worker, he'd make love then make coffee.
He took me home on the big holidays.

On weekends, with his parents, we saw plays.
We saw everything except that we were gay.

VIII

"What did sex have to do with politics?"
Susan, my first, wrestled me to the floor
after her two-set win: six/one, six/four.
She was privileged, both pretty and rich.

Though I wasn't in love with her riches,
the idea that she passed was seductive.
We escaped the closeted coaches' judgment.
She was younger, but had already had

stacks of lovers: boys, girls, even a divorced
mother. Both she and her sister lost their
virginity to their older brother.
She said, "*It* had nothing to do with *it*."

I didn't know what *it* she meant, or
pretended I didn't, as I licked and kissed.

IX

We saw everything except that we were gay.
Or, I saw everything except the way
around being gay. So I took to bars,
Donna Summer and Gloria Gaynor.

But I liked the stone butch I met better,
who by day flipped hamburgers and at night
was a chest-taped male impersonator.
Nothing ever happened with her, but I

paid the cover charge again and again
though I didn't speak to any new lesbians.
For cover, I'd take my closeted friends.
We danced shackled together like prisoners.

Eleanor, R., Nat, Virginia, or me—
One of us had to be the first to lead.

X

I licked and kissed her in a bathroom stall
as a line of sisters wound down the hall,
Joey's eyes shut against the light green walls.
I drank the warm juices in, swallowing

sips of her like heroin, swallowing
her pride, still unable to summon
any of mine. Months after that kiss
she'd scold me in the Acropolis

for something I'd never heard of that she
loudly termed my *goddamambivalence.*
I snapped back that she was too serious
and imagined leaving her for good right there.

I didn't. I was too in love and scared—
thousands of years up in the chalky air.

XI

One of us had to be the first to lead:
Eleanor R., Natalie B., Virginia
Woolf, Elizabeth R., Elizabeth B.,
Hedda and Alla Nazimova,

Debbie Reynolds, Gertrude Stein, Amelia,
Willa Cather, Cheryl, Whitney Houston,
Sylvia Beach, Billie Jean, Martina,
Jodie Foster, Marion Dickerman,

Lisa, Elizabeth Cady Stanton,
Lesley Gore and Susan B. Anthony,
Bessie, Babe Didrikson, Val, Anne Murray,
Barbara Jordan and life-long companion,

Yourcenar, Colette, Marlene, H.D.—
the minds I admired, the strong-bodied.

XII

Thousands of cheers filled the chalky air
in the hot Dalton School gymnasium.
Joey sipped cola and chewed Aspergum.
The speaker railed against the oppression

of gay/straight/black/white/Latina women.
They called a break. We hit the streets, like a gang, in
our "Sisterhood Is Powerful" buttons.
I was firmly a not-quite believer,

while Joey's button seemed to protect her.
At Sixtieth and Lex, I doubled over.
Outside things were different. I could see
that people could see. But that didn't seem

to bother Joey, whose hand lay on my knee,
a gesture I thought was only about me.

XIII

The minds I admired, the strong-bodied,
the women who had started my fire,
all in the impregnable closet with me,
shackled together, caged by the same wire.

I was, at the time, just turning twenty
and lacked the mettle to try to unbend
thousands of years of history of women.
And so, like many women before me,

I let other women come out before me.
It wasn't that I had a wicked itch,

for I had long before gladly scratched *it*,
but I was still afraid of the language.

It was in the closet that the words took form
and with them I went forth in uniform.

XIV

I thought the gesture was only about me.
We made our way through Greek islands by boat:
Joey in a chair; I, crossed-legged and tortured
as Crane, reading his poems on a heap of rope.

I don't remember the other two women
except they were straight and Canadian.
That night after dinner and too much wine
I went to one (with blue eyes?) with the hope

of blurring the line between her kind and mine.
I found Joey walking with a cup of coffee.
I still hear the metronome of her steps,
that morning quiet as our empty bed.

The old man waves to me through iron bars
on his window and I wave back at him.

XV

And so I went forth in uniform.
Through iron bars, the old man waved to me.
I left home, an ill-equipped bride-to-be
and lay in an attic under beamed eaves.

I befriended Mike with the good hash pipe.
They called the next panel, "New Lesbians."
Then came Bob, but before him was Phil.
What does sex have to do with politics?

We saw everything except that we were gay,
or pretended we didn't, as we licked and kissed.
One of us had to be the first to lead,
thousands of years up in the chalky air.

The minds I admired, the strong-bodied—
I thought the gesture was only about me.

Nominated by Marilyn Hacker

BOWEN

fiction by EVAN CONNELL

from THE THREEPENNY REVIEW

HE CAME out of a skeletal midwestern town beside the Mississippi and his favorite novel was *Huckleberry Finn*. Instead of floating down the river on a raft he joined the merchant marine, but until the day he stripped himself naked on a cliff overlooking the Pacific and just after dawn stepped forward to eternity he imagined himself as Huck—only more sophisticated and intelligent, maddened by genius.

I first saw him in Paris, seated on an old-fashioned trunk in the hotel suite of a famous Southern author, grande dame of American literature. He had begun writing a novel about his voyage to New Guinea aboard the freighter *Pelican* and he had come to pay homage, perhaps to divine the secret of her eminence. I remember that he sat motionless on the ancient steamer trunk and his eyes were crystal gray.

Three years later I saw him in California. *Voyage of the Pelican* had been published with unusual success. Reviews were excellent. He had been interviewed on radio and television. A movie producer was going to option the book. Several paperback houses were interested in reprint rights. He told me it was selling better than anybody expected. He had married a porcelain English goddess named Felicia, they were buying a little house in a eucalyptus grove near the Golden Gate, and he believed his days as a merchant seaman were over.

About that time he met another dislocated midwesterner, Willie Stumpf, in O'Leary's bar and grill. Stumpf had inherited a few thousand dollars, he admired Bowen's novel and thought the two of them should publish a literary magazine. He would be the publisher. Bowen could be the editor-in-chief. They discussed it until O'Leary's closed. Bowen said the magazine should be called *Octopus* because nothing escapes the grasp of this remarkable creature, and they ought to publish it quarterly. Willie Stumpf said that was a great idea, he would rent an office. They shook hands. Both of them were very drunk.

Marriage turned out to be more expensive than Bowen anticipated; he learned that women require all sorts of things. Then, as if by magic, Felicia became pregnant. He was astonished and dismayed. It seemed to him that life was happening too quickly. Next, the Hollywood producer rode off into the sunset without a word of explanation, as movie producers tend to do. Bowen had started another novel and after contemplating the situation he decided to ask his New York publisher for an advance. The publisher agreed, although with some reluctance, and the advance was rather stingy, considering those good reviews. Then Willie Stumpf discovered that because *Octopus* would cost quite a lot to print, there might not be enough left over to pay the editor-in-chief's salary. Bowen cursed the universe with particular emphasis on Hollywood producers, New York publishers, and Willie Stumpf, after which he got drunk as he often did when fortune showed her ugly face, and concluded that his days as a merchant seaman were not over.

Aboard the oil tanker *Gulfport* somewhere west of Jalisco he missed a step on a gangplank and fell to the deck with such force that he split a kneecap. When I saw him next he was limping, but cheerful. Insurance had taken care of the medical bills, he and Felicia now had a charming daughter, Willie Stumpf had promised $300 a month as soon as *Octopus* showed a profit, and a national travel magazine had commissioned him to write about the San Francisco waterfront. As if this were not enough, *Voyage of the Pelican* would be translated into Swedish. It was strange and wonderful how one's luck could change.

He wrote a colorful description of the waterfront for which he was handsomely paid, so he got drunk and bought a dog. Every now and then somebody who had read the novel or the waterfront essay would compliment him. Once in a while a stranger asked for his autograph. His name appeared in newspapers. A

93

columnist said he was the best writer in California. The public library asked him to give a reading. Felicia was happy. Day by day their tiny daughter Aurora grew more beautiful. Except for the fact that he was having trouble with the second book, life could hardly be better.

The first novel had almost written itself so he did not understand why *Harvest* should be so difficult, but the longer he worked on it the more dissatisfied he became. Ideas evaporated. Words would not fall into place. No sooner did he write a line than he scratched it out. The narrative had no logic. Emotions that he tried to evoke seemed false. He began to wonder if he might be arguing against himself, if consciously he might be opposing his unconscious. He remembered a comment by Jung to the effect that a faulty interpretation encourages feelings of stagnation, opposition and doubt. This, he said, was exactly how he felt, and he thought a change of scene might give him a new perspective on the novel. Unexplored streets, unfamiliar faces—if he could get away for a couple of weeks he might interpret the problem correctly.

He went to Mexico. In Oaxaca he rented an airy whitewashed room with a big overhead fan, a view of the plaza, and a window screen to keep out mosquitoes. He decided to stay for a month because it seemed like a perfect place to work on *Harvest* and life south of the border was cheap.

Oaxaca, he discovered, was full of pleasant surprises. Scarcely had he gotten settled when he met a Sacramento kindergarten teacher on vacation, with the result that he didn't get very much sleep and found it hard to concentrate on the manuscript. Then, during the second week, Oaxaca turned unpleasant. Eighty dollars vanished from his duffel bag. He suspected the chambermaid because she had a key to the room and she avoided looking at him. After a few more days, exasperated and restless, unable to work on the book, he came home. Although he had lost eighty dollars he did receive something in exchange—a stomach disorder that would afflict him the rest of his life.

The first issue of *Octopus* appeared with the title of an essay on Baudelaire printed upside down. Nobody could understand how this happened. The printer claimed it was not his fault. The proofreader said everything had been rightside up when she went over it. The poetry editor, Troy Dasher, said he had nothing to do with printing the magazine, he merely accepted or rejected poems, so he was innocent. Wendy, the part-time associate editor who read unpromising manuscripts, wrote letters of rejection, and made coffee, said she had nothing to do with it. Willie Stumpf accused Bowen, who, as editor-in-chief, must have neglected his duties. This annoyed Bowen, who said he had done everything expected of an editor-in-chief. Besides, it was the publisher himself who had delivered the final proofs to the printer. Why hadn't the publisher bothered to look at what he was delivering.

All of them adjourned to O'Leary's bar where the argument continued. After enough drinks Willie and Bowen vowed to settle the matter outside, so everybody marched across the street to a parking lot. O'Leary's bartender telephoned the police station, which was not far away. A policeman walked over to investigate. The publisher and the editor-in-chief, between insults, had begun shoving each other, so Troy Dasher attempted to separate them just as the policeman arrived and mistook Dasher for the cause of the trouble. In spite of being a poet, Dasher was heavily muscled. When some unknown party grabbed his arm he flung the assailant against a parked car. The entire staff of *Octopus,* as well as the printer, was then escorted to the police station, where the publisher, editor-in-chief, and poetry editor were charged with fomenting a public disturbance.

Not long after this incident a small paperback house bought *Voyage of the Pelican,* which was good news, although Bowen had been expecting a sale to one of the international giants. The first printing would be 10,000 copies instead of perhaps ten times that many, but the size of the printing was unimportant. If the paperback drew a large audience they could go back to press.

Meanwhile he continued to work on *Harvest* and he predicted that it would do even better than the first book. It was going to be a very long novel about midwestern America with dozens of significant characters. Because of the length and complexity there were technical problems, but he felt confident that he would soon have everything under control. In order to receive the advance he had signed a contract, but he wanted his agent to negotiate with the publisher for better terms. This novel, he said, might very well be a classic.

Bad luck came visiting once again. Outside of O'Leary's one night he was stopped by a derelict who asked for money. He responded by calling the bum a bum, and for declaring the obvious truth he got his nose smashed. Nature had endowed him with a beak in place of a nose and the assault crumpled it. However, on his craggy midwestern face it did not seem inappropriate. He never had been vain, not in the usual sense, and except for the humiliation he felt at having his nose bloodied in a street fight the grotesque encounter meant very little. He was vain only of his talent.

The technical problems, whatever they might have been, were at last resolved and he mailed his second book to New York. The manuscript probably weighed as much as a metropolitan phone book because he said it was almost nine hundred pages long. He looked forward to an excited call from his agent, but she did not finish reading it for nearly a month. Then she sent a note explaining that the office had been swamped and she would let him know as soon as there was any news from the publisher.

After a long silence he heard from New York. It had been accepted.

By coincidence, the publication date of *Harvest* was his twenty-ninth birthday. A celebration seemed like a good idea, and O'Leary's bar was the logical place. Bowen invited everybody and told the Canterbury Bookshop to provide a stack of copies, which he would autograph.

He began drinking before the party started. In the past he had been able to drink throughout an evening with amiable sobriety, but he had done it too often. His body could absorb no more. His eyelids drooped and his mouth hung open. In a display of arrogance or contempt he propped his feet on a table, patted his crotch and mumbled that he had written a superb book, a masterpiece. Among the guests was another writer he had always liked; but now, focusing on him, Bowen deliberately belched.

Harvest failed to attract much notice. When the first book came out he was identified as a promising young writer, but not this time. Reviewers were disappointed. One or two offered tepid praise and expressed hope for his next work. When I saw him a few months later I asked if there had been any movie interest. He said an important director was reading it.

He was angered and puzzled by the reaction to his second novel. He had visited a number of bookstores to discuss it with the clerks and he urged them to promote it, even to suggesting window displays, and he autographed every copy in stock so that none could be returned to the publisher. He telephoned book critics to complain that they had not understood what it was about. He said they were fools who could not appreciate anything more complex than a children's story with a moral set in italics. Originality befuddled them. He explained all of this while slumped in a corner of O'Leary's patio drinking beer. Finally the waitress asked him to hold his voice down and keep his boots out of the flowers.

When another issue of *Octopus* rolled off the press everything was rightside up, but Willie Stumpf felt dissatisfied. He thought more copies could be sold if the magazine had cartoons and Bowen told him he should be marketing codfish instead of literature. As a result, the next issue was indefinitely postponed.

Still, the planets must have been aligned in Bowen's favor. A philanthropic organization dedicated to helping artists, writers and musicians awarded him a three-month fellowship at a bucolic retreat in southern California. He had not applied for it; indeed he had never heard of the organization which awarded these fellowships, but he saw no reason to decline a gift. The fellowship did not provide for wives or children, so Felicia and Aurora would stay at home.

When I next saw Bowen he was asleep in a Santa Monica hospital. He had told me to call the foundation if I happened to be in the neighborhood, so I did and was informed that he had been taken ill. At the hospital they directed me to his room. The door was open. When I saw him lying on his back with his face the color of parchment and his hands folded on his chest and that beak of a nose jutting from the blanket like the prow of a sunken ship, I thought he had died. I hurried down the corridor and talked to a nurse. She said he was asleep. I said he might be dead, or almost dead, and perhaps she ought to have a look, but she insisted he was taking a nap. I went back to the room. He had not moved and he resembled a corpse, but I could hear a gentle snoring.

A few days later he was out of the hospital. I found him in a rustic cabin where he was busily typing up a short story. Life in the cabin had stimulated him to write stories, he said. As for the illness, an ulcer had developed during his tenure as editor-in-chief of *Octopus* but it didn't amount to much. It gave his stomach something to think about other than the mysterious Mexican ailment.

He wrote five or six stories while he lived in the cabin. His agent had sold one to a men's magazine for a respectable amount by the time Thanksgiving came around, but the others were gathering rejection slips. An excerpt from his celebrated first novel had appeared in a textbook on the art of writing, which was complimentary, but payment was meager, and royalties had declined to the point that Bowen referred to them with amazement. His ulcer muttered, his entrails bubbled with the Oaxaca flux, and the bank had warned him about overdrafts. He no longer sounded cheerful.

He told me that he had a recurrent dream of silver dollars littering the beach while he floated indolently from one shining heap to the next. He said it was a marvelous dream. Awake, he dreamed that some New York literary panjandrum would discover his neglected second novel, catapulting it to the peak of the best seller list where it stayed month after month. He imagined Hollywood executives wondering if he could be persuaded to write a movie script. Telegrams from Lotusland offered rich contracts, each proposal more extravagant than the last. His career had opened like a morning glory. Why should it fade? He compared himself not unfavorably to Conrad and Melville.

Felicia handed him a cigar on Christmas Day. Bowen was not thrilled. I heard that on the day after Christmas he sold a pint of blood.

And I heard about his affair with the olive-eyed Eurasian girl, Wendy, part-time associate editor of *Octopus*. She had come to the golden state of California looking for adventure. She was in her twenties, although she seemed no more than fifteen, and she must have become pregnant not long after Felicia.

Felicia learned about Wendy. I do not know what she said to Bowen, but he moved out of the eucalyptus grove and into Willie Stumpf's apartment where he was less than welcome. After a series of drunken arguments during which Bowen called his host an illiterate huckster, a mediocrity, a bumpkin, a cultural adolescent, a cartoon-lover, an undergraduate intellectual with a tin ear, and whatever else came to mind, he was evicted. He then lived for a while in the vacant garage of another friend where he started to write an existentialist novel about his experiences aboard the tanker *Gulfport*. His duffel bag and a few other possessions lay on a shelf alongside some camping equipment, a used battery, assorted wrenches, sections of pipe, garden hose, and a sack of fertilizer. His desk was a packing crate. The author himself could be observed seated in a canvas chair on the oil-soaked concrete, fashionably dressed in dungarees, moccasins, and a San Francisco Giants baseball cap. On warm days he typed without a shirt, exhibiting a flaccid paunch for whoever cared to look.

Occasionally he interrupted work on the novel to write a travel essay, which he could do without much effort by recalling the odors and sounds and activities of distant ports and by describing in humorous, picturesque language the human flotsam he had met. And he wrote sketches of small town life, affecting the style of Sherwood Anderson. A few of these sketches sold to midwestern journals, but they reeked of forgery. What animated Bowen to write at a level beyond understanding was the mythic quality of life at sea.

Felicia at last relented, so he moved back into their untidy little house among the trees. When they were first married she had attempted to cook and she had managed to keep the house reasonably clean, but now the center of what had drawn them together was sliding askew. She had put on fifteen or twenty pounds that sagged like tallow from her delicate bones, and her English porcelain face was beginning to wrinkle. Somebody described her as a premature grandmother. Day and night she served spaghetti, Bowen said, and she was feeding Aurora peanut butter sandwiches. He could remember what he had loved about her once upon a time, but it no longer affected him. He, himself, was noticeably less attractive. He had lost a front tooth and in order to save money he did not have it replaced; or perhaps he took pride in his raffish appearance—the reincarnation of Huck.

Now and then some newspaper asked him to review a book, usually a novel about the sea. When *Voyage of the Pelican* was first published he had been called upon frequently, and because he knew the subject his criticism was perceptive. But little by little his reviews grew venomous, as though he resented competition. Then he began to mention his own work while commenting on the work of someone else, so that calls for his service had become less frequent.

However, the gods of Olympus look indulgently on poets and dancers and sculptors and scribblers. Bowen must have been a favorite because he was offered the position of writer-in-residence for a year at a distinguished New England college. Living quarters would be furnished, he would be required to teach a workshop once a week, the rest of the time would be his own. Felicia, Aurora, and the baby could go with him. It sounded like an easy job, the salary would more than pay his bills, and campus life was relatively civilized. He remembered his days at the state university—tweedy professors and sycamore trees and football games and bonfires and pretty girls everywhere—so it did not take him very long to decide. Most of all he liked the promise of so much free time. He hoped to complete his *Gulfport* novel before the academic year ended.

Bowen's reign as writer-in-residence did not go well. It did not begin auspiciously, nor did the situation improve. At a cocktail party intended to welcome him and the new artist-in-residence he got drunk, he neglected to zip his fly after a visit to the men's room, he attempted to kiss a glamorous young teacher of Romance Languages, and he called the artist-in-residence a comic book illustrator who couldn't paint a catsup bottle. At another ceremonial affair he again drank too much and called the wife of the Dean of Admissions a babbling frump. And it was said he became involved with one of the girls in his literary workshop. The college no doubt was relieved when he went back to California.

A few months later Felicia stabbed him. According to what she told friends, he used vulgar language and threatened to strangle her so she picked up a bread knife to protect herself but he paid no attention, which is how it happened. Bowen's account was different. They had argued, so in order to get away from her he went for a walk in the eucalyptus grove. When he got back to the house she came at him with a steak knife in each hand. Whatever happened, Felicia called the police, who dispatched an ambulance to the scene of the crime, and Bowen was rushed to the hospital because he did not have very much blood left.

When I saw him he looked better than he did in Santa Monica. He was flat on his back again but he sounded optimistic. He did not blame Felicia. Neither did he blame himself. I asked how he was getting along with *Gulfport*. He stared at the ceiling with a thoughtful expression and licked his lips as though anticipating a drink. Oh, he said, there were a couple of problems, nothing important. And the ulcer? Oh, nothing to worry about. On the doorstep of middle age with a bad kneecap, watery entrails, fading eyesight, a missing tooth, an explosive stomach, quite possibly a damaged liver, and now a couple of stab wounds, he seemed to think himself invulnerable.

Bowen's publisher rejected *Gulfport*. He was shocked. He had been expecting a large advance. Thousands in the bank would solve nearly all of his problems. There would be no more arguments with Felicia about paying the bills. He would buy a roll of tarpaper and fix the leak in the roof. He would visit the dentist. He would pay off the mortgage. He would get a new muffler for the car which thundered and smoked like an old diesel and swayed through the eucalyptus as though the tank had been filled with whiskey. He might even get a new car. Thousands in the bank would restore his confidence, which had been unspeakably abused. *Gulfport* was a major book, he insisted, maybe the best novel written in America during the past fifty years. The rejection made no sense. And he disparaged a recent novel that had been critically praised, saying the author had a tin ear and the critics should be reviewing science fiction.

The longer he thought about being rejected, the angrier he became, and having worked himself into a rage he decided to commit suicide. His death should be a lesson not only to the idiots at the publishing house but to all the newspaper hacks who had dismissed his second book. After he was gone they would realize their mistake. He pointed out that *Remembrance of Things Past* had been rejected by an editor with a tin ear.

So, one night when the moon was full, he wandered away from the house with a bottle of whisky, a bottle of sleeping pills, and a copy of the scorned manuscript tucked under his arm. When he came to an appropriate site overlooking San Francisco Bay he seated himself and uncorked the whiskey. Some time later he opened the bottle of sleeping pills, washed them down, and stretched out with *Gulfport* clasped to his breast. He would not be found until the next day, which was unfortunate because his death would seem more tragic if searchers discovered his body beneath a full moon, but it couldn't be helped. Next day a peaceful corpse would be found among the towering eucalyptus. News that Bowen had killed himself would stun the literary world. It would be the subject of intense discussion from Greenwich Village to Beverly Hills, and posthumously his novel would be published to enormous acclaim.

I never knew the source of Bowen's romanticism, which had about it the appealing innocence of another era. Stern-wheel paddleboats roiled the Mississippi not long before he was born and perhaps he could see them churning around the bend. Whatever the cause, he lay down that night dizzy with expectations of immortality.

He awoke on a bright sunny morning with birds twittering through the eucalyptus grove and found himself covered with vomit. The pills had made him sick. The pages of his manuscript were scattered, so he crawled around collecting them, and then he decided to read the opening of *Gulfport* to see if it was as brilliant as he thought. The first page proved that he had not been mistaken so he read the next page, and the next, and he did not stop until he had finished the opening chapter. It was good. Here and there a few lines might be improved but they were easy enough to fix, so he went back to the house, took a shower, and started to work.

When we talked about the bungled suicide he remarked that he couldn't do anything right. I don't even know how to kill myself, he said.

He resembled the youth with crystal gray eyes who sat on a steamer trunk in a Paris hotel, but it was no more than resemblance. His eyes appeared rheumy, as though something inside was melting. He wore glasses for reading. His fine tawny hair was a disorganized cobweb. His mouth had assumed the peculiar expression of habitual drinkers and his missing tooth no longer seemed raffish, only disagreeable.

The god of misfits looked down upon Bowen with pity, or maybe it was the god of malice. *Voyage of the Pelican,* by now half forgotten in the United States, was sold to a Dutch publisher. But a short time afterward Bowen's agent called to explain that there had been a misunderstanding. The terms were not as generous as first believed. In fact, the advance against royalties would be little more than a gesture.

He vanished. He had done this before when he was discouraged or enraged, so Felicia paid no attention. Somebody told her that he was loitering around the waterfront trying to wheedle drinks and money from strangers. She seemed unconcerned.

When I saw him again he wanted to talk about the town where he had grown up. He ran the fingers of one hand through his uncombed hair and said the town lay on a marshy point thick with osier. He described the Methodist church and a feed store and chicken coops behind the houses and a Bible with gilt edges. He could remember antimacassars on the sofa in the parlor where shades were always drawn against the afternoon sun, willow branches touching the river, red-winged blackbirds, an old steamboat landing at the foot of Main Street. He talked about people gathering to watch a channel dredge that groaned and thumped and spouted sandy mud. In August the creeks ran dry, he said, and his grandmother would sit on the porch swing with a rag dipped in camphor tied around her head. He remembered whippoorwills and wild geese and the south wind and a clock ticking in the public library. And while I listened I had no idea what he meant. He was talking to someone else—some biographer commissioned to preserve each fragment of his mosaic. His mother belonged to the Epworth League and she had a pink conch shell that gave out the roar of a barbarous foreign sea. His father worked as a Rock Island brakeman. And at the time it made no sense. I understood that he was trying to explain something, but only he knew what it was.

Then he said he might ship out again. He thought he would write another realistic novel like *Voyage of the Pelican*. His stomach lapped over his belt.

Nobody was surprised when Felicia divorced him. Bowen himself was not surprised; he cheerfully admitted that he had not been a faithful husband, that he drank too much, that he had not earned enough. What seemed to trouble him most was the failure of literary critics to understand the significance of his work and public indifference to everything he had written since that first novel. He mentioned Hart Crane plunging into the Gulf of Mexico.

103

That was the last time I talked with Bowen. Considering the number of beer bottles he left on the cliff he must have spent quite a while up there. Just when he made his decision is a mystery because he was alone. Sometime after dawn he took off his clothes and folded them. In each moccasin he placed an empty bottle and before the final step he put on his glasses. When I heard about the glasses, which lay on the sand near his body, I wondered why he had worn them, but of course he wanted to see where he was going.

Nominated by The Threepenny Review

MARABOU

fiction by JOY WILLIAMS

from THE PARIS REVIEW

THE FUNERAL of Anne's son Harry had not gone smoothly. Other burials were taking place at the same hour, including that of a popular singer several hundred yards away whose mourner fans carried on loudly under a lurid, striped tent. Still more fans pressed against the cemetery's wrought iron gates screaming and eating potato chips. Anne had been distracted. She gazed at the other service with disbelief, thinking of the singer's songs that she had heard now and then on the radio.

Her own group, Harry's friends, was subdued. They were pale, young, and all wore sunglasses. Most of them were classmates from the prep school he had graduated from two years before, and all were addicts, or former addicts, of some sort. Anne couldn't tell the difference between those who were recovering and those who were still hard at it. She was sure there was a difference, of course, and it only appeared there wasn't. They all had a manner. There were about twenty of them, boys and girls, strikingly alike in black. Later she took them all out to a restaurant. "Death . . . by none art thou understood. . ." one boy kept saying. "Henry Vaughan."

They were all bright enough, Anne supposed. After awhile he stopped saying it. They had calamari, duck, champagne, everything. They were on the second floor of the restaurant and had the place to themselves. They stayed for hours. By the time they left, one girl was saying earnestly, "You know, a word I like is *interplanetary.*"

Then she brought them back to the house, although she locked Harry's rooms. Young people were sentimentalists, consumers. She didn't want them carrying off Harry's things, his ties and tapes, his jackets, anything at all. They sat in the kitchen. They were beginning to act a little peculiar, Anne thought. They didn't talk about Harry much, though one of them remembered a time when Harry was driving, and he stopped at all the green lights and proceeded on the red. They all acted as though they'd been there. This seemed a fine thing to remember about Harry. Then someone, a floppy-haired boy who looked frightened, remembered something else, but it turned out that this was associated with a boy named Pete who was not even present.

About one o'clock in the morning, Anne said that when she and Harry were in Africa, during the very first evening at the hotel in Victoria Falls, Harry claimed that he had seen a pangolin, a peculiar anteater-like animal. He described it, and that's what it was clearly, but a very rare thing, an impossible thing for him to have seen really, no one in the group they would be traveling with believed him. He had been wandering around the hotel grounds by himself, there were no witnesses to it. The group went on to discuss the Falls. Everyone could verify the impression the Falls made. So many hundreds of millions of gallons went over each minute or something, there was a drop of four hundred feet. Even so, everyone was quite aware it wasn't like that, no one was satisfied with that. The sound of the Falls was like silence, total amplified silence, the sight of it exclusionary. And all that could be done was to look at it, this astonishing thing, the Falls, then eventually stop looking, and go on to something else.

The next day Harry had distinguished himself further by exclaiming over a marabou stork, and someone in the group told him that marabous were gruesome things, scavengers, "morbidity distilled" in the words of this fussy little person, and certainly nothing to get excited about when there were hundreds of beautiful and strange creatures in Africa that one could enjoy and identify and point out to the others. Imagine, Anne said, going to an immense new continent for the first time and being corrected as to one's feelings, one's perceptions in such a strange place . . . And it was not as though everything was known. Take the wild dogs for example. Attitudes had changed utterly about the worth of wild dogs. . . .

Abruptly, she stopped. She had been silent much of the evening, and she felt that this outburst had not gone over particularly well. Harry's friends were making margaritas. One of them had gone out and just returned with more tequila. They were watching her uncomfortably, as though they felt she should fluff up her stories on Harry a bit.

Finally one of them said, "I didn't know Harry had been to Africa."

This surprised her. The trip to Africa hadn't worked out particularly well, but it hadn't been a disaster either, it could very well have been worse. They had been gone a month, and this had been very recently. But it didn't matter. She would probably never see these children again.

They sat around the large kitchen. They were becoming more and more strange to her. She wondered what they were all waiting for. One of them was trying to find salt. There was no salt? He opened a cupboard and peered inside, bringing out a novelty set, a plastic couple, Amish or something, she supposed the man was pepper, the woman salt. They were all watching him as he turned the things over and shook them against his cupped hand. Anne never cooked, never used anything in this kitchen, she and Harry ate out, these things were barely familiar to her. Then, it was really quite a normal gesture, the boy unscrewed the head off the little woman and poured the salt inside onto a saucer.

Someone shrieked in terror. It was the floppy-haired boy, he was yelling, horrified. Anne was confused for an instant. Was Harry dying again? Was Harry all right? The boy was howling, his eyes were rolling in his head. The others looked at him dully. One of the girls giggled. "Uh-oh," she said.

Two of the boys were trying to quiet him. They all looked like Harry, even the boy who was screaming.

"You'd better take him to the emergency room," Anne said.

"Maybe if he just gets a little air, walks around, gets some air," a boy said.

"You'd all better go now," Anne said.

It was not even dawn yet, of course, it was still very dark. Anne sat there, alone in the bright kitchen in her black dress. There was a run in her stocking. The dinner in the restaurant had cost almost a thousand dollars, and Harry probably wouldn't even have liked it. She hadn't liked it. She wanted to behave differently now for Harry's sake. He hadn't been perfect, Harry, he had been a very troubled boy, a very misunderstood boy, but she had never let him go, never, until now. She knew that he couldn't be aware of that, that she had let him go now. She knew that between them, from now on, she alone would be the one who realized things. She wasn't going to deceive herself in that regard. Even so, she knew she wasn't thinking clearly about this.

After some time, she got up and packed a bag for Africa, exactly the way she had done before. It was a gray duffle. The contents could weigh no more than twenty-two pounds. When she was finished, she put it in the hallway by the door. Outside it was still dark, as dark as it had been hours ago, it scarcely seemed possible.

Perhaps she would go back to Africa.

There was a knock on the door. Anne looked at it, startled, a thick door with locks. Then she opened it. A girl was standing there, not the *interplanetary* one but another one, one who had particularly relished the dinner. She had been standing there smoking for awhile before she knocked. There were several cigarette butts ground into the high-gloss cerulean of the porch.

"May I come in?" the girl asked.

"Why no," Anne said, "no you may not."

"Please," the girl said.

Anne shut the door.

She went into the kitchen and threw the two parts of the salt shaker into the trash. She tossed the small lady's companion in as well. Harry had once said to her, "Look this is amazing, I don't know how this could have happened actually, but I have these spikes in my head. They must have been there for awhile, but I swear, I swear to you, I just noticed them. But I got them out! On the left side. But on the right side it's more difficult because they're in a sort of helmet, and the helmet is fused to my head see. Can you help me?"

She had helped him then. She had stroked his hair with her fingers for a long, long time. She had been very careful, very thorough. But that had been a unique situation. Usually, she couldn't help him.

There was a sound at the door again, a determined knocking. Anne walked to it quickly and opened it. There were several of Harry's friends there, not just the girl, but not all of them either. "You don't have to be so rude," one of them said.

They were angry. They had lost Harry, she thought, and they missed him.

"We loved Harry too, you know," one of them said. His tie was loose, and his breath was sweet and dry, like sand.

"I want to rest now," Anne told them. "I must get some rest."

"Rest," one of them said in a soft, scornful voice. He glanced at the others. They ignored him.

"Tell us another story about Harry," one of them said. "We didn't get the first one."

"Are you frightening me?" Anne said. She smiled. "I mean, are you trying to frighten me?"

"I think Harry saw that thing, but I don't think he was ever there. Is that what you meant?" one of them said with effort. He turned and as though he were dancing, it looked as though he were dancing, moved down the steps and knelt on the ground where he lowered his head and began spitting up quietly, like a baby. The black grass winked and glittered with it.

"Harry will always be us," one of them said. "You better get used to it. You better get your stories straight."

"Good night," Anne said. She did not feel frightened. There was an ugly sound in her head was all. It seemed to be falling through her, filling her.

"Good night, *please*," they said, and Anne shut the door.

She turned off all the lights and sat in the darkness of the house. Before long, as she knew it would, the phone began to ring. It rang and rang, but she didn't have to answer it. She wouldn't do it. It would never be that once, again, when she'd learned that Harry died, no matter how much she knew in her heart that the present was but a past in that future to which it belonged, that the past, after all, couldn't be everything.

Nominated by Robert Phillips

MY MOTHER'S SHOES

by ROBERT LOVE TAYLOR

from THE SOUTHERN REVIEW

A BOY OF TWELVE, the year my father was dying, I used to go out to the garage during the summer evenings, just after dusk, and put on a pair of my mother's high heels. I found them in a grocery sack of my sisters' and my outgrown clothes to be given to the Salvation Army. Black leather sling pumps of the style fashionable in the previous decade, the forties, they did not seem badly worn, and they were not so large on me that they would slip off when I walked in them, not with the strap buckled to the last notch. I walked out of the garage in them, and when I reached the street, I could see the cars whizzing past on Robinson Avenue, a half-block away. In the other direction, at the end of a two-block-long row of bungalows, lay a dark blankness.

This blankness was in fact a park, Edgemere Park, where in the daytime I might have gone to climb trees or wade in the warm water of a shallow creek. But at night the park looked faraway and menacing, a shimmering deep pool of darkness. And so I went no farther than the end of the driveway, standing as long as I dared, breathing in the sweet night air. It was a strange, eerie time. Neither a gifted nor a dull child, I craved getting by, preferably unnoticed, but there I stood, risking discovery and certain ridicule—and for what? For the pleasure of it. It pleased me. I don't know why.

Sometime during that autumn the shoes disappeared. The Salvation Army must have picked them up while I was in school. I was sorry to see them go. We never seemed to have enough money, and now that my father had stopped working, there would be even more stringent economies. Mother wasn't likely to throw away another pair of shoes soon. I regretted the loss, but by this time my father's illness had become severe and I imagined that my deprivation might have been ordained as a way of making me pay attention to him and take up the role, as directed by my mother, of man of the family.

Mother worked full-time at Kerr's Department Store and served as our father's nurse all the months of his decline. We children did little to help her. After all, she did not tell us, not for the longest time, that he was dying. He worked too hard, she always said, and when he came home from his office at Oklahoma Gas & Electric one hot July afternoon and said he didn't feel so well, she said he just needed to catch up on his rest. We—my two sisters and I—believed her. But he never went back to work at all. By the end of the summer he seldom left the back bedroom. Some months later we were told he had cancer. I do not know if there was ever any pain. He was a silent, grim man, then as before. At Christmas he went to the hospital and after a few weeks was operated on, and we thought that would be the end of the trouble. We have to hope and pray for the best, Mother said. After the operation, he stayed in the hospital another three weeks before coming home. His body afire with secret wanton rot, he survived the remainder of the winter, lasted through the spring, and died on June 21, 1954, two days after his fortieth birthday, in his bed. Now at last he would rest, my mother said.

The Edgemere section of Oklahoma City where we lived was nowhere near the edge of any mere, which an elementary school teacher had told us was an old-fashioned word from England that meant sea. The park two blocks from our house, with its trickle of red water, was bordered by pleasant, quiet neighborhoods of modest but comfortable homes, most of them one-story, built during the boom years of the twenties, made of red or buff brick, their roofs pitched and pointed to resemble, though surely not intentionally, the little houses that cuckoo clocks inhabited. A few of the buff-brick houses had wrought-iron trim around the windows and along the front steps. Ours was one of these.

The garage sat apart from the house, in the far corner of a small backyard. This garage was filled with my father's things, his

111

electric saw and worktable with its assortment of hammers, nails, screwdrivers, hacksaws, handsaws, drills, and odd tools I never knew the names for. There was no space left for the car. A black Ford, kept shiny and clean by my father, it sat in the driveway alongside my mother's well-trimmed forsythia.

During the warm months, my father labored Saturdays in the yard, mowing and trimming and raking and seeding and fertilizing constantly—so it seemed to me—and our grass was thicker and greener than all our neighbors'. In the cooler months, he went to the garage, kept the jigsaw whining, the sawdust thick in the air. He was skillful, I'm sure, and the solitary labor must have appealed to some deep, long-standing need to quarantine himself. For a time he made little cut-out figures, caricatures he had painstakingly traced from books and transferred to plywood—Dutch boys, hillbillies, cowboys, Old Black Joes, and Aunt Jemimas, which he then sanded, painted at last with brilliant colors, and attached to wrought-iron spikes so that they could be stuck in the ground as decoration for gardens and yards. A gardening supply store where my father bought his fertilizer took some of them on consignment, and a few actually sold, but one day—this would have been a summer several years before his illness—we saw him unloading them from the trunk of the car. There must have been a hundred of them. He installed a few in our yard and rested the others neatly in a corner of the garage.

From the age of ten, I was a paperboy, throwing the *Daily Oklahoman* in the mornings and the *Oklahoma City Times* in the afternoons. My route consisted of an area about fifteen blocks to the south of Edgemere, an older section of the city where graceful old mansions faced tree-lined streets. The trees, mostly sycamores and elms, were the tallest in the city, their intertwined branches making bowers pleasant to pass beneath in the early morning, the light just beginning to flicker through the fat, shiny leaves. Best of all, however, was the depth of the winter before daylight, the tall windows in the mansions still dark, the inhabitants warm in their big beds. I felt as if I owned the streets and the houses, and the life in them could not begin until I had thrown the last newspaper.

The residents of those fifty-year-old mansions I rarely saw. When I called for my monthly payment, servants dressed in black-and-white uniforms came to the door. I seldom saw a car at any of these houses, though they had broad asphalt driveways, brick-columned porticoes alongside the house for rainless, snowless departures and arrivals, and large garages in back, some with apartments above the stalls. Servants lived in these garage apartments, I imagined, or poor relations.

In my family's bungalow in Edgemere, my sisters shared one bedroom, and, after my father took to his bed, I shared the bunk beds in my bedroom with my mother. The small back room, the master bedroom, was scarcely big enough for a double bed. All the rooms had a decidedly cramped feel to them. My father did not, we were constantly reminded, make a lot of money working for OG&E. Mother sold curtains and draperies at the uptown branch of Kerr's, about a dozen blocks from our house. Until my father no longer needed the car, she walked to work every day. There must have been some disability insurance, sick pay from OG&E, but this was not spoken of. My *Oklahoman* money, minus a small weekly allowance, went into my mother's purse.

As I began my route on one of the coldest of winter mornings that year of my father's dying, I saw a figure coming in my direction on the sidewalk about a block away. I stopped dead in my tracks. It was a woman, walking slowly in her high heels, as if afraid of slipping on a patch of ice. There was no ice, though a dusting of snow lay on the frozen lawns of the mansions. The woman wore a long coat with a fur collar. She didn't wear a hat, and her hair was whipped back and forth across her face by the wind. I took her to be my mother's age, or a little younger. At the corner she looked up. That must have been when she saw me for the first time. She stopped abruptly, on the verge of stepping down from the curb into the street. I looked away and began to move again, taking the next folded paper from my bag. I was about a half-block from the corner. After throwing the paper onto the next porch, I looked again for the woman and saw her walking away from me, rapidly, almost running. By the time I came to the corner she was nowhere to be seen.

In the days that followed, I thought little of this near-meeting. I was in the eighth grade, in junior high school, and one of the first boys in my class to persuade a girl to wear his identification bracelet as a sign of love. I had plenty of distractions. In the evenings that we did not go to the hospital to visit my father, I

113

worked hard to complete my assigned chores before my older sister Lila had done hers so that I could beat her to the phone and, in the half-hour allotted to me, listen to my girlfriend, a fast and furious talker, tell me about the day we had experienced more or less together. After that, I joined my younger sister Sandra in our small living room and sat with her before the television set, doing my homework during the commercials and low points in the programs.

Mother went to the hospital every evening, leaving just after supper and returning in time to tell us to brush our teeth and get ready for bed. My sisters and I visited on Tuesday and Thursday evenings, and on Sunday afternoons. Because we had talked so little to him when he was in good health, conversation now seemed unnatural. Usually he was asleep, and we worked on our homework while our mother, with her chair pulled up close to his bed, read the latest *Look* or *Life*.

On some of the evenings when Mother went alone to the hospital, instead of calling my girlfriend or watching television I went back to my room, happy for the time alone there. I liked to read books that I had been given to understand were classics, *The Count of Monte Cristo, 20,000 Leagues under the Sea, The Call of the Wild, Riders of the Purple Sage*. Now and then I was distracted from my reading by the sight of something of my mother's that she'd left hanging on the railing of the bunk bed or on top of the chest of drawers, a pair of nylon stockings or a blouse or underwear. I thought wistfully of the hot summer nights I'd put on her shoes and walked to the end of the driveway and back. And I remembered the woman I'd seen on my paper route, the way she'd walked slowly in the high heels, the fur collar of her coat fluttering in the wind. It was almost as if I believed her to be the self I'd left behind in the summer, the nightwalker in my mother's shoes. I hoped that I would see her again.

One evening I found a strange book on my desk. It was hardbound, black, and at first I thought it was a Bible. But when I picked it up I saw that its title was *Cancer: A Guide*. I sat down and read of a mystery in the blood, a secret born with birth itself, hidden in the dark reaches of gut and bone. I looked at illustrations that might have been of caverns, clouds, tunnels. Then, hearing the door of my father's room open, I knew Mother was coming and so I quickly closed up the book, turned out the light, and bounded up onto the top bunk. I heard her go into the bathroom, and then, my eyes adjusted to the dark, I watched her come into my room, the curves of her body pressing against her flowing nightgown. She believed I was asleep and settled herself quietly in the lower bunk. It was a strange feeling, hearing her breathing. There was a little whimpering sound she made, almost as if she were crying, but it wasn't the same and it never lasted long.

I rose well before her, sliding down from the bunk quietly. I liked seeing my mother sleeping. She slept on her side, facing the wall. It was comforting somehow, seeing her there, sleeping so soundly.

The book *Cancer: A Guide* appeared only that one evening and then disappeared. I guessed my mother must have left it there accidentally and had reclaimed it.

A few days after this, I saw the mysterious woman on my paper route as she walked down the driveway from the garage apartment in back of a gray granite mansion. It was cold and clear, the sky still dark, and stars glimmered through the bare branches of the trees. I stepped behind an evergreen hedge and listened to the sound of her high heels tapping on the concrete. When she came to the end of the hedge she turned in my direction and I decided it best to start moving again.

We almost collided.

She towered over me. Light from the streetlamp made her face very white. I had surely misjudged her age. She must have been closer in years to my older sister than my mother, though certainly no teenager. There was anger in her eyes, but she looked at me for only an instant before spinning around and stepping quickly back towards the garage. Unaccountably, I stayed there watching her. She wore the fur-collared coat, black patent-leather high heels, and carried a large black purse strapped over her shoulder. The coat looked gray in that dim light, the fur collar a dull yellow. When she came to the staircase that led up to the garage apartment, she looked back, though only for an instant, before hurriedly ascending. Now I saw something other than anger in her quick look. I imagined it was a sense of longing, of complicity, and I felt a powerful desire to follow her. But she was gone, and no lights shone from the apartment's windows.

I began to dream of her all day, picturing her as she paused at the foot of the stairs. In my mind I followed her, rose with her into a room dark like the caverns I'd seen in my mother's secret book of cancer.

What's wrong with you, my girlfriend asked during lunch in the cafeteria. Is your father . . . worse?

He was not worse, I said with some vehemence, believing I spoke the truth, for hadn't he always had this sickness in his blood?

She picked up her tray and left. At the end of the day she pressed into my palm my identification bracelet.

I began to live for my mornings among the dark mansions, the thick trunks of the sycamores, the webbed branches, and the last of the winter night sky. The woman I stalked was not, I told myself, my secret sickness, my birthright, not the mystery that lay ready to devour me, body and soul. She was a mystery, yes, a riddle, but restorative, luxuriant, lavishly life-giving.

Mercy Hospital was a three-story white stucco building shaped like a *U*. The Sisters of Mercy, in their old-fashioned black habits, their strange white hats with the upswept, pointed brims, stood behind the reception desk and patrolled the hallways. Watching one of them drift past in the hallway, I imagined her as a young girl, packing away dozens of dresses to be sent to the Salvation Army, then cutting off all her beautiful long hair, shaving her head smooth. It was a peculiarly romantic notion.

We were not Catholics. Mercy Hospital was less expensive than others and closer to our home. Mother took my sisters and me to the First Baptist Church for Christmas and Easter services, but we belonged to no church.

One evening when we entered my father's hospital room, we saw a nun standing alongside his bed, hovering over him. She was tall, and the way she leaned forward you could see her thin ankles and the backs of her well-worn mannish shoes.

Mother motioned for my sisters and me to wait outside.

They're converting him, Lila said as we waited in the hallway. That's why they let him in here in the first place, so they can take advantage of him and make him a Catholic.

Mother won't let them do that, Sandra said.

I agreed with Sandra.

116

Maybe something's wrong, I said.

Brilliant, Einstein, Lila said.

A chubby, red-faced nun came up to us and asked if she might help us find somebody.

He's in there, Lila said harshly.

The nun smiled sweetly and glided away. She had a pretty face, her large eyes clear and blue, and she had looked at me, I thought, with interest.

Mother appeared, gestured for us to come back into the room. The tall nun stood alongside our father's bed, pale and still in her black shoes.

I'm Sister Luke, she said with a pleasant smile. Please come over here.

We had advanced to the center of the room. Mother hung back at the doorway. On the other side of the room, by the windows, my father's roommate lay on his side with the sheets pulled over his head. My father was propped up in bed, but his eyes were closed. No one had shaved him, and the bristles on his cheeks were white and shimmery.

Your father wants to say something to you, Sister Luke said. You'll have to come closer, though.

My sisters, always less ready to obey, stayed where they were, but I did as the nun said. She took hold of my wrist and then with her other hand grasped my father's hand and placed it in mine. His hand was cold. It felt light as a feather. He looked at the nun and then at me.

Son? he said.

It's your son, Mr. Smalley, the nun said. Do you want your glasses on?

He began to pull on my hand, as if to raise himself up.

He wants to hug you, the nun said to me.

I love you, Larry, my father said as I leaned down to receive his embrace. He held me tight, pressing his bristly cheek against mine. When he let go, the nun called for my sisters, who approached him together, as if afraid to go alone. After pulling each of them down into his embrace and professing his love, he sighed heavily and looked at the nun.

There, now, she said, that didn't hurt at all, did it.

The morning after that visit a whiter light shone from one of the windows of the garage apartment. The curtains were pulled

117

back, and I could see the blank gray of the ceiling. In a little while I saw the woman herself. Staring out into darkness from inside a lighted room, she could not have seen me, but I jumped back behind the hedge that had hidden us from each other the day before and waited a few seconds before daring to peek around it.

The light in the window had gone out and she was coming down the stairs. At least I thought I saw her. It was dark, and I did not wait around. I heard the tapping of her heels, but kept my eyes trained on the darkness ahead.

I began to get up earlier and ride my bike straight to the mansion before picking up the morning papers. I stood the bike behind the hedge and crept along the driveway towards the garage apartment. Sometimes the light in the window was on, sometimes not, but even through the darkened panes I imagined I saw movement, deeper shades of darkness that took human form, became a woman, possibly more than one woman. Once she came to the window in a white dress, stood there for what seemed a long time. Another time she appeared in bright red.

Days grew longer, warmer. By the time I came to the end of my paper route, the morning darkness was a faint, rosy grayness. Buds began to swell and glisten at the extremities of the sycamore branches. My father was home again, again in his bed in the corner bedroom. At last we were told he had cancer. But we must never lose hope. Mother bought him a new pair of pajamas made of a lustrous royal-blue material that she must have thought cheerful, but its brilliancy made him look paler than ever. We visited him in the evenings just as when he was in the hospital, entering his room one at a time, Lila first, then me, then Sandra, and sat out our time in a metal folding chair by the side of the bed. He did not speak of his love again, nor pull me to him for a hug. Most of the time he was sleeping, even when propped up, his head hanging to one side and his mouth open.

When it came time to collect at the mansion belonging to the garage apartment, I stood in the bright and broad hallway and gazed at a grand blue-carpeted staircase with white banisters. At the staircase landing a pair of tall, deep-set windows rose up, their white curtains held in place along the sides by a thick golden rope. The air smelled clean and dry.

A few times while waiting, I walked softly and swiftly to the staircase, clasped the smooth banister, and took several steps up, my heart beating wildly, my breath quickening. How easy to continue, climb first to the landing, turn, then ascend the remaining steps to the upper rooms. But, only slightly out of breath, I was back in position near the front door by the time the servant, none the wiser, returned with my money.

School days passed in a blur. I did enough schoolwork to get by, neither failing nor excelling, and I was friendly enough only to keep from being considered odd, without inviting confidence. My teachers remembered Lila, a poor student, frequently in trouble for passing notes or talking in class, and they must have found my mild and quiet diligence a relief.

My father lay in his bed, thin and pale in his blue pajamas. I studied his nose, the blunt tip, the dark hairs extending from his nostrils. Mother didn't have time to shave him daily, and I could see the silver bristles on his cheeks. His fingernails had grown as long as a woman's.

His life was a mystery to me. I knew his birthday, June 19, 1914. I knew he had been born in Stillwater, where his father once owned a small grocery store near the college. He did not attend college. He was twenty-four years old when he married my mother, who was eighteen, just out of high school. This would have been in Oklahoma City. They met, I always understood, on a blind date. There was an older half-brother, Uncle Ferris, in insurance out in the Texas Panhandle, who sent a Christmas card every year. My father's father died of natural causes a few years after my birth, and his mother, my grandmother, lived with a sister in Tulsa. I had been only a few times to the office where my father worked. I remembered it as a large gray room with dozens of desks, a big black typewriter on each desk, fluorescent lights hung from chains all along the ceiling. My father's desk looked like all the others.

I told my mother I did not want to visit my father again. It was a waste of time, since for all I could tell he neither knew nor cared whether I was there or not. I would go again when he was awake, when he recognized me.

If he did not sleep, she said, then he would likely be in great pain.

If I did as I wanted, she said, I would regret it the rest of my life.

One early spring morning as I reached for my shoes in the dark closet, my hand happened to fall upon something silky. It was one of my mother's slips, and, on an impulse that I did not stop to question, I held it up before me. It would fit me, I thought. Just as her shoes fit me so well last summer, this slip would fit me now.

She was breathing deeply, sound asleep in my bottom bunk. It was still dark outside, dark in the room. There was no rush to get ready. I had been rising a good hour and a half earlier than I needed to in order to put in my time at the apartment window. In a jiffy, I took off my shirt and jeans and, after a moment's hesitation, my underwear too. I then tiptoed back into the room, found the panties she'd left on the railing at the foot of the bunk bed, and returned with them to the closet. Listening closely for signs of a change in her breathing and hearing only the same steady rhythm as before, I stepped quickly into the panties, thrilled by the strange smoothness, and then pulled the slip up until I could get my hands through the straps. I rolled up a pair of my socks and tucked them in the spaces for breasts. The fit was fine, as I had hoped. If only I had her shoes, the pretty sling pumps I'd worn last summer. And a dress. Why shouldn't I wear a dress?

I tiptoed back into the room. Sometimes she left her shoes under the bed, but this time she hadn't. Nor had she left her dress on the doorknob. I might find a dress, or a skirt and blouse, in the bathroom dirty clothes hamper, but of course there would be no shoes in there. I had no choice but to go to the back bedroom.

I thought of my father, saw in my mind's eye the blunt nose, the wiry hair in his nostrils, the long fingernails, his open mouth sucking in the air. What if he woke at night, what if these were his waking hours, and I found him wide-eyed, lucid in his wonderful blue pajamas, staring at me? It could not be so, I decided. He was sick. Medicine would keep him in a deep, deep sleep.

I stepped out into the hallway. My sister's bedroom was directly across from mine, the door open. I heard deep breathing, a small whimpering sound like the one my mother made sometimes. I might have gone in their room after one of Lila's dresses, but it seemed more likely that Sandra or Lila would wake up than our father.

I had no more than an hour, I figured, until the darkness would begin to give way to morning light. Quickly then, I approached the closed door of the back bedroom. It opened quietly and I shut it behind me, stood dead still, one hand on the doorknob. I could hear my father's breathing and the ticking of the clock on his nightstand. The air smelled stale almost sour.

His bed was in the corner of the room, placed so that he slept facing the door, with the windows behind him. Just inside the door, to my right, was the chest of drawers, and on my left, no more than six feet from my father's bed, the closet. I knew all this by memory, but I could see well enough, after a few seconds, to take it all in. How was it that this darkness was so transparent? His blinds were pulled up, he never wanted them down. That might have accounted for it. Would the moon still have shone at that early hour of the morning? Light from a streetlamp? I saw him clearly, clearer than I wanted to. His head was turned towards me, his mouth closed, and he was staring right at me.

But I saw no sign of recognition in his eyes. Could he be asleep with his eyes open? His face, even with the mouth closed, looked as expressionless as when he slept. I held my breath, froze, not taking my eyes off him. Something suddenly flashed forth from his eyes. I never saw anything like it. It must have been pain, it might have been terror. It lasted only a second. Then his eyes squeezed shut.

I prayed that they might stay shut, even if it meant he was dead. God have mercy, I wanted that dress, those shoes.

The eyes did stay shut, the mouth dropped open, the blue pajamas shimmered in the filmy dark. He began to snore softly.

At the closet I took the first dress I touched, then leaned down and found my mother's high heels. In the bathroom I stepped into the dress. It went on smooth over the slip, it felt fine, there was the faint scent of my mother, and I smoothed the bodice, the skirt, looked at the dark image of myself in the mirror, the breasts rising the way they were supposed to, the dainty collar trimmed with lace. Then I eased my feet into the high-heeled shoes and when I stood up I had my balance.

I had to watch my step. There were no carpets in our halls and in spots the floor was likely to creak. I kept to one side, on tiptoe, glad of my last summer's practice in wearing high heels. Once in the kitchen, I crossed directly to the back door, unlocked it, opened it as quietly as I could. Then I stepped out into the last of the darkness.

Such a strange, fearsome elation! The leaves on the frail mimosa tree in our backyard looked burnished and lush, the grass glistened, the black Ford sat in the driveway, gleaming and terrible and monumental. I stayed on the grass, the high and narrow heels of my mother's shoes sinking ever so slightly into the ground, the tapered skirt brushing against my shins, the smooth slip cool across my knees, but even as I stepped around the Ford, letting my fingers graze the cold steel, I knew that I was not going to stop when I came to the end of the yard. This was different from last summer. A lovely, dangerous world lay before me, a universe secret and dark and forever. Edgemere! The whirring cicadas might have been the rustling wings of angels—I did not stop to think whether fallen or not. There must have been a chill in the air, but I did not feel cold.

The little houses sat hunched and still, the street curved gently down to the park, and every step took me deeper into the mystery of myself. The high heels resounded on the concrete. I let them sing out. I didn't look back. Ahead of me the trees of the park swayed and shook, as if sweeping the sky of the last of its stars. Resplendent, I was going down into that beautiful darkness.

And that is where I went. That is where I wanted to stay.

When the school year ended, my sisters and I were shamed into helping with the care for my father. Sandra and Lila shaved him and I helped Mother bathe him. She showed me the tube that curled from his penis into a bag beneath the bed, and how to empty the bag and change it. During this last phase, Mother grew more lively and cheerful, a change I attributed to our aid, but it may simply have been relief in knowing that the end was near. At any rate, I felt good about helping my mother, and, unlike my sisters, was not disgusted by my father. He seemed to me more like a great raggedy doll than the grim and distant father I'd known, who in my mind was already dead, might have died the moment he'd seen me coming into his room in search of my mother's dress and shoes. After that, he'd lost the power to frighten me. I grew fond of him.

At the funeral, a Baptist minister obtained by the funeral home spoke of God's love and the sacrifice of His only begotten son. He went on and on. My father, dressed in his gray business suit, lay in front of the altar in a copper-colored coffin with beige satin lining. I had gone with my mother to choose it, an economy model more sturdy than beautiful. My grandmother and her sister, white-haired ladies with canes, and Uncle Ferris, the half-brother from the Texas Panhandle, accompanied by a woman whose platinum-blond hair fairly glowed from beneath a tiny black pillbox hat and veil, sat alongside us in the family mourning area, a booth hidden from the other viewers by shaded glass. In the chapel proper a few people sat scattered about, a neighbor or two, some fellow workers at OG&E, I supposed.

Way out on the far north side of the city, the cemetery had almost no trees. The hot wind blew hard. My grandmother and great aunt wore black stiff-looking dresses. My mother wore navy blue, not the dress I'd worn, but the shoes were the same. She had tied a black scarf around her hair and bought black scarves for my sisters, a black clip-on bow tie for me. I heard Uncle Ferris tell Mother that it was a shame the way lives drift apart. He was holding the blond woman's hand, and she pressed her other hand down on top of her little pillbox hat while the wind kept lifting its black net veil.

The woman in the window never undressed before me, understand. This was no striptease. Nor did I hope for one. If it was myself I looked for, saw, desired, then it was enough to see her in full regalia, just like me, in my own way, when I circled Edgemere Park in my mother's shoes, a soft spring breeze pressing the skirt against my legs.

After my father's death, when I took up my position near the hedge and looked upward into the woman's window, I began to feel afraid—not of being discovered, it was more as if I feared *not* being discovered. Even when this modest fear became purer, more general, more intense, as it shortly did, I kept up the ritual. It became a test of my courage.

Then one morning a man appeared in the window. I drew back, thinking him my father. He was thin, stark naked, his body very white, hairless, the penis thick and risen. Turning away from the window, I saw him leaving the apartment, dressed now in a gray suit like the one my father was buried in, his black shoes shining. I ran to the station house, certain that he followed me, but he did not.

In a dream, my father wanted to tell me something, something important, but he could not say it, and I woke with tears flooding my eyes, with the keen sense that he had been here, here in my room, close.

I woke possessed by restlessness. It was only two o'clock, but I rose, made my way through the dark house to the back bedroom. I had no illusion that my father would be there. At first I thought my mother might not be asleep, and I waited behind the door, listening for sounds. But it was very quiet in there. When at last I thought it safe enough to peek around the door, I could see nothing at all. I stepped inside, stark naked, silent in my bare feet on the smooth planks of the floor, and made my way to the closet by touch. Then I stood very still until my eyes adjusted to the dark. My mother slept to one side of the bed, facing the wall. A breeze blew through the open window and the air smelled clean and fresh. She had scrubbed the room top to bottom and put up lacy curtains.

I dressed in the garage. When I was halfway to the park, a car came towards me and I jumped behind the nearest shrubbery. The car drove past without slowing down. It was not a police car, but I was badly frightened. I had certainly been seen, and wouldn't I be reported now as a prowler, a peeping Tom? I took off the heels and began to run back to the house, hitching up the tight skirt above my knees.

A light was on in the kitchen window. I crept up to it and peeked in. My mother sat at the kitchen table in her robe. She smoked a cigarette and sipped from a coffee cup.

I slipped back to the garage, took off the skirt, the blouse, and hung them carefully on my bicycle handlebars. It would have been smart, I realized, to have brought a change of clothes with me to the garage. Mother might not have missed me. Something else had awakened her. She would not have thought to check my room. Restored to jeans and T-shirt, I could wait until daybreak;

throw my papers as usual, then appear at breakfast as if nothing out of the ordinary had happened. She would not miss the clothes, she had other skirts, other shoes, and there would be plenty of time after she had gone to work for me to return what I'd taken.

Then I saw the row of paper sacks and remembered: my father's clothes. She had set the sacks out in the hall and asked me to carry them to the garage, six of them altogether. I had leaned them against the closed door alongside the unsold yard ornaments, and now I went to them and found a shirt, a pair of slacks, a belt. Nothing fit, but I rolled up the trouser cuffs, the sleeves of the white shirt, pulled the belt in as tight as I could. It was not the same as wearing my mother's clothes. There was no transformation. I felt foolish.

But I could ride my bicycle in them, and that is what I did, placing my mother's clothes in the basket attached to the handlebars and slowly walking the bike to the edge of the driveway before jumping onto it and pumping as though my life depended on it. The loose-fitting trousers flapped in the wind like flags. I rode without thought of destination, whipping around the park and onto dark side streets. I wanted only to be far away from that house, far from the light of that window, that kitchen where my mother sat in a haze of cigarette smoke, making her way back from the dream that had awakened her, a dream like my own, I imagined, a dream of my father.

Then I came to the streets lined with tall trees and dark mansions. Out of breath, my legs aching, I stopped, dismounted at the driveway that led to the garage apartment. There was no light in that window, but I waited, sitting on my knees in the grass beside the hedge. After a while, rested, I took my mother's clothes from the bike basket and put them on again. As I folded my father's clothes, tears came to my eyes. I had an image of my mother doing the same thing, folding one shirt after another, the white shirts he'd worn to work, the useless socks, the absurd ties, the boxer shorts. Still the sacks filled up, six of them. And then there was no more and she stopped, she looked into the closet, she closed and opened the empty drawers. What was I looking for? What did I imagine I would find there? The sadness of these questions overwhelmed me. I sobbed furiously. Then I stopped.

He is not here, I told myself, my father is dead and I am not my mother.

I stepped away from the hedge, took a deep breath, walked up to the front door of the mansion. The bell rang out so loud I was sure that all the world heard it. But nobody answered. I rang it again and again but nobody answered. I tried the door. Locked, naturally.

And so I walked boldly to the side of the house, passed through the brick-columned portico, my mother's shoes clicking on the asphalt drive-way, and then I stood poised at the steps that led up to the entrance of the garage apartment, my hand on the cool wrought-iron railing. I hesitated only a moment before ascending. The night air was warm and sweet. The trees seemed to whisper, every breeze-touched leaf a tongue. I understood that secret language. It spoke of my beauty. Each step I took seemed further proof of it, a beauty born of my own grief, of a sorrowfully personal mortality. To live was no more than a fatal birthright. The miracle lay curled in the blood alongside the calamity.

I reached the door, knocked loudly, waited, knocked again. No light, no sound. I tried opening the door. Like the other, it was firmly locked. No one would open it, no one was inside. The realization seemed final, absolute.

I turned away and knew that I would go there no more. Day was breaking by the time I stepped back inside my parents' house, but everyone was sound asleep. I had plenty of time to change into my own clothes, ride again to the mansions and deliver the morning newspapers.

What else is there, after all, but to go back to the small, safe houses of our mothers and fathers, rest ourselves as long as we can in that sad clarity, that somber subduing light? We live on the edge of a fathomless dark sea. No mansion on earth can contain us.

All the rest of that long summer of my fourteenth year, day broke in our house as naturally as sin. In the garage, awaiting the Salvation Army, the row of paper bags filled with my father's clothes sat next to the stacks of his toothless hillbillies, his grinning Aunt Jemimas. Inside the house, my mother rested nightly in the bedroom my father had occupied, and my sisters, dead to

126

the world, afloat in their own dark dreams, their cagey sick-
nesses, slept on and on. Son and brother, I vowed to stay with
them. You're the man of the house now, my mother kept saying,
and so I was.

Nominated by The Southern Review

YARN WIG

by LOIS-ANN YAMANAKA

from MICHIGAN QUARTERLY REVIEW

My madda cut our hair so short.
Shit, us look like boys, I no joke you.
I mean more worse than cha-wan cut.
At least cha-wan cut get liddle bit hair
on the side of your face.
Us look almost bolohead'
and everybody tease us, *Eh boy,*
What time? or *Eh boy,*
what color your panty?

I figga my madda sick and tired
of combing our long hair every morning.
She make us all line up
and us sit one by one on her chair
by her make-up mirror. She pull
and yank our hair just for put um
in one ponytail, but I tell you
she pull um so tight,
our eyes come real slant
and our forehead skin real tight.
Ass why now we get boy hair.

One time we stay walking home from school
and Laverne Leialoha calling us snipe
because us Japanee and we get rice eye
she say. Then her and her friend write

S-N-I-P on the road with white chalk
they wen steal from school.
Us dunno if she teasing us
SNIPE for Japanee or
SNIP for our boy hair.

My madda she start for feel sorry
for us but what she can do?
She no can make our hair grow back
all long again. But she go down Ben Franklin
one day and come home with plenty black yarn,
the thick kine. She make us yarn wigs,
I no joke you, with short bangs
and long, long yarn hair in the back,
all the way to our okole.
Just like the high school cheerleaders or
like Cher on the Sonny and Cher Show.
My sistas and me make the yarn hair
come in front then we flip um back
like Cher do.

The other day my madda took us store
and all us wen wear our yarn wigs in the car.
We stay letting the yarn blow out the window
cause so long. But when we was ready
for go out, I wen fast kine pull off
my yarn wig. Shame, eh? More better
they tease me. *Eh, boy* than *Eh, yarn for hair.*

My sistas, they so stoopid,
they wear their yarn wigs in the store.
The lady at the soda fountain
tell, *Oh ma goodness! So cute!*
Harriet, try come, try come,
and the lady from the fabric side
come running over. *Oh-la cute yo daughtas!*
I kinda stay thinking maybe
I should of wore my yarn wig too.
The fabric lady tell my madda,
You made um? Oh you so cle-va wit yo hands!

And they so adora-bull.
My sista start bringing her hair
in the front and acting like Cher.
My other sista pull all her hair on one side
and start acting like she looking
for split ends and her too go fling
her hair back. Me, I start feeling
more bolohead. I look at myself
in the soda fountain mirror
and order my vanilla coke.
My sistas begging my madda
buy yellow and orange yarn
for make like Bewitched and Lucy.
Me, I pulling my bangs real hard
and the hair by my neck.
Gotta grow longer.
Fast.

Nominated by Michigan Quarterly Review

ISLAND OF THE RAPED WOMEN

by FRANCES DRISCOLL
from VOLT

There are no paved roads here and all of the goats
are well-behaved. Mornings, beneath thatched shelters,
we paint wide-brimmed straw hats. We paint them
inside and outside. We paint very very fast. Five
hats a morning. We paint very very slow. One hat
a week. All of our hats are beautiful and we all look
beautiful in hats. Afternoons, we take turns:
mapping baby crabs going in and out of sand, napping,
baking. We make orange and almond cake. This requires
essence and rind. Whipped cream. Imagination.
We make soft orange cream. This requires juice
of five oranges and juice of one lemon. (Sometimes
we substitute lime for the lemon. That is also good.)
An enamel lined pan. Four egg yolks and four ounces
of sugar. This requires careful straining, constant
stirring, gentle whisking. Watching for things not
to boil. Waiting for things to cool. We are good
at this. We pour our soft orange cream into custard
cups. We serve this with sponge cake. Before
dinner, we ruffle pink sand from one another's hair.
This feels wonderful and we pretend to find the results
interesting. We all eat in moderation and there is no
difficulty swallowing. We go to bed early. (Maybe, we

even turn off lights. Maybe, we even sleep naked. Maybe.)
We all sleep through the night. We wake eager from dreams
filled with blue things and designs for hats.
At breakfast, we make a song, chanting our litany
of so much collected blue. We do not talk of going
back to the world. We talk of something else
sweet to try with the oranges: Sponge custard.
Served with thick cream or perhaps with raspberry sauce.
We paint hats. We paint hats.

Nominated by Volt

THE CHAMBER

by STUART DISCHELL

from COLORADO REVIEW

"For years I waited for this to happen to me.
It was my precious secret, the affair I imagined
Before falling asleep. Then my dreams would
Terrify me. All night I swam in my sheets.
Sometimes thinking about the future, I would rise
In my office and knock the wooden door or the frame
Of the window. Looking down I would see one
Rolling across the street or being pushed
With a patient smile. Then I would knock
Wood again. It went on this way for years.
People believed I was merely superstitious.
A funny little man with peculiar habits.
That's the way people treat artists. Yet,
I understood their behavior—I had nothing
To offer. Once I won a trip to London.
I went alone. I was grateful for the double seat
And even had the stewardess bring me double portions.
When we landed at Heathrow, I would not stand up.
I waited until the passengers left the plane
And still I would not stand up.
The stewardess asked if there was a problem.
When I told her she could not hear me.
I watched as she watched my lips and frowned.
An attendant came and lifted me into a wheelchair.
He chatted at me. I liked his British accent.
Near the baggage claim area I felt the urge

133

To rise. I don't remember what I told him
But he stopped the chair. He shouted for me
To stop but I broke into a trot, took my bag
From the carousel, and climbed into a taxi.
Everyone watched as I sped away. I was amazing.
That was the first of what are called episodes.
Others are less memorable yet always occurring
In some public place: a museum, a restaurant,
A rest room. And people always wanted to help.
I did not mean to disappoint them or refute
Their kindness. I can still see that dear, tricked
Look cloud their faces as I made my recovery.
But they were not relieved. I found myself
Told not to enter certain establishments,
The proprietors acting downright hostile.
I never said a word. I just lowered my head,
The bald spot glaring back their own reflections.
Eventually, I was fired from the firm where I worked.
My superiors believed I was no longer promising
And that I had a bad effect on the younger men
Just up from college. They called it retirement.
Now I am doing what I have always anticipated.
At night the various moths are attracted
To the light of the window. I draw them in my mind.
Here is the lesson I have learned from life:
I took the wrong road but finally came home.
I read somewhere about a statue inside
A stone. This is what I have done. My work
Of art. I have carved at myself these many years
While I have posed for a statue inside a stone."

Nominated by Edward Hirsch, David Rivard

RIDERS TO THE SEA

fiction by MARIA FLOOK

from BOMB

Bᴇʟʟ ᴡᴀs fighting a sex hangover as he fixed a fried egg sandwich. He was feeling unsettled and wanted to line his stomach before he resumed his evening schedule at the Narragansett. He scored the egg with a spatula; the gold pillow wobbled then steadied, its lacy albumen white as a doily.

His knees turned hollow and tensed back each time he remembered the CVS girl from the other night. They parked the car at the Cliff Walk. He let her out of the passenger side and she came right along with just her fingertips alert in the palm of his hand. Her jeans had zippers at the ankles and she ripped each tag, one cuff then the other. The twilight lingered reflected on the sea. She made him acknowledge his first view of her, the labia's pink crest, sudden, symmetrical as a tiny valentine. Then he looked away. He felt it in the small of his back, in his legs, he felt the sting in the arches of his feet.

He adjusted the toaster. The electric twists glowed. Then a neighbor kid ran past the window, notching left and right and screaming in crimped bleats. Bell snapped the dial on the stove and went outside. Some neighbors had stepped onto their lawns to see whose boy was having the trouble. Bell looked down the string of white clapboard houses which ended on First Beach; nothing had changed much since he was small. He tucked the spatula inside the mailbox and followed the people down to the water. A group had assembled at the edge of the sea; a few men waded in ankle-deep. Thirty feet out, a wind-surfer tacked back and forth in silent, accurate swipes.

135

The woman was face-down, her chestnut hair filtered forward then pleated back in the calm water. The waves came in like clear rolls of Saran before puddling on shore. The sea hardly tugged her. A wreath of suds, pearly as BBs, surrounded the body and tagged the rocks. He couldn't see her face or guess her exact age. She was wearing a cocktail dress stitched with fancy beadwork. Sewn in undulating lines over her hips, the beads reflected the sun in shifting gradations of light like the contrasting whorls in polished marble. This marble effect made her look like something which had toppled from a pedestal. The woman rode back and forth in six inch increments over the pebble sheet. Bell saw it was the agitation of the brine, the brine forced through the cores of the miniature beads on the woman's dress which had created the foamy scud on the surface of the water.

Bell was living at home again with his mother and his sister Christine, coming back to Newport after three months in a Navy brig at Portsmouth, Virginia. He had hoped to wrangle some duty in his home town. He asked for the Construction Battalion Unit where he could do his hitch building piers or grouting the swimming pools on base. Instead, he had been assigned to the Naval Supply Center in Norfolk. He never shipped out. He never looked down at the chop from deck or followed sea birds until they disappeared on the horizon line. He worked on a terminal in the bowels of a warehouse, cataloguing dry goods and food supplies for the carriers. He couldn't tell the weather, what clouds stumbled overhead, tinting the sea. All day, he was under the fluorescents.

He began to do some wagering, and some simple pilfering. It wasn't much, just what he could get into Eric's Plymouth once or twice over weekends. Mostly, it was cases of cigarettes which they sold to Richmond Vending. After his time in the brig, he wasn't surprised by the General Discharge. It's abrupt language was stinging even without being accusatory. He accepted that. In just two lines of print it was all over.

He tried to adjust to hours in his mother's house—scents from the kitchen, yeast cakes soaking, knotted rolls swelling like broken knuckles, the floor always gritty with cinnamon sugar. He hated to hear the same low thump of the radiator building with steam, the pipes knocking room to room, and then subsiding. The vision of the drowned woman was a refreshing surge, washing through the catalogue of family accessories in his childhood house. Even the public landmarks of the town, which he had always respected, added a cloying poignancy to his return. All of his old haunts flipped before his eyes like lantern slides or stereoscopic pictures: the old Viking Look Out Tower, the Mt. Hope Bridge with its green lanterns, then the Providence skyline, the State House with its needle spire injecting the horizon.

The crowd on the beach had adjusted to the visual impact and had started vocalizing. A man questioned the idea of an actual drowning, the woman could have been dumped. They said she must be a Boston whore down for the weekend. There were always illicit odd jobs during the off season when summer boutiques fell back on drug trafficking. Motel bars hired girls to do some modeling; they arranged elevated runways by just lining up three or four billiard tables. There were one or two video pioneers manufacturing hard core. They were working out of the Sheraton, and the same up at the Ramada. Bell's stomach was still empty, but he wasn't hungry. He felt weighted, almost sleepy; the abrasive slushing of the waves over the beaded dress was hypnotic. Because the woman had washed ashore so close to his house, he couldn't resist thinking it might be a commentary on his arrival. He studied her body. Bell saw she had a little mole half way up her thigh, just at the hem of her short dress. He saw it, then flicked his gaze farther out. It was restful to study the horizon, letting it snag and scurry. Then he looked back at the woman.

An Emergency vehicle drove up the beach. The paramedics flipped her over and tried to revive her, by rote theory, before lifting her onto a gurney. The wheels of the gurney left tiny furrows in the sand, but the tide was coming in, erasing wide crescents. Bell was impressed, but he couldn't figure out what left him astonished. He envied the woman's anonymity. Her suspended identity enriched a ballooning awareness, a raw knowledge—that nothing has meaning.

He thought of a bar trick he liked to perform for the girls. He could do it all night with just a pack of Salems and a sixty-five cent Krazy Wand bottle. He takes a drag and fills a giant, erotic bubble with exhaled smoke. It drifts into the tables of ladies. The mirrory circle swirls, quivers eye level, like the taut lining of a dream, the same dream, until it erupts and the smoke disperses.

When he returned to the house, his mother was in the kitchen stirring a pot, her hand making a figure eight, then tapping, then twisting. The spoon on the enamel rim resonated on the spinal nerves and Bell walked over and took the spoon out of his mother's hand. She took it back. Divorced from his father for years, she was still upset if she sometimes saw him on the street. She told Bell that she had met his father at one of the rotaries and they had to steer around the circle together for a few moments, jockeying for position. Bell told her to pretend that his father doesn't exist. She reminded Bell that they lived on an island, after all, and they couldn't always avoid one another, could they?

Then he heard his sister, Christine, drive up the oyster shells with her boyfriend Miller. Christine worked days at Raytheon. She seemed different since he'd last seen her. It wasn't anything he could put his finger on. Her face was a peculiar contradiction; she looked both expectant and sullied. As if expectancy itself was what tainted her. Bell didn't imagine she could have changed too much since high school. She maintained a serious, collegiate aura although she didn't go on to college. She had a habit of biting her lower lip, organizing her thoughts with her teeth clamped down on the same red swell. In Bell's absence, she had joined the local Latin League, going to monthly pot lucks with some steeped-in-culture oldsters and scholarly kids interested in the Roman lifestyle. She tried to explain to Bell about the saturnalia. Then, she was a new member of the Newport Community Theater where she had been asked to star in a one act play. She showed Bell the flyers advertising the production. 'Kristine Bellamy in Riders to the Sea, by Irish playwright J. M. Synge.'

Her name had been spelled with a "K." Bell approved of the change, telling her he never liked the "christ" in her name. He saw that she carried a spinning wheel back and forth to the rehearsals. The first night he was home, he watched his sister leave the house with the little wooden contraption, a wheel and a spindle. It gave him a start. Yet, she was still wearing her David Bowie tour jacket, scuffed leather, scabby at the elbows, a relic of the seventies. The spinning wheel lost its clout against the rock 'n' roll souvenir and the contrast pleased Bell.

Christine introduced Bell to her new boyfriend, Miller, who she had met at the Community Theater. Miller explained to Bell how he changed the colored spots and moved the flats back and forth with a crew of aspiring teen-aged actors who didn't always get the parts they wanted. "Idle brats," Miller called them. Miller came often to the house to prompt Christine and help her rehearse her lines for Riders to the Sea. Bell wasn't pleased to have Miller around when he wanted to settle in with his mother and sister.

Bell described the drowned woman on First Beach and waited for the women's reactions. Christine looked at him and saw he was evaluating her, so she didn't say anything. His mother asked him one question: Did we know the girl? Then she went next door to discuss the news with her neighbor who had signaled to her through the facing kitchen window.

When it was just the three of them, Miller admitted he wished he had seen the drowned woman. "Nothing like a body in the surf," Miller said.

"What do you mean, nothing like it? Are you crazy?" Christine asked.

Bell squinted at Miller, trying to see where this was going and he pushed it along. "Miller's right about that. It's a seventh wonder."

"An impressive sight, isn't it?" Miller asked. "More lyrical than a body on dry land. Like a message in a bottle. There's a mysterious connection, a romantic spell, like a tryst between the victim and the person who finds her. Who found the woman?"

"A kid."

Miller said, "Yeah, well, but you were down there. You had a part."

"I felt that," Bell said, "like I'm initiated."

"Exactly! It's a tingle," Miller said.

"She was like some dish from Atlantis," Bell went on, teasing his sister.

Miller discussed local catastrophes, boats going down, a couple of notable shootings, Sunny von Bulow, and the six or seven yearly leaps from bridges.

"Hey, who writes the Crime Report, is it you?" Christine rolled her script into a tight tube and pointed to Miller who had seated himself at the kitchen table.

Miller talked all that time but never looked directly at Bell. He talked about the drowned woman as if he was teaching a class on it. And Miller looked too old for Christine. He had stiff ashy hair

139

which formed three or four stalactites across his shoulders. He smiled at Christine, showing teeth which were harnessed in clear plastic fencing, some kind of invisible orthodontics to correct an overbite. A progressive decision for a man his age, he told Bell. Miller slouched with his legs extended deep under the kitchen table, a posture, Bell believed, which should be reserved for family members only.

When Miller stretched his arms over his head, Bell glimpsed a peculiar device belted at his waist. He wore some kind of hospital gizmo. It was a tiny box, the size of a pack of Winston Kings. A small display screen shimmered while an emerald dot was pulsing to prove its battery pack was A-okay or to provide some other light-coded information. Bell was trying to remember what he knew about modern medical technology when Christine told Bell that the box was Miller's "Insulin Infusion Pump." The pump regulated a steady feed of insulin through a little tube taped to Miller's abdomen. The idea disturbed Bell; he wasn't alarmed about the man's problem, but he realized Christine had been privy to this tube inserted in Miller's belly. Bell saw that this high-tech malady might be an attraction for Christine. Christine had always suffered from the moral surges of someone like Clara Barton. Her lovers seemed to have chronic maladies, a skin condition or a joint replacement. Then, she dated new arrivals, Cuban boys and Cape Verdeans with English as a second language; there was always some obstacle she enjoyed tackling.

The current thing, a diabetic stage technician. For someone suffering a condition, Miller appeared self-assured and arrogant. Thin and sallow, he looked utterly confident, svelte even, in his underweight condition. His smile, reinforced with plastic brackets, had a sinister depth. He had Christine up against the GE, kissing her, the buzz of the Freon increasing. Bell took the keys to the car and looked back once, hoping his sister had disentangled, but she wasn't rushing for his sake.

He drove his mother's car the full perimeter of the island. He went up West Main Road watching the late sun touch long ribbons on the bay, wakes from tankers and little frothy bows behind pleasure boats. He came back on East Main, seeking blue splints of the Sakonnet all the way down. He drove out Ocean Drive where breakers crashed against the jetties in bright crescents, glassy as chandeliers. He loved the spectacle of the sea, the ornament of its lighted spray against notches of granite. After seeing something like that, he sought the smeary ambiance of a tavern. It was the tiled bar at The Narragansett, black and white inches of cracked ceramics like a littered shoreline and stale spills puddled around the table legs.

"They're all gone now, and there isn't anything more the sea can do to me." Christine was just coming in the door, home from Raytheon. She was in character, the keening voice of an Irish matron whose sons have all been drowned. Her authority always surprised Bell. She took the spinning wheel from the closet and went into the living room. Bell watched as she placed it on the floor and the wheel revolved slowly. It was like something he might see at the helm of a small ketch. She wanted to rehearse while spinning a snag of yarn and she asked him if he would read the lines and cue her.

"This play is in Irish?" he asked her.

She told him, "Don't be stupid, of course it's English, but it lilts. I'll show you." She recited a phrase, an insistent querying dirge. "Everything sounds like a question," she told him. "The words go up at the end, the sentences just keep ascending like climbing switchbacks."

"No kidding?" he said.

"There's someone-in after crying out by the seashor-ir," she recited. The words were echo-y, lifting at the final syllables.

"Okay," he said.

"He's gone now, and when the black night is falling I'll have no son left me in the whar-ald," her voice climbed and faltered, climbed again.

Bell read from the script like a mechanic running his eyes over a Parts and Service ledger in the Metric System, rubbing his chin with the back of his wrist. Christine enjoyed his shyness and she let him founder.

" 'Riders to the Sea' is supposed to be a tragic play," she told him. She wanted to share the winey taste of the lines, and she told him the words should feel exciting on the tongue like capers or wild mushrooms.

He asked her, "Why are they doing this one? Why not the usual 'West Side Story?' What about 'Hair'? "

141

"This is a real play," she told him. "You know, there are just two themes in life. No musical soundtracks necessary."

"What themes?"

"Love and death."

"When did you decide this?" he asked her.

"We're all born with the secret," she told him.

Christine wasn't just teasing. Her remark emerged whisper-smooth, the way a U-2 rises all glossy and serene in the middle of a giant swell.

"Real drama," she told him, "Is pain kept brewing all the weeks before the curtain goes up so that no one can misinterpret pain as performance. It's supposed to be pain alive."

He wanted to get out of the house. Christine was tilting something. She looked pale and eerie, but maybe this was from working deep in the windowless complex at Raytheon.

He cued her lines. It was a depressing story. All the men drown and the women are left weeping before a rough-hewn coffin. "This is a little hard to swallow," he told her. He told her that he was happy she was just practicing at it when sooner or later it gets dark on its own. "Don't ask me what I saw in jail. Not just the crowd on the inside, I'm talking about the families who come to visit. Talk about the sad truth."

Christine nodded, she was trying to picture the unhappy relations queuing up outside the prison doors. "I would have visited you, Bell, if it wasn't Virginia. Didn't I come to see you all the time at the Training School?"

"I'm not complaining," he told her. He was wondering. Maybe acting in a tragic one act play can make a girl responsible and wary. "This Miller dude," Bell told her, "what's the story with him?"

Christine turned her face to the window to secrete her grin. The beach light touched her profile as it reached into the house, splicing through glass curtain pulls and lifting the grain on the woodwork. Bell saw Christine was pleased that he worried about her, or perhaps she was pleased, simply, when she thought of Miller.

She began again. This time her voice was too high, the sing-song of leprechauns. She halted mid-sentence and started over. Finding the right pitch, she recited a long passage and tried her

142

best to keen at an appropriate octave, with the complexity of a vibrating cello string, the way her director had explained it should sound.

He was in the first booth at the Narragansett Tavern. He liked to watch the door sweep open and ratchet slowly back. He glimpsed the harbor outside, a dense stand of masts like a glaring aluminum atrium. The girl from the CVS drug store was rolling a ball point over the curve of his knee, inking a burning dot on the stiff denim of his line-dried jeans. The other week,he had found her sorting the magazines in the front of the store. Stacking the older issues on a trolley. He asked her what she did with the old issues. Do they get recycled? He took a heavy issue of Computer Shopper out of her hands, thick as a phone book. She didn't say anything as the weight was transferred. She looked back in a steady, instinctive perusal of his face the way a bird and its worm exchange a moment of awakening.

"We send them back on the truck," she said after a while. She looked pretty young. But youth is a pie with many slices. She told Bell, "I can punch out for an hour at about seven-thirty. Come get me if you want. Or do you just want one of these periodicals?"

"I'll be back," he had told her. He was smiling. He liked the way she had said "periodicals," as if she was some kind of librarian. No names were exchanged. He didn't tell her his name was Bellamy, Bell for short, and she seemed just as happy to stand, unidentified, in the center aisle surrounded by waist-high stacks of glossies.

She was finished writing her telephone number along his inside seam and he told her, "You could have spared my mother the annoyance. Besides, I have a photographic memory."

"Really? Well, what's my number then?" she said. She flattened her palm against his eyes.

He recited the telephone number.

"God, that's scary," she said. She didn't look scared.

"Lucky try," Bell said. It was easy to please this girl. He didn't have to encourage her. She sat next to him pushing her cuticles back as if her fingertips were a key to everything. She wasn't like Christine who might get bored without conversation. Christine might demand to play cards or challenge him to match historical data from the last three decades of rock 'n' roll. Christine once asked him, "Who was the first truly androgynous star?"

"Mick Jagger," he said.

"Oh come on, he imitated Little Richard."

"Are we talking about eyebrow pencil? Patent leather?"

"No, you know, it's like they could be singing to boys *or* girls."

"James Brown."

"I don't think so," she said. "He goes almost in drag, he's got that cape. But that's not what I'm talking about."

"You're right, James Brown is too athletic. Slides across the stage on his knees. You mean someone like Bowie." He thought this was what she was leading up to. Her idol.

"A chiffon scarf can say so many things. Around someone's neck, it's innocence. But chiffon tied around the waist, you know, drifting there, it's so decadent!"

"Christine—"

"God," she said, laughing, "the roots are deep, really. It goes back to ancient culture, like the saturnalia."

When he was in the company of a thriving slut like the CVS girl, why was he dragging his sister into it, trying to nestle her image against the drug store clerk? The CVS girl already failed to intrigue him beyond his first inspiration which was never a thrill if left entirely to its own design. He might go with the CVS girl again. For a couple of hours, park on a side street near the Cliff Walk. Relief, without an immediate rekindling of tension, is often a disappointment.

Never calling it forth, still he saw the dark fleck on the drowned woman's thigh. Its tiny circumference seemed to recur in his vision like a vitreous floater or a snag in the retina. He faced his companion. She wet her lips and waited. He spoke and her eyes squeezed shut in tight winces of approval. She agreed. It didn't matter what he was saying.

His father was standing in the kitchen holding a heavy paper bag. The bag was leaking from its bottom folds and Bell could see from its dripping mass that it must be some two-pounders. His mother had the big speckled kettle whining on the stove. Christine was peeling the wax paper from a pound of butter. She put the pale block in a saucepan and adjusted the gas until the flame

144

steadied. She set the burner very low, using her expertise so that each flame kept separate lifting from the jets, like the beads of a blue necklace. The butter started to slide in the pan.

"To celebrate," his father announced.

Bell looked at his mother, but she didn't seem put out by the intrusion. She accepted his father's presence in her kitchen now and again the way she was tolerant of plumbers, electricians, painters, anyone she had to incorporate into her household for small allotments of time until maintenance was complete, a repair job finished. She showed no familiarity, yet she tried to stand at ease, without knotting her apron too tight as she might do in moments of distress.

"Supper is a surprise," she said.

"Are you staying to eat, then?" Bell asked his father.

"Oh, no. I just brought these over for you and Chrissie. Your mother's got one there, if she desires."

Bell lifted a heavy lobster out of the paper sack. "This one's mine," Bell said, trying to keep the talk going. "And for you, Christine?" Bell reached into the bag and pulled another one forth. "This one's seen it all." Bell held the lobster high so everyone could admire it.

"His big claw looks funny," Christine said, seeing the lobster's aggressive, thumping arms, its large, palsied claw.

"It's a fighter," his father said, looking back and forth between his son and daughter. "Vinnie Pazienza."

"The Paz." Bell was smiling.

"12th round," Christine said, "Ding." She lifted the lid off the big pot.

The lobsters went in the kettle and the water stilled for a moment before churning back. Bell's father said his goodbyes. Bell walked him out to the street and drummed the trunk of the car as he drove away. When he went back in the house, Christine was arranging newspaper over the kitchen table, opening the sections and layering the wide sheets. "Look at that," she said to Bell, her fingertip touched the newsprint. It was a picture of the drowned woman at First Beach. The photo was from Con-Temp, a temporary office pool where she had been on the roster for a year. The woman's name was Kelly Primiano, from Medford.

"Irish Italian," Bell's mother said. "Where was her luck that day?"

145

"If she's half Italian that cancels out the luck factor right there," Bell said.

"Says here she wasn't drunk. No bones broken." Christine read the print. "Her parents say she was a good swimmer. They taught her in Marblehead every summer."

"You can be an excellent swimmer, but if it's too far to swim, you might as well not know how," Bell said.

"Are you saying she tried to swim the cove?"

"Maybe she was pushed off a skiff," Bell said. "Anything—"

Christine read some more, "There wasn't any fluid in her lungs."

Bell dropped his face down to the sheet of newsprint. "Shit. She didn't drown, then. See what I'm saying?"

"She wasn't *dressed* for the beach; it must have been something awful. Maybe she just slipped and hit her head on the rocks," Christine said.

Bell looked at the face in the newspaper. Her hair was twisted in two elegant braids high over her forehead as if she was going to the opera. He thought she looked Lace Curtain but must have crossed the tracks at some point in time.

"Says here, she was engaged," Christine said.

Bell said, "Is that so? Who was the lucky guy? Davey Jones? Man 'O' War in her trousseau. Honeymoon cruise on the Titanic." He listed the possibilities until his mother set the lobsters in the center of the table. Bright shells steaming, long red whiskers tilted at odd angles like sweep second hands on a nightmare clock.

Bell discovered a Navy friend had been reassigned to The Naval Underwater Systems Center in Newport, a good job in combat research and electromagnetics. The assignment came with a nice duplex in re-landscaped Naval Housing. Bell left messages for his friend, teasing him about his fat job, but none were returned. He thought he would drive over there and he decided to take Christine and Miller. Maybe they would be sandblasting a destroyer at Pier I and Christine could take a look at that. He drove his mother's Buick and Christine pounded the center arm rest closed so that they could all sit in front. Cracker crumbs and stale cookies sifted over the vinyl, and Bell wondered why his mother's world was always defined by bread stuffs, a branny litter of sweets and biscuits.

Miller complained about the sweets and he teased Christine, accusing her of trying to tempt him.

"You can't eat a cookie?" Bell asked Miller.

"It isn't the best thing for Miller," Christine said.

There we are, Bell was thinking, Clara Barton. Then Christine was taking it even farther, suggesting that Miller's desires didn't reside in cup cakes and candies. Christine seemed electrified, giggling each time Bell turned the wheel and his elbow knocked her. Women love to be centered between two men. It makes them feel on top of the world. Now and again, even with the motor humming, Bell heard a blip from Miller's tummy pack.

He turned into Gate Seventeen, but there were some MPs checking decals and stickers. They weren't letting vehicles come on base. An official Bronco tugged around the Buick and headed down the road leading to Coddington Cove, but Bell was directed to turn his car around.

Slow flushes bloomed and receded, bloomed again at Bell's throat and over his cheekbones. He didn't give the fellow his name or rank, or bother with explanations about his past connections with the Navy. He turned the car around and drove away. Christine cleared her throat. She tried one small apologetic cough to relieve a general indignant feeling, but it didn't help.

Miller said, "Anyone drives on base, what's the problem, Bellamy?"

Of course it had nothing to do with Bell's General Discharge. There was probably some reason why they were sending people away. They might have the pot-sniffing dogs going around, or maybe they were spraying grass seed on the lots or painting the curbs. Bell told them, "Do we care? Do we need this crap?"

"Let's forget it," Christine said.

Miller said, "I don't understand. Since when do they send people away?"

Christine tried to shush him, but he stopped on his own and fiddled with the lapels of her blouse. Bell tried to ignore it. It was jokey and innocent, but it irritated him when it went on for too long. He drove through town and stopped in the Almacs parking lot. He got out of the car and walked across to the CVS. He came back with the girl. She trotted behind him removing

147

her grey smock. She looked bewildered but pleased, shaking her head, letting her curls flop side to side. She scanned the parking lot to see who might acknowledge her. She knew she was leaving her job for this impulsive, hotted-up guy and it must look interesting. Imagine, a man coming in the store, tearing her free from her maddening job? She told them she had been collecting the expired Easter cards from their plexiglass bins then sorting and inserting new cards for Mother's Day.

She started right in. "I *hate* working the card display. It takes me forever. I have paper cuts, see these poor fingers? You know, the envelopes—like fucking razors!"

Christine and Miller shifted to the back seat. The CVS girl took her place beside Bell. Bell revved the engine and thumbed the radio dial as everyone settled in. He turned out of the parking lot onto Bellevue Avenue. "Well, what do you want to do?" he said, but he was just being polite.

"What about the Green Animals?" Christine said.

"Christine, how many years have you been going to see Green Animals? Every single year of your life, am I right?" Bell said.

"It's beautiful there," she told him.

The CVS girl said, "Are you talking about those sculpted bushes? I've never been up there to see those."

"Forget it," Bell said.

They drove past the famous mansions, most of them acquired by the state. Bell slowed the car as they approached the driveway where an heiress had steered a sedan over her chauffeur as he opened a gate. It was an old love story but it afforded new remarks as they rolled past the spot. The murder location gave them a giddy surge as they left Bellevue's heavy arbor and the street jogged onto Ocean Drive. They were out of the proper town and snaking up the shoreline. The sea's white light washed through the windshield.

"Well? How many times have we driven out here? Only a zillion times," Christine said to Bell, but her remark drifted. They were looking at the first glimpse of the sea at the turn-around at Bailey's Beach. There was a strong, sweet scent coming in through the open window. It was the narcotic spell of early plankton blooming. Bell understood that the plankton bloom was a biological phenomenon having to do with chlorophyll and photosynthesis. It was a simple process impelled by the sun, but he

148

felt indirectly involved. As if by some collective subconscious, the sea's "self" and Bell's dreamy stasis culminated in this deep rejuvenation. He argued that anyone born and raised beside the sea must suffer. He felt his lust grow razor-y, his daydreams intensify, wavering through harsh stages of melancholy.

"A sign of spring," Bell said, trying to subdue an explosive coronary rhythm which started to crush the breath from him. The scent was so luscious, he rubbed his hand over his face as if dusting sugar from his lips.

"It intoxicates me," Christine admitted to Miller. "You never think of the sea as a kind of garden, all floral like this."

"It's peaking," Bell said, "like a thousand water lilies—"

"I don't see lilies. Where?" the CVS girl said. Miller leaned over the front seat and tapped her shoulder. She turned and shrugged in benign agreement. She wrinkled her nose once, puffed in and out trying to track the scent that Bell was describing. "Everything smells like *Giorgio* to me," she told them. "A lady was spritzing it on herself at the counter."

They parked the car in the empty lot at The Beach Club, a private string of pastel cabanas, still boarded up for the winter. There was a stiff wind, but the sun felt strong, falling in broad plackets of peachy light. The sand was extraordinarily hot for a day in mid spring, and the heat rose to shin-level. They walked four abreast, the women in the middle.

"He basically *kidnapped* me!" the CVS girl told Christine.

"God, what did your boss say?"

"What was she going to say? Bell looked intense," the girl said. "I didn't think we were going for a walk on the beach! I would have stayed where I was. I make four seventy-five. That's an hour," she confided to Christine, but she punched her small fist into Bell's side, digging her thumbnail into his ribs and cranking it a quarter turn.

"Here," Bell told them. He climbed onto a grouping of boulders and granite formations which made a natural breakwater into the sea. Giant ledges of rusty shale ascended like drunken stairways right and left. The surf sliced over the misshapen pillars and sloshed into its hollows dragging ropes of effervescent foam. Sudsy lines extended far out. The water was so aerated, the place smelled of extra oxygen. A central configuration of rocks formed irregular bleachers around a deep chamber where the sea

149

crashed inward, doubled its pressure and shot upwards through a narrow fissure. The small opening was like a whale's breathing hole. The place was called Spouting Rock, a local perch for teens who used its unpredictable force for threats and dares.

Christine sat down beside the blow hole. She rubbed her fingertips over its stony lip, inserting her pointer to the second knuckle. She looked distracted by something far out on the water as she fingered the blue-black opening. Her fingers probed and swirled over the slick rock until the men couldn't hide their discomfort.

The CVS girl pulled her jersey over her head to feel the sun. She was wearing an underwire bra, and its ribs rode up until her breasts were sliced across, making four even lumps out of two. She tugged the bra back in place and threw her shirt at Bell. He caught the jersey before it fell into the water. Christine looked at Miller to gauge his reaction, or she was trying to find her own response. She unbuttoned her top button and lifted her shirt off. Bell thought she was just trying to keep up.

He didn't want to stare at her and he studied the water. A large bank of waves was coming in and it would cause some action at Spouting Rock. It was so utterly familiar, these procedures. He saw the undertow pull back and the surface flatten. For a few seconds, nothing. The swell ascended in frothy notches, wobbled and shuddered in a dead halt before beginning its advance. Building a high curl, its wall looked green and corrugated as a carport awning. Bell thought of the drowned woman, her beaded dress, variegated and marbled like the rocks, as if she herself might have broken off this reef and washed onto First Beach.

"Here it comes," Bell shouted out, pulling his sister to her feet. The sea crashed into the trough, smacking the planes of rock like pistol shots. The level ascended, rising up until the full force of the wave exploded from the crevice where Christine had been seated. The spray shot up twelve feet, feathered left and right in different tugs of wind. The girls squealed and the men yanked them out of its circle. Miller touched his hip to see if his insulin pump was wet. It had been spared. The CVS girl saw it; she recognized the box. "Hey, I've seen one of those at work," she told Miller. "Is that one of those electronic blood pressure kits, is that it? Have you got hypertension?"

150

Miller started to explain to the girl. He walked her over to the craggy shale ladders. He put his arm around her bare neck, letting his wrist swivel on her shoulder as he talked. He strummed her hair away from her eyes and pulled her close, into his medical confession.

"He's telling her his symptoms," Christine said.

"What are his symptoms?"

"Weakness, blurred vision. He could go blind, you know?"

"He just looks lovesick, if you ask me," Bell said.

Christine watched her boyfriend with the other girl. Christine was smiling. Bell admired this. He didn't feel like walking over there to claim the CVS girl for himself or to get Miller back on her account. Christine walked out a tiny natural bridge to another huge boulder. Bell followed her out. She was reciting lines when he came up beside her. The wind erased her words and she turned around in the other direction. She faced her brother.

"They're carrying a thing among them and there's water dripping out of it and leaving a track by the big stones."

"Don't you know your lines by now?" Bell had to yell.

"Leaving a track by the big stones," Christine repeated.

"Must you always—"

She was laughing. *"The big stones*—just like these," she said. She toed the granite with her sneaker.

He watched her profile, the wind lifted her weft of blond hair until it flared level. "What are we doing here with these people?" Bell asked her. "These geeks? What are we doing here? With them?"

"Oh, Christ," she said, looking out at the water. She was trying not to listen.

He squared before her. He put his arms around her waist, crossing his fists at the small of her back. He cinched his wrists tighter and held her without the imprint of his hands. She was beneath his chin. "What are we doing?" he said.

"Meaning?" she said. Her eyes looked startled, the pupils swirled open but she kept her face level, steadied. The slight translucent down at her hairline was electrified by the sun; her eyelashes blazed like tiny welders arcs.

She bent her knees and crawled out from under his arms. She laid her palms flat against his biceps and shoved him lightly

151

across the rock. She told him, "You're just getting adjusted to home. Shit. Everything's a Three-Ring, that's what you used to say."

Miller was calling to them. He was having some sort of panic spasms and his arms windmilled in two directions.

Bell went down to where he was standing.

"She's fucking with me, man," Miller said. "She's took my insulin pump and won't let me have it."

Christine descended carefully from the boulder. She reached under her shorts and tugged the elastic leg of her panties, letting it snap.

"So you took it off? Are you supposed to take it off? What happens to your blood?" she said.

"I was showing it to her," Miller said.

Christine said, "Since when do you disconnect it?"

"Wake up, Chrissie," Bell said.

"What do you mean, wake up?" She looked at her brother and back to Miller. She saw Miller was wearing his Nike sweats inside out.

Miller said, "It was nothing, Christine. Just nothing."

"Not worth the effort?" Bell said.

Miller didn't protest the assumption.

"Since when do you take it off for that?" Christine said.

Bell examined his sister. Then he looked for the CVS girl and saw her leaning against the car in the beach parking lot. Her arms were crossed tightly at her bosom, the way girls fold their arms when they're ready to go home.

"Is that your gizmo? Right there?" Bell pointed to a rocky ledge where the girl had propped the insulin pump. He lifted it off the granite niche and tossed it to Miller. It fell in a weightless arc and landed in the water. The little box drifted back and forth in one of the frothy gullies between land and sea.

"Nice," Miller said. "That's just wonderful. Just what am I dealing with here? Do you have the hard cash to replace something like that? That's what I'm asking—"

"Did we ask you to get undressed?" Bell told him.

Christine looked over at the CVS girl and waved. The girl knew it was a snub; she shifted her legs and looked in the other direction.

"Maybe you can get the box."

"That's crazy. I've got the insurance. Let's just travel. I'm ready," Miller told them.

"Tell you what. I'll race you for the cost of that thing. Swim out, touch the mooring at Bailey's, turn around, get back. Ten minutes. If you win, I pay for the machine. Even-steven. Time us, Christine." He pulled his jersey over his head and the wind snapped it until he wadded it down.

Miller turned to Christine but her eyes were squinting and unreceptive. Her face showed a refined acknowledgement of something. Miller said, "Does your brother want me to race him to that mooring? Is he serious?" he said.

"That's the request," Bell said.

"Sorry, my friend," Miller said. He tried to edge past Bell.

Bell put his arm out. He grabbed Miller's throat, half-serious, pinching the windpipe with his thumb and middle finger. Bell wiggled the ribbed cartilage left and right, like a toilet paper tube, until Miller started coughing. Bell might be reaching his maximum capacity for self-control and the other man recognized that Bell was nearing this boundary.

Miller pushed his sweats down and stepped out of them. He marched around the ledge of rock, searching for a way down into the trough. The water was rough. He turned back. "Fuck you," he told Bell but he was looking at Christine. "I'm not going in that Mix-master to please you."

"What about Christine? Here's your chance to make it up," Bell said. He was marching Miller backwards on the ledge.

"You want me to jump in that icy water?"

"Does he have to?" Christine said.

"It's a free world," Bell said. "Do whatever you want." He turned away from Miller and let the two of them discuss it.

A retired couple, exercising their dog, arrived at Spouting Rock. The dog climbed the boulders, its nose brushing side to side for mollusk scents. The couple were surprised to see Miller without his clothes.

"The Polar Bear Club, are you?" the man asked Bell. He had to shout over the surf.

"That's right," Bell told him. "The initiation stage. It's a closed session, try not to gawk."

The man stopped coming when he heard Bell's tone. He watched from a distance. Bell's grave, no-nonsense dementia was

153

beginning to show. He was shifting his legs, stepping in place. He clenched his fists at intervals and some surface veins had engorged along his pectoral ledge, his dark nipples flared. The stranger steered his wife by her elbow and they walked off. The dog raced ahead.

Christine found her shirt and slipped it over her head. Bell looked at his sister's lover; his penis was screwed close inside the scrotum, his teeth were clacking, an inaudible chatter of strikes and pauses as he pulled the fleecy side of his sweatpants right side out.

"Pants on, pants off. Can't decide what to do with it?" Bell said.

"You're sick!" Miller said, shivering in large, convulsive shrugs as he dressed.

Bell looked out at the sea. A tanker was coming in by Brenton Reef; it was carrying a full load and rested flat as a domino. Closer in, there was something in the water. A pale form rolled on the waves, taupe-colored, like a raincoat. Bell watched the waves fill the fabric in fleshy billows before shooting past. He remembered the way the drowned girl filled his thinking, devoured that entire morning when he found her and kept eating into his mind, even now, days later. The garment surged forward on a swell, it took the curve of a hip, then flattened as the wave eased underneath.

"What is that?" Miller said.

"Something or somebody?" Christine said.

"It's just a sailcover. A tarp, I guess. It's trash. This is becoming a nautical waste heap. Jesus—what comes and goes in the water. Things wash up and you don't always need dental records to figure it out," Bell said. He studied the ragged sheet as it opened and folded, accenting the voluptuous depths which carried it forward. He was taking his shoes off, toeing one heel loose then the other. He pushed his jeans down.

"What are you doing? You can't swim today," Christine told her brother. "The water's too cold."

Miller said, "Oh, but it was okay for me—"

"I'm going in." Bell removed his jockeys and dove from the rocks into the sea. Christine picked up his briefs and collected them in her right hand. She walked to the end of the jetty to keep sight of him. He was swimming towards the mooring, but he swam right past its rusty sphere and shifted in another direc-

154

tion. He headed towards the mysterious cloth. He swam in smooth aggressive strokes as if he could swim a long time, perhaps he could swim far beyond any return to land. He wasn't trying to worry his sister, but he knew she waited. He felt her longing like a vibration in the water. It seemed to help his rhythm; his kicking was silky and powerful although he was getting tired.

The scrap was a loose-weave sheet used to repair dragger nets, something makeshift and discarded. It's grommets were knotted with nylon wire that feathered in the surf like a colossal hydra. Bell circled the torn square as if it was marker for a particular disaster in a man's life. Its ghost outlines flowered, palpitated and contracted in mockery of the living. He tried to sink it. Free it from its endless float. He shimmied onto the netting, but it disappeared under his weight, retreated to the deep like a frightened pneuma. It wrapped his ankle as he kicked, fanned out behind him like a train, then swirled to the surface again.

The Irish girl floated, lofted in his retina's mirror-y sea. Seeing that kind of thing once was plenty. Her body, its helpless curve against the shore, everything, even the tiny decals on her fingernails. Glossy as a photograph. Her body washed in, it conformed to a few general expectations, but her spirit collected or dispersed, where? He couldn't imagine. He had no imagination for *that*. Ordinary silver nitrate could never etch a picture of heaven. He preferred to think of the live girl, her summers at Marblehead. What was her line of work? Was she in the profession? Did her innocence cease-up, suddenly, or was it a gradual decline?

Bell tried to gather the unmanageable netting and tow it into shore. Despite its transparency, its coarse knots, the sheet was too difficult to maneuver and he had to leave it. He worked to get back to the rocks. The rip current made swimming hard. When he pulled himself out of the water his flesh was pink from the effort, he felt a tingle of sweat beneath the crystallizing salt scum. He picked up his jeans and put them on, forgetting his underwear. Christine twirled the waistband on her pointer finger and let them sail. Miller tried to lead Christine back to the car. Her dramatic handling of her brother's briefs made Miller question out loud his luck with women. Why did Christine have to insult him with such inventive gestures? Miller told Christine, "I'm going. Now. Fish or cut bait." She waited for Bell to lace his shoes.

155

Christine looked at her brother and smiled. She started to recite her lines, her voice silky and true to her role. *"There does be a power of young men floating around in the sea—"*

Miller touched his forehead with the back of his knuckles. "You're a sad story. The two of you. You're both really sad."

At the car, the CVS girl climbed in the back seat with Miller and Christine rode in front. The girl wanted to return to her job and Bell let her off at the drug store. He drove down Memorial Boulevard. He watched his sister's profile and bounced the heel of his hand on her knee. "Christine. Green Animals?"

"The topiary? You want to go there? You're not just being nice?"

Bell told her he was giving it another chance.

She smiled and watched the other way. "Look, there's Pop," she said, pointing to a car in the next lane. She started to wave but her father didn't see her. "In his own world," she said.

"It's the same world," Bell said.

Miller jumped out at the next intersection and he left the car door swinging. Bell watched the light change, then he shoved the gas pedal just-so until the door came back and the lock caught.

Nominated by Pat Strachan

MY FATHER, DANCING

fiction by BLISS BROYARD

from GRAND STREET

MY FATHER AND I used to dance together in the kitchen be-
fore dinner. I grew up with the kitchen radio always on, tuned to
a local R&B station. The habit got started with the dogs; my
mother said the music kept them company when we were all
away for the day. When I was small enough still to like being
picked up, I shimmied in my father's arms while he performed
an improvised two-step. Later I squirmed out of his grasp and
made up my own steps, ducking out of the way of pots as my
mother moved from refrigerator to sink to stove.

When I was old enough to be snuck into bars—"She's with
me," my father would tell the bouncer with a sly grin—we con-
tinued dancing to the sounds of stompy live bands. At these bars,
dancing was serious business. We sat at a table, a bottle of beer
in one hand, the fingers of the other tapping out a rhythm, the
bony crack of our thumbs on the edge of the table giving an ac-
cent sharp as a cymbal crash. And then we were up, pushing our
chairs back, no word exchanged, but both responding to some
tightening of rhythm or a deepening in the bassline. That mo-
ment reminded me of the way our dogs on the beach would sud-
denly begin to run down the sand at a breakneck clip, running
toward something that seemed to be attached by an invisible
string to a part of them not yet bred out.

I relied on this silent method we had of communicating, so I
didn't know how to talk to my father when he was lying in a hos-
pital bed, slowly dying of cancer. I hung over him, unable to

157

leave, like an insect caught in a spider's web, thrashing uselessly. I watched for the tiniest movement, a gesture, a raising of his eyebrows, anything that would tell me about what I meant to him.

On those dance floors over the years, we told each other more about ourselves than in any conversation. I mimicked my father's movements, and when I had gotten it right, I felt suddenly that I had been dropped into his body for a moment and knew his pleasure at pushing out on the floor a rhythm that brought the music inside of him. I used these occasions to test him, too. As my body grew and pushed out in new places, I wriggled these parts and tried on different movements, the way I would try on new clothes. He was my first male audience, and I used him as a mirror to understand what I looked like to the world. His eyes told me what worked and what was too much, until I settled into a rhythm that suited me. It seemed natural that I should learn these lessons from him. Once my father told me that he wanted to be the first man to break my heart, because then he could ensure that at least it would be done gently. I thought about this during one of the many hours I spent sitting next to his hospital bed holding his hand. As I waited for some sign that he was aware of me, I thought it had boiled down to this: all I wanted from him was a simple squeeze of his fingers. As I waited and did not receive any sign, I realized that he was breaking my heart and it wasn't gentle at all.

My mother would watch our dancing at these bars from the table. Usually a woman friend would have joined her, and they would talk, their mouths lifted to each other's ears, hands cupped to their faces like they were telling secrets. My mother liked to dance too, and at times, when I was younger, I wondered if she was jealous. But now I could see that she must have liked to watch us, her husband and the daughter they had made, proving out there on the dance floor the success of their lives together.

Sometimes in the hospital my father and I talked. Or rather, he talked. He told stories about when he was young, women he dated before he met my mother, friends he had who were, I knew, now dead. As he spoke, he stared slightly below and to the left of the television set. Once I moved behind him so I could match my line of sight with his. Maybe, I thought, the sunlight coming in from the large windows was catching this patch of white wall and giving it a suggestive sheen. But it just looked blank to me. It seemed he was seeing his life projected onto this wall and was giving it voice. I listened for my name and, when I didn't hear it, told myself that he just hadn't gotten to me yet. Once in a while he turned toward me and asked if it was time to go yet. I misunderstood the first time and tried to reassure him with what would become my mother's and my refrain, "I'm right here. I love you."

"Oh, stop with your bromides!" he answered. "I'm a busy man. Get the car and let's go. Let's go! Let's go!"

I quickly learned to lie and would say that we were leaving any minute. He would forget after a while or go back to telling stories about his life.

One day, while I was riding the bus to the hospital, a blind man sat in the seat across from me. I noticed him at first because of his sunglasses, which were French and very expensive, and which I had coveted in a shop earlier in the summer. Then I noticed his stick and wondered if someone had helped him pick out the glasses. As we rode, he rubbed his foot up against the pole separating his seat from the seats next to him and also stroked it furtively with the back of his hand, from knee to shoulder height. The other riders stared out the window or read or focused blankly on the space in front of them. It struck me that the blind man was trying to make sense of the world around him. As I watched him, I thought about sitting with my father in the hospital, about how I continued to bump up against the fact of him lying there, through my conversations with the nurses about his temperature, his platelet count, and how the night had gone, through the hospital food that we ordered for him, though he couldn't eat it, and which I ate. When his friends came to visit, I waited for them to turn back from the windows as they wiped the tears from their eyes. I struggled to see the shape of what would happen as it loomed, invisible, in front of me.

Sometimes I saw things too clearly. One day my mother and I were helping my father roll onto his side so that the nurse could rub lotion on his behind, where the bedsores were worst. I held his thigh firmly to keep him in place. His lower body had become bloated with fluid. My mother cradled his shoulders in a

159

hug to keep him on his side and said, "Come on honey. Hug me back. That's it." When I removed my hands, their imprint remained, each finger clearly outlined. My hands are large, like my father's. He once said we were descended from road workers and our palms were made to crush rocks. The sight of my mark on him shocked me out of the inertia into which fear had pushed me in the recent days. I looked at the mark again and glanced at my mother and the nurse, guiltily, lest they had seen what I had done. I rubbed my father's thigh, trying to erase my fingermarks. This was not the impression I wanted to make.

After my mother and the nurse left the room, I sat on the edge of my father's bed and held his hand between mine, so that my hands were flat and covered his completely, front and back. His hands didn't seem so large anymore. The skin had the softness that babies and old people share. I thought, "Here is something useful I can do. I can protect this hand." I talked of things we would do when he got out of the hospital. How we would dance together again. I told him that I had discovered a new band for us called Tower of Power. They had a terrific horn section and good conga drumming too. Maybe tomorrow, after he had rested, I would play the tape and we could crank up the bed. He could dance, I told him, the way we danced in the car during long trips, just moving his shoulders and clapping out rhythms.

When I walked into his room the next morning, my father asked me to come to his bedside. He hadn't said anything to me directly in days. He pointed toward the closet and whispered, "My pants."

I pulled down a pair of sweat pants that were folded on the top shelf. "Here they are, Dad. They're right here," I said. I shook them out and handed them to him.

Then I took the tape out of my pocket and put it on the player, the volume turned low. "This is the band I told you about yesterday," I said. "They're called Tower of Power." I pulled the folding chair out from the corner, opened it, and placed it close to his bedside. I tapped my palms in time to the music on the top of his blanket. My father stared down at the sweat pants in his lap. I turned up the volume a little more. He turned the pants slowly in his hands, pushed his fingers through the cuff of one leg and looked up at me.

"You want to put them on?" I asked.

160

"Yes. Yes," he said. His voice was hoarse with annoyance, as if I'd asked an unreasonable question.

"Dad, I don't think that would be a good idea. You have all these tubes down there." He pushed the sheet covering him down to his belly. I tried to pull it back up. "I don't think I could get them over the tubes."

"Get some money from Mommy." His voice was low and hard to hear over the tape player. I craned my neck forward so our faces were very close, and smelled the heady staleness that had become my father's scent. Each time I smelled it, the truth of him lying there flashed through me like a painful forgotten memory. "Get twenty dollars," he said, "and give it to one of the attendants to go buy some nail clippers. Harry would do it. You know, the little guy with the mustache."

"Nail clippers? You want to cut your nails?" I saw that they had gone unattended.

"No, no. Why can't you listen?" He clenched his jaw and spoke through his teeth in a harsh whisper. "To cut the tubes. You can cut the tubes with nail scissors."

I tried to explain that I couldn't cut the tubes, that he needed to stay there until he was stronger. My voice had a whining hysteria to it as I hid my fear behind the cover of an urgent rationality.

"No, Kate. I need to go home." Morphine had made his pupils very large. He looked as if he were trying to stay awake.

The rails on the hospital bed were raised. I stood up to rest my hands on either side and lean over him. I told him that I knew he wanted to go home and added that he would go home soon but he had to stay here for now and get better. "Dad, don't you want to get better?" The panic I had been trying to hide crept into my voice and filled the white room. There was nothing in the room to absorb it: no colorful rug, no family photos on the wall. The knickknacks my mother was always discovering at flea markets were not covering these tables. There was only a naked cleanliness and order. Everything was white, and the machines around his bedside were ticking in an urgent steady tempo. I looked out into the hallway for someone to interrupt this moment. My father stared up at me, his expression shamelessly pleading, like that of a junkie. I have always had trouble telling people "no," and I realized that my father knew this and that that was why I had been singled out to take him home.

"I can't, Dad," I said again, as much for myself as for him.

One of his hands rested on the bed rail next to the folding chair where I had been sitting. He now gripped the rail with both hands and tried to pull himself to a sitting position. He placed one hand over the other and rose toward me. His head hung back loosely from his neck. As he pulled harder, his torso began to twist toward one side of the bed. Under his arm's lean covering of fat and skin, I could see the stringy fibers of his muscles stretching. "Dad!" I said, not being able to stand it anymore. I rushed for the button to elevate the head of his bed. The hand rails slipped through his fingers. He sank back and the rising mattress caught him.

He looked at me and reached out, swatting the empty air as if trying to bat away some invisible adversary. His hand settled on my shoulder, and I was surprised by the strength in his fingers as he pulled me toward him, bringing my ear to his mouth. I was conscious of keeping my face relaxed as his scent pressed in on me again.

"Please!" he said, and there was nothing I could do for him. I drew my head back and lifted his hand from my shoulder. His arm hung suspended between us for a moment. His watch, the strap secured on the tightest hole, slid down toward his elbow. Finally his hand dropped to his side.

The cassette was still going, and the saxophonist played a bluesy solo. It was the kind of thing my father liked. The intensity of the music heightened. The sax player blew slow high notes. I got up from my father's bedside, walked across the room, and looked out the window. I placed my hands on the sill and rocked my weight gently from foot to foot.

Soon after my father was diagnosed, we went together to the movies in Harvard Square. We were early and he took me to one of the small parks in the Square to show me a band he had discovered. The band was made up of two guys on drum kits, another on rhythm sticks, and a fourth who played two conga drums. The musicians stacked rhythm over rhythm surrounding a collaborative beat. One drummer stood apart from the others. With his head down and his long brown hair curtaining his face, he took his tempo from half-time to double-time and then back again. His arm hung in the air for a moment and then struck down on the drumskin as he provided his accent to the general beat. My father and I had looked at each other and smiled because we both understood this musician's sophisticated intentions.

I stood back from the windowsill and closed my eyes. I swung my arms in half-circles around my body, letting them knock into my hips before they reversed direction again. My movements in this room so far had been small and apologetic. My father lying motionless in bed made me walk, literally, on tiptoe. He was changing slowly before my eyes, but my body had been tensed as if something was going to happen at any minute. I took a deep breath and let it out through my lips in a noisy hiss. I wanted to take us back to that park.

With my eyes still closed, I rocked my hips back and forth, and the ticking of the machines around my father's bedside blended into the rhythm of the music. We were standing on a patch of grass, and the band was lit by some lanterns hanging low in the maple trees around us. Our drummer saw us and waved one drumstick. We started to dance.

My father took up the drummer's alternative, while I started with the universal beat. He liked to begin with the complex rhythm, to pay tribute to intelligence, to make it known that the drummer was heard. Younger and less experienced, I tarried in the solid underlying rhythm and was content to let my father accent me. He shuffled to the double-time and showed the drummer that he had some tricks too. He sang "Ooh! Ooh!" through the purse of his lips. His right leg was thrust out in front of the left and he shifted his torso forward, with a jaunty lift of his hip.

"Come on," he said to me. "Try it for a minute. You can always go back." At first I faltered, following the rhythm too closely. My tongue was pressed against the corner of my mouth in concentration. My father laughed at me and, in imitation, furrowed his brow. "Kate, you're trying too hard," he said. "I'll show you." I thought, and lightened my step, and left him behind. I lingered and loafed in the hollows between the beats. I skittered along the edge of the melody, swaggering from note to note. "Yes," I heard faintly. "Yes."

163

The tempo increased and I began to spin around. Using my right foot to propel me, I turned faster and faster on my left leg. I opened my eyes briefly, and the flowers lining the hospital room and the machinery crowding my father's bedside dissolved into the scene. There was a garden in the small park, and the machines became tall bushes, their tubes stretching out into thin, fragile branches.

I closed my eyes again. As I turned faster and faster, the sight of my father hunched over, watching me, grew blurred, and the clapping of his hands became a sustained clatter. Other people began to surround me. They yelled "Do it! All right!" Then I was in a place alone with the music. My feet didn't feel the ground. I knew the music was going to stop before it actually did. I stopped too, catching myself all at once with my right leg exactly on the beat.

I opened my eyes, and as when you wake up from a vivid dream and still expect to be in its setting, I was surprised and disappointed by my surroundings. I was still in the hospital room. My father lay cranked up in the bed, his eyes fixed on the blank wall. The door to the hallway was open. A nurse walked by, and an orderly wheeling a cart of food came in and out of view. I so expected to see an audience in the doorway, wide-eyed and shocked that I had been dancing in my father's hospital room, that for a moment I doubted I had been moving at all.

I sat back down in the folding chair and, out of breath from spinning, leaned forward, resting my forearms on my knees. I moved forward a little more so that I was in my father's view. "Dad!" I called out. "Guess what, Dad?" I waited for a gesture, a focusing of his eyes, for his eyes to close. In the park, he had clapped out staccato rhythms. I clapped in front of his face. He closed his eyes. I leaned back in my chair.

My mother walked into the hospital room. She put down her purse and hung up her coat on the hook on the back of the closet door. She looked at me expectantly. I hadn't said anything yet, and my silence made her come to my side and take my hands.

"What is it, honey? Is there news? Did the doctor come by?"

She bit down on her lower lip to hold in the rest of her words while she waited for me to speak. Half-formed sentences clamored in my head: about my father wanting to leave, Harvard Square, dancing, all those dance floors. I wanted to tell her how at one time I knew what it felt like to be him, and now I couldn't even stand to look into his eyes, because it seemed that what he saw was none of us, but his own death staring back at him. I took a breath and started to cry.

"What is it?" my mother asked again, her fingers tightening around my hands.

"I've been here all along," I said, "but I don't know where he's gone to."

Her grip loosened, and she let her head fall forward. After a moment, she patted and stroked the back of my hand. "I know," she said. "I know."

A few months later, when I walked into my parents' house, the air smelled slightly sweet. It reminded me of the smell when my father had come in from playing football on the beach or when we sat around in the kitchen having a beer together after a night out dancing. I heard some movement in the dining room. My mother was out for the day visiting an old friend in New Hampshire. I called out "Hello." Our Labrador retriever, George, appeared around the corner with her bowl in her mouth. She looked up at me and thumped her tail against the doorway. I could faintly hear music, a drum and someone singing, but I couldn't make out the words. My mother must have left the radio on for the dogs.

I walked into the dining room and noticed the Revolutionary War rifle hanging over the mantel.

"Gift from an old friend." I heard my father's voice. I turned around the room looking for him. "Talked him out of killing himself."

"Dad?"

"Antique dealer now."

"Are you here?" I walked into the living room.

"This rug." His voice came from far away. I looked down to the rug under my feet.

"Saw it at a yard sale . . . when we were first married."

I knelt down to touch the rug.

"It had just started to rain."

"Dad?"

"Felt we had to save it."

165

I'd always loved this rug with its border of cabbage roses. When I was little I would stand on my father's feet and he would dance at my command. "Hop to that flower, Daddy," I would say, pointing to a rose in the opposite corner. He would jump to the designated flower, and I would press against him, wildly laughing. "Now that flower, Daddy," and he would leap again. "Faster, faster," I'd say, and we would leap from rose to rose as I clung to him, never wanting to let go.

I stood up and walked to the bookcase in the corner of the room where the stereo was kept. After leafing through some of the albums stacked next to it, I picked out an Afro-Cuban record of my father's, by Tito Puente, and put it on. I turned the volume up loud. The music began with a conga drum beating the air and a woman's voice blaring out. The singer did not sing words. I listened to the voice expand and contract and could hear the singer experiment with the feeling of the sounds moving around in her mouth, the rush of air through her throat. I heard her breath force through the small space of a kiss. I turned back to the center of the room, and there was my father dancing on the rug of overblown roses, his arms clasped tightly to his chest.

Nominated by Lily Frances Henderson

IMHOTEP

by YUSEF KOMUNYAKAA

from HARVARD REVIEW

His forehead was stamped with *Administrator*
    of the Great Mansion. Unloved in the
        Crescent City, I sat in a bathtub

with a straightrazor that spring day.
    Desire had sealed my mouth
        with her name. I asked,

"What do full moons & secret herbs
    have to do with a man's heartache?"
        But this sage from the island of Philae

just smiled. Here before me stood the Son
    of Ptah. Dung beetles & amethyst . . .
        cures for a mooncalf,

flaccidity, bad kidneys, gout,
    & gallstones. What he knew
        about the blood's map

went back to the court
    of King Zoser. Something
        beneath this dream

was scored by voices passing
    outside my front door, a rap song
        thundering from a boogie box.

I wasn't dead. This Homeric healer
    from the Serapeum of Memphis
        lingered in the room.

I folded the blade
    back into its mother-of-pearl
        handle, laughed

at the noisy street, at a yellow moth
    beating its wings into dust
        against the windowpane.

Nominated by Sharon Olds

MY STUDENTS

by LISA LEWIS

from AGNI

I get tired teaching the students I have now.
Most of them have failed the class before,
And they don't listen to me; they ask the same
Questions over and over like the senile.

I walk into the classroom on time every day.
I write funny things on the board, and I'm hurt
When no one laughs, though I know my students
Are stupid; I grade their papers.

It's hard to say things they'll understand.
Someone always manages to look puzzled.
I ask for questions and they make it clear
They don't have any. They're ready to go home.

I wonder what they do at home but I'd never ask.
They haven't heard of any of the new movies.
I have had many students before who seemed
Horny; but these students are not even horny.

At my house I never want to think about students.
At my house the two Dobermans and the pit bull
Set the pace. They don't appreciate
Students calling to find out their assignments.

When students bring me presents, I don't like them
And can't use them. I don't burn incense.
I don't wear a charm bracelet. I won't eat food
Except from legally licensed facilities.

Sometimes one of my students gets a crush on me.
He lets me know on the course evaluations,
Or maybe he tells me the day of the final.
He steals peeks while he writes his essay,

Trying to size up my reaction. He wants to know
If he will get an A for noticing my attractions.
I give him an A, but I was planning to anyway.
I do have some integrity.

I am sorry my students never seem to get better.
I do what I can to get them to read the chapters.
I do what I can but nothing matters to them.
I have read the chapters many times.

They can't see themselves as I see them.
Their hands tremble because I make them nervous.
Their breath smells of rotten spice
When they ask me how they're doing in the class.

I wanted them to save the world.
They're not going to do that. My students don't want
To hear me hint around about their saving the world.
My students think I am full of shit.

They watch me close in case I give them shit.
What they don't know is how pissed off I am
I can't just *be* them again, since I did a better job.
I only needed a little help, getting started.

Nominated by Jennifer Atkinson

THE CRYING HOUSE

fiction by LINDA HOGAN

from THE MISSOURI REVIEW

"THE HOUSE IS CRYING," I said to her as steam ran down the walls. The cooking stove heated the house. Windows were frozen over with white feathers and ferns. It was a long week of cooking, and there was no music.

"The house can withstand it," Bush said. She stepped outside and brought in an armload of wood. I caught the sweet odor of it and a wind of cold air as she brushed by me. She placed a log in the stove. It was still damp and when the red hands of flame grabbed it, the wood spat and hissed.

I didn't for a minute believe the house could withstand it. I knew already it was going to collapse. It was a wooden house, dark inside, and spare. The floors creaked as she swept about, still wearing the cold. The branches of trees scraped against the windows, trying to get in. Perhaps they protested the fire and what it lived on.

Bush unjointed the oxtails and browned them in suet. She worked so slowly, you would have thought it was swamp balm, not fat and backbone, that she touched. I thought of the old days when oxen with their heavy hooves arrived in black train cars from the dark, flat fields of Kansas, diseased beasts that had been yoked together in burden. All the land, even our lost land, was shaped by them and by the hated thing that held them together as rain and sunlight and snow fell on their toiling backs.

The shadows of fish were afloat in the sink. Bush did her own hunting then, and she had a bag of poor, thin winter rabbits. She

171

removed their fur the way you'd take off a stocking. She dredged them in flour. In the kitchen, their lives rose up in steam.

Day and night she worked. In her night clothes, she boiled roots that still held the taste of mud. She stirred a black kettle and two pots. In her dark skirt, she cut onions. I didn't understand, until it was over, what it was she had to do. I didn't know what had taken hold of her and to what lengths she must go in order to escape its grip.

She had black hair then, beautiful and soft. She folded blankets and clothing and placed them on the floor in the center of that one dark room. She took down the curtains, shook out the dust, washed them in the sink and hung them on lines from wall to wall. All the while, bones floated up in broth the way a dream rises to the top of sleep.

Your mother entered my dreaming once, not floating upward that way, but crashing through, the way deer break through ice, or a stone falls into water, tumbling down to the bottom. In the dream, I was fishing in Lake Grand when the water froze suddenly, like when the two winds meet against each other and stop everything in their path, the way they do in waking life, the way they left a man frozen that time, standing in place at the bank of Spirit River. In the dream, your mother was beneath ice in the center of the lake. I was afraid of her. We all were. What was wrong with her we couldn't name and we distrusted such things that had no name. She was a deep and magnetic force like the iron underground that pulls the needle of a compass to false north and sets it spinning. My heart beat fast. The part of me that was awake feared I was having a heart attack, but I could not shake myself out of the dream.

Whatever your mother was in that dream, it wasn't human. It wasn't animal or fish. It was nothing I could recognize by sight or feel. The water became solid and the thing she was, or that had turned into her, pulled me toward it, out across the ice. I was standing, still and upright, drawn out that way to the terrible and magnetic center of what I feared. I reached an arm, as if to grab for anything that might stop me, but nothing was there, and I slid across the glaring surface of ice. Standing like a statue, being pulled that way, helpless and pale in the ice light, old stories I'd heard from some of the Cree began to play across my mind, stories about the frozen heart of evil that was hunger, envy, and

172

greed, and how it tricked people into death or illness. The only thing, finally, that could save them was to find a way to thaw it, to warm it back into water.

But where your mother, Hannah Wing, stood was at the bottomless passage to an underworld. And there was no thawing to it.

Bush had struggled with your mother's ice-cold world. There was the time she heard you crying in the house when you were not there. I heard it, too, your voice, crying for help, or I would not have believed her. It was a chilling sound. Bush turned desperate as a caged animal, wanting to get you out of the clutch of the nameless thing that held you.

In her battle with that underworld, whatever it was, Bush didn't win, but she didn't lose either. It was a tie, a fragile balance that at any time could go either way. That was why she cooked the mourning feast. That was why she baked the bread and soaked corn in lye and ashes until it became the sweetest hominy, and who would have believed such a caustic thing could sweeten and fatten the corn. That was why she cooked the wild rice we harvested two years earlier with Frenchie pole-ing in the canoe. The rice was the most important thing; you had gone with us that fall day, wrapped in cotton and with netting over your face so that the little bugs and dust wouldn't bother you as we drifted through the plants, clicking the sticks that knocked rice into the boat.

And when Bush opened the jar of swamp tea, it smelled like medicine to me. It smelled like healing. It was what we needed. It reminded me of the days when the old women put eagle down inside wounds and they would heal.

Bush is a quiet woman, little given to words and she never takes kindly to being told what to do. So while she prepared the feast, I let her be, even when she did a poor job on the rice soup. I knitted and sat in the chair by the window and looked outside, straight at the face of winter. There was a silence so deep it seemed that all things prepared for what would follow, then and for years to come, years when the rest of us would be gone, when the land itself would tremble in fear of drowning.

The windows had frozen over so it was through ice that I saw them coming, the people, arriving that cold Sunday of the feast. Across ice, they were like shadows against a darkening winter

173

evening, and the ice shifted as they approached. Wind had blown snow from the surface of the lake. In places the ice was shining like something old and polished by hands. Maybe it was the hands of wind, but the ice shone beneath their feet. I scraped the window with my fingernails and peered out. Jarrell Illinois, gone now, wore a miner's headlamp even though it wasn't quite dark, and the others walked close to him, as if convinced that night had fallen. As they drew closer, I saw that their shadows and reflections walked alongside them like ghosts or their own deaths that would rise up and meet them one day. So it looked like they were more. My breath steamed the window, I remember. I wiped it again for a better look.

Some of the people were wrapped in the hides we used to wear, others wore large wool coats, or had blankets wrapped around them. They walked together like spirits from the thick forest behind winter. They were straight and tall. None of them talked.

"Here they come," I said. Bush, for a change, was nervous. She stirred the iron pot one last time, then she untied her hair. It was long and thick. Hair is a woman's glory, they say, and hers fell down her back. The teakettle began to sing as if it remembered old songs some of us had long since forgotten. Its breath rose up in the air as she poured boiling water over the small oval leaves of swamp tea. The house smelled of it and of cedar.

"Look at that," I said. "They look beautiful."

Bush bent over the table and looked out the window as the people came through a path in snow. The air was shimmering in the light of the miner's lamp and a lantern one woman carried. She wiped her hands on her apron. And then they came through the door and filled up the crying house. Some of them stamped their feet from the habit of deep snow, their cheeks red with cold. They took off their boots and left them by the fire. They greeted us. Some of them admired the food or warmed their hands near the stove, and all of them looked at the pictures of you that sat on the table, but after greeting us, they said very little. After all the years she'd lived here, they were still uncomfortable around Bush. They had never understood her. To get them to her banquet, she'd told them this was her tradition, and it was the only thing that could help her. There wasn't one among

174

us who didn't suspect that she'd made this ceremony up, at least in part, but mourning was our common ground and that's why they came, out of loyalty for the act of grief.

Bush put a piece of each kind of food in her blue bowl for the spirits, wiped her hands on her apron, and took the bowl outside. When she left the doorway and went out, heat rose from the bowl, going up like a story carried to the sky, begging any and all gods in the low clouds to listen. The aching joints of my hands told me it was a bone-chilling, hurting cold, the worst of winters, and the temperature was below zero. Bush held up the bowl for the sky to see, for the spirit of ice, for what lived inside clouds, for the night wind people who would soon be present because they lived on Fur Island and returned there each night. I could barely make out her shape in the newly swirling snow, but when she came back in, she smiled. I remember that. She smiled at the people. As if a burden was already lifted.

One by one the people took their places, settling into chairs or on the couch that was covered with a throw I had made, or they sat at the long table. They hadn't been there before and so they looked around the little, now-stripped house with curiosity. It was stained wood and wallpaper. There were places where rain had seeped through. It was lighter without curtains than it had been a few days before.

When Bush served up the food, it came to me that I didn't want to eat. I was a large woman then, I loved my food, but I must have known that eating this meal would change me. I only picked at it.

At first, we hardly spoke except for a few exchanges of small talk, then there was just the sound of forks on plates, spoons in bowls. We were such quiet eaters that when the wind died down for a moment you could hear the snow hitting against the wood of the house, dying against the windows, tapping as if it, too, was hungry and wanted in. I could only think of the island where she lived, the frozen waters, the other lands with their sloping distances, even the light and dust of solar storms that love our cold, eerie poles.

There was moose meat, rice, and fish. The room was hot. There were white-haired people, black-haired, and the mixed-bloods in colorful clothes. Frenchie was there, dressed in a blue dress. It was low cut and she wore rhinestones at her neck, and

175

large rubber boots. We were used to her way of dress, so we didn't think it was strange attire. We just believed she was one kind of woman on top and another below the waist.

It was so damp and warm inside, the wallpaper, full of leaves, began to loosen from the moist walls. It troubled my mother, Dora-Rouge, who sat with her back against the wall. She was always an orderly woman and accustomed to taking care of things. When Bush wasn't looking she tried to stick it back up, holding edges and corners with her hands until it became too much for her so she sat back down and took the fine bones out of her fish and placed them together on the side of her plate in a neat arrangement.

Jarrell Illinois took some tobacco out of the tin and pinched it into his cheek and smiled all around the room.

The house grew smaller. It settled. The floors sloped as if they knew the place would soon be abandoned, the island quiet and alone with just its memory of what had happened there, even the shipwreck of long ago.

I don't know how to measure love. Not by cup or bowl, not in distance either, but that's what rose from the iron pot as steam, that was the food taken into our bodies. It was the holy sacrament of you we ate that day. We ate from evening through to near light, or as light as it gets in winter. The fire cast shadows on the walls as most everyone cleaned their plates. The old men picked the bones, then piled them up like ancient tellers of fortune. They ate the bowls empty, clear to the bottom. By then, people were talking and some even laughing, and there was just something in the air, and that night, in front of everyone, Bush cut her long hair. It held a memory of you and she had to free it.

And when the dishes were all piled up, she went to the middle of the room where she had placed her earthly goods, then gave each diner present some part of her world. It was only your things she parted with unwillingly, holding them as if she dreaded their absence, and now and then a tear would try to gather in her eye, but she was fierce and determined. She gave away your handmade blanket, t-shirt, shoes, socks—gave one here, one there. Some of the people cried. Not only for her, or for you, but for all the children lost to us.

That was how I came to have the cradleboard Bush beaded for you in the dim light of the house that cried. It is made of soft

176

buckskin with red and blue beads. I leave the small doll laced inside it. It's been this way all these years. Inside the smaller bag is your hair and nail clippings. Your mother, Hannah Wing, did not save your stem, so it was all Bush, who loved you so, could think to close inside, to call you home again to us, and it worked.

Then she gave her quilts away, and the hawk feathers that had survived both flood and fire. She gave the carved fish decoys my son Harold made. They were weighted just right to drop through ice and lure many a slow and hungry winter fish. No one else had weights as good as those. She gave her fishing poles and line, and her rifle. She gave the silverware. At the end she stood there in her white sleeping gown for she'd even given what she wore that day, the black skirt, the sweater.

With all the moisture of cooking and breath, the door froze shut, and when the people were ready to leave, John Husk struggled to open it until finally it gave. And when they went through it each person carried away a part of her. She said it was her tradition. No one questioned her out loud or showed a hint of a doubting face, though they knew she had created this ceremony for the ending of her grief.

They came to love her that night. She'd gone to the old ways, the way we used to live. From the map inside ourselves. Maybe it reminded us that we had made our own ways here and were ourselves something like outcasts and runaways from other lands and tribes to start with.

When they left through the unstuck, pried-open door, night had turned over. The vast white silence of winter was broken only by the moaning sound of the lake.

I was glad to remain in the hot kitchen with Bush, but I watched the others walk away with their arms full. Going back that morning, in the blue northern light, their stomachs were filled, their arms laden with blankets, food, and some of the beaver pelts Bush had stolen and been arrested for—from the trappers who had trespassed the island. Anything that could be carried away, they took. Frenchie pushed a chair before her across the ice, leaving the track of wooden legs in shining lines. Beneath her coat, she wore Bush's black sweater over the dress and rhinestones. But the largest thing they carried was Bush's sorrow. We all had it, after that. It became our own. Some of us

177

have since wanted to give it back to her, but once we felt it we knew it was too large for a single person.

They walked through the drifts that had formed when the wind blew, then they seemed to merge with the outlines of trees. I was worried, thinking as they neared the mainland, that Frenchie might fall into the warm spot where the lake never freezes. Others had fallen before her.

When the people were no longer in sight, Bush went outside to get the bowl. It was empty and there were no tracks. Or maybe the wind had covered them. But a bowl without its soup is such a hopeful thing, and like the bowl, Bush was left with emptiness, a place waiting and ready to be filled, one she could move inside and shape about her. And finally, she was able to sleep. She had made her grief small and child-sized, one that would slide its hand inside one of ours and walk away with us, across the frozen water.

After that, she didn't talk about you any more, or wear black. But we did. We were the ones who began to wear black, not to defy ghosts as in other days, but out of pain. And after that, we were never together without you in our hearts. Your absence sat at every table, occupied every room, walked through the doors of every house.

The next evening, Bush said it was time for me to leave. "Go on," she said, handing me my coat and hat. I hesitated. She had little more than a few pieces of firewood and some cooking pots. She had given away even the food. She saw me look about the house at what wasn't there. I sipped hot tea. We'd slept near each other for warmth the night before, my bear coat over us. Once Bush sat up and said, "This coat is singing." I told her it was just the sound of ice outside the door.

I must have looked worried. "I'll be fine," she said, holding up the coat to help me into it.

At least, I remember thinking, if she'd kept her long hair she would be warmer. But I said, "What about me? It's getting close to dark." She wasn't fooled. She knew I walked late at night just to hear the sounds of winter and see the sky and snow. She handed me my gloves and hat. I left unwillingly. It was all I could do to go out the door. I felt terrible leaving her in all that emptiness. I guess it was her sadness already come over me. I wanted to cry but I knew the wind, on its way to the island where it lived, would freeze my tears.

I took my time getting home. Above me there were the shimmering hints of light. The sky itself was a bowl of milk.

Four days later, food and blankets appeared at Bush's door. She never knew who left them and there were no tracks on the ice. But I was beside myself with worry, and one night that worry got the best of me. I laced up my boots and went back over the frozen water. She was thinner, but she looked happy, and she didn't argue when I opened this bear coat I've always worn and wrapped it around the both of us. We walked together back to the mainland. The only sound was our feet on ice, the snap and groan of the lake. We were two people inside the fur of this bear. She said she could see the cubs that had lived inside and been born from this skin, and I said, "Yes."

Nominated by Wally Lamb, David Romtvedt

WHO DO YOU LOVE

fiction by JEAN THOMPSON

from AMERICAN SHORT FICTION

IT WAS AN itch in her mouth. She had to say it. "I love you."

His eyes were closed. The lashes fluttered, a brief, involuntary code: SOS.

"You don't have to be embarrassed. Relax. Hey, it's just me. It's just how I feel right this minute. You feel any way you want to."

"I feel fine."

"Well, that's good. It's fine to feel fine. Don't mind me, I'm just happy."

He laughed and patted her arm. Then he picked up the arm by the wrist, as you would a sack, and moved it off his chest. He pushed the bedsheets aside and stood up.

"Where are you going?"

"Bathroom."

She listened to his footsteps, then the gargle of the plumbing. He wasn't coming back to bed. Well, OK. She hopped up also. He was sitting at the kitchen table, reading *TV Guide*. Annoyed at the lack of morning newspapers, she imagined. She would offer to go out for them. She would offer to subscribe. What was the matter with her? She wasn't even sure yet if she liked him very much. "Hungry?" she asked, brightly.

"Not really."

"Belgian waffles. Steak and eggs. Fresh-squeezed juice. Homemade jam. Denver omelet."

"I'm not that hungry. Honestly."

"I want to smother you with food. Smother you, then lick it off. Just kidding. I'll make coffee. So you're one of those no-breakfast guys."

"Sometimes I eat breakfast. But if I eat when I'm not really hungry, I don't respect myself in the morning."

He said it to be funny, so that she could smile. She had to remind herself that she'd really only said one wrong thing.

They both had coffee. She fixed herself toast. She was ravenous. She was almost impatient for him to leave so that she could eat all she wanted, something sickening and unbreakfastlike, cold spaghetti or a whole box of Girl Scout cookies. They talked a little about work and something else that didn't matter. She was looking at him, trying not to be obvious about it, like taking little sips from a glass of water. She was trying to put all his different faces together. His ordinary daytime face, and the one that hung overhead in bed like a blurred moon, and now this rumpled morning one. It didn't matter what she looked like. He wasn't watching her.

"What are you thinking?" she asked, the next time there was silence. "What are you thinking about, right now?"

"Women are always asking you that."

"And men never tell you."

"Well, women always want you to say, 'I was thinking about you, darling.' Or, 'About us.' Anything else is a wrong answer."

"No, no," she protested. "Whatever you say is fine. Anything at all. Spill it."

"Well, I *was* thinking about you."

"Oh-oh."

"It wasn't anything bad. Why would you think it was bad? I like you. It's just that sometimes you—"

"Interrupt people. Finish their sentences. Talk too much. Try too hard."

"We just need to take things slow," he said, not unkindly.

"Oh, yes." She was relieved that it wasn't anything worse. She knew everything else would be easy. If that was the worst thing he was going to say, she could sit there patiently, smiling, agreeing to everything, waiting for him to leave. Once he was gone she could do whatever she wanted. Cry, stare at herself in the mirror until she was as ugly as she chose to be. She would call herself

181

idiot, fool, jerk. She waited with perfect serenity, curious even as to how he would extricate himself.

"Well," he said, finally.

*

Her name was Judy Applebee. She was thirty-two years old and she worked in an office that coordinated human services for the city. The office directed programs for latchkey kids and meals for the elderly, hot lines for battered women and drug addicts, ghetto basketball leagues, emergency shelters, urban minigardens, home winterization assistance. There were programs to help the deaf get telephone equipment and to aid the illiterate in filling out tax returns, others that gave horseback riding lessons to crippled children or provided them with foster grandparents, or served Thanksgiving dinner to recent immigrants.

Judy's friends would say to her. "It must be rewarding to make an impact, to really help people with their problems." Judy would shrug and say she supposed so. Her friends thought this was modesty, one more proof of how virtuous her work was. But Judy knew better. Her office did not solve anyone's problems. It only took the edge off misery so that misery could be endured. Her job was not to eradicate poverty, but to tend and manage it as you would a crop. Her job was to make poverty more tolerable. Sometimes she imagined the city's misery as water backed up in a dam, passive but threatening, and herself as a kind of engineer, monitoring the pressure, opening sluices and closing valves. If you supplied one old woman with transportation to the doctor's, then the teenage prostitutes or the Vietnamese refugees living in church basements would somehow be appeased. The wave of human suffering would not crest that day. Often she felt there was no point in giving people what you thought they needed, when they would never get what they wanted. They wanted fish fries, new automobiles, Florida vacations; they wanted their cancers to shrivel and their children to thrive. People wanted good luck. They wanted the lottery, not human services.

And if you were serious about changing anything, you would shut the office down. Allow misery to become intolerable, let it boil over the lip of the dam and come down hard on everything. Of course she and those like her would be the first targets. The

182

poor hated the doling out and apportioning she did, the grudging gifts of half a mouthful. They hated waiting in line, they hated being orderly and deserving. Since when did *rich* people deserve what they had? The poor hated the office itself, the neat walls and airless corridors and stink of thrift about the place, meant to convince them how little there was to give. They would destroy it gladly. Judy was unsure why it gave her such satisfaction to imagine this. She supposed she felt guilty for having problems less monumental than those she saw at work, inadequate, unworthy problems.

She was a pretty woman, although she knew she had the sort of looks that would not hold up forever: fair, fine-boned, brittle, she had long nervous hands and a quick smile. "Judy dresses like a social worker," her friends said despairingly. Her light hair was long and artless, her nails were blunt, her shoes comfortable. She attracted men who would have been uneasy with a more decorative woman. With these men she had serious conversations about whatever the men wished to talk about: politics, technology, literature. She usually agreed with them. There was no reason not to. Those things hardly mattered to her. She agreed with them so they would like her. She was too anxious to be liked, she knew that. People could tell, and then they secretly despised you for it.

She was often unhappy for no reason at all. What right did she have to be unhappy? She was stern with herself about this. She was healthy, well fed, a citizen of a highly developed nation. Each day she consumed more of the earth's resources than some people did in a year. She had family and friends. Why should she spend whole evenings weeping into a towel? Or dug into a nest on the couch, watching the most inane, grating television she could find, sunk in idiocy and uselessness? It was true that she was alone. None of the men she agreed with had amounted to much over time. She thought she would like to have children. Of course she was not unique in any of this. So many overeducated women her age were alone that it hardly seemed worth complaining about.

Once she swallowed a handful of Valium and drank most of a bottle of red wine and waited for something to happen. She was pretty sure she wouldn't die, but if she did at least she would not be around to reproach herself for it. She supposed what she wanted was to wake up in a hospital, surrounded by concerned friends and efficient nurses. "Judy, we had no idea," her friends would say. The nurses would hush everyone, tell her when to chew, swallow, roll over, sleep. She would sleep as long as she wanted in a white-gauze world. She would be helpless.

She had fallen into a muddy, thick-headed dream when the phone rang. It kept on ringing. Since she was not dead, she had to answer it.

"Judy?" The voice was so small it fit in her ear. "Honey? Did I wake you up?"

It was her mother. "Kind of," Judy said. She couldn't hear herself say it. Her voice dropped into the silence like a stone in a well.

"Honey? Your phone must be going out."

"No, I'm here." The inside of her mouth tasted dead, even if the rest of her wasn't.

"Maybe it's my phone. We got a new phone for the den. Nothing ever works the way they say it will. How are you?"

"I'm dying."

"Darling, don't talk like that," said her mother briskly. "Everybody has those days."

Judy felt sweat rolling under her clothes, everywhere all at once. She leaned over the edge of the bed and vomited, thin, sour purple vomit.

"Dying never helps anything," her mother went on. "Cheer up. Most people are just about as happy as they make up their minds to be. You were always such a happy child."

"No, I wasn't. I was afraid of everything."

"Hold on," said her mother. The phone exploded in Judy's ear, a series of bludgeoning sounds. Her mother came back on the line. "That's much better. Darling, I should let you get some sleep. It's good to hear your voice. Call us. We worry when we don't hear from you."

"Why?" asked Judy. Then it was morning. It was fifteen minutes before the time she usually got up for work. The vomit had dried on the floorboards by her bed, leaving a small tidal pool of food particles. So that much had really happened. She wasn't sure about any of the rest of it. She was afraid it had, and that her worst fears were confirmed. She was emotionally invisible. It made no difference what she thought or felt or said. Others looked at her and saw what they had always seen. They thought she was happy. Most people were just about as happy as other people decided they should be.

She went into work that day. There was no reason not to. She threw up as soon as she got there. The path between her head and stomach was a subway line traversed by shrieking, incessant trains. It was that day she made a discovery. She did not feel compassion for the poor, or even that much guilt. She envied them because they were allowed to be unhappy.

She was interviewing a client. The client's name was Mrs. Sturgis. "And how have you been?" Judy marveled to hear herself, sprightly, banal, her lips twitching in a passable smile. Was there no part of her that was genuine?

"Praise Jesus, no worse," replied Mrs. Sturgis, belligerently. Mrs. Sturgis had breast cancer and bone cancer. Parts of her body kept dropping away. She wore a sticky blond wig to cover her bare scalp. Her pale eyes were flat with pain. She had four children, two of whom were diabetic, and a husband who drank. If you wanted pure suffering, she was perfect.

"We need to update your profile," said Judy, wondering just what combination of fear and hope and calculation allowed Mrs. Sturgis to praise the deity. "Is your husband working?"

"Oh, *him*," said Mrs. Sturgis, twisting her clamplike mouth tighter.

Judy waited, but this was all the eloquence Mrs. Sturgis had to offer. Judy was used to dragging answers from her. It was as if Mrs. Sturgis begrudged letting any more of herself be taken away, even words. "Well, when was the last time he worked?"

"Know when he *says* he worked," said Mrs. Sturgis, meaningfully. She shifted her fatty shoulders. Her bosom shifted a moment later, like a sack of sand. Before the cancer she had probably been big, fleshy. Now she was sucked dry.

"Well, we have to put something down."

"Put down I never saw any money. Him and his stories."

"Three months," Judy wrote, recognizing this as a new, dangerous edge she was approaching: indifference, arbitrariness, spite. In similar fashion, she dealt with the questions about the childrens' doctor and Mrs. Sturgis's prescriptions.

Mrs. Sturgis sat, squat and unblinking. This was what was left of a human face, after you shoved it around enough. Her skin was

185

freckled, dusty, worn thin. She looked impossibly ugly and she knew it. She saw it in other people's faces. Her own stare only reflected that back again. Oh God, this woman, Judy thought, sick with feeling. How could anyone have problems compared to hers? How could you have problems if they didn't show? How could you refuse to pity Mrs. Sturgis? But I do. Judy's head was grinding and her stomach clenched. I do refuse, she said inwardly. I dislike and fear you.

"Coffee," said Mrs. Sturgis, out of nowhere. "Isn't coffee bad for you?"

"It's not particularly good for you."

"They say it gets into your brain," said Mrs. Sturgis severely. "I'm giving it up."

Judy waited for one of them to say more. When that didn't happen she stared at Mrs. Sturgis, who stared back. There was nothing particularly rude about it. They could have been two cats.

Of course she should have agreed with Mrs. Sturgis. Should have told her of miraculous cures effected by caffeine-eschewing sufferers. Told her it would keep her last few healthy cells from peeling away. Chat her up. Be human. Here's your chance. Judy said nothing. That was how she knew she must hate Mrs. Sturgis. It must be hatred, when you withheld something that cost you so little.

"Well, that should do us," said Judy. She reached for a paper clip, then another. "Did you get your vouchers? Your receipts?"

She watched Mrs. Sturgis begin to gather her vinyl handbag, her rain boots, her lumpy brown overcoat, and finally her body, that loose bundle of treacherous parts. She rolled and heaved and limped. The office humanely provided Mrs. Sturgis cab fare for her visits. The trip to and from the cab would probably kill her.

In the midst of her preparations, Mrs. Sturgis paused. "Doctor said I have a nervous bowel," she announced, a little grandly.

"Oh, dear."

"It's a sensitivity thing," said Mrs. Sturgis.

When she'd finally gone, Judy went to the window. It was November and the sky was thin and watery, the wind steady. Old newspapers and smaller, gaudier trash skittered along the sidewalks. The city was scoured by wind. People were caught by it like so much garbage. It was a long time before Mrs. Sturgis emerged four stories below. Her coat flapped in the wind like something broken. One hand was clasped to her head and it threw her off balance, slowed her even further. Judy realized she was afraid her wig would blow away, and even this did not move her.

Judy watched Mrs. Sturgis until she stumped around a corner out of sight. She was tingling with hatred. It exhilarated her. People expected to be hated here, and now she could oblige them. She hated them because they were ugly, ill, hopeless, all the reasons you ought to pity them. Pity was only failed love. Pity exhausted you. Hatred made you feel powerful. You could never pity anyone enough to do any good, but you could hate them all you wanted. She went back to her desk, feeling much steadier, and worked calmly through the rest of the day.

*

"I hate to see you so unhappy all the time," he said.

"I'm not," Judy protested. "I'm only unhappy when it makes sense to be. When something goes wrong or just when I get tired of being happy."

"Tired of being happy. Why would anyone feel that way?"

"Well, sometimes I do. Nobody has to believe it."

They were sitting at Judy's dining room table. She'd cooked dinner and she'd made way too much food. Broccoli sagged in a volcanic lake of crusting cheese sauce. The cooling steak seeped blood.

He pushed his chair back from the table. She knew he would leave now. No one was ever hungry enough to stay as long as she thought they should. But he said, "Have you ever thought about going to see somebody?"

"What do you mean?" She knew exactly what he meant.

"Like a counselor. Somebody who's good at thrashing out problems. Sometimes it helps to have someone you can talk to."

"I'm talking to you. Right now."

He smiled and lowered his eyes. Mistake. He didn't want to be her therapist. She wouldn't want him to be.

Still, she couldn't let it go. She asked him just what sort of problems he thought she had.

"Like I said. You aren't happy."

187

"Happy is an attitude. It's not something you have to have."

"Sure it is. Why not?"

"Character building."

"That's stupid. Look, drop it. Forget I said anything. You know, this was one of the top ten great all-around meals. Maybe Number five. No, four."

"You can't do this. You can't tell me how sick I am, and then leave."

"Did I say sick? I wish I could stay, but I only keep upsetting you."

"Bullshit."

He said, "I'm so stuffed, I don't think I'll need to eat again for a week."

After he'd gone Judy ate the rest of the broccoli and two pieces of pecan pie. She did the dishes, soaped them carefully and scalded them clean. She was not the sort of woman who threw dishes. She tidied the rooms, switched on the stereo, and turned off all the lights. In the darkness the stereo hummed green. There was a red dot of light to show the power was on.

The record was an old one. It was old when she got it, at a garage sale. The date, if there ever was one, had rubbed off the jacket long ago, but it was mid-to-late hippie. She sat on the floor with her arms clasped around her knees, watching the red and green. The beat thumped. The guitars grabbed notes and held them far out in the empty air—*I'm coming, I'm coming*—for a long, long time.

> *Who—do you love?*
> *Who—do you lo-ove*
> *Come on and take a little*
> *Walk and tell me*
> *Who do you love*

The singer had a hoarse, throaty, bad-boy's voice. The song made Judy feel she was on the brink of something dangerous, a high cliff or a dark pit. She turned the volume up one notch past what the neighbors would bear. The record was scratched, and silvery balls of static jumped from it. Still the sound came through, urgent, menacing, hard. All the other love songs were sugary. She supposed that was why she liked this one. Judy wondered where the singer was now, if he'd grown paunchy and middle-aged or died from cocaine, if he was the one who'd loved someone, or if that was just the song. It didn't matter. Somebody had once loved somebody else, and the echo of it still reached her ears. Judy gripped her knees, harder. "Who do you love, who do you love," she sang along under her breath. She knew she didn't love anyone at all.

*

The psychologist asked her what she saw as the main problem in her life. "I cook too much food," Judy said.

She was looking for another job. The psychologist, who was careful not to give outright advice, suggested she put it on her list of life decisions. He talked about burnout and making positive changes. Judy thought it was a nice way of saying that she herself was beyond hope, but she could at least get it together at work. And burnout was another way of saying you hated people.

For a while Judy was excited about the idea of a new job. She updated her resume, she read the want ads. She considered going back to school. She imagined herself emerging with a new degree, a new woman, barking orders and building empires. Then she realized she did not want to be anything in particular, at least not enough to work at it. When she considered what would really please her to do all day, she thought of making deliveries for United Parcel Service. She liked the idea of driving a van busily from place to place, wearing a neat, anonymous brown uniform. People would be glad to see her because she brought them things. She stopped sending out her resume. She tore up her list of life decisions.

One evening, shopping at an expensive store, she wondered what it would be like to work in a place where people had lots and lots of money. The store was decorated grandly for Christmas. There were small trees trimmed with Italian lights and set on pedestals. The vaulted ceiling, three stories high above the main floor, glittered with glass and silver globes, silver stars and bows and swags of silver roses. The carpeting smelled of perfume. The Muzak played the very classiest sort of Christmas car-

189

ols, medieval arrangements performed by harpsichord, oboe, and flute. Everywhere she looked were soft heaps of things and expensive surfaces.

"Can I help you?"

She had strayed too close to one of the counters and a salesclerk materialized. The clerk was as splendid as the rest of the store. All the clerks were like that, pretty women who dressed like rich ones. Judy stared at the clerk. She was young, younger than Judy, with a prim, small-featured face. She wore a high-necked gray dress, severely fashionable, which made her look like a long gray tube. Her hair was white blond, sheep's fleece in a storm. Silver shells hung in her ears. The face was painted raspberry, slate, blue, mocha. Amazing. To think that this face and Mrs. Sturgis's belonged to members of the same species. Judy watched the face begin to crease and pucker, and realized she had not answered.

"I'd like—" She cast about her. She seemed to have washed ashore in small leather goods. Her eye took in ranks of billfolds, coin purses, cigarette cases, eyeglass cases, in sober brown calf, red and navy and turquoise and gray and butter yellow leathers, paisley and embroidered fabrics, the hides of exotic animals, too much of everything. "—to look at wallets," Judy said, and the salesclerk turned noncommittal once more. It was a sort of code. Anyone too dazzled to get the words out would be hustled through the door.

The clerk handed over wallet after wallet, waiting while Judy pretended to examine them. The clerk's fingernails were polished, ten raspberry crescent moons. The nails tapped, out of rhythm with the medieval carols. It was plainly a boring transaction for both of them. No one would expect a clerk to pity or love or hate the customers.

It was then that she caught sight of her own face in one of the ever-present mirrors. She should not have been surprised. She looked the way she always looked in such stores. Her hair was as lank as if she'd sprayed it with a hose. Her face was bare, shiny, more unnatural somehow than the clerk's layers of cosmetics. The flesh was spread unevenly over the bones, like cold butter on bread. Her best sweater sagged at the neck. Her waistline was sloppy. Self-image, the psychologist said, and maybe this was

190

what he meant. She was so ugly that she would never be allowed
the luxury of treating anyone with indifference.

"I'd like to see that one." Judy pointed, and when the clerk's
back was turned she flopped one of the wallets into her open
purse.

This is a suicide attempt, Judy thought. If anyone had seen her
they'd wait until she reached the door to arrest her. She knew
that much. There would be phone calls, lawyers, disgrace. "Judy,
we had no idea," people would say, or maybe they wouldn't say
anything at all.

The clerk saw nothing. She had the kind of face that saw noth-
ing very easily. A few moments later Judy said, "I'm afraid I just
don't see the kind I want." Ridiculous statement. She couldn't
have imagined any other possible kind of wallet. The clerk looked
nearly as bored as she would have been if Judy had bought
something.

"I like your hair," said Judy, surprising both of them. She felt
powerful in her ugliness, like Mrs. Sturgis, forcing people's eyes
to her.

The clerk touched a hand to her hair, as if to remember just
what shape it had taken. "Thank you."

"Is it expensive?"

"You mean—the perm?"

"I guess so." She was stalling for time, not wanting to leave and
reach the door. "I keep meaning to do something about mine."

Judy giggled and touched her own hand to her hair. If she had
a wig, like Mrs. Sturgis, she could take it off.

She imagined the clerk was hesitating between polite escape
and polite small talk. But the clerk leaned toward her and shook
her head violently, ranking her fingers through her white curls.
They blurred in the air like a miniature snowstorm, then settled
back into place undisturbed. "Look," said the clerk. "See what
you can do. Everybody in the world should have hair like this,
but in all different colors."

On the way out Judy forced herself to slow down, dawdle, pre-
tend she was interested in silk scarves and crocodile handbags.
She eyed the doors. No one official-looking waited there, but she
knew these people made every effort to be unobtrusive and to
look normal, just as she did.

Even the music sounded expensive, Judy thought, as a swell of it lifted her toward the triple bank of glass. She walked to meet them, head up, like the last scene in a movie. She kept a little smile in one corner of her mouth, ready for the moment when the hands would descend on her. She would arch her eyebrow, questioning. Some mistake? Afraid not, miss.

Beyond the glass the city dusk lay like a blue pool. The carol was a stately one, "Adeste Fideles," a triumphal march. The glass swung toward her.

And then she was outside. Nothing had happened. Without the frame of warm light the street was only dark. She leaned up against the rush of the late shopping crowds and touched the wallet inside her purse. Of all the things to steal, an empty wallet. It was like a bad joke. Nothing had happened. She was still invisible.

*

He said, "I want to help you. I really do."

She had been crying steadily for ten minutes. She was crying to keep him awake. "Help me do what?"

"Feel better about things. Enjoy life."

"Like one big goddamned Pepsi commercial."

"I truly think there's something chemically wrong with you. One of those drug things."

"Caffeine."

"Huh?"

"So what's wrong with *you?* What's wrong with a man who can fall asleep while someone's crying?"

"Am I asleep?"

Judy raised herself up on one elbow. "Why do you want to help me?"

"Because you need it."

"Not good enough."

He yawned and pulled the sheet over his head. "Nothing's ever good enough for you."

"Do you love me?"

The sheet stopped its billowings. He sighed. "Does it matter so much what I say?"

"I guess not."

They were both quiet then. After a while she heard his breathing lengthen. The body under the sheet relaxed into sleep.

This time she cried silently. Tears ran down her throat and burrowed into the sheets. With great caution, she twitched the blankets away from him, little by little, until she uncovered him down to his feet. Her eyes adjusted to the dim, underwater light from the hall, and she could see him clearly. He looked blue. Like something newly born or newly dead, fished out of the depths.

The house was chilly, and she put on a sweatshirt, sweatpants, thick cotton socks. Goose bumps were forming on his legs and arms. Funny how skin led this independent life. She thought of Mrs. Sturgis's skin, thin as Kleenex, bombarded by radiation from outside, cancer from within.

She padded out to the kitchen. She sat down at the table, pulling the chair up hard, thump.

Bastard.

She slipped on her shoes, fetched her coat and gloves and keys and wallet. She thought about shooting him, or setting the bed on fire, and knew she would settle instead for some small meanness. She turned on the stereo, set the volume on high, and positioned the record. She was out the door and at the elevator when the first crash of music reached her. She imagined she heard it falling all the way down the shaft after her.

It was past midnight, and no one was on the street when she stepped outside. There had been a hard frost. The ground was covered with it and the sidewalk glazed. Rings of frozen vapor surrounded the streetlights. Her street had trees and boxy hedges and buildings that sat like fists on little squares of lawn. It was considered a safe neighborhood. All that meant was that people left you alone. What was so safe about that?

She set off walking. She was still crying a little, weak, sick, furious, not caring what happened to her as long as it was his fault. This is a suicide attempt, she thought, aware she was being childish and that nothing she did made sense anymore. She would freeze to death or be raped or murdered or all of these, and that would make her happy.

Of course, if you walked far enough in any direction the city provided you with an unsafe neighborhood. On the larger streets cars still rolled through the path of their own headlights. From time to time one of these honked at her, or someone shouted something from a window. A tavern sign winked out on a corner as she watched. Across the street two Puerto Rican boys, out too late, chased each other down the broken sidewalk on skateboards. A thin sleet began to tap. Not too far from here the real decay began, warehouses as tall and black as vertical tombs, gangs of rats, steel gates pulled across steel doors, blind windows.

By her elbow, a voice said something in hard, efficient Spanish.

Judy's heart billowed up, then fell back to her knees. A woman sat in a doorway. You could tell it was a woman by her voice. Her face was grimed and blackened, her eyes veined like cracked eggs. A knit hood was pulled down over her head, and a baseball cap over that. The rest of her was layers of flapping rags.

Judy bent closer, close enough to catch the smell. "Do you speak English?"

"Shit."

Judy regarded the face. The mouth gummed and spat more Spanish. What was it she kept trying to see in faces? Something human.

The Puerto Rican boys had crossed the street and racketed up to them. Their skateboard wheels cut trails in the frost. "Eh, it's Grandma," one of them said. He might have been as old as eleven, thin and woolly-haired. He danced with cold and excitement. "Grandma say give her a dollar."

"Grandma nasty," said the second, smaller boy. "She piss on herself."

"Talk nice, dickface. Lady, Grandma say she hungry."

"Grandma say, Piss on everybody!"

"How do you say that in Spanish?" Judy asked. The old woman's tongue kept darting in and out of her mouth, a surprising pink. She didn't look at any of them, but addressed the cement. The smaller boy giggled and retreated. The older boy took it up again, sounding almost patient:

"A dollar."

"You should go to a shelter," said Judy. Which of them did she mean? The cold was making her thickheaded. She felt as if the four of them were the only people awake in the city and everyone else was iced in sleep. She wondered about the boys, if they had stolen the skateboards, if that was what they had instead of homes. "Ask her if she wants to go to a shelter," she said, but at the same time her hand closed around the wallet in her coat pocket. She drew it out, seeing the older boy's green eyes come closer, realizing two things simultaneously: that the boy would take it, and that it was the wallet she had stolen, still empty except for its protective leaf of tissue.

Something collided with the back of her legs, hard, at the same time the boy snatched at her hands. The next instant they were flying away on the skateboards, calling to each other in shrill, excited voices. The sleet was coming down in a fine curtain now, and their figures blurred in the distance, dissolving.

The old woman was laughing into the curb, a sound full of ancient spit. "Yes, funny," Judy agreed. "Joke."

She started back the way she'd come, back to the man who did not love her. Well, OK. She didn't particularly love herself. When she reached the apartment house her legs were as numb as stumps, her hair full of ice. The city birds were calling, their voices small in the gray air.

She opened the apartment door cautiously. He was asleep on the couch, the blankets dragged into a cocoon around him. The record lay in two pieces on the floor, a perfect, jagged crack, like something in the comics.

She had begun to shiver. She peered over the edge of the blankets to look at his face. Sleep made it appear slack, as if a pin that held it together had come loose, and anger, amusement, indifference, all the things that made him recognizable, had dropped away. Human? Yes, she decided, and her shivering increased, her heart started up like a drill in her chest, painfully, dangerously. There was no reason not to love anyone.

Nominated by Molly Giles, C. E. Poverman

SKUNK DREAMS

by LOUISE ERDRICH

from THE GEORGIA REVIEW

W HEN I was fourteen, I slept alone on a North Dakota football field under the cold stars on an early spring night. May is unpredictable in the Red River Valley, and I happened to hit a night when frost formed in the grass. A skunk trailed a plume of steam across the forty-yard line near moonrise. I tucked the top of my sleeping bag over my head and was just dozing off when the skunk walked onto me with simple authority.

Its ripe odor must have dissipated in the frozen earth of its winterlong hibernation, because it didn't smell all that bad, or perhaps it was just that I took shallow breaths in numb surprise. I felt him—her, whatever—pause on the side of my hip and turn around twice before evidently deciding I was a good place to sleep. At the back of my knees, on the quilting of my sleeping bag, it trod out a spot for itself and then, with a serene little groan, curled up and lay perfectly still. That made two of us. I was wildly awake, trying to forget the sharpness and number of skunk teeth, trying not to think of the high percentage of skunks with rabies, or the reason that on camping trips my father always kept a hatchet underneath his pillow.

Inside the bag, I felt as if I might smother. Carefully, making only the slightest of rustles, I drew the bag away from my face and took a deep breath of the night air, enriched with skunk, but clear and watery and cold. It wasn't so bad, and the skunk didn't stir at all, so I watched the moon—caught that night in an envelope of silk, a mist—pass over my sleeping field of teenage guts

196

and glory. The grass in spring that has lain beneath the snow har-
bors a sere dust both old and fresh. I smelled that newness be-
neath the rank tone of my bag-mate—the stiff fragrance of damp
earth and the thick pungency of newly manured fields a mile or
two away—along with my sleeping bag's smell, slightly mil-
dewed, forever smoky. The skunk settled even closer and began
to breathe rapidly; its feet jerked a little like a dog's. I sank
against the earth, and fell asleep too.

Of what easily tipped cans, what molten sludge, what dogs in
yards on chains, what leftover macaroni casseroles, what cellar
holes, crawl spaces, burrows taken from meek woodchucks, of
what miracles of garbage did my skunk dream? Or did it, since
we can't be sure, dream the plot of *Moby-Dick,* how to properly
age parmesan, or how to restore the brick-walled, tumbledown
creamery that was its home? We don't know about the dreams of
any other biota, and even much about our own. If dreams are an
actual dimension, as some assert, then the usual rules of life by
which we abide do not apply. In that place, skunks may certainly
dream themselves into the vests of stockbrokers. Perhaps that
night the skunk and I dreamed each other's thoughts or are still
dreaming them. To paraphrase the problem of the Chinese sage,
I may be a woman who has dreamed herself a skunk, or a skunk
still dreaming that she is a woman.

In a book called *Death and Consciousness,* David H. Lund—who
wants very much to believe in life after death—describes human
dream-life as a possible model for a disembodied existence:

> Many of one's dreams are such that they involve the
> activities of an apparently embodied person whom one
> takes to be oneself as long as one dreams. . . . What-
> ever is the source of the imagery . . . apparently has
> the capacity to bring about images of a human body
> and to impart the feeling that the body is mine. It is, of
> course, just an image body, but it serves as a perfectly
> good body for the dream experience. I regard it as
> mine, I act on the dream environment by means of it,
> and it constitutes the center of the perceptual world of
> my dream.

Over the years I have acquired and reshuffled my beliefs and
doubts about whether we live on after death—in any shape or

form, that is, besides the molecular level at which I am to be absorbed by the taproots of cemetery pines and the tangled mats of fearfully poisoned, too-green lawn grass. I want something of the self on whom I have worked so hard to survive the loss of the body (which, incidentally, the self has done a fairly decent job of looking after, excepting spells of too much cabernet and a few idiotic years of rolling my own cigarettes out of Virginia Blond tobacco). I am put out with the marvelous discoveries of the intricate biochemical configuration of our brains, though I realize that the processes themselves are quite miraculous. I understand that I should be self-proud, content to gee-whiz at the fact that I am the world's only mechanism that can admire itself. I should be grateful that life is here today, though gone tomorrow, but I can't help it. I want more.

Skunks don't mind each other's vile perfume. Obviously, they find each other more than tolerable. And even I, who have been in the presence of a direct skunk hit, wouldn't classify their weapon as mere smell. It is more on the order of a reality-enhancing experience. It's not so pleasant as standing in a grove of old-growth red cedars, or on a lyrical moonshed plain, or watching trout rise to the shadow of your hand on the placid surface of an Alpine lake. When the skunk lets go, you're surrounded by skunk presence: inhabited, owned, involved with something you can only describe as powerfully *there*.

I woke at dawn, stunned into that sprayed state of being. The dog that had approached me was rolling in the grass, half-addled, sprayed too. The skunk was gone. I abandoned my sleeping bag and started home. Up Eighth Street, past the tiny blue and pink houses, past my grade school, past all the addresses where I had baby-sat, I walked in my own strange wind. The streets were wide and empty; I met no one—not a dog, not a squirrel, not even an early robin. Perhaps they had all scattered before me, blocks away. I had gone out to sleep on the football field because I was afflicted with a sadness I had to dramatize. Mood swings had begun, hormones, feverish and brutal. They were nothing to me now. My emotions had seemed vast, dark, and sickeningly private. But they were minor, mere wisps, compared to skunk.

I have found that my best dreams come to me in cheap motels. One such dream about an especially haunting place occurred in a rattling room in Valley City, North Dakota. There, in the home of the Winter Show, in the Rudolph Hotel I was to spend a week-long residency as a poet-in-the-schools. I was supporting myself, at the time, by teaching poetry to children, convicts, rehabilitation patients, high-school hoods, and recovering alcoholics. What a marvelous job it was, and what opportunities I had to dream, since I paid my own lodging and lived low, sometimes taking rooms for less than ten dollars a night in motels that had already been closed by local health departments.

The images that assailed me in Valley City came about because the bedspread was so thin and worn—a mere brown tissuey curtain—that I had to sleep beneath my faux fur Salvation Army coat, wearing all of my clothing, even a scarf. Cold often brings on the most spectacular of my dreams, as if my brain has been incited to fevered activity. On that particular frigid fall night, the cold somehow seemed to snap boundaries, shift my time continuum, and perhaps even allow me to visit my own life in a future moment. After waking once, transferring the contents of my entire suitcase onto my person, and shivering to sleep again, I dreamed of a vast, dark, fenced place. The fencing was chain-link in places, chicken wire, sagging X wire, barbed wire on top, jerry-built with tipped-out poles and uncertain corners nailed to log posts and growing trees. And yet it was quite impermeable and solid, as time-tested, broken-looking things so often are.

Behind it, trees ran for miles—large trees, grown trees, big pines the likes of which do not exist in the Great Plains. In my dream I walked up to the fence, looked within, and saw tawny, humpbacked elk move among the great trunks and slashing green arms. Suave, imponderable, magnificently dumb, they lurched and floated through the dim-complexioned air. One turned, however, before they all vanished, and from either side of that flimsy-looking barrier there passed between us a look, a communion, a long and measureless regard that left me, on waking, with a sensation of penetrating sorrow.

I didn't think about my dream for many years, until after I moved to New Hampshire. I had become urbanized and sedentary since the days when I slept with skunks, and I had turned inward. For several years I spent my days leaning above a strange desk, a green door on stilts, which was so high that to sit at it I bought a barstool upholstered in brown leatherette. Besides, the entire Northeast seemed like the inside of a house to me, the sky small and oddly lit, as if by an electric bulb. The sun did not pop over the great trees for hours—and then went down so soon. I was suspicious of Eastern land: the undramatic loveliness, the small scale, the lack of sky to watch, the way the weather sneaked up without enough warning.

The woods themselves seemed bogus at first—every inch of the ground turned over more than once, and even in the second growth of old pines so much human evidence. Rock walls ran everywhere, grown through and tumbled, as if the dead still had claims they imposed. The unkillable and fiercely contorted trees of old orchards, those revenants, spooked me when I walked in the woods. The blasted limbs spread a white lace cold as fire in the spring, and the odor of the blossoms was furiously spectral, sweet. When I stood beneath the canopies that hummed and shook with bees, I heard voices, other voices, and I did not understand what they were saying, where they had come from, what drove them into this earth.

Then, as often happens to sparring adversaries in 1940's movies, I fell in love.

After a few years of living in the country, the impulse to simply *get outside* hit me, strengthened, and became again a habit of thought, a reason for storytelling, an uneasy impatience with walls and roads. At first, when I had that urge, I had to get into a car and drive fifteen hundred miles before I was back in a place that I defined as *out*. The West, or the edge of it anyway, the great level patchwork of chemically treated fields and tortured grazing land, was the outside I had internalized. In the rich Red River Valley, where the valuable cropland is practically measured in inches, environmental areas are defined and proudly pointed out as stretches of roadway where the ditches are not mowed. Deer and pheasants survive in shelter belts—rows of Russian olive, plum, sometimes evergreen—planted at the edges of fields. The former tall-grass prairie has now become a collection of mechanized gardens tended by an array of air-conditioned farm implements and bearing an increasing amount of pesticide and herbicide in each black teaspoon of dirt. Nevertheless, no amount of reality changed the fact that I still *thought* of eastern North Dakota as wild.

In time, though, *out* became outside my door in New England. By walking across the road and sitting in my little writing house—a place surrounded by trees, thick plumes of grass, jets of ferns, and banks of touch-me-not—or just by looking out a screen door or window, I started to notice what there was to see. In time, the smothering woods that had always seemed part of Northeastern civilization—more an inside than an outside, more like a friendly garden—revealed themselves as forceful and complex. The growth of plants, the lush celebratory springs made a grasslands person drunk. The world turned dazzling green, the hills rode like comfortable and flowing animals. Everywhere there was the sound of water moving.

And yet, even though I finally grew closer to these woods, on some days I still wanted to tear them from before my eyes.

I wanted to *see*. Where I grew up, our house looked out on the western horizon. I could see horizon when I played. I could see it when I walked to school. It was always there, a line beyond everything, a simple line of changing shades and colors that ringed the town, a vast place. That was it. Down at the end of every grid of streets: vastness. Out the windows of the high school: vastness. From the drive-in theater where I went parking in a purple Duster: vast distance. That is why, on lovely New England days when everything should have been all right—a spring day, for instance, when the earth had risen through the air in patches and the sky lowered, dim and warm—I fell sick with longing for the horizon. I wanted the clean line, the simple line, the clouds marching over it in feathered masses. I suffered from horizon sickness. But it sounds crazy for a grown woman to throw herself at the sky, and the thing is, I wanted to get well. And so to compensate for horizon sickness, for the great longing that seemed both romantically German and pragmatically Chippewa in origin, I found solace in trees.

Trees are a changing landscape of sound—and the sound I grew attached to, possible only near large deciduous forests, was the great hushed roar of thousands and millions of leaves brushing and touching one another. Windy days were like sitting just out of sight of an ocean, the great magnetic ocean of wind. All around me, I watched the trees tossing, their heads bending. At times the movement seemed passionate, as though they were flung together in an eager embrace, caressing each other, branch

201

to branch. If there is a vegetative soul, an animating power that all things share, there must be great rejoicing out there on windy days, ecstasy, for trees move so slowly on calm days. At least it seems that way to us. On days of high wind they move so freely it must give them a cellular pleasure close to terror.

Unused to walking in the woods, I did not realize that trees dropped branches—often large ones—or that there was any possible danger in going out on windy days, drawn by the natural drama. There was a white pine I loved, a tree of the size foresters call *overgrown*, a waste, a thing made of long-since harvestable material. The tree was so big that three people couldn't reach around it. Standing at the bottom, craning back, fingers clenched in grooves of bark, I held on as the crown of the tree roared and beat the air a hundred feet above. The movement was frantic, the soft-needled branches long and supple. I thought of a woman tossing, anchored in passion: calm one instant, full-throated the next, hair vast and dark, shedding the piercing, fresh oil of broken needles. I went to visit her often, and walked onward, farther, though it was not so far at all, and then one day I reached the fence.

Chain-link in places, chicken wire, sagging X wire, barbed wire on top, jerry-built with tipped-out poles and uncertain corners nailed to log posts and growing trees, still it seemed impermeable and solid. Behind it, there were trees for miles: large trees, grown trees, big pines. I walked up to the fence, looked within, and could see elk moving. Suave, imponderable, magnificently dumb, they lurched and floated through the dim air.

I was on the edge of a game park, a rich man's huge wilderness, probably the largest parcel of protected land in western New Hampshire, certainly the largest privately owned piece I knew about. At forty square miles—25,000 acres—it was bigger than my mother's home reservation. And it had the oddest fence around it that I'd ever seen, the longest and the tackiest. Though partially electrified, the side closest to our house was so piddling that an elk could easily have tossed it apart. Certainly a half-ton wild boar, the condensed and living version of a tank, could have strolled right through. But then animals, much like most humans, don't charge through fences unless they have sound reasons. As I soon found out, because I naturally grew fascinated with the place, there were many more animals trying to get into the park than out, and they couldn't have cared less about ending up in a hunter's stew pot.

These were not wild animals, the elk—since they were grained at feeding stations, how could they be? They were not domesticated either, however, for beyond the no-hunt boundaries they fled and vanished. They were game. Since there is no sport in shooting feedlot steers, these animals—still harboring wild traits and therefore more challenging to kill—were maintained to provide blood pleasure for the members of the Blue Mountain Forest Association.

As I walked away from the fence that day, I was of two minds about the place—and I am still. Shooting animals inside fences, no matter how big the area they have to hide in, seems abominable and silly. And yet, I was glad for that wilderness. Though secretly managed and off limits to me, it was the source of flocks of evening grosbeaks and pine siskins, of wild turkey, ravens, and grouse, of Eastern coyote, oxygen-rich air, foxes, goldfinches, skunk, and bears that tunneled in and out.

I had dreamed of this place in St. Thomas, or it had dreamed me. There was affinity here, beyond any explanation I could offer, so I didn't try. I continued to visit the tracts of big trees, and on deep nights—windy nights, especially when it stormed—I liked to fall asleep imagining details. I saw the great crowns touching, heard the raving sound of wind and thriving, knocking cries as the blackest of ravens flung themselves across acres upon indifferent acres of tossing, old-growth pine. I could fall asleep picturing how, below that dark air, taproots thrust into a deeper blankness, drinking the powerful rain.

Or was it so only in my dreams? The park, known locally as Corbin's Park, after its founder Austin Corbin, is knit together of land and farmsteads he bought in the late nineteenth century from 275 individuals. Among the first animals released there, before the place became a hunting club, were thirty buffalo, remnants of the vast Western herds. Their presence piqued the interest of Ernest Harold Bayne, a conservation-minded local journalist, who attempted to break a pair of buffalo calves to the yoke. He exhibited them at county fairs and even knit mittens out of buffalo wool, hoping to convince the skeptical of their usefulness. His work inspired sympathy, if not a trend for buffalo yarn, and collective zeal for the salvation of the buffalo grew until by 1915 the American Bison Society, of which Bayne was secretary, helped form government reserves that eventually more than doubled the herds that remained.

The buffalo dream seems to have been the park's most noble hour. Since that time it has been the haunt of wealthy hunting enthusiasts. The owner of Ruger Arms currently inhabits the stunning, butter-yellow original Corbin mansion and would like to buy the whole park for his exclusive use, or so local gossip has it.

For some months I walked the boundary admiring the tangled landscape, at least all I could see. After my first apprehension, I ignored the fence. I walked along it as if it simply did not exist, as if I really was part of that place which lay just beyond my reach. The British psychotherapist Adam Phillips has examined obstacles from several different angles, attempting to define their emotional use. "It is impossible to imagine desire without obstacles," he writes, "and wherever we find something to be an obstacle we are at the same time desiring something. It is part of the fascination of the Oedipus story in particular, and perhaps narrative in general, that we and the heroes and heroines of our fictions never know whether obstacles create desire or desire creates obstacles." He goes on to characterize the Unconscious, our dream world, as a place without obstacles: "A good question to ask of a dream is: What are the obstacles that have been removed to make this extraordinary scene possible?"

My dream, however, was about obstacles still in place. The fence was the main component, the defining characteristic of the forbidden territory that I watched but could not enter or experience. The obstacles that we overcome define us. We are composed of hurdles we set up to pace our headlong needs, to control our desires, or against which to measure our growth. "Without obstacles," Phillips writes, "the notion of development is inconceivable. There would be nothing to master."

Walking along the boundary of the park no longer satisfied me. The preciousness and deceptive stability of that fence began to rankle. Longing filled me. I wanted to brush against the old pine bark and pass beyond the ridge, to see specifically what was there: what Blue Mountain, what empty views, what lavender hillside, what old cellar holes, what unlikely animals. I was filled with poacher's lust, except I wanted only to smell the air. The linked web restraining me began to grate, and I started to look for weak spots, holes, places where the rough wire sagged. From the moment I began to see the fence as permeable, it became something to overcome. I returned time after time—partly to see if I could spot anyone on the other side, partly because I knew I must trespass.

Then, one clear, midwinter morning, in the middle of a half-hearted thaw, I walked along the fence until I came to a place that looked shaky—and was. I went through. There were no trails that I could see, and I knew I needed to stay away from any perimeter roads or snowmobile paths, as well as from the feeding stations where the animals congregated. I wanted to see the animals, but only from a distance. Of course, as I walked on, leaving a trail easily backtracked, I encountered no animals at all. Still, the terrain was beautiful, the columns of pine tall and satisfyingly heavy, the patches of oak and elderly maple from an occasional farmstead knotted and patient. I was satisfied and, sometime in the early afternoon, I decided to turn back and head toward the fence again. Skirting a low, boggy area that teemed with wild turkey tracks, I was just heading toward the edge of a deadfall of trashed dead branches and brush, when I stared too hard into the sun, and stumbled.

In a half crouch, I looked straight into the face of a boar, massive as a boulder. Cornfed, razor-tusked, alert, sensitive ears pricked, it edged slightly backward into the covering shadows. Two ice picks of light gleamed from its shrouded, tiny eyes, impossible to read. Beyond the rock of its shoulder, I saw more: a sow and three cinnamon-brown farrows crossing a small field of glare snow, lit by dazzling sun. The young skittered along, lumps of muscled fat on tiny hooves. They reminded me of snowsuited toddlers on new skates. When they were out of sight the boar melted through the brush after them, leaving not a snapped twig or crushed leaf in his wake.

I almost didn't breathe in the silence, letting the fact of that presence settle before I retraced my own tracks.

Since then, I've been to the game park via front gates, driven down the avenues of tough old trees, and seen herds of wild pigs and elk meandering past the residence of the gamekeeper. A no-hunting zone exists around the house, where the animals are almost tame. But I've been told by privileged hunters that just beyond that invisible boundary they vanish, becoming suddenly and preternaturally elusive.

There is something in me that resists the notion of fair use of this land if the only alternative is to have it cut up, sold off in lots, condominiumized. Yet the dumb fervor of the place depresses me—the wilderness locked up and managed but not for its sake; the animals imported and cultivated to give pleasure through their deaths. All animals, that is, except for skunks.

Not worth hunting, inedible except to old trappers like my great uncle Ben Gourneau, who boiled his skunk with onions in three changes of water, skunks pass in and out of Corbin's Park without hindrance, without concern. They live off the corn in the feeding cribs (or the mice it draws), off the garbage of my rural neighbors, off bugs and frogs and grubs. They nudge their way onto our back porch for catfood, and even when disturbed they do not, ever, hurry. It's easy to get near a skunk, even to capture one. When skunks become a nuisance, people either shoot them or catch them in crates, cardboard boxes, Hav-A-Hart traps, plastic garbage barrels.

Natives of the upper Connecticut River valley have neatly solved the problem of what to do with such catches. They hoist their trapped mustelid into the back of a pickup truck and cart the animal across the river to the neighboring state—New Hampshire to Vermont, Vermont to New Hampshire—before releasing it. The skunk population is estimated as about even on both sides.

We should take comfort from the skunk, an arrogant creature so pleased with its own devices that it never runs from harm, just turns its back in total confidence. If I were an animal, I'd choose to be a skunk: live fearlessly, eat anything, gestate my young in just two months, and fall into a state of dreaming torpor when the cold bit hard. Wherever I went, I'd leave my sloppy tracks. I wouldn't walk so much as putter, destinationless, in a serene belligerence—past hunters, past death overhead, past death all around.

Nominated by Philip Booth, Michael Martone

OVER ALL

by THOMAS RABBITT

from PLOUGHSHARES

> *Gored by the climacteric of his want*
> *He stalls above me like an elephant.*
> —Robert Lowell

Stalls? I'd have wondered, *Has he died at last?*
Like Antony's self-pity: *I am dying, Egypt, dying.*
Like Nelson Rockefeller undoing Happy on his hooker.
Like a stuck pig who hasn't seen the dripping knife,
Kemal Pasha's grunting, grunting, till his air gives out
And leaves me trapped and scared beneath him,
If he be rich and all our children blond . . .
If he be dead and I am found like this . . .
If, if, if . . . Whatever death this man fears most
It can't be this, caught under the obscene collapse
Of cooling flesh and blood and hair and bone.
One can feel the lost already beginning to rot.
Worse, one feels oneself going soft, then gone.
In the dresser mirror the small slice of him bursts
And glows and then grows quickly gray as ash
And one thinks, while waiting, Would it be better now
Or worse to have had that mirror hung above the bed?
So, when they called me from the hospital to say
He'd collapsed in a cab on his way to Logan
And was DOA in the ER at MGH, I thought:
That's O.K. That's great. Thank God the old fart
Didn't die on me, didn't die at six a.m.
When we were fucking, or in the shower, or at breakfast.

He didn't die on me! He rolled off. Dressed and left.
Still, I'll have to go downtown, I'll have to face
Confessing that I can identify his last remains.

Nominated by Ploughshares

A PORTRAIT OF THE SELF AS NATION, 1990–1991

by MARILYN CHIN

from ZYZZYVA

> *Fit in dominata servitus*
> *In servitude dominatus*
> *In mastery there is bondage*
> *In bondage there is mastery*
> *(Latin proverb)*

> *The stranger and the enemy*
> *We have seen him in the mirror.*
> *(George Seferis)*

Forgive me Head Master
but you see, I have forgotten
to put on my black lace underwear, and instead
I have hiked my slip up, up to my waist
so that I can enjoy the breeze.
It feels good to be *without*,
so good as to be salacious.
The feeling of flesh kissing tweed.
If ecstasy had a color, it would be
yellow and pink, yellow and pink
Mongolian skin rubbed raw.
The serrated lining especially fine
like wearing a hair-shirt, inches above the knee.
When was the last time I made love?
The last century? With a wan missionary.

Or was it San Wu the Bailiff?
The tax-collector who came for my tithes?
The herdboy, the ox, on the bridge of magpies?
It was Roberto, certainly,
high on coke, circling the galaxy.
Or my recent vagabond love
driving a reckless chariot, lost
in my feral country. *Country,* Oh I am
so punny, so very, very punny.
Dear Mr. Decorum, don't you agree?
It's not so much the length of the song
but the range of the emotions—Fear
has kept me a good pink monk and poetry
is my nunnery. Here I am alone in my altar,
self-hate, self-love, both self-erotic notions.
Eyes closed, listening to that one hand clapping—
not metaphysical trance, but fleshly mutilation—
and loving *it,* myself and that pink womb, my bed.
Reading "Ching Ping Mei" in the "expurgated"   (1)
where all the female protagonists were named
Lotus.
Those damned licentious women named us
Modest, Virtue, Cautious, Endearing,
Demure-dewdrop, Plum-aster, Petal-stamen.
They teach us to walk headbent in devotion,
to honor the five relations, ten sacraments.
Meanwhile, the feast is brewing elsewhere,
the ox is slaughtered and her entrails are hung
on the branches for the poor. They convince us, yes,
our chastity will save the nation—Oh mothers,
all your sweet epithets didn't make us wise!
Orchid by any other name is equally seditious.

Now, where was I, oh yes, now I remember,
the last time I made love, it was to *you.*
I faintly remember your whiskers
against my tender nape.
You were a conquering barbarian,
helmeted, halberded,
beneath the gauntleted moon,

210

whispering Hunnish or English—
so-long Oolong went the racist song,
bye-bye little chinky butterfly.
There is no cure for self-pity,
the disease is death,
ennui, disaffection,
a roll of flesh-colored tract homes crowding my imagination.
I do hate my loneliness,
sitting cross-legged in my room,
satisfied with a few off-rhymes,
sending off precious haiku to some inconspicuous journal
named "left Leaning Bamboo."
You, my precious reader, O sweet voyeur,
sweaty, balding, bespeckled,
in a rumpled rayon shirt
and a neo-Troubadour chignon,
politics mildly centrist,
the *right* fork for the *right* occasions,
matriculant of the best schools—
herewith, my last confession,
(with decorous and perfect diction)
I loathe to admit. Yet, I shall admit it:
there was no Colonialist coercion,
sadly, we blended together well.
I was poor, starving, wartorn,
an empty coffin to be filled,
You were a young, ambitious Lieutenant
with dreams of becoming Prince
of a "new world order," Lord
over the League of Nations.

Lover, destroyer, savior!
I remember that moment of beguilement,
one hand muffling my mouth,
one hand untying my sash—
On your throat dangled a golden cross.
Your god is jealous, your god is cruel.
So, when did you finally return?
And . . . was there a second coming?
My memory is failing me, perhaps

you came too late,
(we were already dead).
Perhaps, you didn't come at all,
you had a deadline to meet,
another alliance to secure,
another resistance to break.
Or you came too often
to my painful dismay.
(Oh how facile the liberator's hand.)
Often when I was asleep
You would hover over me
with your great silent wingspan
and watch me sadly.
This is the way you want me—
asleep, quiescent, almost dead,
sedated by lush immigrant dreams
of global bliss, connubial harmony.

Yet, I shall always remember
and deign to forgive
(long before I am satiated,
long before I am spent)
that last pressured cry,
"your little death."
Under the halcyon light
you would smoke and contemplate
the sea and debris,
that barbaric keening
of what it means to be free.
As if we were ever free,
as if ever we could be.
Said the judge,
"Congratulations,
On this day, fifteen of November, 1967,
Marilyn Mei Ling Chin,
application # z-z-z-z-z,
you are an American citizen,
naturalized in the name of God
the father, God the son and the Holy Ghost."
Time assuages, and even

the Yellow River becomes clean . . .

Meanwhile we forget
the power of exclusion   (2)
what you are walling in or out—
and to whom you must give offence.
The hungry, the slovenly, the convicts
need not apply.
The syphilitic, the consumptive
may not moor.
The hookwormed and tracomaed   (3)
(and the likewise infested).
The gypsies, the sodomists, the mentally infirm.
The pagans, the heathens, the non-
denominational—
The coloureds, the mixed-races and the reds.
The communists, the usurous,
the mutants, the Hibakushas, the hags . . .   (4)

Oh connoiseurs of gastronomy and *keemun* tea!
My foes, my loves,
how eloquent your discrimination,
how precise your poetry.
Last night, in our large, rotund bed,
we witnessed the fall. *Ours*
was an "aerial war." Bombs
glittering in the twilight sky
against the Star Spangled Banner.
Dunes and dunes of sand,
fields and fields of rice.
A thousand charred oil wells,
the firebrands of night.
Ecstasy made us tired.

Sir, Master, Dominatrix,
Fall—was a glorious season for the hegemonists.
We took long melancholy strolls on the beach,
digressed on art and politics
in a quaint wharfside cafe in La Jolla.
The storm gazed our bare arms gently . . .

213

History has never failed us.
Why save Babylonia or Cathay,
when we can always have Paris?
Darling, if we are to remember at all,
let us remember it well—
We were fierce, yet tender,
fierce and tender.

Nominated by Rita Dove

Notes:

1) "Ching Ping Mei"—Chinese erotic novel.

2) Exclusion—refers to various "exclusion acts" or anti-Chinese legislation which attempted to halt the flow of Chinese immigrants to the U.S.

3) Hookworm and tracoma—two diseases which kept many Chinese detained and quarantined at Angel Island.

4) Hibakushas—scarred survivors of the atom bomb and their deformed descendants.

TWICE REMOVED

by RALPH ANGEL

from VOLT

Not even sleep (though I'm ashamed of that too).
Or watching my sleeping self drift out and kick harder, burst
   awake, and then the nothing,
leaf-shadow, a shave and
black coffee, I know how a dream sounds.

This ease. This difficulty. The brain that lives on a little longer.
   The long
commute (not even what happened back then—this sort of
giving up with no one around and therefore
no charge for anything).

No word. No feeling
when a feeling wells up and is that much further.
Cupola and drumming, from the inside, holes open up a sky no
   thicker than cardboard.
You, the one I'd step over. You, whom I care for

and lie to, who doesn't want to, either, not even this failure
(having grown so used to it), the wreck that still
seeps from a stone, sinks down among the roots and, in their
   perfect darkness, such bloom.
No name for it. No place inscribed with its own grief,

where the grass resists, and I too
resist.

No place to get to. No place to leave from. No place where those times,
and times like these, are allowed to die.

Nominated by James Harms, David Rivard

AGE OF REASON

fiction by JEWEL MOGAN

from ONTARIO REVIEW

Nana read to them under her bed lamp as she always did when their grandaddy, whom they called Grundy, was working late at the market. She read for Rachel something from her photo-copied church materials that she felt was suitable for eleven-year-olds, while Tolliver made gentle flopping movements with his limbs, occasionally throwing his leg over Nana, putting his fingers into her ears and his, taking the fingers out, lacing his fingers together, crooning to himself sleepily. He sensed when the moral of the piece had been hammered out and said, "Now. My turn."

"Not yet. Shh."

He shushed. He was exceedingly well-mannered for a four-year-old. Their grandmother finished reading the material—it had to do with the gifts of the Spirit—and Tolliver reached over to the bedside table for his book, *Jesus Loves Me*. Rachel, nestling closer to her Nana, listened to this story too, although she had heard it a hundred times. She decided she would read the words backwards. She liked to do this when they were riding around. She liked to be Alice in Backwards Land and read billboards and signs backwards. She and her brother rode around a lot with Grundy and Nana. When Grundy was one with the Spirit they rode all kinds of places, him talking fast and loud, there and back, and Nana lots of times not saying a single word, which their grandaddy never noticed. When he was that way they visited church friends and prayer groups one behind the other, attended every revival for miles around. She often wondered what they would pick up and do next. On the good side, they went to Putt-Putt or the Dairy Queen when they were not doing church things. Once, on a day that was a dream come true, they drove to Dollywood! They were in paradise for an unforgettable eight hours.

At one of their picnics to Standing Stone State Park, Grundy had been inspired and had run around shouting, "I understand every thing! I understand every thing!" And something about the universe, the universe. He shouted many other holy things, like "Two men will be out in the field; one will be taken and one will be left. Two women will be grinding meal; one will be taken and one will be left." And, "Ha. Ha. Safe are the blessed in the bosom of the Lord!" and he and Nana sang. He kind of shook Nana into singing, shouting, "Good God, woman, does anything move you? I am moved by every thing!" After they ate lunch, Nana got him to calm down by them praying in tongues until he was slain in the Spirit and it turned into a short nap. Rachel and Tolliver wanted permission to go and look at the waterfall. They waited, watching his jerky movements as he slept. When he was waking up, Rachel (she knew to do this) had crept up to him softly on her knees and spoken to him gently. He had screamed.

They were always changing. They changed houses. Once they just moved down the street. They changed cars, but only one rattletrap for another, changed telephone numbers most of all, changed friends within their church. Her grandaddy had never changed occupations; he had always been a butcher. But he had worked at all the supermarkets in Cumberland County, there not being more than half a dozen big grocery stores in these mountains. He rearranged the furniture, the contents of the garage, and the car trunk over and over. He carried butchering tools around in the trunk—an extra cleaver and big knives. Recently she had watched him add a hatchet and a long-handled ax to the cleaver and knives. He wasn't happy at the market where he was now, but he had told Nana he'd just as well stay there for the two years until his retirement or the Rapture, whichever came first. The Rapture had just been invented at that time, and their whole church was beginning to buzz about it.

They never changed churches. They all spent endless hours in Jesus' one house while games went unplayed, races unrun. They could have been taking giant steps or petting puppies. Not their own puppies—they had no pets—but Whatzit, the Neilsons-next-door's dog, had puppies. Five wriggling, cuddly, adorable little puppies. She would give anything to have any one of them, especially the one with two white feet. She could sit and watch him and pet him by the hour.

In church there was body twisting and clapping, love-shouts and singing, nasal trembly, sing-songy singing. Tolliver slept through even the noisiest parts of it, stretched out on the wooden pew, but Rachel would alternately doze and jolt awake until it felt like she was sitting on pins and needles and she wanted to scream. Her legs were so jerky they wanted to run for miles and her body wanted to throw itself down in lush grass and roll around. When they had the chance, how feverishly they played on the Neilsons' lawn before darkness descended. She thought she would like Sheila Neilson's church, First United Methodist. It sounded kind and strong. But, no, they never changed churches. She hoped that when they were taken up, God's heaven would be more interesting than His house.

She had been able to attend the same school in spite of all their changing: the beloved big-little school whose library she had squeezed dry from Aladdin to Oz, starting with the animal books. All the books were perfect. There were only grades of perfect and superperfect. *The Little House on the Prairie* by Laura Ingalls Wilder, for example, as dear as it was, couldn't compare with *Caddie Woodlawn* by Carol Ryrie Brink. The magic names of the authors, often repeated reverently to herself, were part of the unshakableness of the titles. She, too, would have three names when she grew up. Several times a year she checked out *Caddie Woodlawn* just to see if it was still as good, and it almost always was. She sometimes checked it out and back in on the expiration date unread. It was important just to have it near her, on her bed, or the table or chair next to the bed. She always brought Caddie along on their trips.

Caddie slipped away to join Tom and Warren on the back step. They sat together, and Nero lay close to their feet. Out by the barn, Robert Ireton was strumming his banjo and singing softly. Something something something. Then *Behind the barn there*

219

*were northern lights, long white fingers shooting up in the black-
ness of the sky; and the three adventurers were overcome by that
delicious weariness which suddenly overtakes one at the end of an
outdoor day.*

"Em sevol suseJ," she murmured, as Nana read *Jesus Loves Me*
and Tolliver put his hands palm to palm, prayerlike. She
watched, fascinated, as he placed thumb to forefinger on each
hand and made graceful movements with them, like his hands
were two deaf people talking to each other. Jesus loves Em. She
called herself that sometimes. Backwards me.

She looked up from the pillow to Nana's sweet saggy face.
There was a small permanent indentation in Nana's lower lip
where in cold weather she tore at the tiny tatters of skin with her
teeth or sometimes with her fingertips, repeatedly peeling off
skin. Rachel watched the depression in her lip move as her lips
moved. Nana never changed anything about herself. She wore
the same two or three outfits all the time. She sighed a lot over
the world and people's troubles. When her voice would trail off
without finishing its sentence, you had to finish it for her, but
usually, you knew what she meant to say. You couldn't rush Nana.
When you did, she would always say, "I can't think. . . . I can't
think. . . ." When Grundy frowned, Nana frowned. When he
laughed, she smiled.

Rachel hungrily kissed her grandma six times on the side of
her face. She was getting drowsy, so she said goodnight and went
to bed before *Jesus Loves Me* was over.

Between the short simple sentences of the book the grand-
mother could hear the schoolhouse regulator on the opposite wall
limping. She had told Ernest, her husband, that it was limping.
It was going tock-TICK tock-TICK all night long, she had told
him. He told her, "If it's out of beat, it's not enough for me to
hear." Later, he said, "I adjusted it very slightly." She could hear
it now, going tock-TICK tock-TICK again. She guessed it was out
of beat just enough to distract her, but not enough to cause it to
stop beating.

Tolliver was still singing to himself as she read. When she fin-
ished his story he wandered into salad talk, gradually diminishing
to a whispered conversation with himself. The whispers floated
up to the bed lamp and he watched them with fixed, luminous

220

eyes. Suddenly he was asleep. She switched off the lamp and was already lonesome for him. There would be a few precious minutes before Ernest came home. In the dark she lifted Tolliver's hand, so yielding it frightened her, took her breath away. She kissed his fingers, brooded, prayed fervently with his fingers to her moving lips. She put him to bed in his own small room. Then she went back to her bed and lay still, gave herself over to silent crying which she stifled immediately Ernest came in.

He was not one in the Spirit at this time, so they greeted each other as she expected, solemnly and shortly. He took off his pants and shirt, which always smelled of blood, balled them up with his underwear, threw it all into the clothes basket. When he was not in the Spirit he would not shower. A shower would not make him clean, he said. When he *was* in the Spirit he showered twice a day and he seemed to want sex nearly every day. Tonight he put on his pajamas and rolled solidly into her flank and into sleep. She took up crying again. It was two years since the children's mother, their daughter, died, and their father deserted the family.

She couldn't see the face of the clock on the opposite wall. It was that dark in the bedroom. Ernest liked it pitch black. She wouldn't be surprised, even if she had light, if that clock wouldn't turn its face away from her on purpose so she couldn't see the time. TOCK-tick. TOCK-tick. The times were turning out so bad. The time for the Rapture had come and gone. It had been a bitter disappointment to her and Ernest and a large segment of their church that nothing had happened. She prayed now over the new date that had been set, not for the Rapture, but for the End. It was coming very soon, the day after Easter. Would it be by fire, this time? Oh, then the clocks would throw their hands to their faces in terror.

It was hours until she slept.

But now everything was fresh and young.
"A magic time of year," Caddie called it to herself. She loved both spring and fall. At the turning of the year things seemed to stir in her, that were lost sight of in the commonplace stretches of winter and summer.

The long long Palm Sunday service was over. Tolliver was still in his Wal-Mart suit and tie—Midget Man, Rachel called him on

221

Sundays when he was dressed like this—and she was in her new navy blue long cotton dress with a high ruffled neck, long sleeves with ruffles at the end, white stockings, and black patent-leather shoes. Her hair was in two pigtails with bows on the ends to match her dress. Nana was wearing her gray and white long-sleeve meeting dress and white patent-leather bag that was turning yellow where she held it.

They were driving out into the country; Grundy said it was a surprise where they were going. He had on a brand new suit of a pinkish-brown color and a purple tie. Maybe it was the tie that made the suit look pink. He was in the best mood she had ever seen him. He sang swingy gospel songs and when he couldn't think of any more songs, he sang made-up ones: "Safe are the blessed in the bosom of the Lord" and "Jib jibber-jibber jab, and jab jabber-jabber jib!" And laughed, Ha-Ha! Tolliver laughed his head off with him. She heard that silly rhyme and Tolliver's piping laughter all that night after they got home and went to bed.

They had left the main highway with its gray limestone outcroppings on either side that seeped water all the year around, but more so in the spring. The country road they were on was leading back into green hills. It was so beautiful out the car windows. Cornfields were shooting up all over and every so often they would glimpse a white farmhouse, tall and narrow, tucked back in the fold of two hills as they rounded a bend in the road. Between two other hills she saw the spider web of a tiny train trestle and a dark green river underneath. Then suddenly, they were turning in at one of those narrow farmhouses.

"Dunk knows you are coming for the lamb?" Nana asked worriedly.

"It's waiting for me. He's selling off half of his lambs next week. I got in on a good thing. He's giving me wholesale slaughter price on it."

"A lamb?" Rachel asked. "Are we going to get a lamb?"

"For our Easter dinner," said Nana.

It was a little boy lamb, and he was the most precious thing Rachel had ever seen or imagined in her most tumultuous rush of maternal love for the Neilsons' puppies, or Whatzit, or her baby dolls. His eyes! And his white woolly body, delicate little legs, and tiny hooves. You could still pick him up! although Dunk said he was as grown as he could be and still be called a lamb. His

222

little cries! He was unbelievable. On her knees, Rachel hugged him and stroked his thick yielding wool and gently dug her fingers into it. She longed to take him home for her own and care for him. All that she would do for him went through her mind in vivid flashes. She pictured his bed in a wooden box of straw in the corner of the garage next to the warm water heater, and the milk, and other as-yet-undetermined things she would feed him—she wasn't sure what lambs ate—and the purple and pink ribbons she would put around his neck. . . . And violet-colored bows! She would put violet bows on his precious woolly ear-flops. Neither she nor Tolliver had ever had a pet. Tolliver hugged him hungrily, too, said Ahhhh, put his head down on the lamb's neck and nuzzled the wool. They couldn't stop admiring all that whiteness and those melting eyes, his panting sides, his flanks.

But they weren't going to take him home. Not alive, anyway. Grundy had parked around the back of the barn and Dunk pointed out a spot for him to do the slaughtering that had a wooden table and a faucet and trough. Grundy got his white coat and tools out of the trunk. After he got the coat on, he took off his pants from underneath the coat. He took off his shoes and socks also.

No one watched, not even the farmer. Dunk's wife gave Tolliver and Rachel some lemonade and they sat on the back steps of the house with their heads drooping. They could hear Grundy behind the barn praying out loud over the animal with his gift of tongues, spinning webs of words, hanks, strings of loud words from the Bible and his own mind, while the lamb bleated every now and then. Rachel imagined that the cries must be very strong back there, but weakened by the time they reached the steps where she and Tolliver sat. Then there weren't any more sounds. Her heart was pounding heavily and she wanted to die instead of the lamb or even along with it, never feeling another thing, never having to lie awake waiting to go to sleep, never having to eat or drink again. Nothing worse than this could ever possibly happen to her. How long, she wondered, would a person have to go without eating to die?

On the way home nobody said a word except Tolliver. He chattered to himself from the time they started out. Rachel kept telling him under her breath, "Shut up. Oh, shut up." He probably never once thought of the ice chest of meat in the trunk, and he fell asleep halfway home. Grundy was out of the Spirit now, as far out of it as she had ever seen him. When he was not in the Spirit you would think he would get some peace. But it was the other way around. He would be sadder than sad. He would be the gloomiest man you ever saw. Down in the mullygumps, Nana said, sighing. He was deep in the mullygumps now, Rachel could tell by the slump of his body over the steering wheel, and his silence. Nana was leaning against the window, eyes closed, but she was not asleep. Rachel was learning to read them better, quite cunningly sometimes. It was a trick she herself used, pretending to sleep so she would not have to talk to him. They rode endless miles. The sun was gone and massive clouds on the horizon to which they were traveling were flexing their slow, heavy muscles.

"Rachel, you asleep?"

She didn't answer.

"Nana, you asleep?"

No answer.

"Nana!"

She answered him faintly, flatly, like the lamb's bleat.

"Are you prepared?"

"I've been ready for it."

"Since it will fall the day after Easter, I think we should wait until Easter Sunday to prepare the children."

"I don't think we should tell them anything. Let them enjoy Easter. We have to pray and expiate our sins, but they are innocent babes. They will be sinless before the Lord and taken up that way." The idea of the Rapture had hit their church and caught on like wildfire. Many were given the gift of tongues, prophesy, and healing. Nana herself had been almost miraculously raised out of her worthlessness and she felt urgings that she had been given the gift of prophecy. She had many messages to reveal, such as a Russian invasion of Germany, the death of Saddam Hussein in July of 1992, and the conversion of China. She prophesied these and other events aloud in church. None of the prophecies came true, and her self-esteem plunged to a lifetime low. Looking back, she should have prophesied that too, since she was too sinful to merit the gift of the Spirit. Neither did the Rapture occur on the expected date. The new date of annihilation gave her some hope, as death now seemed the only appropriate punishment for her sins and failures.

"Will it be like a fireball destroying the whole earth?" she asked.

"A big flash. You won't know it's happening except for a few seconds. Then it will all be over."

"Praise God."

"When I was nine years old I set my own clothes on fire. And ran from myself. Seemed like an eternity but it was only a few seconds. My mother smothered the fire."

Nana looked at his stony profile and it flitted briefly through her mind that he might be crazy. But no, they thought too much alike, and she knew she wasn't crazy. It was natural for death to dominate your thoughts when you reached a certain age. And it was fitting that the End-Time should come now, when the world lay helpless in the hands of evildoers.

"Safe are the blessed in the bosom of the Lord," Ernest said, echoing her thoughts.

"Amen. Rebuke me not, O Lord, in thy wrath, nor chastise me in thy fury," she groaned.

So they were still talking about it, and the day after Easter was going to be the day. You never knew what was going to happen in this world. Rachel did not think her Nana was sinful, but of course, Nana knew best. If Nana had sins . . . She began to be very worried about herself, because she knew that she herself was in deep sin. It was that she had drawn in almost every library book in the school library. It was something like reading backwards, something she couldn't keep from doing. Nobody knew about it yet. Only one of the drawings had been reported so far, and so the librarian was not overly concerned. Wait until they found out. The drawings were in pencil. Maybe she could erase them starting tomorrow during library period. She would have to be very careful not to get caught. It had been so easy to do it. In every book that she checked out and brought home, over the last year, she had done the drawing. Even *Caddie Woodlawn*. She kissed the book cover fervently. She would erase *Caddie Woodlawn* the instant she got home.

The drawing was basically the same: it was usually a man's profile and a woman's facing one another, sometimes a woman's and a woman's, or a man's and a child's. From the forehead of one to

225

the other she drew dotted lines. That was it. Except sometimes there was a word or words on the dotted lines. The words were teeny and did not get very far from the head of the one thinking them. She was grateful to know that she had a week to return the damaged books to their original state—she was an optimist, she knew she could do it—and to prepare herself for the End with prayers and fasting. Fasting would be no problem. She knew she would not want to eat during the coming week, especially would she not be able to eat lamb roast on Easter Sunday.

The weekdays of Passion Week were a swiftly moving cloud of agony marked by uncertainty, fear, and furtive forays into the library at every odd moment of her schoolday. She checked out the limit of books every day—five—and returned the five from the previous day. During her lunch hour and Library Period, a space of only twenty minutes on Monday and Friday, she riffled pages, thousands of pages, in the fiction section. As early as Tuesday Mrs. Kniffin began looking at her suspiciously and she had to be more careful, piling her gym clothes on top of the open page and applying her big gum eraser in tiny strokes of her fingers while she gazed out of the window. Finally Mrs. Kniffin caught her in the bookstacks searching frantically through *Amelia Bedelia* and asked her what was going on. How could she tell Mrs. Kniffin that her eternal soul was hanging in the balance? Like the worst kind of criminal, she had thought out her alibi ahead of time. She told the librarian that she was taking a correspondence course in speed reading, adding a lie to her burden of sin.

The week was awful for Nana and Grundy, too. Nana gnawed her lower lip till it bled. She either walked around and around the house or sat in her chair near the window. Grundy was high and low, high and low. He shouted to himself as he did when he was in the Spirit, but the shouts were like an animal dying. When he got too low, he went to bed. He missed two days of work, lying in bed, praying, laughing and crying. Easter Sunday dawned glorious, a beautiful day, bursting with life, that second-to-last day of life on earth. Their church service was three hours long. People were high and low. They hung on to each other and the preacher, laughed and cried, praised God and sang songs.

Nana cooked, but no one ate much except Tolliver, who stuffed himself on roast lamb and potatoes on top of speckled malted milk balls, candy eggs, and a chocolate bunny that he ate after church. He ate just exactly like there was no tomorrow. He had been eating that way for several months and he was getting to be a loveable little dumpling. Rachel foresaw that he would be a fat teenager. She corrected herself. He would have been a fat teenager. She stayed awake most of the night, planning tomorrow's final assault on the library.

Easter Monday her grandfather took the day off again. After some deliberation, Rachel was sent to school. She insisted on it, because she had not yet finished her erasures and she must find a way to cover the authors R through Z in a single day, and *that* only if she was to be allowed to finish the school day before the End came.

Three o'clock came and she didn't get finished; that is, she finished the fiction, but there was a scattering of other books she had read, nonfiction, that she didn't get to. These included some important, unforgivable ones, like the big *Encyclopedia of Music*, that she had forgotten about until this very day, this last day. It was too late now. She went straight home and did not go out to play with Sheila Neilson. She hovered around Nana who was in her gray and white print meeting dress. Grundy paced around the house, stopping once to grasp her and almost smother her against his stomach and say, "Child, I love you," and then did the same to Tolliver, who was playing with miniature cars on the rug. Rachel hugged Grundy back but she did not feel loving to him, had not felt the same toward him since the day they went to Dunk's farm. The eternity of the evening passed, Tolliver fell asleep on the couch. Rachel was allowed to stay up until midnight, then she was sent to bed. She climbed into bed with faintly rising hopes. After all, it was midnight. That meant the day of judgement must have passed. At the very least, she had one more day of expiation in the library. And she could finish it in one more day. She fell soundly asleep. When she awoke the next morning, no one had waked her up for school. She looked outside at the beautiful morning and ran to Tolliver's bed. "Wake up, Tolliver, wake up!" He grunted and turned. "It didn't happen. It didn't happen," she breathed.

They were on the road again later in the morning. Nana had on her gray and white print meeting dress, just as if she had slept in it, and she carried her Bible. Grundy was more grim than she had ever seen him. He had kept her out of school. Although she

227

wished she could have gone to school on this particular day to finish up in the library, Rachel's heart was rejoicing. The End had not come on two consecutive deadlines, and she was beginning to think that it would not come just yet. She had Caddie Woodlawn with her in the car. The hills had never looked so green. The sky had never looked so blue. They passed one farmyard with a clothesline of bright quilts, one with big stars and another with hooked-together circles. Tolliver was singing that crazy song. "Jib jibber-jibber jab and jab jabber-jabber jib!"

Grundy ordinarily did not tell them where they were going, but this morning he did. "Children," he began, grasping the wheel of the car tighter and shifting a little to be able to talk over his shoulder, "the Lord spoke in my dream last night, just as plain as I am talking to you now, and He said that all of us in this family are saved, and that He invites us to come to Him today. He wants us. He calls us to the Kingdom today, for behold now is the acceptable time, now is the time of salvation. . . ." He went on with some other sayings that tumbled on and on over the back seat but which they did not understand. "Safe are the blessed in the bosom of the Lord!" It sounded like his regular self but not exactly. Rachel listened closer, joy guttering in her heart, but she could not make out what he was talking about.

"Where are we going, Grundy?"

"Rachel, child, we are going to the Lord." He had to explain it over and over to them. "We are answering the call of the Lord. It is time. The time is here."

"How are we going to the Lord?"

"Through the dark valley we will pass on to glory!"

"Today?"

"Yes, today, today, our resurrection day! Oh, praise God with the tongues of angels! Thank you, Lord, for this trial by fire, even as you commanded Abraham!"

"Praise God," Nana said.

This is not real, she told herself. Nothing is going to happen to us.

Suddenly Caddie flung herself into Mr. Woodlawn's arms. "Father! Father!"

It was all she could say, and really there was nothing more that needed saying. Mr. Woodlawn held her a long time, his rough beard pressed against her cheek. Then with his big hands, which were so delicate with clockwork, he helped her to undress and

228

straighten the tumbled bed. Then he kissed her again and took his candle and went away. And now the room was cool and pleasant again, and even Caddie's tears were not unpleasant, but part of the cool relief she felt. In a few moments she was fast asleep.

"Is something going to happen to us? Are we going to die?"
"There is no other way to enter blessedness."
Nothing is going to happen to us. Yes, he is going to kill us
That is what he means. He is going to kill us.

"Massacre!" breathed Mother, laying her hands against her heart. Her face had gone quite white.
"No, Harriet, not that word," said Father quietly.

She opened the book and there was a drawing she had not caught. She must have done two in *Caddie Woodlawn.* A man and child faced each other in profile with faint dotted lines in between with no words on the lines. She rubbed and smudged the drawing with her fingers until it was obliterated and the spot was just a black slur and then a black-outlined hole showing the white of the next page through it. Her eyes were acting funny. The words were sliding around on the pages, then off the pages as she turned them searching for an answer. She went quickly to the last page. The story was over. She was going blind. The last sentence, like an iron bar, hung suspended over half a page of white space. Maybe she could get it off and keep the story from ending. She pried up the last line, bent it upward, but it would not let go. She pulled and it finally snapped off in the middle.
"Nana," she asked, "are you going, too?"
"Yes, Rachel. It's time. We are going to cross over."
"Can't we—can't we think about it some more? Oh, can't we take it to the Lord in prayer?" Please. Please!
"I can't think. . . . I can't think. . . . Ernest. . ."
"Rachel," Grundy interrupted. "Nana and I have chosen this way for her and me. We have made our choice. Tolliver doesn't have a choice because he is not yet of the age of reason but we are sure he wants to go with us."
"I want to go with you and Nana," said Tolliver.
Grundy continued, "You are past the theological age of reason, Rachel, and the Lord commanded me to give you a choice. He compels me under penalty of His wrath to let you choose."

Rachel slid sideways and whispered harshly to Tolliver, "They are going to kill us! Tell them you don't want to go!"

"No. I want to go with Grundy and Nana." He began to cry.

This is not real, she thought. Yes it is. He means to kill us all. "Nana—" She burst into tears and leaped forward to hug Nana's neck. Nana was already turned toward her, and patted Rachel's hair and hands as she cried for several miles. They were now on the main turnpike heading east. Rachel knew this highway very well. She dried her tears on the shoulder of Nana's gray and white dress. "Did you say I could choose?"

"You have the choice of going with us to the Lord or staying behind."

"Go with us, child," urged Nana, with her face shining, not from being happy, but from something like a battle she had finally won. "You will never suffer again. You will be in Paradise."

"Come on, Rachel," said Tolliver, brightening up. "Nana, will it be like Dollywood?"

It would all be over quickly if she went with them. A few slashes of horror and then she would never have to wonder what was going to happen to her next. She wanted to be obedient to God and her grandfather. God and Grundy merged in her mind. She thought about it for a few more miles in the silence of the humming, hurtling car.

There was that matter of the unfinished erasures. She was certain that if she had to go to God today He would forgive her and give her credit for doing the best she could. She was a logical thinker, even under stress. Her grandmother always said that Rachel had been given the gift of wisdom by the Spirit. But in the end her choice was not made rationally. It was made on the basis of what he had killed when he killed the lamb. That precious pet that in her fantasy she had called *her* lamb, he had killed. Why?

"I want to stay alive."

They put her out on the side of the road with what she knew and with her copy of *Caddie Woodlawn* and her grandmother's Bible.

Nominated by Ontario Review, Maxine Kumin, Joyce Carol Oates

IN BROAD DAYLIGHT

fiction by HA JIN

from THE KENYON REVIEW

WHILE I was eating corn cake and jellyfish at lunch, our gate was thrown open and Bare Hips hopped in. His large wooden pistol was stuck partly inside the waist of his blue shorts. "White Cat," he called me by my nickname, "hurry, let's go. They caught Old Whore at her home. They're going to take her through the streets this afternoon."

"Really?" I put down my bowl, which was almost empty, and rushed to the inner room for my undershirt and sandals. "I'll be back in a second."

"Bare Hips, did you say they'll parade Mu Ying today?" I heard Grandma ask in her husky voice.

"Yes, all the kids on our street have left for her house. I came to tell White Cat." He paused. "Hey, White Cat, hurry up!"

"Coming," I cried out, still looking for my sandals.

"Good, good!" Grandma said to Bare Hips, while flapping at flies with her large palm-leaf fan. "They should burn the bitch on Heaven Lamp like they did in the old days."

"Come, let's go," Bare Hips said to me the moment I was back. He turned to the door; I picked up my wooden scimitar and followed him.

"Put on your shoes, dear." Grandma stretched out her fan to stop me.

"No time for that, Grandma. I've got to be quick, or I'll miss something and won't be able to tell you the whole story when I get back."

We dashed into the street while Grandma was shouting behind us. "Come back. Take the rubber shoes with you."

We charged toward Mu Ying's home on Eternal Way, waving our weapons above our heads. Grandma was crippled and never came out of our small yard. That was why I had to tell her about what was going on outside. But she knew Mu Ying well, just as all the old women in our town knew Mu well and hated her. Whenever they heard that she had a man in her home again, these women would say, "This time they ought to burn Old Whore on Heaven Lamp."

What they referred to was the old way of punishing an adulteress. Though they had lived in New China for almost two decades, some ancient notions still stuck in their heads. Grandma told me about many of the executions in the old days that she had seen with her own eyes. Officials used to have the criminals of adultery executed in two different ways. They beheaded the man. He was tied to a stake on the platform at the marketplace. At the first blare of horns, a masked headsman ascended the platform holding a broad ax before his chest; at the second blare of horns, the headsman approached the criminal and raised the ax over his head; at the third blare of horns, the head was lopped off and fell to the ground. If the man's family members were waiting beneath the platform, his head would be picked up to be buried together with his body; if no family member was nearby, dogs would carry the head away and chase each other around until they ate up the flesh and returned for the body.

Unlike the man, the woman involved was executed on Heaven Lamp. She was hung naked upside down above a wood fire whose flames could barely touch her scalp. And two men flogged her away with whips made of bulls' penises. Meanwhile she screamed for help and the whole town could hear her. Since the fire merely scorched her head, it took at least half a day for her to stop shrieking and a day and a night to die completely. People used to believe that the way of punishment was justified by Heaven, so the fire was called Heaven Lamp. But that was an old custom; nobody believed they would burn Mu Ying in that way.

Mu's home, a small granite house with cement tiles built a year before, was next to East Wind Inn on the northern side of Eternal Way. When we entered that street, Bare Hips and I couldn't help looking around tremulously, because that area was the territory of the children living there. Two of the fiercest boys, who would kill without second thoughts, ruled that part of town. Whenever a boy from another street wandered into Eternal Way, they'd capture him and beat him up. Of course we did the same thing; if we caught one of them in our territory, we'd at least confiscate whatever he had with him: grasshopper cages, slingshots, bottle caps, marbles, cartridge cases, and so on. We would also make him call every one of us "Father" or "Grandfather." But today hundreds of children and grown-ups were pouring into Eternal Way; two dozen urchins on that street surely couldn't hold their ground. Besides, they had already adopted a truce, since they were more eager to see the Red Guards drag Mu Ying out of her den.

When we arrived, Mu was being brought out through a large crowd at the front gate. Inside her yard there were three rows of colorful washing hung on iron wires, and there was also a grape trellis. Seven or eight children were in there, plucking off grapes and eating them. Two Red Guards held Mu Ying by the arms, and the other Red Guards, about twenty of them, followed behind. They were all from Dalian City and wore home-made army uniforms. God knew how they came to know that there was a bad woman in our town. Though people hated Mu and called her names, no one would rough her up. Those Red Guards were strangers, so they wouldn't mind doing it.

Surprisingly, Mu looked rather calm; she neither protested nor said a word. The two Red Guards let go of her arms, and she followed them quietly into West Street. We all moved with them. Some children ran several paces ahead to look back at her.

Mu wore a sky-blue dress, which made her different from the other women who always wore jackets and pants suitable for honest work. In fact, even we small boys could tell that she was really handsome, perhaps the best looking woman of her age in our town. Though in her fifties, she didn't have a single gray hair; she was a little plump, but because of her long legs and arms she appeared rather queenly. While most of the women had sallow faces, hers looked white and healthy like fresh milk.

Skipping in front of the crowd, Bare Hips turned around and cried out at her, "Shameless Old Whore!"

She glanced at him, her round eyes flashing; the purple wart beside her left nostril grew darker. Grandma had assured me that

233

Mu's wart was not a beauty-wart but a tear-wart. This meant that her life would be soaked in tears.

We knew where we were going, to White Mansion, which was our classroom building, the only two-storied house in the town. As we came to the end of West Street, a short man ran out from a street corner, panting for breath and holding a sickle. He was Meng Su, Mu Ying's husband, who sold bean jelly in summer and sugar-coated haws in winter at the marketplace. He paused in front of the large crowd, as though having forgotten why he had rushed over. He turned his head around to look back; there was nobody behind him. After a short moment he moved close, rather carefully.

"Please let her go," he begged the Red Guards. "Comrade Red Guards, it's all my fault. Please let her go." He put the sickle under his arm and held his hands together before his chest.

"Get out of the way!" commanded a tall young man, who must have been the leader.

"Please don't take her away. It's my fault. I haven't disciplined her well. Please give her a chance to be a new person. I promise, she won't do it again."

The crowd stopped to circle about. "What's your class status?" a square-faced young woman asked in a sharp voice.

"Poor peasant," Meng replied, his small eyes tearful and his cupped ears twitching a little. "Please let her go, sister. Have mercy on us! I'm kneeling down to you if you let her go." Before he was able to fall on his knees, two young men held him back. Tears were rolling down his dark fleshy cheeks, and his gray head began waving about. The sickle was taken away from him.

"Shut up," the tall leader yelled and slapped him across the face. "She's a snake. We traveled a hundred and fifty *li* to come here to wipe out poisonous snakes and worms. If you don't stop interfering, we'll parade you with her together. Do you want to join her?"

Silence. Meng covered his face with his large hands as though feeling dizzy.

A man in the crowd said aloud, "If you can share the bed with her, why can't you share the street?"

Many of the grown-ups laughed. "Take him, take him too!" someone told the Red Guards. Meng looked scared, sobbing quietly.

His wife stared at him without saying a word. Her teeth were clenched; a faint smiled passed the corners of her mouth. Meng seemed to wince under her stare. The two Red Guards let his arms go, and he stepped aside, watching his wife and the crowd move toward the school.

Of Meng Su people in our town had different opinions. Some said he was a born cuckold who didn't mind his wife's sleeping with any man as long as she could bring money home. Some believed he was a good-tempered man who had stayed with his wife mainly for their children's sake; they forgot that the three children had grown up long before and were working in big cities far away. Some thought he didn't leave his wife because he had no choice—no woman would marry such a dwarf. Grandma, for some reason, seemed to respect Meng. She told me that Mu Ying had once been raped by a group of Russian soldiers under Northern Bridge and was left on the river bank afterwards. That night her husband sneaked there and carried her back. He looked after her for a whole winter till she recovered. "Old Whore doesn't deserve that good-hearted man," Grandma would say. "She's heartless and knows only how to sell her thighs."

We entered the school's playground where about two hundred people had already gathered. "Hey, White Cat and Bare Hips," Big Shrimp called us, waving his claws. Many boys from our street were there too. We went to join them.

The Red Guards took Mu to the front entrance of the building. Two tables had been placed between the stone lions that crouched on each side of the entrance. On one of the tables stood a tall paper hat with the big black characters on its side: "Down with Old Bitch!"

A young man in glasses raised his bony hand and started to address us, "Folks, we've gathered here today to denounce Mu Ying, who is a demon in this town."

"Down with Bourgeois Demons!" a slim woman Red Guard shouted. We raised our fists and repeated the slogan.

"Down with Old Bitch Mu Ying," a middle-aged man cried out with both hands in the air. He was an active revolutionary in our commune. Again we shouted, in louder voices.

The nearsighted man went on, "First, Mu Ying must confess her crime. We must see her attitude toward her own crime. Then we'll make the punishment fit both her crime and her attitude. All right, folks?"

"Right," some voices replied from the crowd.

"Mu Ying," he turned to the criminal, "you must confess everything. It's up to you now."

She was forced to stand on a bench. Staying below the steps, we had to raise our heads to see her face.

The questioning began. "Why do you seduce men and paralyze their revolutionary will with your bourgeois poison?" the tall leader asked in a solemn voice.

"I've never invited any man to my home, have I?" she said rather calmly. Her husband was standing at the front of the crowd, listening to her without showing any emotion, as though having lost his mind.

"Then why did they go to your house and not to others' houses?"

"They wanted to sleep with me," she replied.

"Shameless!" Several women hissed in the crowd.

"A true whore!"

"Scratch her!"

"Rip apart her filthy mouth!"

"Sisters," she spoke aloud. "All right, it was wrong to sleep with them. But you all know what it feels like when you want a man, don't you? Don't you once in a while have that feeling in your bones?" Contemptuously, she looked at the few withered middle-aged women standing in the front row, then closed her eyes. "Oh, you want that real man to have you in his arms and let him touch every part of your body. For that man alone you want to blossom into a woman, a real woman—"

"Take this, you Fox Spirit!" A stout young fellow struck her on the side with a fist like a sledgehammer. The heavy blow silenced her at once. She held her sides with both hands, gasping for breath.

"You're wrong, Mu Ying," Bare Hip's mother spoke from the front of the crowd, her forefinger pointing upward at Mu. "You have your own man, who doesn't lack an arm or a leg. It's wrong to have others' men and more wrong to pocket their money."

"I have my own man?" Mu glanced at her husband and smirked. She straightened up and said, "My man is nothing. He is no good, I mean in bed. He always comes before I feel anything."

236

All the adults burst out laughing. "What's that? What's so funny?" Big Shrimp asked Bare Hips.

"You didn't get it?" Bare Hips said impatiently. "You don't know anything about what happens between a man and a woman. It means that whenever she doesn't want him to come close to her he comes. Bad timing."

"It doesn't sound like that," I said.

Before we could argue, a large bottle of ink smashed on Mu's head and knocked her off the bench. Prone on the cement terrace, she broke into swearing and blubbering. "Oh, damn your ancestors! Whoever hit me will be childless!" Her left hand was rubbing her head. "Oh Lord of Heaven, they treat their grandma like this!"

"Serves you right!"

"A cheap weasel."

"Even a knife on her throat can't stop her."

"A pig is born to eat slop!"

When they put her back up on the bench, she became another person—her shoulders covered with black stains, and a red line trickling down her left temple. The scorching sun was blazing down on her as though all the black parts on her body were about to burn up. Still moaning, she turned her eyes to the spot where her husband had been standing a few minutes before. But he was no longer there.

"Down with Old Whore!" a farmer shouted in the crowd. We all followed him in one voice. She began trembling slightly.

The tall leader said to us, "In order to get rid of her counter-revolutionary airs, first, we're going to cut her hair." With a wave of his hand, he summoned the Red Guards behind him. Four men moved forward and held her down. The square-faced woman raised a large pair of scissors and thrust them into the mass of the dark hair.

"Don't, don't, please. Help, help! I'll do whatever you want me to—"

"Cut!" someone yelled.

"Shave her head bald!"

The woman Red Guard applied the scissors skillfully. After four or five strokes, Mu's head looked like the tail of a molting hen. She started blubbering again, her nose running and her teeth chattering.

A breeze came and swept away the fluffy curls from the terrace and scattered them on the sandy ground. It was so hot that some people took out fans, waving them continuously. The crowd stank of sweat.

Wooooo, wooooo, woo, woo. That was the train coming from Sand County at 3:30. It was a freight train, whose young drivers would toot the steam horn whenever they saw a young woman in a field beneath the track.

The questioning continued. "How many men have you slept with these years?" the nearsighted man asked.

"Three."

"She's lying," a woman in the crowd cried out.

"I told the truth, sister." She wiped off the tears from her cheeks with the back of her hand.

"Who are they?" the young man asked again. "Tell us more about them."

"An officer from the Little Dragon Mountain, and—"

"How many times did he come to your house?"

"I can't remember. Probably twenty."

"What's his name?"

"I don't know. He told me he was a big officer."

"Did you take money from him?"

"Yes."

"How much for each time?"

"Twenty *yuan*."

"How much altogether?"

"Probably five hundred."

"Comrades and Revolutionary Masses," the young man turned to us, "how shall we handle this parasite that sucked blood out of a revolutionary officer?"

"Quarter her with four horses!" an old woman yelled.

"Burn her on Heaven Lamp!"

"Poop on her face!" a small fat girl shouted, her hand raised like a tiny pistol with the thumb cocked up and the forefinger aimed at Mu. Some grownups snickered.

Then a pair of old cloth-shoes, a symbol for a promiscuous woman, were passed to the front. The slim young woman took the shoes and tied them together with the laces. She climbed on a table and was about to hang the shoes around Mu's neck. Mu elbowed the woman aside and knocked the shoes to the ground.

The stout young fellow picked up the shoes, and jumped twice to slap her on the cheeks with the soles. "You're so stubborn. Do you want to change yourself or not?" he asked.

"Yes, I do," she replied meekly and dared not stir a bit. Meanwhile the shoes were being hung around her neck.

"Now she looks like a real whore," a woman commented.

"Sing us a tune, Sis," a farmer demanded.

"Comrades," the man in glasses resumed, "let us continue the denunciation." He turned to Mu and asked, "Who are the other men?"

"A farmer from Apple Village."

"How many times with him?"

"Once."

"Liar!"

"She's lying!"

"Give her one on the mouth!"

The young man raised his hands to calm the crowd down and questioned her again, "How much did you take from him?"

"Eighty *yuan*."

"One night?"

"Yes."

"Tell us more about it. How can you make us believe you?"

"That old fellow came to town to sell piglets. He sold a whole litter for eighty, and I got the money."

"Why did you charge him more than the officer?"

"No, I didn't. He did it four times in one night."

Some people were smiling and whispering to each other. A woman said that old man must have been a widower or never married.

"What's his name?" the young man went on.

"No idea."

"Was he rich or poor?"

"Poor."

"Comrades," the young man addressed us, "here we have a poor peasant who worked with his sow for a whole year and got only a litter of piglets. That money is the salt and oil money for his family, but this snake swallowed the money with one gulp. What shall we do with her?"

"Kill her!"

"Break her skull!"

"Beat the piss out of her!"

A few farmers began to move forward to the steps, waving their fists or rubbing their hands.

"Hold," a woman Red Guard with a huge Chairman Mao badge on her chest spoke in a commanding voice. "The Great Leader has instructed us: 'For our struggle we need words but not force.' Comrades, we can easily wipe her out with words. Force doesn't solve ideological problems." What she said restrained those enraged farmers, who remained in the crowd.

Wooo, woo, wooo, woooooooooooo, an engine screamed in the south. It was strange, because the drivers of the four o'clock train were a bunch of old men who seldom blew the horn.

"Who is the third man?" the nearsighted man continued to question Mu.

"A Red Guard."

The crowd broke into laughter. Some women asked the Red Guards to give her another bottle of ink. "Mu Ying, you're responsible for your own words," the young man said in a serious voice.

"I told you the truth."

"What's his name?"

"I don't know. He led the propaganda team that passed here last month."

"How much did you make out of him?"

"None. That stingy dog wouldn't pay a fen. He said he was the worker who should be paid."

"So you were outsmarted by him?"

Some men in the crowd guffawed. Mu wiped her nose with her thumb, and at once she wore a thick mustache. "I taught him a lesson, though," she said.

"How?"

"I tweaked his ears, gave him a bleeding nose, and kicked him out. I told him never come back."

People began talking to each other. Some said that she was a strong woman who knew what was hers. Some said the Red Guard was no good; if you got something you had to pay for it. A few women declared that the rascal deserved such a treatment.

"Dear Revolutionary Masses," the tall leader started to speak. "We all have heard the crime Mu Ying committed. She lured one of our officers and one of our poor peasants into the evil water,

240

and she beat a Red Guard black and blue. Shall we let her go home without punishment or shall we teach her an unforgettable lesson so that she won't do it again?"

"Teach her a lesson!" some voices cried out in unison.

"Then we're going to parade her through the streets."

Two Red Guards pulled Mu off the bench, and another picked up the tall hat. "Brothers and sisters," she begged, "please let me off just for once. Don't, don't! I promise I'll correct my fault. I'll be a new person. Help! Oh, help!"

It was no use resisting; within seconds the huge hat was firmly planted on her head. They also hung a big placard between the cloth-shoes lying against her chest. The words on the placard read:

I am a Broken shoe
My Crime Deserves Death

They put a gong in her hands and ordered her to strike it when she announced the words written on the inner side of the gong.

My pals and I followed the crowd, feeling rather tired. Boys from East Street were wilder; they threw stones at Mu's back. One stone struck the back of her head and blood dropped on her neck. But they were stopped immediately by the Red Guards, because a stone missed Mu and hit a man on the shoulder. Old people, who couldn't follow us, were standing on chairs and windowsills with pipes and towels in their hands. We were going to parade her through every street. It would take several hours to finish the whole thing, as the procession would stop for a short while at every street corner.

Bong, Mu struck the gong and declared, "I am an evil monster."

"Louder!"

Dong, bong—"I have stolen men. I stink for a thousand years."

When we were coming out of the marketplace, Cross Eyes emerged from a narrow lane. He grasped my wrist and Bare Hips' arm and said, "Someone is dead at the train station. Come, let's go there and have a look." The word "dead" at once roused us. We, half a dozen boys, set out running to the train station.

The dead man was Meng Su. A crowd had gathered at the railroad a hundred meters east of the station house. A few men were examining the rail that was stained with blood and studded with bits of flesh. One man paced along the darker part of the rail and announced that the train had dragged Meng at least twenty meters.

Beneath the track, Meng's headless body lay in a ditch. One of his feet was missing, and the whitish shinbone stuck out several inches long. There were so many openings on his body that he looked like a large piece of fresh meat on the counter in the butcher's. Beyond him, ten paces away, a big straw hat remained on the ground. We were told that his head was under the hat.

Bare Hips and I went down the slope to have a glimpse at the head. Other boys dared not take a peep. We two looked at each other, asking with our eyes who should raise the straw hat. I held out my wooden scimitar and lifted the rim of the hat a little with the sword. A swarm of bluebottles charged out, droning like provoked wasps. We bent over to peek at the head. Two long teeth pierced through the upper lip. An eyeball was missing. The gray hair was no longer perceivable, as it was covered with mud and dirt. The open mouth filled with purplish mucus. A tiny lizard skipped, sliding away into the grass.

"Oh!" Bare Hips began vomiting. Sorghum gruel mixed with bits of string beans splashed on a yellowish boulder. "Leave it alone, White Cat."

We lingered at the station, listening to different versions of the accident. Some people said that Meng had gotten drunk and dropped asleep on the track. Some said he hadn't slept at all but laughed hysterically walking in the middle of the track toward the coming train. Some said he had not drunk a drop, as he had spoken with tears in his eyes to a few persons he had run into on his way to the station. In any case, he was dead, torn to pieces.

That evening when I was coming home, I heard Mu Ying groaning in the smoky twilight. "Take me home. Oh, help me. Who can help me? Where are you? Why don't you come and carry me home?"

She was lying at the bus stop, alone.

Nominated by Michael Bendzela

MY FATHER'S PLACE

by KIM R. STAFFORD

from HUNGRY MIND REVIEW

A FEW DAYS after my father, poet William Stafford, died, I was sleeping alone at the house of my parents, when something woke me at around four A.M. My mother, who was away, had told me of this effect, for she, too, had been awakened since his death at my father's customary writing time. As I opened my eyes, the moon was shining through the bedroom window. But that wasn't it. The house was still, the neighborhood quiet. The house wanted me to rise. It was the hour, a beckoning. There was a soft tug. Nothing mystical, just a habit to the place. The air was sweet, life was good, it was time.

I dressed, and shuffled down the hall. In the kitchen, I remembered how he would make himself a cup of instant coffee, and some toast. I followed the custom, putting the kettle on, slicing some bread my mother had made, letting the plink of the spoon stirring the coffee be the only sound, then the scrape of a butter knife. And then I was to go to the couch, and lie down with paper. I pulled the green mohair blanket from the closet, turned on a lamp, and settled in the horizontal place where my father had greeted maybe ten thousand mornings with his pen and paper. I put my head on the pillow just where his head had worn through the silk lining.

What should I write? There was no sign, only a feeling of generosity in the room. A streetlight brightened the curtain beside me, but the rest of the room was dark. I let my gaze rove the walls—the fireplace, the dim rectangle of a painting, the hooded

243

box of the television cabinet, a table with magazines. It was all ordinary, suburban. But there was this beckoning. In the dark of the house it felt as if my father's death had become an empty bowl that was filled from below, like the stone cavern of a spring that brimmed cold with water from a deep place. There was grief, and also this abundance. So many people had written to us saying, "Words cannot begin to express how we feel. . . ." They can't? I honored the feeling, for I, too, am sometimes mute with grief. But words *can* begin to express how it is, especially if they can be relaxed, brimming in their own plain way.

I looked for a long time at the bouquet of sunflowers on the coffee table beside the couch. I remembered sunflowers are the state flower of Kansas. I remembered my father's poem about yellow cars. I remembered how, the night before, we had eaten the last of his third summer planting of green beans.

For a time, I thought back to the last writing my father had done at this place, the morning of August 28. As often, he had begun with a line from an ordinary experience, a stray call from an insurance agent trying to track down what turned out to be a different William Stafford. The call had amused him, the words had stayed with him. And that morning, he had begun to write:

"Are you Mr. William Stafford?"
"Yes, but. . . ."

As often, he started with the recent daily news from his own life, and came to deeper things:

Well, it was yesterday.
Sunlight used to follow my hand.
And that's when the strange siren-like sound flooded
over the horizon and rushed through the streets
of our town. . . .

But I wasn't delving into his writing now, only his writing life. I was inhabiting the cell of his habit: earlier than anyone, more ordinary in this welcome, simply listening.

The house was so quiet, I was aware distinctly of my breathing, my heart, how sweet each breath came into me, and the total release of each exhalation. I felt as if my eyes, too, had been "tapered for braille." The edge of the coffee table held a soft gleam from the streetlight. The jostled stack of magazines had a kind of sacred logic, where he had touched them. Then I saw how each sunflower had dropped a little constellation of pollen on the table. The pollen seemed to burn, so intense in color and purpose. But the house—the house didn't want me to write anything profound. The soft tug that had wakened me, the tug I still felt, wanted me to be there with myself, awake, awake to everything ordinary, to sip my bitter instant coffee, and to gaze about and to remember. I remembered how my father had said once that such a time alone would allow anyone to go inward, in order to go outward. Paradoxically, he said, you had to go into yourself in order to find the patterns that were bigger than your own life.

I started to write ordinary things. And then I came to the sunflowers, and the spirit of the house warned me this could be told wrong if I tried to make something of it. It's not about trying. It's not about writing poems. It's not about achievement, certainly not fame, importance. It's about being there exactly with the plain life of a time before first light, with breath, the streetlight on one side of the house and the moon on the other, about the worn silk, the blanket, and that little dusting of pollen from the sunflowers.

My head fit the dent in the pillow, the blanket warmed my body, my hand moved easily, carelessly with the pen. I heard the scratch on paper. If this was grieving, it was active in plain things. I found myself relishing the simplest words, mistrusting metaphor, amused by my own habits of verve with words, forgiving myself an occasional big thought:

> . . . to pause at the gate to take off the one big shoe
> of his body and step forward light as wind . . .

I could forgive myself because there was this abundance in time and place and habit. And then I had a page, I closed my notebook, and I rose for the day. There was much to do, but I had done the big thing already.

Who will take my father's place in the world of poetry? No one. Who will take his place in this daily practice of the language of the tribe? Anyone who wishes. He said once the field of writing will never be crowded—not because people can't do important work, but because they don't think they can. This way of writing beckons to anyone who wishes to rise and listen, to write without fear of either achievement or failure. There is no burden, only a beckoning. For when the house beckons, you will wake easily. There is a stove where you make something warm. There is a light that leaves much of the room dark. There is a place to be comfortable, a place you have worn with the friendly shape of your body. There is your own breath, the treasuries of your recollection, the blessings of your casual gaze. What is this way of writing, of listening easily and telling simply? There is the wall, the table, and whatever stands this day for Kansas pollen in your own precious life.

Nominated by Naomi Shihab Nye

SONG

from BRIGIT PEGEEN KELLY
from THE SOUTHERN REVIEW

Listen: there was a goat's head hanging by ropes in a tree.
All night it hung there and sang. And those who heard it
Felt a hurt in their hearts and thought they were hearing
The song of a night bird. They sat up in their beds, and then
They lay back down again. In the night wind, the goat's head
Swayed back and forth, and from far off it shone faintly,
The way the moonlight shone on the train track miles away
Beside which the goat's headless body lay. Some boys
Had hacked its head off. It was harder work than they had
    imagined.
The goat cried like a man and struggled hard. But they
Finished the job. They hung the bleeding head by the school
And then ran off into the darkness that seems to hide
    everything.
The head hung in the tree. The body lay by the tracks.
The head called to the body. The body to the head.
They missed each other. The missing grew large between them,
Until it pulled the heart right out of the body, until
The drawn heart flew toward the head, flew as a bird flies
Back to its cage and the familiar perch from which it trills.
Then the heart sang in the head, softly at first and then louder,
Sang long and low until the morning light came up over
The school and over the tree, and then the singing stopped. . . .
The goat had belonged to a small girl. She named
The goat Broken Thorn Sweet Blackberry, named it after

The night's bush of stars, because the goat's silky hair
Was dark as well water, because it had eyes like wild fruit.
The girl lived near a high railroad track. At night
She heard the trains passing, the sweet sound of the train's horn
Pouring softly over her bed, and each morning she woke
To give the bleating goat his pail of warm milk. She sang
Him songs about girls with ropes and cooks in boats.
She brushed him with a stiff brush. She dreamed daily
That he grew bigger, and he did. She thought her dreaming
Made it so. But one night the girl didn't hear the train's horn,
And the next morning she woke to an empty yard. The goat
Was gone. Everything looked strange. It was as if a storm
Had passed through while she slept, wind and stones, rain
Stripping the branches of fruit. She knew that someone
Had stolen the goat and that he had come to harm. She called
To him. All morning and into the afternoon, she called
And called. She walked and walked. In her chest a bad feeling
Like the feeling of the stones gouging the soft undersides
Of her bare feet. Then somebody found the goat's body
By the high tracks, the flies already filling their soft bottles
At the goat's torn neck. Then somebody found the head
Hanging in a tree by the school. They hurried to take
These things away so that the girl would not see them.
They hurried to raise money to buy the girl another goat.
They hurried to find the boys who had done this, to hear
Them say it was a joke, a joke, it was nothing but a joke. . . .
But listen: here is the point. The boys thought to have
Their fun and be done with it. It was harder work than they
Had imagined, this silly sacrifice, but they finished the job,
Whistling as they washed their large hands in the dark.
What they didn't know was that the goat's head was already
Singing behind them in the tree. What they didn't know
Was that the goat's head would go on singing, just for them,
Long after the ropes were down, and that they would learn to
    listen,
Pail after pail, stroke after patient stroke. They would
Wake in the night thinking they heard the wind in the trees
Or a night bird, but their hearts beating harder. There
Would be a whistle, a hum, a high murmur, and, at last, a song

The low song a lost boy sings remembering his mother's call.
Not a cruel song, no, no, not cruel at all. This song
Is sweet. It is sweet. The heart dies of this sweetness.

Nominated by Marianne Boruch, Mark Jarman, Joyce Carol Oates, Maura Stanton

PRACTICING DEATH SONGS

by ADRIAN C. LOUIS

from THE ANTIOCH REVIEW

My woman leaves to visit her brothers.
I sit in the yard drinking Pepsi.
A solitary red star blinks
and a one-eyed coyote screams
a sententious sermon
from a nearby hill.
The mothering smoke from woodstoves
wends across the reservation
and gathers the ghost
of a white girl I loved.
It's so hard to remember her face
because she had the most perfect body
I have ever seen.
Because of the spurned sun
of our generation
and the drugs in our blood
we always stuttered our prayers of life.
We were married to the wind
and it blew the flesh from our bones.
I met her outside the Student Union
in Berkeley in '68 where she
was screeching a folk song
like some grade-B Baez.

My loins were clean-young
and in deep need of scarring.
She'd die of fright if she saw me now.
Small blotches of wisdom
have tainted my soul.
I know now the essential tawdriness
and tiredness of lust.
I now know that my girl dog
can bark prayers to Jesus.
I know the weight of the shadows
have withered my soul
and soon will shatter my heart.
That is why I am practicing death songs.

Nominated by Sandra McPherson

WATERMELON TALES

by KHALED MATTAWA

from THE KENYON REVIEW

January. Snow. For days I have craved
　　　　　watermelons, wanted
　　　　　　　to freckle the ground with seeds, wanted
to perform an ancient ritual:
　　　　　　　Noontime, an early
　　　　　summer Sunday, the village
chief faces north, spits seven mouthfuls, then
　　　　　　　fingers a cycle
　　　　　around the galaxy of seeds.

Maimoon the bedouin visited in
　　　　　　　summer, always with
　　　　　a gift: a pickup truck-load
of watermelons. "Something for the
　　　　　　　children," he explained.
　　　　　　　Neighbors brought wheelbarrows to
fetch their share. Our chickens ate the rest.

　　　　　　　His right ear pricked up
　　　　　close, my father taps on a
watermelon, strokes as though it were
　　　　　　　a thigh. Then he slaps.
　　　　　　　"If it doesn't sound like your hands
clapping at a wedding, it's not yours."

Men shake the chief's hand,
　　　　　children kiss it. Then all file

behind him when he walks back. No one
　　　　talks until the tomb
　　　　of the local saint. The rich
place coin sacks at his feet, the poor leave
　　　　cups of melon seed.

　　　Maimoon also brought gazelle meat,
gazelles he ran over with his truck.
　　　　His daughter, Selima,
　　　　said he once swerved off the road
suddenly, drove for an hour until
　　　　he spotted six. He hadn't
　　　　hit one when the truck ran out
of gas. Thirty yards away the gazelles
　　　　stood panting, and he
　　　　ran to catch one with bare hands.

Two choices, my father's doctor tells us:
　　　　transplant or six months
　　　　of pain. Outside the office,
I point to a fruit stall, the seller
　　　　waving off flies with
　　　　a feather fan. My father
strokes, slaps, and when I lift the melon
　　　　to my shoulder, says
　　　　"Eleven years in America
and you carry a watermelon
　　　　like a damn peasant."

　　　Uncle Abdallah buries
a watermelon underneath the
　　　　approach of the waves—
　　　　"Like a refrigerator
down there." It's July, a picnic at
　　　　Tokara Beach. We're
kicking a ball around when
my brother trips hard on the hole. He's
　　　　told to eat what he'd
　　　　broken too soon. I watched him
weep and swallow pulp, seed, salt, and sand.

253

Her shadow twice her
height, the village sorceress
walks to where the chief has spit. She reveals
size of the harvest,
chance of drought, whose sons will wed
whose daughters, and names of the ill whose
ailments will not cease.

Selima started telling the gazelle
tale while my mother had her sit
in a tub. With soap,
my mother scrubbed the girl's scalp,
tossing gray handfuls of foam against
the white tile. She then
poured kerosene on Selima's
hair, rubbed till lice slid down the girl's face,
combed till the tines
of the comb filled with the dead.

Selima married. My mother sent her
a silver anklet,
a green silk shawl, and decided
against an ivory comb. My father paid
the sheikh to perform
the wedding. A week later
at his door, the sheikh found three water-
melons and a gazelle
skin prayer rug, a tire mark
across the spot where he would have rested his
head in prostration.

I cut the melon we bought
into cubes, strawberry red. But they were
dry, almost bitter.
After the third taste, my father
dropped his fork. He gazed at the window
for a while, then spent
the rest of the day in bed.

Nominated by Joan Murray, Naomi Shihab Nye

'ORITA ON THE ROAD TO CHIMAYÓ

by LISA SANDLIN

from SHENANDOAH

Wʜᴇɴ Good Friday fell in March, it often snowed, and next day *The New Mexican* ran shots of pilgrims trudging into the white flurry, heads bent, cold hands shoved up their sleeves. But this Friday landed three weeks into April. The sky glowed like a turquoise bowl—from the Sangres to the Jemez mountains, over the piñon hills, over the tiny, toiling people. They streamed from the south, from Pojoaque and Santa Fe, even Albuquerque, walking the sides of the highway to keep out of the way of cars.

Back here, on this particular jog of a shortcut off U.S. 285, they had to keep out of the way of three young firemen who were running to Chimayó. The firemen wore gym shorts and football jerseys cut off at the ribs. One wore a turned-round *Dodgers* cap. They had dark, slim-muscled legs without much hair and their stomachs were flat now, but not for so much longer. Their barrel chests would plump out. They called to people *Gangway!* or they ran around them so close that people jumped over, stumbling and sliding on the gritty shoulder.

Fireman sweat would have flicked on Catherine Sachett—a woman with the long, sad face of an El Greco count—but the firemen hadn't caught up to her yet. Catherine dedicated the first mile of her pilgrimage to exorcising her ex-husband. She was well now, except for those traces of Pete. Her sickness and the loss of her breasts had just . . . erased him. First to go was his

255

great jackass laugh, then eye contact, then his voice faded so that she kept after him, repeating, What? What, babe? He had managed to make love to her after the operation, give him that. And it wasn't that he turned her around; she liked it that way. It was how he touched her—his hands fast, lifeless, quickly withdrawn. Sitting up, she'd clutched the pillow to hide her face and cried, "Oh please, where's my husband?" A few days later Pete disappeared for real, giving Catherine, in a backhanded way, her lone advantage: her rage at him outweighed the fear of cancer.

She used to dress up in dreams—sequined minis, always Caribbean blue—slip in the C-cup breast forms, and go kill Pete. Shooting him was good for her, she found: fury and pain swarmed from her belly, her forehead, from far down beneath her scars. She woke up with a wetness on her body, broken through the skin like dew.

Catherine sighed and shooed her ringless hands around. *Out of here, out.*

She'd promised her second mile to the sick people she visited now. To Loretta, Dolores and Roy, curled like children in wide white beds. And the third mile was for. . . . In Mexican Spanish everything little—*chico*—can be made even littler. *Chiquito, chiquitito,* that just means something's really there. Catherine Sachett hardly knew it but she was walking a part—*lo mas chiquitito* part—of the third mile for herself, because she was still alive.

Sweat from those running firemen did flick on Benny Ortiz, and he hurled them a few words. Benny was a hot-looking guy but jittery, a twenty-seven-year-old weightlifter with no Life Plan. Sometimes, really pumped, with four or five guys psyching him, he freaked himself—glided from under the iron and spread into the mirror's thin brightness. His mother thought he was walking the pilgrimage because her folded hands trapped him into it; let his father come back to them. Right. What Benny really wanted—what he'd ask for in Chimayó's little *sanctuario*—was the guts to tell his mother to give it up. Tune in. Get some strength. The old man wasn't ever coming back. Once, Benny'd gone to a house where his father was staying with a girl and her baby. He'd brought a bear for the kid; hey, it was his brother. And the girl—Benny could still picture her dead spider eyelashes—told him not to come around again. His father shrugged, winked, like he'd fix it later. Who's asking? At seven, Benny knew the rule: don't ask your father for nothing. He shot a swift finger to fireman number 19's back.

About that time, as Benny's finger still goosed number 19, the wind jacked up. Light started sliding from the blue bowl sky.

Because the sky had darkened, it was easy to see the man fly up as the car veered to the shoulder and caught him. He was wearing a white shirt and a white straw cowboy hat like a real Mexican and he sailed up in a gainer, except his arms weren't tucked but flung out. He landed on his back well off the road, on a piece of ground tended by a tall piñon. The driver wavered, and then nosed the car—low-slung Buick, metallic green—back on the road.

Two of the firemen pirouetted in their tracks and took out after the Buick. The third, once he wasn't mesmerized by the flying man, spotted a roadside cross held up by some decent-sized rocks. Should he EMT the poor guy now or bust that fucker's back window? *Smoke one POW! right down the pipe.*

"Hold on, don't move him!" he called, scooped up a rock and ran off.

Catherine Sachett found the victim first, on a hard swell of ground behind the piñon. She knelt beside the hurt young man, a boy really, of eighteen or nineteen. The next person to run up—a man about Pete's age but with an easy brow—took one look, repeated after Catherine, *Ambulance*, and sprinted out toward U.S. 285 for help.

The hip was mangled, but worse, the boy seemed not to feel it. He didn't respond when she pressed her palm to his groin, through his raveled jeans, which were growing wet and red. He gazed up at Catherine as to a face in an alarming dream.

Aquí está, oh no, Brother Teo, the historian, whom he'd always displeased. Though Brother begged him to memorize the blessed lives, the boy could never remember which saint had burned, which had been ripped by lions, which had her breasts sliced off, which sat old and feeble in the temple door repeating to the heedless, *Love one another*. Brother Teo reported him to his mother. Then they exchanged expressions, Brother departing, eased, to coach the soccer team, and his mother's face drawn long and sad. When he saw how sad she looked, the boy thrashed.

257

With one hand, Catherine stroked his chest until he calmed and even smiled at her. With the other, she pressed a clean handkerchief to the bleeding. She didn't know much first aid, but growing up in Santa Fe had taught her some Spanish. The wind was rising; she bent close. *"Dígame, chulo, cómo te llaman?"*

The boy told her, his tone straining a beat, urgent, and he gestured. Verdiano, his name was Verdiano. When he flashed a nervous smile, his kid mustache looked even wispier, like a teenage Zorro's, and he stared up at her with eyes that were big, dark and clear. But he didn't know where he was, she could see that. Other pilgrims discarded their staffs in the ditch, tracked over from the road, and gathered by the piñon, asking questions. One old man, his cheek stapled in on itself in a deep scar, crossed himself and hunkered down at the boy's head. "Hey, let's get the wind off him," he said. Those who'd happened to be on this shortcut shuffled together, elbow to elbow.

Turning his head slowly to take them in, Verdiano murmured, *"Frío, hermanos."* He spoke so familiarly that people hurried to pull off sweatshirts and windbreakers. When Benny Ortiz stripped off his MANPOWER T-shirt, a couple of women raised their eyebrows. The staple-faced man, already squatting, took it on himself to receive the clothes, duckwalked a step, and spread them on the boy. He tucked some gray sleeves beneath the boy's worn-down Chihuahua heels.

Swiveling his head again, Verdiano addressed them, *"Gracias . . . Gracias."* He fixed on Catherine. Her hollow cheeks, how lines were worn all around her eyes but not her mouth made him comfortable. Catherine told the bystanders, "He says he could have lived in the trailer with the others, but to save rent he slept in the restaurant's storeroom, so then the only thing anyone tells him is what table to clean. He says he hasn't talked in six months."

"Escucha, Ms. U.N.," Benny growled, "save the translation." Benny didn't usually put himself forward; didn't pay. But he was ruffled. He was upset. Who died and left her boss? Pectorals bulged as he knelt down, squinting at the anglo woman. Bony, they never stopped dieting. Raw eyelids.

"You a nurse?" he asked her. To keep focused, he really bored in on her. Because there was one little more thing—the way the boy said *Cold, brothers* barbed his chest. Benny'd been hit by an urge he didn't know what to do with—to make sure the kid got warm now, got an ambulance, got a doctor with some brains.

"I'm not a nurse," the woman said. Benny craned around at the bystanders. "Anybody here a doctor or an EMT?" Everybody shook their heads. "Bunch of plumbers," he muttered; the woman heard. She cocked her head at him, asking, "Look, you know first aid? You want to do this?"

Benny jerked back; hey, not him. And for making fun of how he didn't know anything—he'd give her the needle back. He jutted his chin at her. "You got a pretty good hold of his privates there."

She spread her fingers so the blood seeped through, then closed them up again. People winced and murmured over the injured boy, whose olive face was a shocky white, like they were seeing it by moonlight. The handkerchief was soaked—a woman in a sunhat offered another.

Benny passed the handkerchief, then spoke in the kid's ear. He couldn't keep the anglo woman from hearing, but he could let her know she wasn't included in any way. "Bro. Ambulance'll be here soon. Don't talk." The kid nodded at the English, smiled, turned his head until he located Catherine's sad face, and began to talk.

They were startled by the boy's thanking them for listening. "It's that . . . I feel like talking," he said. He looked from Catherine to Benny and his eyes softened and he choked. The onlookers flinched, but no blood came up. He just cleared his throat and started to talk again. He told them about his family back in Mexico, his four little sisters and his mother who was tranquil now that an aunt had died and left them two rooms in her house. He told about his *novia*, his sweetheart, who was sick. She coughed too much and when the wind blew she had to lie down. Her name was Ana Luz and she sewed Ford seat covers, Verdiano said, and though he had family, she had no one but him. "Thank you, señores, but I'd better stand up now. 'Orita," he said, meaning he'd stand right this second, in this tiny bit of now. His head lifted as though the rest of him would follow but it didn't and his mauve lips formed an O. For a moment, they thought he might cry out.

Verdiano knew he had something urgent to do but not what it was. Then Brother Teo's exasperated voice lanced his confusion.

259

Staving him off respectfully with *Sí, hermano*, oblivious of his own fingers rising in a jerky ripple, Verdiano cast about in his jumbled memory for a saint to report on. Who came to his aid, inching forward with eager, earthy hands, but the least likely of luminaries—Simplicio.

Simplicio was a kitchen worker, just like him. Simplicio was a kitchen worker to the priests but he took no vow himself because he loved a girl and wanted her, and besides, he was mostly Indian and couldn't read.

Benny, who'd ordered Verdiano, "C'mon lay back, man," recoiled at the sight of the kid's hands. They reminded him of caught fish quivering. "Hold here," the bony woman urged him to take over. *Why'd she do that if she thought he was so stupid?* Benny held his breath when he received the rag, feeling the trickle, the suggestion of a beat *thum . . . thum . . .* under his pressure. The woman captured Verdiano's hands and smoothed them down. She asked the whole crowd to go through what pockets they had left for another handkerchief, and then resumed pressing the wound. She passed the soaked rag to Benny, who couldn't help squeezing it and shuddering before he threw it away.

"Una vez," Verdiano said, "when the cook's knife slipped and cut the back of his hand and the little strings there, Simplicio put down some carrots and clamped the cook's hand between his. When he let go the strings were whole and the bloody cut sealed pale pink like baby veal." "Hijo, like veal!" exclaimed the staple-cheeked man, and the boy turned up his eyes toward the voice and smiled. "Just like, señor," he said. "Y otra vez, the cook's helper spilled boiling fat on his shins and feet. Simplicio knelt down and blew on the burns. He rubbed some spit on the blisters. They went away. That time the cook told the head priest who told the bishop who called Simplicio before him and ordered him not to do those things anymore."

Wind tossed a piece of Verdiano's hair on and off his forehead until Benny licked his fingers and combed it back. Every so often another curious pilgrim on this shortcut would cross to see what was happening behind the piñon, see the boy on the ground and stay. At first the people had shifted foot to foot, anxious. They scanned the sea of hills, the piñons, the arroyos, stared hard toward the highway they knew was on the other side. But then

260

they'd just crept in closer to hear the story. What else could they do? All run off in a crowd to get an ambulance? If somebody didn't hear a phrase, Catherine repeated it in English. Verdiano would wait for her to finish before he went on. Talking genuinely calmed him, though the corners of his mouth crusted white.

"One day when Simplicio was coming back from the garden with onions and garlic, he heard a scream from the church wall where some masons were plastering on a scaffold. A man was falling, so Simplicio stopped him. He didn't save him because he'd been forbidden; he just stopped him upside down in the air."

"How did he do that, Verdiano?" asked the woman in the sunhat. The jaunty pink bow on her hatband had come undone and straggled in the wind.

"Lo mismo," the boy said, licking his lips. The same as before. "It's good to hear my name called." He breathed in deeply, breathed out deeply, like a fat man after a fine dinner, and said it again, "It's so good to hear my name."

The little wind-tears flying out of his eyes roused a world in the sunhat woman's head. She should have had children this boy's age. Those children, her own blood, now found themselves alone, hurt in some strange land, like this boy. Tenderly she promised, "Listen, Verdiano, we're here." The staple-faced man asked, "So what happened?" The woman shushed him, "Let the child save his strength."

"Did Simplicio save the mason?" the staple-faced man still wanted to know.

"Bastard," the woman whispered.

Verdiano meant to gesture as he spoke, but his hands moved apart from his words; that frustrated him. He shrugged and lay them on his chest, as though they were gloves he'd taken off.

"Simplicio had to go ask permission to save the man," Verdiano told them. "He was only a kitchen worker. So the mason stayed in the air upside down while Simplicio found the bishop. When he doffed his hat, he saw how his hands were dirty from the garden; abashed, he hid them behind his back. He would obey his superior. Yet . . . he wanted to save the mason. The man surely had a wife and children to feed. And then. Then . . . he craved *Say the truth, Simplicio you crave the time during these occasions when all runs out and all flows in. Simplicio lowered his head and advanced. 'Do I save this man, your grace, or let him fall?' he asked the bishop. 'I told you to stop doing these things,' the bishop said. Simplicio begged, 'I can't help it, holiness, they go where I do.' 'Nevertheless, you don't have qualifications.' " Verdiano took a long time saying that word *cal-i-fi-ca-ci-o-nes;* once he'd gotten it out, he seemed spent. His lids fluttered, showing the whites of his eyes. People groaned.

Benny cursed, thumped Verdiano's chest, hollered at the woman across from him. "Fix it, fix it, lady, get a new rag or somethin'!" She looked at him—*híjole, what eyes, like bruises*— unzipped her yellow sweatshirt, reached under a T-shirt, and handed him one of two round pink jobs with pooches like sofa buttons on them. She applied the other to the bleeding—it fit perfect.

Connection, Catherine knew too much about why people stick around not to sense a connection. She'd seen them, patients who'd become friends, holding on at seventy-nine pounds, waiting for the grandbaby, the son on the midnight plane. Catherine cupped her free hand to call him back. "Verdiano!" She really had to yell. "Verdiano! This long story! Do you mean you left your novia in Mexico waiting for you?"

Verdiano returned. "But that's it," he said. The chalk corners of his mouth frowned in dismay, stretching the wispy mustache; the clear brown eyes spilled. The sunhat woman gasped: it was true, as her sisters lamented—*y porque?*—why were you asked to stand the pain of your children? "Sí, mi novia," Verdiano said, "I left her in Mexico, hanging in the air."

Catherine understood the beauty of resignation—a way to go forward—but now she found herself coughing up its other half, the beauty of not being resigned. As a plain matter of fact, she would not allow this situation to exist. "Do something," she commanded to no one in particular. The wind whistled; a fat, wet snowflake landed on the piñon. She looked at the muscled man across from her. All Benny's features had screwed together, except for his bottom lip, which hung loose. It had just sunk in what the woman had given him, that the pooch was supposed to be a nipple. Her gaze seared each bystander, and returned to the staple-faced man at Verdiano's head. "Do something for this boy!" she shouted.

The crowd began emptying their pockets, but because they were pilgrims that day on a route with nothing to buy, they didn't have much money. The young man, goosebumped as a turkey but such a body, the sunhat woman noted, nodded gruffly toward Catherine, so they stuffed the money for Verdiano in her yellow sweatshirt pocket.

Benny said, "Look, bro. That's for your girl," but Verdiano didn't understand so he put it in Spanish *pa tu novia*, and then Verdiano tried to touch his white cowboy hat in thanks but it had blown away long since and besides, his hands were gone. He only closed his eyes, showing how long and thick his black lashes grew, and opened them again.

The old man with the scar still wanted to know about Simplicio, did he save the mason or not?

Benny crowded the narrow old face. "Cost you to find out, jodido. How much you got?"

The sunhat woman raised a dyed eyebrow and said about the old man, her husband, "Ése? He owns seventy-nine apartments in Santa Fe."

"*Cállete, mujer*, what does that have to do with anything?"

"And five houses all on the same street. Y one por acá way up on the hill. That one has a historical plaque."

The old man blinked and shifted a little in the wind, like a stunted piñon.

Benny pulled out his pockets so the wind would flap them. "Anybody else here got money?" Everybody said *No, Uh uh*, that was it. They'd given it all. For a minute, like he was straining at the limit—two-hundred-seventy-five pounds of iron chin-high and wobbling—Benny couldn't figure what to do. But then *Eeee, this is it, I'm a genius*, he loomed over the old man. All the shivering still didn't make his muscles look any smaller. "Give him a house, Mr. Monopoly."

"A house?" The old man looked at the people and they looked back at him. "Give my house? That I worked all my life for?" He thrust out his hands so they could see the pad of callous from holding the trowel, but that was years ago and the people saw only smooth skin.

"Well, let him live there, then. Give him some rent."

"Yeah, rent." "Rent's okay." People were nodding.

The old man's eyes got slick and his face as chamisa green as the spring roadside. He held his stomach down with both hands. All the time his face was working, rubbery, like the staple was being pried open. "Evaristo, que pasa!" cried his wife, "are you having a coronary?"

Coughing, Evaristo managed to sputter, "A year's free rent."

Benny gave him some breathing room, smiled. "No, you don't get it. As long as he wants."

Evaristo grunted. "It hurts, it really hurts like I swallowed a cleaver, five years," he said.

The bystanders applauded. Catherine informed Verdiano, whose face, by now as white as a Japanese dancing girl's, didn't change. Two more spring snowflakes lumbered down; everybody hugged their own arms. "Look, take this." Catherine gave her sweatshirt to Benny who tugged it on, the cuffs hitting him mid-arm, zipped it up tight, and by main force did not look to see how level the pocket on her T-shirt lay.

Once he'd made the hard decision, old Evaristo's next one was surer. "He can live in the little casita on Scissors Street, the first one I bought in 1952. Let him bring his novia there. Cómo se llaman?"

All the rest had gone past Verdiano like so much chatter, like restaurant conversation; he couldn't quite attend to it. But, *novia*, Verdiano heard. "Ana Luz," he said.

"No, not that house!" Evaristo's wife had his number. "That one is falling down."

"Hey, a little mud." Her husband threw out his arms. "I will provide." Saying it, he was an actor, but with the little sentiment echoing, bouncing off people's impressed faces, he began to believe, *un poco, un poquito*, you know? He liked how it sounded. He cleared a single snowflake above Verdiano's head. "I will provide."

"They'll have children, Evaristo." His wife enlarged the world—now Verdiano and Ana Luz had dear little babies the ages her grandchildren should be. "Get them a new roof, a washer-dryer. Some carpet, entiendes? Some of that champagne color, it goes with everything."

Evaristo's half-face bloomed out. "I will provide it, no problem."

Benny grumbled, "Okay, you paid, you can ask now."

The old man was blank. Ask what? Ay, the curse of old age, he couldn't remember anything he needed to know. "Ask what?" he said.

"The story. Did Simplicio get the mason down or not?"

So they turned to Verdiano and asked him and he was about to answer when the car drove up.

A green Buick with the back window smashed coasted to the ditch. Those runner firemen, they'd caught up to her. One scared her foot off the gas with a rock hurled through the rear window; the other two ran alongside until the car stopped rolling. They had to make her raise her head off the wheel and hear what they were telling her. They had to get her to unlock a door. They had to talk her into unclenching her fist and giving them the car keys. It took some time but finally they'd made her do all those things. Then they slid in and turned the car around.

Three men in wet gym shorts lunged out the doors and dragged over a girl by the tender part of her arm. The crowd melted back, all except Evaristo's wife who pointed a red finger, "Mira. Look at the blood all over her headlight. Look at the dent! It was her, all right." A hissing noise came from the people and just then a cop car approached and they cheered. "Hey! Hey! Here they come," people yelled, and "It's about time," and "Where's the ambulance?" but even though a fireman loped out from behind the piñon, semaphoring and whistling, the cop car drove right by. "Eeee, those guys are more stupid than dirt," the fireman said. He left the girl and took off chasing the cruiser.

Another fireman hauled her through the crowd of people right up to the hurt boy. She took a lot of little steps because her white lace mini cut any natural stride and her white high heels made her sink and trip over the uneven ground. A second after the girl stumbled by, they could smell her. She smelled like piña coladas and peach daquiris and crème de menthe with shaved chocolate and amaretto sours with extra cherry juice. She stared down at Verdiano, her huge brown eyes smudged all around with flicks of mascara.

Nobody said anything. Some of them stood on their toes to see what she was going to do. They thought the girl would fall on her knees in her white Easter mini, clench her hands and cry. Say she didn't see him. Say it was an accident, she didn't mean to hit him. Never in a million years did she . . . that's what they were expecting. But the girl just curled her lip, breathed through her mouth, and tried to back up. Her wide eyes kept jerking away from the boy on the ground to the people around her; she twisted her head like someone was poking her with a stick.

Finally a fireman narrowed one eye and bobbed his heavy head two or three times to show how serious he was. "If he dies, you're a murderer," he pronounced to the girl. The bystanders agreed with him. They had some names for her and they weren't just mumbling; they were making sure she heard. Somebody reached past the fireman and shoved her. "Hey, don't do that," another person said and shoved her back. Evaristo's wife dug two red fingernails into the girl's lace shoulder blades, giving her a pinch. This one here, this very girl broke her children, never even looked back as they bled on the road. "Little puta hit and run," she accused. The girl whimpered.

The girl and the whimper made Benny Ortiz kind of sick. Couple of years ago it might have been fun to shove her, but not now. The kid was still going to be lying here with most of his blood leaked out, wasn't he? Benny made the first speech of his life. "Hey, back off," he told the bystanders. "She's lost it. Like if your dad was poundin' your mom and you hit him with the steam iron, then when he woke up you swore you didn't. I mean, you stared at that iron and you really, truly believed you didn't. It's too big to handle. Look at her, man, she ain't got her lights on."

But nobody paid much attention. "Mira, kid," a fireman hooked his thumb at the girl and spoke past Benny to Verdiano. "This is the one did it to you." People stopped muttering and watched to see what would happen.

Verdiano opened his velvet eyes on the girl. Pink, the most delicate pink, a drop of red in an ocean of white, tinged his cheeks. "Ana Luz," he said.

The fireman yelled in frustration. "No, no, man, wake up! This is the one *hit you!*"

"Ana Luz, I can smell your cough syrup."

The girl surged back, but the fireman had her clamped.

"It's good you drank it because the wind is blowing."

Nonononono she shook her head, her pretty face contorted.

The sunhat woman cried, "You little bitch hit and run! You ought to get down on your little puta knees and beg him you're sorry." With that, the woman stepped up and pushed her to her knees, so that when she fell forward the girl's black-smeared cheek touched the boy's white one.

Verdiano's eyes glittered. His chin was trembling. How had she managed to find him? His *novia*, all dressed up. After a grinding day shift, she must have sneaked in at night to make this dress. He could see how it must have been. Ana Luz with her bowed neck, hiding far in the back where the seat cover foreman never inspected, her foot speeding the machine's pedal. For her health he had walked the pilgrimage, but now this. Softly, through a froth of rosy bubbles, Verdiano praised her name. "Ana Luz. Who could have done this but you?"

It was like the girl had been electrocuted. She leapt to her feet and broke the fireman's grasp. Flailing her arms, she beat her way through the bystanders, who reeled back from her blows, her scent of curdled sugar. She made it to her car, where a fireman leaned leering against the Buick's door. The girl threw back her head and howled.

Evaristo hoisted himself up and limped over to her. He was just her height. First he got her by the shoulders and gave her a few shakes, then he talked to her. After a while he took the girl's arm like they were crossing a busy street or he was escorting her down the aisle in her soiled Barbie bride dress and he walked her back to Verdiano.

The girl's face kept changing. Her eyebrows would draw together and apart, from wide and blank her eyes would focus. Finally her shoulders sagged. She wiped her face with her hands, looked down at Verdiano, and her red lips parted like a little slit heart.

Verdiano's brow furrowed the slightest degree, as if he were listening hard. He breathed in, eating the rose bubbles. Then, like someone taking his picture told him to stop jostling around and get serious—c'mon freeze for the camera—he was still. People drew forward, waiting for him to let the breath out, but Verdiano kept it.

The girl's eyes rolled back then, and they had to grab her and hold her for maybe ten more minutes until the cop car, with ambulance trailing, screeched up in a fishtail stop. The doors burst open, and two state cops sprang out. Taking his time, a fireman slid from the back seat and bent over to massage his hamstrings.

Flashing and whooping ("Aw, man, what *for*," said a fireman), the ambulance sprayed them with grit and pebbles. People kneeled down where Verdiano had lain, picking through the pile of sweatshirts and windbreakers to find their own. Shrinking the world to regular size—oh much better—Evaristo's wife sent a prayer for the *pobrecito*, the little *mojado* dead so young, and set about provoking her husband. "Bueno, that dump on Scissors Street, you got your rent back, are you happy?"

Evaristo blew on his hands and rubbed them, rubbed his face, yeah, he was still there. "Hey don't call it that, okay?" It wasn't a bad house, brought in $475 a month, even with no screens and pipes you had to put hot towels on in the winter. His first house, in 1952. For seven years, after he returned from the service, he saved for it. A million adobes he'd laid, a million cinderblocks fit and grouted, miles of scaffolding climbed, saving up for it, his little cornerstone. Yeah, he decided, he was glad to have his *casita* back.

Benny peeled off Catherine's yellow sweatshirt; it was way stretched out. He found his bloody T-shirt in the pile. People who'd carried staffs retrieved them from the ditch, and stood by the road trying to clear their heads before they continued their walk.

Who felt like going seven more miles to Chimayó?

Nobody, but were they supposed to turn around and walk back to Santa Fe? With all the world heading the other way? Besides, the day was warming up again. The wind had dropped. The sky was lightening into blue ribbons, and see—there on the wavy piñon hills a little gold was shining.

"Poor kid," a fireman crossed himself before jamming on his *Dodgers* cap. Another one slapped his flat belly which would soon be fat and did a few calf stretches. They all ran off, slim muscles prancing, "Híjole," a voice carried back to the last two left, "this damn weather is so crazy."

Catherine lowered herself to the roadside and propped her head on her knees. She needed to sit a while, calm her breath. As she wiped her streaming face with the hem of her T-shirt, she saw the muscleman shoot her a glance. He stood in the dusty road shifting his weight, rubbing his forehead. Then he squatted down, and barely meeting her eyes, held out her pink breast. Because his face was so serious, she didn't laugh—though it was funny how he handled the foam rubber. With unease but with respect. Reluctant but wanting something—like Simplicio advancing on the bishop.

When the woman smiled to herself, Benny found her face less weary, her eyelids less scraped, less blue, her wide mouth harmless. In order to stick the breast in her sweatshirt pocket, she had to remove a wad of money. "Uh oh," she said, fanning the bills of Verdiano's collection.

An idea had struck Benny—it was just that *'orita,* he couldn't shape words—could they find Ana Luz? Because the money belonged to Ana Luz, and of all the people there, Verdiano belonged to him and to this woman. She had no breasts. She really had no breasts. Benny was having this crazy sensation of his hand reaching out, simultaneously seeing in his mind how it would be—smooth, sealed, her pink chest. Like it would hurt him to touch it. And what was weird was he didn't flinch, didn't grimace. She was clasping his wrist, whether to slap him back or to keep him with her, Benny couldn't say. He couldn't get out even one word. It was like he'd been falling, hurtling down head first, only to be stopped mid-air and set down . . . shocked, dizzy, dumbfounded by the rescue.

Nominated by Shenandoah

THE LINE

by RAYMOND FEDERMAN

from ALASKA QUARTERLY REVIEW

at first one could stand in line almost anywhere people didn't really mind too much if one cut in front of them though there were always some who objected when overtaken particularly those who were under the impression that they stood near the head of the line but even these people did not object too vehemently since the line was not moving very fast or for that matter often hardly moved for long periods of time and since no one could tell where it was going but people waited anyway patiently and goodhumoredly and more were coming all the time in endless processions after all it was a good line a pleasant line a decent line even though in places people allowed gaps holes in it looseness and laxness as the line weaved stretched meandered out of sight thicker here thinner there single or double file here triple even quadruple there in fact in various places it was more like a social

270

gathering or a human press as people crowded around
in circles as if preparing for a town meeting or a
debate or getting set for a choir or a game after all with
such little progress forward and so much time to wait
people moved about the line up and down in and out
casually and freely stopping along the way to chat with
neighbors old friends or distant relatives cousins or
uncles they had not seen in years all sorts of people
with whom one had had dealings or commerce as the
saying goes before joining the line but also to chat with
the new acquaintances made in line as one moved
about leisurely from place to place up and down for
indeed the mere fact of being in line seems to create a
friendly atmosphere a sense of sincere congeniality
and solidarity among the liners as they were called
therefore those who made a fuss when someone
squeezed past them would be sneered at and even
booed by those being by-passed since the line was
endless in both directions and it was impossible to
determine where it started where it originated and
where it ended therefore it was ridiculous on the part
of anyone to want to claim a legitimate place in it or
insist on any priority of standing for what would be the
point of declaring oneself ahead of anyone else that
would certainly be futile yet some people kept moving
up the line overtaking others squeezing in front of them
or by-passing them but without any hurry or sense of
urgency these people were merely moving up or giving
themselves the impression of moving from one place
in line to another nearer to the head simply for the
sake of moving forward without any specific reason or
purpose hoping perhaps that eventually they would be
first in line a vain hope of course because the more
people there were moving up the line the further away
the head would be for obviously as these people
squeezed in front of others the further away the head
would be pushed so that in fact a step forward in this
case really meant two steps backward for while certain
people moved forward others moved in the opposite
direction falling back in line so to speak away from the
head because frankly they did not care where they
stood in the line and so they would loaf about or mill
around in groups in and out of the main stream

271

forming circles to gossip or tell jokes or listen to the
stories which were circulating up and down the line
funny stories about what people did in line to pass the
time or how others had forgotten why they came to the
line and yet continued to wait simply because they had
nothing else to do or how some people truly believed
they knew where the line was going groups could be
seen standing around laughing at the curious objects
people had brought with them to the line for instance
the bed on wheels on which an old man was lying in
his nightgown and which he pushed along with a cane
as if paddling a canoe just to keep up with the line or
the little desk and chair and even a calculating machine
an accountant kept lugging along so he could continue
to do his numbers as he waited in line ah what dumb
things people do while waiting in line one could hear
muttered all over but it was the jokes especially that
attracted most attention and caused the greatest
hilarity one joke in particular kept being repeated up
and down the line the one about the fellow who sees
a funeral procession going slowly down the street with
two hearses and a gentleman holding a huge muzzled
dog in leash and behind them a long line of men all
wearing black the puzzled onlooker asks the
gentleman with the dog why are there two coffins in
this ridiculous funeral oh replies the man with the dog
the first coffin is my mother-in-law and the second my
wife ah I see says the curious man okay but why
the dog oh the dog answers the gentleman pulling at
the leash he killed both of them ah exclaims the
inquirer could I borrow your dog for a few hours well
you better get in line mister the mourner with the mean
dog retorts with a large grin on his face some of these
jokes were not very funny but this one kept being told
over and over because it seemed so appropriate to the
situation though some people claimed they had heard
it before probably those who had been in the line from
the beginning and heard that joke when they first
arrived for it was said that the joke was as old as the
line itself and it was indeed a very old line some people
had been in the line so long they could not remember
when they first joined as a matter of fact the line had
been going for such a long time that many died while

waiting and had to be buried on the spot special crews
were appointed to dig graves and perform the burial
rites but there were also happy occasions on the line
for instance people falling in love and getting married
or children being born or birthdays and anniversaries
being celebrated it was very interesting to observe how
the line not only changed shape constantly but also
changed mood how it fluctuated from sad to happy or
vice versa and this as a result of the many activities
that were going on in the line so that it could be said
that the line changed moods as often as it changed
shape sometimes it was joyful lively full of playfulness
and other times it was sad gloomy somber anguished
but in general the line was calm and uneventful simply
moving along in its ordinary but disorganized fashion
becoming thinner here or thicker there and usually this
because someone had stopped to tell a story or a joke
and a crowd had gathered or elsewhere someone had
just finished telling a story or a joke and those who had
been listening were now moving on or sometimes if
there was a tree or a wall along the way or some other
such natural or man made structure that cast a
shadow on a sunny day or gave a bit of protection
from the wind on a cold day or from the rain on a
stormy day then people would gather under that tree
or line up near that wall or huddle next to that structure
and wait consequently the line would become thinner
and lax in that spot lazy as it were for there was no
great urgency or unnecessary impatience in the line
even though arguments would sometimes flare up
about nothing in particular and even occasional fist
fights for no apparent reason simply that someone's
foot had been stepped on and no immediate apology
offered and quickly a shove would result followed by
an even harder retaliatory shove and then a fist would
strike someone's ribs or someone's nose and for a few
moments there would be turmoil and agitation in the
line until the people around the disturbers would
restore a semblance of order and calmness with pleas
insistent pleas of please let's keep the line moving and
gradually the line would resume its careless progress
as casually as before the disturbance quickly forgotten
and the disturber politely forgiven in general then one

could say that it was not a bad line on the contrary a
good decent honest line perhaps a bit too chaotic but
nonetheless adequate a line to which people could
come without apprehension and once in line without
having to complain too much about being stuck there
for the main concern in line was civility and generosity
many had come to the line quite unprepared not
having anticipated the fact that it would be a slow
endless process so that waiting would be in vain just
as progress would be in vain therefore they had not
brought with them the essential in food and clothing to
last or continue to last in line so that food drinks and
clothing would be shared generously among the liners
it was not unusual to see groups of people who had
never met before eating from the same picnic basket
or drinking from the same bottle or handing pieces of
clothing or blankets to people who suffered from the
cold more than others especially during the night after
sundown but particular care was given to the young
and the very old for there were people of all ages in
the line male and female of course and of all ways of
life educated and illiterate rich and poor this was
apparent from the clothes and manners of certain
people many races and colors were also present in line
but usually these people preferred to stay together in
bunches in remote parts of the line naturally there were
also people of different religious beliefs this was evident
from the discussions and arguments having to do with
questions of morality for one of the major concerns of
all the people present was the morality of the line and
when disagreements occurred on this question the line
would become extremely agitated though it should be
noted that not all discussions had to do with morality
or theology in some places people would get together
to sing songs in unison while in other places someone
would suddenly stand on a box to make a speech or
deliver a lecture and people would gather around to
listen to the speaker or argue with him there were
always people ready to argue about anything for the
sake of a good argument while others who did not
care to listen to these impromptu speeches would
shout keep the damn line moving but since no one
really payed much attention to these dedicated liners

274

they would simply by-pass those gatherings and move on but usually most people preferred the one-to-one conversation moving with the flow of the line two people would casually talk about anything in particular where one is from what one does in life talk about the family about the wife who didn't want to come to the line or talk about the children or reminisce about one's childhood in other words the usual banalities of life occasionally one could hear an intellectual discussion or a critique of the latest artistic fad but it should be stated that not everyone in line was willing to engage in conversation many preferred to remain silent facing the back of the person in front extremely serious in their waiting quietly performing their role as liners of course since the line moved extremely slowly and in no apparent direction many people would drop out if not permanently at least temporarily sometimes simply to rest along the way and watch the others in line go by or else to take a nap many could be seen stretched on the ground soundly asleep during the day and naturally at night too however there were some who complained all the time saying that it was hopeless that we will never get there but in general most people seemed resigned to the slowness and indeterminacy of the line in fact some people who had previous experience with other lines said that in spite of its disorganization and purposelessness this was a rather good pleasant line perhaps the best line they had ever joined and this because of its casualness and lack of regulations for indeed in spite of its disorder this line was remarkably smooth and easy going and as such acceptable to most though many feared that one day unexpectedly out of the blue so to speak it would be announced that everyone in line should stand in alphabetical order and this would immediately cause an incredible mess a frightful state of disorder for the commotion that would result from the fact that one would have to change place and move either forward or backward depending on the spelling of one's name would create not only chaos but irritation and anguish and consequently the line would turn ugly full of animosity as people would not hesitate to ask others with whom they had had a friendly relationship for their identification cards in order to ascertain that they were in the correct place according to the first letter of their last names and one would probably hear people shouting to others your name begins with a T get the hell back or someone would say in a somewhat embarrassed tone of voice my name starts with a B I have to move ahead of you and it would not be rare nor surprising for some people to accuse others of lying about their names or of using false names just to be ahead of them therefore this line which had been so good and so flexible would rapidly degenerate into an angry state of mutual suspicion simply because of alphabetical ordering for there would be order now in the line oh yes indeed order unhappily

Nominated by Alaska Quarterly Review

FICTION AND THE
INNER LIFE OF OBJECTS

by CHARLES BAXTER

from THE GETTYSBURG REVIEW

for Irving Massey

ABOUT A THIRD of the way through Ivan Turgenev's second
novel, *Home of the Gentry* (1859), the hero, a luckless man
named Lavretsky who has been experiencing a painful marriage
and who will soon fall in love with a woman as unsuited to him as
his wife has been, pauses for a moment to observe the flow of
natural events outside in an open field. Lavretsky, we are to un-
derstand, has not been a particularly gifted observer at any time
in his life, at least until now. His slight taint of obtuseness prob-
ably accounts for his tendency to love people who cannot love
him back.

Because this is a Russian novel of the mid-nineteenth century,
Lavretsky's gift of sight occurs on an estate. He is between
scenes and is feeling bored and lazy. For the first time, it seems,
he is paying some attention to things he cannot touch or eat. (The
narrative has somewhat slyly let us know that he is overweight.)
Feeling calmly indolent in the middle of his unharvested crops,
he begins to listen to gnats and bees. Half lost in all the vegeta-
tion, he sees brightly burnished rye and the oats that have
formed (in Richard Freeborn's translation for the Penguin edi-
tion) "their little trumpet ears." Out of habit, he returns his con-
scious attention to himself and thinks immediately of his
miserable romantic attachments, but then, as if his perspective
has been subtly adjusted, he looks again at the objects in front of
him.

All at once the sounds die, and Lavretsky is "engulfed" in silence. He looks up and sees "the tranquil blue of the sky, and the clouds floating silently upon it; it seemed as if they knew why and where they were going."

Russian literature is rich in moments when wisdom arises out of indolence, but this one seems unusually eerie to me. Lavretsky has lost his industry, or rather his industriousness, and in this pre-industrious state he can see self-contradicting objects that are metaphorically both ears and trumpets, producers and receivers of sound that are playing only in his imagination. In his laziness, Lavretsky gives up his feeling and thinking to the objects that constitute his environment, and in this air-pocket of silence the clouds acquire consciousness and a sort of ontological intelligence. The passing of the clouds feels slightly god-haunted, although no god is visible anywhere in the scene.

It seems important to me to resist reading this episode through what we may know about Wordsworth or English Romantic poetry, or epiphanies, or psychoanalysis and Zen Buddhism. The twentieth century has built up a powerful set of intellectual shortcuts and devices that help us defend ourselves against moments when clouds suddenly appear to think. To say that clouds know something is already to sound a little mad. Lavretsky has given away some of his emotional and intellectual autonomy, and suddenly the things surrounding him have their own thoughts and feelings—not necessarily Lavretsky's—and in this reduction of the human scale, Lavretsky's misery disappears. Lavretsky has momentarily recognized an integrity in nature that was invisible as long as he made himself gigantic with pain and problems. Lavretsky's misery will reappear because the plot demands it, but this moment will function as a benchmark—at least for the reader, if not for Lavretsky—against which to measure the size of his feelings.

In this century, the fiction with which we have grown familiar has tended to insist on the insentience and thoughtlessness of things, if not their outright malevolence. Generally things have no presence at all except as barriers or rewards for human endeavor. When nature is given something like a face to look back at humans, as it often is in Conrad's stories and novels, the expression on that face is typically one of straightforward hostility. Or at least what seems to be hostility: the violence of nature—its typhoons and uninterpretable remoteness—is what nature flings back at men who are deeply involved in the project of imperialism. If, as Conrad often insists, imperialism is a kind of rape of nature, then it should be no surprise that man's violence is visited upon him in return, coming the other way as a force field of unknowingness, the "sullen, dumb, menacing hostility," for example, that Lena perceives in the forest in *Victory*. This often leaves Conrad's characters in a highly specified nowhere where the only option is not to grant objects much visibility of any kind, as in Winnie Verloc's repeated assertion in *The Secret Agent* that "most things did not bear very much looking into."

I want to trouble this topic because I think that contemporary fiction has gradually been developing a fascinated relationship with objects that parallels in some respects the concerns of the ecological movement. It is as if things are again, after a war of about eighty years, making visible a correspondence to human feelings, but only under certain circumstances. The truce, if there is one, is probably conditional. To say that the realms of objects and humans may be collaborative, however, is to risk an obvious sentimentalism in the face of continued human violence against the earth; and to say that things may be "making visible a correspondence to human feelings" still sounds slightly mad and wrongfully acquisitive. John Ruskin's concept of the pathetic fallacy is deeply implicated in such responses.

Madness, like many conditions, has to be culturally defined, and one can see a part of that definition being formulated in Ruskin's delineation of the pathetic fallacy in 1856. In this essay, Ruskin takes it upon himself to define what he calls an "unhinged" literary response to nature by analyzing certain metaphors that writers employ. What Ruskin asserted as an aesthetic working-principle became an informal aesthetic law in the twentieth century. My interest here is not so much to argue against that law as to ask how it came into existence in the first place.

Things, Ruskin says, should not be made to reflect the emotions of the observer. In poetry and prose, human emotions should not be allowed to discolor the integrity of observed phenomena. Although Ruskin would not have put it this way, his objection is to an overspillage of human expression onto the things that surround the individual. Ruskin's claim in this chapter of

Modern Painters that the projection of human feelings on things is fallacious, untrue, morbid, and frightful has all the violence of an ideology that is meant to put certain kinds of poets in their place. His examples are interesting. One is two lines from a poem by Oliver Wendell Holmes:

> The spendthrift crocus, bursting through the mold
> Naked and shivering, with his cup of gold.

Curiously enough, Ruskin does not object to "naked and shivering" but to "spendthrift." The crocus, he says, is *not* spendthrift but "hardy." It does not give away, apparently, but instead hoards. Ruskin finds the poem's metaphor for the plant's economic life mistaken and, as he says, "untrue." But in eliminating one metaphor for plant life—"spendthrift"—Ruskin substitutes another metaphor—"hardy"—without appearing to recognize that the inescapability of metaphors and figurative language is part of the problem that he is trying to correct. Evidently the crocus is more like a young Victorian gentleman or banker than an undisciplined and sentimental squanderer of a fortune.

In another example, from a novel by Charles Kingsley, Ruskin quotes with considerable distaste the phrase "cruel, crawling foam" and argues that as a phrase it is "unhinged." Of course Ruskin's point is clear enough. He is simply observing that when people say that the "storm is raging," for example, there is no real rage in the storm. The rage is human and is projected upon the storm. Human attributes cross a boundary line and are wrongfully stitched to the nonhuman.

In his pleasantly irascible way, Ruskin is doing his best to define a problem that is considerably larger than he is. He is describing the distortion of perceptions that (he believes) occurs when someone has what he calls "violent feelings." Violent feelings, he says, produce a "falseness in all our impressions of external things." Feelings, or as he says "souls," can be compared to things, but the separateness of the feelings and the things must be maintained; in his opinion Dante maintains this distance but Coleridge does not. The result is what Ruskin calls a "morbid" effect in Coleridge. The world's integrity can be saved (by implication) through the deployment of a discriminating sensibility.

At certain times of day, Ruskin's love of sanity is lovable, as is his hope that the worlds of human consciousness and nature can be made figuratively distinct. Behind his anger is a certain understandable squeamishness, a distaste for any kind of aesthetic confusion. He desires clarity. And there is a sense also behind his words that he is entering a battle that he suspects he is going to lose. Ruskin sees nature being entered, mucked around with, and violated for the purposes of what he thinks is second-rate poetry—cheap effects and paltry lyricism.

Everywhere Ruskin looks, he sees the human presence expanding. Objects are being shamelessly taken over, *used*, for an easy poetical effect, which is imperialism at the level of aesthetics. Objects are being forced to go to work, are being *employed* to carry their burden of human feeling. No one is leaving objects alone anymore—not in industry, or in literature. Ruskin wants to stop this expansionism and confusion of realms, but he has to do so by bracketing violent feelings and the atrocities that give rise to them and putting them to the side somewhere. In a rather English manner, he seems to want to deny that when people look at things, things look back. He is thus resisting both emotional violence and the Being that gazes out from objects. His assumption is that all emotional violence arises out of sensationalism and a carelessness in the notation of feeling. For him, emotional confusion is by its very nature violent. All this, as I have said, is understandable and even lovable, and it has the sound of someone sitting in a comfortable study and saying that there will be no war, there must not be a war, even as the guns of the twentieth century start blasting away, and the terms of the war are announced by the John-the-Baptist of apocalypse, Friedrich Nietzsche.

Ruskin's essay on the pathetic fallacy takes its place in a larger quarrel about the division of literary property in the nineteenth century. At about the time of the rise of the English novel, a marker or borderline begins to appear in literary consciousness that makes the relationship between the inner life of human beings and the inner life of objects almost exclusively a matter for poetry. It is as if all the speaking about the terms of the relationship between people and the spirit within things will occur in poetry and poetics or in almost uncategorizable writing such as theosophy. We begin to hear about these matters from Wordsworth and Baudelaire, Rilke and Yeats and Vallejo, Madame Blavatsky and Rudolf Steiner. (Steiner's observations that anyone can intuit an individual spirit poking the water upward underneath each wave, or that there are some experiences that make the mind resemble an anthill, travel so far beyond the pathetic fallacy that, in his writing, philosophy demands a religious leap of faith.)

Virtually all myths, fables, and allegories assert that there is an inner life to things—that things speak to us—but with the advance of science and historical materialism, to say nothing of commercial culture, the life of objects is defined as either poetic or surreal or a base-line assumption of insanity. In the case of Marx, the only life an object has consists of its life as a commodity, tossed back and forth in the tidal ebb and flow of capital. By the late nineteenth century, it is as if the division of realms has become absolute: poetry gets the spirit, and fiction gets the material. Modern lyric poetry is assigned to track the fate of the inner life, while fiction is stuck with consciousness and material objects, neither of which speaks to the other. The stages of this process are all outlined by the Spanish philosopher Ortega y Gasset in his wonderful *Meditations on Quixote*. Don Quixote, he says, is the spirit of epic poetry who hears all things speaking; Sancho Panza is the practical materialist, the spirit of the rise of the novel. Cervantes's novel is the thunderous and comic announcement that Don Quixote is about to be supplanted in human history by Sancho Panza. Poetry, displaced by prose, can keep its heroism and its madness, but prose will be delegated to speak about material life. Poetry gets the spirit and hears it speak but is called mad; prose fiction is given a landscape of dead objects and is rewarded for writing about these things with a popular acclaim, a mass audience.

In any case, following this model, one can understand why, when Don Quixote is dying and has regained his lucidity, Sancho Panza wants him to be his old self again—heroic and mad and epical. Sancho is going to be stuck with a paunch and a world of mute things. So much the worse for him, but he *has* survived, in the way that laboratory science has survived its unruly parent, alchemy, and for some of the same reasons. Marxism survives Hegelianism until something turns up to displace dialectical materialism. Everyone remembers Sancho Panza's tears at the deathbed of Don Quixote. Materialism without ideals, mad or not, weeps. Deprived of a quest, it is consigned to centuries of weeping. Don Quixote and Sancho together are the two parts of a whole that speaks beautifully and memorably and comically. Separated, they die in different ways.

An interlude: during a particularly harsh period in my life, I was living in a rented room in Buffalo, New York. At the time, I was trying to convince myself that I loved someone I did not really love. All my emotions seemed willful and tired, like a muscle that has been overtrained. The city of Buffalo seemed to me a visual representation of the futility of all human endeavor. Like many people in my condition, I was broke all the time but did not care. Money was for others. At least, I thought, I have my cigarettes and books and enough food to live on. From day to day my personality was probably insufferable. One way or another my friends suffered it.

I had a new idea, it seemed, every five minutes. When friends came to Buffalo, I gave them a tour of the cemetery, which was, to be fair, a local attraction. I woke up at night hearing serious accusations against my life and would read D. H. Lawrence or Hegel until sunrise. I tried to silence these accusations by reading voices of massive explanation, the masters of intellectual volume. The only ideas that seemed worthy to me were those that were desperate or excessive. All my ideas about sex were inflamed. Sexually, I wanted to be a laboratory animal.

We are talking now about the psychology of private obsession, rented rooms, student life, high unsupported intellectuality, balconies with a good view that are attached to no building. It is a mode of existence that interested Dostoyevsky. In our own time Don Delillo has written about it. Somehow I cannot think about this kind of life without seeing cigarettes and smoke and drugs as part of it, as if Faust and the dark powers must always be invoked. I do not know how I knew that thinking-at-the-frontiers required cigarettes. I just knew smoke figured into it.

One night, coming back to my rented room at about three in the morning after a particularly excruciating romantic encounter, I turned on the light in my room and saw the chair I usually sat in. This chair had high padded arms and was upholstered in what I remember as worn pale-green polyester fabric, very much in the taste of my landlady, Mrs. Zachman. I looked at the chair and

283

the desk and the bed, and I began weeping as one weeps under such circumstances. The content of my thought was both alcoholic and sentimental. Nevertheless, my fit had a particular content. It was Sancho Panza trying to cross over into Don Quixote, and it had to do with the belief that things would take care of me. These things, the chair and the desk, would hold me and carry me at those times when humans would not.

People in a traumatized state tend to love their furniture. They become ferociously attached to knickknacks. Laura and her love for her glass menagerie in Tennessee Williams's play will have to stand for a whole platoon of the dispossessed for whom objects have come alive. To write about these spiritual conditions, an author might do better to describe the furniture than to describe the consciousness of the person entering the room. The things carry the burden of the feeling. They do not when our emotions are placid, but when our emotions are violent, they must.

In an age of violent emotions, objects become as expressive as the people who live among them. Anglo-American fiction, unlike poetry, has been slow to arrive at this recognition. It wants to contain objects and material but to give all the feelings to the human characters. The resulting effect of articulated will and passion in the void of pure consciousness is one of the great modes of Modernist fiction. The rise of delineated consciousness in fiction, powerful and solitary as it grasps for a handle on the world, is so apparent in the twentieth century that it needs no further elaboration from me. My intention in the remainder of this essay is to single out certain passages of fiction that I love, where objects rather than people are expressive or even sentient. Behind these moments I hear John Ruskin clearing his throat, but I think that Ruskin's clarity of categories operates best in moments of nonviolence free of atrocity. For this and other reasons I think of the pathetic fallacy not so much as a dated concept but as a critical urban pastoral.

For years, each time I read the "Time Passes" section of *To the Lighthouse*, it puzzled me. These twenty-four pages of Virginia Woolf's prose struck me at one time as somehow both fey and bizarre. I understood—I was a graduate student—how Woolf wanted to reincorporate material objects in fiction with what she called a "luminous halo" and how her quarrel with the novels of

Arnold Bennett had to do with the manner in which objects appeared in fiction. She concluded that Bennett was a crude materialist and that this produced in his novels an offensive knowingness about worldly things. What she wanted, by contrast, was the spiritualization of the world of objects.

All the same, "Time Passes" looked odd no matter how I read it. The sheer writerly heroism of the section, its courage, eluded me. With the snobbery of middle-age, I now believe that an understanding of this rather singular interlude is aided by a reader's experience of or feeling for immediate—even personal—decay. Having gotten over being young is an aid in reading it.

The main character in the section is the Ramsay house, vacated by the Ramsays, as it gradually loses its integrity and form. The other two actors are darkness and wind. Human beings are, in this section, secondary to objects and spirits. There is a cleaning woman, Mrs. McNab, and her helper, Mrs. Bast, both of whom appear late in the section to clean things up, but when the members of the Ramsay family are mentioned, their names and their actions appear within brackets.

Death, often violent or sudden, is held within these brackets: Mrs. Ramsay's sudden death from an unnamed illness; Prue Ramsay's death in childbirth; Andrew Ramsay's death in the First World War. These calamities are narrated with a shocking offhandedness. The narrative consciousness of *To the Lighthouse* refuses to dwell on them. They are the stuff of trauma, and in the world of this novel they are in some fundamental sense nonnarratable. Beyond stating the bare facts, trauma declines to speak of itself. The odd purity of true suffering, in this case, is that it is resolutely undemonstrative; unless our sensibilities are corrupt, the facts must always be the sufficient shock. Any narrative inflation of pain is an exploitation of it and a betrayal of its nature. In this novel the death of the spirit cannot be housed narratively in the flesh where that death occurs but must move into the dwelling place of the body, the house itself.

What happens in this section tonally has a touch of fable, horror movie, and children's story. In passages such as the following I hear a voice almost unknown to the Modernist novel:

> Only through the rusty hinges and swollen sea-moistened woodwork certain airs, detached from the

285

body of the wind (the house was ramshackle after all) crept round corners and ventured indoors. Almost one might imagine them, as they entered the drawing-room questioning and wondering, toying with the flap of hanging wall-paper, asking, would it hang much longer, when would it fall?

I recognize this voice. It says, "Now listen, children." At some outer limit of pain, innocence is being allowed to enter through a back door, a secret entrance. Abstract qualities are given human form at the same time that humans lose it:

Loveliness and stillness clasped hands in the bedroom, and among the shrouded jugs and sheeted chairs even the prying of the wind, and the soft nose of the clammy sea airs, rubbing, snuffling, iterating, and re-iterating their questions—"Will you fade? Will you perish?"—scarcely disturbed the peace, the indiffer-ence, the air of pure integrity, as if the question they asked scarcely needed that they should answer: we re-main.

As the members of the family die, the house is invaded by wind and rain and darkness. We are witnessing the soul of a house as it expires. The feeling in these passages is wonderfully and beautifully peculiar. As saucepans rust, the mats decay, and the toads invade the interior, and as the lighthouse watches "with equanimity" while the house is undermined, all forms of the pa-thetic fallacy are put on display. But, if I can put it this way, what is being projected onto the house is not a human feeling, but a god's. Spirits give life, but in this case they also rot. The tone of the sentences mixes wonderment and incantation; it is a tone I am familiar with from children's literature, but the English novel does not to my knowledge display it with high seriousness until this moment. This leap-to-childhood does not feel regressive to me so much as desperate and enterprising. Some ancient source of wonder has to be traced back to its origin if life is to be sus-tained at all. If humans are to suffer spirit-death, things will too. By this means the "something" that lies behind our objects will be glimpsed:

But there was a force working; something not highly conscious; something that leered, something that lurched; something not inspired to go about its work with dignified ritual or solemn chanting.

This "something" has to be tricked out of hiding. Solemn chanting will not do the trick, but (at the level of style) fable, lyric, whimsy, lushness just might. The "something" spied in this passage is not malign; but it does not gaze with equanimity either, as the lighthouse does. It is a dead god being brought back to life in the revival of things in which it can find habitation. As the house is restored, so is the presence that lies behind it.

For any number of reasons, I find this section of *To the Lighthouse* wildly, almost insanely, courageous. In a voice invoking magic, it equates housekeeping with religion. It says that taking care of things, both natural and man-made, is the way back to the reconstitution of the spirit, and it gives a sentience to objects as the containers of that spirit. It declares a truce between humans and objects, and it observes that if any group effects the repair, it will probably be women, women who have never read Descartes, who would not understand Descartes if they did read him. Against the absolute separation of man and thing, the mind-body dichotomy tormenting Mr. Ramsay, we just might place a therapeutic incomprehension. "One wanted," Lily Briscoe thinks, "to be on a level with ordinary experience. . . ."

The solemn and lyrical zaniness of "Time Passes," its cast of characters of rats, frogs, wind, darkness, and spirit, makes it immune, I think, to skepticism and epistemological badgering. The person who asks, "How do you *know* that loveliness and stillness clasped hands in the bedroom?" is immediately recognizable as a fool; the question is absurd in a way that the assertion of the clasped hands is not.

In *To the Lighthouse* the reconciliation of matter and spirit is managed at such a high level of psychic virtuosity that one holds one's breath while reading it. Aesthetically, it almost does not happen, in the same way that James Ramsay is almost not reconciled to his father as they sail out to the lighthouse in the closing pages of the book. James wants to kill his father, knife him for his emotional coldness and his other crimes against the spirit. But

287

the winds fill the sails at the last moment, Mr. Ramsay says, "Well done!" and James "was so pleased that he was not going to let anyone share a grain of his pleasure." Opportunistic violence is bracketed at last and removed from the scene of narrative.

The fragility of these narrative instances can hardly be over-stated. I do not find anything much like it, certainly in American writing, for another two decades. What happens instead is a narrative interest in the anger of objects, the fierce hostility of things to man and his enterprises. A few examples will have to stand for what I take to be a larger field of activity.

Here is Malcolm Lowry's Consul in *Under the Volcano*, sitting in a bathroom, drunk, and gazing at the insects on the wall:

> The Consul sat helplessly in the bathroom, watching the insects which lay at different angles from one another on the wall, like ships out on the roadstead. A caterpillar started to wriggle toward him, peering this way and that, with interrogatory antennae. A large cricket, with polished fuselage, clung to the curtain, swaying it slightly and cleaning its face like a cat, its eyes on stalks appearing to revolve in its head. . . . Now a scorpion was moving slowly across towards him. Suddenly the Consul rose, trembling in every limb. But it wasn't the scorpion he cared about. It was that, all at once, the thin shadows of isolated nails, the stains of murdered mosquitoes, the very scars and cracks of the wall, had begun to swarm, so that, wherever he looked, another insect was born, wriggling instantly toward his heart. It was as if, and this was what was most appalling, the whole insect world had somehow moved nearer and now was closing, rushing in upon him.

The Consul expresses insects. Having been expressed, they return to him, to their insect home, his heart. They are grotesque, of course, not only because they are hideous but also and especially because they hate him. He is defined—he defines himself—as a character who refuses to love. Therefore he gets the insects. They are like tiny violence-prone fates.

Thomas Pynchon's Byron the Light Bulb (in *Gravity's Rainbow*) travels from bulb babyhood to a tour of the world's systemic cartels, including the light cartel, Phoebus. In Pynchon's encapsulated light bulb *Bildungsroman,* Byron, who is immortal, sees the truth of the human systems but "is condemned to go on forever, knowing the truth and powerless to change anything. No longer will he seek to get off the wheel. His anger and frustration will grow without limit, and he will find himself, poor perverse bulb, enjoying it. . . ."

As in much of Pynchon, this Olympian understanding leads to an immobilized rage. It is now power rather than capital that moves in a tidal ebb and flow, and—in a very Foucaultian manner—one's understanding of the system is essentially paralytic. Anger and frustration expand to fill any space available to house them.

Another way of saying this is to argue that the speech and the feelings traded between human beings and objects, both animate and inanimate, have something to do with a contract. The contract's language is not always easy to decipher; nevertheless, it concerns how humans will employ the things that come to hand. In what I can make out of this contract, as it becomes visible in twentieth-century fiction, the earth is described (in a traditional metaphor) as a home. When greed, violence, and the various other human vices begin to make the home unhomelike—in German, *unheimlich*—the uncanny erupts out of things that were once silent. Objects are forced to speak, to become visible as thoughtful, when the home is endangered. The double meaning of *unheimlich* as both *unhomelike* and *uncanny* is a traditional puzzle. Freud worried over it in his "On the Uncanny" and saw it, in part, as the estrangement of the familiar. We might describe the uncanny here as "the speaking or thinking of mute, thoughtless things."

Certainly it arises, as Ruskin predicted it would, from emotional violence and extremity. The examples I have cited so far all have warfare—the First World War, the Spanish Civil War, and the Second World War—deeply painted in the background. In some cases, again in fiction, where warfare or imperialism are not explicitly implied, the hidden subject may be described as soul-theft. This tradition is very strong in Russian literature and finds its great artist in Nikolai Gogol, whose work tracks and shadows the soul as it is bought and sold, and in whose work objects seem to be living a giddy life of their own. Leo Tolstoy, too: in the first section of "The Death of Ivan Ilych," Pavel Ivanovich suffers the pranksterish rebellious springs of the chair he sits on, while Praskovya Fedorovna, the grieving widow, gets her shawl stuck on the side of a table. These are not accidents; the objects want it that way. Loveless, petty functionaries, in Tolstoy's account, come face to face with the perversity of inanimate objects, beginning with their sickening bodies and going on from there. The trading and buying of souls enlivens the uncanny in Andrei Bely, Mikhail Bulgakov, and Vladimir Nabokov as well; in Nabokov's *Bend Sinister,* located in a police state where the dictator Paduk is doing his best to acquire the soul of the philosopher Adam Krug, Krug's friends, the little things, haplessly sing tunes to him he can only half-see and half-hear:

> The stove crackled gently, and a square clock with two cornflowers painted on its white wooden face and no glass rapped out the seconds in pica type. The window attempted a smile. A faint infusion of sunshine spread over the distant hill and brought out with a kind of pointless distinction the little farm and three pine trees on the opposite slope which seemed to move forward and then to retreat again as the wan sun swooned.

If this is the pathetic fallacy, whose pathos is it? The internal narrator's? Krug's? Nabokov's? These floating perceptions have a detachment that is so complete that they have a feeling of weightlessness, an immunity to gravity. In this sense they have the god-feeling of "Time Passes," a forthright and almost vehement innocence, the song the angels sing that cannot for all of its beauty relieve the torments of human life.

Perhaps such innocence must be brought out by dualities, by an opposition of brutality or violence. I began this essay by arguing that objects can speak back to us and let us know their thoughts in fiction suffused with a tone of balance and equilibrium, but I am suspicious of that claim because its best examples are not found in fiction but in poetry. It may be that the native tension of narrative fiction is more conducive to an edgy relation to things, a set of mutually accusing voices.

Still—and here I wander guilelessly into a major problem of philosophy—it is recognizable that a tree or a sidewalk café viewed by a person in love are not the same objects when viewed by a person with congestive heart failure. Conventionally we say that the tree is *viewed* differently by those two people. But it takes a third person to say so. In the kind of fiction I have been discussing here, it is not a matter of the tree being viewed differently. The tree itself is different.

The word "setting," especially as it is used in fiction-writing textbooks and workshops, has a drab, dutiful quality, a feeling of something always already-there. Worse, it may be assumed that setting is objective, that it "helps" or "shapes" a story. In the way that I am describing them, however, the objects and things surrounding fictional characters have the same status as the characters themselves, and an equal portion of energy. Setting, then, is *not* just a place where action occurs, any more than the earth is a prized location where our lives happen to happen. Setting in its psychic extensiveness projects a mode of feeling that corresponds to, or contrasts with, the action. The way that setting is usually taught in fiction-writing classes results in the fictional equivalent of a curtain that rises on a stage set with one desk, one potted plant, and a stairway reaching toward empty air. What surrounds the characters can be and often should be as expressive as the action, but no law or formal entitlement dictates that it should always express the feelings of the characters. Too often, however, it does. Let us call this the fallacy of the objective correlative. In the fallacy of the objective correlative, the setting can *only* express the feelings of the characters. A sad man sees sad trees. A murderer gazes upon a murderous lake.

This kind of one-to-one equivalency makes John Ruskin's ideas about the pathetic fallacy seem sensible all over again. If objects reflect *only* the characters who look upon them, they have nothing to tell us. In such cases, they function as mirrors serving to enlarge—once again—the human realm. But if there is a feeling characteristic of our time, it is that the human realm needs no further enlargement; it is already bloated, in many senses at once. If a mountain exists only to express human feeling, it is no longer itself—dangerous, unknowably beautiful, and absolutely nonhuman. Malcolm Lowry's Consul does see versions of himself wherever he looks, but Lowry himself is careful to include other points of view in the novel to readjust the perspective and to let other versions of nature speak. Lowry does not let his character

291

dictate the terms of the novel's telling. The Consul's presence makes *Under the Volcano* possible, but the novel also requires his absence from time to time. I think it also requires his death, or at least his sacrifice; he is a character who must die, or at least be thrown away, so that the novel *about* and around him can live.

Is there such a condition as an expressive background of speaking objects that are heard by a reader but not by the characters themselves? Virginia Woolf points us in this direction, as does Nabokov, but in contemporary American fiction few examples suggest themselves. We are too often in the presence of characters and narrators who dictate the terms under which things, or the world itself, may speak. More often, things are not allowed to speak at all; they are every bit as inarticulate as the characters who acquire and despise them.

Examples of the mute object, broken on the thematic wheel, are so common that they do not command much attention, but objects that speak over the heads of characters directly to readers are so uncommon in fiction that the prevalence of this form of knowing and saying in the work of William Maxwell deserves some notice. Modesty and a variety of innocence that is never naive replace the usual forms of worldliness and willfulness in this fiction, which is often stuck in the Midwest and stuck, too, at a particular time, the 1920s and '30s. Its rather astonishing love for its characters—astonishing only for its size and generosity—may be a function of its nostalgia, but in this case nostalgia acts as a perpetual questioning of what constituted the place that a person could once call "home." It is probably consistent with this questioning that most of Maxwell's characters are fated to fall in love with the wrong thing or the wrong person. They experience love just long enough to know what love is; then the object of that love, being wrong, is removed. (In this respect his work bears a single, odd resemblance to that of Toni Morrison.)

In Maxwell's *Time Will Darken It*, Nora Potter, the young woman who will fall in love with a married man, Austin King, is located at the center of what would be in other respects a conventional narrative—if the town where it occurs, Draperville, Illinois, were not so articulate. But in this novel, because everything is loved, everything speaks. The "mindless, kindless voice of nature," as the narrator calls it, speaks through the heat, the locusts, the rain, and the bric-a-brac. Spoken only to the

292

reader, it bypasses the characters. One example from many will have to suffice:

> The house was so still that it gave her the feeling that she was being watched, that the sofas and chairs were keeping an eye on her to see that she didn't touch anything that she shouldn't; that she put back the alabaster model of the Taj Mahal and the little bearded grinning man (made out of ivory, with a pack on his back, a folded fan, and his toes turned inward) exactly the way she found them. The locusts warned her, but from too far away. The clocks all seemed preoccupied with their various and contradictory versions of the correct time.

This passage begins with Nora's feelings, but it has more feelings than Nora does, and by the time the paragraph is over, Nora is insufficient to explain them. She has been diminished just enough so that the locusts can speak without being heard by her. The passage notices that the little bearded man made out of ivory has toes turned inward, but it is unclear whether Nora notices that. Here, she is one thing in a field of things. And she is about to violate those things, without being quite aware that she is doing so. If we have caught the feeling of the scene, we probably know that Nora is going to suffer eventually, that things (in this case, in the form of fire) will have their revenge for her interference.

In his tender, antiheroic fiction, Maxwell lovingly puts his characters in their places; like Turgenev's Lavretsky and like Chekhov's characters, they slowly learn what it means to have a sense of scale. In the only way that matters, they are humbled by being placed in proximity to objects that, in Turgenev's words, "seem to know where they were going."

In two other contemporary stories, objects acquire humaneness when humans themselves cannot possess it. In Cynthia Ozick's "The Shawl," a story about a concentration camp, the shawl takes on the burden of nurturing Magda, a malnourished infant, and becomes a breast and a womb and a house. The electric fencing around the death camp, as if disturbed by the role it plays, hums with "grainy sad voices." In Tim O'Brien's "The Things They Carried," about Vietnam, the soldiers transfer all their feelings to the objects they "hump," as the narrative has it: feeling, dispossessed by humans, moves quickly into the nearest receptacle willing to house it.

A final interlude (or a postlude): My stepfather liked on winter weekends to repair broken furniture, and he often gave me the responsibility for holding his tools while he did the work. Because he was a man of small patience and terrible temper, but with a high vision of himself, he would turn screws or hammer nails with a bland expression on his face that revealed almost nothing. Only his skin revealed his feelings: it grew redder and redder as his fury against inanimate objects increased. Holding his tools, I thought: He is a steam engine, and he is going to explode any minute now.

He never cursed and hardly spoke while doing these tasks. He took himself as an upper-class, lapsed Protestant very seriously. But when he exhaled, he exhaled through his nose in regular three-second intervals, exhalations of the purest rage, utterly machinelike, so much so that I cannot now hear the distant sound of a stamping plant or a production line without thinking of my stepfather. Holding his tools, I felt sorry for the screws and the nails. They screamed and squeaked as they fell under my step-father's interest.

Outside my window is an apple tree. It is August as I write these sentences. For the last few days a squirrel has been foraging in the tree, and sometimes it descends low enough on one of the branches in front of my study window to take a good look at me. It can stare at me for two minutes without moving. Then it goes back to its business, as I do to mine.

We do not spray the tree, and the apples growing there are mostly green or wormy. During the time that I have been writing this essay, the apples have been falling to the ground in the backyard. Every now and then, writing a sentence, I have heard the sound of an apple hitting the earth. Before the sound of that impact, there is a breath, a swish, as the fruit drops through the branches and leaves. It is not a sigh but sounds like one. This sound has nothing to do with my current moods, but I listen for it, and I have been counting the number of apples that have fallen during the last ten pages of this essay. There have been eighteen.

Nominated by Robin Hemley, Robert Phillips

INVENTING THE FILIPINO

by FATIMA LIM-WILSON

from THE KENYON REVIEW

Let's celebrate the yoyo-makers.
Before you named it "Walking the Dog"
And "Cat's Cradle," our folks
Climbed trees, those agile monkeys,
Knocking down the day's meal
With the world's first yoyo
Created from twine, a skull-
Sized stone and the spittle
Of gods. What about that jeep
That bounced on the moon? We
Thought of that, too. From
The war's heap you left behind.
When you first landed there
In '69, bouncing like the kids
You are, tossing lunar balls,
Our Miss Philippines pinned on,
Demurely, Miss Universe's crown.
She now rides horses, up and down,
Her makeup artist strategically
Throwing buckets of water
Between her breasts. We have more
Elvises than we can count. And of
Course, our very own Marie Antoinette,

Who has only you to thank
For the shape of her ankles.
We're a graceful lot, you know.
Great dancers in G-strings,
Especially under dim red
Lights. We'd like to join you
Someday, very much. And so
We sway to our sad-sweet songs,
Longing to be the fifty-first appendix.
Till then we'll fly your flag
Half-mast, over all the hot air
From that blasted god
Thrashing his chains, underground.

Nominated by Ha Jin, The Kenyon Review

JOURNAL OF THE THOUSAND CHOICES

by SUSAN WHEELER
from O•BLĒK

I Dinner

So that's what you've got in your back pocket.
Come over here. And when she moves to her left
the Missouri courthouse behind her looms into view until
you are distracted by her collar, alive as it seems.

II Job

The acacia at the bayou bloomed a thousand times,
a thousand times. A small librarian
born to better things sang I see the moon and the moon
sees me. The townspeople, caught off guard, watched
the lobe suspiciously. The tower tolled a dozen chimes—
it tolled for thee.

III Relations

She wanted burgers but before they had even hit the grill
a police car pulled up in front of the restaurant and two
cops bolted in with fire arms out.

IV City & State of Origin

Land in malachite, eyeball the sediment, stratify the
limonite. What breather breaks the churt, the flint?
What arrow bursts obsidian? I have a dollar bub
the pyrite rains round here like gold.

V Canned Goods

Lassia found her skating and skating around
the Tyrolean pond in circles. Herr Settembrini
had but just left her,
and Lassia became shy at her new ruddiness.
The words alarmed at the larynx,
the steam of the blade on the ice,
the rise of the fruit at her chest,
the falling of water, the roar.

Here, unwrap the cigar and cut it like so.

VI School

Châteaubriand this, châteaubriand that.
Like pekinese sniffing at table,
Mr. Lewis and his electric organ spun
the stuff of a thousand halls.

Nominated by O·Blēk

298

THE WAY IT FELT
TO BE FALLING

by KIM EDWARDS

from THE THREEPENNY REVIEW

THE SUMMER I turned nineteen I used to lie in the backyard and watch the planes fly overhead, leaving their clean plumes of jet-stream in a pattern against the sky. It was July, yet the grass had a brown fringe and leaves were already falling, borne on the wind like discarded paper wings. The only thing that flourished that summer was the recession; businesses, lured by lower tax rates, moved south in a steady progression. My father had already left, but in a more subtle and insidious way. After his construction company failed he had withdrawn, into some silent world. Now, when I went with my mother to the hospital, we found him sitting quietly in a chair by the window. His hands were limp against the armrests and his hair was long, a rough gray fringe across his ears. He was never glad to see us, or sorry. He just looked calmly around the room, at my mother's strained smile and my eyes, which skittered nervously away, and he did not give a single word of greeting or acknowledgment or farewell.

My mother had a job as a secretary and decorated cakes on the side. In the pressing heat she juggled bowls between the refrigerator and the counter, struggling to keep the frosting at the right consistency so she could make the delicate roses, chrysanthemums, and daisies that bloomed against the fields of sugary white. The worst ones were the wedding cakes, intricate and bulky. That summer, brides and their mothers called us on a regular basis, their voices laced with panic. My mother spoke to them as she worked, trailing the extension cord along the tiled floor, her voice soothing and efficient.

Usually my mother is a calm person, levelheaded in the face of stress, but one day the bottom layer of a finished cake collapsed and she wept, her face cradled in her hands as she sat at the kitchen table. I hadn't seen her cry since the day my father left, and I watched her from the kitchen door, a basket of laundry in my arms, uneasiness rising around me like slow, numbing light. But it was all right, she was all right. After a few minutes she dried her eyes and salvaged the cake, removing the broken layer and dispensing with the plastic fountain which spouted champagne, and which was supposed to rest in a precarious arrangement between two cake layers held apart by plastic pillars.

"There." She stepped back to survey her work. The cake was smaller but still beautiful, delicate and precise.

"It looks better without that tacky fountain, anyway," she said. "Now let's get it out of here before something else goes wrong."

I helped her box it up and carry it to the car, where it rested on the floor, surrounded by bags of ice. My mother backed out of the driveway slowly, then paused and called to me.

"Katie," she said. "Try to get the dishes done before you go to work, okay? And please, don't spend all night with those dubious friends of yours. I'm too tired to worry."

"I won't," I said, waving. "I'm working late anyway."

By "dubious friends" my mother meant Stephen, who was, in fact, my only friend that summer. He had spirals of long red hair and a habit of shoplifting expensive gadgets: tools, jewelry, photographic equipment. My mother thought he was an unhealthy influence, which was generous; the rest of the town just thought he was crazy. He was the older brother of my best friend Emmy Lou who had fled, with her boyfriend and 350 tie-dyed tee shirts, to follow the Grateful Dead on tour. Come with us, she had urged, but I was working evenings in a grocery store, saving my money for school, and it didn't seem like a good time to leave my mother. So I stayed in town and Emmy Lou sent me postcards I memorized—a clean line of desert, a sky aching blue over the ocean, an airy waterfall in the intermountain west. I was fiercely jealous, caught in that small town while the planes traced their daily paths to places I was losing hope of ever seeing. I lay

300

in the backyard and watched them. The large jets moved in slow silver glints across the sky; the smaller planes droned lower. Sometimes, on the clearest days, I caught a glimpse of skydivers. They started out as small black specks, plummeting, then blossomed against the horizon in a streak of silk and color. I stood up to watch as they grew steadily larger, then passed the tree-line and disappeared.

After my mother left I went inside, where the air was cool and shadowy and heavy with the scent of sugar flowers. I piled the broken cake on a plate and did the dishes, quickly, feeling the silence gather. That summer I couldn't stay alone in the house; I'd find myself standing in front of mirrors with my heart pounding, searching my eyes for a glimmer of madness, or touching the high arc of my cheekbone as if I didn't know my own face. I thought I knew about madness, the way it felt, the slow suspended turning as you gave yourself up to it. The doctors said my father was suffering from a stress-related condition, brought on by the failure of his company. They said he would get better. But I had watched him in his slow retreat, distanced by his own expanding silence. On the day he stopped speaking altogether I had brought him a glass of water, stepping through the afternoon light that flickered on the wooden floors he had built himself.

"Hey, Dad," I had said, softly. His eyes were closed. His face and hands were deeply tanned from the construction work, but where his shirt opened in a V his skin was soft and white and pale. When he opened his eyes they were clear blue, as blank and smooth as the glass in my hand.

"Dad?" I said. "Are you okay?"

He did not speak, then or later, not even when the ambulance came and took him away. He did not sigh or protest. He had slid away from us with apparent ease. I had watched him go, and this was what I knew: madness was a graceless descent, the sudden abyss beneath an ordinary step. *Take care* I said each time we left my father, stepping from his cool quiet room into the bright heat outside. And I listened to my own words, I took care too. That summer, I was afraid of falling.

Stephen wasn't comfortable at my house and he lived at the edge of town, so we met every day at Mickey's Grill, where it was cool and dark and filled with the chattering life of other people. I al-

301

ways stopped in on my way to or from work, but Stephen sometimes spent whole days there, playing games of pool and making bets with the other people who formed the fringe of the town. Some of them called themselves artists, and lived together in an abandoned farmhouse. They were young, most of them, but already disenfranchised, known to be odd or mildly crazy or even faintly dangerous. Stephen, who fell into the last two categories because he had smashed out an ex-lover's window one night and tried, twice, to kill himself, kept a certain distance from the others. Still, he was always at Mickey's, leaning over the pool table, a dark silhouette against the back window with only his hair illuminated in a fringe of red.

Before Emmy Lou left, I had not liked Stephen. He was eight years older than we were, but he still lived in a fixed-over apartment on the second floor of his parents' house. He slept all morning and spent his nights pacing his small rooms, listening to Beethoven or playing chess with a computer he'd bought. I had seen the dark scars that bisected both his wrists, and they frightened me. He collected a welfare check every month, took valium every few hours, and lived in a state of precarious calm. Sometimes he was mean, teasing Emmy Lou to the edge of tears. But he could be charming too, with an ease and grace the boys my own age didn't have. When he was feeling good he made things special, leaning over to whisper something, his fingers a lingering touch on my arm, on my knee. I knew it had to do with the danger, too, the reason he was so attractive at those times.

"Kate understands me," he said once. Emmy Lou, the only person who was not afraid of him, laughed out loud and asked why I'd have any better insight into his warped mind than the rest of the world.

"Can't you tell?" he said. I wouldn't look at him so he put his fingers lightly on my arm. He was completely calm, but he must have felt me trembling. It was a week after my father had been taken to the hospital, and it seemed that Stephen knew some truth about me, something invisible that only he could sense.

"What do you mean?" I demanded. But he just laughed and left the porch, telling me to figure it out for myself.

"What did he mean?" I asked. "What did he mean by that?"

"He's in a crazy mode," Emmy Lou said. She was methodically polishing her fingernails, and she tossed her long bright hair over her shoulder. "The best thing to do is pretend he doesn't exist."

But Emmy Lou left and then there was only Stephen, charming, terrifying Stephen, who started to call me every day. He asked me to come over, to go for a ride, to fly kites with him behind a deserted barn he'd found. Finally I gave in, telling myself I was doing him a favor by keeping him company. But it was more than that, of course.

One night, past midnight, when we were sitting in the quiet darkness of his second story porch, he told me about cutting his wrists, the even pulse of warm running water, the sting of the razor dulled with valium and whiskey.

"Am I shocking you?" he had asked, after awhile.

"No. Emmy Lou told me about it." I paused, unsure how much to reveal. "She thinks you only did it to get attention."

He laughed. "Well, it worked," he said, "didn't it?"

I traced my finger around the worn pattern in the upholstery. "Maybe," I said. "But now everyone thinks you're crazy."

He shrugged, and stretched, pushing his large thick hands up toward the ceiling. "So what?" he said. "If people think you're crazy, they leave you alone, that's all."

I thought of all the times I had stood in front of the mirror, of the times I woke at night, my heart a frantic movement, no escape.

"Don't you ever worry that it's true?"

Stephen reached over to the table and held up his blue plastic bottle of valium. It was a strong prescription. I knew, because I had tried it. I liked the way the blue pills slid down my throat, dissolving anxiety. I liked the way the edges of things grew undefined, so I was able to rise from my own body, calmly and with perfect grace.

Stephen shook a pill into his hand. His skin was pale and damp, his expression intent.

"No," he said. "I don't worry. Ever."

STILL, ON THE DAY the cake collapsed, I could tell he was worried. When I got to the pool room he was squinting down one cue at a time, discarding each one as he discovered warps and flaws.

"Hey, Kate," he said, choosing one at last. "Care for a game?"

We ordered beer and plugged our quarters into the machine, waiting for the weighty, rolling thunk of balls. Stephen ran his hand through his long red beard. He had green eyes and a long, finely shaped nose. I thought he was extremely handsome.

"How goes the tournament?" I asked. He'd been in the play-offs for days, and each time I came in the stakes were higher.

Stephen broke, and dropped two low balls. He stepped back and surveyed the table. "You'll love this," he said. "Loser goes skydiving."

"You're kidding," I said, remembering the plummeting shapes, the silky streaks against the sky. "You know, I've always wanted to do that."

"Well," Stephen said, "keep the loser company, then."

He missed his next shot and we stopped talking. I was good, steady, with some competitions behind me. The bar was filling up around us, and soon a row of quarters lined the wooden rim of the pool table. After a while Teddy Johnson, one of the artists in the farmhouse, came in and leaned against the wall. Stephen tensed, and his next shot went wild.

"Too bad," Ted said, stepping forward. "Looks like you're on a losing streak, my friend."

"You could go fuck yourself," Stephen said. He was tense, but his voice was even, as though he'd just offered Ted a beer.

"Thanks," Ted said. "But actually, I'd just as soon ask Kate a question, while she's here. I'd like to know what you think about honor, Kate. Specifically, this: Do you think an honorable person must always keep a promise?"

I shot again. The cue ball hovered on the edge of a pocket, then steadied itself. There was a tension, a subtext that I couldn't read. I sent my last ball in and took aim at the eight. It went in smoothly, and I stepped back. There was a moment of silence, and we listened to it roll away into the hidden depths of the table.

"What's your point, Teddy?" I asked, without turning to look at him.

"Stephen is going skydiving tomorrow," Ted said. "Or so he promised."

"Stephen, you lost?" I felt betrayed, and wondered why he hadn't told me about it when I first came in.

"It was a technicality," Stephen said, frowning. "Ridiculous, in fact. I'm the better player." He took a long swallow of beer.

304

"What bullshit," Ted answered. "You're graceless in defeat, you know."

Stephen was quiet for a long time. Then he put his hand to his mouth, very casually, but I knew he was slipping one of his tiny blue valiums. He tugged his hands through his thick hair and smiled.

"It's no big deal, skydiving. I called today and made the arrangements."

"All the same," Ted answered, "I can't wait to see it."

Stephen shook his head. "No," he said. "I'll go alone."

Ted was surprised. "Forget it, champ. You've got to have a witness."

"Then Kate will go," Stephen said. "She'll witness. She'll even jump, unless she's afraid."

I didn't know what to say. He already knew I wasn't working the next day. And it was something to think about, too, after a summer of sky-gazing, to finally be inside a plane.

"I've never even flown before," I told them.

"That's no problem," Ted answered. "That part is a piece of cake."

I finished off the beer and picked up my purse from where it was lying on a bar stool.

"Where are you going?" Stephen asked.

"Believe it or not, some of us work for a living," I said.

He smiled at me, a wide, charming grin, and walked across the room. He took both my hands in his. "Don't be mad, Kate," he said. "I really want you to jump with me."

"Well," I said, getting flustered. He didn't work, but his hands were calloused from playing so much pool. He had a classic face, a face you might see on a pale statue in a museum, with hair growing out of his scalp like flames and eyes that seemed to look out on some other, more compelling, world. Recklessness settled over me like a spell, and suddenly I couldn't imagine saying no.

"Good," he said, releasing my hands, winking quickly before he turned back to the bar. "That's great. I'll pick you up tomorrow, then. At eight."

When I got home that night my mother was in the kitchen. Sometimes the house was dark and quiet, with only her even breathing, her murmured response when I said I was home. But usually she was awake, working, the radio tuned to an easy-

305

listening station, a book discarded on the sofa. She said that the concentration, the exactness required to form the fragile arcs of frosting, helped her relax.

"You're late," she said. She was stuffing frosting into one of the cloth pastry bags. "Were you at Stephen's?"

I shook my head. "I stayed late at work. Someone went home sick." I started licking one of the spoons. My mother never ate the frosting. She saw too much of it, she said, and hated even the thick sweet smell of it.

"What is it that you do over there?" she asked, perplexed.

"At work?"

My mother looked up. "You know what I mean," she said.

I pushed off my tennis shoes. "I don't know. We hang out. Talk about books and music and art and stuff."

"But he doesn't work, Kate. You come home and you have to get up in a few hours. Stephen, on the other hand, can sleep all day."

"I know. I don't want to talk about it."

My mother sighed. "He's not stable. Neither are his friends. I don't like you being involved with them."

"I'm not unstable," I said. I spoke too loudly, to counter the fear that seemed to plummet through my flesh whenever I had that thought. "I am not crazy."

"No," said my mother. She had a tray full of sugary roses in front of her, in a bright spectrum of color. I watched her fingers, thin and strong and graceful, as she shaped the swirls of frosting into vibrant, perfect roses.

"Whatever happened to simple white?" she asked, pausing to stretch her fingers. This bride's colors were green and lavender, and my mother had dyed the frosting to match swatches from the dresses. Her own wedding pictures were in black and white, but I knew it had been simple, small and elegant, the bridesmaids wearing the palest shade of peach.

"I saw your father today," she said while I was rummaging in the refrigerator.

"How is he?" I asked.

"The same. Better, maybe. I don't know." She slid the tray of finished roses into the freezer. "Maybe a little better, today. The doctors seem quite hopeful."

"That's good," I said.

306

"I thought we could go see him tomorrow."

"Not tomorrow," I said. "Stephen and I have plans already."

"Katie, he'd like to see you."

"Oh, really?" I said sarcastically. "Did he tell you that?"

My mother looked up from the sink where she was doing dishes. Her hands were wet, a pale shade of purple that shimmered in the harsh overhead light. I couldn't meet her eyes.

"I'm sorry," I said. "I'll go see him next week, ok?"

I started down the hall to my room.

"Kate," she called to me. I paused and turned around.

"Sometimes," she said, "you have no common sense at all."

SECRETLY I HOPED for rain, but the next day was clear and blue. Stephen was even early for a change, the top of his convertible down when he glided up in front of the house. We drove through the clean white scent of clover and the first shimmers of heat. Along the way we stopped to gather dandelions, soft as moss, and waxy black-eyed Susans. Ted had given me his camera, with instructions to document the event, and I spent half the film on the countryside, on Stephen wearing flowers in his beard.

The hangar was a small concrete building sitting flatly amid acres of corn. The first thing we saw when we entered was a pile of stretchers stacked neatly against the wall. It was hardly reassuring, and neither was the hand-lettered sign that warned CASH ONLY. Stephen and I wandered in the dim, open room, looking at the pictures of skydivers in various formations, until two other women showed up, followed by a tall, gruff man who collected $40.00 from each of us, and sent us out to the field.

The man, who had gray hair and a compact body, turned out to be Howard, our instructor. He lined us up beneath the hot sun and made us practice. For the first jump we would all be on static line, but we had to practice as if we were going to pull our own ripcords. It was a matter of timing, Howard said, and he taught us a chant to measure our actions. Arch 1000, Look 1000, Reach 1000, Pull 1000, Arch 1000, Check 1000. We practiced endlessly, until sweat lifted from our skin and Howard, in his white clothes, seemed to shimmer. It was important, he said, that we start counting the minute we jumped; otherwise, we'd lose track of time. Some people panicked and pulled their reserve chute even as the first one opened, tangling them both and fall-

307

ing to their deaths. Others were motionless in their fear and fell like stones, their reserves untouched. So we chanted, moving our arms and heads in rhythm, arching our backs until they ached. Finally, Howard decided we were ready, and took us into the hangar to learn emergency maneuvers.

We practiced these from a rigging suspended from the ceiling. With luck, Howard said, everything should work automatically. But in case anything went wrong, we had to know how to get rid of the first parachute and open our reserves. We took turns in the rigging, yanking the release straps and falling a few feet before the canvas harness caught us. When I tried it, the straps cut painfully into my thighs.

"In the air," Howard said, "it won't feel this bad." I got down, my palms sweaty and shaky, and Stephen climbed into the harness.

"Streamer!" Howard shouted, describing a parachute that opened but didn't inflate. Stephen's motions were fluid—he flipped open the metal buckles, slipped his thumbs through the protruding rings, and fell the few feet through the air.

Howard nodded vigorously. "Yes," he said. "Perfect. You do exactly the same for a Mae West—a parachute with a cord that's caught, bisecting it through the middle."

The other two women had jumped before but their training had expired, and it took them a few tries to relearn the movements. After we had each gone through the procedure three times without hesitation, Howard let us break for lunch. Stephen and I bought cokes and sat in the shade of the building, looking at the row of planes shining in the sun.

"Have you noticed?" he asked. "Howard doesn't sweat."

I laughed. It was true, Howard's white clothes were as crisp now as when we had started.

"You know what else, Kate?" Stephen went on, breaking a sandwich and giving half to me. "I've never flown either."

"You're kidding?" I said. He was gazing out over the fields.

"No, I'm not." His hands were clasped calmly around his knees. "Do you think we'll make it?"

"Yes," I said, but even then I couldn't imagine myself taking that step into open space. "Of course," I added, "we don't have to do this."

"You don't," said Stephen, throwing his head back to drain his soda. He brushed crumbs out of his beard. "For me it's my personal integrity at stake, remember?"

"But you don't have to worry," I said. "You're so good at this. You did all the procedures perfectly, and you weren't even nervous."

"Hell," Stephen said. He shook his head. "What's to be nervous? The free fall is my natural state of mind." He tapped the shirt pocket where his valium was hidden.

"Want one?" he asked. "For the flight?"

I shook my head. "No," I said. "Thanks."

He shrugged. "Up to you."

He pulled the bottle out of his pocket and flipped it open. There was only one pill left.

"Damn," he said. He took the cotton out and shook it again, then threw the empty bottle angrily into the field.

We finished eating in silence. I had made up my mind not to go through with it, but when Howard called us back to practice landing maneuvers, I stood up, brushing off the straw that clung to my legs. There seemed to be nothing else to do.

I was going to jump first, so I was crouched closest to the opening in the side of the plane. There was no door, just a wide gaping hole. All I could see was brittle grass, blurring, then growing fluid as we sped across the field and rose into the sky. The force of the ascent pushed me against the hot metal wall of the plane and I gripped a ring in the floor to keep my balance. I closed my eyes, took deep breaths, and tried not to envision myself suspended on a piece of metal in the midst of all that air. The jumpmaster tugged at my arm. The plane had leveled, and he motioned to the doorway.

I crept forward and got into position. My legs hung out the opening and the wind pulled at my feet. The jumpmaster was tugging at my parachute and attaching the static line to the floor of the plane. I turned to watch, but the helmet blocked my view. I felt Stephen's light touch on my arm. Then the plane turned, straightened itself. The jumpmaster's hand pressed into my back.

"Go!" he said.

I couldn't move. The ground was tiny, an aerial map, rich in detail, and the wind tugged at my feet. What were the commands? Arch, I whispered. Arch arch arch. That was all I could

309

remember. I stood up, gripping the side of the opening, my feet balanced on the metal bar beneath the doorway, resisting the steady rush of wind. The jumpmaster shouted again. I felt the pressure of his fingers. And then I was gone. I left the plane behind me and fell into the air.

I didn't shout. The commands flew from my mind, as distant as the faint drone of the receding plane. I knew I must be falling, but the earth stayed the same abstract distance away. I was suspended, caught in a slow turn as the air rushed around me. Three seconds yet? I couldn't tell. My parachute didn't open but the earth came no closer, and I kept my eyes wide open, too terrified to scream.

I felt the tug. It seemed too light after the heavy falls in the hanger, but when I looked up the parachute was unfolding above me, its army-green mellowing beneath the sun. Far off I heard the plane as it banked again. Then it faded and the silence grew full around me. I leaned back in the straps, into air. Four lakes curled around the horizon, jagged deep blue fingers. All summer I had felt myself slipping in the quick rush of the world, but here, in clear and steady descent, nothing seemed to move. It was knowledge to marvel at, and I tugged at the steering toggles, turning slowly in a circle. Cornfields unfolded, marked off by trees and fences. And still the silence; the only audible sound was the whisper of my parachute. I pulled the toggle again and saw someone on the ground, a tiny figure, trying to tell me something. All I could do was laugh, drifting, my voice clear and sharp in all that air. Gradually, the horizon settled into a tree line a quarter of a mile away, and I was falling, I realized, falling fast. I tensed, then remembered and forced myself to relax, to fix my gaze on that row of trees. My left foot hit the ground and turned and then, it seemed a long time later, my right foot touched. Inch by inch I rolled onto the ground. The corn tunneled my vision and the parachute dragged me slightly, then deflated. I lay there, smiling, gazing at the blue patch of sky.

After a long time I heard my name in the distance.

"Kate?" It was Stephen. "Kate, are you okay?"

"I'm over here." I sat up and took off my helmet.

"Where?" he said. "Don't be an idiot. I can't see anything in all this corn."

310

We found each other by calling and moving awkwardly through the coarse, rustling leaves. Stephen hugged me when he saw me.

"Wasn't it wonderful?" I said. "Wasn't it amazing?"

"Yeah," he said, helping me untangle the parachute and wad it up. "It was unbelievable."

"How did you get down before me?" I asked.

"Some of us landed on target," he said as we walked back to the hanger. I laughed, giddy with the solidity of earth beneath my feet.

Stephen waited in the car while I went for my things. I hesitated in the cool, dim hangar, letting my eyes adjust. When I could see, I slipped off the jumpsuit and black boots, brushed off my clothes. Howard came out of the office.

"How did I do?" I asked.

"Not bad. You kind of flapped around out there, but not bad, for a first time. You earned this, anyway," he said, handing me a certificate with my name, and his, and the ink still drying.

"Which is more than your friend did," he added. He shook his head at my look of surprise. "I can't figure it out either. Best in the class, and he didn't even make it to the door."

I didn't say anything to Stephen when we got into the car. I didn't know what to say, and by then, anyway, my ankle was swelling, turning an odd, tarnished shade of green. We went to the hospital. They took me into a consulting room and I waited a long time for the x-ray results, which showed no breaks, and for the doctor, who lectured me on my foolishness as he bandaged my sprained ankle. When I came out, precarious on new crutches, Stephen was joking around with one of the nurses.

It wasn't until halfway home, when he was talking nonstop about this being the greatest high he'd ever had, that I finally spoke.

"Look," I said. "I know you didn't jump. Howard told me."

Stephen got quiet and tapped his fingers against the steering wheel. "I wanted to," he said. His nervous fingers worried me, and I didn't answer.

"I don't know what happened, Kate. I stood right in that doorway, and the only thing I could imagine was my chute in a streamer." His hands gripped the wheel tightly. "Crazy, huh?" he said. "I saw you falling, Kate. You disappeared so fast."

"Falling?" I repeated. It was the word he kept using, and it was the wrong one. I remembered the pull of the steering toggle, the slow turn in the air. I shook my head. "That's the funny thing," I told him. "There was no sense of descent. It was more like floating. You know, I was scared too, fiercely scared." I touched the place above the bandage where my ankle was swelling. "But I made it," I added softly, still full of wonder.

We drove through the rolling fields that smelled of dust and ripening leaves. After a minute, Stephen spoke. "Just don't tell anyone, okay, Kate? Right? It's important."

"I'm not going to lie," I said, even though I could imagine his friends, who would be unmerciful when they found out. I closed my eyes. The adrenalin had worn off, my ankle ached, and all I wanted to do was sleep.

I knew the road, so when I felt the car swing left, I looked up. Stephen had turned off on a country lane and he was stepping hard on the gas, sending bands of dust behind us.

"Stephen," I said. "What the hell are you doing?"

He looked at me, and that's when I got scared. A different fear than in the plane, because now I had no choice about what was going to happen. Stephen's eyes, green, were wild and glittering.

"Look," I said, less certainly. "Stephen. Let's just go home, okay?"

He held the wheel with one hand and yanked the camera out of my lap. We swerved around on the road as he pulled out the film. He unrolled it, a narrow brown banner in the wind, and threw it into a field. Then he pressed the accelerator again.

"Isn't it a shame, Kate," he said, "that you ruined all the film?"

The land blurred; then he slammed the brakes and pulled to the side of the deserted road. Dusk was settling into the cornfields like fine brown mist. The air was cooling on my skin, but the leather of the seat was warm and damp beneath my palms.

Stephen's breathing was loud against the rising sound of crickets. He looked at me, eyes glittering, and smiled his crazy smile. He reached over and rested his hand on my shoulder, close to my neck.

"I could do anything I wanted to you," he said. His thumb traced a line on my throat. His touch was almost gentle, but I could feel the tension in his flesh. I thought of running, then

312

remembered the crutches and nearly laughed out loud from nerves and panic at the comic strip image I had, me hobbling across the uneven fields, Stephen in hot pursuit.

"What's so funny?" Stephen asked. His hand slid down and seized my shoulder, hard enough to fix bruises there, delicate, shaped like a fan.

"Nothing," I said, biting my lip. "I just want to go home."

"I could take you home," he said. "If you didn't tell."

"Just drive," I said. "I won't tell."

He stared at me. "You promise?"

"Yes," I said. "I promise."

He was quiet for a long time. Bit by bit his fingers relaxed against my skin. His breathing slowed, and some of his wild energy seemed to diffuse into the steadily descending night. Watching him I thought of my father, all his stubborn silence, all the uneasiness and pain. It made me angry suddenly, a sharp illumination that ended a summer's panic. The sound of crickets grew, and the trees stood black against the last dark shade of blue. Finally he started the car.

When we reached my mother's house he turned and touched me lightly on the arm. His fingers rested gently where the bruises were already surfacing, and he traced his finger around them. His voice was soft and calm.

"Look," he said. There was a gentle tone in his voice, and I knew it was as close to an apology as he would ever come. "I have a bad temper, Kate. You shouldn't provoke me, you know." And then, more quietly, even apprehensively, he asked if I'd come over that night.

I pulled my crutches out of the back seat, feeling oddly sad. I was too angry to ever forgive him, and I was his only friend.

"You can go to hell," I said. "And if you ever bother me again, I'll tell the entire town that you didn't jump out of that plane."

He leaned across the seat and gazed at me for a second. I didn't know what he would do, but it was my mother's driveway and I knew I was safe.

"Kate," he said then, breaking into the charming smile I knew so well. "You think I'm crazy, don't you?"

"No," I said. "Not crazy. I think you're just afraid."

I was quiet with the door, but my mother sat up right away from where she was dozing on the couch. Her long hair, which reached the middle of her back, was streaked with gray and silver. I had a story ready to tell her, about falling down a hill, but in the end it seemed easier to offer her the truth. I left out the part about Stephen. She followed me as I hobbled into the kitchen to get a glass of water.

I didn't expect her to be so angry. She stood by the counter, drumming her fingers against the formica.

"I don't believe this," she said. "All I've got to contend with, and you go and throw yourself out of a plane." She gestured at the crutches. "How do you expect to work this week? How in the world do you expect to pay for this?"

"Oh, Lord," I said, shaking my head. Stephen was home by now. I didn't think he would bother me, but I couldn't be sure.

"Working is the least of my problems," I said. "Compared to other things, the money aspect is a piece of cake."

And at that my eyes, and hers, fell on the counter, where the remains of yesterday's fiasco were still piled high, the thick dark chocolate edged with creamy frosting. My mother gazed at it for a minute. She picked up a hunk and held it out to me.

"Piece of cake?" she repeated, deadpan.

My mouth quivered. I started laughing, then she did. We were both hysterical with laughter, clutching our sides in pain. And then my mother was shaking me. She was still laughing, unable to speak, but there were tears running down her face too, and when she hugged me to her I got quiet.

"Kate," she said. "My God, Katie, you could have been killed."

I held her and patted awkwardly at her back.

"I'm sorry," I said. "Mom, it's okay. Next week, I'll be as good as new."

She stepped back, one hand on my shoulder, and brushed at her damp eyes with the other hand.

"I don't know what's with me," she said. She sat down in one of the chairs and leaned her forehead against her hand. "It's too much, I guess. All of this, and with your father. I just, I don't know what to do about it all."

"You're doing fine," I said, thinking about all her hours spent on wedding cakes, building confections as fragile and unsubstantial as the dreams that demanded them. My father sat, still and silent in his white room, and I was very angry with him. I wanted to tell my mother this, to explain how the anger had

314

seared away the panic, to share the calmness that, even now, was growing up within me. Eventually, I knew, I would forgive my father. Whatever had plunged him into silence, and Stephen into violence, wouldn't find me. I had a bandaged ankle, but the rest of me was whole and strong.

My mother pulled her long hair away from her face, then let it fall.

"I'm going to take a bath," she said. "You're okay, then?"

"Yes," I said. "I'm fine."

I went to my room. The white curtains lifted, luminous in the darkness, and I heard the distant sound of running water from the bathroom. I took off all my clothes, very slowly, and let them lie where they fell on the floor. The stars outside were bright, the sky clear. I knew that even now Stephen was home, making fun of the jumpmaster, and telling his friends how it felt to step into air. I knew I wouldn't see him again, and I was glad. I leaned against the window sill. The curtains unfolded, brushing against my skin in a swell of night air, and what I remembered, standing there in the dark, was the way it felt to be falling.

Nominated by The Threepenny Review

BETWEEN THE POOL AND THE GARDENIAS

by EDWIDGE DANTICAT

from THE CARIBBEAN WRITER

SHE WAS very pretty. Bright shiny hair and dark brown skin like mahogany cocoa. Her lips were thick and purple, like those African dolls you see in Port-au-Prince tourist store windows, but can never afford to buy.

I thought she was a gift from Heaven when I saw her on the dusty curb, wrapped in a small pink blanket, a few inches from an open sewer. She was like baby Moses in the bible stories they read to us at the Baptist Literary class. Or baby Jesus who was born in a barn and died on a cross; with nobody's lips to kiss he went. She was like that. Her still round face. Her eyes closed as though she was dreaming of another place.

Her hands were bony and there were veins so close to the surface that you could rupture her skin if you touched her too hard. She probably belonged to someone, but the street had no one in it.

I was afraid to touch her. Lest I might disturb the early morning sun rays, streaming across her forehead. Maybe she was some kind of *wanga*, an illusion fixed to trap me. My enemies were many and crafty. The girls who slept with my husband while I was still grieving my miscarriages. They might have sent that vision of loveliness to blind me, so that I never find my way back to a place that I totally plucked from my life when I got on that broken down mini-bus, and left my village two weeks ago.

She was wearing an embroidered little green dress with the letters R-O-S-E on the butterfly collar.

She looked the way I'd imagine all my little girls would look. The ones my body could never hold. The ones that somehow got suffocated inside me and made my husband wonder if I was killing them on purpose.

I called out all the names I wanted to give them. Helene, Nicolette, Malene, Laflorette, Nadine, Jacqueline, Karine.

I could give her all the clothes I'd sewn for them. All these little dresses that went unused. I could rock her in silence in the middle of the night, rest her on my belly, and wish she were inside.

I saw on Madame's television that a lot of poor city gals threw out their babies, because they couldn't afford to feed them. Back in the upper parts of Haiti—the beautiful mountains of Jacmel— where I come from, you can't even throw out the bloody clumps that shoot out of your body after your child is born. It's a crime and your whole family would consider you a criminal if you did it. You have to give every piece of flesh a name and bury it under your favorite tree, so the world don't fall apart around you.

In the city, I hear they throw out whole children. On door steps, in garbage bags, gas stations, sidewalks. In the two weeks I'd been in Port-au-Prince, I had never seen such a child. Until now.

But, Rose. My, she was so clean. Like a tiny angel, sleeping after the wind had blown a lullaby into her little ears.

I picked her up and pressed her cheek against mine. I felt her coldness.

"Little Rose," I whispered as though her name were a secret.

She was like the edible little puppets we played with as children—mangoes we drew faces on and then called by our nicknames.

She didn't stir or cry. She was like something that was thrown aside after she became useless to someone.

317

When I pressed her face against my heart, she smelled like the scented powders in Madame's cabinet.

I always said my mother's prayers at dawn, welcoming the years which were slowly bringing us closer. For no matter how much distance death try to put between us, my mother always comes to visit me. Sometimes, in somebody else's voice. Sometimes, in somebody else's face. Other times, in my dreams.

One night I saw three women leaning over my bed.

"That's Therese," my mother said. "She is the last of us left."

Mama had to introduce me to them, because they had all died before I was born.

There was old hunchbacked Aunt Rezia who died giving birth to my father. Aunt Grace who was shot by her lover—an old woman name Tonia. Then, there was baby Céline who was aborted with the silver tip of Grandpapa's cane.

Je vous salue, Marie. I pray thee Mary. Mother of God. Forgive us poor sinners. Amen. I always knew they would come back and claim me to do some good. Maybe it was with this child.

I carried Rose with me to the outdoor market in Croix-Bossale. I swayed her in my arms like my own sleeping dove.

"Ah, what a sweet baby."

In the city, even people who come from your own village don't know you. Or care about you. They didn't notice that I had come the day before, with no child. Suddenly, I had one and nobody asked a thing.

In the maid's room, at the house in Petionville, I laid Rose on my cot and rushed to prepare their lunch. Monsieur and Madame—Duvalierist Haitians—sat on their terrace and welcomed the coming afternoon, by sipping my soursop juice.

They liked the fact that I trekked to the market, every day before dawn, to get them a taste of the real Haiti, away from their gilded bourgeois life.

"She's probably a mambo," they said when my back was turned. "It's that voodoo nonsense that's holding us Haitians back."

I sat Rose on the kitchen table as I dried the dishes.

I had a sudden desire to explain my life.

318

"Tu vois, bebe. You see, baby. I loved that man at one point. He was very nice to me. I was a virgin when I married him. He made me feel proper. Next thing I know, it's ten years with him. I'm old like hell at twenty-seven and he's got ten babies with ten different women. I just had to run."

I pretended that it was all mine. The terrace with that view of their private beach and the holiday ships cruising in the distance. The large television system and all those meringue and zouk records with conch shell sounds on them. The bright paintings with white winged horses that might be outright convenient in Haiti. The pool that the sweaty Dominican man cleaned three times a week. I pretended that it all belonged to us: him, Rose, and me.

He and I made love on the grass once, but he never spoke to me again. Rose listened with her eyes closed, even though I was telling her things that were much too strong for her ears.

I tied her with the apron around my waist, as I fried some plantains for the evening meal. It's so easy to love somebody, I tell you, when there's nothing else around.

Her head fell back just like any other infant. I held out my hand and let her black curls tickle the lifelines in my palm.

"I'm glad you're not one of those babies that cry all day long. All little children should be like you. I'm glad you don't need changing and all that trouble either. You're just like a perfect child, *pa vray?"*

I put her back in my room when they came home for their late dinner. As soon as they went to sleep, I took her out by the pool and told her the stories.

"You don't just join a family without knowing what you're getting into. *Chérie,* you got to know some of the history. You got to know that we pray to Ezili who loves men like men love her, because she's all mulatto and Haitian men seem to love her kind. You've got to look into your looking glass on All Saints Day, because you might see faces there that knew you, even before you ever came into this world."

I fell asleep rocking her in a chair that wasn't mine. I knew she was real when I woke up the next day and she was still in my arms.

319

She looked the same as she did when I found her. She continued to look like that for three days. After that, I had to bathe her constantly to keep down the smell.

I had an uncle who bought pigs' guts in Jacmel to sell at flea markets in Croix-Bossale. She began to smell like that. Then, she began to smell like the stuff that comes out of the guts before they're spiced and cooked.

I bathed her more often but the mistress' perfume wasn't helping. I was tempted to take her back to the street where I'd found her, but I felt like I'd done disturbed her rest and had taken on her soul as my own personal responsibility.

I left her in a shack behind the guest house, where the pool man kept his tools. Three times a day, I visited her with my hand over my nose. I watched her skin grow moist and sunken in some places, then ashy and dry on others. It seemed like she had aged in four days, as many years as there was between me and my dead grandmother.

I knew I had to act with her, because she was beginning to attract flies and I was keeping her spirit from moving on.
I gave her one last bath and slipped on a little yellow dress that I'd sewn while praying that one of my little girls would come along further than three months.
I took Rose down to the yard behind the house. I dug a hole in the garden. I wrapped her in the little blanket I'd found her in, covering all but her face. She smelled so bad that I couldn't even bring myself to kiss her without choking on my breath.

I felt a grip on my shoulder as I lowered her into the ground. At first I thought it was Monsieur or Madame, but they were away on one of their trips to Miami, or some place like that.
Rose fell from my hands as he forced my body around.
"What are you doing?" asked the Dominican.
His face was a deep brown, but his hands were paled and wrinkled by the pool's chlorine.
He looked down at the baby, lying in the dust. She was already sprinkled with some of the soil that I had dug up.

"You see, I saw these faces in my dreams—"

I could have started my explanation in a million ways.

"I go already. I call the *poste* on you. The *gendarmes*. The police. They coming," he said. "I smell that rotten flesh. I know you kill the child and put it in the garage."

I thought I heard a little soca in the sway of his voice.

"But you made love to me," I pleaded.

"You cannibal. It's a child."

He only kept his hands on me because he was afraid I would escape.

I looked down at Rose and imagined her teething, crawling, fussing, and just carrying on.

Over her little corpse, we stood, a country maid and a Spaniard groundsman. I should have asked him his name before I offered him my body.

We made a pretty picture standing there. Rose, me, and him. Between the pool and gardenias, waiting on the law.

Nominated by The Caribbean Writer

EATING THE ANGEL, CONCEIVING THE SUN: TOWARD A NOTION OF POETIC THOUGHT

by SHEROD SANTOS

from AMERICAN POETRY REVIEW

IN THE LAST lectures Heidegger gave before retiring from the university in 1952—the first he'd been permitted to give since the end of the Second World War—he embarked on a series of meditations on the endlessly riddling subject of thinking.[1] During the course of those lectures he would form the opinion that science doesn't think, that pure thinking lies closer in fact to the ground of poetry, and that the only thing worth thinking about is what is truly unthinkable. One can't say for sure to what degree, or with what inflection, he might have intended that secondary sense which "unthinkable" carries in English—that sense of the dark, the repressed, the forbidden—but for the moment anyway we'll allow that meaning to play alongside the more ordinary one of what is simply unimaginable. (After all, Heidegger was barred from teaching for having been drafted into the Nazi's people's militia.) And if, indeed, it's true that thinking lies closer to poetry than science—by "an abyss of essence," as the lectures conclude—then perhaps there's something to be learned about

322

thinking, of which we presumably know little, by asking some questions about poetry, of which we presumably know a lot. Perhaps, as well, there's something to be learned about poetry's art by inquiring into the famously extrasensory manner by which it's known to think.

But where to begin? Since some form of thinking inevitably precedes the physical act of writing out a line of poetry, however automatic or spontaneous it seems, then our questions should probably begin with that period before the words are scratched to life. That is, what do we know beforehand when we sit down to write a poem? At what level is it consciously determined what our poem will think about? And when, in advance, we do already have a "subject" in mind, what does it mean, as so often happens, when the poem decides to pursue some wholly different inclination?

Those questions all point to an ongoing problem poets face, the problem of choosing a subject: do we choose it, or does it choose us? The weight of historical evidence would seem to suggest the latter (as true for Hopkins as it was for Reverdy, or so their testimony would have us believe), though this is a lesson our institutions still tend to overlook; in fact, the bulk of recent commentary on poetry, with its narrowly defined theoretical codes, appears to proceed from an opposite assumption, and supports the impression that poetry, like criticism, is bounded by forethought and caution. But poems will often prove least responsive when we've decided in advance what we want them to say. And is it truly misleading when poets claim (as they often do) that we're most engaged, most "called into being" (in Heidegger's phrase), in those very moments when we're only discovering *as we write* what we're actually writing about? And even then, even in those most halcyon times, aren't we actually discovering a meaning it's safe to say we weren't in possession of moments before?

The answer to those questions would seem to locate meaning *elsewhere,* somewhere beyond the poet's reach, an idea fraught with murky implications for the already mysterious process of writing. And yet, in deference to that possibility, and in apparent contradiction to that age-old advice handed out like gospel in our writing schools—"Write about what you know the best"—this essay will attempt to propose a somewhat rash alternative: "Write about what you know the least, about that which you find the most unthinkable." As Heidegger explained it in a metaphor derived from Rilke, it's only then that we're caught "in the draught" of thinking, that "we are, somewhat like migratory birds . . . caught in the pull of what draws [us]." In other words, I would like to propose that we shift our emphasis from the *thought about* to the *thinking* itself; or, to pose it in the form of a paradox, that we shift our emphasis to a kind of thinking which thinks about what cannot be thought.

If there's any value to this proposition, and any at all practical advantage to be had from our considering it, then the issue hinges on what, for the poet, declares itself as truly thought-provoking. And here Heidegger devises a rather plain, if elusive, distinction: "Some things are food for thought in themselves, intrinsically, so to speak, innately. And some things make an appeal to us to give them thought, to turn toward them in thought: to think them." We might probe more deeply into these puzzling maxims by calling to mind, however briefly, two of the more celebrated examples of "thinking" poems this century has produced, Rainer Maria Rilke's *Duino Elegies* and Wallace Stevens' *Notes Toward a Supreme Fiction*. With a ferociously chastened sweep of the hand—part Shakespearean, part young Werther—Rilke's epic of yearning begins:

Who, if I cried, would hear me among the angelic
orders? And even if one of them suddenly
pressed me against his heart, I should fade in the strength of his
stronger existence.
>   (translated by J. B. Leishman and Stephen Spender)

And so in those much-quoted opening lines—lines, we're told, that arrived unbidden as the poet paced the windy bastions of Schloss Duino in the winter of 1911—Rilke introduces a figure of thought, an angel, a figure he quickly comes to see he will never be able to think,

For Beauty's nothing
but the beginning of Terror we're still just able to bear,
and why we adore it so is because it serenely

disdains to destroy us. Each single angel is terrible.
And so I keep down my heart, and swallow the call-note
of depth-dark sobbing.

Rilke's fearsome creatures serve, I think, as an example of that
which Heidegger claimed was innately "food for thought," for
their aerial presence becomes, in time, the obverse of, and the
nourishment for, our deepest spiritual hungers. In the grand Pla-
tonic sense, his angels represent an out-reaching form of educa-
tion (from *educere: e—*, "out," + *ducere*— "to lead"); rather than
turning us inward (that neo-Romantic notion of the solitary, solip-
sistic life), angels lead us out of ourselves: What, in them, gives
us to think is precisely what is lacking in us; what, in them, gives
us to think is therefore wholly unthinkable. "Angels . . . surpass
us in action," Rilke remarks in a letter to Karl von der Heydt,
"precisely as much as God surpasses them" (*Briefe aus den
Jahren 1907–1914*). And then, in a letter to his Polish translator:

> The Angel of the Elegies is the creature in whom that
> transformation of the visible into the invisible we are
> performing already appears complete. . . . The Angel
> of the Elegies is the being who vouches for the recog-
> nition of a higher degree of reality in the invisible.—
> Therefore "terrible" to us, because we, its lovers and
> transformers, still depend on the visible.
>
> (*Briefe aus Muzot*)

If angels bear the measure of our own inadequacy, they also
affirm the quiet dignity of all our noblest aspirations. Because of
that, their distance from us functions as both a promise and a
reproach, and it's through that nagging paradox that they pro-
vided Rilke "food for thought," and in surprisingly literal ways. If
we ever hope to attain them—and in Rilke it's their exemplary
nature that's both "terrible" and attractive—we must take them
into ourselves, we must feed off their examples, we must, so to
speak, eat angel. In other words, if we can't enter them through
our thoughts, then perhaps they can enter us (in an oddly con-
ceived transubstantiation) through the vehicle of our bodies:
"This world, regarded no longer from the human point of view,
but as it is within the angel, is perhaps my real task" (*Briefe aus*

325

den Jahren 1914–1921). This isn't exactly anthropophagy, cannibalism, consuming the other animal, but it is a kind of theophagy, a consuming of god or the divine, a commonplace if still curious aspect of most religious experience (*i.e.*, the Eucharist in Roman Catholic and Eastern Orthodox Christianity). And like all truly religious spirits, Rilke sees his charge as decidedly unequivocal, as if uttered from a celestial voice—"You must change your life" ("Archaic Torso of Apollo")—which meant no less than setting his thoughts on a "higher degree of reality"; which meant no less than standing in the draught of a thinking toward something that simply can't be thought.

One sign of how agonizing this labor would be is the fact that, following those first clairvoyant lines, it would take another decade before he would ever finish the *Elegies*. And even then they would come to him fitfully, almost against his flagging will, in two brief but electrifying blocks of time—periods of "monstrous obedience," as he later described them—in 1912 and 1922. Rilke once said of Tolstoy that he "made a dragon out of life so as to be the hero who fought it." By the same light it might be said that Rilke made an angel out of human imperfection so as to be, like Jacob, the mortal destined to wrestle with it.

If those "deadly birds of the soul" provided Rilke "food for thought," then it might be argued that, for Wallace Stevens, Reality belonged to that second category Heidegger describes, of things that "appeal to us to give them thought." And what in Reality appeals to Stevens is the very fact that it's *outside thought*, that, in his words, it's "inconceivable": "Not to be realized because not to/Be seen, not to be loved or hated because/Not to be realized" (*It Must Be Abstract*, canto VI). That explains the nature of Reality's remoteness, its inaccessibility to us and our language; and yet, as the very first canto reminds us, there it stands, "The inconceivable idea of the sun," "Washed in the remotest cleanliness of a heaven/That has expelled us and our images," appealing, as it were, to give it thought, to turn toward it in thought, to think it—though *it*, paradoxically, is that which finally "Must bear no name . . . but be/In the difficulty of what it is to be." Unlike Rilke's angels, Stevens' Reality never becomes a "food for thought" for the simple reason that nothing in it is consumable (in the way, for example, that an angel's death-consciousness is), nothing in it is exemplary. It exists beyond the moral order, and only through the distortions of our own sadly projected egos do we turn it to such purposes. In Stevens' cosmology, we're faced with the knowledge that the womb of God is amoral and wholly indifferent to our presence in the world. On the other hand, Reality remains something toward which our thoughts are drawn, drawn in spite of the crippling fact that "poisonous/Are the ravishments of truth," those very thoughts we think it with, "fatal to/The truth itself" (canto II).

In fact, applying Heidegger's terminology, we might say that Stevens' poem isn't "about" Reality at all—for language falls short of capturing Reality by the very degree that it's brought to bear—it's about Reality's withdrawal, about our own strangely implacable desire "to have what is not," to think what is finally unthinkable. Here's Heidegger again:

> What must be thought about turns away from man. It withdraws from him. But how can we have the least knowledge of something that withdraws from the beginning, how can we even give it a name? [A name like Phoebus, Stevens reminds us, "a name for something that never could be named."] Whatever withdraws, refuses arrival. But—withdrawing is not nothing. Withdrawal is an event. In fact, what withdraws may even concern and claim man more essentially than anything present that strikes and touches him. . . .

As Stevens comments in his *Letters*, "The poem is a struggle with the inaccessibility of the abstract," though abstract here means, not opposed to concrete, but separate from, withdrawing.

So let's just ask all over again: When we sit down to write, what do we intend to do, and how do we intend to do it? More importantly, how does one go about putting oneself "in the pull" of thinking? The question of our somehow choosing our subjects Heidegger puts to rest: "What is thought-provoking, what gives us to think, is then not anything that we determine, not anything that only we are instituting, only we are proposing." Or, as he states it more crisply in his gnomic poem/essay "The Thinker As Poet," "We never come to thoughts. They come to us."

And yet who among us, at one time or another, hasn't had the impression of choosing the thing we'd like our poem to say? At

327

the same time, who among us hasn't had the impression, on just such occasions, of the poem starting to veer away, with a mind of its own, toward its own set of strict concerns? In the year that Germany invaded Poland, W. H. Auden concluded his poem "September 1, 1939" with the premonitory line, "We must love one another or die"; fifteen years later he revised that line to read, "We must love one another and die." In the tragic arc between those versions one can chart the brutal disillusionment of our century; and one can begin to understand how poetry works to undermine our conscious intentions. For within that single syllable "or" lay the basis for the liberal humanist hopes Auden harbored in those days; but within that subversive alternative "and" lay a darker intuition, a thought beyond the reach of thought, the unthinkable prospect that world events issued from the chaos of the human heart. Applying Heidegger's maxim, it may be said that Auden came to the first version of the poem, the second version came to Auden. Of the original he would later remark that it was "the most dishonest poem I have ever written."

And here is where I'd like to suggest, in yet another departure from common sense, that therein lies the crux of the matter, the one perhaps sure distinction, quantitative issues of verse aside, one can draw between poetry and prose: its stubborn, inborn, implausible resolve to tell the truth, however incongruous, however insufferable the telling may be. Poetry, like dreaming, seems intent on saying those very things we're most determined to hide—even from ourselves. Or, to put it more directly: The poem revises the poet, not the other way around.

Two offhand but not unrelated comments may shed some light on this (admittedly) odd idea. The first one comes from a letter Elizabeth Bishop wrote to Robert Lowell, about some difficulties she'd encountered with a piece of prose: "That desire to get things straight and tell the truth—it's impossible not to tell the truth in poetry, I think, but in prose it keeps eluding me in the funniest way." The second one comes from an interview with Richard Wilbur: "I know a lot of people, poets, who are not consciously religious, but find themselves forever compromised by their habit of asserting the relevance of all things to each other. And poetry being a kind of truth-telling (it's pretty hard to lie in poetry), I think that these people must be making, whether they like it or not, what are ultimately religious assertions."

It's almost impossible to lie in poetry, both poets tell us paren-
thetically, as though it's the most obvious thing in the world?
What, exactly, are we to make of this? To get at some kind of an
answer, I'd like to pursue a rather round-about analogy. In
Freud's writings on hysteria, we learn that there are moments in
childhood which inscribe themselves so indelibly on us, that
we're doomed to repeat, in ways that may be a mystery to us,
their inherent patterns and forms. The French philosopher Jean-
François Lyotard has even suggested that what we call "style" in
writing is just such a case of hysterical repetition—an irrepress-
ible urge to assert a pattern repeatedly. This simplifies matters
far too much, but while setting aside the question of illness (the
mind's complexities are not, by nature, a "disorder," however in-
scrutable they appear to be), I'd like to suggest that a poet's re-
lation to the poem is, in many ways, oddly correspondent to the
hysteric's relation to memory—Mnemosyne, remember, is the
Mother of the Muses. At least it's correspondent to the degree
that the *process* of writing—over and against one's *intentions* in
writing—makes "telling a lie" impossible, just as the willed devi-
ation from a hysterical pattern is instantly erased, or overridden,
once the will relents: "We must love one another or die" be-
comes "We must love one another and die." The conscious will
stands corrected in time by the unconscious impulse to tell the
truth. The correspondence deepens when we realize the poem's
unspoken charge is to awaken memory to motion again, to recol-
lect the remembranced body into the present tense, as a child-
hood trauma is gathered by the body into the hysteric's living
here and now. As Heidegger continues, in the name of poetry:

> Memory thinks back to something thought. But when
> it is the name of the Mother of the Muses, 'Memory'
> does not mean just any thought of anything that can be
> thought. Memory is the gathering of thought upon
> what everywhere demands to be thought about first of
> all. . . . That is why poesy [poetry in the Greek sense
> of *poiesis*] is the water that at times flows backward to-
> ward the source, toward thinking as a thinking back, a
> recollection.

This is the same distinction Freud draws between reminiscence,
which he calls storytelling, and memory, which he calls remem-

bering back to the origin of the story. It may be that Rilke considered a similar point of origin when, in the first *Elegy*, he referred to "the suspiration,/the uninterrupted news that grows out of silence." And Stevens may have thought along parallel lines when, in "Man and Bottle," he likened the violence of poetry, nature, and the human mind:

> The poem lashes more fiercely than the wind,
> As the mind, to find what will suffice, destroys
> Romantic tenements of rose and ice.

But, one asks, where does it come from, all this "uninterrupted news"? Toward what does the direction backwards lead? What lies behind that revisionist fury of poem and mind? And who are those we gather together in our moments of recollection? Pursued far enough, one answer to all those questions is, of course, the dead. As we know, for Stevens "Death is the Mother of Beauty"; for Rilke, it appears to be the Mother of Love as well: "Only from the side of death," he writes, "only from the side of death, I believe, is it possible to do justice to love."

To philosophize is learning how to die, says Montaigne. And Hélène Cixous: "You need something that dies to give birth to writing. . . . Writers have a foreign origin, they don't know what it is, but someone is calling them backwards." Rilke remains, first and foremost, a poet of the dead, and time after time in the *Elegies* we see the access they provide him to his wildly "foreign origin," we see the almost physical power they have to call him back. The root of that power, and the death that in his case (we might conjecture) gave "birth to writing," derive from the fertile, loamy soil of his finally unthinkable childhood, a world that must have been to him no less daunting an object of thought than "those deadly birds of the soul." The following, from J. F. Hendry's *The Sacred Threshold*, provides a frightening glimpse into that secreted world:

> René's hair was still long, as was a custom of the period, and he played with dolls. Even during the rare birthday parties, when he was allowed to entertain other children, or else play at 'cooking' by himself, his pursuits were inclined to be feminine. . . . Indeed un-

til he was five, in accordance with [his mother's] grim pretence that he was not himself but a reincarnation of the daughter lost in infancy, René had to wear girl's clothes, and behave like a girl. He would stand outside the door and knock. When his mother called out, 'Who is it?', he would squeak 'Sophie.' And when he entered, wearing a little housefrock with rolled-up sleeves, he was Mama's little Sophie, whose hair had to be plaited, so she should not be confused with the naughty boy. . . . Later she would ask him what had happened to 'Sophie' and venture the opinion that 'Sophie' must be dead. This Rilke would strenuously deny.

. . . If he could, René said, he would have been a girl for her sake. He enjoyed dressing up and standing before the mirror, until the day he became terrified because the girlish image was more real than he.

Here was a child who carried within him the living presence of his dead sister; or perhaps more accurately, here was a child who carried within him his own secret, suppressed identity, while the living presence of his dead sister took over the features of his external life. In either case, the gulf between appearance and reality, essence and identity, surface and interior, proved enormous and, as one can imagine, unthinkable in Rilke. In light of that, one can see the *Elegies* as an almost wholly involuntary effort to think that forbidden thought:

> Who shows a child as he really is? Who sets him
> in his constellation and puts the measuring-rod
> of distance in his hand? Who makes his death
> out of gray bread, which hardens—or leaves it there
> inside his round mouth, jagged as the core
> of a sweet apple?. . . . Murderers are easy
> to understand. But this: that one can contain
> death, the whole of death, even before
> life has begun, can hold it to one's heart
> gently, and not refuse to go on living,
> is [and note the word he chooses here] inexpressible.
>
> *(Elegy IV)*

Once more I'll ask the question with which this essay began: What do we know beforehand when we sit down to write a poem? It may be that what we know, what's essential to know, is that very thing we cannot know: the "inexpressible" in Rilke, the "unthinkable" in Heidegger, the "inconceivable" in Stevens. For who hasn't been struck, while struggling to recall some fragment of the past, by the sudden impression of sifting through ash; and then, by the slowly dawning realization that who we are is composed of what, perhaps only what, we can never reclaim from that rubble. It may be that *that's* the thing which poets know, the presence of that marked, presiding loss, the thought beyond the reach of thought, the thought toward which our thoughts all turn when we're in the draught of thinking. Perhaps in the face of just such quandaries, Paul Valéry, at the end of "Poetry and Abstract Thought," felt so suddenly awed by the frightful complexities of the poet's task:

> Try to imagine . . . what the least of our acts implies. Think of everything that must go on inside a man who utters the smallest intelligible sentence, and then calculate all that is needed for a poem by Keats or Baudelaire to be formed on an empty page in front of the poet.
>
> Think, too, that of all the arts, ours is perhaps that which co-ordinates the greatest number of independent parts or factors: sound, sense, the real and the imaginary, logic, syntax, and the double invention of content and form . . . and all this by means of a medium essentially practical, perpetually changing, soiled, a maid of all work, *everyday language,* from which we must draw a pure, ideal Voice, capable of communicating without weakness, without apparent effort, without offense to the ear, and without breaking the ephemeral sphere of the poetic universe, an idea of some *self* miraculously superior to Myself.
>
> *(translated by Denise Folliot)*

"An idea of some *self* miraculously superior to Myself"? Isn't that the thought which Rilke himself was struggling to form when he paced the bastions of Schloss Duino in the winter of 1911? And

332

what Stevens imagined in that "strong exhilaration/Of what we feel from what we think, of thought/Beating in the heart, as if blood newly came, //An elixir, an excitation, a pure power" (*It Must Be Abstract*, canto III)?

And so once again we come in proximity of angels. I suppose in some way it might be said that angels have been the implicit subject of all that we've considered here. For what is Heidegger's unthinkable thought which recedes as we approach it—but an angel? And what is that huge, untouchable loss which Rilke felt so much more powerfully than his physical life—but an angel? And what is memory? childhood? death? and what, after all, is the unconscious itself—but spaces filled with those winged, invisible spirits who are borne within us, as in dreams? And what, in Valéry, is that figure of the poet while making a poem, "an idea of some *self* miraculously superior to Myself"—but another form of angel?

We move among shadows, we move among shades, but from whom or what those presences come remains a lifelong mystery to us; and not to solve that mystery, but to continually think us back to it remains an enduring necessity of poetry. It seems appropriate, then, that we conclude this essay with Wallace Stevens, with the one poet who—in our ruthlessly skeptical, postmodern age—has taken it upon himself to reinstate the critical role that angels play in the hearts and imaginations of us all. For his work proposes, not some final deconstruction of the angelic orders, but a new conception of those grandly human longings which angels signify within our lives; not a domestication of *potentia* for poets and angels alike, but a restoration of the pathos that derives from their joined reciprocal powers; not the overthrow of some wearied heavenly space, but the breaking ground for a new habitation as unthinkable and, for poetry's sake, as restorative as any idea of God.

Summoned by absence, reasoned by negation, on an evening we're told the angels have fled, Stevens' mnemonic seraphim return to us—even as they appear to be taken away—our sheer blind appetites for existence itself, for the unsayable center that awakens a towering voice within us:

Air is air.
Its vacancy glitters round us everywhere.

333

Its sounds are not angelic syllables
But our unfashioned spirits realized
More sharply in more furious selves.

And light
That fosters seraphim and is to them
Coiffeur of haloes, fecund jewellers—
Was the sun concoct for angels or for men?
Sad men made angels of the sun, and of
The moon they made their own attendant ghosts,
Which led them back to angels, after death.

....

. . . Evening, when the measure skips a beat
And then another, one by one, and all
To a seething minor swiftly modulate.
Bare night is best. Bare earth is best. Bare, bare,
Except for our own houses, huddled low
Beneath the arches and their spangled air,
Beneath the rhapsodies of fire and fire,
Where the voice that is in us makes a true response,
Where the voice that is great within us rises up,
As we stand gazing at the rounded moon.

Note

Martin Heidegger, *What Is Called Thinking*, translated by Jay Glenn Gray (New York: Harper Colophon, 1968).

Nominated by David Baker, Christopher Buckley, Edward Hirsch

NASH

fiction by JON BARNES

from THE GEORGIA REVIEW

WE CALLED HIM Uncle Nash, though he wasn't blood. My mother told me once, or else I overheard it from the women as they talked among themselves, how a favorite aunt had married a man from Mississippi and brought him back to her homeplace in the Kiamichi Mountains. She died soon after, as people often did in such stories, but Nash stayed on, tending his crops on the banks of the Mountain Fork River. By the time I came on the scene he was ancient, almost blind, dying in pieces. Not fit for much more than watching over a sickly boy, as he often did when my mother went to work at the Idabel five-and-dime.

I think about him more and more these days, especially in the mornings, but I haven't told the Angel as I promised her I would. She's back to reading self-help books and says talking about how I grew up might help save our marriage or at least get us back to sleeping together. God knows what she would make out of Nash. Or of me. The Angel is so hungry to understand. Last night, over dinner, she told me I had a "father thing"—that everything would be okay if I would just see the child inside. She looked up at me, nervous and expectant, like I was some vault door ready to clang open, but I just said something nasty about her Unitarian friends and got up to leave.

I sweated out the petulance in a yup-bar down on the river, dancing nasty with a skinny woman with scared eyes. A reggae band was up from Houston, and she pressed against me on the crowded floor, rocking back and forth on the balls of her feet while the band—homeboys all—did their Rastaman acts. She flitted around in her peasant frock, but I caught her peeking into the crowd for whoever was supposed to care. By the middle set, she'd roped her arms around my waist and pressed her head hard against my chest. She called me a no-neck sonofabitch when I didn't want to take her home.

It was after two before I slipped into our bedroom.

The Angel took me in her arms, as always, stroked my hair. She made no noise as she cried, and her tears were warm against my neck. But they cooled as they trickled down my chest, and soon my skin itched and burned as if it had been brushed with acid. Such is the Angel's love, her corrosive compassion. What an obscene Pietà we made: her shivering as she held my weight, me willing myself not to scratch.

Now, the Angel sleeps. I could wake her, but I never do. I'm up at five, at the Y by the time it opens at 5:30—too early to see the mirrors in her eyes. Sometimes, if I'm running early, I watch her for a moment or two. She sleeps like a child: on her side, one knee drawn in so close that it almost touches her throat. The Angel is best when she sleeps.

*

I remember his skin. It was gray, translucent, and malleable as wax. Sometimes I'd stand beside him and he'd press against his forearm with a crooked yellow thumbnail and I'd watch as the dark crescent of blood welled up. Even his blood was different from mine, sweet as sugar and dark as the iodine solution he put on my cuts. Then he'd laugh and wipe the blood away on the bib of his overalls, and we would go in and eat Vienna sausage and dill pickles while we watched *Days of Our Lives* on the black-and-white Zenith my mother had given him.

As I drive into the city, I wonder what Nash would have made of all of this. The exit ramp carves a white arc above the deserted railyard; maybe he'd look down and judge the pillars too fragile for his liking, the speed too fast to make sense. I downshift and surge onto the ramp, rear tires breaking on the turn, and realize most likely he'd point with a crooked finger—the wide Red River shuddering past the cotton land to the east, the marsh hawk hanging above the cane and ragweed and twisted track—and laugh his snaggle-toothed laugh.

For a moment the city is laid out whole and full of promise, reflecting the orange light and blue-gray haze like a Houston or Dallas, not another dying river town. But the illusion never holds. I pass into the shadows between buildings, their ground-floor windows boarded up or covered with butcher paper, their walls papered with handbills warning of the Papist-Zionist conspiracy, the coming of the Antichrist. Up on Texas Street, a few pharmacies are still in business, but the markets are gone. Five-and-dimes advertise blonde wigs and Jheri Kurl for the blacks who can't make it out to the malls. Presiding over all is the Bank of Commerce, the glittering twenty-story tombstone that rises unfinished above the river. A year and a half since the bank went under and construction stopped, the top five floors are still a maze of rusting girders and guy wires. A friend of mind is still trying to rent out the bottom fifteen floors.

Across the street, though, is the dark granite façade of the old Petroleum Tower. Oil's come and gone, but you can still have lunch at the private club on the top floor. For a time, I spent every Friday there, pressing flesh, listening to the old fucks hold court. We sat together in groups of five and six, and the black waiters kept our glasses full while we talked of sweet crude pushing forty dollars a barrel, fifty dollars—the curve rising higher and higher, a bridge to the sky. All that was keeping us pressed to the earth were the oil leases we held in our pockets, a meaty ache swelling by the day.

Why we didn't see that the Arabs could ream us just by opening a spigot, I don't know. My senior partner, whose father had sunk the first wells in Caddo Lake back in the thirties, considered himself old money and went Chapter 13 in six months. He wound up with barely enough to settle in a Phoenix retirement village, then died within the year. I scrounged a job as a middle manager at a trucking company. "Sick Transit," according to my partner: a feeble joke even for a dead man.

I pass the Tower, driving slow. My reflection ripples across stone.

Hip abductor . . . leg raise . . . leg press . . . lat pull down. Incline press . . . lateral raise . . . overhead press . . . duo hip ma chine. Stations of the Cross. Mirrors ring the Nautilus room. You can see yourself from many angles, check your technique, watch the gleaming cams turn beneath the fluorescent lights.

Since I ripped my biceps last year, I go easy in the mornings: light weight and heavy reps for definition, careful technique. Still, my triceps seem to pull away from the bone. The veins in my arms are swallowed in fat. My hands are as weak as a boy's. The bucks with the big arms say be patient, let it come to you, but I'm at the Y three times a day now—Nautilus in the morning, basketball and ab work at noon. The free weights I leave for evening when there are spotters. Two years ago, a man was killed in the next room, an early morning lifter like myself. They found him lying on the bench, a 220-pound barbell across his throat, his face black, his lip bitten clean through. They called it an accident, but I was never sure, having felt the temptation beneath the iron bar: to push it till it gives, then let go.

I strain against the incline press, rep after rep, until I taste metal on the back of my tongue, flakes of copper and brass, and it feels that something deep inside my chest is pulling in two. I cough. Sometimes I am short of breath.

The Angel has asked to come, but this is not her place. One by one, my compatriots drift in to begin their sets. A bulked-up fireman straps weights around his waist and does pull-ups until his face is red and contorted with pain. A slender man pushes out multiple sets on the overhead press. His mouth quivers each time he lowers the weight, as if he is trying not to cry. A bull dyke straddles her lover on the fly machine, grasps the slender woman's exhausted arms when they can no longer lift the weight. Together they force another three reps. Their skin is mottled blue and red, their lips swollen and dry. Outside, the sun rises above the skyline; the eastern windows flame orange. No one breaks the silence. Even at seven o'clock, when the secretaries and executive-types descend, I hear only the slap and clank of weights, a sound that builds on itself, layer on layer, until we seem to labor in an ancient metalworks, trapped in the guts of a lumbering machine. The Angel has no business here.

Even though he had arthritis and a pin in his hip from a fall that happened years before, Uncle Nash usually went on foot, walking in a half-blind stagger that turned into an odd sort of lope once he picked up steam. He must have spent half of each day walking—it was three-quarters of a mile from his house on the river to the mailbox at the top of the ridge. He checked his mail religiously, though the box was usually empty except for sales circulars from the stores down in Idabel and Broken Bow. The days I stayed with him, when my asthma was bad, we looked forward to the mail all morning. We would struggle up the slope, through a corridor of big pine, past the pasture my father leased, our shoes crunching in the loose gravel. Every fifty feet or so, we'd stop to catch our breath, but we'd usually time it right to say hello to Trudi Hunkapillar, the mail carrier. She was a Cherokee my mother's age, and when I told Uncle Nash I wanted to marry her, he nodded his head and said she'd make a good wife.

In the spring, and again in fall, my father and his friends would work the cattle. Uncle Nash would walk up the hill to watch. I'd follow them around, helping the best I could, though I was always a step too slow. My father, an impatient man when young, was tall and thin with corded muscles that seemed to vibrate and hum like a powerline in the wind. He made his living working swing shift in the paper mill down at Valliant, driving a forklift, but for some reason he never forgot how his grandfather had homesteaded in Indian Territory, had run cattle on the open range. He had about thirty scrubs running on the land he'd leased. Never made a dime. All I heard growing up was talk of a 1,000-acre spread, a remuda of fine-blooded horses, an open sky—but each time we moved, it was closer to the paper mill, where the air tasted like sulphur.

Still, my father was good with a lat-rope, and even though he wasn't a big man, he could throw a 450-pound yearling with little effort. One of his friends would throw a half hitch around the calf's back feet, and together they would pull its body taut. My job was to bear the knife and alcohol, and I would watch as my father would douse the scrotum, then make the cut with the sharp sheep's-foot blade. The calf would bawl and tense against

339

the rope, but always quieted when my father pulled the balls down and stripped the flesh away. Another quick cut and he tossed them across the grass, one after the other.

One fall—I must have been ten or eleven—my father picked out the smallest calf, handed me the rope and told me to get after it. I never had much problem roping, but throwing the calf was something else again, and the calf and I waltzed across the corral as I tried to get enough nerve to reach over its back to grab its foreleg and flank. The calf's sharp hooves scraped my shins, and I fell; my father and his friend Emmett laughed and finished their cigarettes. Finally, though, my father jumped down from the fence and told me to set my feet and jerk as he'd shown me.

Unfortunately I had no stamina when I was young, and no courage, so when Emmett laughed again, an edge came into my father's voice. It ended the same as always: with my father pushing me aside, then throwing the calf himself, a little higher and harder than necessary, so that the calf hit the ground with a solid thump and did not move. As I crawled out of the corral, Nash called me over, told me to dust off, and we walked down to his shack on the river while they finished the job.

Nash was not like the rest of us. He never was in good shape, apparently, and even in youth he never did what the other men did. He had lived on the banks of the Mountain Fork River for fifty years but had no stories of gigging flathead catfish down at the White Dog Hole or running lines in spring. We cut cane poles and fished for sun perch instead, like colored women fishing off a bridge. I thought he was teasing when he told me he'd never killed a deer. A couple of squirrels was all, he said, back in Mississippi when he was a boy.

Instead, he tended his garden, hoeing between his rows each morning, stirring up the soil every couple of days with his old push-plow. He was proud of his cantaloupes. One summer, he grew one that weighed nine pounds—the Idabel newspaper sent a photographer. He kept the clipping nailed above the stove. People treated him well enough, I suppose, but those Saturdays we went to the co-op together to buy fertilizer and seed, I noticed that they looked at him differently than they did at my father— there was always a smile behind their smiles, an irony. They made me nervous, those big, slab-muscled men who grinned at us. I never knew what they saw.

A strange thing happened, that fall evening we came down from the corral. When I could breathe easier and the mist started to rise over the river, Nash turned off the TV, gave me a washtub to carry, and had me follow him back up the ridge to the corral. The men were gone. Slowly, Nash sifted through the cowshit and dust for the testicles. He examined each he found, turning them over in his hands before he dropped them in my tub. "Your daddy cuts them cords too high," he said.

We cleaned them best we could, and Nash breaded and fried them up. I didn't want to eat them at first, but Uncle Nash told me they would make me strong. He cooked up a mess of squash to go with them, and we ate while Huntley and Brinkley gave the weekly body counts. It's hard to know what really happened and what I've just made up, but I remember looking up and finding him watching me. He didn't say a thing, but I felt my chest opening up, and I knew that everything I was or would be was laid out before his eyes.

A few hours later, my mother was there to drive me home. I pressed against the passenger-side door and stared up at the trees that flickered past, my arms and shoulders tingling with the glide and swell of muscle.

*

Each morning, Louis meets me at the warehouse gate and parks my car inside. He's an unrepentant Tom, better than any I've seen. He drops his push broom the moment I turn in, jogs over in a loose-jointed lope, wearing a shit-eating grin. He's fifteen years older than I am, pushing fifty, but he still looks like a kid, pudgy and somehow unformed. Morning, Mr. Tollett, he says, drawling out each syllable as he reaches for the keys. Before he gets in, he steps back, admires the Saab. He opens the door with exaggerated care, then lays a dropcloth across the leather. I follow him as he eases the Saab inside. "How much this car?" he asks as he drapes the parachute silk over the hood. I tell him, as I have twenty times before, and he stands stock still and stares at the ceiling, whispering to himself as if he's adding and subtracting in his head. I'm going to have a car like this, he says. I tell him to save his money.

341

They hate Louis here. Whites call him Tollett's nigger, and they spend their work breaks complaining about the black bastard they can't get fired. He makes them nervous, reminds them that management can do anything it damn well pleases, including replacing them with an idiot who'll work for $4.10 an hour. He drives the blacks apeshit for the same reason, since they know the whites are secretly pleased to have Louis here—living, breathing proof of the superiority they feel, but can no longer voice. Even Marcus has been trying to get me to fire Louis, though he knows the score. Instead, I halved Louis' pay and gave him the company van to drive so he could pick up donuts for us on his way to work.

Marcus is already at work by the time I get in. He looks up from the computer monitor just long enough to nod hello. He's a big black man, built like a cannonball. He started with the company on the loading docks, worked his way up. He'd been here fifteen years when I slipped into the slot above him, and he taught me the ropes, never seeming to hold it against me. Company man.

Every summer we played softball together on the management team. Marcus was the only black we had, the only athlete other than myself. He'd played his college ball down at Grambling in the sixties and was still in good shape, his arms and shoulders heavy with muscle. I thought for a while that he might see me for what I was, since we got along on the field just fine, and I always liked the fact that the outfielders backed up against the fence for both of us. But each time Louis comes into the office looking to run an errand in the van, or asking permission to wax the Saab, Marcus just looks at me, the corners of his lips turning up, frozen halfway between a grimace and a smile. "You're a pair," he says.

A half-dozen times I've almost called him on it, asked him what the hell he means, but I've always let it go. Louis embarrasses him—nothing I have to be ashamed of. Distance isn't always a bad thing. At any rate, Marcus says little to anyone, though I came back from lunch one day and found him with a rangy white guy, a forklift driver from third shift I never liked. Turned out he'd been a lurp, though he looked like somebody's alcoholic uncle, and Marcus, who had been Air Cav, talked half the afternoon of X-ray and Albany, Sin City and the A Shau. I closed my office door, but I could still hear them—though what they said made as little sense as a TV tuned to a foreign station.

*

Stories don't come easy to me. I'm built different from the Angel
and her friends, I guess. They always amaze me, those wan din-
ner guests of hers—so quick to spill their guts, men as well as
women. Confession is their secret sign, weakness a Masonic
handshake. The bigger the sin, the better. They will listen to any-
thing so long as it leaves them feeling world-weary, yet somehow
noble inside. I remember the fat man who sat at my table one
night and cried as he explained how he liked to hurt little animals
because his mother had rejected him. And they listened to him,
the Angel and her friends, even as he described the cur he'd
found and how he had burned its feet. The Angel hugged the fat
man then, but all I could think of was how easy it would be to slit
his throat.

The Angel tells her own stories. I am a good man, though trou-
bled, she says. I love her no matter what. Why else have I stuck
around all these years? she asks. She brushes the hair from her
eyes and smiles, content in her revenge.

Reflections are the Angel's stock in trade, the currency she
deals. Love her, protect her, and she will spin for you a picture of
yourself that you couldn't construct in your wildest dreams. And
she'll hold that glowing image of you no matter what, and call it
love, while all the time the distance between what you are and
what she believes you to be grows and grows, till each time you
look in her eyes you realize you've become a photographic nega-
tive of the man you see, twisted and dark, nailed to her illusions.

It's harder and harder to remember the beginning. Her hair
was ash-blonde then, like a rain cloud in the sun. Weekends at
North Texas State, we'd make the long drive back south to Barks-
dale AFB to visit her father. He was career Air Force, chief mas-
ter sergeant—a small man, but with muscle that bunched and
coiled under his skin when he moved. The Angel was a daddy's
girl from way back. By the time we hit the Louisiana line she'd
be talking in her little-girl lisp, ready to fly into his arms the
second we passed the guardhouse. At night, they snuggled up
watching TV, her arm thrown across his shoulders. Sometimes
she would play with his close-cropped hair. I never got used to
seeing her that way. At college, she was passionate enough,

343

though pious as ever. In her father's house, we didn't kiss good night.

But I'll give her father this—he kept his end of the bargain. He wouldn't deny his little girl anything, even me. He didn't care for me, of course. The Angel and I have had troubles from the beginning—he surely heard the stories of my leaving, my coming back. The rages. So I drank his liquor and chatted politely and learned how to hit a golf ball. He died in a car crash in West Germany not long after we married.

The Angel mourns him still, I think. And for me, it's harder and harder to remember why I hated him. Sometimes I watch the B-52's lumber into the air above Barksdale, black smoke pouring from their engines as they burn off water. I always laugh and say his name. It seems a fond thing to do.

*

Noon. The Y awaits. A new set of games. Already, I know, the men have gathered on the basketball courts to begin their slow, awkward contests. I imagine the slap of hard fouls, a muttered curse. The ball thumps against wood like a heartbeat. In the corridors, the balding men suck in their guts as they pass; thirty-five-year-old women put their hair in ponytails and giggle like schoolgirls. Married, divorced, doesn't matter—they come together in a swirl and dance straight out of high school, but their hearts are shrewd as they ponder whether to stand pat or to trade up. I worry about being late.

Louis sweeps the parachute silk off the Saab with a practiced flair. He almost bows as he hands me the keys. But in midcurtsey he sees something out of the corner of his eye, and then he is off, arrowing across the warehouse floor like a dog springing after a car. He is already outside by the time I catch up to him, a black silhouette against the blinding sun.

"What the fuck you doin'?" he screams at the two black teenagers he's got cornered against the chain-link fence. They look at him, point toward downtown. "Goin' Mickey D's, man," the shirtless one says.

"Lyin' motherfucker."

I grab Louis' arm, motion for the two boys to take their shortcut. Louis pulls out of my grip. I grab him again, using both hands this time, and pull him tight. We stand like two dancers,

Louis quivering, breathing hard. His hair scratches my cheek. His shirt-collar smells of old sweat and bacon grease.

The boys make the main gate; one turns and gives us the finger. I laugh, slap Louis on the back. We're a pair, Marcus says. Louis doesn't move. "Fuckin' turds," he whispers close to my ear. "Fuckin' turds."

After the boys have turned the corner, Louis relaxes some and I slowly release my grip. Five or six men from the warehouse have circled around us to watch the fun. The story of how Louis treed two more niggers will make the rounds this afternoon. I pull away, dust off. A greasy handprint marks the front of my shirt.

"Goddamn it, Louis. Go fetch me a fresh shirt."

Louis looks at me, then at the circle of men surrounding him. He mumbles something under his breath and lopes off to the office. The first-shift foreman, a big bearded man, looks at me and grins and shakes his head. I grin, too.

Louis told me a story once about how he'd grown up in Zwolle, the son of a respectable black man, not a field nigger like I'd guessed. His father had a degree from Grambling, worked in the courthouse, and one Sunday morning on the way to church, the man and boy came across an old colored man passed out in the middle of the road. Louis took one look at the old man sprawled out in the red-clay dust and puke, clutching his bottle of Garland Pride, and turned away. "But my daddy slap me 'side the head," Louis told me. "He say, 'You look at that shit. Don' you turn your head. You look at that shit.'"

*

There have been affairs. A petroleum engineer—a sad, slender woman—three times a week at a hot pillow off I-20. A convention whore or two. The latest, last December, the new girl in accounting.

She reminded me of the Angel, when we were young: old family, Christian school, recently married. Why she was slumming at a trucking company, I never understood. Nor did I understand why it was that she had lunch with me, or why we spent the gray afternoon at the house she and her husband were building on the lake. A cold rain had chased the contractors off. The drywall was up in the master bedroom, though still in the process of being taped and floated. Gypsum dust hung in the air. We spread the painter's dropcloth on the floor. She was ardent enough, made the appropriate noises at the right times, but I could almost hear the workout tape playing in her head. Suddenly, though, she flipped me onto my back and rode me as she stared straight ahead, the reflections of the windows and the winter light in her eyes.

We drove back on Hart's Island Road, following the levee into the city. I looked out my window as timberland gave way to cotton, then melted into subdivisions. The streetlights were on, but most of the houses were dark, lit only by the Christmas decorations woven around the burglar bars in their windows.

"Pagan lights," she said in a child's lisping singsong. "Pagan lights." It was the only time she broke the silence, and I did not ask her what she meant.

I drove home, still overfull of the taste and scent of her, but I thought of the Angel and our first time there in her father's bed. The night is still a blur of bourbon and Benzedrine, and I remember only vaguely the Angel saying that she was leaving. I do not know how the knife came to be in my hand, or how the sheep's-foot blade was opened. But I remember holding her tight, and the cutting of her. A small scratch beside one eye, then the other, and I drew her down upon me, silent and trembling in shock, the membrane that she had made so much of stretching and tearing at last. I remember my Angel's eyes. The blood on her cheeks, and below.

*

Nash spoke of Revelation. He told it as a kind of bedtime story, only at night. The mist would hang above the river, and I would lie on my pallet and wheeze and listen to his strange voice speak of End Time, a lake of fire, how our Rapture bodies would be made whole and shining. Fire from the sky, he would say, and all that night I would watch the crest of the western ridge, waiting for the sheet of flame. Even now there is a pounding in my throat every time a firetruck comes by.

Nash fell apart, piece by piece. They took his left foot, then his right arm below the elbow. He hopped around his garden then,

346

and hoed left-handed, guiding the handle with his hook. When they took his legs, he spent his life savings on a garden tractor and widened his rows so he could drive between.

In a few years, I grew out of my asthma, just as Uncle Nash had said I would, and I never went back to the shack on the river. Instead, I grew strong, played ball, negotiated the slippery crevices of sex. From time to time, I would pass the old man as he rode his tractor into town—he would wave, but I never stopped. Once or twice, we ran into one another at the co-op, and the old man would grin, and I would mumble a word or two. A casual betrayal, but it was never the same between us. My shame was in the way, layer on layer, a shell that hid the weakness we both knew was there. He died when I was off at college.

Things wind down. Even the Angel suspects. We've spun on this axis of need and hate for fifteen years, screaming at each other, grasping at each other, bored out of our heads. She's going back to school next fall at the LSU branch, talking about getting a teaching certificate. This summer she's retaking English comp, of all things. Just to get her feet wet, she says, but she's all fired up, talking about Janet, her airhead instructor just out of Texas A&M. The Angel hands me her papers to read with expectant eyes, but I know it's just for show. The words will stay hers, no matter what I say.

Last night, before our fight, she was reading aloud: "Define a term or concept with which your audience may be unfamiliar," and she just looked at me, and it was like her eyes cleared for a second as all the possible words she might make clear scrolled down in front of her face. For a second she was sadder and more beautiful than I have ever seen her, and in that second I could have spoken. Then it was gone, and she smiled, but her eyes were brittle mirrors, looking in.

*

The big men lift at night. They stalk from station to station, attacking each machine like wolves going for a kill. There is not much talk amid the grind and clank of metal, though some train together in twos or threes, screaming at one another for encouragement. A big black man lifts alone, pushing out each bench press without a word. Several of us watch him, count the plates on the bar: 320 pounds. I slap on too much weight, throw it up until my breath comes in gasps and my shoulders feel like they're pulling in two.

At home, the Angel stands at her window and whispers the count of cars gone past.

Nine-thirty. A garbled voice over the intercom tells us that the Y will close in fifteen minutes. I'm the only one left to hear. I start down the narrow steps to the locker rooms.

Travis Street is empty. I walk down the sidewalk to the Saab, each step bringing the grind of bone on bone. My knees feel as if they've filled with silt. There's the smell of tar and pigeon shit. (High overhead in hidden roosts, their heartbeats thrum.) Styrofoam cups clatter over the pavement. As I near my car, I hear music, look up. Down the alley, on the third floor of the old Brill building, yellow light filters from a dance studio. A tinny recording of a fiddle drifts down from an open window. Twirling, the cloggers flash into view, disappear—old men and women with orange bandannas around their necks, remote as windup toys or a television glimpsed through a neighbor's half-closed curtain.

When I turn, he is there. Black kid—white T-shirt, baggy cut-offs, no shoes. Across the street, hunched over his bicycle, watching me. His reflection shimmers in the plate glass windows. I feel my lats spread as I glance over my shoulder, ready to fight. But this is no setup. The street is empty behind me.

I open the trunk to the Saab, throw in my gym bag. He watches me. He is slender, all arms and legs, his skin the color of wet tree bark. Twelve, maybe thirteen. I open the car door, get in. I keep expecting to hear his pitch: rock in vial, dime bag of grass, the whore down on Fanin Street. Silence. He looks at me, expressionless. There is a scar—about two inches long, shaped like a teardrop—on the inside of his right arm.

I start the Saab, pull out slowly. He pedals his bike down the sidewalk, following. I make the turn onto McNeil Street—he follows. I turn onto Texas Avenue, driving slow. The boy barrels along, racing me, racing his reflection in the storefront windows. The streetlamps glow yellow and green. I shift into third, testing him. I hear his breath, the clatter of the bike chain, hum of tires on concrete. We pass the courthouse, the black-spiked fence which guards the Confederate Memorial. The Stars and Bars hangs limp above the floodlights.

There is a red light at Spring Street, right before the Texas Street bridge. I pause before turning right, look at him. The boy leans against the Petroleum Tower, trying to catch his breath. The granite is purple as a bruise. He stares at me, waiting.

The light turns. He cuts in front of me as I turn, almost grazing the bumper, heads up the steep pavement into the yellow mist above the river.

*

Home. I run warm water into the bathroom sink, cup my hands under the faucet, wet my face. I look up. Droplets of water hang in my eyebrows, my eyelashes, my mustache, the stubble on my cheeks. Behind me, through the open door, the bedroom unfolds inside the mirror, where the Angel sleeps, curled up like a child.

I wonder sometimes if you choose the kind of man you want to be, and if so, when those choices come. Would it be possible, if you had the nerve, to simply reach inside, push a bloody hand past bowel and bone to take hold of that part of yourself that's not forgiven, and bring it up into the air, into the light, to see if anything there has somehow remained solid and whole?

I lean forward into the mirror, study my face. I lean closer, looking for Nash's eyes, though I know he wasn't blood.

Nominated by The Georgia Review

THE TRIUMPH OF THE PRAGUE WORKERS' COUNCILS

fiction by EUGENE STEIN

from THE IOWA REVIEW

1. Thieves Like Us

The auction at Sotheby's of European political memorabilia was under way. Jessica Neumann had come to New York from Chicago on the off-chance some Situationist material might turn up. Elaine Friedman had come from Massachusetts for precisely the same reason.

Jessica found herself behind the main auditorium, in front of the long wooden table where the next few lots had been placed before being auctioned. Elaine was already there.

Nothing on the table much interested Jessica—Popular Front claptrap and reactionary fodder—but on a chair nearby she spotted a pile of posters and pamphlets. She sifted quickly through the pages, and halfway through, she found a single, handwritten sheet of paper. She recognized the handwriting at once—it was Guy Debord's; Debord was one of the Situationists' leading ideologues. The document, evidently the rough draft for a communique issued during the occupation of the Sorbonne in May 1968, called upon workers to occupy a Renault plant in Lyons.

Inside a large box filled with political buttons, meanwhile, Elaine Friedman had found, tucked all the way at the bottom, a

350

small jewel box with a rusty clasp. She finally managed to open the box and took out a small handmade silver pendant. She opened the pendant and inside was a tiny painting of Charles Fourier.

Jessica tried to stifle a cry when she saw what Elaine was holding, but a small moan escaped. And then, softly: "Tatiana."

"Yes," Elaine agreed. She turned over the jewel box. A label from a store in Brussels was pasted to the bottom.

"We'll go together," Jessica said.

"Of course."

They recognized each other; they'd both attended a symposium on the Situationists a year before, in Toronto. While the guard was distracted by an old woman who insisted on bringing her Lhasa apso into the auction room—"He has very good taste," the woman maintained—Jessica managed to sneak the Debord manuscript into her program, and Elaine dropped the pendant into her pocket. She left the jewel box but copied down the Brussels address.

2. The Proletariat as Subject and as Representation

In 1968, when Jessica was fourteen, she spent the summer with her Uncle Rene, who lived in Paris. (Her father's family originally came from Alsace, and Jessica had grown up speaking French and German.) A few months earlier, Jessica's cousin Michelle had been one of the students who seized control of the university of Nanterre. The Nanterre occupation had sparked the entire May uprising in France. Michelle gave her younger cousin books to read—Hegel, Marx, Lukacs, Bakunin—and patiently worked through them with her; brought her to cafes, where dialectical materialism was debated; and accompanied her to a birth control clinic. That summer Jessica slept with a boy for the first time, and she became a Situationist, and somehow the joys of revolution and sexual freedom merged in her mind, so that she couldn't tell where one left off and the other began.

Back in Chicago, her teacher asked her to do a book report, and when Jessica got up in front of the class, she announced that she was going to consider the entire Paris rebellion in her text. She proceeded to give a Situationist analysis of the May events.

She said that late capitalism really represented the dictatorship of the commodity; that *things* ruled and were young; that modern society as a whole constituted a spectacle, and the spectacle marked the triumph of the commodity; that by their very contemplation of the spectacle, human beings were controlled, subjugated, made passive, isolated.

When she finished, most of the class just looked at her, blankly. In the back of the room, the single black student in the class gave her the black power salute. He hadn't really understood her talk, but he had the sense her heart was in the right place. The teacher hadn't understood what she'd said either, and failed her.

A month later she was told she could erase the F if she gave another book report, this time on an actual book. Jessica chose Willa Cather's *The Professor's House*. She said Cather was America's most underrated novelist. She said the characters were beautifully realized. She said the book was a brilliant dissection of alienated labor and the emptiness of bourgeois life, and then she segued into an analysis of the recent invasion of Czechoslovakia by the Russian, Polish, East German, Hungarian, and Bulgarian armies. She explained that the Bolshevism/"communism" of Eastern Europe was just another form of state capitalism; that modern life was marked by the banality of work and the pauperization of play; that a revolution *of everyday life* was needed. The black student stood up in the back of the room and applauded. This time he got the jist of it. The teacher failed her again.

She was given one last chance to give a book report. Jessica chose *Huckleberry Finn*, and said simply that Huck and Jim showed how much pleasure awaited us if we could rupture the spectacle of racism and the racism of spectacle.

The teacher was now frightened by Jessica and even more frightened by the black student in the back of the room, who she believed might riot at any moment; this time she gave Jessica an A.

3. The Big Sleep

The plane touched down in Brussels during a light drizzle. It was late, so the two women took a cab to a small hotel Jessica knew, ate a light supper of bread and cheese, and then sat in front of the brick fireplace in the common room, nursing their wine. They compared notes: their lives, their lovers, their sense of the mysterious past forever receding . . . And they talked about Tatiana, about her art and her loneliness, and especially about her masterpiece, "Triumph of the Prague Workers' Councils, 1956/1968."

Elaine told Jessica that her boyfriend had recently left her for a Trotskyist nymphomaniac, and Jessica shared her pain.

The next day they rose early, ate breakfast, and then went out into the Brussels morning. The sky was as gray as the alley cat who lived behind the hotel and fed on scraps of garbage. Elaine and Jessica walked along the rue du Chêne, past the Manneken-Pis (a fountain of a small boy urinating, and one of Brussels' most important sights). The store, which sold rare books, antiquities, and memorabilia, had just opened when they arrived. The tiny, ancient Flemish owner was still hanging up his coat.

He turned around and looked at them. He spoke in English, lightly accented. "Can I mebbe perhaps to help you?"

"We're interested in the work of Tatiana—" Elaine never even got to finish the sentence.

"Everybodde want piece of Tatiana," the man told them. "Last week, another wooman, rich wooman come. I have nothink."

"There was another woman here?" Jessica asked.

"Yes, a third wooman. There was a third wooman."

"What did you tell her?" Jessica pressed him.

"I got neckless from old man. Eisenberg. He die. He love Tatiana."

The man went on to say that he had sold the necklace to a European collector who made frequent trips to the U.S., that Eisenberg had a son, and yes, he had an address . . . now where had he put it . . . Eventually he found the slip of paper.

Elaine and Jessica rushed to the address. The son was sitting down to a late breakfast but consented to talk to them. Yes, his father had fallen in love with Tatiana in the sixties. He was an accountant who had done her taxes the year she lived in Paris. No, the pendant was the only gift he'd ever received from her. Yes, he'd heard of the collages. No, he'd never seen them. Yes, a third woman had asked him these same questions. She was actually an old client of his father's. The son gave them the address of the woman, who lived in Paris and who had left her card. And they might want to look up another friend of Tatiana's, the son said, a Monsieur Roche, who also lived in Paris, near the Luxembourg Gardens.

They took the bullet train to Paris and were there by lunch time.

"Tatiana was everything to everybody," said Roche, when they tracked him down. He would have looked dapper in his dapper new gray suit, if not for the beads of sweat that had formed above his upper lip. He spoke excellent English. A ceiling fan overhead chopped the air and made vaguely threatening noises, but did little to cool the overheated apartment. The light streaming into Roche's living room filtered through a lattice-work he'd just had built for his orchids and left shadows the shape of a cobweb on the walls of his flat. The orchids were large and almost obscenely suggestive with their gaping mouths. There were packages and shopping bags all over the room; Roche had done quite a bit of shopping lately. "She could be whatever she wanted or needed to be," he continued. "Her paintings are the same way."

"About her collages," Elaine prompted gently . . .

"You're after the 'Prague,' aren't you?" Roche asked.

They were noncommittal.

"Maybe it's better that it's never found," he said. "This way it exists for all of us. And no one can take it away."

"Have you ever seen it?" Jessica wondered.

"Never."

"He's lying," Jessica said later.

"Hmm," Elaine temporized.

A heavyset man seemed to be following them when they left Roche's apartment, but he disappeared after a few blocks.

Jessica and Elaine went back to their hotel on the rue des Ecoles. That night, they stayed up late, drinking brandy, talking. Jessica said she no longer considered herself a Situationist. In the last few years she had begun reading the works of some 20th century Italian ultra-anarchists—anarchists so opposed to authority that they viewed *any* organization as inherently fascistic. Consequently, these anarchists never formed political groups, but recommended instead that individuals attack the state privately and anonymously. It was a lonely sort of life, Jessica conceded, and

354

she felt a certain kinship with Tatiana. Jessica had never settled down anywhere for long and in fact made her living as a court stenographer.

Elaine Friedman was an assistant professor of art history at Smith. She had done her dissertation on Situationist art, and the art still spoke to her powerfully. She said she felt it was her duty to keep the collages out of museums at all cost, because a museum represented a hierarchical, managerial, bureaucratic approach to art—the antithesis of Tatiana's message.

Jessica went to sleep, but Elaine stayed up a little longer, reading a book on non-Euclidean geometry she'd found in the night table in her hotel room. At last she went to the bathroom down the hall to brush her teeth before going to bed. She left her room unlocked since she'd only be gone for a minute or two. She returned to her room and noticed that the door was open a bit more than she'd left it. Probably the wind, she surmised. She went into her room and turned to lock the door. Suddenly she felt a sharp, intense pain in her left temple, as someone smashed something on her head. She dropped on her knees and saw a pair of beautiful blue women's shoes before she sank into unconsciousness.

4. Watch out for Manipulators! Watch out for Bureaucrats!

Elaine Friedman considered Tatiana one of the most important artists of the century, and certainly one of the most essential. Tatiana was not the first to insist that true art and true revolution could only be realized when art and revolution merged; but she was the first to show *how to make it happen.*

Tatiana Basho Malevich was the single member of the Situationist International who lived behind the Iron Curtain. She was born in Leningrad during the Nine Hundred Days siege to an artistic and bohemian family; her father was a great admirer of Japanese haiku, as her middle name attests. She settled in Moscow as a young woman, and lived there until 1969, when she was placed, against her will, in a psychiatric hospital sixty kilometers outside of Vladivostok. A cousin of Casimir Malevich, the Russian Suprematist painter, she linked up with the French Situationists when she accompanied an exhibition of Malevich's work that

355

toured Europe. She absorbed much from her cousin's book *World Without Objects*, but grounded his rather ethereal aesthetic philosophy in a rigorous anarcho-Marxist skepticism.

Her fame as an artist rests largely on the half dozen collages she made in Moscow in 1968 during a single one-month burst of creativity, and which she managed to smuggle out of the country. Distraught over the collapse of the May rebellion in Paris and the brutal repression of the Czechs that August, Tatiana (she preferred to be called by her first name) decided she would rewrite history. She would imagine a world where workers rose up against their overlords, and where revolution was never hijacked by bureaucrats, juntas, Leninists, or spectacle. The six collages in the "Triumph" series were the happy result of Tatiana's reverie.

"Triumph of the Paris Communards, 1871," was a take-off on Goya's "The Burial of the Sardine." But where Goya saw madness in carnival revelers, Tatiana saw freedom. The Situationists had long maintained that true revolution could be seen as festivity, as passionate, spontaneous play. The collage depicts a Commune that has defeated the Prussians. Drunk with joy and liberty, Paris throws itself the biggest party in history. Reds predominate in the collage—the red of blood, the red of wine, the red of revolution. Tatiana gave the work to her father, who lived in Finland, and whom she apparently adored.

The first collage she actually completed was "Triumph of Brook Farm/Fourier Phalanx, 1843," which showed an imagined tableau of Nathaniel Hawthorne, Margaret Fuller, and Albert Brisbane cavorting naked. It is presently in the collection of a Japanese industrialist.

Next she constructed "Triumph of the Peasants/Eternal Council of Mühlhausen, 1525." The collage posited that the uprising of South German peasants led by Thomas Münzer was actually successful. Luther, who had opposed the rebellion and supported the princes, was shown in a stockade. The collage found its way to East Germany, which, from time to time, embraced the Peasant Uprising as an important forerunner to the Communist state. Consequently, the collage was shown occasionally at the Museum für Deutsche Geschichte, until an anarchist snuck in and wrote the name "Erich Honeker" on Luther's dunce cap. Twelve weeks went by before any of the curators noticed. Tatiana was delighted, purportedly, when word reached her in Siberia, but the collage was subsequently put back into storage. After the collapse of the

German Democratic Republic, the collage was shipped to the Städtisches Kunstmuseum in Bonn, where a curator declared it "not worthy of exhibition."

Tatiana would probably consider that a compliment, Elaine reasoned.

"Triumph of the Barcelona Anarchists, 1937," showed POUM revelers joyfully hanging Franco, Mussolini, and Stalin by the heels. It was sent to Franco as a birthday present—Tatiana had a wonderful sense of humor—and is presumed to have been destroyed.

Next Tatiana made her most dangerous collage, the one that probably got her sent to Siberia. "Triumph of the Kronstadt Sailors, 1921" showed the seamen tossing Lenin and Trotsky into the Baltic Sea. "All power to the soviets" was stenciled, in Russian, underneath the collage; on top Tatiana wrote (with her blood, some say) "Workers of all Nations, Unite!" Criticizing the Communist Party by invoking Marx—criticizing the Party for not being communist enough—well, it was simply too much of an affront. A day after the collage was first exhibited in Norway, Tatiana was hospitalized. It is undeniable that Tatiana was emotionally disturbed, plagued by visions, occasional hallucinations, and (justifiable?) paranoia; moreover, the events of 1968 had plunged her into a nearly psychotic depression. Still, Brezhnev called her "the most dangerous woman in Moscow," (see Andropov's *Memoirs*) and the political reasons for her hospitalization seem clear. Tatiana's own mental illness simply made it easier for the Kremlin.

The last collage she made, "The Triumph of the Prague Workers' Councils, 1956/1968" was actually the most important of all. The "Prague" and "Kronstadt" collages were both thought to be lost when Situationist headquarters in Oslo were set on fire by either Stalinists, neo-Nazis, or careless children. But the "Kronstadt" collage had recently turned up in a stall on Portobello Road, in London, and Elaine and Jessica believed the "Prague" was extant as well.

5. Not Another Movie About Two Women on the Road

Madame LaGrange, the woman who'd given her card to Eisenberg's son, had recently come back from New York, her con-

357

cierge assured them, but was indisposed and wasn't seeing visitors. Jessica and Elaine needed to kill some time. Jessica wanted to see the new Godard film, so she could revile it, and Elaine wanted to go to the Beaubourg museum, which she abhorred. The discussion grew rather heated. Elaine was angry anyway, because Jessica refused to believe someone had attacked her the night before, even though the pendant was now missing. In fact, Jessica started laughing when Elaine mentioned the beautiful pair of shoes.

So Elaine called Jessica a fascist, and Jessica called Elaine a Shelepinite with Nashist tendencies, and they both started crying, and wiped the corners of their eyes with tissues, and started laughing through their tears, and hugged each other very tight. And after that, everything was all right.

"'Elaine the fair, Elaine the lovable, / Elaine, the lily maid of Astolat,'" Jessica recited.

"My father used to say that," Elaine remembered.

6. Alphaville, a Film by Jean-Luc Godard

They saw the special compu-gendarmes everywhere they went in Paris. A small boy used a slingshot against one of the CD-ROM-aided policemen, then made his escape, swinging from one building to another, using the clotheslines that connected each building to its neighbor and that reminded Jessica of cables linking PCs into a computer network.

"Tarzan versus IBM," Jessica noted.

The sky was as gray as in Brussels, and as the afternoon wore on, the light shortened, until it seemed to Elaine as though the city were being filmed in black-and-white. Or perhaps, when the light slanted just so and left a pool of shadow lapping up against their feet, it reminded her of one of Goya's dark etchings. Paris, City of Pain.

They walked along the Seine, and it looked like every body of water Jessica had ever seen, dirty, as dirty as Lake Michigan or the Hudson, the Hamburg Hafen or the Mediterranean. "It's always the same water," Jessica told Elaine.

The compu-gendarmes patrolled every street corner, serving their master, Big Memory, as the total computer vector that dom-

358

inated France had come to be called. The cops arrested anyone who refused to conform; they patrolled against *difference,* which Prime Minister LePen had outlawed.

"Maybe it's best that Tatiana didn't live to see this," Elaine mused.

"What are you talking about? She's still alive," Jessica reminded her.

Elaine was embarrassed. "I forgot." But it was easy to forget . . . Tatiana had been released only recently from the mental institution that had been her home for more than two decades, and now she lived quietly in Moscow, refusing to see any visitors.

That night Jessica, who was pursuing a master's degree in library science in her spare time, broke into Big Memory's cavernous files with a password she'd bought on the black market in Montparnasse. She managed to find the subfile on Situationist subversives, and by carefully tracking down every mention of the "Prague," she soon established that the collage still existed.

"I knew it," Elaine said. "I knew it."

In fact, all the evidence indicated the "Prague" was right there in Paris. If only they knew where to look . . .

A warning light started blinking on the computer Jessica had rented. The compu-gendarmes, probably alerted by an internal security mechanism, were trying to track her down. Jessica turned off the machine before they could trace her.

7. Untitled

"The Triumph of the Prague Workers' Councils" was Tatiana's most important work, for it described and invoked—possibly, some mystic anarchist-pagans claimed, it even summoned into being—Situationist utopia: workers/consumers would establish local councils in factories and communes around the world; the non-bureaucratic, participatory councils would confiscate the productive forces of society, and thereby the proletariat as a revolutionary class *would seize history.*

Authority and hierarchy would simply vanish. Poof . . .

Only a handful of people had ever seen the "Prague" before its disappearance. All vouched for its almost mesmeric appeal; but it

359

was a kind of upside-down mesmerism that challenged passivity, that smashed and ruptured the spectacle.

Elaine dreamt of the "Prague," often. But once it was found, how could she keep it from becoming just another spectacle? "The long lost 'Prague'"—just one more commodity—grist for the capitalist mill. Like the "Kronstadt" collage, set in a little alcove in the National Gallery, garnering quaint praise from *The Tatler* and *Time* . . .

The two women decided to go out on the town. Jessica dressed up in a short denim skirt and blue high heels.

Elaine was horrified. "Your shoes—!"

Jessica looked down at her feet and then back up at Elaine. "You don't really think. . ."

"I don't know what to think. Do you swear? Do you swear you didn't do it?"

"Tell me, Elaine," said Jessica, very gently, "what can women such as we find to swear *on*? On the graves of our mothers, who loved us, but mistreated us, because they mistreated themselves? On the graves of our fathers, who worked too hard for too little money, and whom we can never respect, even though we're moved profoundly by their sacrifice? On the Bible, on the Torah, which we don't believe in? On Marx, who grew old and orthodox and, ultimately, bourgeois with his mathematics? On what, Elaine? On what?"

And Elaine loved Jessica then, loved her because they were very much a pair, because Jessica was the only one who understood what Elaine's life had been all about.

"Swear on the life—not the grave—of Emma Goldman," Elaine told her finally. "And Bessie Smith. Swear on cold ripe peaches on hot August days. Swear on *My Antonia*."

"I swear," Jessica said.

"I believe you," Elaine said.

8. The Plot Thickens

Jessica stood there, in the middle of the room, with her gun.

Madame LaGrange sat on the couch, calmly smoking a cigarette, and wearing a beautiful blue kimono. Monsieur Roche, next to her, fidgeted nervously. Madame LaGrange's obese chauffeur, Jacques, sat quietly on an easy chair off to the side.

Elaine watched it all, and it seemed to her that she'd watched it all before.

"I supposed you're wondering why I've called you all here," Jessica said.

They were.

"Madame LaGrange went to Belgium as soon as she heard about the pendant," Jessica began. "But the pendant had already been sold. When Madame heard it would be auctioned at Sotheby's, she flew to New York to bid on it. She arranged with a corrupt Sotheby's employee to stash the pendant in a box of worthless buttons, where Elaine chanced upon it."

Madame LaGrange blew a perfect smoke ring into the air, then smiled enigmatically.

"Meanwhile, Madame LaGrange had encouraged the relationship between her chauffeur and Monsieur Roche," Jessica went on.

Monsieur Roche began chewing on his nails.

"Relationship?" Elaine asked.

"Of course. They were lovers," Jessica explained. "But Jacques had a secret. Madame LaGrange had slowly and quite deliberately addicted him to heroin. Once he was addicted, he was bound to her forever. In fact, he was her slave. She knew that Monsieur Roche knew more about the collages than he let on, and she knew Jacques would come in handy one day."

Jacques sat very still on the easy chair, impassive and thoughtful. A single tear fell from his left eye and splashed on his cheek. His chauffeur's hat was perched at a rakish angle.

"Madame LaGrange was certain Roche held the key to the 'Prague.' Now was the time to act. Using Jacques as her intermediary, she offered money to Monsieur Roche, a great deal of money, and Monsieur Roche, who had guarded the 'Prague' honorably and courageously for many years, finally broke down. He needed the money for his sister's kidney transplant and to pay for Jacques's stay at a drug rehabilitation clinic. With the money in hand, Roche also treated himself to a new suit and the various parcels we saw in his apartment."

"Don't forget the trellis for my orchids," Monsieur Roche reminded them. "That was very important too."

361

"Right. And one more thing. Madame LaGrange knew whoever had the pendant would eventually come to Roche. All she had to do was wait. When we left Monsieur Roche's apartment, Jacques tailed us. He was the heavyset man we saw behind us."

"I knew he looked familiar," Elaine said.

"Madame LaGrange was the woman in the blue shoes who knocked you out, Elaine. At first I didn't believe you," Jessica admitted. "I thought you'd concocted the story so you wouldn't have to share the necklace with me. But when I saw that Madame LaGrange, my evil double, my twin, only wore blue, I realized she was the culprit."

"But why?" Elaine asked, turning from Jessica to Madame LaGrange. "Why?"

"I have my reasons," said Madame LaGrange, quietly but with steely determination.

"She was jealous of Tatiana," Jessica proposed. "At first I thought she wanted the collage for political reasons. Or because she respected Tatiana's artistic vision. Or even as an investment opportunity to hedge against inflation. But now I know it was simply jealousy. Remember Eisenberg?"

"Yes. The old man who died. Tatiana's accountant."

"Accountant?" Madame LaGrange spit out the word. "Perhaps you mean the greatest fiduciary mind of the century."

"Yes, Eisenberg was a genius," Jessica acknowledged. "A master of oil depletion allowances, tax-shelters, and depreciation. He raised inventive bookkeeping to an art, and in fact lectured occasionally at the Sorbonne before he retired to Brussels. Madame LaGrange loved him. But he loved *Tatiana*. Madame never forgave Tatiana. She swore revenge. And what was her revenge? She would deprive the world of Tatiana's work. She wanted the collage, *so she could annihilate it*. And she visited Eisenberg's son, simply to find out if there was anything else of Tatiana's she could destroy."

"That's why you wanted the collage?" Monsieur Roche accused Madame LaGrange, his voice breaking with sorrow, his eyes brimming over with tears. "To ruin something so beautiful? God forgive me."

"It's not too late," Jessica said. "The collage still exists. Madame LaGrange couldn't bring herself to destroy it."

"I wanted to," Madame LaGrange told them, and for the first time a hint of sadness crept into her voice. "I wanted to so badly. But it's very powerful. More powerful than I. . ."

"Thank God," Monsieur Roche muttered.

"God—or revolutionary Marxism," said Jessica. "You be the judge."

"I have to see it, Jessica, I have to," Elaine begged. "Where is it?"

"Well, I can't be sure—but I suspect it's behind those curtains." Jessica pointed to the blue damask satin that draped the windows behind Elaine.

9. Martian Time Slip

They were alone in the Bois de Boulogne, where the red and yellow irises bloomed, and where the yellow and purple lilies were just beginning to bud.

They were alone with the collage, which was covered with heavy brown paper.

Together they unwrapped it. Together they propped the collage against a tree. Together they stepped back. Together they looked.

The collage conflated the Budapest Workers' Council of 1956 and the Prague Spring of 1968; together, Czechoslovakia and Hungary pushed back the Soviet army. The councils were triumphant. The last capitalist was hung with the guts of the last bureaucrat. True socialism reigned.

Jessica took another step back. "My God, it's beautiful. The colors. . ."

"They're *playing*," Elaine said reverently.

In a startling reversal, Tatiana depicted the common people, leisured and happy, gamboling like a court of aristocrats. There were masquerade balls, coquettes, archery contests, jazz ensembles, and in one corner, a Los Angeles beach party and volleyball game.

But the most interesting effect was the middle of the collage, where a kind of vacancy or telescoping occurred. Tatiana had cut a hole in the canvas, and covered it with clear cellophane; and somehow, miraculously, Tatiana had succeeded in bending the

363

space-time continuum, so that through the center, the viewer could peer into another universe. Not metaphorically—*actually*. The other universe was actually visible.

"They talk about rupturing the spectacle," Elaine reflected, "but I never knew they meant it literally."

"I read something somewhere—that anarchism is a kind of miracle," Jessica told her. "The intrusion of another world into this one."

They looked through the cellophane and they saw the other universe. And what they saw was unspeakably beautiful. Unspeakable, because there were no words to describe it. Only mathematics could describe it: anarchism, socialism, freedom, fraternity raised to the infinite power.

But they could not pass through.

10. Liebestod

A wind crept up and swept over them and over the flowers, and then Jessica took out her gun and pointed it at Elaine.

Nervously: "Jessica, what are you doing?"

"I love you, but I can't trust you."

Elaine was trembling. "Of course you can."

"How can an anarchist trust anyone but herself?" Jessica asked sadly.

"I'd never do anything to hurt the collage," Elaine said. "I'd protect it. I would." She was desperate.

"Anyone can be corrupted. I have to guard the 'Prague.' For future generations. They'll know what to do with it."

"But all we've been through—"

"Exactly. All we've been through. Which means you'll understand what I have to do. You're the only one who *can* understand. . ."

"Yes, I see," said Elaine, after thinking for a moment.

Jessica fired twice. One bullet went into Elaine's abdomen, the other hit her chest.

Elaine fell to the ground. Jessica knelt by her side. And then Elaine took out a revolver. And aimed— Not at Jessica— At the collage. She fired six times, and when she stopped firing, there was nothing left.

"I had to, Jessica. I couldn't trust you, either. I couldn't let it be put on display somewhere. It's safer this way."

"Yes," Jessica said. "Of course." What courage, she marveled. What commitment.

"The expropriators are expropriated," Elaine said, with a little laugh, but the laughter turned into coughing, and the cough turned into choking.

Jessica took Elaine's hand and kissed it. "I've never loved anyone as much as I love you."

"Swear?" Elaine said, the blood in her throat making her gurgle.

"I swear on the life—not the grave—of Emma Goldman. And Bessie Smith." Jessica kissed Elaine's red lips. "I swear on cold ripe peaches on hot August days. I swear on *My Antonia.*"

"We saw something," said Elaine, content, and then she died.

Note: Any portion of this short story may be reproduced, even without asking permission, even without mentioning the source.

Nominated by The Iowa Review

AGAINST SINCERITY

by LOUISE GLÜCK

from AMERICAN POETRY REVIEW

SINCE I'm going to use inexplicit terms, I want to begin by defining the three most prominent of these, as they'll be used in what follows. By *actuality* I mean to refer to the world of event, by *truth* to the embodied vision, illumination, or enduring discovery which is the ideal of art, and by *honesty* or *sincerity* to "telling the truth" which is not necessarily the path to illumination.

V. S. Naipaul, in the pages of a national magazine, defines the aim of the novel; the ideal creation, he says, must be "indistinguishable from the truth." A delicious and instructive remark. Instructive because it postulates a gap between truth and actuality. The artist's task, then, involves the transformation of the actual to the true. And the ability to achieve such transformations, especially in art that presumes to be subjective, depends on conscious willingness to distinguish truth from honesty or sincerity.

The impulse, however, is not to distinguish but to link. In part the tendency to connect the idea of truth with the idea of honesty is a form of anxiety. We are calmed by answerable questions, and the question "Have I been honest?" has an answer. Honesty and sincerity refer back to the already known, against which any utterance can be tested. They constitute acknowledgement. They also assume a convergence: these terms take for granted the identification of the poet with the speaker.

This is not to suggest that apparently honest poets don't object to having their creativity overlooked. For example, the work of

Diane Wakoski fosters as intense an identification of poet with speaker as any body of work I can think of. But when a listener, some years ago, praised Wakoski's courage, Wakoski was indignantly dismissive. She reminded her audience that, after all, she decided what she set down. So the "secret" content of the poems, the extreme intimacy, was regularly transformed by acts of decision, which is to say, by assertions of power. The "I" on the page, the all-revealing Diane, was her creation. The secrets we choose to betray lose power over us.

To recapitulate: the source of art is experience, the end product truth, and the artist, surveying the actual, constantly intervenes and manages, lies and deletes, all in the service of truth. Blackmur talks of this: "The life we all live," he says, "is not alone enough of a subject for the serious artist; it must be a life with a leaning, life with a tendency to shape itself only in certain forms, to afford its most lucid revelations only in certain lights."

There is, unfortunately, no test for truth. That is, in part, why artists suffer. The love of truth is felt as chronic aspiration and chronic unease. If there is no test for truth, there is no possible security. The artist, alternating between anxiety and fierce conviction, must depend on the latter to compensate for the sacrifice of the sure. It is relatively easy to say that truth is the aim and heart of poetry, but harder to say how it is recognized or made. We know it first, as readers, by its result, by the sudden rush of wonder and awe and terror.

The association of truth with terror is not new. The story of Psyche and Eros tells us that the need to know is like a hunger: it destroys peace. Psyche broke Eros's single commandment—that she not look at him—because the pressure to see was more powerful than either love or gratitude. And everything was sacrificed to it.

We have to remember that Psyche, the soul, was human. The legend's resolution marries the soul to Eros, by which union it—the soul—is made immortal. But to be human is to be subject to the lure of the forbidden.

Honest speech is a relief and not a discovery. When we speak of honesty, in relation to poems, we mean the degree to which and the power with which the generating impulse has been transcribed. Transcribed, not transformed. Any attempt to evaluate

367

the honesty of a text must always lead away from that text, and toward intention. This may make an interesting trail, more interesting, very possibly, than the puem. The mistake, in any case, is our failure to separate poetry which sounds like honest speech from honest speech. The earlier mistake is in assuming that there is only one way for poetry to sound.

These assumptions didn't come from nowhere. We have not so much made as absorbed them, as we digest our fathers and turn to our contemporaries. That turning is altogether natural: in the same way, children turn to other children, the dying to the dying, and so forth. We turn to those who have been dealt, as we see it, roughly the same hand. We turn to see what they're up to, feeling natural excitement in the presence of what is still unfolding, or unknown. Substantial contributions to our collective inheritance were made by poets whose poems seemed blazingly personal, as though the poets had performed autopsies on their own living tissue. The presence of the speaker in these poems was overwhelming; the poems read as testaments, as records of the life. Art was redefined, all its ingenuities washed away.

The impulse toward this poetry is heard in poets as unlike as Whitman and Rilke. It is heard, earlier, in the Romantics, despite Wordsworth's comment that if he "had said out passions as they were, the poems could never have been published." But the idea that a body of work corresponds to and describes a soul's journey is particularly vivid in Keats. What we hear in Keats is inward listening, attentiveness of a rare order. I will say more later about the crucial difference between such qualities and the decanting of personality.

Keats drew on his own life because it afforded greatest access to the materials of greatest interest. That it was *his* hardly concerned him. It was a life, and therefore likely, in its large shapes and major struggles, to stand as a paradigm. This is the attitude Emerson means, I think, when he says: "to believe your own thought, to believe that what is true for you in your private heart is true for all men—that is genius."

That is, at any rate, Keats's genius. Keats wanted a poetry that would document the soul's journey or shed light on hidden forms: he wanted more feeling and fewer alexandrines. But nothing in Keats's attitude toward the soul resembles the proprietor's investment. We can find limitation, but never smug limitation. A great innocence sounds in the lines, a kind of eager gratitude that passionate dedication should have been rewarded with fluency. As in this sonnet, dated 1818:

WHEN I HAVE FEARS

When I have fears that I may cease to be
Before my pen has gleaned my teeming brain,
Before high-piled books in charactry,
Hold like rich garners the full ripened grain;
When I behold, upon the night's starred face,
Huge cloudy symbols of a high romance,
And think that I may never live to trace
Their shadows, with the magic hand of chance;
And when I feel, fair creature of an hour!
That I shall never look upon thee more,
never have relish in the fairy power
of unreflecting love!—then on the shore
of the wide world I stand alone, and think
Till love and fame to nothingness do sink.

The impression is of outcry, of haste, of turbulent, immediate emotion that seems to fall, almost accidentally, into the sonnet form. That form tends to produce a sensation of repose; no matter how paradoxical the resolution, the ear detects something of the terminal thud of the judge's gavel. Or the double thud, since the sensation is especially marked in sonnets following the Elizabethan style, ending, that is, in a rhymed couplet: two pithy lines of summary or antithesis. "Think" and "sink" make, certainly, a noticeable rhyme, but they manage, oddly enough, not to end the sonnet like two pennies falling on a plate. We require the marked rhyme, the single repeated sound, to put an end to all the poem's surging longing, to show us the "I," the speaker, at a standstill, just as the dash in the twelfth line makes the necessary abyss that separates the speaker from all the richness of the world. Consider, now, another sonnet, akin to this in subject and rational shape, though the "when" and "then" are here more subtle. The sonnet is Milton's, its occasion, the fact of blindness, its date of composition, 1652:

WHEN I CONSIDER HOW MY LIGHT IS SPENT

When I consider how my light is spent,
Ere half my days in this dark world and wide,
And that one talent which is death to hide
Lodged with me useless, though my soul more bent
To serve therewith my Maker, and present
My true account, lest he returning chide,
"Doth God exact day-labor, light denied?"
I fondly ask. But Patience, to prevent
That murmur, soon replies, "God doth not need
Either man's work or his own gifts; who best
Bear his mild yoke, they serve him best. His state
Is kingly: thousands at his bidding speed,
And post o'er land and ocean without rest:
They also serve who only stand and wait."

When I say the resemblance here is sufficient to make obvious the debt, what I mean is that I cannot read Keats's poem and not hear Milton's. Someone else would hear Shakespeare: neither echo is surprising. If Shakespeare was Keats's enduring love, Milton was his measuring rod. Keats carried a portrait of Shakespeare everywhere, even on the walking tours, as a kind of totem. When there was a desk, the portrait hung over it: work there was work at a shrine. Milton was the dilemma; toward Milton's achievement, Keats vacillated in his responses, and responses, to Keats, were verdicts. Such vacillation, combined with inner pressure to decide, can be called obsession.

The purpose of comparison was, finally, displacement; in Keats's mind, Wordsworth stood as the contender, the alternative. Keats felt Wordsworth's genius to lie in his ability to "[think] into the human heart"; Milton, for all his brilliance, showed, Keats thought, "less anxiety about humanity." Wordsworth was exploring those hidden reaches of the mind where, as Keats saw it, the intellectual problems of their time lay. And these problems seemed more difficult, more complex, than the theological

370

questions with which Milton was absorbed. So Wordsworth was "deeper than Milton," though more because of "the general and gregarious advance of intellect, than individual greatness of mind." All this was a way for Keats of clarifying purpose.

I said earlier that these sonnets were like in their occasions: this statement needs some amplification. The tradition of sincerity grows out of the blurring of distinction between theme and occasion; there is a greater emphasis, after the Romantics, on choice of occasion; the poet is less and less the artisan who makes, out of an occasion tossed him, something of interest. The poet less and less resembles the debating team: lithe, adept, of many minds.

In the poems at hand, both poets have taken up the question of loss. Of course, Keats was talking about death, which remains, as long as one is talking, imminent. But pressingly imminent, for Keats, even in 1818. He had already nursed a mother through her dying and had watched her symptoms reappear in his brother Tom. Consumption was the "family disease"; Keats's medical training equipped him to recognize its symptoms. The death imminent to Keats was a forfeit of the physical world, the world of the senses. That world—this world—was heaven; in the other he could not believe, nor could he see his life as a ritual preparation. So he immersed himself in the momentary splendor of the material world, which led always to the idea of loss. That is, if we recognize movement and change but no longer believe in anything beyond death, then all evolution is perceived as movement away, the stable element, the referent, being what was, not what will be, a world as stationary and alive as the scenes on the Grecian urn.

In 1652, Milton's blindness was probably complete. Loss makes his starting place; if blindness is, unlike death, a partial sacrifice, it is hardly a propitiation: Milton's calm is not the calm of bought time. I say "Milton's" calm, but in fact, we don't feel quite so readily the right to that familiarity. For one thing, the sonnet is a dialogue, the octet ending in the speaker's question, which Patience answers in its six sublime lines. In a whole so fluent, the technical finesse of this division is masterfully inconspicuous. It is interesting to remark, of a poem so masterful, so majestic in its composure, the extreme simplicity of vocabulary. One-syllable words predominate; the impression of mastery derives not from

371

elaborate vocabulary but from the astonishing variety of syntax within flexible suspended sentences, an instance of matchless organizational ability. People do not, ordinarily, speak this way. And I think it is generally true that imitations of speech, with its false starts, its lively inelegance, its sense of being arranged as it goes along, will not produce an impression of perfect control.

And yet there is, in Milton's poem, no absence of anguish, As readers, we register the anguish and drama here almost entirely subliminally, following the cues of rhythm. This is the great advantage of formal verse: metrical variation provides a subtext. It does what we now rely on tone to do. I should add that I think we really do have to rely on tone, since the advantage disappears when these conventions cease to be the norm of poetic expression. Education in metrical forms is not, however, essential to the reader here: the sonnet's opening lines summon and establish the iambic tradition, with a certain flutter at "consider." No ear can miss the measured regularity of those first lines:

> When I consider how my light is spent
> Ere half my days in this dark world and wide. . . .

The end of the second line, though, is troubled. "Dark world" makes a kind of aural knot. We hear menace not simply because the world is described as "dark," alluding both to the permanently altered world of the blind and, also, to a world metaphorically dark, in which right paths cannot be detected. The menace felt here comes about, and comes about chiefly, because the line that has been so fluid is suddenly stalled: a block is thrown up, the language itself coagulates into the immobile, impassable dark world. Then we escape; the line turns graceful again. But the dread introduced is not dissolved. And in the fourth line we hear it again with terrible force, so that we experience physically, in sound, the unmanageable sorrow:

> And that one talent which is death to hide
> Lodged with me useless. . . .

"Lodged" is like a blow. And the next words make a kind of lame reeling, a dwindling. As I hear the line, only "less" receives less emphasis than "me." In these four words we hear personal torment, the wreckage of order and hope; we are carried to a place as isolated as Keats's shore ever was, but a place of fewer options. All this happens early; Milton's sonnet is not a description of agony. But loss must be vividly felt for Patience's answer to properly reverberate.

The most likely transformation of loss is into task or test. This conversion introduces the idea of gain, if not reward; it fortifies the animal commitment to staying alive by promising to respond to the human need for purpose. So Patience, in Milton's sonnet, stills the petulant questioner and provides a glimpse of insight, a directive. At the very least, corrects a presumption.

Great value is placed here on endurance. And endurance is not required in the absence of pain. The poem, therefore, must convince us of pain, though its concerns lie elsewhere. Specifically, it proposes a lesson, which must be unearthed from the circumstantial. In the presence of lessons, the possibility of mastery can displace the animal plea for alleviation.

In Milton's sonnet, two actions are ascribed to the speaker: he considers, and, when he considers, he asks. I have made a particular case for anguish because we are accustomed to thinking the "cerebral" contradictory to the "felt," and the actions of the speaker are clearly the elevated actions of mind. The disposition to reflect or consider presumes developed intelligence, as well as temperamental inclination; it further presumes adequate time.

The "I" that considers is very different from the "I" that has fears. To have fears, to have, specifically, the fears on which Keats dwells, is to be immersed in acute sensation. The fear that one will cease to be is unlike the state of chronic fearfulness we call timidity. This fear halts and overtakes, it carries intimations of change or closure or collapse, it threatens to cancel the future. It is primal, unwilled, democratic, urgent; in its presence, all other function is suspended.

What we see in Keats is not indifference to thought. What we see is another species of thought than Milton's: thought resistant to government by mind. Keats claims for the responsive animal nature its ancient right to speech. Where Milton will project an impression of mastery, Keats projects a succumbing. In terms of tone, the impression of mastery and the impression of abandon

373

cannot co-exist. Our present addiction to sincerity grows out of a preference for abandon, for the subjective "I" whose impassioned partiality carries the implication of flaw, whose speech sounds individual and human and fallible. The elements of coldness to which Keats objected in Milton, the insufficient "anxiety about humanity" correspond to the overt projection of mastery.

Keats was given to describing his methods of composition in terms implying a giving-in: the poet was to be passive, responsive, available to all sensation. His desire was to reveal the soul, but soul, to Keats, had no spiritual draperies. Spirituality manifests the mind's intimidating claim to independent life. It was this invention Keats rejected. To Keats, the soul was corporeal and vital and frail; it had no life outside the body.

Keats refused to value what he did not believe, and he did not believe what he could not feel. Because he saw no choice, Keats was bound to prefer the moral to the divine, as he was bound to gravitate toward Shakespeare, who wrote plays where Milton made masks. Who wrote, that is, with an expressed debt to life.

It follows that Keats's poems feel immediate, personal, exposed; they sound, in other words, exactly like honesty, following Wordsworth's notion that poetry should seem the utterance of "a man talking to men." If Milton wrote in momentous chords, Keats preferred the rush of isolated notes, preferred the penetrating to the commanding.

The idea of "a man talking to men," the premise of honesty, depends on a delineated speaker. And it is precisely on this point that confusion arises, since the success of such a poetry creates in its readers a firm belief in the reality of that speaker, which is expressed as the identification of the speaker with the poet. This belief is what the poet means to engender: difficulty comes when he begins to participate in the audience's mistake. And on this point, we should listen to Keats, who intended so plainly that his poems seem personal and who drew, so regularly and so unmistakably, on autobiographical materials.

At the center of Keats's thinking is the problem of self. And it is on the subject of the poet's self that he speaks with greatest feeling and insight. Those men of talent, he felt, who impose their "proper selves" on what they create, should be called "men of power," in contrast to the true "men of genius," those men who, in Keats's view, were "great as certain ethereal chemicals

374

operating on the mass of neutral intellect—but they have not any individuality, any determined character." Toward the composition of poems that would seem "a man speaking to men," he advocated the opposite of egotistical self-awareness and self-cultivation; he recommended, rather, the negative capability he felt in Shakespeare, a capacity for suspending judgment in order to report faithfully, a capability of submission, a willingness to "annul" the self.

The self, in other words, was like a lightning rod: it attracted experience. But the poet's obligation was to divest himself of personal characteristics. Existing beliefs, therefore, were not a touchstone, but a disadvantage.

I referred, some time ago, to our immediate inheritance. I had in mind poets like Lowell and Plath and Berryman, along with many less impressive others. With reference to the notion of sincerity, it is especially interesting to look at Berryman.

Berryman was, from the first, technically proficient, though the early poems are not memorable. When he found what we like to call "himself," he demonstrated what is, to my mind, the best ear since Pound. The self he found was mordant, voluble, opinionated, and profoundly withheld, as demonically manipulative as Frost. In 1970, after *The Dream Songs* had made him famous, Berryman published a curious book, which took its title from the Keats sonnet. The book, *Love and Fame*, was dedicated "to the memory of the suffering lover & young Breton master who called himself 'Tristan Corbière.'" To this dedication, Berryman added a parenthetical comment: "I wish I versed with his bite."

We have, therefore, by the time we reach the first poem, a great deal of information: we have a subject, youth's twin dreams, a reference, and an ideal. But this is as nothing compared to the information we get in the poems. We get in them the kind of instantly gratifying data usually associated with drunken camaraderie, and not with art. We get actual names, places, positions, and, while Berryman is at it, confessions of failure, pride, ambition, and lust, all in characteristic shorthand: arrogance without apology.

It can be said of Berryman that when he found his voice he found his voices. By voice I mean natural distinction, and by distinction I mean to refer to thought. Which is to say, you do not find your voice by inserting a single adjective into twenty poems. Distinctive voice is inseparable from distinctive substance; it cannot be grafted on. Berryman began to sound like Berryman when he invented Mr. Bones, and so was able to project two ideas simultaneously. Presumably, in *Love and Fame*, we have a single speaker—commentator might be a better word. But the feel of the poems is very like that of *The Dream Songs;* Mr. Bones survives in an arsenal of sinister devices, particularly in the stinging, undermining tag lines. The poems pretend to be straight gossip, straight from the source; like gossip, they divert and entertain. But the source deals in mixed messages; midway through, the reader is recalled from the invited error:

MESSAGE

Amplitude,—voltage,—the one friend calls for the one,
the other for the other, in my work;
in verse & prose. Well, hell.
I am not writing an autobiography-in-verse, my friends.

Impressions, structures, tales, from Columbia in the thirties
& the michaelmas term at Cambridge in 36,
followed by some later. It's not my life.
That's occluded and lost.

On the page, "autobiography-in-verse" is a single ladylike word, held together by malicious hyphens.

What's real in the passage is despair. Which owes, in part, to the bitter notion that invention is wasted.

The advantage of poetry over life is that poetry, if it is sharp enough, may last. We are unnerved, I suppose, by the thought that authenticity, in the poem, is not produced by sincerity. We incline, in our anxiety for formulas, to be literal: we scan Frost's face compulsively for hidden kindness, having found the poems to be, by all reports, so much better than the man. This assumes our poems are our fingerprints, which they are not. And the pro-

376

cesses by which experience is changed—heightened, distilled, made memorable—have nothing to do with sincerity. The truth, on the page, need not have been lived. It is, instead, all that can be envisioned.

I want to say, finally, something more about truth, or about that art which is "indistinguishable" from it. Keats's theory of negative capability is an articulation of a habit of mind more commonly ascribed to the scientist, in whose thought the absence of bias is actively cultivated. It is the absence of bias that convinces, that encourages confidence, the premise being that certain materials arranged in certain ways will always yield the same result. Which is to say, something inherent in the combination has been perceived.

I think the great poets work this way. That is, I think the materials are subjective, but the methods are not. I think this is so whether or not detachment is evident in the finished work.

At the heart of that work will be a question, a problem. And we will feel, as we read, a sense that the poet was not wed to any one outcome. The poems themselves are like experiments, which the reader is freely invited to recreate in his own mind. Those poets who claustrophobically oversee or bully or dictate response prematurely advertise the deficiencies of the chosen particulars, as though without strenuous guidance the reader might not reach an intended conclusion. Such work suffers from the excision of doubt: Milton may have written proofs, but his poems compel because they dramatize questions. The only illuminations are like Psyche's, who did not know what she'd find.

The true has about it an air of mystery or inexplicability. This mystery is an attribute of the elemental: art of the kind I mean to describe will seem the furthest concentration or reduction or clarification of its substance; it cannot be further refined without being changed in its nature. It is essence, ore, wholly unique, and therefore comparable to nothing. No "it" will have existed before; what will have existed are other instances of like authenticity.

The true, in poetry, is felt as insight. It is very rare, but beside it other poems will seem merely intelligent comment.

Nominated by Jack Marshall, Arthur Smith

CAPITALISM

by MARK LEVINE

from COLORADO REVIEW

It's a kind of reflex, taking the fall.
If you listen closely you can hear me.
The flier says
Put your ear to the page, get let in
on a secret.

Giselle has wires looped round her ankles and wrists.
It's me who is her choreographer. It's me working
the cranks.
I learned from playing with wind-up toy soldiers
on the edge of the table.
Rat-a-tat.
I learned from the wind-up soldier.

I've sat in the kitchen
too long.
My eyes get hot and wet and I start
making up reasons.
Such as "Indifferent Nature" or "Thirty
days hath September."

I'm not ready to go.
Time's up and I want
to stay.
I'm stamping my feet, pasting bread in my ears.
The buzzer continues.

Giselle has forgot what it's like
to move.

She just hangs there, getting fed, her joints swelling
some, but not bad.
"Giselle," I say—I am rubbing her with a butterfly net—
"The train needs its coal, and coal is a lot
like diamonds."

Bending my knees when I speak. More a shovel
than a lover.

Giselle invokes the nineteenth century.
She thinks her wires are
invisible wires.
She thinks her wires are wings.
She will not be compared to a summer's day.

But Giselle—
Does the War Machine not love you?
Are you not crammed with things
that the War Machine needs? Are your people not
a hungry people?
Do officers not bang their heels on the dining-car table?
Is the name of this dance
not "Giselle"?

Stay as you are, Giselle,
thinking of Nature, thinking of
God.
Forget that it's me that winds you up.

The Industrial Revolution is dreaming, Giselle.
There are more of you where I come from.

Nominated by Colorado Review

LOST BRILLIANCE

by RITA DOVE

from BLACK WARRIOR REVIEW

I miss that corridor drenched in shadow,
sweat of centuries steeped into stone.
After the plunge, after my shrieks
had diminished and his oars sighed
up to the smoking shore,
the bulwark's gray pallor soothed me.
Even the columns seemed kind, their murky sheen
like the lustrous skin of a roving eye.

I used to stand at the top of the stair
where the carpet flung down
its extravagant heart. Flames
teased the lake into glimmering licks.
I could pretend to be above the earth
rather than underground: a Venetian
palazzo or misty chalet tucked into
an Alp, that mixture of comfort
and gloom . . . nothing was simpler

to imagine. But it was more difficult
each evening to descend: all that marble
flayed with the red plush of privilege
I traveled on, slow nautilus
unwinding in terrified splendor
to where he knew to meet me—

my consort, my match,
though much older and sadder.

In time, I lost the capacity
for resolve. It was as if
I had been traveling all these years
without a body,
until his hands found me—
and then there was just
the two of us forever:
one who wounded,
and one who served.

Nominated by Brenda Hillman

MORICHES

fiction by DEAN SCHABNER

from WITNESS

THE NIGHT my parents met—and according to my father, the night I was conceived—two black men were lynched a mile outside Pineton, Mississippi. My father was in Pineton trying to get a man to sell him a dog, a Jack Russell terrier. My father was a twenty-one-year-old blond guy from New York. He had some money from his great aunt. He was spending it. That was 1957 and he had a little English sports car that broke down a lot. He was driving it around the country and he was in Pineton because a man in Hattiesburg told him about these dogs and this Pineton guy who bred them.

My mother was a tall black woman. She sang in the church; she wanted to be a singer. My father saw her in the street after he'd finally convinced the man to sell him one of the dogs. He was sitting on a bench with the puppy between his feet and she walked by. This is what he told me: She looked at the dog, then at him and he stood up and almost bowed. He had to stop himself. He had curly yellow hair and a band of freckles across his nose and cheeks. He said, Do you know a mechanic?

She looked at his face. I got all this from my father. It was a story he loved to tell, how she rolled her eyes away from him, how her lower lip pushed her mouth up and then how she rolled the words off her lips and laid them out in front of him. You got a problem?

My father nodded at the car and she looked at it a minute.

I got my brother works on cars, she said. You don't want to take your car to him.

382

Why not? my father said. Isn't he any good?

She looked at him a minute, standing almost perfectly still. Then she told him how to get there.

He asked her to go with him, but she wouldn't, so he followed her directions. The car fought every bit of the way down the dusty narrow roads between the scrub pines. The dog slept in his lap. It was tiny and warm between his legs.

Her brother was a lot older than she was. His hair thinned back off his forehead and he listened to my father like he was speaking a foreign language, like not a word of it, hardly even the sound of it meant anything to him. He was my uncle, I guess, but I never met the man.

When my mother showed up, my father was working under the hood of the car in front of her brother's shop. She watched my father put the motor back together. He'd taken off his shirt. It was hot as hell there, he told me, and the sweat ran off him. When he finished it was sunset. He turned the switch and it lit up, the engine's buzz hot in the yard. She'd listened to him talk. My father told me he never knew what all he said. He ran his mouth. He always did when he was doing something. So I could hear him cursing the car some, talking to it, coaxing it and talking, too, to whoever was around him, about the sky, the weather, launching into a story about some exploit, something silly you never got to hear because it was all broken up by the curses and coaxes and moving on to something else. She listened to it, holding the puppy, playing with it, and when he started the car up, when it sat there quivering like a dog ready to hunt, she stood up, the terrier in her hands.

You want to take a ride? he said.

She went, and I was conceived out in some field outside Pineton, my mother sitting on my father's lap on the trunk of the car and the stars sharp in the hot still night.

My mother was twenty and wanted to get out. She wasn't going to wait for a second chance. It might sound bad, but I know my father never thought of it that way. She left with him that night, and he cut short his cross-country trip to come back to New York. She tried to find work singing until she got too big with me. My father went to NYU and worked part-time jobs. My mother stayed home with me until I was big enough to take to rehearsals or leave with somebody. She got to be pretty well-known for a while, but by then my father had taken me out to the Moriches, on Long Island, where he went to work doing research on ducks. I grew up out there, in a little house between two duck farms. I heard those birds day and night, wanking at each other. I smelled their shit so much I almost didn't notice it anymore. The stink of it probably got in my hair, which was kinky, like my mother's, but some weird dusty yellow. I let it grow in a bush on my head.

At first my father took me around with him to the farms. He'd walk around the coops, now and then picking up a duck, looking into its eyes, ruffling its feather, pinching a quill or two between his fingers. They all looked sick to me. Wozniak. Olczyski. The men would follow him, watching him. My father was thin and though his clothes were just as worn as theirs, he had a sharpness about him the farmers didn't. I knew he was in control. They looked all the same to me. Big men, fleshy, with round pasty faces, their hairlines lost to the top of their heads, at least from my angle. And slow-moving. I was always glad to get back in the car with my father, to have it be just us.

In 1974, when I was a junior, I started seeing Claudette Reux. She was in choir, too. Her skin was white and her hair was a brown you might not notice on another girl, but when she pushed it back out of her face or gathered it up quickly in her hands to braid it, her arms in a jagged halo around her head, it seemed like the only hair she could have.

Late that fall she'd been hit by a car when she was riding her bicycle. She wasn't hurt bad, but she busted up her mouth and chipped a tooth. After she got the stitches out she guarded her smile. I saw her one night, around Christmas, at a party. I started talking to her: we were teasing each other, but even when she laughed she tried to keep her lips closed. A couple of times she put her hand up to cover her open mouth.

I said, What, you got a cat you're keeping in there?

For a minute she had this queer look, then she smiled her smile—her lips opened and I saw the tooth. That was when I went off for her. Not that I hadn't been looking at her in chorus, listening for her voice, pulling it out of the other sopranos. But that night her face was so pretty, and there was that chipped tooth.

It was winter and we used to hang out in the barn in back of Wally Kryzyrsky's. That was where it started between us. A bunch of kids hung out there. It had been Wally's father's shop, but his father died. His tools were still there, dusty, some of them rusting out, and Wally liked to throw them around, tear the place up. It was somewhere to go to hang out and get high where it was warm.

There was a bunch of us there, and she came in with a friend of hers. She had an old fur coat on. The longer we were there the more we kept looking at each other. When I finally smiled at her, she smiled back, showing me that broken tooth between her pretty lips. I felt like she'd given me something.

I walked her home through the fields behind Wally's, and the bay muck scent hung in the air with the duck shit. But close to her I smelled lemon, like she'd just torn one open with her fingers.

I never knew what people thought about my father and me then. We lived in that little house as long as I can remember, and whenever we saw my mother it was in the city. We'd go hear her sing and then maybe go out with her. I was blond, my eyes were brown. I had my father's color but my mother's features, like she was hiding under my skin.

What I'm talking about is my mother. That she's black. None of the white kids called me nigger, though they did the other black kids. My father cured duck diseases and that made him pretty popular in the Moriches. I went wherever I wanted to and nobody turned me away. That winter there had been riots up west, in Bellport and C.I. I remember the guys in our school looking at each other, but nothing happened.

Claudette and I fucked for the first time on our back porch, while my father was off at work. It had been cold that morning, but rain started to fall toward noon and fog rose off the creek at the back of our yard. The dampness held the duck smell down. It was a week after we'd really started going together. We cut out at lunch and went to my house and the musty old couch on the porch.

I understood my father being able to tell his story over and over. That day with Claudette Reux—I see her smile; I taste the gum she spit out as we went up the two wooden steps. I hear the ducks and the creak of the couch. It doesn't matter what anything's been like since.

There was no coaxing, no fooling, no faking this to get that between us. She spat out that gum into the dirt beside the stairs and when I kissed her standing there she moved me, just a lean, towards the couch. I didn't need anything more than that.

Even though I thought about her all the time, everything else fell in place. My grades went through the roof. My history teacher talked to me about colleges. My science teacher talked to me about marine biology. I thought about those things, too, and it all seemed to have weight. I felt like I had weight and the strength to carry it. Claudette and I talked about the duck farms closing, the houses being built everywhere up west, the grubby little shopping centers that straddled the road in Shirley and were spreading out to us. I started feeling like I loved everything that was going to be gone.

My father had given up the research stuff by then. He taught school in Riverhead. Biology. Everybody thought he was young to be my dad. He was steady with another teacher up there, Sally. She was a redhead, in her late twenties; later on he married her.

One night the four of us, Claudette and I and the two of them, ate dinner together. Afterwards we sat and talked, or listened to my father talk. We drank beer and Claudette and I held hands under the table. My father put on the records of my mother singing. The albums of blues tunes and spirituals, just her, a sax and a piano, were his favorites, and he winked at me. That was all. He didn't tell the story—just the wink. I didn't know what Sally knew.

That wink was the way he and I had always lived. The night Martin Luther King was shot we were sitting, my father and I and his friend Darryl Brown, in my father's VW, listening to the news to get the baseball scores. We had the windows open— Darryl Brown was smoking a cigar, hanging his arm out the window and puffing the smoke out into the cool night. My father was talking about St. Louis and how good he thought they could be. He kept turning his head around to me. What was I, ten? Then it came on and we sat there, the three of us, listening.

Well, that just about fucks things, my father said. What do you think, he said to me. Doesn't that just fuck things no goddamn end?

We went back to our house and the two of them got drunk on dark rum. It tasted like tar to me, but I took it when my father pushed his glass towards me. He told the story of my mother that night, though Darryl Brown knew it, I'm sure. The Jack Russell was still alive then, and he watched the three of us sitting around the kitchen table from the couch where he liked to sleep. That dog, my father said, pointing to him. That dog is who you have to thank. Without him, everything would be different. He said it over and over.

Whenever Claudette asked me about my mother I told her she was a singer, and she didn't live with us, but that my dad and she were friends and that they'd never been married. All that was true. I never heard him bad-mouth her.

That night we were sitting around, and when it got late, my father and Sally went to his room. Before I knew it I had Claudette on my lap, her skirt around her waist and my pants undone. I was up inside her, rocking her on the edge of the seat when the door opened and my father came out. His hair was messed up and his shirt was half unbuttoned and out of his pants. He looked confused and he kind of waved at us as he went to the bathroom. He kept his face turned away, squinting his eyes like we were a light and he had just woken up. Claudette didn't move away. If anything, she let herself down on me a little more and she held me in there. We stayed still while he was in the bathroom, just looking at each other. Her cheeks were red and her lips looked dark and big, like I'd smeared them a little. When my father closed the door to his room she took in a deep breath and hugged me. I felt like that was what I wanted from life—to be inside her and have her head on my shoulder, her lips on my neck, and have my father a little embarrassed, closing the door behind him.

One week when the weather was starting to get nice, we skipped out and went into the city. It was Claudette's idea. She wanted to see the North and South American Indian museum that had just opened. We slept on the train in.

Maybe none of this means anything to you. When I started going out with Claudette I was sixteen. I'd been living with my father, alone with him, for more than ten years. It was me and him, like we were brothers or something. He had his job. I had

387

school. I didn't really know what it was like to be looked at the way other kids' parents looked at them, that fear and confusion and anger about losing control over this life they had made. When my father talked to me it was just to talk.

We went to the Indian museum and looked at oars and weapons, pipes and fabulous ceremonial clothes. Hats made of animal heads and cloaks covered with feathers and beads. In one room were pale buffalo skins with paintings on them that told stories. The horses and men were awkward, but they were individuals, too; you could tell them apart and they told a story that must have said something about the people who lived inside.

Claudette held my hand. We hugged and kissed. I stole a grasp of her bare side under her sweater, or I touched her cheek, her hair. The museum was quiet. Guards stood around together, talking, joking. We couldn't hear what they were saying, but their deep laughs rose to the high ceilings and echoed up there like thunder in the hills.

When we got to the shrunken heads she let go of my hands. She leaned close to the glass, then put her hands on the case. There were a dozen of them and they looked like rotten pears or apples; the eyes were closed, the noses and mouths wrinkled into the rest of the brownness. Most of them had long dark hair knotted up on their heads. Claudette's breath steamed the glass and one of the guards clapped his hands twice. We both looked at him and he shook his head. Claudette stepped away from the case.

You look at these guys, they could be looking back at you, she said. What would make you want to—She shook her head. Why would you want to take somebody and shrink up their head, then hang it around and look at it all the time?

I don't think they looked at them all the time, I said.

She looked at the case, then at me. Could you?

They thought it was medicine, I said. Power or something.

I'll bet it is. Something like that, she said. She stepped back close to the heads. This one, she said, pointing at one on the top row. There was a pattern of scars on the cheek, and the eyelids seemed about to open, like the eyes had just rolled up: like the guy heard something and wanted to see it. We stood there awhile but he didn't open up. Their world must be so different, she said, and she put her arm around me.

388

We rode a bus downtown. The streets were lighting up and the sky was going black. She sat close to me. I remember kissing her for minutes, holding her under her coat and then looking around the bus like I'd come up from underwater. I felt like a seal. I felt on that bus like I knew what life was about and had it in my hand. And those guys sitting around us, looking away. Hurrying, even as they sat in their seats. Reading the papers about scandals and shit. It looked to me like they'd forgotten they were alive.

We walked around the village looking at menus posted in the windows of restaurants. There were students from the university, and bums and old hippie types. But then there were other people who seemed to be looking around, like it was all there for them to see.

We ate Indian food. She said, We might as well stick with it, right?

I started to say it wasn't the same Indian, but she rolled her eyes and gave a quick grab at my side to tickle me.

We had no idea what to eat, but we piled it on. Big puffs of bread, little rolls of potato and peas, and strange-shaped fried things we could only guess at. We ate everything they put in front of us. A dish of meat and potatoes stewed in hot, thick green sauce. Bright red chicken. Little bowls of red onions, lentil sauce, some brown sweetish stuff. I didn't know what the hell it was then, but she and I gobbled it all up and then sat stunned with the food in our bellies. We blew our noses. My tongue felt like it was swelled twice its size. I could hardly get a word out around it.

There was nobody else in the place but an old couple by the door. The waiters stood together at the window to the kitchen in the back. They talked to each other, soft in their own language. After a while one brought over a pot of tea and two cups. He said, Tea, putting the word out delicately between us the way he put out the cups and the blue china pot.

When we went outside she took my arm and said, Now what? I didn't know, and that was when I saw my mother across the street. She had her collar turned up, but she didn't walk like she was cold. She was talking to a man, looking around. She saw me, too, then, and said my name and laughed.

You don't call me when you come in anymore? she said as she crossed the street. The man stood on the curb a moment, then followed her across the street.

Claudette was looking at her, and she edged away from me.

My mother gave me a kiss, holding my hand in hers as she did. She introduced the man she was with as Charles Turner, her bass player, and she said, This is my son. Claudette slipped her arm out of mine. I looked at her and she was staring at my mother. Her mouth was just open and her tongue was at that chipped tooth. I touched and she jerked her head at me. I said, Mom, this is Claudette.

Hi, honey, I hear you've got a voice in you, my mom said, and she put out her hand. Claudette took it, but she glanced at me as she did.

Even though she's my mom I can say this. She was a very beautiful woman when she was young. In the picture on her first record, I thought of her that way. A gown off her shoulders, a black-and-white shot, the light on her cheeks, her eyes, her shoulders, the skin across her chest. She's holding the microphone, her lips forward in a soft kiss as she sings. Her voice is naturally deep, but her range is high and strong. Like I said, she was famous. Then she started singing with some different people—avant garde. She didn't sing the standards anymore. That night, when Claudette Reux slipped her hand out from my arm I saw the age coming in my mother's face and the way she was spreading into her shoulders and her hips.

She said she was singing that night. We were coming to hear her, of course. We went. She got us a table on one side of the room, where we could see everything. It was a little club, in a basement, a V-shaped room with the stage at the point and the bar across the back. In between was jammed with little tables, waitresses in black dodging around them, balancing trays of drinks over their heads. Everybody in the place was talking but us. We weren't saying a word.

When I looked at Claudette I was scared. I was just hoping my mom would come out and sing soon. Claudette was as tough as I'd ever seen her then. She was looking that place in the eye, like everybody who was paying no attention to her was actually facing her down. She was ready for it. I touched her arm and it was cold. Fucking stone, I thought. She was as white as that, and the club light just made her more pale.

The band came out. A sax, piano, Turner on bass and a drummer. They wore bright-colored clothes, African stuff. The sax player had a pointed face and his afro grew back off his head like there was wind blowing at him. The first song started out pretty, a melody that sang a lullaby. Then the sax player started soloing, and he tore it all apart, like a kid too hungry to go to sleep. I'd grown up with it and I love it, I really did, but when I looked at Claudette, she was braced against it like the same wind that was blowing the sax player's hair back was hitting her. When they stopped I said, It's like getting knocked around the ocean.

She just looked at me and I smiled. She turned to the band again, then back at me.

The sax player flipped the mike up and introduced my mother, who came out through the crowd. Everybody was clapping, turning around to see her. She was serious and she bowed her head when she got on stage.

The piano and bass started, a slow beat that rocked in and out of rhythm. The drums came in, steadying it out, but when the sax started up, it seemed to tug the rhythm out again. There was this beat, but everything was going against it. The sax was raw, edgy; he heard the beat and he was fucking with it, like a street tough fucking with some guy.

When my mother started to sing, Claudette put her hand on my leg. Her voice was as deep as the horn's, but it was full and smooth. She didn't sing words, and everything made sense. She rose out of the tune and pulled the rest of them into the air with her.

After the set, she sat with us and talked to Claudette about singers, then paid for our cab to the station. Claudette took my mother's kiss as she put us in the taxi, but she didn't sit close to me. That back seat was huge, and slick as ice.

You played her records for me and never told me? she said somewhere on that ride. You told her about me and you couldn't tell me about her? She could have been punching me. I felt the bruises swelling and watched the city going by.

She slept most of the ride out curled up in the seat. I guess I must have slept, too. I don't know.

Claudette didn't go to school the next day. When I called her, there was no answer, and later, her mother told me she was in bed.

When my father fell asleep that night I went to the back porch and smoked a joint, listening to the ducks muttering in their sleep. For a change, the salt from the creek smelled stronger than their shit. I tried to think of Claudette coming around the side of the house. I'd be able to see her white skin. I'd hear her sneakers in the grass, on the gravel of the walk to the steps. She'd say Hey at the screen door and she'd come in. I wouldn't have to move or say anything until she sat down beside me. Then we'd talk low to each other, wrapped up together.

Until then when I thought about myself, it all seemed a piece. Maybe it was a secret between my father and me, something that made us separate. Maybe that was how I thought of it. On our trips to see my mother, the whole world seemed different—busy, full, the streetlights, clubs and faces, the kind of hipsters who only glanced at our life in the Moriches on their dash out of the Hamptons. There was no way to talk about it to the people I knew out there. I didn't have a name for what I was—black or white—and I guess I'd let myself think because of that, that nobody else did either. Even now, talking about it, I lose the words, the simple direct words that everybody else thought of it in, and that I'd kept out of my head. I watched the moon, big and yellow as it settled into the branches of the trees across the creek.

The phone rang in the kitchen. I let it ring some, then went in and answered it. She said, Are you all right?

Claudette, I said. Are you coming back to school?

Yeah, I'm coming back.

There was a fuss from next door, feathers rustling, wanking, clattering of duckbills. Then it quieted down.

Can I come around? I said.

What do you think?

I rested my forehead against the window. It was cool and slightly damp. I closed my eyes. When I opened them, the moon was down in the black branches across the water and as I watched, it slipped away behind one of the duckhouses over there.

I don't know why I called you, she said. I'm thinking about you and it hurts. It's keeping me up. Every time you looked at me you lied.

I heard her breath against the phone.

I'll see you in school, she said, and she hung up.

When I woke up it was late enough that the sun was starting to burn off the mists and dew from the night before. It wasn't hot really, but there was something about it that wrapped around me. I don't know what I was thinking. I don't think I knew then, either. I walked through the fields up to Main Street, then along east to school. I didn't have my books or anything with me. I know I didn't think about that.

The halls were crowded. It was fourth period. I went straight to the music room. Most of the kids were already there. Claudette was standing by herself at the piano, looking at some sheet music. Then she tore a little piece of paper out of her notebook and spit her gum into it. She crumpled the paper up in her hand, and as she turned to throw it out she saw me, standing just inside the door. I nodded at her and she threw the gum out.

Mr. Melonae came out of his office at the back of the room and told us we were going to start with the Bach. She went to her place and I found mine. I looked on with Alfred Kammen, who I'd sung next to since second grade. Melonae hit a couple of chords to give us the notes. Claudette was hitting them to herself. I could see her feeling the vibrations in her throat, listening inside her head. Then she looked at me, all of a sudden, like I had just touched her. I couldn't look away. For a minute I was standing next to her. I smelled the lemon and the beat-up fur coat, and I could hear the notes in her throat.

Melonae said, Let's begin, and counted out the beat. They all started. Alfred Kammen beside me, his voice hitting the notes as though there were piano keys inside him. But Melonae heard something and stopped it. He ranted a minute, then said, Now again, and can we have everyone this time, Miss Reux? She flushed and looked at him, away from me for the first time. Alfred Kammen nudged me, stuck the music at me. I read it through quick and when we started again I sang, and I heard Claudette's voice, full and dark in the center of the sopranos.

I didn't see her again and I didn't try to. I went to my classes. At lunch I went outside, walked to the deli and got a sandwich, which I wolfed down sitting on the steps outside the store. I didn't go back to school. I just didn't want to hear the teachers carrying on.

When my father came home I told him I'd cut out. I don't know what I expected from him. He said, So what happened? I

393

told him it was no big deal and he let it go at that. He said something about the basketball playoffs, the game that night, and whether we'd be able to get it on the TV.

We were watching that game when Claudette came around. I knew when I heard the knock at the back door that it was her. She'd come inside the porch when I got out there. I opened the door but she stayed out in the darkness.

What are you doing? she said.

Watching the game, I said. I stood a minute, then I just felt stupid. I went out into the darkness with her. The night was warmer than I thought it would be. Except for the TV it was quiet.

She sat down on the couch and I sat there too, but not up close to her. Then I moved a little.

You sounded good today, I said. Is Melonae going to give you that solo in Bach?

He had me in after school, to hear me on it, she said. He kept correcting me, making me go back. Her head was down, but she was looking at me. She kept her voice low, and I leaned closer to her.

He'll give it to you, I said, keeping my voice just as low as hers. I wanted to feel it touch her. I wanted it to go get her for me, to put me back inside her. I said, He wouldn't work with you if he was going to give it to somebody else. You know, I can hear you out of all of them, I can hear them following you. Melonae can hear that, too, anybody can.

I'm supposed to blend in, she said.

Not if they're not hitting it, I said. I put my hand on her thigh, her shoulder, then her neck. I felt the few loose strands from her braid, and with my thumb I touched her cheek.

She lifted her face a little and turned out of my hand, but she caught it in her own and held it there, in midair. I've got to think about this, she said.

Nothing's changed, I said.

She stood up and walked to the screen. She put her face up close to it, then she came back to me. She knelt and put her hands on my thighs. I feel like I've been lied to, like you thought you couldn't trust me.

She started to get up but I put my hands on her shoulders. I brought her closer to me and leaned forward to her. She's just my mother, I whispered. I'm no different.

394

That's not what I'm talking about. She was crying, not hard; she was fighting it, holding it tight in her eyes, her cheeks and her lips. It hit me, the salt smell of her tears, like seasickness. She wiped one eye, then the other with the back of her hand. I've got to go home, she said.

I'll walk you.

She let me. We woke the ducks cutting through the field and along the creek behind my house. The moon was high and small, white as a tooth, I took her hand for a ways. At her house I took it again. Then she went in.

My father had fallen asleep on the couch. The game was over, the news done. Some old movie had started. I shut it off and my father opened his eyes. He looked at me and sat up. He rubbed his cheeks then looked at me again. His face was queer, pasty, his hair rumpled and his eyes red.

Who won? I asked.

He looked at the black screen. I fell asleep at halftime, he said.

I started to go out to my room, but my father, still sitting on the couch started to talk, and I stopped in the door to listen. He didn't look at me, but I guess he knew I was still there. He could talk softly, but he kept his voice solid; he caught you by the arm and held you, pulled you close to him where you could smell his breath.

When I looked at your mother the first time, I didn't think anything but what a beautiful girl she was, he said. There was an instant there when she wasn't anything but beautiful. I think about that, when I see her again after a while, or when I listen to her sing. It's just beauty for an instant—then everything else comes in and I don't know which is right. He rubbed at his hair. I hope you can figure it out, he said. I always thought you came out of that moment when I didn't see anything but—He looked at me and it was like I was inside his dream with him; we were both young and the world was beauty. I guess I didn't see anything but what I wanted to see, he said.

Why'd you leave Mom? I said.

I didn't ever leave her, he said. She was doing one thing and I was doing another.

What if she wanted to come back?

It's not like that, he said. Your mother and I, we weren't ever like, married. We weren't ever the way you see people here. We loved each other, but a lot of it went through you.

Did she ever want me?

She always wanted you. She still does. I thought you knew all this.

Yeah, I guess I do, I said. I'm just thinking about it.

With Claudette?

With her and everything.

My father stood up, picking up his shoes as he did. He stopped by me on his way to his room. You want to know what I say? Think about her and forget all that everything. Good night.

I didn't turn on the light in my room. I opened the window an inch or two. The ducks were restless in the warm night. I could hear them rustling their feathers, shifting their feet in the sand and feed and shit they stood around in. I heard my father, in his room, undress and get into bed. I slipped off my shoes and went back out to the living room. I found that first album my mother put out. I put the thick heavy disk on the turntable and turned the volume on so low, it was barely louder than the muttering of the ducks in their sleep. All I needed was the hint of it. I felt Claudette's hand on my thigh, that night when we saw her, and I thought, There's no line between Claudette and everything else, the way my father said. My mother's voice was whispering in my ear. I thought, The only line is the one I've drawn myself. Now it was a circle around me that I wanted to step out of. There was no world of beauty, just one where ducks chattered in their sleep and on warm nights you breathed the thick air off the stinking salty creeks.

Nominated by Witness

GOOD AND BAD

fiction by LUCIA BERLIN

from SO LONG (Black Sparrow Press)

NUNS TRIED HARD TO teach me to be good. In high school it was Miss Dawson. Santiago College, 1952. Six of us in the school were going on to American colleges; we had to take American History and Civics from the new teacher, Ethel Dawson. She was the only American teacher, the others were Chilean or European.

We were all bad to her. I was the worst. If there was to be a test and none of us had studied I could distract her with questions about the Gadsden Purchase for the whole period, or get her started on segregation or American imperialism if we were really in trouble.

We mocked her, imitated her nasal Boston whine. She had a tall lift on one shoe because of polio, wore thick wire-rimmed glasses. Splayed gap teeth, a horrible voice. It seemed she deliberately made herself look worse by wearing mannish, mismatched colors, wrinkles, soup-spotted slacks, garish scarves on her badly-cut hair. She got very red-faced when she lectured and she smelled of sweat. It was not simply that she flaunted poverty . . . Madame Tournier wore the same shabby black skirt and blouse day after day, but the skirt was cut on the bias, the black blouse, green and frayed with age, was of fine silk. Style, cachet were all-important to us then.

She showed us movies and slides about the condition of the Chilean miners and dock workers, all of it the U.S.A.'s fault. The ambassador's daughter was in the class, a few admirals' daughters. My father was a mining engineer, worked with the CIA. I knew he truly believed Chile needed the United States. Miss Dawson thought that she was reaching impressionable young minds, whereas she was talking to spoiled American brats. Each one of us had a rich, handsome, powerful American daddy. Girls feel about their fathers at that age like they do about horses. It is a passion. She implied that they were villains.

Because I did most of the talking I was the one she zeroed in on, keeping me after class, and one day even walked with me in the rose garden, complaining about the elitism of the school. I lost patience with her.

"What are you doing here then? Why don't you go teach the poor if you're so worried about them? Why have anything to do with us snobs at all?"

She told me that this was where she was given work, because she taught American History. She didn't speak Spanish yet, but all her spare time was spent working with the poor and volunteering in revolutionary groups. She said it wasn't a waste of time working with us . . . if she could change the thinking of one mind it would be worthwhile.

"Perhaps you are that one mind," she said. We sat on a stone bench. Recess was almost over. Scent of roses and the mildew of her sweater.

"Tell me, what do you do with your weekends?" she asked.

It wasn't hard to sound utterly frivolous, but I exaggerated it anyway. Hairdresser, manicurist, dressmaker. Lunch at the Charles. Polo, rugby or cricket, *thés dansants*, dinners, parties until dawn. Mass at El Bosque at seven on Sunday morning, still wearing evening clothes. The country club then for breakfast, golf or swimming, or maybe the day in Algarrobo at the sea, skiing in winter. Movies of course, but mostly we danced all night.

"And this life is satisfying to you?" she asked.

"Yes, it is."

"What if I asked you to give me your Saturdays, for one month, would you do it? See a part of Santiago that you don't know."

"Why do you want me?"

"Because, basically, I think you are a good person. I think you could learn from it." She clasped both my hands. "Give it a try."

Good person. But she had caught me earlier, with the word Revolutionary. I did want to meet revolutionaries, because they were bad.

398

Everyone seemed a lot more upset than necessary about my Saturdays with Miss Dawson, which then made me really want to do it. I told my mother I was going to help the poor. She was disgusted, afraid of disease, toilet seats. I even knew that the poor in Chile had no toilet seats. My friends were shocked that I was going with Miss Dawson at all. They said she was a loony, a fanatic, and a lesbian, was I crazy or what?

The first day I spent with her was ghastly, but I stuck with it out of bravado.

Every Saturday morning we went to the city dump, in a pickup truck filled with huge pots of food. Beans, porridge, biscuits, milk. We set up a big table in a field next to miles of shacks made from flattened tin cans. A bent water faucet about three blocks away served the entire shack community. There were open fires in front of the squalid lean-tos, burning scraps of wood, cardboard, shoes, to cook on.

At first the place seemed to be deserted, miles and miles of dunes. Dunes of stinking, smouldering garbage. After a while, through the dust and smoke, you could see that there were people all over the dunes. But they were the color of the dung, their rags just like the refuse they crawled in. No one stood up, they scurried on all fours like wet rats, tossing things into burlap bags that gave them humped animal backs, circling on, darting, meeting each other, touching noses, slithering away, disappearing like iguanas over the ridges of the dunes. But once the food was set up scores of women and children appeared, sooty and wet, smelling of decay and rotted food. They were glad for the breakfast, squatted, eating with bony elbows out like preying mantis on the garbage hills. After they had eaten, the children crowded around me; still crawling or sprawled in the dirt, they patted my shoes, ran their hands up and down my stockings.

"See, they like you," Miss Dawson said. "Doesn't that make you feel good?"

I knew that they liked my shoes and stockings, my red Chanel jacket.

Miss Dawson and her friends were exhilarated as we drove away, chatting happily. I was sickened and depressed.

"What good does it do to feed them once a week? It doesn't make a dent in their lives. They need more than biscuits once a week, for lord's sake."

Right. But until the revolution came and everything was shared you had to do whatever helped at all.

"They need to know somebody realizes they live out here. We tell them that soon things will change. Hope. It's about hope," Miss Dawson said.

We had lunch in a tenement in the south of the city, six flights up. One window that looked onto an airshaft. A hot plate, no running water. Any water they used had to be carried up those stairs. The table was set with four bowls and four spoons, a pile of bread in the center. There were many people, talking in small groups. I spoke Spanish, but they spoke in a heavy *caló* with almost no consonants, and were hard for me to understand. They ignored us, looked at us with amused tolerance or complete disdain. I didn't hear revolutionary talk, but talk about work, money, filthy jokes. We all took turns eating lentils, drinking *chicha*, a raw wine, using the same bowls and glass as the person before.

"Nice you don't seem to mind about dirt," beamed Miss Dawson.

"I grew up in mining towns. Lots of dirt." But the cabins of Finnish and Basque miners were pretty, with flowers and candles, sweet-faced Virgins. This was an ugly, filthy place with misspelled slogans on the walls, communist pamphlets stuck up with chewing gum. There was a newspaper photograph of my father and the minister of mines, splattered with blood.

"Hey!" I said. Miss Dawson took my hand, stroked it. "Sh," she said in English. "We're on first name basis here. Don't for heaven's sake say who you are. Now, Adele, don't be uncomfortable. To grow up you need to face all the realities of your father's personae."

"Not with blood on them."

"Precisely that way. It is a strong possibility and you should be aware of it." She squeezed both my hands then.

After lunch she took me to "El Niño Perdido," an orphanage in an old stone ivy-covered building in the foothills of the Andes. It was run by French nuns, lovely old nuns, with fleur-de-lis coifs and blue-grey habits. They floated through the dark rooms, above the stone floors, flew down the passages by the flowered courtyard, popped open wooden shutters, calling out in bird-like voices. They brushed away insane children who were biting their legs, dragging them by their little feet. They washed ten faces in a row, all the eyes blind. They fed six mongoloid giants, reaching up with spoons of oatmeal.

These orphans all had something the matter. Some were insane, others had no legs or were mute, some had been burned over their entire bodies. No noses or ears. Syphilitic babies and mongoloids in their teens. The assorted afflictions spilled together from room to room, out into the courtyard into the lovely unkempt garden.

"There are many things needed to do," Miss Dawson said. "I like feeding and changing babies. You might read to the blind children . . . they all seem particularly intelligent and bored."

There were few books. La Fontaine in Spanish. They sat in a circle, staring at me, really blankly. Nervous, I began a game, clapping and stomping kind of game like musical chairs. They liked that and so did some other children.

I hated the dump on Saturdays but I liked going to the orphanage. I even liked Miss Dawson when we were there. She spent her time bathing and rocking babies and singing to them, while I made up games for the older children. Some things worked and others didn't. Relay races didn't because nobody would let go of the stick. Jump rope was great because two boys with Down's syndrome would turn the rope for hours on end without stopping, while everybody, especially the blind girls, took turns. Even nuns jumped, jump jump they hovered blue in the air. Farmer in the Dell. Button Button. Hide-and-go-seek didn't work because nobody came home. The orphans were glad to see me; I loved going there, not because I was good, but because I liked to play.

Saturday nights we went to revolutionary theatre or poetry readings. We heard the greatest Latin American poets of our century. These were poets whose work I would later love, whom I would study and teach. But then I did not listen. I suffered an agony of self-consciousness and confusion. We were the only Americans there; all I heard were the attacks against the United States. Many people asked questions about American policy that I couldn't answer; I referred them to Miss Dawson and translated her answers, ashamed and baffled by what I told them, about segregation, Anaconda. She didn't realize how much the people scorned us, how they mocked her banal communist clichés about their reality. They laughed at me with my Josef haircut and nails, my expensive casual clothes. At one theatre group they put me on stage and the director hollered, "OK *Gringa*, tell me why you are in my country!" I froze and sat down, to hooting and laughter. Finally I told Miss Dawson I couldn't go out on Saturday nights anymore.

Dinner and dancing at Marcelo Errazuriz's. Martinis, consommé in little cups on the terrace, fragrant gardens beyond us. A six course dinner that began at eleven. Everyone teased me about my days with Miss Dawson, begged me to tell them where I went. I couldn't talk about it, not with my friends nor my parents. I remember someone making a joke about me and my *rotos*, "broken" meant poor people then. I felt ashamed, aware that there were almost as many servants in the room as guests.

I joined Miss Dawson in a workers' protest outside the United States Embassy. I had only walked about a block when a friend of my father's, Frank Wise, grabbed me out of the crowd, took me to the Crillon Hotel.

He was furious. "What in God's name do you think you are doing?" He soon understood what Miss Dawson didn't . . . that I had not the faintest idea of politics, of what any of this was about. He told me that it would be terrible for my father if the press found out what I was doing. I understood that.

On another Saturday afternoon I agreed to stand downtown and collect money for the orphanage. I stood on one corner and Miss Dawson on another. In only a few minutes dozens of people had insulted and cursed me. I didn't understand, shifted my sign for "Give to El Niño Perdido," and rattled the cup. Tito and Pepe, two friends, were on their way to the Waldorf for coffee. They whisked me away, forced me to go with them to coffee.

"This is *not* done here. Poor people beg. You are insulting the poor. For a woman to solicit anything gives a shocking image. You will destroy your reputation. Also no one would believe you are not keeping the money. A girl simply can't stand on the street unescorted. You can go to charity balls or luncheons, but physical contact with other classes is simply vulgar, and patronizing to them. Also you absolutely cannot afford to be seen with someone of her sexual persuasion in public. My dear, you are too young, you don't understand. . . ."

We drank Jamaican coffee and I listened to them. I told them I saw what they were saying but I couldn't just leave Miss Dawson alone on the corner. They said they would speak to her. The three of us went down Ahumada where she stood, proudly, while passersby muttered *"Gringa loca"* or *"puta coja,"* crippled whore, at her.

"It is not appropriate, in Santiago, for a young girl to do this, and we are taking her home," was all Tito said to her. She looked at him with disdain, and later that week, in the hallway at school she told me it was wrong to let men dictate my actions. I told her that I felt everybody dictated my actions, that I had gone with her on Saturdays a month longer than I had first promised. That I wasn't going any more.

"It is wrong for you to return to a totally selfish existence. To fight for a better world is the only reason for living. Have you learned nothing?"

"I learned a lot. I see that many things need to change. But it's their struggle, not mine."

"I can't believe you can say that. Don't you see, that's what is wrong with the world, that attitude."

She limped crying to the bathroom, was late to class, where she told us there would be no class that day. The six of us went out and lay on the grass in the gardens, away from the windows so no one could see that we weren't in class. The girls teased me, said that I was breaking Miss Dawson's heart. She was obviously in love with me. Did she try to kiss me? This really made me confused and mad. In spite of everything I was beginning to like her, her dogged naive commitment, her hopefulness. She was like a little kid, like one of the blind children when they gasped with pleasure, playing in the water sprinkler. Miss Dawson never flirted with me or tried to touch me all the time like boys did. But she wanted me to do things I didn't want to do and I felt like a bad person for not wanting to, for not caring more about the injustice in the world. The girls got mad at me because I wouldn't talk about her. They called me Miss Dawson's mistress. There was nobody I could talk to about any of this, nobody to ask what was right or wrong, so I just felt wrong.

It was windy my last day at the dump. Sand sifted into the porridge in glistening waves. When the figures rose on the hills it was with a swirl of dirt so they looked like silver ghosts, der-

403

vishes. None of them had shoes and their feet crept silently over the soggy mounds. They didn't speak, or shout to each other, like most people do who work together, and they never spoke to us. Beyond the steaming dung hills was the city and above us all the white Andes. They ate. Miss Dawson didn't say a word, gathering up the pots and utensils in the sigh of wind.

We had agreed to go to a farm workers' rally outside of town that afternoon. We ate *churrascos* on the street, stopped by her apartment for her to change.

Her apartment was dingy and airless. The fact that her hot plate for cooking was on the toilet tank made me feel ill, as did the odor of old wool and sweat and hair. She changed in front of me, which I found shocking and frightening, her naked, distorted blue-white body. She put on a sleeveless sundress with no brassiere.

"Miss Dawson, that would be all right at night, in someone's home, or at the beach, but you just can't go around bare like that in Chile."

"I pity you. All your life you are going to be paralyzed by What Is Done, by what people tell you you should think or do. I do not dress to please others. It is a very hot day, and I feel comfortable in this dress."

"Well . . . it makes me not comfortable. People will say rude things to us. It is different here, from the United States. . ."

"The best thing that could happen to you would be for you to be uncomfortable once in a while."

We took several crowded busses to get to the *fundo* where the rally was, waiting in the hot sun and standing on the busses. We got down and walked down a beautiful lane lined with eucalyptus, stopped to cool off in the stream by the lane.

We had arrived too late for the speeches. There was an empty platform, a banner with "Land Back to the People" hanging askew behind the mike. There was a small group of men in suits, obviously the organizers, but most of the people were farm laborers. Guitars were playing and there was a crowd around a couple dancing *La Cueca* in a desultory fashion, languidly waving handkerchiefs as they circled one another. People were pouring wine from huge vats or standing in line for spit-roasted beef and beans. Miss Dawson told me to find a place at one of the tables, that she would bring our food.

I squeezed into a spot at the end of a table crowded with families. Nobody was talking politics, it seemed that these were just country people who had come to a free barbeque. Everyone was very, very drunk. I could see Miss Dawson, chattering away in line, she was drinking wine too, gesticulating and talking very loud so people would understand her.

"Isn't this great?" she asked, bringing two huge plates of food. "Let's introduce ourselves. Try to talk to the people more, that's how you learn, and help."

The two farm workers we sat by decided with gales of laughter that we were from another planet. As I had feared, they were amazed by her bare shoulders and visible nipples, couldn't figure out what she was. I realized that not only did she not speak Spanish, she was nearly blind. She would squint through her inch-thick glasses, smiling, but she couldn't see that these men were laughing at us, didn't like us, whatever we were. What were we doing here? She tried to explain that she was in the communist party, but instead of *partido* she kept toasting the "*Fiesta,*" which is a festive party, so they kept toasting her back, "La Fiesta!"

"We've got to leave," I said but she only looked at me slack-jawed and drunk. The man next to me was halfheartedly flirting with me, but I was more worried about the big drunk man next to Miss Dawson. He was stroking her shoulders with one hand while he ate a rib with the other. She was laughing away until he started grabbing her and kissing her, then she began to scream.

Miss Dawson ended up on the ground, sobbing uncontrollably. Everyone had rushed over at first, but they soon left, muttering "Nothing but some drunken *gringa.*" The men we had sat by now ignored us totally. She got up and began to run toward the road; I followed her. When she got to the stream she tried to wash herself off, her mouth and her chest. She just got muddy and wet. She sat on the bank, crying, her nose running. I gave her my handkerchief.

"Miss Perfect! An ironed linen handkerchief!" she sneered.

"Yes," I said, fed up with her and only concerned now with getting home. Still crying, she staggered down the path toward the main road, where she started to hail down cars. I pulled her back into the trees.

"Look, Miss Dawson. You can't hitchhike here. They don't understand . . . it could get us in trouble, two women hitchhiking. Listen to me!"

405

But a farmer in an old truck had stopped, the engine ticking on the dusty road. I offered him money to take us to the outskirts of town. He was going all the way to downtown, could take us all the way to her house easy for 20 pesos. We climbed into the bed of the truck.

She put her arms around me in the wind. I could feel her wet dress, her sticky armpit hairs as she clung to me.

"You can't go back to your frivolous life! Don't leave! Don't leave me," she kept saying until at last we got to her block.

"Goodbye," I said. "Thanks for everything," or something dumb like that. I left her on the curb, blinking at my cab until it turned the corner.

The maids were leaning on the gate talking to the neighborhood *carabinero*, so I didn't think anyone was home. But my father was there, changing to go play golf.

"You're back early. Where have you been?" he asked.

"To a picnic, with my history teacher."

"Oh, yes. What is she like?"

"OK. She's a communist."

I just blurted that out. It had been a miserable day; I was fed up with Miss Dawson. But that's all it took. Three words to my father. She was fired sometime that weekend and we never saw her again.

No one else knew what had happened. The other girls were happy she was gone. We had a free period now, even though we would have to make up American history when we got to college. There was nobody to speak to. To say I was sorry.

Nominated by Molly Giles

ALFRED CHESTER: GOODBYE TO CHRISTENDOM

by EDWARD FIELD

from EXQUISITE CORPSE

Exept for some juvenilia from his early Paris years, most of Alfred Chester's reviews and literary essays were written between 1962 and 1964, a period when he was one of the most sought after and talked about writers on the New York literary scene. This was in sharp contrast to the neglect a few years later, after he had rejected writing criticism as a betrayal of his talents, and then had progressively withdrawn when his book of short stories, *Behold Goliath* (1964), and his novel, *The Exquisite Corpse* (1967), failed to get more than cursory critical attention.

In the early fifties in Paris, he had served briefly as Book Review Editor for a little magazine called *Merlin*, edited by Alexander Trocchi. But a projected essay on James Baldwin and Ralph Ellison for *Merlin* never materialized. In 1953, an essay on Djuna Barnes, "Watchman, What of the Day?" appeared in the Dutch magazine, *Litterair Paspoort* #VIII, along with an interview. Both have only survived in the Dutch translation, and therefore the versions, retranslated into English and included in the volume of his essays, *Looking for Gent;, Literary Essays & Reviews* (Black Sparrow Press, 1992), are twice removed from the language of the original and, necessarily, mere approximations.

407

Even allowing for this double distortion, the Djuna Barnes piece is clearly juvenilia, and even might be a clever term paper, one that perhaps had received praise from the teacher, and that Chester had brought to Paris with him when he dropped out of Columbia Graduate School in 1951.

But the interview with Hans de Vaal, a young Dutch writer he met in Paris, is a more interesting document. It has clearly been worked over, for Chester's answers are too long and elaborate to be spontaneous. But as an expression of the young Alfred Chester's ideas and enthusiasms it has special significance in light of later developments: for instance, he speaks of Countess Elizabeth de Breza, the disciple of Chopin and piano teacher whom he is to write about so vividly in his story "Head of a Sad Angel." Furthermore, it is startling to see the beginning of his fascination with Paul Bowles, who led him to Morocco, and madness, 10 years later. And *The Exquisite Corpse*, the novel that he is to write there, will be a vivid demonstration of the very ideas he discusses with de Vaal in this interview, where he speaks about the novel as "a continually changing entity." He even defines for de Vaal the Pirandellian ideas about madness and identity that obsessed him throughout his life and were so crucial to his thinking.

The Dutch, an extraordinarily open-hearted people, if somewhat overidealistic and naive, even innocent, to our eyes, are always the first to accept everything new from America, and here we see the interviewer taking the young author as seriously as he took himself. But the interviewer's pomposity is clearly a game, for going out for coffee at the end of the interview seems as important to him as the discussion of literature. Ah, the Dutch, how charming and civilized they are. When Alfred Chester died in 1971, I first learned of it when someone sent me a clipping from a Dutch newspaper. He was remembered there, even after years of silence, whereas in his own country the death of an important writer was ignored in the press.

Locating a copy of this early publication in Amsterdam was for me a small adventure of literary sleuthing—though nothing special, I am assured by academic friends, in the life of a research scholar. For over a decade, I've made it a project to collect and type out Alfred Chester's marvelous letters for future publication. In transcribing the correspondence with Theodora Blum

(McKee), I came across several mentions of an essay and interview to come out in Holland in a literary magazine. Alfred was terribly broke at the time and reported to her on March 3, 1953, that he was being "paid 2500 frs. for an article on *Nightwood.*" (In old francs, this sum translated into about seven dollars.) Again, on April 17, 1953 he wrote, "*Litterair Paspoort* came out with my photo and five large pages all about me." Reference was also made in a letter of November 22, 1953, of a recent story in *Elsevier's Weekblad,* a more popular Dutch magazine, about the literary expatriates in Paris: "There on page 25 you will see a picture of me among many thousand other American writers." And here the fledgling author lists the literary people he knew in Paris that year. "I am the queer-looking bit standing between a North Korean Don Juan and Austyn Wainright. Sitting below me is Jean Garrigue and to her right is Miss Alice Jane Longee of Limerick, Maine (the backer of *Merlin*). At the extreme right is C. Logue, the human diphthong. Above him is Miss Mobile, Alabama (Eugene Walters), and above her is George Plimpton. To GP's left is William Pene DuBois, partly obscured by James Broughton (whose film opens soon in London) and to Broughton's right is William Gardner Smith who they tell me publishes in Pocket Books. As you can see, I have arrived." This was only a year after Alfred Chester's first publication, an essay "Silence in Heaven," in *Botteghe Oscure,* but he was already making enough of a name for himself among the expatriate literati in Paris to merit inclusion in the photo.

The mention of the publication in Holland was a slim enough clue, but a year or two later, when I was visiting my sister who lives in The Hague, I made a trip into Amsterdam, less than an hour by train, to inquire at one of the libraries about *Litterair Paspoort* in which the interview and essay had reportedly appeared. But I was not overly hopeful of locating an obscure little magazine that had probably only existed for a few issues nearly forty years before.

I was not encouraged by my first attempts: The libraries I visited either did not have the magazine in their collections, or were closed for remodeling. Finally, I was directed to the main library of the University of Amsterdam, a bland, modern building which lay in the heart of the tourist belt with its merchant houses on picturesque canals, and which I had passed many times before on the No. 2 tram from Central Station to Leidseplein and never noticed. I doubted that they would allow someone with no academic credentials to simply go in and use the facilities. New York University only allows me, even as an alumnus, to use its library if I pay a fee.

But the Dutch were extraordinarily civilized about this too, and treated me as seriously as they would a visiting scholar, instead of a crazy American with a wild idea. And predictably helpless, I was unable to read the instructions in Dutch on the computerized file catalogs, but a librarian patiently punched in the request for me—research librarians are a remarkable breed. When the file of *Litterair Paspoort* glowed on the screen, and under Issue #VIII of 1953, the name of Alfred Chester in the Table of Contents, I will confess my hair stood on end and my heart beat, as if I had gotten a communication from The Beyond.

In a few minutes, the issue itself was delivered across the counter into my hands. I looked at it for a long time, this magazine the size of *Harper's* or *Encounter*, with a photo I had never seen of a young Alfred Chester, before spreading it face down on the glass table of the photocopying machine, feeding my *quartje* into the slot and pressing the "Print" button.

Until the early sixties in New York, the only critical prose Alfred Chester had written, after the Barnes piece, were reader's reports for The Book of the Month Club (on whose legal-size forms he also wrote long letters to friends). But this latter job was simply one of his desperate free-lance devices to earn some money, just as he had once written a dirty novel for a few hundred dollars for Olympia Press in Paris. He had never seriously considered turning pro, for in spite of his delight in appearing in the literary group photograph, like many in his generation he was an extremist about Literature, and a believer in Art as Redemption. It may sound strange to today's generation that one should write for posterity, rather than immediate recognition, but, in that not-so-long-ago-time before it became perfectly acceptable to aim at celebrity, we all shared a general contempt for writers who "sold out," and expected a true artist to reject fame even if it pursued—as, later, in Morocco, Alfred Chester rebuffed a Time Magazine reporter and photographer who persisted in trying to interview and photograph him (yet afterward, how bitterly he resented his book not getting attention). Occasionally, though, his scorn of writers of his generation who wrote for television and the movies seemed less idealism than jealousy. As he wrote from Paris in February 8, 1954 to Theodora Blum: ". . . it is kind of unpleasant to be getting nowhere what with Eugene [Walters, who had had a short story done on television] and Manny [Rubin, an old classmate who was writing movie and TV scripts] and James Baldwin (to Hollywood yet for 25 Gs) rolling it in hand over fist."

Generally, after thirty, one can't help beginning to feel like this, especially if you're still living in poverty, struggling to pay the rent, while around you your peers are advancing their careers, or at least settling down to the serious adult business of raising a family. In 1959, 30-year-old Alfred Chester returned to New York after nearly a decade in Paris—to "face reality"?, deal with unfinished business?, to grab for the gold ring of success? His novel, *I, Etc.*, after years of work, was still an enormous, shapeless manuscript, from which he rescued various chapters to reshape as short stories. He was still in 1959 committed only to fiction, and continued to write startling stories, among them "From the Phoenix," about the recent breakup with his long-time boyfriend who had left him and gotten married. Though he had had no problem producing his first novel, *Jamie Is My Heart's Desire,* (published in 1956, but written several years earlier), he had struggled for years since then, agonizing over his inability to complete another. But, as if fiction wasn't enough or he was trying to expand his horizons, he also dabbled at playwriting, and wrote four one-acters of a projected series. (One of these has survived, and has been issued as a pamphlet by Kent State University.)

The irony was that the minute he turned to criticism, editors started telephoning him, and he was faced with the shocking but undeniable fact that as a critic he was a rising star on the scene. Though flattering, this was very hard for him to swallow. But understandable—Alfred's critical prose was high powered, racy, and iconoclastic. He was called a "sport" in the critical field for his original, off-center, ruthless, and devastating analyses. To a certain extent one could call this approach to reviewing Literary Criticism as Entertainment, just as Tom Wolfe a few years later invented the essay of Social Criticism as Entertainment.

411

Editors soon expected from him more than book reviews; they wanted controversial re-assessments of major literary figures that they could feature. He was willing to oblige them, and produced, one after another in the next two years, essays on Updike (a famous roasting), Nabokov, Burroughs, Rechy, Albee, Salinger, Genet and others. He worked with great intensity, laboring for long hours through draft after draft, often resorting to dexamils, a then-easily obtainable version of speed that gave him *sitzfleisch* at the typewriter.

Whether it was Norman Podhoretz, editor of *Commentary*, or William Phillips of *Partisan Review*, who first enlisted him in the criticism racket is hard to establish. It was probably *Partisan*, though the essay on Updike appeared first in *Commentary* which came out monthly, and only later that year was the Henry Miller piece published in the quarterly *Partisan Review*. I ought to emphasize that *Commentary* at that time was not the stodgy parochial journal it is today, but like *Partisan Review*, was one of the hippest possible organs on the New York intellectual scene.

But *Partisan* was not so hip as to allow some of Alfred's more outré remarks on Miller. Deleted by the editors after Miller's line, ". . . having taken on his (Miller's) six-incher, she will now be able to take on stallions, bulls, drakes, St. Bernards," was Alfred's reaction that ran: "Six-inches? Eeek! Ooh-ooh! Help!" Or something close to that—I was laughing so hard when he read it to me in manuscript, I may not have got the exact words. That summer *Partisan* further demonstrated its prissy puritanism by rejecting his Genet-like story, "In Praise Of Vespasian." "Our objection is not to the subject or its detail but rather to the rhapsodic treatment. The piece is very well written but the writing is more celebratory than analytical or just plain fictional-prosaic," they wrote. This is so obvious an evasion it doesn't need any analysis. Perhaps it was just typical of the hypocrisy of the time, even in the highest intellectual circles. Thank God for Gay Liberation, is all I can say.

His attacks on and ridicule of some of these major authors was not expedient. He continued to express doubts about them in his correspondence. A year after the essay on Salinger had appeared, he wrote that "his spiritual quest leads nowhere." And his put-down of Burroughs (whom he had gotten to know in Tangier) was confirmed in a letter to Norman Glass on May 3, 1964: "My review of *Naked Lunch* is true. I looked through the book at Paul's [Bowles] the other day. I also listened to some taped cutups (boring) . . . I don't like his easy assimilation of the vocabulary of Industry and Wall Street. Remember, remember, he is the Burroughs Adding Machine. With them, of them, against them,. He is the world of science and mechanics . . . He obviously believes in assimilating the machine and using it to personal advantage."

Of course, with criticism taking over Alfred's life, his fiction had to suffer,and it was with a feeling of loathing for the literary marketplace that he turned his back on his New York success and left for Morocco in the summer of 1963. But even there he had to eat, and was forced to continue to write reviews, though less frequently. Besides the study of Jean Genet for *Commentary*, he reviewed *Candy* by Terry Southern and Mason Hoffenberg, and a last, but enthusiastic piece on Truman Capote's *In Cold Blood* for *Book Week*, at that time a supplement of the *NY Herald Tribune*. Richard Kluger, the editor, also offered him $100 a throw for a monthly column, a significant sum in Morocco at that time, enough to live on for a month.

A vivid picture of Alfred Chester at work on the Genet essay (during the holy month of Ramadan) is given in letters he wrote from Morocco:

January 20, 1964 "My Genet essay tears everything down, the whole of western civilization. It must be there by the 1st, and my column is due today for the *Trib* and I haven't even begun it. I want to write about Mailer as a postscript to the Genet. The Genet says that when Christ died in the 19th Century, Europe woke from a sweet dream with a bloody knife in its hand. It couldn't face its guilt, 2000 years of godless murder so it had to go on believing in dead institutions. *Freud comes briefly to Europe's rescue with his brilliant diversion. He makes guilt personal; though he too denies God, he fouls from the target by making it possible for a man to ignore history in favor of his childhood. We pay attention to our mouths and anuses (tr. assholes). What a relief to be guilty of nothing worse than coveting mama. (And what a perfect totalitarian weapon psychoanalysis potentially, if not actually, is. It reduces all opposition to expressions of personal and misdirected hostility. It makes all protest*

413

infantile.) . . . On and on goes my inexorable logic, until the coup: Hitler had the genius to turn Christianity inside out, to make that of which the Christians were most guilty into the ideals of a new order. Conquest, murder, betrayal, all the crimes of man that had been for twenty centuries blessed by God, again received the blessing, and along with it the blessing of bread."

(The fascinating thing about this and the following quotes from the piece he is writing, and my justification for reproducing them in full, is that all this material was deleted by the editors of *Commentary* from the essay as published. Unfortunately, the original manuscript, which Alfred said was three times as long, thirty pages, has disappeared. Knowing him, I'm sure he would have rewritten all these pieces for his collected essays, and put back much of the deleted material, as well as adding to it, if he were alive.)

Later in the same letter, in his eternal identity crisis, he writes: "I just have never faced myself, really. That probably sounds so boring to you, but it is causing me gigantic anguish. Even my criticism. All I ever do in it is try to show the writers up. I am campier than Rechy, beater than Blitoughs, more brainy than Nabokov, more zen than Salinger, etc., etc. All you have to do is turn the dial and I'm it. Even all this is just because of Genet probably. I'm Genet now. Is there any hope of ever being Alfred?"

It is nevertheless true that if his stories sometimes seem to be written by different authors, as critics have noted, in his essays we hear a single, unmistakable, authoritative voice. But after the lapse into self pity, he returns sure-footedly to the Genet essay: "When one looks back at the slaughtered of Christendom—the American Indians, the Negroes, the Moslems, the Christians themselves, the Asiatics and Africans—six million Jews are a drop in the bloody bucket. Hitler was no uncouth accident in the ladylike history of Europe. He *was* the history of Europe, he *was* Europe merciless up to its very last gasp. And if we don't know of the crimes of the humanists, it is probably only because the humanists won the war . . . To a melody by Mozart, enter Jean Genet, whom François Mauriac has accused of being in league with the devil."

And later: "I finally ran out of dexamils and to my surprise I went right on working, just as many hours and just as

414

clearminded. Lots of coffee though. I don't need liquor either, though I might if I started on a novel. I can't write at all with kif except analytical horrors.

"Tuesday. Strange you mention the golden chalice. I use it in the Genet. I say: *He holds the golden chalice in his hands but he knows the Holy Water has dried out of it leaving a crust of blood around the edges.* I thought I was making up the expression as an image of the cup, the holy grail. But I guess I wasn't. Yes, I think it is the cup of the tarot, since I've always assumed, or was told, that the tarot cup is the grail. . . . *But no one can be thrown out of civilization because each man contains the whole and tells the truth about the whole. A state executes in order to disavow everyone's guilt. The execution of Eichmann, for example, makes all the rest of us seem innocent, when in fact the only honorable and honest thing would be to have the whole human race hanged in Jerusalem.* Do you think *Commentary* will be amused by that?"

And on January 29, 1964— "It is eight p.m. and I've been at the Genet since eight in the morning and yesterday and forever and it is supposed to be there this week and I'm exhausted. It gets more and more brilliant, but I hate it more and more. And the letter comes from Irving Rosenthal in Marrakech saying money is absolutely the only justification for writing essays and book reviews in which case you don't tell your friends about it. So I've written him a letter (Hitler being his favorite hate) beginning Mein lieber Adolf and telling him I didn't know the law. And that if he was cold there was a surplus of fuel at Auschwitz. But it's made me depressed because it's true and I'm working like a dog . . . What I say in the Genet is just telling the truth. He (Genet) is making the real Christian ideals—murder, pillage, treachery and robbery—into his own ideals. As he's in jail he has nothing to lose. It takes me thirty pages to say it, but that's a good sign. I'm beginning to get my wind back. I don't come out in farts now, but in streams of shit. Note how long my letters are . . . From last part of essay: *America is Europe's knight in shining armor. But the love-starved maiden needs something a lot warmer in her arms than a coffer of jewels. Beauties have been known to fall in love with beasts before; or, as Confucius said, a hot dragon is more fun in bed than a cold dollar bill...*I really need a rest after this."

". . . Dris woke me at five this morning and I finished the Genet in time to get it to the post office before noon when it closed for the weekend . . . The Genet is called, "Goodbye to Christendom." [It was published as "Looking for Genet."] I do hope they print it. It will bring me $300 and cause a little stir."

It is easy to see why he called it "Goodbye to Christendom" and why *Commentary* had to rename it when they threw out that whole aspect of the essay. Besides the unlikelihood of a Jewish magazine publishing an attack on Christianity, they probably did not appreciate that he was writing from outside the Christian world, from the liberating vantage point, for a Jew, of a Moslem country.

"I read it over this morning and could hardly believe how good it was though it reads like I'm in the middle of a nervous breakdown. It must be the dexadrines I use to keep going. I alternated between dex and librium as you can't get dexamils here. At night I had gin and kif to unwind with . . . The Genet is really an apologia per mia vita. It tries to explain my dybbuk . . . The essay is really such a vicious attack on everything except Genet, you, God and myself, that I don't even know whether they'll have the nerve to print it.

". . . By the way, my Genet ends up talking about Kennedy. I quote Mailer's passage about the subterranean river of American life. *It was out of this river that the assassin's bullet came, regardless of who pulled the trigger or why. We accept, with the authorities, the guilt of the lonely psychopath because it tells a truth if not a fact. It dramatizes the refusal of Unreason to be silenced any longer by man's Europe's, idea that he, Reason, rules the world. Humanism, however pretty, isn't for us because nature isn't human, and man willy nilly is of nature. Nature is unreason and God. It is the madness that runs through our lives and connects us to the stars in a way no rocket ship can ever duplicate. It connects us to all living things and to ourselves. To name this madness Holy doesn't promise peace or prosperity; it promises only a reason for being, a reinvestment of life into the dead matter of which the universe is now composed. Nice, yes?"* But in a later letter, he adds: "I feel as if mama's going to slap me hard for writing such mean things."

Writing a column for the *New York Herald Tribune* aimed at a mass readership was at variance with Alfred's image of himself as a writer for the literary few, but he could not ignore the fact that he was being widely read for the first time. It disturbed him, and he wrote me in February 19, 1964: "Edward, am I going mad or is it possible that people do actually write nasty things about me in newspapers? . . . Someone called Jimmy Breslin . . . writes: 'Behan at least tries to write for the entertainment of the reader. He is not some outlandish homosexual trying to sound off on human destiny between paragraphs about his boyfriends.' I just read that and I thought that man is talking about me . . . I keep thinking I am mad. I mean, suddenly I think How can I write about being poor, and Dris, in the *Herald Tribune*?" But the columns brought him some diverting correspondence: A theatre group in Washington D.C. asked for permission to stage one of them, paying him $5 per performance, and a psychiatrist wrote, "Dear Scabrous Fungus Collector . . . I'd order you to douse the glim of your horrible light in darkness if I had the power and if I didn't like the twisted macabre stuff. . ."

But with the upheavals of his life in Tangier, encompassing stormy relations with his boyfriend, feuds with the Bowleses and others of the literary colony, bouts of near starvation, breakdowns and strange ailments, the "monthly" *Book Week* column came out only sporadically. And as he started to concentrate on writing a new novel, which eventually became *The Exquisite Corpse*, he devoted less and less time to criticism and the column, dropping this kind of work entirely after he suffered a final psychotic attack.

When he returned from Morocco to New York in the winter of '65–'66, he began his novel *The Foot*, much of which has been lost. And as his mental state deteriorated and he embarked on desperate voyages, his literary production became sporadic. There is firm evidence that he wrote a story called "Trois Corsages," about his three friends, Harriet (Sohmers) Zwerling, Susan Sontag, and Irene Fornes, but this too has been lost, along with most of his unfinished and unpublished works. In his madness, I believe he destroyed much correspondence and many manuscripts himself, but some things were in the hands of his agent, Ted Chichak of the Scott Meredith Agency, who now denies any knowledge of their whereabouts.

After much erratic wandering, Alfred Chester settled in Israel sometime in 1970, where he wrote a final essay, "Letter From

417

The Wandering Jew," that was never published. (It exists thanks to Theodore Solotaroff who photocopied it when it was submitted to him at Harper & Row by the same Ted Chichak who refuses to search his files for surviving manuscripts.) If Alfred Chester's charm has disappeared, along with his sense of humor, (either due to a state of mental deterioration or on his way to death), this final essay reveals a new identity, no longer worried about who he was, whether he had an "I" or not. To paraphrase his early mock-formulation, *oh m'encule, donc je suis,* he now suffered, therefore he was. Unexpectedly for such a previously elegant, often humorous writer, he let out, at the end of his life, a hurt, angry bellow of rage and despair at a world he couldn't stand, almost Celine-like, not caring what anyone thought, and mixing large complaints with petty gripes—it was all the same to him by now. With a sour, don't-give-a-shit tone, he did not try to pretty up his feelings, and snarled and snapped unreasonably at his imagined persecutors. And the fact that he sent this piece to his agent meant he wanted the world to listen. As a record of his last lonely years, when he rejected his friends, as well as the literary world he was part of, it is unique testimony.

In a commentary in *The New York Review Of Books*, that could apply just as well to all of Alfred Chester's critical work, Gore Vidal wrote that he ". . . was a glorious writer, tough as nails, with an exquisite ear for the false note: his review of Rechy's *City of Night* is murderously funny, absolutely unfair and totally true, a trick that only a high critic knows how to pull off."

Nominated by Exquisite Corpse

LILACS ON BRATTLE STREET

by GAIL MAZUR

from PARTISAN REVIEW

On the brick sidewalk; pale clusters
of purple stars, picked carelessly
from nineteenth-century yards
by rootless flirtatious students,
tossed away, darkening, after a brief fling
with nature and the city's literary past . . .

Brattle Street. "Tory Row." This afternoon,
I could almost think nothing's changed—
clouds of May cherry blossoms, pink dogwood,
the mellow blown tulips—so peaceful,
Longfellow himself might be strolling here,
lost in Dante, *nel mezzo del cammin.* . . .
or Margaret Fuller, her father's only son,
breaking from studies in Greek and Latin,
not yet awakened to love, not yet drowned . . .

A small boy tears past me, his arms full
of lavender plunder, lilacs he's bringing home
for his mother. I like his face
on which little but joy is written,
yet I have to invent a darkness in it,
as if, moments ago, he was dragging

419

his sneakered feet, desperate to forget
what his teacher said, something about Chernobyl.
She'd pointed to it on the roll-down Hammond map.
He was swept for the first time by the question,
What if nothing lasts?

I make this innocent boy, this thief,
think my thoughts about nuclear ash
blowing across Kiev, across our ancestors.
I see him in the stunned classroom, terror
that passes when the bell rings, but we know
it will return now, over and over,
the too-bright light, eye-widening
what if—
what if everything in his world that matters
were colorless, empty, gone
like the wooden synagogues of Poland,
everything—the Victorian schoolhouse,
its airy unfair cage of gerbils; the 5 & 10
where he buys his models; his sister,
his sister waiting for him now on the front steps;
the houseplant his mother named for him yesterday
while she watered it—"begonia"—its pink flowers
in the front window beside the gray cat
watching for him, too, planted there,
we think, since morning, since he left for school—
reliable, wily;
                and his room upstairs,
his Marvel comics, his painted bookcase,
the plastic dinosaurs lined up on its shelves
like disguised lead soldiers—the fierce
triceratops, the mastodon, the inchling
woolly mammoth—replicas he loves from the set
his grandfather *May his soul rest in peace*
sent him last year . . .

Nominated by Robert Pinsky, Lloyd Schwartz

BIRMINGHAM, 1962

by DIANN BLAKELY SHOAF

from THE LOUISVILLE REVIEW

Barely affluent, we always had maids.
    One worked a few months then left for Detroit,
the next for a husband's home town; another
    took her children and returned to an elderly
mother living beneath a rural tin roof,
    having found cities and their men "no good."
I was a good girl, they all told me so
    when I'd stand by their ironing boards, dipping
my fingers in a bowl of water to sprinkle

    on my father's shirts, my mother's lace-wristed
blouses, the pale dresses I wore to church.
    The TV murmured with husky-voiced women
in negligees; I was admonished to listen
    to what preachers told me, to remember
that Jesus was watching always. I watched
    black hands guiding roasts out of ovens,
turning pieces of chicken in skillets
    of sizzling oil, noticed the rough pink

of blisters and scars. These hands dressed me
    each morning; I imagined they loved me.
One August afternoon, my mother home late,
    back from a bridge party, shopping. Delores
had missed the last bus. We drove for miles
    through heat-steaming streets to a part of town

I'd never been to; the houses grew smaller
    and closer together. Peeling paint.
No real driveways, or yards. Then nothing

    but rows of small brick apartments,
"projects," as if someone had named them
    for school. Heat shimmered from roof tops;
as we pulled to the curb, my mother locked both
    our doors, I heard a kitchen radio playing hymns
and saw in the red sun boys my own age
    stripped to their briefs, alarmingly white
against their skin, laughing while pummeled
    by water from the corner hydrant they'd opened.

Nominated by Andrew Hudgins, Roger Weingarten

MASK SERIES

by CAROL SNOW

from DENVER QUARTERLY

1.

The hills and I would exchange qualities.
(In my need.)

Which frank, which masked?

If I were over there by the boats?

2. *If I were over there by the boats?*
(displaced . . . 'withdrawn' . . .)

          Or drawn to memory by a vague memory
of walking to the front of a crowded room to receive
(a laurel leaf stapled to a postcard) my prize
in the contest of naming a series of natural objects
placed in a box, a closed box: by touch alone,

day after day in camp: 'pinecone', 'chestnut', 'burr',

'?': deep in the blindness of the inside of the box (apart, in a
   kind of *listening;* the glaring, the dusty
world, displaced . . . 'withdrawn' . . .)?

*

Tethered — by touch — to the level
of form (the fingers, stubbed at form, all attention at the edges)

to recognize — by touch — by a likeness
of form (which is not *to remember*):

where the eyes were looking was *for*.

    Bereshith . . . [In the beginning . . .]

    God wanted to behold
    God . . .

    and turned to fragments . . .

(A card I found at the back of a drawer — the leaf
then dry, yet fragrant.)

3. *Which frank, which masked?*

facing (as hills),

engrossed—

The expression of looking at — beautiful, 'available' —

                               "Beatrice
gazing upward and I on her. . ."
Beatrice in suso, ed io in lei, guardava . . .

Passing men,
the woman does more than look down or aside;
she looks away and also changes the shape of her mouth.

424

Dearest.

The thought of you looking away and fear
rose in me —as shame rises — as into lack.

                                       And trees seemed
hollow, then — all glory, all

attention, drained out — drained
suddenly as though violently

poured —

     Rabbi Isaac said,
     "The light created by the Blessed Holy One in the act of
        Creation
     flared from one end of the world to the other
     and was hidden away."

     . . . Rabbi Judah said,
     "If it were completely hidden
     the world would not exist for even a moment!
     Rather, it is hidden and sown like a seed
     that gives birth to seeds and fruit . . .
     Since the first day it has never been fully revealed. . ."

David — having climbed the stairs
to bed, his breathing a little
'pronounced' (recognizably his breath) — David

pulling the fabric of the nightdress down
over the curve of my thigh (he loves)
and stroking the soft flannel.

4. *The hills and I would exchange qualities./ (In my need.)*

But 'assume', not 'exchange': "I would assume/
qualities of the hills.//

Solidity. Glory. Repose (in my need)."

But not

'qualities', rather,

'attributes' . . .

Nominated by Brenda Hillman

JACINTA

Fiction by CHARLES D'AMBROSIO

from STORY

T HEY WERE married in a small white church upon a hill—that was true, a fact, but it was also a phrase Dorothy often repeated to herself, a phrase that gave her a sense of fairy-tale beginnings. The church was in LaConner, Washington. Below the hill, in all directions, low fields filled with tulips, a sea of red and yellow and purple flowers washed in waves by the coastal wind. Dorothy had timed the date of their wedding to coincide with the first blossoming of the tulips, a quilt of color stitched together by a network of dikes that held the emerald water of the Skagit River in check. Dorothy wore a simple white dress with a sweetheart neckline and an illusion veil fastened over her eyes by a coronet of pearls and intricately-woven baby's breath. She felt herself hover, weightless as a high, white cloud, as she swept down the aisle on the arm of her father—he was a PR man for Weyerhae-user, and it was through him, at a Logging Days Festival in Ray-mond, that she'd met Bill. They said the traditional vows, straight from the Catholic ceremony. A quiet, plainspoken man, Bill must have found the cadence of the ceremonial language frilly and or-nate, unfamiliar. He seemed almost embarrassed by the lan-guage, and there was something tentative, unsure, in his delivery. This didn't worry Dorothy, although she'd just found out she was pregnant. Bill didn't know he was a father when he said, "I do."

She told him on the way down old Highway 99. When he didn't respond immediately, Dorothy cracked her window and let

427

the air blow her veil back: it lifted from her face, fluttering through the cab.

"Say something," she said.

Bill lifted a hand from the steering wheel and gestured helplessly—that hand worked like a conductor's baton, a silent thing whose smallest movements orchestrated emotion, and Dorothy often misread him.

"Are you disappointed?" she asked.

"No," Bill said. "Not at all."

"Her name's Jacinta."

"Who?"

Dorothy patted her stomach. "The baby."

"It might be a boy," Bill said.

"I don't feel that it is," Dorothy said. "I have a sense."

"Jacinta." Bill rolled the word over in his mouth.

"It's a stone," Dorothy said. "Also a flower, the hyacinth."

It all had happened so quickly: she was married, she was pregnant. Only yesterday, it seemed, she was meeting Bill in Raymond. That was a year ago September and the summer light was sweet and lingering. Across the field there was a refreshment stand where the Kiwanis was selling blue slushies and corn dogs on sticks and fat wedges of watermelon. Bill and Dorothy were wandering away, out toward the edge of the fairgrounds, past the big billowing striped tents and the rickety Ferris wheel, past the straw-and-dung smell of the paddock, out to where Bill's truck was parked in the gravel lot. Night was coming and the arc lights above pearled the darkening sky with blue halos and her father's voice was floating over the public address, faint and sad, so far away. She was slouching down in the truck and Bill was talking. He was chewing gum and his jaw tensed. He was rolling the sleeves of his flannel shirt into tight doughnuts around his upper arms. Soon the distant lights were shutting off and people were wandering into the lot. She was closing her eyes and leaning forward in the cab, offering her lips to the dark.

Afterward, she'd found her father in the front seat of his car with a can of Oly and a cigarette, the long, dead ash curling down. When she opened the door, it fell into his lap. They sat silently in the empty lot and Dorothy listened to a man laughing happily and to the ring of coins falling as someone counted change. Her father remained silent and withdrawn all the way back to Annie Wright, a girl's prep school in Tacoma. The school had a certain cachet in her mother's mind because Mary McCarthy had spent some time there; her mother hoped Dorothy would pursue Mary McCarthy one step further and attend Vassar. Her mother worshipped Culture and things "back East" and gave everyone the impression that she was suffering some kind of terrible exile. In the circular drive, her father shifted into park and let the car idle. He sipped his beer and in the dim light his lips stood out, moist and red in a face otherwise old and gray. Dorothy could see the dark silhouettes of her dormmates drifting across the curtained windows.

"You know dear," her father said. "I don't love your mother." He finished his beer and then pried two triangular holes in the top of another. "Isn't that a hell of a thing?"

She had waited for an explanation, but there was none.

All that year Bill left work early on Fridays and drove north from Hood River to visit Dorothy in Tacoma. There was a small state park on the tip of Vashon Island where he pitched a tent and slept after he'd returned Dorothy to the dorm just in time to make her midnight curfew. In his hair and the rough wool of his Pendleton shirts was always the smell of wood smoke and salt-water. Her friends knew of the affair and envied Dorothy: the thought of a man camped out on a wooded island across the water struck them as deeply, incredibly romantic. They all had the idea, at Annie Wright, that they'd been locked away in a tower to languish unloved forever.

Bill and Dorothy moved to a small white house at the end of a dusty access road that wound through an apple orchard owned by Homer Jorgenson, a man Bill had known all his life. Homer had built the house for his parents, built it himself during the war, requisitioning the wood with a lie—telling the government he needed the lumber to rebuild a barn blown over by a storm that had howled up the Columbia Gorge that spring. Homer—who'd never married—had given Bill a job as an overseer, running the orchard. Homer was sixty years old, an angular man who looked as though he'd been carved into his current hard shape by a constant wind, by slow erosion, by long resistance; when he stood still, his body leaned forward slightly, like a scrub pine perched on a sea cliff. His solitary life had not made him fussy, the way

429

some men get. He'd lived on the same eight hundred acres of apple orchard all his life and so had his father and grandfather before him, and there was something in that continuity that sat contentedly in Homer's bones; deep down he knew exactly what he had to do—laying out and lighting smudge pots all night to ward off a sudden frost, tracking and killing a cougar that had come down the mountains and attacked the few head of cattle he kept.

As a wedding gift, Homer had fixed up the little house: he'd rolled a fresh coat of thick white paint over the interior walls, he'd installed a new gas stove and reglazed the front windows and cleared the chimney of a bird's nest. When Bill and Dorothy entered their new home for the first time, the nest, as neatly woven as a wicker basket, sat alone on the dinner table, and in the hollowed center were two keys twisted together by a blue ribbon: one key worked the front door and the other opened the gun cabinet. In the cabinet, they'd found a bottle of champagne floating in a bucket of lukewarm water. It was a nice gesture, they'd just arrived late. Dorothy loved the little house, but something about it felt boxy and austere, the idea of a man who lived alone. She immediately set about cluttering the walls with pictures and mirrors and, in the kitchen window, she arranged her collection of Japanese fishing floats, globes of colored glass used to buoy drift nets. For a few hours every day, late in the afternoon, when the sun slanted over Mt. Hood in a fan of cloud-broken light, "God's light" as it was called, the floats lifted the plain white room out of itself, into another realm, giving it the bright, swimming color of a church awash with the blues and reds and greens of stained glass windows.

Early one morning, not long after they'd settled in, Bill was sitting on the porch with a cup of black coffee and his Freedom Arms 454, a sidearm with enough stopping power to drop a bear at thirty yards. Dorothy heard the report in her dreams as Bill, between sips of steaming coffee, shot a yearling not twenty feet from their doorstep. He'd winched the doe upside down from the branch of the single apple tree in their yard and was gutting it when she came out onto the porch. Close by the trees were black and shadowy but far off the leaves shimmered a dewy silver in the sunlight. The apples were still green on the branch. Bill slit the doe's throat and the blood spilled to the ground as if from a

430

spigot. The knife he used shone in the morning sun, a knife, it seemed to Dorothy, from some kind of ancient lore—the silver blade, a shaft of light as Bill plunged it hilt-deep into the doe's dark belly and opened the interior to the sun, pulling the gut wide open and allowing the light to pour in as if that were his only intention all along. Then the entrails fell out, hot and steaming, on the wet, green grass.

Homer had heard the shot echo and walked up through the trees from his place. He looked at the doe and the bloody grass and then scratched his head, running his fingers through his thick white hair. Dorothy had noticed about Homer that he always combed his hair, that it always smelled of some pomade and stood stiffly and neatly in place, no matter what hour of the day. It suggested, to Dorothy, a childhood habit. She imagined that his bed was made each morning, too.

"Young," Homer said.

"Year or more," Bill said. Sunlight caught the glistening fat and for an instant the doe looked like tallow hanging from the tree, a burning candle twisting gently n the wind.

Bill wrapped the soft heart in a scrap of newspaper.

"Like to clear the dragline ditch out front," Homer said. "Drainage is bad."

"Be right on it," Bill said. "Soon as I'm done here."

Dorothy's breasts and the swelling curve of her belly showed through her thin, gauzy robe. She saw Homer staring, and the exposure gave her a pleasant sensation. Bill looked, too. A light wind blew, and in the quiet, for a moment, it was as if her presence were somehow at issue. Dorothy crossed her arms in front of her, almost to break the spell and help the men resume their discussion. Homer looked across the orchard in the direction of Mt. Hood, a white cone of snow carved like a cameo against the clearing blue sky.

Bill said, "How about some coffee?"

When Dorothy ducked inside, Homer said, "This wasn't really necessary."

Bill squinted. "It was there. Snuck up on me."

"That's no reason."

"Well," Bill said. "It's done."

Dorothy came out of the house with two cups. Her feet were bare and the blades of grass, tender spring growth, soft and damp, felt pleasant against her skin. She had lately been feeling bloated and dull, a heavy, waddling thing, but the grass brushing beneath her feet momentarily relieved her of that, and lifted her spirits.

"Your husband here's getting a nesting urge. Some kind of sympathetic deal. Happens to men."

Bill said, "This'll come in handy when you're laid up, Dot."

"Are you promising to cook?" Dorothy asked.

He wiped his hands on his trousers. "I don't know that I'm saying that."

"I'll cook," Homer said. A lifelong bachelor, he'd acquired a kind of domestic felicity that made him, at times, seem feminine. Dorothy had borrowed cups of sugar and flour from Homer and traded recipes with him, walking back and forth along the worn dirt path between the two houses; he didn't seem at all out of place when he wrapped the strings of an apron around his waist and stood before a kitchen stove crowded with simmering pots, a smudge of baking soda on his forehead. But it was more than this, more than a man with a whisk in his hand, more than a man bent over the counter to pick a piece of shell from a cup of egg whites; alone for so long, he had taken up the role because there was no one to assign it to.

"I make a good venison stew," he said. "We can freeze up a batch."

"That'd be nice," Dorothy said.

"I'd've rather married you," Bill said, "had I known your secret talents."

"What's that supposed to mean?" Dorothy asked.

Bill said, "Hell, I don't know."

The doe turned a slow circle, winding and unwinding in the wind.

"There's more coffee on, you want it," Dorothy said.

When she walked away, she felt the men watching her; she was intensely aware of how wide she'd gotten, how heavy and over-ripe. Their scrutiny made each footstep awkward and calculated; she thought she might stumble. She wanted to feel weightless and walked immediately to the back of the house, where she began filling the claw-footed tub. With the water running, she went back to the kitchen for a cup of tea. A trail of blood marked her path, perfect red prints of her big toe and the wide flat pad of her foot, like a strange animal, moving across the linoleum, the pine planks, the carpet, the tiles in the bathroom. The bright oxygenated blood had seeped through the wet grass. She grabbed a washcloth from the kitchen sink, scrubbed the stains away as best she could, and when the tub was full, she lowered herself into the water, briefly felt buoyant and free of burden, and then, awkwardly, she reached forward and washed her feet.

Jacinta was born in August and she died a year later without ever speaking a word. She had learned to walk, she had learned to climb the couch and scale the kitchen chairs, with Bill teaching her, praising her handholds, urging her on, taking delight in her wordless joy. A few days after her first birthday she drowned in a shallow tin trough full of rainwater. Early in the afternoon, she climbed over the lip of the trough and when Bill found her, she was floating face down, her short blond hair curling away from her head like weeds in the clear water. Dorothy was frosting an apple spice cake when Bill ran across the yard holding Jacinta in his arms like a bundle of dripping rags. He set her on the dining table and unzipped her pink jumpsuit. He bent down. He plugged her nose and placed his mouth over hers and breathed into her. Jacinta's stomach inflated with every entering breath and then flattened again. A slight sound of exhaling, a secret whisper could be heard in the quiet room as Bill's breath flowed back out through her lifeless mouth. He rose up and drew breath, then went back down, as if to place a kiss on her lips. Festoons of limp party streamers twirled lazily above Bill, streamers from several days ago and a small celebration they'd had. Dorothy gripped the back of Bill's shirt as he tried to breathe life into Jacinta. He began pounding his fist against her baby's heart. A gurgle of water spilled from her lips. Dorothy called Homer. Homer called for an ambulance. Bill kept at it for half an hour, breathing, pounding, pumping her stomach to clear her windpipe, when at last the ambulance arrived from town. Even then, Bill wouldn't stop. Finally, Homer put a hand on his shoulder, then pulled hard. Bill looked up. He seemed surprised to see anyone else standing there.

"There's nothing you can do," Homer said. "She's dead."

Bill glanced back at Jacinta, and for a moment he seemed like a brave man, the kind of man who would walk away and never look back again, and then he looked directly at Dorothy.

433

"Who the hell are you staring at?" he said. His hands were trembling, and he clutched the seams of his pant legs to calm them.

Dorothy went out the door, shocked into silence. It had rained hard the night before, but now the sun was out and a strong steady wind blew through the trees. Shadows shifted like living things on the grass. With a house in the middle of an orchard, it was difficult to know where the yard ended and the world began—rows and rows of apple trees angled away into a shimmering, sun-lit infinity. She stopped at the trough. It was no bigger than a washtub. A few green leaves floated on the surface, and when she looked in, Dorothy saw her face, reflected on the still surface and framed in white clouds. She believed then—or later, maybe—that Jacinta had seen her own reflection floating on the surface, too, a round face drifting with the mirrored blue and white of the sky, and that she had tried to follow her image up into the heaven, and instead went down into the darkness, where she drowned. Dorothy walked to the barn and found an awl. She punched a single small hole in the trough, a hole the size of a star. She watched the blue sky and the white shifting clouds pour out onto the lawn. The water drained slowly. She bent down and cupped her hand under the tiny flow and drank from the water as it dribbled away between her fingers. She stayed until the trough was empty.

The ambulance had pulled away on the road toward town, moving slowly, its lights off. Dorothy returned to the house. Homer leaned against the kitchen counter, his hands folded. Bill sat on the couch, gazing at the white wall in front of him. He had not spoken since the paramedic lifted Jacinta's perfect and lifeless form from a puddle of water on the table and carried her, still dripping, to the ambulance.

"If it hadn't rained," Dorothy said.

"It did rain," Bill said. His voice was calm. "It rained all fucking night."

Dorothy stuck a leftover birthday candle in the center of the cake and held a match to the wick. The tiny flame rose around the black wick in the shape of two hands folded in prayer. She felt pitiful. "God," she said. Bill looked up at her as if he were blind and had only heard a slight movement in the corner of the

434

room. Dorothy would have preferred anger, outrage, anything but this calm that came from some heartless place Bill had discovered in himself.

"Let's sing," Dorothy said. The kitchen was flooded with a wash of red and blue and green light from the floats lined along the sill. "Okay, we don't have to sing. Maybe singing's not a good idea." She started to cry. "I don't know why not, though."

Bill left the house, kicking the screen door off its hinge. Homer held Dorothy by the shoulders, then hugged her. The candle still burned in the cake.

Homer rocked Dorothy in his arms, and she could feel the spare, necessary arrangement of him—the bone, the muscle, the rough skin where his face scraped against her temple. She saw over his shoulder the alarm clock, and the time blinked off and on, a green insult. A clean wind pushed at the curtains, and she could smell Scotch broom in the air. She heard a train whistle echoing in the Gorge. A dog barked, and then there was a long silence. Dorothy listened. It was quiet for a long time, but she imagined new sounds already out there, moving toward her, crossing that wide space.

"That candle's going to go out," Homer said.

He wet his fingers with spittle and pinched the flame. He eased Dorothy down on the couch and then went to work in the kitchen. He started two new potatoes in a pan of boiling water and chopped fresh parsley and shaved slivers of garlic. He set two stick matches in his mouth and sliced open an onion. "Keeps the tears away," he said, chewing on the matchsticks. He fried a chunk of bacon and dipped two small rainbow trout in the fat and rolled them in cornmeal and cooked them quickly in an iron skillet alive with the sizzle of grease.

"You want to talk, go ahead," Homer said. "I'm listening."

The garlic and onion went with a thick pad of butter into another pan and when they were ready Homer cut up the potatoes and put them in.

Dorothy absently traced the molded ear of Jacinta's favorite doll—one that wept when you filled a little reservoir in its head with water. Her daughter was gone, but here was the dumb doll, here was the kitchen sink with the brown splotch of mineral stain, here was the wide plank floor of soft pine that still had the same pocked surface it had yesterday, and the day before, making

435

of it a map of rearranged sofas and chairs, of the places people had sat and talked and eaten and loved and fought in the forty years since the house was built.

Homer set a plate in front of Dorothy. He put a white paper napkin on her lap and a fork in her hand. He said, "Eat."

"What about Bill?" she asked.

"Just eat. He'll come back."

Dorothy ate; it was enough to move her mouth over something solid.

Later that night, Dorothy went into the barn. She unhooked a wool blanket from a nail on the wall and sat beside Bill. He was curled up. A bottle of vodka lay tipped over and empty at his side. His hair was matted with dirt and straw and white molted feathers, and from his mouth, pressed against the ground, a dark drool-stain spread in the dirt. He kicked the hard-packed earth with the toe of his boots as if he were trying to prod an answer from it. Dorothy bent down to him and turned his face. His nose was bleeding. His lips were caked with crumbs of dirt. She brushed them clean and kissed them. His breath was a damp, sour wind rising from within the cavern of his mouth.

In the weeks following the funeral, Dorothy began attending daily mass. She wasn't so much religious as spiritual, and with the church, she shopped her way through the dogma, tossing out what she considered old and rotten, keeping what was ripe and beautiful. She didn't need rules written in stone; she was there for the slant of light through the lofty row of windows, the blue hush of votive candles in the quiet moments before the first mournful intonations of the Latin High Mass began—there was something about a dead tongue speaking, that she loved, and the words, loosed from the weight of meaning, floated free, a music in which she could drift forever.

Bill mended section fences, roofed the barn, and drank in the early evenings with the migrants. He'd start with them in the afternoon and come home and continue drinking in his chair, balancing his glass on the arm and watching Dorothy, silently, as she cooked dinner. He kept his liquor in the unlocked gun cabinet and when he was finished for the night he returned his glass and the spoon he used as a swizzle, both unwashed, to the shelf, next to his bottle. Once, when Dorothy had washed the glass and

436

spoon, Bill blew up at her, angry in the calm way that had become his manner—he squeezed her arm so tightly that a bruise in the shape of his thumbprint showed purple and yellow just below her shoulder. His eyes held some kind of unfocused enormity, but all he said was, "Don't. Don't. Don't." Now, when he watched her work over the stove, his blank eyes bearing down, Dorothy was afraid; and in her fear, she became forgetful, letting things burn to black or boil limply in the pan until the water was nearly gone.

Upstairs, in bed, with a wind whistling through the chinking in the walls, or the windows rattling, or the hazy light of town hovering above the trees, or a sliver of gold moon slipped into a corner pane, or the slow red blinking of a jet from Portland passing up and out of her view, Dorothy would lay still, alert. She was uncomfortably aware of her body, keeping it frozen in a single position until, heavy and numb, time itself seemed to stop. Nightly, for several weeks, Bill took her—no kisses, no real touching, no tentative exploration, he'd turn her over and enter her with a quick stab from behind and jerk hastily above her buttocks and, when done, withdraw immediately and fall asleep. Dorothy would remain awake. She began spending most nights awake on a wicker love seat, beneath the window. She'd look at her husband, buried in the quilt. He'd be smiling, as if there'd been a joke; he often smiled in his sleep, in the silent hours when she watched. Toward dawn, she'd fall asleep, and there would be dreams, dreams of sun and sand and the shadow of something, a fox or coyote, but in the morning, there was always nothing.

One morning she stayed after mass to visit with the parish priest, Father McGill. Grains of rice from a wedding had settled into the black gummy tar that lined the seams of the sidewalk, and Dorothy stood outside, after the blessing, as the parishioners filed away, each placing a hand still wet with holy water in Father's pink palm; there were always a few men who attended daily mass, but only, it seemed, out of some lack of vigor—jobless, retired, crippled, lonely. Mostly, it was a congregation of women who wore old shabby clothes that dated from the last days of their happiness, women who wore black and mourned losses that were lost, irrevocably, years ago. As Dorothy watched them, she worried about becoming one of those crazed, wounded women who always wore hats in the old manner and arrived before mass to kneel in a long wooden pew and pray solemnly, muttering aloud, with a bowed head, alone in their lunatic sorrow.

When they were by themselves, Dorothy said, "Can I talk with you, Father?"

"Of course," he said.

He touched her elbow and guided her back into the church, into the cool, dark air, and together they walked up the aisle, genuflecting before the altar. To Dorothy, it seemed strange to do this when no one was around, to kneel and cross herself in the empty church, like a kind of mime show. Father McGill led her across the sanctuary, through a door; he offered her a card chair, and they sat together in the sacristy.

"Would you like to make a confession?" Father asked.

"No," Dorothy said, "that's not why I've come. I'm not here about me."

She knew the church from her seat in the nave and had never stood in the sanctuary and certainly had never entered the vestry, this back room where the priest slipped on his soutane and knotted tight his cincture. She looked around. A frayed veronica hung from the wall, a replica, obviously—it was from one of the stations of the cross, but Dorothy couldn't remember which. Cases of novitiate wine were stacked in a corner. A plastic bag lay on the counter—white wafers with a blue twist-tie pinching the neck of the sack closed.

Father McGill waited patiently.

"You know our daughter died," Dorothy said.

"Yes," Father said.

"Since then our marriage has been difficult."

She knew she needed to talk about her body, needed to talk about the relationship Bill had with it; he had stopped his nightly taking of her, no longer touched her at all, but the fear she felt had not gone away.

Father fingered the tassled tip of his cincture. "How so?"

"I'm afraid that I will have to leave him." Dorothy had not considered the possibility until the words were spoken aloud. Looking at Father McGill, the words sounded cruel and harsh, and she wanted them back immediately.

"A marriage is not a thing to abandon lightly."

438

"Every breath is a crisis," she said. "When he's around, I can't breathe."

"Your daughter's death has placed a terrible strain on your relationship," Father said. He looked at her benevolently. His hands were folded in his lap. "Is it possible that time itself will mend it?"

"I don't know," Dorothy said.

"She died in August, if I remember. It's now March. Eight months."

"It feels longer."

"Tragedy always does. The Mass itself is two thousand years old."

Dorothy realized she did not want to speak about this in religious terms. She wanted practical advice. She looked at Father McGill and then at the counter with the bag of wafers. Crystal cruets of wine and water rested in a silver tray. Behind Father was a door that led outside.

"I suppose you're right," Dorothy said.

"Of course," Father said. He stood and opened the door. Light poured in and lit up the green walls of the sacristy. It was an ugly, small room. Dorothy had only once in her life entered the home of a blind person, and it, too, had been painted this same unpleasant green.

"Stay with him," Father said. "He needs you."

Every morning Bill drove the rutted two-track through the orchard in an old Ford flatbed loaded with migrants and day pickers and before coming home he stopped nightly at the row of dirty white shacks and bet on the cockfights. Through the kitchen window, in the fading light of early evening, Dorothy would see the trail of bleached white dust rising from the road and know Bill was headed for the fights. El Blanco, the Mexicans called him. They'd cordoned off a patch of packed dirt with chicken wire and stakes of light gauge rebar and the men sat around the ring on old barrels and wooden boxes and car seats. The cocks fought until one of them sliced open the other's throat with tiny razor blades attached to their feet. When it grew dark, someone would pull a car or two up to the ring and turn on the headlights, and the men would sprawl on the hoods, and their drunken shouts and cries would rise in a plume of dust and echo across the orchard for Dorothy to hear.

Bill had started an affair with a young Mexican girl and told Dorothy. His confession seemed calculated to drive her away. Dorothy had visited the girl once and come away with nothing. She had not gone to threaten the girl or warn her or cause a scene. She had gone because she loved her husband with a love that had never been in question, and she wanted to know about him, about his secret life, his Mexican girl and the cockfights, and what it was, possibly, that he had found in the dusty compound of white shacks—that world of clotheslines fluttering and alive with hand-washed shirts and dungarees, of trikes tipped over in the dirt, a bent front wheel turning slowly in the wind. The girl hardly spoke English, but Dorothy got the impression, as she listened to the mangled sentences, that this girl had dreams of a lasting relationship with Bill; there was a cloudy hint of covetousness in her words, a hint of washing machines, of running cars, of a charmed life in the house of the gringo foreman. It all sounded proud and bitter and aggressive to Dorothy.

Later that night, when Bill got home and took up his seat, he began to cry. He didn't make a sound. His shoulders didn't heave. His lips didn't quiver. Tears fell slowly from his clear blue eyes, drop by drop, as though ice were melting, and then dried on his face. He did not wipe the tears away.

Dorothy knelt at the foot of his chair. "Bill?"

He stared past her, unmoved. Dorothy reached for Bill's shoulder; he slapped her hand down.

"Don't touch me," he said.

"I want to talk," Dorothy said.

"Talk," he said.

"I don't want to just talk to nothing," she said. "This can't go on."

"Sure it can," Bill said. "It can go on forever."

She went back to the stove and stirred a pot of squash.

"You're always watching me, you're always looking at me," she said. He was looking right at her, his steady stare bore down, but Dorothy had the impression he wasn't listening. She continued anyway. "I'm starting to feel crazy a lot. I don't feel like anything I do is free. Everything, every move is wrong. I'm afraid of you."

His silence belittled and dismissed her words. From the shelf above the sink, she took one of her floats, a green float with a flawed seam, a float her sister had sent her from Seattle, and pitched it at the wall behind Bill. The glass shattered and rained to the floor.

Bill sipped from his drink. "Your aim is off."

She sat up with Homer and Bill that night. When Homer came around, things were better; he drank heavily but only seemed to mellow, to grow gentle as the night wore on, sinking into himself and settling there, comfortably. When Bill ranted, dropping into his private shorthand, Homer was always careful to nod knowingly and sympathetically to Dorothy, letting her understand she was not entirely alone. She was grateful—Homer had kept Bill busy around the orchard, and when work fell slack, they went to the mountains; he got Bill involved with the Mt. Hood Search and Rescue Team, and together they had climbed Mt. Adams and Mr. Rainier. Bill always came home calmed after one of their climbs, as if the mountain were still in him, a high peak on which he stood, looking down from that distance at the daily life he lived.

Bill and Homer talked, dreamily, of a trip to Nepal. Together, they seemed to know every mountain in the world, and when they talked, growing excited, there seemed to be a freedom in the planning of things that would never be. Himalaya, Bill said, meant the home of snow.

"Why go so far?" Dorothy asked.

Quoting Mallory, Bill said, "Because it's there."

Dorothy frowned. "That's dumb," she said.

"There's no other reason," Bill said. "You go because they're there. If they weren't there, where would you go? What if everything was flat? Where would you go then? You'd go nowhere, right, because every place would be the same."

"You're not making sense, Bill."

"Maybe not to you," he said but decided to try again. "If everything was flat and the same, you'd never have to go anywhere because nothing anywhere else would be different, you'd be like God, everywhere and fucking nowhere in particular."

"Sounds like hell," Dorothy said. She got up and fixed another drink. She realized she didn't really care what Bill said as long as he kept talking.

"That's right," Bill said.

"Me," Homer said, "I've got to go because I'm getting old. I'm on my next-to-last switchback." He smiled at his own corniness. He bit an ice cube. "You live alone, you don't notice life passing by so much."

Dorothy sat down, crossing her legs; her shorts hitched up along her thigh. She did not find it unpleasant to be exposed, to be looked at. When she met Homer's eye, he averted his face. He shifted his feet.

"Home of snow," he repeated. "A Piper Cub crashed on the summit of Mt. Hood about ten years ago. It got lost in a cloud cap. Don't know what it was doing up there."

"Trying to see the summit," Dorothy offered.

"Can't see anything in a cloud," Homer said. "They crashed going about ninety, I guess. The plane flipped, and when they released their seat belts, they fell on their heads. These guys were businessmen, they had on business suits." Homer poured out two fingers of scotch "It snowed every day for a week, no one could get to them. Five feet of snow covered the airplane, and that was their good luck. The snow kept them warm inside their buried plane. They survived."

"Thank God for snow," Bill said.

"That plane's still up there, right?"

"Yeah," Bill said. "Still." He stared into his glass.

That night was like other nights, nights when he would talk of mountains, mountains that he'd never seen but knew were out there just as men once knew the edge of the world waited beyond the horizon. Bill came alive when he talked of mountains, of climbs, of snow—especially snow: he would talk about powder snow, corn snow, rotten snow, of suncrust and windcrust and rime and hoarfrost, of firn mirror and the way slope angle and sunlight will create a brilliant sheen of glacier fire; he'd seen this once, a bright golden ribbon of fire showing a path right up the mountain to the summit; and he spoke of sun cups and fields of nieves penitentes on higher elevations, columns of snow, like nuns in a church, slanting with a slight forward bow toward the midday sun. He talked of spindrift, of cornices, of silver thaw when an inch of ice coats everything so that rocks seemed to be made of glass and trees are encased in crystal. "Nothing moves," he said. "If anything moves, it cracks. You can hear the crashing like breaking glass. Everything shatters." Time holds still in the higher elevations, he would say. "That high, that cold, things don't change. They're preserved. Even the body, when it drops to ninety degrees—two, three heartbeats a minute, that's all. You can't know if a man's alive then." Time is visible, you can see it, he would insist, as wind currents pass over the snow and leave their shape behind in the form of drifts and cornices, like waves that curl and never break.

"Snow ghosts," Homer said.

"They look like people," Bill said.

He went to the gun cabinet and poured another drink. He looked at Homer and said, "Me and her, we don't sleep together anymore."

"Please, Bill," Dorothy said.

"You want my wife." He sipped his drink. "I see you looking. I've seen you before."

Bill swallowed his drink, set the spoon in the glass, and placed the works in his cabinet.

"I'm tired," he said. "Good-night."

When he'd gone upstairs, Dorothy said, "He doesn't mean it."

"You sleep together?" Homer said.

"No," Dorothy said, embarrassed. "He makes a show of driving me away, when that isn't what he means. He wants me around, to witness everything."

A while later, Dorothy said good-night to Homer. He bent forward to kiss her, an awkward, dry kiss, and then instantly vanished into the stand of cedar between their homes. Dorothy went upstairs. She walked in front of Bill, crossing the path of his stare. Slowly she undressed herself. She unbuttoned her blouse and let it slough to the floor. She let her breasts fall from the cups of her bra and then stood there, holding them. The nipples hardened under her fingers. She felt her own touch and caress travel the length of her body. She stepped out of her shorts and faced Bill.

"You didn't go with him?" he said.

She sat on the edge of the bed. After Jacinta was buried, Bill had gone through the house, removing her clothes, her toys, her crib; he'd taken down all the pictures from the walls and the snapshots pinned with magnets to the fridge; he'd torn them up in a monstrous frenzy. There had been one large, framed studio portrait of Jacinta on the wall above Dorothy's dresser; it was a portrait that Dorothy remembered from long lazy afternoon naps when she and Jacinta would lie in the bed, and a shaft of light, solid with drifting dust, would cut through the window; when Bill destroyed the picture, a clean, white space remained on the wall, and the blank so unnerved Dorothy that she had taken a bucket and sponge and scrubbed the entire surface. Still, now, it seemed to float there for a moment. She dismissed the apparition as an optical trick.

Dorothy had purchased an open bus ticket to Seattle, where her sister lived, and twice in the past month she'd gone to the station. It was a small dingy station, little more than a ticket window and a wooden bench with an ashtray at one end, full of gum wrappers and cigarette butts and chewed toothpicks; behind the bench was a row of rental lockers. She had folded her ticket and slipped it into a small travel bag she kept stowed in one of the lockers. At certain moments in her day, she would think of the depot, of her locker and her ticket to Seattle, but in the two times she'd gone to town, the reality of the dingy station frightened her away.

The second time she stood outside the door, frozen. Inside, a soldier sat slumped on the bench, his green duffle on the floor, a pair of headphones in his ears; a little girl with stringy blond hair fingered the coin slot of the candy machine, looking for change; her mother stood by a large window that fronted the street, looking out, her face freckled by the light pouring through the dirty pane. At her feet rested two suitcases, a naked doll, and a hair dryer.

Dorothy walked away from the station, through town. Day lilies bloomed along the borders of driveways and sidewalks, in little islands on the lawns. The better houses had clipped, square hedges. A good, clearing breeze tossed the chestnut trees, shaking the burred fruit into the street, scratching dryly in the gutters. Children were getting out of school now and running in ragged circles, their coats flapping, their hands waving hectic finger-paint pictures of bunnies and Easter eggs. Mothers, in pairs, strolled along behind. Dorothy slipped past them with her head down.

She walked toward the park above town. Now and then, winded, she looked over her shoulder, taking in more and more of the view as she climbed. Lights came on slowly in the shops and bars. The lowering sun hit Mt. Hood on its western slope, and a shadow spread, cold and blue, over the eastern face. In a sandbox down the hill, some children played tag, spun, dipped, fell, shouted, trying to catch one another. A mother shouted for them to come home. A gang of older kids had set a bonfire in one of the grates. They drank beer and joked, their voices echoing crisply in the cold. The clear evening air had a nip to it; if it got cold enough tonight, Bill and Homer would fill the smudge pots with oil, and the fires would smolder and burn in the orchards, glowing orange and blue in the hills that sloped to the Gorge, keeping the early buds alive.

A train whistled in the Gorge, across the Washington side of the river. At this distance, the river looked still; the Columbia was wide, more like a lake than a river flowing toward the Pacific. A yellow beacon flashed in the shipping lane, marking a safe depth for the boats from Japan, Venezuela, Greece. Voices from town carried up to the park. Dorothy heard a thick ring of keys jangling against a lock. A stoplight changed, green. A container ship edged out into the lane, its bulky black hull visible only in outline now, a darker thing than the night. The decks were lit, the men moving around, small and shadowy, but it was the hull Dorothy watched, down below, black, cutting the water. Hood River wasn't a port exactly, but it was only forty miles through the Gorge to Astoria, and then there was open sea, the Pacific, just over the rough Columbia Bar.

When she returned home that night, she heard Bill's voice upstairs. She knew instantly what was going on, but it was too late for betrayal, too late for hurt, too late for scenes. She set her purse on the counter and slipped off her coat. She tied an apron around her waist and inspected the fridge; two thick steaks thawed in a metal pan, the white butcher paper stained with pink juice. She took them out, placed them on the slotted broiler pan, and set the temperature. She could hear the soft pad of bare feet upstairs, the toilet flushing, the water washing down through the pipes. She understood vaguely that she was broken and could offer no resistance, that her life was a dream, and that whatever

445

happened was perfectly all right. She stabbed the steaks with a fork and salted them and slipped them in the oven, setting the timer on the stove.

Bill came downstairs. "You were gone."

"Town," she said.

He sat at the table. She placed a fork and knife and napkin in front of him.

"She can't stay up there all night," Dorothy said.

"No, I guess not." Bill was turning shy, soft; it was an old comic routine, a bedroom farce, and the familiarity drained him, momentarily, of his ferocity.

"Yolanda," he called upstairs.

She came down. She'd combed her hair, and in the hall light, it shone raven and dark, almost blue. She hesitated in the kitchen, looking around, and then touched Bill's shoulder on the way out.

Dorothy served dinner. She ate in silence, cutting the meat into small, precise pieces, listening to the tines of her fork scrape the plate, to the serrated edge of the knife saw the steak, watching the shadow of Bill's hand rise and fall across the table. When they had finished, she cleared their plates and began to clean up. Bill fixed a drink and hovered behind her, leaning against the counter. He sipped from his glass and the ice clinked and Dorothy felt the sound at the base of her neck. It travelled down her spine.

"What were you doing in town?"

A fleck of pepper, she noticed, floated in the rinse water. She pinched it out with her finger.

"You done talking forever?"

She worked a washrag over a fork, even though it was already clean.

"Funny," Bill said. But he didn't say what he found funny.

Dorothy had the vague impression that if she kept washing, if she kept reaching into the sink and turning on the faucet and scrubbing the knives and forks, then Bill would recognize her, he would see in her something old and familiar, and she would be saved.

"What the hell," Bill said. He bit down on an ice cube. It cracked loudly in his open mouth.

446

She imagined herself mixing batters, spooning blueberries in muffin tins, baking breads and rolls, roasting a chicken, a stew simmering on the stove. She imagined lining the cupboards with fresh paper and ironing Bill's good shirts and fanning magazines out across the coffee table. She imagined running the vacuum, picking up shirt pins, paper clips, buttons, bending over to pocket a penny, which, after all, might be the lucky one.

She lifted a plate from the sink and then braced herself. She felt his anger coming before it arrived, a sudden stillness. His fist landed on the side of her face, near the eye. The plate sank back through the suds, into the water. She turned from the force of the blow. His fist was still clenched, and he raised it to his mouth, biting into a whitened knuckle. He dropped his hands to his sides and began to shudder convulsively in a pained mimicry of someone crying; there were no tears in his eyes, they were dry, drier than stone.

"Hold me," he begged.

The embrace was only the memory of an embrace, a lesson learned and repeated rote-like. He had hit her, but it was too late for them to touch. Bill sat down in his chair, and Dorothy walked out the door. Spiderwebs spread across the path, holding in their threads some of the light rain that had begun to fall. Dorothy broke through them blindly.

When Homer answered his door, immediately he asked, "What happened?" But he knew. He sat Dorothy down in an old rocking chair that had been his grandfather's. He pushed the chair back and forth and said, "You can stay here if you want."

"I'm leaving."

"I wish that wasn't so."

"I can't remember anything anymore. Nothing, you know?"

Homer disappeared into his kitchen and brought back a damp cloth. He'd slipped two ice cubes in the center, and now he held the bundle to her swelling eye.

"I wish there was some revelation," Dorothy said. "Something you could tell me about Bill that I don't already know."

"There's no excuse."

"It's not just the baby."

Dorothy had never been above the first floor of the house, but she had been right: Homer's bed was neatly made, a thick blanket bought from the Umpquas was spread crisply over the mat-

447

tress, and two pillows with bright green cases lay beneath the headboard, strangely waiting. Homer had been so long alone that Dorothy had half-imagined he might have dispensed with one of the pillows, gotten rid of it as unnecessary, an extravagance, a charade. But he had two pillows, and he also had nightstands with identical shaded lamps flanking either side of the bed.

She went to the bathroom. A black comb rested on the lip of the sink. Two clean towels were stacked on top of a silver radiator. On the wall next to the bathtub hung a picture of Jacinta. Homer was holding her aloft, above his head, in the backyard beside the apple tree. That apple tree, Homer had said, was the first in the orchard, planted by his grandfather, a sapling ordered from a catalogue. Beside the picture of Jacinta was an old tintype from the days when the whole world was recorded in a mild golden hue; Homer's grandfather stood over the sapling, proudly pointing at its tiny, bare, twig-like branches. Behind him, the far background was vague, but closer in there was a clear-cut field of stumps. The shadow of the photographer crept into a corner of the picture, a dark hooded shape that gave the scene a feeling of silence.

In the bedroom, the windows were open.

"Don't cry," Homer said. "Everything's going to be fine."

He clasped her waist and bent to kiss her at the open throat of her blouse. When he folded back the fabric and ran a finger under the lacy fringe of her bra, her chest heaved in a sudden stutter; she trembled from the cold and the simple exposure. The curtains lifted. A brown-and-white feather floated across a small writing desk and sailed to the floor. Homer shut the windows, and Dorothy continued undressing. When she was naked her skin seemed incredibly white, like something long buried. Homer eased her down on the edge of the bed and asked, "Are you sure?" It wasn't really a question she could answer. Homer undressed, hanging his shirt in the closet, draping his slacks over the back of a chair. A quarter fell from the pocket and rolled in circles and wobbled to a stop beneath the bed.

Dorothy had returned home and was waiting for daybreak when the call came—a party was lost in a freak spring snowstorm that had wrapped around the western face of the mountain.

448

While Bill dressed upstairs, Dorothy started coffee. In a sort of ritual trance, scrubbing dishes in a slow, circular motion, she continued where she left off the night before. Islands of cold grease whitened on the plates. She ran them under the scalding water and watched the islands thaw and loosen and slide away. She wiped a rag over a plate and was aware, suddenly, that she always cleaned in a counterclockwise motion, as if cleaning were the reverse of time, an action against it. Beyond the kitchen window, a fringe of morning glory clung to the window frame; beyond that, Dorothy saw nothing but a murky gray light. Her reflection was still solid in the window, the mess of red hair, the white slope of her throat as it curved from sight. A gray bruise shut her left eye. Dorothy caught herself staring and, with a dull shock of recognition, turned away, reaching into the warm water for another dish.

As he dressed, Bill ran through the next twenty-four hours in his mind, visualizing the operation, seeing it all, down to the moment of triumph and success. He had done this countless times before, often in search of people he knew but mostly looking for strangers—which was worse, since he couldn't anticipate how they thought or what they might know about survival. The members of the lost party were Christians from a bible camp in Portland, and because it was spring, Bill guessed, they had foolishly relied on a sense of the season's benevolence—climbing the mountain in lightweight gear, praising God as they went, and perhaps this snow, on Easter weekend, had reminded them of the Resurrection or the lamb or the wings of angels in flight. Bill Hughes had seen enough trailside cairns—he'd built a few himself from scree and talus and two crossed sticks—to know how futile it was to address a personal God in such situations.

For Bill, there was no such thing as being lost; there were only varying degrees of uncertainty. The party had left base camp two days ago—that meant seven thousand feet, maybe eight, eight-five. A margin of a thousand feet, two thousand at the most; the rule was, stay put. People driven on by hysterical hope weren't found until the summer thaw—bones, a jackknife or compass—or years later, frozen in their final attitude, hunched like fetuses in a womb of ice. Or they were never found—a dream, a thing to wonder about, forever. He'd made the ascent before, had stopped counting his climbs after one hundred, and he'd seen people—

damned fools—do it in tennis shoes and shorts late in the summer. Hardly thinking, a scenario took shape: heavy spring snow would have a lot of creep, new wet snow contained little air, and he thought of breathing space, of chest compression, of snow rising up and then closing around the ribs like a vice.

Above Bill's nightstand, worked in crochet, hung a framed quote from Ben Franklin. "Some are weatherwise," it read. "Some are otherwise."

Dorothy had been through this before, too. Depending on the situation, and there were so many variables—variables of experience and age, faith and determination, sudden shifts in weather—Dorothy knew that hope lasted undiminished for twenty-four hours. She had learned this from Bill. Everyone had twenty-four hours—after that time, hypothermia was the big killer: falling body heat, slurred speech, memory lapses, uncontrollable shivering that slowly settled into a stunned numbness, loss of consciousness. "At a body temperature of ninety degrees," Bill had told her, "the heart only beats three times a minute." Twenty-four hours—beyond that time, hope and optimism were loans, borrowed notes that were often repaid in disappointment and regret long after. She knew about this, too. The letdown after a failed rescue was unbearable. All the women, the wives and members of the church guild, would gather in one house or another, preparing food for the men, aware of the helplessness, the poverty of their effort—brewing coffee, baking, fixing stew and sandwiches, answering phones, praying, waiting—the women did what they knew how to do, and none of it really mattered. They felt this, and the air was always charged with avoidance: the women spoke of garage sales, TV soaps, canning. Talking, they were like explorers searching for a low pass, some way around the mountain, which rose among them, looming in their midst like a kind of silence.

Dorothy wiped her hands on her apron and flicked on the radio. Their bedroom door shut. Bill pounded across the floor above. Dorothy listened as he lurched down the stairs, her heart synced to each descending step.

Bill stood in the doorway, filling the frame.

"Can I fix you something to eat?" Dorothy asked.

"I've got to go, Dot," Bill said. He was defending himself against her objections. He expected resistance; Dorothy didn't offer any. Bill kicked open the screen door and let it slap shut.

450

"There's no choice about it," he said.

"I understand," she said and reached in the sink and scrubbed another dish. She placed it to dry in the rack. Robins sang in the old, gnarled apple tree, a gray shadow in the backyard. Other things were becoming visible—the wheelbarrow on its side, the yellow webbing of a chaise, the blue rim of a plastic bucket. Silver pools had formed in the shallows after last night's heavy rain.

Bill turned his wife toward him and saw that she was crying. Her pain was a million miles away; he smudged a tear from her face with his thumb. Then he held his thumb to Dorothy's mouth, and Dorothy sucked the tear away, tasting the salt, feeling Bill's rough skin rasp her wet lip.

Bill lifted his hands and looked at them as though he were vividly picturing something he was holding. He dropped his empty hands. The scent of cold, wet cedar swept into the kitchen as he slammed the door shut. He gunned the truck in the driveway. Clouds of blue exhaust spewed from the tail pipe and the rumbling engine rocked the chassis like a cradle. While the engine warmed, Bill hurled logs from the woodpile into the bed, weighting it for traction. Lilac branches whipped his windshield as he sped away, turning onto the road toward town.

Dorothy leaned against the sink. She plunged her hands through the surface of graying suds and felt for another dish, but she was finished. She pulled the plug and watched the water suck down and vanish. Then she cleaned the drain trap.

Late in the afternoon, she caught a ride into town with Homer. All the storefronts had been decorated with Easter scenes, rabbits hopping through fields of green grass, a Jesus hovering above an empty tomb, ascending through the clouds. She felt the slight pressure of Homer's palm in the curve of her hip as he guided her across the street. The windows of the bar were blackened at sidewalk level except for a peephole in the shape of a diamond. Homer held the door for her. A few old men turned to the sudden light, squinting, then bending back down to their beers. Behind the bar, the grill spattered, thick smoke curling beneath the clogged vent. Dorothy had met the bartender once. Talbot? She didn't think so. A cousin, a nephew. He flipped a burger, then shuffled down along the bar, wiping a rag in the well. He said hello to Homer and looked at Dorothy.

"I'm Dorothy Hughes," she said. "Dot Hughes, Bill's wife—we met once."

"Dotty," he said, remembering. "Got some kids up there."

The other men looked up but turned away on contact. The bar had a drowsy, wartime feel; shame, lethargy, as only the unfit remained behind, isolated, knowing why.

"You heard anything?" Homer asked.

"Just the radio and the paper," the bartender said. "No calls, not so far."

He squeezed the rag dry, a trickle of rust brown water. Dorothy ordered a hamburger. The bartender returned to the grill, flipped a burger, pressed grease from it. Over his shoulder, he said, "I'd expect something soon." He flattened two buns on sizzling pads of butter, speaking to himself now, into the weak updraft as the gray smoke fanned in lazy arabesques.

Homer went to the phone and made a call. Dorothy's plate came.

"On the house," the bartender said.

It felt good to eat. She ate slowly. The afternoon *Oregonian* was delivered and she examined a copy, the front page, the facts. She searched for familiar names among the list of the missing but found none. Her eyes scanned the bold black headline words, then sank between them, into the white spaces. She drew a picture of the mountain, gouged it out with a pencil. Inside it she wrote:

Dot
Dotty
Dorothy

She ordered another beer, and looked for Homer; he was still on the phone. This was where Bill would come, where the rescue team would come, after. If they failed, the men would stay on the mountain longer, two, three, sometimes four days, way beyond what was reasonable. They would be afraid to admit the truth, so they would remain up there, searching, grimly silent, determined, alone in their world. No one wanted to be the first to give in, and when they finally returned, past all delusions, they would keep together at a back table.

"I don't want you to go," Homer said.

"You?" Dorothy said. "It's impossible."

He nodded. "I'll send along what you need."

"I'll be fine."

She had only what was in her travel bag, in the locker. Her floats she'd left behind, and she knew Bill would take them down, begin dismantling her presence as he had Jacinta's, until there was no trace left of either of them. The kitchen, without the floats, would be a plain white room, a little shabby and small. Her very first float, a sea-worn shade of blue, she'd found nestled in a tangle of seaweed on the beach at Cape Alvarez; over the years, she'd picked up the floats in junk stores and flea markets and rummage sales, and she could still remember, for each, the day of discovery. Often she wondered what calamity had cut the float loose, what accident had torn the net, half a world away, so that the float would break free and drift in the current across the Pacific and finally wash ashore, a jewel found on the beach saved at someone's home, treasured for a while, and cast off again—she had always romanticized high seas and sharks and capsized trawlers.

The light outside the bar was shocking in its whiteness, and Dorothy stood for a moment, stunned and shielding her eyes. She crossed the street. In the waiting room, she found her travel bag. People were going places this weekend. It was Easter. A few little girls were dressed in frilly outfits, with white cotton tights and puffy skirts and dainty gloves, the fingertips of which were already smudged with diesel black dirt from everything they touched in the dingy station.

"I might come visit you," Homer said.

"Please." Dorothy lifted her travel bag.

"Bill's going to ask where you are. He'll want to know."

"Tell him whatever you think's right."

She boarded the bus and waved to Homer from her window. The bus pulled away from the curb, and she held a headrest to steady herself. As the bus rose out of the Gorge, toward the highway, and north, Dorothy watched the mountain. She knew little about what the men actually did up there. Often at lower elevations they used dogs, but in that high white country, swept by blizzard winds and blanketed in snow, trails of scent or sight were hard, if not impossible, to pick up, and when they were, they didn't last and were easily lost. She knew the men used long alu-

453

minum poles and ran them into the snow, plunged them down deep through the soft layers, hoping for contact, hoping to reach into something solid. Resistance gave them energy, kindled hope, often only to find a buried rock, cracked ice, earth. As time wore on, the slightest evidence gave life to the most outlandish expectations. Ruts and hollows appeared as footsteps wandering across the blank white fields and clouds shifting in the sky threw down swift dark shadows that seemed moving and alive. Drifts in the snow took on the shape of huddled bodies and the wind whistling over a rock outcropping was heard as a faint cry for help. Or, in those sudden, muffled silences that sometimes close over a mountain, when the wind dies and everything is held in a crystal quiet, a man might hear his own pulse and mistake it for the heartbeat of another.

Nominated by Karen Bender

FROM *AVA*

by CAROLE MASO

from CONJUNCTIONS

AVA IS A living text. One that trembles and shudders. One that yearns. It is filled with ephemeral thoughts, incomplete gestures, revisions, recurrences and repetitions—precious, disappearing things. My most spacious form thus far, it allows in the most joy, the most desire, the most regret. Embraces the most uncertainty. It has given me the freedom to pose difficult questions and has taught me how to love the questions: the enduring mystery that is music, the pull and drag of the tide, the mystery of why we are here and must die.

No other book eludes me like *AVA*. It reaches for things just outside the grasp of my mind, my body, the grasp of my imagination. It brings me up close to the limits of my own comprehension, pointing out, as Kafka says, the incompleteness of any life—not because it is too short, but because it is a human life.

AVA is a work in progress and will always be a work in progress. It is a book in a perpetual state of becoming. It cannot be stabilized or fixed. It can never be finished. It's a book that could be written forever, added to or subtracted from in a kind of Borgesian infinity. Do I ever finish putting things in order? Can I assign a beginning to affection, or an end? Every love affair returns, at odd moments, as a refrain, a handful of words, a thrumming at the temple perhaps, or a small ache at the back of the knee. *AVA* is filled with late last-minute things—postscripts, post-postscripts.

I come back to writing continually humbled and astonished. I do not pretend to understand how disparate sentences and sen-

455

tence fragments that allow in a large field of voices and subjects, linked to each other quite often by mismatched syntax and surrounded by space for 265 pages, can yield new sorts of meanings and wholeness. I do not completely understand how such fragile, tenuous, mortal connections can suggest a kind of forever. How one thousand Chinese murdered in a square turn into one thousand love letters in the dying Ava Klein's abstracting mind, or how the delicate, coveted butterflies Nabokov chases on the hills of Telluride become a hovering and beautiful alphabet. I cannot really speak of these things. As Michael Palmer said of one of his volumes of poetry, "the mystery remains in the book." I can discuss only the writing of *AVA*.

I was promoting my novel *The Art Lover*. I was flying places, meeting people, connections were constantly being made and broken. I felt strange and estranged the way I do during such times, with all the reading, all the talking into black microphones, all the pat replies to the same questions. Because I must write every day, I continued to write then, though I could manage only one or two sentences a time. The next entry, some time later, would be another sentence, often unrelated to the one that had come before. I was using language as an anchor and a consolation, enjoying the act of simply putting one word next to another and allowing them to vibrate together. Most days it was my only pleasure. Shortly after the book promotion, North Point Press, scheduled to do my next book, *The American Woman in the Chinese Hat* and also *The Art Lover* in paper, folded. These books made the rounds at commercial houses where so-called literary editors displayed the ignorance and lack of vision I have now become more accustomed to, with their love of safety and product and money. But I was still capable of being shocked by them then. I kept writing in pieces. I was scheduled to escape to France and had sublet my apartment when a death prevented me from leaving the country. The fragments piled up. Keeping the notebooks going, I began to travel the world in my own way. Among the many voices I had accumulated I began to hear a recurring voice, an intelligence if you will. She was a thirty-nine-year-old woman, confined to a hospital bed and dying, yet extraordinarily free.

I cannot say what direction her story would have taken had it not been assuming its final form during the terrible weeks of the

Persian Gulf War. It was my first war as an adult and like everyone I watched the whole awful thing live on TV. War as a subject permeates the text of *AVA*, but more importantly war dictates the novel's shape. A very deep longing for peace, one I must admit I had scarcely been aware of, overwhelmed me as I watched the efficient, precise elimination of people, places, things by my government. My loathing for the men who were making this and my distrust for male language and forms led me to search for more feminine shapes, less "logical" perhaps, since a terrible logic had brought us here, less simplistic, a form that might be capable of imagining peace, accommodating freedom, acting out reunion. I was looking for the fabric of reconciliation. Something that might join us. I was determined not to speak in destructive or borrowed forms any longer. But what did that mean? I began to ask the question of myself, "What could she not ask of fiction and therefore never get?" I began one more time to ask what fiction might be, what it might do and what we might deserve, after all. Traditional fiction had failed us. Did we dare presume to dream it over? To discard the things we were given but were never really ours?

In an attempt to ward off death with its chaos and mess, traditional fiction had flourished. Its attempts to organize, make manageable and comprehensible with its reassuring logic in effect reassures no one. I do not think I am overstating it when I say that mainstream fiction has become death with its complacent, unequivocal truths, its reductive assignment of meaning, its manipulations, its predictability and stasis. As I was watching the war it became increasingly clear to me that this fiction had become a kind of totalitarianism, with its tyrannical plot lines, its linear chronology and its characterizations that left no place in the text for the reader, no space in which to think one's thoughts, no place to live. All the reader's freedoms in effect are usurped.

In an ordinary narrative I hardly have time to say how beautiful you are or that I have missed you or that—come quickly, there are finches at the feeder! In a traditional narrative there is hardly any time to hear the lovely offhand things you say in letters or at the beach or at the moment of desire. In *AVA* I have tried to write lines the reader (and the writer) might meditate to, recombine, rewrite as he or she pleases. I have tried to create a place to breathe sweet air, a place to dream. In an ordinary narrative I barely have the courage or the chance to ask why we could not make it work, despite love, despite everything we had going. In an ordinary narrative I probably would have missed the wings on Primo Levi's back as he stands at the top of the staircase. And Beckett too, during the war, hiding in a tree and listening to a song a woman sings across the sadness that is Europe.

"The ideal or the dream would be to come up with a language that heals as much as it separates." When I read this line by Hélène Cixous, I knew she was articulating what I was wordlessly searching for when I began to combine my fragments. "Could one," Cixous asks, "imagine a language sufficiently transparent, sufficiently supple, intense, faithful, so that there would be reparation and not only separation?" And yes, isn't it possible that language instead of limiting possibility might actually enlarge it? That through its suggestiveness, the gorgeousness of its surface, its resonant, unexplored depths, it might actually open up the world a little, and possibly something within ourselves as well? I agree with Barthes when he says that the novel or the theater (and not these essays by the way) are the natural setting in which concrete freedom can most violently and effectively be acted out. That this is not the case for the most part, in fiction at any rate, is a whole other matter relating back to the "literary" editors who have entered a covert, never discussed and possibly not even conscious conspiracy to conserve the dead white male aesthetic. Women, blacks, Latinos, Asians, etc., are all made to sound essentially the same—that is to say, like John Cheever, on a bad day. Oh, a few bones are thrown now and then, a few concessions are made to exotic or alternative content, but that is all.

All experience of course is filtered through one's personality, disposition, upbringing, culture (which is why I know we do not all sound like John Cheever). Truth be told I was never much for ordinary narrative, it seems. Even as a child, the eldest of five, I would wander year after year in and out of our bedtime reading room, dissatisfied by the stories, the silly plot contrivances, the reduction of an awesome, complicated world into a rather silly sterile one. When my mother was reading stories I would often wander out to the night garden, taking one sentence or one scene out there with me to dream over, stopping, I guess, the incessant march of the plot forward to the inevitable climax. Only when it came time for poetry did I sit transfixed by the many moments of beauty, the astounding leaps and juxtapositions. These seemed to me much closer an approximation of my world, which was all mystery and strangeness and wonder and light.

Back then my remote father grew roses. The tenderness of this fact, and the odd feeling I had that he cared more for these silent, beautiful creatures than he did for us, always intrigued and oddly touched me. It was what my childhood was: random, incomprehensible, astounding events, one after the next. I cherish this image of my father. And because I have never wholly understood it I gave Ava's father the task of growing roses. Unlike my father, Ava's father survived Treblinka. He gives Ava a penny a piece for each Japanese beetle she can collect from the garden. The Germans sold the dead Jews' hair for fifteen pennies a kilo. There were piles of women's hair there. Fifty feet high. Ava in her innocence and purity, holding her clear jar of beetles, says, "Yes, we'll have to make holes for air." The book is built on waves of association like this. There is a rose called "Peace." A rose called "Cuisse de Nymphe Emue"—that's "Thigh of an Aroused Nymph." It blooms once unreservedly, and then not again.

I have attempted in some small way to create a text, as Barthes says, "in which is braided, woven in the most personal way, the relations of every kind of bliss: those of 'life' and those of the text, in which reading and the risks of life are subject to the same anamnesis."

Back to my mother reading stories those long-ago nights. Another thing I did was to detach the meanings from the words and turn them into a kind of music, a song my mother was singing in a secret language just to me. It was a rhythmic, sensual experience as she sang what I imagined were the syllables of pure love. This is what literature became for me: music, love and the body. I cannot keep the body out of my writing; it enters the language, transforms the page, imposes its own intelligence. If I have succeeded at all you will hear me breathing. You will hear the sound my longing makes. You will sense in the text the body near water, as it was then, and in silence. Not the body as it is now, in Washington, D.C., next to obelisks and pillars and domes, walking it seems in endless circles and reciting the alphabet over and over. That will show up later; the body has an incredible memory.

My hope is that you might feel one moment of true freedom in *AVA*. That the form, odd as it may at first seem, will not constrict

459

or alienate, but will set something in motion. I am always just on the verge of understanding here, which is the true state of desire. Perhaps you will feel some of this enormous desire for everything in the world in the fragments of this living, changing, flawed work. And in the silence between fragments.

"Almost everything is yet to be written by women," Ava Klein says, moments before her death.

Let us bloom then, unreservedly.

There's still time.

MORNING

Each holiday celebrated with real extravagance. Birthdays. Independence days. Saints' days. Even when we were poor. With verve.

Come sit in the morning garden for awhile.

Olives hang like earrings in late August.

A perpetual pageant.

A throbbing.

Come quickly.

The light in your eyes.

Precious. Unexpected thing.

Mardi Gras: a farewell to the flesh.

You spoke of Trieste. Of Constantinople. You pushed the curls from your face. We drank Five-Star Metaxa on the island of Crete and aspired to the state of music.

Olives hang like earrings.

A throbbing. A certain pulsing.

The villagers grew violets.

We ran through genêt and wild sage.

Labyrinth of Crete, mystery of water, home.

On this same street we practiced arias, sang sad songs, duets, received bitter news, laughed, wept.

Green, how much I want you green.

We ran through genêt and wild sage.

You are a wild one, Ava Klein.

We were working on an erotic song cycle.

He bounded up the sea-soaked steps.

She sang like an angel. Her breast rose and fell with each breath.

Night jasmine. Already?

On this slowly moving couchette.

Not yet.

Tell me everything that you want.

Wake up, Ava Klein. Turn over on your side. Your right arm, please.

Tell me everything you'd like me to—your hand there, slowly.

Pollo allo Diavolo. A chicken opened flat. Marinated in olive oil, lemon juice. On a grill. A Roman specialty.

Up close you are like a statue.

After all the dolci—the nougat, candied oranges and lemon peel, ginger and burnt almonds, anisette—my sweet . . . after walnut biscotti and lovemaking, Alfred Hitchcock's *Vertigo*. . . . Francesco, what was conspiring against us, even then?

This same corner I now turn in bright light, in heat and in some fear, I once turned in snow and the mind calls that up reminded of—

The way you looked that night, on your knees.

Reminded of: a simple game of Hide and Seek. Afterwards a large fire.

461

Sundays are always so peaceful here.

A child in a tree.

August.

I dream of you and Louise and the giant poodle, Lily, and the beach.

But it is not of course that summer anymore.

August. They sit together on a lawn in New York State in last light-bent, but only slightly.

Come quickly, there are finches at the feeder.

Let me know if you are going.

The small village. I could not stay away. My two dear friends. Always there. Arms outstretched, waiting.

A dazzle of fish.

My hand reaching for a distant, undiscovered planet.

Through water.

Where we never really felt far from the sea.

He kept drawing ladders.

We dressed as the morning star and birds.

He bows his head in shadow. He turns gentle with one touch. In the Café Pourquoi Pas, in the Café de Rien, in the Café Tout Va Bien where we seemed to live then.

We were living a sort of café life.

Let me describe my life here.

You can't believe the fruit!

I'd like to imagine there was music.

Pains in the joints. Dizziness. Some pain.

A certain pulsing.

She's very pregnant.

I'd like to imagine there was music in the background.

And that you sang.

What is offhand, overheard. Bits of remembered things.

Morning. And the nurses, now. Good morning, Ava Klein.

Ava Klein, Francesco says, helping me on with my feather headdress.

Brazil, 1988; Venice, 1976; Quebec, 1980.

Determined to reshape the world according to the dictates of desire—

Where we dressed as the planets and danced.

Spinning. To you—

Charmed, enchanted land.

Chinatown. A favorite Chinese restaurant. The way he held my hand. As if it were a polished stone. Steam and ginger. News that the actress you most wanted had agreed to the part and financing had come. On the street, rain, a yellow taxicab. I love you.

He bounded up the sea-soaked steps.

Music moves in me. Shapes I've needed to complete. Listen, listen hard.

It's cool at this hour—morning. How is it that I am back here again, watering and watering the gardens?

And you are magically here somehow.

A heartbeat away.

We have a curious way, however, of being dependent on unexpected things, and among these are the unexpected transformations of

Poetry.

And he is here in front of me asking, Qu'est-ce que tu bois?

Blood and seawater have identical levels of potassium, calcium and magnesium.

Wild roses and rose hips.

The rose.

Qu'est-ce que tu bois?

Summer in New York. I'm thirsty.

I say "water" in my sleep. I'm thirsty. You bring me a tall glass of water and place it by my bed.

And one is reminded of: We were driving from New York City up the Saw Mill Parkway toward the Taconic and listening to the *Wanderer* Symphony of Schubert on the radio. I begged you to slow down, but as slowly as you drove, we were still losing it in the static, long before it finished.

You are a rare bird.

And I had to complete it in my head.

Which is different from hearing it completed on WNYC.

Though I sang it LOUD. All the parts.

It was completing itself, in midtown Manhattan without us.

Though I knew the ending and tried to sing it LOUD, without

You are beautiful

forgetting any of the important parts.

How is this for a beginning?

There is scarcely a day that goes by that I do not think of you.

Turn over on your side.

My heart is breading.

New York in summer.

The Bleecker Street Cinema. Monica Vitti on the rocks.

Danilo laments the U.S.A. He says we have forgotten how to be Americans.

Maria Ex Communikata gets ready for the midnight show.

The Bleecker Street Cinema closes for good. And suddenly it is clear,

We are losing.

The scales tip.

Please invoice me. Input me. Format me. Impact me.

The bullet meant for Ricardo hits Renee instead. The bullet meant for target #1 hits baby Fawn. A bullet kills Daryl, honor student.

We will go to the river. We will rent a boat.

There were flowers each day in the market in Venice.

And how your hands trembled at a gift of exquisite yellow roses, so beautiful, and pas cher, Emma.

To hear you say japonica in your British accent once more.

Tell him that you saw us.

Because the corner of Broadway and West Houston is everyone's in summer.

I think of his life. That somewhere else it was completing itself. Somewhere outside my reach. Without me.

Though there was no way for me to know, unlike Schubert's *Wanderer*, how it was going to be played out.

Somewhere a young girl learns how to hold a pencil. She writes A.

To sing the endless variations on the themes he set up.

Thirty-five years old. Aldo.

Because the guandu, Ana Julia's favorite food, when we could finally bear to use it was no longer good. Expiration date: 1989.

I might turn the corner and there will be Cha-Cha Fernández walking a Doberman pinscher.

I can see it all from here.

Rare butterflies.

Nymphets by the pool.

Danilo, working out an unemployment scam for himself. Plotting a trip to Prague. Can you come?

The *Prague*, the *Paris*, the *Jupiter*, to name a few. Can you come?

I miss Czechoslovakia sometimes.

I'll probably never see you again.

Of course you will.

I might look up and there will be the Fuji Film blimp.

Or Samuel Beckett in a tree.

They are singing low in my ear, now. In the morning garden.

He grew old roses.

So what's the war about? someone asks. In brief.

Impact me. Impact me harder.

She finds herself on her thirty-third birthday on a foreign coast with a man named Carlos.

Never stop.

He is worried the city will get better—but not for awhile, and not before it gets worse.

The man on the TV wants them to freeze his head while he is alive, and to attach his brain to another body sometime later, when they find the cure for his incurable brain tumor.

How are you Ava Klein?

What answer would you be interested in other than the truth?

Make a wish.

The blue and purple in your black hair, Carlos. . . .

Danilo is writing a love story where the beloved makes the mistake of not existing.

Ava Klein, you are a rare bird.

Because decidedly, I do not want to miss the grand opening scheduled for early winter, still some months away, of the new Caribbean restaurant down the block that will serve goat.

Or the cold. Or the Beaujolais Nouveau.

And so: Monday: chemotherapy. Tuesday: reiki. Wednesday: acupuncture. Thursday: visualization. Friday: experimental potion, numbers one through twelve. Monday: chemotherapy.

This room. White curtains to the floor. Wide pine panels. Painted white. Like the room in a dream.

The iris, Marie-Claude, like you, so glowing and grave.

Thank you for the tiger lilies.

In an attempt between 1968 and 1970 to fashion a perfectly round sphere, he made three thousand balls of mud, all unsuccessful;

I wrote you fifty love letters.

She has lived to tell it. How to make the family challah: sugar, flour, oil, kosher salt, eggs, honey.

I ran through broom and wild sage.

We took the overnight train.

You are a wild one, Ava Klein.

The men hung swordfish in the trees to dry. Sword snouts. Teeth in the trees.

He spoke of Trieste, of Constantinople. He pushed the curls from his face, thought of buying a hat perhaps. My first honeymoon. It was how the days went.

The changing of the guard.

In Crete, a gold-toothed porter.

She sang like an angel. Her breast rose with each breath.

I needed to travel.

Aida sits in the day's first square of light.

I love your breasts.

It was Rome. I was twenty, and you were forty, almost. You were making a film of the *Inferno*. I laughed imagining the task. I was a graduate student. A student of comparative literature. I held

467

your giant hand. You pressed me against a broken wall in the furnace called August. I kissed you. Or you kissed me.

Yes, but it is not that August anymore.

And in 1971 the artist carved 926 sculptures from sugar cubes.

That evening he led me into the circular room.

A woman named Yvette Poisson dancing in a glass bar in the seaside resort in winter.

A perfect gray sea. Grayness of the days.

Let me know if you are going—

Snow fell on water.

We took the overnight train. He kissed me everywhere. Shapely trees passing in the windows.

A beautiful landscape. Imagined in the dark.

The way his body swelled.

Trees that looked like other things.

He tries to conserve moments of existence by placing them in biscuit boxes.

At the feeder, goldfinches.

Danilo, my Czech novelist, with his deep mistrust of words. His fear of the Russians. His love of Nabokov.

And Flaubert is *not* Madame Bovary, students, I don't care what he says.

The Empire State Building is working overtime emoting in colored lights for every cause known to man: international children, the Irish, hostages, Fourth of July.

Václav Havel: Everywhere in the world, people were surprised how these malleable, humiliated, cynical citizens of Czechoslovakia, who seemingly believed in nothing, found the tremendous strength within a few weeks to cast off the totalitarian systems in an entirely peaceful and dignified manner. We ourselves are surprised at it.

Strange the way the joy keeps changing.

I remember the smell of rosemary and thyme in a young man's hair.

It was a kind of paradise, Anatole.

He makes a record on which he tries to remember the lullabies he might have heard as a child.

The morning nurse singing, Let me know if you are going to Central Park. Lunch break 12:30.

I hear water. You come around the rounded stone fountain. Ça va? I say. And you nod.

At La fontaine des Quatre Dauphins in Aix, where I wept.

To see your beautiful head turn.

To see your beautiful head turn once more.

But we've already lost so much.

The heat of a plot. I'm beginning to detect the heat of the plot.

García Lorca feigning death.

Václav Havel comes to town. Danilo tries to meet him on this, his triumphant visit. Havel, being pushed out for five minutes at a time here, there to speak with American dignitaries. Also with Frank Langella, Paul Simon, Carly Simon, etc., John Irving in the corner. (Nobody wanted to talk to him.) This one, that one-poor Havel. Danilo looks pained.

It was as if we had come in on a conversation midway. That was the kind of beginning it was.

The late verses of Neruda vary widely in tone and texture. Their fluctuating musical impulses require a looser structure woven together less by the uniformity of lines than by the dying poet's sensibilities.

A stroll around the park. While the weather's still fine. The ginkgo trees in fall.

Un, Deux, trois.

A simple game of Hide and Seek.

Danilo to his last, crazy lover: I'm going to take the garbage out. And she responds, What, you're going to see Gorbachev now? She shakes her head. Go then!

Turn over on your side.

And it will seem like music.

A blue like no other.

Maria Regina remembers the fascists: They told us to mount the stairs two at a time.

Often there is nowhere to go but forward or back. It is hard to stay here in one place and especially at moments like these.

I am afraid the news is bad, Ava Klein.

Now in America, they call this coffee. But I remember coffee. . . .

A simple game of Hide and Seek.

The giant head of Françoise Gilot in stone. We took photographs, though photographs were not allowed. Marie-Claude and Emma and Anatole and me, smiling in the bright light and so much sea, in the room called Joie de Vivre.

The Picasso Musée. Antibes.

He was on his way to see Gorbachev when we met for the first time on the street. It seems that all along we were neighbors.

Ten, eleven, twelve. . . .

I kiss you a thousand times.

Making mysterious La Joconde faces next to Françoise Gilot one afternoon.

Vladimir Nabokov: The book you sent me is one of the tritest and most tedious examples of a trite and tedious genre. The plot and those extravagant "deep" conversations affect me as bad movies do, or the worst plays and stories of Leonid Andreyev, with whom Faulkner has a kind of fatal affinity. I imagine that this kind of thing (white trash, velvety Negroes, those bloodhounds out of Uncle Tom's Cabin melodramas, steadily baying through thousands of swampy books) may be necessary in a social sense, but it is not literature . . . (and especially those ghastly italics).

The emblem is for a group called Missing Foundation. An upside-down champagne glass with the champagne crossed out. The party's over is what the emblem stands for. And everything points to it—that the party is over.

Would you like to have a perfect memory?

Because there is still Verdi and sunlight and the memory of that man on the Riviera—and when memory goes it is replaced maybe with beautiful, floating, free, out of context fish. Orange in deep blue with tails like feathers.

Or Samuel Beckett learning to fly.

Vitello Tonato: Boneless veal roast, white wine, anchovies, capers, tuna, a sprig of thyme.

It's a hot and lovely day. No humidity—odd for this city. A clear sky, high clouds. And the weather is for everyone.

What's the rush then?

Unable to get to you, Marie-Claude and Emma, any other way right now, I dream of the fish in your stone pond. I send you a report of the weather.

We are making a day trip to Cap d'Antibes. How much we wish you were here!

Also recalls his grandfather: he is gnawing on the end of an anisette biscuit with the perfect pointy teeth he acquired right before his death.

After sex, after coffee, after everything there is to be said—

The hovering and beautiful alphabet as we form our first words after making love.

And somehow I'm still alive.

Danilo swearing that in the next book he'll do something easier, less ambitious, more suitable to his talent.

So many of the old places: Sabor, Felidia, Trattoria da Afredo.

Café Un, Deux, Trois.

In Venice. In August. At the mouth of the Saluti. . . . A celebration because *the plague is over*! So much joy.

They were going to go to the river. She brought chayote and plátano.

There was a man whose name was Whistle.

The small light a candle can give. The face flushed.

That's an almond tree. Cherry. Small fig.

A homeless man has fallen asleep in Ann's car on Fourteenth Street when she goes to move it in the morning.

Mr Tunny and his fourteen-year-old grandson were leaving church when they heard the shots being fired. "He was moving very slowly, very gently." A bullet had entered the boy's cheek and exited the left side of the back of his brain.

I see my light dying.

Our destination in those days was always the sea.

Francesco with his silly film quizzes. Asking me one more time where the word *paparazzi* came from.

The choice is made a little mysteriously, in a superstitious manner, not rationally. Still it is made: ultraviolet light, or radiation,

Chinese herbs.

Danilo puts in a good word for modern American medicine.

INTERVIEWER: If you could remember, could keep forever, just one story, what would it be?

FRISCH: Which one? It would not be the story of my life, or a story I have heard, but a myth. I think it would be the myth of Icarus.

Aldo kept drawing ladders. Ladders going nowhere, maybe.

It's OK.

My aunt then, wandering, confused, during the war.

We took the overnight train.

We danced to Price all night long in the circular room. It was 1988. It was France.

You were on holiday.

One night.

It was everything while it lasted.

One night once.

A shining thing.

My father offering pennies for each Japanese bettle.

She sends an envelope of poems.

There is not a day that I do not think of you.

The glittering green of beetles. . . . Hanging on the lip of the yellow rose.

The lemon trees are planted along the garden walls. By and by they will be covered with rush mats, but the orange trees are left in the open. Hundreds and hundreds of the loveliest fruits hang on these trees. They are never trimmed or planted in a bucket as in our country, but stand free and easy in the earth, in a row with their brothers.

Music moves in me. Shapes I've needed to complete. Listen. Listen hard:

I hear a heart beating.

Can it be that our visit was only eight months ago?

I know I am lucky that music moves in me in such a way—and if it has rearranged a few chaotic cells or changed the composition of my blood—but even if it hasn't—still—I have been, of course, extraordinarily lucky.

That night the baby was conceived. In a room called Joie de Vivre.

Where you spoke, Anatole, only once, and in a whisper, of freedom and how much you needed the sky and good-bye—

Swinging on the swing. What shall we name her?

473

Can it be that our visit was only eight months ago? It is so hard to imagine . . . I think even with all the insanity and pain of those days I was happier. I miss you.

Sing to me of Paris and of lost things.

I knew a boy named Bernard Reznikoff. Quiet, carrying a stack of books. Blushing. New York City.

Just once I'd like to save Virginia Woolf from drowning. Hart Crane. Primo Levi from falling. Paul Celan, Bruno Schultz, Robert Desnos, and for my parents: Grandma and Grandpa, Uncle Isaac, Uncle Solly, Aunt Sophie, just once.

In the city of New York. Where I taught school, sang songs, watched my friends come and go. Climbed the pointy buildings. Marveled at all the lights.

Aldo, building cathedrals with his voice.

A man in a bowler hat disappears into thin air. Grandfather.

She was dressed in a gown of gold satin. Suppose it had been me?

She shudders at the sight of a garter belt as if it were a contraption of supreme torture.

I think of him often: Samuel Beckett learning to fly.

Look for this in my shoe.

He waits for disguised contacts who sometimes never come.

A a. B b.

All the bodies piling up on stage.

C.

Like your father you grew old roses.

Snow falls like music in the late autumn.

Home, before it was divided.

A pretty rough show, then, for someone who came to see nudes, portraits and still lifes. It is made rougher still by the inescapable dates on the labels of the stronger images, all of which come from the hopeful ignorant time when it seemed that all that was involved was a kind of liberation of attitude concerning practices between consenting adults in a society of sexual pluralism. Of course the show has its tenderer moments. There are prints of overwhelming tenderness of Mapplethorpe's great friend Patti Smith. There is a lovely picture of Brice Marden's little girl. It is possible to be moved by a self-portrait of 1980 in which Mapplethorpe shows himself in women's makeup, eager and girlish and almost pubescent in the frail flatness of his/her naked upper body. . . .

Let me describe what my life once was here.

Home before it was divided.

. . . The self-portrait as a young girl remains in my mind as the emblem of the exhibition, and the dark reality that has settled upon the world to which it belongs. One cannot help but think back to Marcel Duchamp's self-representation in *maquillage*, wearing the sort of wide-brimmed hat Virginia Woolf might have worn with a hatband designed by Vanessa, with ringed finger and a fur boa. . . .

Come sit in the morning garden for a while. Open the map.

With AIDS a form of life went dead, a way of thought, a form of imagination and hope. Any death is tragic and the death of children especially so. . . . But this other death carries away a whole possible world.

A remote chorus of boys.

Shall we take the upper or the lower corniche?

The way the people you loved spoke—expressed themselves in letters, or at the beach, or at the moment of desire.

Maybe I should go now.

No. Please stay.

Nominated by Kristina McGrath

NIGHT SINGING

by W. S. MERWIN
from THE PARIS REVIEW

Long after Ovid's story of Philomela
    has gone out of fashion and after the testimonials
of Hafiz and Keats have been smothered in comment
    and droned dead in schools and after Eliot has gone home
from the Sacred Heart and Ransom has spat and consigned
    to human youth what he reduced to fairy numbers
after the name has become slightly embarrassing
    and dried skins have yielded their details and tapes have been
slowed and analyzed and there is nothing at all
    for me to say one nightingale is singing
nearby in the oaks where I can see nothing but darkness
    and can only listen and ride out on the long note's
invisible beam that wells up and bursts from its
    unknown star on on on never returning
never the same never caught while through the small leaves
    of May the starlight glitters from its own journeys
once in the ancestry of this song my mother visited here
    lightning struck the locomotive in the mountains
it had never happened before and there were so many
    things to tell that she had just seen and would never
have imagined now a field away I hear another
    voice starting up and on the slope there is a third
not echoing but varying after the lives
    after the goodbyes after the faces and the light

after the recognitions and the touching and tears
  those voices go on rising oh if I knew I would hear
in the last dark that singing I know how I would listen

Nominated by Lisel Mueller, Joan Murray

SALT

by LINDA GREGERSON

from COLORADO REVIEW

Because she had been told, time and
          again,
              not to swing on the neighbor's high hammock,

and because she had time and again gone
          back, lured
              by the older boys and their dangerous

propulsions, because a child in shock (we
          didn't know
              this yet) can seem sullen or intran-

sigent, and because my father hated his life,
          my sister
              with her collarbone broken was spanked

and sent to bed for the night, to shiver
          through the August
              heat and cry her way through sleep.

And where, while she cried, was the life he
          loved?
              Gone before she was born, of course,

gone with the river-ice stored in sawdust,
          gone with the horses,
              gone with the dogs, gone with Arvid Anacker

up in the barn. 1918. My father was six.
                    His father thought Why
          leave a boy to the women. Ole (like "holy"

without the h, a good Norwegian
                    name)—
          Ole had papers to sign, you see,

having served as county JP for years—
                    you
          would have chosen him too, he was salt

of the earth—and Arvid's people needed to cut
                    the body down.
          So Ole took the boy along, my father

that is, and what he hadn't allowed for was
                    how badly
          Arvid had botched it,

even this last job, the man had no luck.
                    His neck
          not having broken, you see, he'd thrashed

for a while, and the northeast wall of the barn—
                    the near wall—
          was everywhere harrows and scythes.

It wasn't—I hope you can understand—
                    the
          blood or the blackening face,

as fearful as those were to a boy, that forty
                    years later
          had drowned our days in bourbon and dis-

gust, it was just that the world had no
                    savor left
          once life with the old man was

gone. It's common as dirt, the story
        of ex-
           pulsion: once in the father's fair

lost field, even the cycles of darkness cohered.
        Arvid swinging
      in the granular light, Ole as solid

as heartwood, and tall . . . how
        could a girl
      on her salt-soaked pillow

compete? The banished one in the story
        measures
      all that might heal him by all

that's been lost. My sister in the hammock
        by Arvid
      in the barn. I remember

that hammock, a gray and dirty canvas
        thing,
      I never could make much of it.

But Karen would swing toward the fragrant
        branches, fleshed
      with laughter, giddy with the earth's

sweet pull. Some children are like that,
        I have one
      myself, no wonder we never leave them alone,

we who have no talent for pleasure
        nor use
      for the body but after the fact.

Nominated by Colorado Review, Alice Fulton, Jim Simmerman

THE WALK

by CHITRA DIVAKARUNI

from PATERSON LITERARY REVIEW

Each Sunday evening the nuns took us
for a walk. We climbed carefully in our black
patent-leather shoes up Darjeeling hillsides looped
with trails the color of earthworms. Below us
the school fell away, the sad green roofs
of the dormitories, the angled classrooms,
the dining hall where we learned to cut
buttered bread into polite bite-size squares,
to eat bland stews and puddings with forks
and spoons. The sharp metallic thrust of the church
spire, small, then smaller, and around it
the town: bazaar, post office, the scab
coated donkeys, dogs nosing through trash,
straggle of huts with hesitant woodfires
in the yards. Though all at a respectful distance,
like the local children we passed, tattered
khaki pants and swollen chilblained
fingers the color of the torn sky, color
of the Sacred Heart in the painting of Jesus
that hung above the staircase with his chest
open, his eyes following us as we filed up
to bed.
      We were trained not to stop and talk
to them, runny-nosed boys and girls with
who-knew-what diseases, not even to wave back,
and, of course, it was improper

to stare. The nuns walked so fast
already we were passing the plantation, the shrubs
lined up neatly, the thick glossy green
giving out a faint wild odor like our bodies
in bed after lights-out. Passing the pickers,
hill women with branch-scarred arms, bent under
enormous baskets strapped to shoulder and head,
the cords in their thin necks
pulling like wires. Back at school although
Sister Dolores cracked the steel refectory ruler
down on my knuckles, I could not drink
my tea. It tasted salt as the bitten inside
of the mouth, and its brown
was like the women's necks, that same
tense color.
             But now we are walking quicker because
it has started drizzling, drops fall on us
from the leaves of the *pipul,* shaped like eyes.
We pull on the hoods of our grey raincoats, we
are prepared for emergencies, we step in time,
soldiers of Christ squelching through vales
of mud, we are singing, as always on walks,
the nuns leading us with choir-boy voices.
O Kindly Light, and then a song
about the Emerald Isle. Ireland, where they grew up,
these two Sisters not that much older
than us. Mountain fog thickens like a cataract
over the sun's pale eye, it is stumbling-dark,
in long black sleeves. We have to take a shortcut
through the upper town. The nuns motion us
faster, faster, an oval blur of hands.
             Honeysuckle over
a gate, lanterns in front windows. In one,
a woman in a blue sari holds a baby, his fuzzy
backlit head against the curve
of her shoulder. Smell of food in the air, *real* food,
onion pakoras, like my mother used to make.
Rain in my eyes, my mouth. Salt, salt. A
sudden streetlamp lights up the nuns' faces,

damp and splotched with red
like frostbitten camellia buds. It prickles
the back of my throat. The woman watches
with wondering eyes as we pass her window
in our wet, determined shoes, singing
Beautiful Killarney, a long line of girls, all of us
so far from home.

Nominated by Paterson Literary Review, George Keithley, Lois-Ann Yamanaka

PARADISE PARK

fiction by STEVEN MILLHAUSER

from GRAND STREET

PARADISE PARK, which was destroyed by fire on May 31, 1924, except for a number of steel and concrete structures that rose eerily from the blackened ruins until they were torn down the following year, first opened its gates on June 1, 1912, on eight and two-thirds acres of the former site of Dreamland, across Surf Avenue from Luna Park. In an era noted for the brilliance and extravagance of its amusement parks, the new park seemed to be presenting itself as a culmination. Even the diminished acreage, with its mere 652 feet of ocean frontage, proved responsible for many of the park's most striking features, for it was immediately clear that Paradise Park was striving to overcome the limitations of space by a certain flamboyance or excess that pushed it in directions never before undertaken in the architecture of amusement parks.

The first sign that the new owner was prepared to respond boldly to the challenge of his rivals was the four-hundred-foot-high white wall that rose about the newly acquired property, dwarfing Luna's main tower, casting its late-afternoon shadow all the way to Steeplechase, and surpassing even the legendary tower of Dreamland, which was said to have been illuminated by one hundred thousand electric lights. In that early era of enclosed amusement parks, Paradise Park was the most visibly and radically enclosed of all. The soaring white wall, composed of staff over a lath-and-iron frame, suggested on the one hand a defiant act of exclusion, an outrageous assertion of privacy, and on

484

the other an invitation, a deliberate titillation or provocation—
the latter most clearly in evidence at the towering top of the un-
adorned wall, which only there, high in the sky, broke into a
profusion of colorful towers, minarets, domes, and spires.

Two openings pierced the mystery of the great wall: an ocean
entrance, across an iron pier and through the grimacing mouth of
an immense clown's face, and the Surf Avenue entrance, through
a soaring arch flanked by sixty-foot dragons. The openings did
not reveal the inside of the park but ushered visitors into a broad,
meandering tunnel that wound its way parallel to the wall for
hundreds of feet before turning abruptly inward to the park itself.
Lit with red, blue, and yellow electric lights, the winding tunnel
was lined on both sides with ball-and-milkbottle booths, carnival
wheels, Moxie stands, curtained freak shows, gypsy palmist tents,
hot roasted corn stalls, phrenology shops displaying maps of
skulls divided into zones, tattoo parlors, penny arcades, shooting
galleries—all of it ringing with the mingled din of tumbling
bottles, rattling balls, Graphophone music, the shouts of barkers
("And a jaunt for joy it is, ladies and gentlemen!"), and the muf-
fled clatter of unseen rides. Scattered among the familiar plea-
sures of Paradise Alley, as the entrance tunnel came to be called,
were a number of new and exciting ones that proved immediately
popular, such as Sky Cars, small electric-traction elevators lined
with black velvet and operated by masked female attendants in
scarlet livery who took customers up to the top of the wall for a
sudden, magnificent view of the park.

Since secrecy was part of the allure of Paradise Park, the elu-
sive creator-manager, who from the beginning surrounded him-
self with a certain mystery, permitted no publicity photos in the
course of an otherwise vigorous promotional campaign. The his-
torian must therefore rely on a scattering of amateur photographs
that focus on particular attractions but give no reliable view of
the whole. Despite the absence of a definitive map or plan, it is
nevertheless possible to reconstruct the early form of the park in
some detail from the many reports, sometimes conflicting, of
early witnesses.

What struck the first visitors, as they emerged from Paradise
Alley into the park itself, was the powerful upward or vertical
thrust. In the bewildering assault of first impressions it was im-
mediately apparent that the park consisted of several levels, to

485

which access was had by numerous stairways, escalators, and electric elevators. Each of the two upper levels was a system of wide iron bridges that intersected at one or more points to form broad plazas, large enough to house booths, cafés, brass bands, and mechanical rides, as well as a variety of exotic attractions: a Zulu village, a Chinese temple, a Javanese puppet theater, a replica of the marketplace of Marrakech, and a reconstructed village of Mbuti pygmies from the Ituri Forest, including forty-five Mbuti tribesmen living in reassembled native huts. The bridges were supported by a system of openwork iron towers, many of which were supplied with stairways and elevators; the entire structure of bridges and supports left a feeling of openness, so that at any point on the ground one could see big slices of blue sky. Fifty-five elevator shafts in the inner walls gave access to every bridge at both levels, and all around the inner wall rose the spiral of an immense railed stairway, which quickly became known as Paradise Road and led to the top of the wall. There people could walk four abreast along a balustrade lined with game booths and food stands and look down at Paradise Park itself, with its crisscrossing bridges, its festive plazas, its roller coaster and Ferris wheel, its exotic villages, its enticing spectacles with casts of thousands, such as the Destruction of Carthage and the Burning Skyscraper; or they could gaze outward at the great beach stretching east and west with its domed and towering hotels, its doubled-decked iron piers, its bathing pavilions—out beyond the lighthouse at Sea Gate in one direction and the sailboats on Sheepshead Bay in the other, and farther still, much farther, for it was said that on a clear day you could see sixty miles in any direction.

Although from the beginning there were critics of the new park, who argued that the vertical emphasis was reminiscent of the world of skyscrapers and elevated railroads from which the urban visitor longed to escape, the response of the public was decisively enthusiastic. Those who frequented the park began to say they could no longer enjoy single-level parks, which seemed too close to the ground; and so successful was the park that a single ride called the Sidewinder, which cost $86,000 to build, drew $375,000 in receipts in the first three seasons.

If the most striking and immediate fact about Paradise Park was its multilevel verticality, its continual invitation to half-glimpsed excitements high overhead, the crowds soon noticed that the park offered, along with familiar amusements, a number of new attractions. One sensation of the opening season was a brand-new mechanical ride called the Nightmare Railway, a development of the scenic railway and Old Mill in the direction of the House of Horrors. Delighted visitors discovered that the great white wall contained an elaborate set of tracks that rose and fell sharply along a dark, twisting tunnel which presented a series of frights: the car, which held twelve people on six benches, went rushing toward immense boulders that collapsed upon contact, approached another car that suddenly swooped overhead on a second set of tracks, experienced a landslide, a flood, an avalanche, and a raging fire, passed through a dragon's den, a mummy's crypt, a haunted graveyard, a cave of malignant dwarfs, and a vampire's castle, and emerged at last in a bright opening two hundred feet above the ground of Paradise Park.

Even more popular than the new mechanical rides was an entirely new group of amusements called Adventures. An Adventure, according to the promotional material, was not a ride but a carefully re-created real-life experience: for ten cents one could enter the Dark Forest and be attacked by a gang of bandits, or step into the Streets of Lisbon and experience the famous earthquake, or wander through Old Algeria and experience the thrill of being surrounded by angry Moslems, tied up in a burlap sack, carried off on the back of a camel, and dangled over a cliff above crashing waves. One of the more popular Adventures was Lovers' Leap, a three-hundred-foot-high rocky cliff (staff over lath and iron) that rose at one corner of the park and offered to daredevil couples a fearful ledge jutting over a thundering waterfall that threw up great clouds of spray; the sound of the roaring water was produced by machines concealed in the artificial cliff and the thick spray was sent up through dozens of holes in the staff. The couples who jumped shrieking into the thundering mist were caught ten feet below in a concealed net that broke their fall lightly and carried them eighty feet down into the swirling mist, where muscular attendants released them and guided them into a descending elevator.

But the single most popular attraction of the 1912 season proved rather surprisingly to be an immense model of the resort itself, done in precise scale and measuring thirty by twenty-five feet. Located on a plaza of the third level and surrounded by roped pedestrian walks supplied with coin-operated telescopes, the model showed Coney Island in May of 1911, just before the fire that destroyed Dreamland. In brilliant detail it replicated the heart of Coney Island from Steeplechase Park to Dreamland, including Surf Avenue, Mermaid Avenue, the host of side streets with their saloons and music halls, their dance pavilions and hotels, their shooting galleries and souvenir shops, and the beach itself with its double-decked iron piers and its bathhouses, all populated by tiny automatons (the brass band played, the man in the straw boater shot the tin duck in the row of moving ducks, the girl on the roller coaster opened her mouth and rolled her eyes). The detail was so scrupulous that the model was said to duplicate every tie in every track of every roller coaster, every waxwork in the Eden Musée, including the pastework pearls of Jenny Lind, and every slat in every rocking chair on the porch of every hotel; and it was rumored that with the aid of a penny-in-the-slot telescope you could see not only the precise replication of every ornate machine in every penny arcade and the minuscule letters of every peepshow entertainment (*Actors and Models, After the Bath, Bare in the Bear Skin, What the Book Agent Saw*), but, through the elegantly duplicated peepshow viewer, the flickering, teasingly vague black-and-white pictures themselves. The highly popular model was the work of Otis Stilwell, a carver of carousel horses who as a hobby made lovingly detailed miniature merry-go-rounds, roller coasters, and funhouses that he sold in a shop on Surf Avenue and who, along with the inventor Otto Danziker, was to prove one of the owner-manager's closest advisers. The miniature Coney Island, which attracted amazed attention as a kind of wondrous toy, served a deeper purpose: by reducing the entire resort to a miniature within his amusement park, the manager was enhancing the size and power of his park, which became a gigantic and marvelous structure stretching away in every direction; at the same time he was inviting the admiring crowds to experience a subtle condescension toward all rival attractions, which were reduced to charming toys.

Like other amusement park entrepreneurs at the turn of the century, the owner-manager of Paradise Park was confronted by the problem of attracting a mass audience hungry for pleasure and excitement while excluding any threat to the supposed values of that audience, such as the prostitutes, gamblers, and gangsters who flourished on every Coney Island side street. By enclosing their parks and hiring enforcement squads, the entrepreneurs were able to exercise unprecedented control, but the astute manager noted a new problem: the new, safe pleasures of the enclosed parks threatened to make them too tame and predictable, to push them in the unfortunate direction of the genteel beer garden. This problem he solved brilliantly by hiring a troupe of eighteen hundred specially trained actors to imitate the rowdiness and vice whose exclusion had left a secret yearning. Hence the park included among its attractions a number of dark saloons, seedy roadhouses, and crooked alleys lined by dubious shops, in which customers could mingle with prostitutes, pickpockets, cutthroats, drunken sailors, pimps, con men, and gangland thugs, assured that the racy language, the shocking costumes, and the terrifying fights which periodically erupted were part of the show. Actresses playing the part of prostitutes were particularly admired by the male and female visitors, who enjoyed seeing at close range the disturbing, thrilling streetwalkers with their invitation to forbidden pleasures that were strictly and safely imaginary. Patrons who themselves became rowdy or offensive were swiftly removed by the very efficient park police, who roamed the grounds in uniform or in disguise. Because the distinction was not always clear between an actor dressed like a sailor with a false tattoo on his forearm and a real sailor with a real tattoo, or an actress with rouged cheeks and brazen eyes strutting along the booth-lined alleys and a factory girl from Brooklyn wearing a new chinchilla coat and a straw hat with a willow plume, a certain heady confusion was experienced by the park's patrons, who began to feel that they too were actors and actresses disguised as seamstresses, schoolteachers, department store clerks, typists, and shopkeepers—roles that they no longer took as seriously as they did in that other world of tiredness.

Among the many disguises in Paradise Park were those of the owner-manager himself, for it quickly became known that the secretive proprietor liked to mingle unseen with the crowds in order to observe the operation of his park at close range, overhear responses to his amusements, and imagine rearrangements and improvements. Disguised as a park workman in cap, shirtsleeves,

489

and vest, an Irish shopkeeper in his Sunday bowler, a uniformed trombone player in epaulets, a city swell in striped pants, bow tie, and straw boater, a bearded Jew in a long coat of black gabardine, the manager would make the rounds of his park, studying the crowd and devising ways to improve congested areas. Once, overhearing a couple complain that the Lovers' Leap was disappointing because the concealed net broke the fall too soon, he had the net lowered by ten feet and discovered that revenues increased. As rumors of his presence persisted, visitors began to search for the disguised owner-manager among the throngs; and people began to wonder a little about the man who walked among them unseen, listening to them, observing them, and seeking to increase their delight.

They knew only that he was an outsider, from Manhattan, who had come late to the amusement-park business and who, it was said, had money to burn. Then a journalist named Warren Burchard wrote a long article that appeared in a special Coney Island supplement of the *Brooklyn Eagle* (August 10, 1912). In the course of analyzing Coney Island amusements, calculating trends, reporting revenues, and discussing patterns of crowd behavior, Burchard devoted several paragraphs to the latest proprietor of "marvelous Coney," Charles Sarabee. Sarabee, Burchard reported, was a native New Yorker who was yet another instance of that peculiarly American phenomenon, the self-made man. Sarabee's father had sold cigars in the shop of a small Manhattan hotel. As a boy Charles had worked long hours in the cigar shop, where by the age of nine he had not only mastered the bewildering array of names, prices, and cedarwood boxcovers, but had begun to arrange cigars in eye-catching displays, the most successful of which was a three-foot-high wire tree hung with Christmas ornaments and high-priced Havanas. At thirteen he went to work as a bellhop at the hotel. There his efficiency, industry, and cleverness endeared him to the manager and earned him a series of promotions starting with desk clerk and ending, when Charles was twenty-one, with the post of assistant manager, in which capacity he introduced a wide variety of improvements, including fruit trees in every lobby and, in every bathroom, up-to-date fixtures in stylish settings: mahogany-hooded shower-baths, heated brass towel-rails, and Ionic pilasters of Siena marble. His big break came several years later when as manager-owner of the hotel he decided to enter a partnership in a new downtown department store. He soon had the controlling interest in three other department stores, but his fortune was made at the age of thirty, when he introduced in his stores a revolutionary idea called the "leisure spot." Sarabee had always had a sharp eye for the behavior of customers, and he had noticed that many of them grew tired and irritable after an hour or two of strolling from department to department and riding elevators and escalators in search of something they thought they wanted but probably didn't need. He knew it was important to keep his customers cheerful and in a free-spending mood, but even more important than this was simply to keep them in the store for as long as possible. Thus arose the idea of leisure spots: small oases of comfort located on every floor, where customers could relax in pleasant surroundings and recover from the tremendous assault on the nervous system represented by the modern department store with its countless treasures temptingly displayed. The leisure spots would attempt to simulate the atmosphere of a cozy living room, with thick armchairs and couches, crocheted pillows, lace antimacassars, mahogany lamp tables on which stood porcelain lamps with tasseled shades, and in one corner a smiling, apple-cheeked young woman in a crisp blue uniform who sold steaming cups of tea and coffee and a variety of tarts, cakes, cookies, and gingerbread. Although the leisure spots took up valuable floor space and proved forbiddingly expensive to install, they turned out to be immensely popular, and after a month it was clear that customers were staying longer and spending more. Rival stores quickly imitated the new device, but Sarabee's leisure spots were always more appealing, and he took care to vary them in order to overcome monotony; in quick succession he introduced leisure spots in the style of an English pub, a Dutch cottage, a Victorian parlor, a Japanese tearoom, and an Alpine chalet. Inspired by his successes, he soon began to introduce more fanciful decors, such as the Amazon jungle, the Italian plaza, the Puritan village, and the hold of a whaling ship, all designed with extreme fidelity, if not to History herself, then to the public's romantic idea of each exotic place. His search for new ideas led him to visit world's fairs and expositions, where the reproduction of exotic places had become fashionable, as well as the big Eastern pleasure resorts that borrowed themes and purchased properties from defunct expositions; and in 1908, on a trip to Coney Island, which he had not visited since his childhood, and where he attempted without success to purchase the old three-hundred-foot-high Iron Tower that had once been the showpiece of the Philadelphia Centennial Exposition of 1876, he was struck by the festive architecture of the three new amusement parks—Steeplechase, Luna, and Dreamland—as well as by the immense, lively, and free-spending crowds. He had been growing a little stale in the department-store business; he needed a new outlet for his energies; the destruction of Dreamland Park by fire in the spring of 1911 was decisive. As the city hesitated to purchase the ruined grounds put up for sale by the Dreamland Corporation, who proposed that the fifteen acres of Dreamland and the fifteen additional acres destroyed by fire should be turned into a public park, Sarabee was able to arrange for the lease of eight and two-thirds acres of the former amusement park, with the stipulation that the lease would be terminated when public development began, an event that was delayed until the administration of Fiorello La-Guardia in 1934, while the remaining acres, during the intervening years, were operated as a parking lot.

With the instinct of a true showman, Sarabee understood that the fatal enemy of amusement is boredom, and he was tireless in his search for new mechanical rides, new spectacles, new thrills and excitements. Working closely with the inventor Otto Danziker, who had designed the Nightmare Railway, Sarabee introduced at least five major rides each season, dismantling any that failed to prove successful. Of the thirteen new rides presented at Paradise Park in the second two seasons (1913 and 1914) before the breakthrough of 1915, one of the most popular was the Swizzler, a three-hundred-foot-high openwork iron column containing a spiral track down which cars holding ten people rushed at terrifying speeds, only to crash through a floor straight into a twisting black tunnel that suddenly burst into light around a bend and revealed that the car was about to rush into a brick wall. At the last second a door in the wall sprung open to reveal a track plunging into a lake, which proved to be an optical illusion projected by tilted mirrors reflecting a movie of rippling lakewater; at the bottom of the track the car slowed and entered a small room that rose into the air—the room was a hydraulic elevator—and released the car into a tunnel that led through suddenly

492

opened doors into a sunny opening at the base of the column. Other successful rides created by Danziker were the Tumbler, the Spider, the Whim-Wham, the Flip, the Lightnin' Lizzie, and the Crazy Wheel—this last a gigantic horizontal ring of steel over one hundred feet in diameter, balanced on a pivot with hanging, swinging seats on the inner and outer rims. Danziker also designed a special Ferris wheel that slowly rotated like a top while turning vertically, and he placed a medium-sized roller coaster on a plaza of the second level, some three hundred feet in the air, which Sarabee promptly advertised as the world's largest roller coaster.

By the end of the third season the box-office take made it clear that Paradise Park had achieved an unprecedented success and had begun to attract a significant portion of the Steeplechase and Luna crowds. The exciting new rides, the lure of the upper levels, the eighteen hundred actors, the sense of being in a place that was unlike any other place on earth but also reassuringly familiar, all this promised a triumphant future, and the outbreak of the European war, which some had feared might harm the amusement business, proved only a further impetus to pleasure. People speculated on the rides already said to be under construction for next season, and a journalist reported, on dubious evidence, that Sarabee was going to unveil an entirely new kind of ride. The rumor was in fact mistaken, for Sarabee and Danziker were planning a number of sophisticated mechanical rides that broke no new technological ground; but in a broad sense the rumor proved to be true, for it was during the last week of the 1914 season that a small incident occurred which led to a startling new development in Paradise Park.

A workman called Ed O'Hearn, who had been sent into the tunnel beneath the Swizzler on a routine check of the track, pulled a handkerchief out of his pocket to wipe some dirt from his face. He dislodged a dime, which began rolling down a packed-earth incline beside the track. O'Hearn had been planning to spend his dime on a hot dog with mustard and sauerkraut, and he hurried after it with his electric lantern. He saw the dime come to a stop some fifteen feet below him, but when he reached the spot, the dime had disappeared. O'Hearn crawled about on his knees and patted the hard earth with his palm. As he did so he was surprised to feel a current of cool air

493

streaming upward. He lowered the lantern and saw a fissure in the earth about two feet long and the width of a finger. When he dropped a flat stone sideways into the crack he counted to twenty before he heard a faint sound. He immediately returned above ground to report to his boss, who sent a message to Sarabee.

An hour later a team of three engineers investigated the crevice and determined that a small limestone cavity existed far beneath the Swizzler but posed no danger to the ride or to the park itself. Sarabee, disguised as one of the engineers, withdrew into a kind of somber brooding. When one of his men tried to reassure him that the park was perfectly safe, Sarabee is reported to have said: "It's all clear now. What'd you say?"

Thus was born the idea that was to give to the history of the amusement park a certain swerve that some found dubious but that no one was able to ignore. All fall and winter the great plans were laid; in his park office on Surf Avenue, Sarabee met daily with Otto Danziker, Otis Stilwell, and the engineer William Engelstein. The project was carried forward with characteristic secrecy, and indeed it remains one of the remarkable facts about Sarabee that he was able to elicit from everyone who worked for him an unfailing loyalty. Two weeks before the start of the new season, red-and-black posters appeared in the windows of restaurants and dance halls, on hoardings and telephone poles, on hotel notice-boards and the walls of bathhouses, announcing a NEW PARADISE PARK: *You Have to See It to Believe It.* On opening day the great entrance remained closed; a barker with cane and striped derby announced from a platform sixty feet high that the park would open one week later, on May 29. Rumor had it that the delay was a promotional gimmick aimed at increasing the air of mystery that surrounded the park; there was talk of a new kind of roller coaster, a more thrilling funhouse; and some said that Sarabee himself, with cane and striped derby, had announced the delay from the platform between the heads of the great dragons that flanked the closed entrance.

The gates opened on May 29, 1915, at eight in the morning; by noon the crowd had exceeded one hundred thousand. People who had visited the park before were puzzled and disappointed. Apart from three new rides, including a splendid Haunted Mountain, a new sideshow consisting entirely of midgets (a midget Fat Lady, a midget Ossified Man, a midget Wild Man of Borneo, a midget Bearded Lady, a pair of midget Siamese twins), nothing about the park seemed new enough to merit the publicity campaign. Visitors did, however, notice a number of odd-looking structures scattered about. Each structure was a rotunda composed of columns with grotesque capitals—grimacing devils, weeping clown faces, winged lions and horses, struggling mermaids fondled by hairy monkeys, three-headed chickens—roofed with a gilt dome, on top of which sat a miniature Danziker merry-go-round turning to barrel-organ melodies. Each of the dozen rotundas contained a central pole, a circle of wooden benches, and a uniformed attendant. When people were seated on the benches, which held as many as forty, the attendant pulled a lever in the pole, causing the platform to descend rapidly through a cylindrical shaft. At the bottom of the shaft the benches suddenly flattened out, the floor began to turn, and whirling, laughing, frightened people began spinning off the edge down any of fourteen chutes that led to a red curtain—and as they passed through the curtain they saw, all around them, as an attendant helped them to their feet at the bottom of the slide, a vast underground amusement park.

This immense subterranean project, with its roller coaster and funhouse, its tents and pavilions, its spires and domes and minarets, all lit by electric lights and alive with carousel music, the shouts of barkers, the rattle of rides, and even the smell of the sea, had been designed by Engelstein with the help of engineers who had worked on the Boston and New York City subway systems, and had been carried out by a force of nearly two thousand Irish, Italian, and Polish immigrant laborers lowered into shafts with pickaxes, shovels, and wheelbarrows, as well as by teams of trained workers who laid charges of dynamite to blast through boulders or operated a hydraulic tunnel-shield designed by Danziker for boring through clay and quicksand. In the course of excavation workmen discovered the jaw of a mastodon, a casket of seventeenth-century Dutch coins, and the rusty anchor of a Dutch merchant ship. The final structure appears to have been a skillful mixture of broad tunnels serving as fairground midways and high, open stretches roofed in reinforced concrete lined with dark blue tiles to resemble a night sky in summer. The completed park included at one end a great beach of white sand and an artificial ocean—in reality a great shallow basin filled with ocean water and containing Danziker's wave machine, which caused long, perfectly breaking waves to fall on the flawless beach. Two immense hotels, a band pavilion, and half a dozen bathhouses lined the beach, and a great iron pier with shops and restaurants under its wooden roof stretched twelve hundred feet into the water. Five hundred seagulls brought down from the upper shore added a realistic touch, though later it was discovered that the birds did not prosper in the subterranean world and gave birth to sickly offspring with wobbly walks and crazed flight patterns, who frightened children and had to be replaced by fresh gulls and hand-painted balsa wood models. High above the beach, and the piers, and the park, and the always burning electric lights stretched the night sky of blueblack tiles, supplied with thousands of twinkling artificial stars and a brilliant moon emerging from and disappearing behind slow-moving clouds beamed up by hidden projectors.

The creation of an underground amusement park with an ocean setting may have been a triumph of engineering, but Sarabee was too shrewd to rely solely on first impressions. His underground park had features that distinguished it clearly from his upper park, so that customers, after the first shock of delight or admiration, did not grow impatient, did not feel cheated. In addition to four new rides, including the wildly popular Yo-Yo, an immense steel yo-yo suspended by a thick cable from a tower and supplied with seats, visitors to Sarabee's Bargain Basement, as the new park good-naturedly came to be called, discovered that many rides and attractions were playful or fiendish variations of familiar amusement park pleasures. Thus the merry-go-round included an all-white horse that turned out to be a bucking bronco, around a high curve the roller coaster left the tracks and soared over a twenty-foot gap to another set of tracks (such at least was the thrilling sensation, although in fact the cars were supported from beneath by hinged beams attached to the coaster frame), the funhouse mirrors turned people into hideous, frightening monsters, and the Ferris wheel, at the climax of the ride, dropped slowly from its stationary supports and rolled back and forth along a track that left room for the bottommost cars to pass unharmed. In the same spirit the architecture was more extravagant—the front roller-coaster cars were supplied with carved dragon's heads, the Old Mill began in the sneering mouth of an ogre, a papier-mâché mountain called the Haunted Grotto opened at a cave flanked by thirty-foot naked giantesses whose legs and arms were encircled by giant snakes—and the stage properties for the actors were more sinister, the actor-drunks rowdier, the false prostitutes more brazen, some going so far as to lure customers into back rooms that turned out to be part of the House of Mirth. The sense that the rides were, in a controlled way, out of control, that they were exceeding bounds, that they were imitating nightmarish breakdowns while remaining perfectly safe, all this proved intoxicating to the crowds, who at the same time were urged to a feverish carnival spirit by the winking electric lights, the artificial night sky, the crash of artificial waves, the sense of a vast underground adventure not bound by the rules of ordinary parks.

Despite the enthusiastic reception of Sarabee's New Paradise Park by Coney Island pleasure-seekers, by journalists, and by a number of distinguished foreign visitors, several critical voices were raised during the first months, and not only from the ranks of observers who might be expected to cast doubt on the new institutions of mass pleasure such as the dance hall, the vaudeville theater, the movie house, and the amusement park. An article in the August 1915 issue of *Munsey's Magazine* praised New Paradise Park for the boldness of its design and the ingenuity of its rides but paused to question whether Sarabee had not pushed the amusement park beyond its proper limit. Such developments as the leaping roller coaster and the rolling Ferris wheel, though of undoubted technological interest, threatened to make people bored with traditional rides and to encourage in them an unhealthy appetite for more extreme and dangerous sensations. It was in this sense that technology and morality became related issues, for a mass audience accustomed to violent mechanical pleasures was in danger of growing dissatisfied with the routines of everyday life and especially with their jobs, a dissatisfaction that in turn was bound to lead to a desire for more extreme forms of release. For finally the carefully engineered mechanical excitements and sensual stimulations of Sarabee's park were not and could not be satisfying, but were in the nature of a cheat, an ingenious illusion that left people secretly restless and unappeased. The unsigned article concluded by wondering whether this abiding restlessness was not the true aim of the great

497

amusement-park showman, in whose interest it was to create an audience perpetually hungry for the unfruitful pleasures he knew so well how to provide.

Even as such questions were being raised by voices skeptical of the new mass culture in general and of New Paradise Park in particular, it was rumored that Sarabee and his staff were at work on new plans, and there were those who said that Sarabee would never rest until he had carried the amusement park to its farthest limit of expression.

The new stage in the evolution of Paradise Park was not completed for two years, during which attendance increased even as war threatened. Unlike the upper park, the underground park was not required to close after the summer season, and Sarabee was able to run it at a profit through mid-November, after which the thinning crowds forced him to close for the winter. In the profitable season of 1916 three new rides appeared in the underground park, including a Ferris wheel supplied with paired carousel horses instead of seats, while in the upper park small signs of a disturbing development first became noticeable. The rides, although still in operation, were no longer replaced by new ones; the high roller coaster suffered a mechanical breakdown and was shut down; here and there a booth stood empty. Although the lawns and paths around the famous rotundas were kept clean and neat, grass grew wild in far corners of the park, and occasional patches of rust appeared on brightly painted steel frames.

It was in the expanded park of 1917 that Sarabee achieved what many called the fulfillment of his dream, although a few voices were raised in dissent. Visitors to the famous underground park discovered, in scattered and unlikely locations—on the beach, in bathhouses, behind game booths, under the roller coaster—some two dozen escalators leading down. The simple escalators led to a second underground level where a puzzling new park had been created—a pastoral park of oak and beech woodlands, winding paths, peaceful lakes, rolling hills, flowering meadows, babbling brooks, wooden footbridges, and soothing waterfalls: a detailed artificial landscape composed entirely of plaster and pasteboard (except for an occasional actor-shepherd with his herd of real sheep), illuminated by the light of electric lanterns with colored glass panes, and inviting the tired reveler to solitude and meditation. This deliberate emphasis on pleasures opposed to those of the amusement park was not lost upon visitors, who savored the contrast but could not overcome a sense of disappointment. That carefully arranged dissatisfaction was in turn overcome when the visitor on his ramble discovered an opening in a hill, or a doorway in an old oak, or a tunnel in a riverbank, all of which contained stone steps that led down to another level, where at the end of rocky passageways with mossy mouths a brilliant new amusement park stretched away.

Here in a masterful mingling of attractions visitors were invited to ride the world's first spherical Ferris wheel; experience the thrilling sensation of being buried alive in a coffin in the Old Graveyard; visit a Turkish palace, including the secret rooms of the seraglio with over six hundred concubines; ride the exciting new Wild Wheel Coaster; visit an exact reproduction of the Alhambra with all its pillars, arches, courtyards, and gardens, including the seventy-five-foot-high dome of the Salo de los Embajadores and the Patio de los Leones with its alabaster fountain supported by twelve white marble lions; enter the world's most frightening House of Horrors with its unforgettable hall of Rats; witness the demonic possession of the girls at the witch trials of Salem; fly through the trees on the backs of mechanical monster-birds in the Forest of Night; ride a real burro down a replicated Grand Canyon trail; visit a bustling harbor containing reconstructions of a Nantucket whaling ship, a Spanish galleon, Darwin's *Beagle*, a Viking long ship, Oliver Hazard Perry's flagship *Lawrence*, a Phoenician trireme, a Chinese junk, and Old Ironsides; see a departed dear one during a seance in the Medium's Mansion; ride the sensational triple-decker merry-go-round; visit a medieval torture chamber and see actor-victims broken on the rack, crushed in the iron boot, and hoisted on the strappado; descend into a replica of the labyrinthine salt mines of Hallstatt, Austria; ride the death-defying Barrel, a padded iron barrel guided by cables along a white-water rapids and down a reconstruction of the Horseshoe Falls composed of real Niagara water; ride the Swirl-a-Whirl, the Hootchie-Kootchie, and the Coney Island Sling; and pay a heartwarming visit to the Old Plantation, where seventy-five genuine southern darkies (actually white actors in blackface) strummed banjos, danced breakdowns, ate watermelons, picked cotton, and sang spirituals in four-part harmony while a benign Master sat on a veranda between his blond-ringleted daughter and a faithful black mammy who from time to time said "Lawdee!"

This continually changing landscape of rides, spectacles, exotic places, and reconstructed cultural wonders was connected by an intricate system of cable cars designed by Danziker, which criss-crossed the entire park and permitted visitors to gain an overview of the multitude of attractions and travel conveniently from one section to another. Danziker had also designed a scale-model sub-way, consisting of roofless cars the size of scenic-railway cars, driven by real engines and underlying the entire park, with twenty-four stations indicated by small kiosks in twenty-four dif-ferent styles, including a circus tent, a Gothic cathedral, a tepee, a Persian summerhouse, a log cabin, and a Moorish palace.

In addition to the striking transportation system, certain fea-tures of the new park drew attention in the popular press, in particular the group of sixteen new mechanical rides invented by Danziker, of which the most successful was the Chute Ball: an openwork iron sphere twenty feet in diameter that rolled along a steep, curving chute while riders inside were seated on twelve benches attached in such a way that they remained upright while revolving on a spindle. It was noted that most of the traditional rides had been carried to further degrees of evolution: in the Double Coaster, specially built roller-coaster cars rounding a turn suddenly rushed from the track and soared unsupported over dangerous gaps onto the track of a second roller coaster, and an immense and swiftly turning Airplane Swing released its planes one by one to fly through the air to a powerful plane-catching machine that resembled an iron octopus. The popular Wild Wheel was seen as a combination of roller coaster and Ferris wheel: along a sinuous coasterlike track rolled a great iron wheel, forty feet in diameter; the wheel's two grooved rims turned along a pair of steel cables that had been suspended at intervals from wrought-iron posts and ran like telephone wires above the entire length of the dipping and rising track; up to one hundred riders sat strapped into wire cages on the inside of the wheel and turned as the wheel turned. But technological process was less evident in the mechanical rides, which at best were clever varia-tions of familiar rides, than in the methods of transportation, in the advanced plumbing system in the public bathrooms, and in minor effects, such as the much-praised pack of mechanical rats in the House of Horrors.

The new park was also praised for its many meticulous reconstructions of cultural landmarks and natural wonders, all of which made the similar attractions of Luna and the expositions seem crude and childish. Sarabee's customers were invited to visit not only the Alhambra, but also the Porcelain Tower of Nanking, the catacombs of Alexandria, the Inca ruins of Cuzco, the hanging gardens of Babylon, and the palace of Kubla Khan, as well as an alp, a fjord, a stalactite cavern, a desert containing an oasis, a redwood forest, an iceberg, a sea grotto, and a bamboo grove inhabited by real pandas. One of the most admired replicas was that of the Edison Laboratory at West Orange, New Jersey, with its three-story main building that contained machine shops, experimental rooms, and rooms for glassblowing and electrical testing, as well as the famous forty-foot-high library with its great fireplace and its displays of thousands of ores and minerals in glass-fronted cabinets, the whole building and its four outbuildings enclosed by a high fence with a guard at the entrance gate; the laboratory was supplied with a staff of sixty actor-assistants, and Edison himself was played by the Shakespearean actor Howard Ford, who was particularly good at imitating Edison's famous naps—after which he would spring up refreshed and invent the phonograph or the electric light. But Sarabee's mania for replication reached its culmination in an immense project that he designed with Otis Stilwell: a sixty-by-forty-foot model in wood and pasteboard of Paris, France, including over eighty thousand buildings and thirty thousand trees (representing thirty-six different species), the precise furnishings of every apartment, shop, church, café, and department store, all the fruits and vegetables in Les Halles and all the fishing nets in the Seine, all the horse-drawn carriages, motorcars, bicycles, fiacres, motor omnibuses, and electric streetcars, every tombstone in Pére Lachaise cemetery and every plant in the Jardin des Plantes, over two hundred thousand miniature waxwork figures representing all social classes and occupations, and at the heart of the little city, an exact scale model of the Louvre, including not only every gallery, every staircase, every window mullion and ceiling decoration, but a precise miniature reproduction of every painting (oil on copper)

501

and its frame (beechwood), every statue (ivory), and every arti-
fact, from Egyptian sarcophagi to richly detailed eighteenth-
century spoons so minuscule that they were invisible to the naked
eye and had to be viewed through magnifying lenses.

The 1917 park was widely regarded as the most complete, most
successful form of the modern amusement park, its final and clas-
sic expression, which might be varied and expanded but never
surpassed; and the sole question that remained was where Sara-
bee would go from here.

Even as the classic park was being hailed in the press, Sarabee
was said to be planning another park, about which he was more
than usually secretive. At about the same time he began to
lose interest in his older parks, which were placed under the
management of a five-man board who were required to report to
Sarabee only twice a year and who concentrated their attention
on the first two underground parks and the pastoral park be-
tween them, while largely neglecting the aboveground park,
which continued to decline. Patches of rust spread on the bridge-
braces, paint peeled on the carousels, weeds grew under the
roller coaster and between lanes of booths; and there were signs
of deeper neglect. In certain stretches of the upper park, guards
were removed and brought below; the remaining guards grew
less vigilant, so that a dangerous element began to assert itself. A
gang of actors, who seemed to have grown into their roles,
prowled the darkened alleyways, where shanty brothels were said
to spring up; and complaints were made against a gang of dwarf
thugs who quit the Nightmare Railway and took up residence in a
dark corner of the park called Dwarftown, where no one ven-
tured after dusk.

Sarabee's new park, which opened in 1920 beneath the classic
park of 1917, puzzled his admirers and caused lengthy reassess-
ments of the showman's career. Here at one blow he did away
with the four central features of the modern amusement park—
the mechanical ride (roller coaster, Swizzler), the exotic attraction
(replicated village, market, garden, temple), the spectacle (De-
struction of Carthage), and the carnival amusement (freak show,
game booth)—and replaced them with an entirely new realm of
pleasures. In a dramatic turn away from meticulous replication,
Sarabee presented to customers in his new underground level a
scrupulously fantastic world. And here it becomes difficult to be

precise, for Sarabee banned photographs and the historian is forced to rely on often contradictory eyewitness accounts, tainted at times by rumor and exaggeration. We hear of dream-landscapes with gigantic nightmare flowers and imaginary flying animals, of impalpable pillars and edible disks of light. There are reports of sudden stairways leading to underwater kingdoms, of disappearing towns, of vast complex structures that resemble nothing ever seen before. Illusionary effects appear to have been widely used, for we hear of high walls that suddenly melt away, of metamorphoses and vanishings, and of a device that made a strong impression: a springing monster suddenly stops in midair, as if frozen, and then dissolves. This last suggests that Sarabee made use of hidden movie projectors to enhance his other effects. The entire park appeared to have been a thorough rejection not only of the replica, the reconstruction, the exotic imitation, which had haunted amusement parks from the beginning, but also of the mechanical ride, which by its very nature proclaimed its kinship with the real world of steel, dynamos, and electrical power even while turning that world into play. Sarabee's new park seized instead on the unreality and otherworldliness of amusement parks and carried fantastic effects to an unprecedented development. But Sarabee was careful to avoid certain traditional elements of fantasy that had become familiar and cozy. We therefore never hear of comfortable creatures like dragons, witches, ghosts, and Martians, or even of familiar elements of fantasy architecture such as pinnacles, towers, and battlements. Everything is strange, unsettling, even shifting—for we hear of lighting effects that cause entire structures to be viewed differently, of uncanny replacements and transformations that resemble scene-shifting in a theater. Machinery appears to have been used solely in a disguised, invisible way; for only the presence of hidden machinery can explain certain repeatedly mentioned phenomena, such as solid islands floating in the air and a mysteriously sinking hill.

The response by the public to Sarabee's new park was curious: people descended, roamed about, uttered admiring sounds, felt a little puzzled, and finally returned to one of the higher parks. The opening-day attendance was the highest ever—over sixty-three thousand in the first two hours—but it quickly became apparent that crowds were not staying. By the second month receipts were far below those of even the uppermost park, in its state of increasing neglect. People seemed to admire the new park but not really to like it very much; they preferred the mechanical rides, the replicas, the booths, the barkers, the hot-dog stands, all of which had been rigorously banished from the new park. Sarabee, always alert to the mood of the crowds, did what he had never done before: instead of making alterations, he launched a mid-season promotional campaign. Attendance rose for one week, then took a dramatic plunge, and long before the end of the season it was clear that the new park was a resounding failure.

Sarabee met with his staff of advisers, who recommended three kinds of remedy: the addition of exciting new rides to enliven the somewhat inert park; the construction of a huge domed amphitheater in the center of the park, to contain twelve tiers of game booths, food stands, shops, restaurants, and penny arcades surrounding three revolving stages on which would be presented, respectively, a funhouse, an old-fashioned amusement park, and a three-ring circus; and the razing of the park and its replacement by an entirely new one on more conventional lines but with brand-new rides. Sarabee listened attentively, rejected all three recommendations, and shut himself up with Danziker and Stilwell to consider improvements that would enhance rather than alter the nature of the park. In an interview given in 1927, Danziker said that Sarabee had never seemed surer of himself than in this matter of the new park; and despite his own conviction that the park was a failure and that Sarabee should listen to the voice of the people, Danziker had laid his doubts aside and thrown himself willingly into Sarabee's effort to save the park, which had already begun to be known as Sarabee's Folly.

The enhanced park opened the next season, to a massive publicity campaign that promised people thrills and pleasures of a kind they had never experienced before; a journalist writing in the *New York Herald* called the new park the most brilliant revolution in the history of the amusement park, with effects so extraordinary that they were worthy of the name of art. The next day a journalist on a rival paper asked scornfully: It may be art, but is it fun? He granted the superiority, even the brilliance, of Sarabee's latest devices, but felt that Sarabee had lost touch with the amusement park spirit, which after all was a popular spirit and thrived on noise, laughter, and rough-and-tumble effects. Within a month it was obvious that the refurbished park was not a success. Sarabee continued to run it at a loss, refused to alter it in any way, and began to spend several hours a day walking in the shifting dream-perspectives of his nearly empty park, which still drew a small number of visitors, some of whom came solely in the hope of catching a glimpse of the famous entrepreneur. And a rumor began to grow that Sarabee was already making plans for an entirely new park, which would surpass his own most stunning creations and restore him to his rightful place as the Edison of amusement-park impresarios.

In the world of commercial amusement, success is measured in profit; but it is also measured in something less tangible, which may be called approval, or esteem, or fame, but which is really a measure of the world's compliance in permitting a private dream to become a public fact. Sarabee, who had made his fortune in department stores and had since made it many times over in his series of unrivaled parks, had always enjoyed the pleasurable sense that his dreams and inspirations were encouraged by the outer world, were so to speak confirmed and made possible by something outside himself that was greater than himself— namely, the mass of other people who recognized in his embodied dream their own vague dreams, who showered him with money as a sign of their pleasure, and for whom he was, in a way, dreaming. His newest park was Sarabee's first experience of commercial failure—his first experience, that is, of losing the world's approval, of dreaming the wrong dream. His peculiar stubbornness may be explained in many ways, but one way is simply this, that he refused to believe what had happened. He kept expecting the crowds to come round. When it became clear they wouldn't, he was already so soaked in his dream that he could not undream it. This is only another way of suggesting that Sarabee, whatever he was, was not cynical; his showmanship, his shrewd sense of what was pleasing to crowds, his painstaking efforts to adjust his inventions in the direction of wider and wider audiences, were only the practical and necessary expression of a cause he thoroughly believed in.

Admirers of Sarabee praised the failed park as a sign of his originality and of his growing independence from the corruptions of mass taste; critics regretted it as a sign of decline, of increasing

505

remoteness from common humanity; but both camps agreed that the failure was a crucial moment in Sarabee's career, a moment that whetted their appetite for his next advance. For there was never any question of that. As Sarabee wandered the shifting illusions of his nearly deserted park, disguised as a weeping clown, or a journalist, or an old man with a cane, who dared to imagine that he hadn't already begun to plan another park?

It was about this time that the board of managers made an effort to save the declining upper park, if only because it served as entrance to the lower levels. Guards in maroon jackets were posted along the paths leading to the rotundas. The high grass was trimmed at the base of the openwork iron towers and under the roller coaster, bare patches were seeded and paths new-tarred, booths cleaned and painted, rust on bridge-braces removed, roller-coaster tracks repaired and old cars replaced with shiny new ones. Only at the far corners of the park, in the dark, twisting alleys of Dwarftown or the decaying lanes inhabited by unsavory actors, did the board abandon its efforts at restoring order and permit a shantytown to flourish among the weeds, the refuse, the broken lights.

Eyewitness accounts of the new park, which opened on May 19, 1923, contradict themselves so sharply that it is difficult to know what was imagined and what was actually there, but the reports all suggest that Sarabee's new level had a deliberately provocative air, as if he had set out to construct a sinister amusement park, an inverted park of dark pleasures. We know that visitors were given a choice: either to pass through the other parks or to descend directly in any of the thirty-six elevators that had been installed on the outside of the great upper wall. Those who chose the new elevators found themselves in large, lantern-lit elevator cars operated by masked attendants costumed like devils. We do not know exactly where the Costume Pavilions were located, although it appears that visitors were urged to assume a disguise before passing through red-curtained archways into an almost dark world. The park was lit only by red and ocher lights that dimly illuminated the midnight towers, the looming buildings and black alleys, where whispers of barkers in dark doorways and bursts of honky-tonk music were punctuated with darker noises—howls, harsh voices, clashes of glass. It was a world both alluring and disturbing, a dark underworld of uncertain pleasures that made people hesitate on the threshold before deciding to lose themselves in the dark.

However exaggerated some of the accounts may be, or confused by the presence of actors and stunt men, it is clear that the park was intended to startle and shock. Many visitors simply left in anger and disgust. But large numbers remained to stroll about uneasily, peering into archways, lingering in the dark alleys, looking about as if fearful of being caught, while still others abandoned themselves utterly to the extreme and dubious pleasures of the park. Such abandonment, such release from the constraints of the upper parks, is precisely what the park seems actively to have encouraged—hence the importance of the Costume Pavilions, which, apart from adding color and humor, served the more serious purpose of encouraging people to assume new identities. The park appears to have deliberately offered itself as a series of temptations; the crowds were continually invited to step over the very line carefully drawn in Sarabee's other parks. The complaints of scandalized visitors resulted in two separate police investigations, each of which turned up nothing, although critics of the investigation pointed out that Sarabee was more than capable of disguising the true nature of his amusements and that in any case the head of the investigations was a former roller-coaster operator in the upper park—a charge that was never substantiated.

In the face of questionable and conflicting evidence it is difficult to know how to assess the many eyewitness reports, which include disturbing accounts of a House of Horrors so frightening that visitors are reduced to fits of hysterical weeping, of funhouse mirrors that show back naked bodies in obscene postures. We hear of smoky sideshows in which the knife-thrower pierces the wrists of the spangled woman on the turning wheel and the sword-swallower draws from his throat a sword red with blood. We hear of rides so violent that people are rendered unconscious or insane, of a House of Eros filled with cries of terror and ecstasy. There are reports of troubling erotic displays in a Palace of Pleasure, where female visitors fitted with special harnesses are said to drop through trapdoors into transparent pillars of glass sixty feet high, which stand in a great hall filled with masked men and women who shout and cheer at the swift but harness-controlled falls that send skirts and dresses swirling high above the hips—an erotic display that is said to take on an eerie beauty as twenty or thirty women fall screaming in the great hall lit by red, blue, and green electric lights. We hear of a Lovers' Leap in which unhappy lovers chain their wrists together and jump to their deaths before crowds standing behind velvet ropes, of a Suicide Coaster built to leave the track at its highest curve and plunge to destruction in a dark field. There is talk of a Palace of Statues divided into a labyrinth of small rooms, in which replicas of famous classical statues are said to satisfy unspeakable desires. We hear of disturbing prodigies of scale-model art, such as an Oriental palace the size of a child's building block, filled with hundreds upon hundreds of chambers, corridors, stairways, dungeons, and curtained recesses, and containing over five thousand figures visible only with the aid of a magnifying lens, who exhibit over three thousand varieties of sexual appetite, and there are reports of a masterful miniature of Paradise Park itself, carved out of beechwood and revealing every level in rigorous detail, from the festive upper bridges with their rides, brass bands, and exotic villages to the most secret rooms of the darkest pleasure palaces in the blackest depths of the lowest level, containing over thirty thousand figures in sharply caught attitudes, the whole concealed under a silver thimble. Even taking exaggeration into account, what are we to make of a Children's Castle in which girls ten and eleven years old are said to prowl the corridors costumed as Turkish concubines, Parisian streetwalkers, and famous courtesans and lure small boys and girls into hidden rooms? What are we to think of deep pleasure-pits into which visitors are encouraged to leap by howling, writhing devils, or of a Tunnel of Ecstasy, a House of Blood, a Voyage of Unearthly Delights? From these and similar reports, however unreliable, it seems clear that the new park invited violations of an extreme kind, and carried certain themes to a dark fulfillment. But the park seems never to have been intrinsically unsafe; rather, the dangers lay in the rides and pleasure palaces themselves, and not in the promenades and alleys, where the costumed crowds were never violent and where serious troublemakers were led away by masked guards and dropped into straw-filled dungeons.

One of the more disturbing features of the new level, which quickly became known as Devil's Park, was the public suicides, which many visitors claimed to have witnessed, although among

508

the witnesses were those who said it was all a hoax performed by specially trained actors. Even the majority who believed the suicides to be real were divided among themselves, some expressing moral outrage and others asserting what they called a right to suicide. The issue was brought to a head by the spectacular death of sixteen-year-old Anna Stanski, a high-school student from Brooklyn who disguised herself as a man in a porkpie hat, pushed her way through the turnstile at the top of the new Lovers' Leap, tore off her hat and set fire to her hair, and leaped flaming from the ledge before anyone could stop her—this at the very moment when a woman in her twenties and a man with wavy gray hair were having their wrists chained together by an attendant. Anna Stanski's fiery death was witnessed by hundreds of visitors, many of whom saw her lying in a field with twisted arms and a broken neck, and it was reported the next day in major newspapers across the country. The park management, forced to defend itself, pointed out that Anna Stanski was a troubled teenager with a history of depression, that those who accused the park of promoting public suicides were now in the odd position of having to admit that Anna Stanski's suicide actually saved two lives, since it discouraged the chained lovers from pursuing their leap, and that the park was no more responsible for her death than the city of New York was responsible for the deaths of those who leaped almost daily from its bridges and skyscrapers. Critics were quick to point out that there was a sharp distinction to be made between the city of New York and an immoral "amusement" that actively encouraged suicide, while others, scornful of the claim that lives had been saved, questioned whether the two so-called lovers were not rather actors hired to stir the passions of the crowd. Their scorn was turned against them by the park's defenders, who argued that if in fact the lovers were actors, then the park could not be accused of encouraging suicide; and they argued further that, in comparison with the number of accidental deaths that occur in all amusement parks and are accepted in good faith as part of the risk, the number of suicides in Sarabee's park, whether staged or real, was trivial and negligible, despite the grotesque attention paid to them by antagonists whose real enemy was not suicide at all but freedom pure and simple. The episode was soon overshadowed by a hotel fire in Brighton, in which fourteen people died, and the murder of minor racketeer Giambattista Salerno in a Surf Avenue seafood restaurant.

Responses to the new park were sharply divided, but even outraged critics who considered the park a moral disgrace admitted that Sarabee, while forfeiting the respect he had earned with his earlier parks, was a shrewd showman who knew how to appeal to the debased tastes of the urban masses. Several commentators made an effort to connect the park with the new postwar freedom, the collapse of middle-class morality, the indiscriminate rush toward pleasure—in short, the collective frenzy of which Devil's Park was but the latest symptom. In an attempt to assess the park and place it in Sarabee's career, one critic argued that it was the embittered showman's cynical response to his failed park: thoroughly disillusioned by failure, Sarabee had created an anti-park, a deliberately crude and savage park pandering to the most despicable instincts of the crowd. This interpretation, which attracted a good deal of attention, was answered incisively in a long article by Warren Burchard, who after an eleven-year silence on the subject of amusement parks returned to the charge and argued that Devil's Park, far from being an exception in Sarabee's career, was the latest expression of an unbroken line of development. Each park, the argument ran, carried the idea of the amusement park to a greater extreme. This remained true even of the failed park, which, despite its rejection of the mechanical ride, moved in the direction of newer and more intense pleasures. The ten-year history of Sarabee's parks, Burchard argued, was nothing less than an uninterrupted movement in a single direction, of which Devil's Park was not simply the latest but also the final development. For here Sarabee had dared to incorporate into his park an element that threatened the very existence of that curious institution of mass pleasure known as the amusement park: namely, an absence of limits. After this there could be no further parks, but only acts of refinement and elaboration, since any imaginable step forward could result only in the complete elimination of the idea of an amusement park. Burchard's argument was taken up and modified by a number of other critics, but it remained the classic defense of Devil's Park, against which opponents of Sarabee were forced to shape their counterarguments.

The moral outrage directed against the new park, the conflicting reports, the rumors and exaggerations, the death of Anna Stanski, all served to pique the public's curiosity and increase attendance, despite the many people who declared they would never return; and such evidence as we have suggests that many of Sarabee's most outspoken opponents did in fact return, again and again, lured by forbidden pleasures, by the protection of masks and disguises, by sheer curiosity.

Even as controversy raged, and investigation threatened, and attendance rose, rumor had it that Sarabee was planning still another park. It was said that Sarabee was working on a ride so extraordinary that to go on it would be to change your life forever. It was said that Sarabee was developing a magical or mystical park from which the unwary visitor would never return. It was said that Sarabee was creating a park consisting of small, separate booths in which, by means of a special machine attached to the head, each immobile visitor would experience the entire range of human sensation. It was said that Sarabee was creating an invisible park, an infinite park, a park on the head of a pin. The intense and often irresponsible speculation of that winter was a clear sign that Sarabee had touched a nerve; and as the new season drew near and the last mounds of snow melted in the shadows of the bathhouses, small weekend crowds began to arrive in order to walk around the famous white wall, to stare at the great gates, the high towers, the covered elevator booths, to hover about the closed park in the hope of piercing its newest secret.

The opening was set for Saturday, June 1, 1924, at 9 A.M.; as early as Friday evening a line began to form. By 6:30 the following morning the crowd was so dense that mounted police were called in to keep order. The eyewitness reports differ in important details, but most agree that shouts were heard from inside the park at about seven o'clock. A few minutes later the gates opened to let out a stream of workmen, concessionaires, actors, spielers, Mbuti tribesmen, ride operators, dwarfs, and maroon-jacketed guards, all of whom were gesticulating and shouting. The first alarm was sounded shortly thereafter, and witnesses claimed to see a thin trail of smoke at the top of the wall. Within twenty minutes the entire park was in flames. The great white wall, a highly flammable structure of lath and staff that had cost a

511

small fortune to insure, quickly became a vast ring of fire; policemen cleared the streets as chunks of flaming wall fell like meteors and threw up showers of sparks. By the third alarm, fire engines were arriving from every firehouse in Brooklyn. As part of the wall collapsed, spectators could see the flaming rides within: the merry-go-round with its fiery roof and its circle of burning horses, the hellish Ferris wheel turning in a sheet of fire, the collapsing bridges, the blackened roller coaster with its blazing wooden struts, the fiery booths and falling towers. Suddenly a cry went up: from one of the rotundas leading to the first underground park, there rose a flock of flaming seagulls, crying a high, pained cry. Some of them flew in crazed circles directly into the crowd, where people screamed and covered their faces and beat the air with their hands.

By nine in the morning firemen were fighting only to contain the raging fire and save neighboring property; hoses poured water on the blistering facades of side-street boarding houses, and a police launch was sent to rescue nine fishermen trapped at the end of a blazing pier. Suddenly a sideshow lion, its mane on fire, leaped over a flaming section of wall and ran screaming in pain into the street. Three policeman with drawn revolvers chased it into a parking lot, where it sprang onto the hood of a parked car. They shot it twenty times in the head and then smashed its skull with an ax. By ten o'clock a portion of ground caved in and fell to the park below, which was also in flames; spectators from the tops of nearby buildings could see down into a pit of fire, which was consuming the two hotels, the six bathhouses, the shops, the restaurants, the underground roller coaster and House of Mirth. The fiery lower pier fell hissing into the artificial ocean, throwing up dark clouds of acrid smoke; and from the flames there rose again a flock of crazed and shrieking gulls, their backs and wings on fire, turning and spinning through the smoke and flames, until at last, one by one, they plunged down like stones.

By noon the fire was under control, although it continued to rage on every level all afternoon and far into the night. By the following morning Paradise Park was a smoking field of rubble and wet ashes. Here and there rose a few blackened and stunted structures: the melted metal housing of a Ferris-wheel motor, the broken concrete pediment of some vanished ride, clumps of curled iron. Somehow—the papers called it a miracle—only a single human life was lost, although innumerable lions, tigers, monkeys, pumas, elephants, and camels perished in the fire, as well as the seagulls of the first underground level. The single body, discovered in the debris of the deepest level and damaged beyond recognition, was assumed by many to be Sarabee himself, an assumption that seemed confirmed by the disappearance of the showman and the discovery, in his Surf Avenue office, of a signed letter transferring ownership of the park to Danziker in the event of Sarabee's death. Some, it is true, insisted that the evidence was by no means conclusive and that Sarabee had simply slipped away in another disguise. Although the cause of the fire was never determined, a strong suspicious of arson was never put to rest; reports from inside the park suggested that the fire had not spread from one level to another but had broken out on all levels simultaneously. The papers vied with one another in proclaiming it Sarabee's Greatest Show, or Another Sarabee Spectacular; the crude headlines may have contained a secret truth. For as Warren Burchard expressed it in a memorable obituary article, the fiery destruction of Paradise Park was the "logical last step" in a series of increasingly violent pleasures: after the extreme inventions of Devil's Park, only the dubious thrill of total destruction remained. Sarabee, the article continued, recognizing the inevitability of the next step, had designed the fire and arranged his own death, since to survive the completed circle of his parks was unthinkable. The historian can only note that such arguments, however attractive, however irrefutable, are not subject to the laws of evidence; and that we know as fact only that Paradise Park was utterly destroyed in a conflagration that lasted some twenty-six hours and cost an estimated eight million dollars in property damage.

It is nevertheless true that the brief history of Paradise Park, when separated from legend, may lead even the most cautious historian to wonder whether certain kinds of pleasure, by their very nature, do not seek more and more extreme forms until, utterly exhausted but unable to rest, they culminate in the black ecstasy of annihilation.

The ruined park was repossessed by the City of New York, which filled in the underground levels and turned the upper level into an extension of the parking lot that covered the remainder of the old Dreamland property; the enlarged parking lot became a public park in 1934 under the administration of Fiorello LaGuardia and has remained a park to this day. Here and there in shady corners of the park, on hot summer afternoons, it is said that you can feel the earth move slightly and hear, far below, the faint sound of subterranean merry-go-rounds and the cries of perishing animals.

In 1926 a paper presented by Coney Island historian John Carter Dixon to the Brooklyn Historical Society revealed that no one called Warren Burchard had ever worked for the *Brooklyn Eagle*. Later evidence uncovered by Dixon showed that the name had been invented by Sarabee as part of a promotional campaign. Although the author of the Burchard articles is unknown, Dixon suggests that they were written by one of Sarabee's press agents and touched up by Sarabee himself, who appears to have had a hand in his own obituary notice.

Nearly seventy years after the destruction of Paradise Park, Sarabee's legacy remains an ambiguous one. His most daring innovations have been ignored by later amusement-park entrepreneurs, who have been content to move in the direction of the safe, wholesome, family park. Sarabee, himself the inventor of a classic park, was driven by some dark necessity to push beyond all reasonable limits to more dangerous and disturbing inventions. He comes at the end of the era of the first great American amusements parks, which he carried to technological and imaginative limits unsurpassed in his time, and he set an example of restless invention that has remained unmatched in the history of popular pleasure.

A book of photographs called *Old New York,* published by Arc Books in 1957 and long out of print, contains fourteen views of Paradise Park: nine pictures of the upper level, including two of Paradise Alley, and five of the first underground level. The one most evocative of a vanished era shows a group of male bathers in sleeveless dark bathing costumes standing with their hands on their hips in the artificial surf before the crisscross iron braces of the underground pier, with its gabled wooden roof, its arches and turrets, its flying flags: some of the men stare boldly and even sternly at the camera, while others, with powerful shoulders and thick mustaches, are smiling in an easy, boyish-manly, innocent way that seems at one with the knee-high water, the pier, the ocean air, the unseen festive park.

Nominated by Joyce Carol Oates

TRACKS AND TIES

by ANDRE DUBUS III

from EPOCH

Y EARS LATER, when I was twenty-six, she said in *The New York Times* you would tie her naked and spread-eagled on the bed, that you would take a bat to her. She said you'd hit her for any reason. But in Haverhill, Massachusetts you were my best friend, my brother's too. I was fifteen and you two were fourteen and in 1974 we walked the avenues on cold gray days picking through dumpsters for something to beat off to. We'd beat off to anything, though I was shy about it and couldn't do it just anywhere.

One February morning we skipped school and went downtown. It was ten or eleven degrees and the dirty snow piled along both sides of River Street had become ice, the air made my lungs hurt and our noses, ears, and fingers felt burned, but you wore your faded blue jean jacket with the green magic marker peace signs drawn all over it. You wore sneakers and thin fake denim pants that looked more purple than blue. It was so cold I pulled the rubberband from my ponytail and let my hair down around my neck and leather-jacketed shoulders. Your hair was long too, brown and stringy. My brother, barely fourteen, needed a shave.

We had a dollar between us so we sat in a booth at Vahally's Diner and drank coffee with so much milk and sugar in it you couldn't call it coffee anymore. The Greek man behind the counter hated us; he folded his black hairy forearms across his chest and watched us take our free refills until we were giddy with caffeine. You went for your seventh cup and he yelled something at you in Greek. On the way out you stole two dollars someone had left on their check under a sugar shaker.

516

You paid our way on the city bus that was heated and made a loop all the way through town, along the river, up to The West-gate shopping center, then back again. We stayed on it for two hours, taking the loop six times. In the far rear, away from the driver, you took out your black-handled Buck knife and carved a peace sign into the aluminum-backed seat in front of you. For a while I looked out the window at all the red brick factory build-ings, the store fronts with their dusty windows, bright neon price deals taped to the bottom and top. Barrooms on every block. I probably thought of the High School Algebra I was flunking, the gym class I hated, the brown mescaline and crystal meth and THC my sister was selling. The bus was warm, too warm, and more crowded than before. A woman our mothers' age sat in her overcoat and scarf in the seat in front of you both. Her back was to you and I'm sure she heard you laughing but she didn't see my brother hunched forward in his seat, jerking back and forth on his penis and coming in no time, catching it all in his hand. I think I looked away and I don't remember what he did with it.

After the bus, we made our way through the narrow factory streets, most of the buildings' windows covered with gray ply-wood, though your mother still worked at Schwartz's Shoe, on the fifth floor, when she wasn't drinking. We walked along the railroad tracks, its silver rails flush with the packed snow, the wooden ties gone under. And we laughed about the summer be-fore when we three built a barricade for the train, a wall of bro-ken creosote ties, an upside down shopping cart, cinder blocks, and a rusted oil drum. We covered it with brush, then you si-phoned gas from a Duster behind Schwartz's and poured it on. My brother and I lit it, air sucked by us in a whoosh, and we ran down the bank across the parking lot into the abandoned brewery to the second floor to watch our fire, to wait for the Boston & Maine, to hear the screaming brakes as it rounded the blind curve just off the trestle over the river. But a fat man in a good shirt and tie showed up at the tracks, then a cop, and we ran laughing to the first floor where we turned on the keg conveyor belt, lay on it belly-first, and rode it up through its trap door over and over.

As we made our way through town it began to snow. My brother and I were hungry, but you were never hungry; you were hawny, you said. One morning, as we sat in the basement of your

517

house and passed a homemade pipe between us, your mother upstairs drunk on Kappy's vodka and Pepsi, singing to herself, you said: "I'm always hawny in the mawnin'."

My brother and I laughed and you didn't know why, then you inhaled resin on your next hit and said, "Shit man, the screem's broken."

"The *what?*"

"The screem. You know, the *screem*. Like a screem door?"

By the time we reached the avenues the snow had blanketed the streets. There were two sisters on Seventh who lived in the projects that always had motorcycles in front of them, and trash, and bright-colored babies' toys. Trish and Terry were older, sixteen and seventeen and so skinny their breasts looked like prunes beneath their shirts, but they had dark skin and long hair and sometimes, if they were high, they'd suck you. But there was a day party on the first floor of their building, and it had only been two weeks since Harry Wright and Kevin McConigle, rent collectors for Fat Billy, both twenty-three or four, beat us up, you and me, just walked us out of a pot party we were both quiet at, walked us off the front porch into the mud then kicked and punched us until they were through. So we kept walking, heading for a street close to the highway where we knew three girls who would fuck if you had wine and rubbers, though after the wine they didn't mention the rubbers.

On Cedar Street, cars spun out snow as they drove from the curb or the corner store. You let out a yelp and a holler and went running after a Chevy that had just pulled away, skidding slightly as it went. You ran low, bent-over so the driver wouldn't see you, and when you reached the back bumper you grabbed it and squatted on your sneakers, your butt an inch or two from the road. And you skied away, just like that, the snow shooting out from under the wheels of the car, out from under your Zayre Department Store sneakers, blue exhaust coughing out its pipe beside you.

In the spring and summer we hopped trucks. A mile from the highway was a crosswalk on Main with a push button traffic signal pole that we three leaned against until a truck came along and one of us pressed the button to turn red. I was the decoy that day, for a white refrigerator truck from Shoe City Beef. It stopped at the line, and I crossed the street jerking my head like

518

a chicken to keep his attention from the mirrors while you two ran around to the back and climbed up on the foot-wide iron ledge at the bottom of its rear doors. As soon as I got to the sidewalk I heard the driver shift from neutral to first, heard him give it the gas. I waited for a car to drive by from the opposite direction, then I ran out into the street behind the truck which was only shifting up to second. You and my brother stood on the ledge waiting, smiling, nodding your heads for me to hurry. I reached the ledge just as the truck moved into higher gear and I grabbed the bolt lock on its back doors and pulled myself up, the truck going faster now, shifting again, dipping and rattling through a low spot in the road. You both held an iron handle on opposite sides of the door so I stayed down, gripping the bolt lock with both hands, sitting on the ledge.

A car horn behind us honked and the driver, some man who combed his hair to the side like a teacher, shook his head and honked his horn again. You gave him the finger and we laughed but it was a scared laugh because the truck wasn't slowing down as it got to the gas stations and Kappy's Liquor near the highway, it was speeding up. Before, we'd jumped off into the grass of the highway ramp, but now we couldn't; he took the turn without leaving third gear and you yelled: "He *knows!* He friggin' *knows!*" My brother wasn't smiling anymore, and he stuck his head around the corner and let the growing wind hit him in the face, run through the hair on his cheeks as he squeezed the handle with both hands and I wanted to stand, to get my feet on something solid, but there was no room and now the driver was in fourth gear, heading north on 495, going fifty, then sixty, then sixty-five. He moved to the middle lane and I tried not to look down at the zip of the asphalt a foot beneath my dangling boots, but it was worse looking out at the cars, at the drivers looking at us like we might be a circus act they should catch sometime. Some honked as they passed so I looked up at you, at the side of your face as you looked around the corner, the June wind snapping your hair back past your forehead and ears, your mouth open in a scream I could barely hear. You smiled and shook your head at my brother then down at me, your brown eyes wet from the wind, your cheeks flushed in a satisfaction so deep I had to look back at the cars behind us, at the six or seven I was convinced would run me over one after the other, after my fingers

519

failed. Miles later, at the toll booths of the New Hampshire line, the truck slowed to a stop and we jumped off exhausted, our fingers stiff, and thumbed home.

That fall you went to the trade school, my brother joined me at the high school, and I saw you six years later in an all-night store in Monument Square. I was buying cigarettes for my college girlfriend. She waited in the car. It was winter. The floor was dirty with peoples' slush and mud tracks, the overhead light was fluorescent and too bright, and I was waiting my turn at the register when I saw you, watching me, smiling as you walked up. You carried a carton of ice cream and a quart of Coke. I had on a sweater and a jacket but you wore only a T-shirt, green Dickie work pants and sneakers. You were taller than me, lean, and your young black moustache and goatee made you look sinister until you started talking in that high voice that hadn't changed since you'd tell us you were hawny in the mawnin'. You said you were living down on the avenues, that you were getting married soon. I said congratulations, then I was at the counter asking for a pack of Parliaments and you touched me on the shoulder, said to say hi to my brother. I said I would. At the door I glanced back at you and watched you dig into your front pocket for crumpled bills. You nodded and smiled at me, winked even, and as I left the store, the cold tightening the skin on my face, I remembered the time your mother went to visit her sister in Nebraska for a whole month. I could never understand why she went alone, why she'd leave her family like that to go off for a visit. Then my mother told me it was detox she went to, some twenty-eight day program in Boston. When I told you I knew, you laughed and said, "Nah," but you swallowed twice and walked away to do nothing in particular.

Six months after I saw you in the store my brother and I got invitations to your wedding. We didn't go.

Four more years and you were dead.

I heard about it after you were buried. They said your wife stabbed you in the back. That was it; she stabbed you. But a year later I was behind the bar at McMino's Lounge and Fat Billy's son, Bill Jr., told me what really happened, that you were cooked, always thinking your wife was cheating on you, always beating her up. That night you ran outside off the porch to go kill the guy you thought she was fucking. This was down on one of

520

the avenues, behind the projects, and you took the trail in back of your house. But your wife opened your black-handled Buck knife and chased after you, screaming. She was short and small, barely five feet, and just as you reached the weeds she got to you and drove it in low, sinking the blade into your liver, snipping something called the portal artery. You went down without a sound. You curled up in a heap. But your wife spent four hours at a neighbor's house crying before they called anyone, and then it was the cops, and you were gone.

I served Bill Jr. another White Russian and for a second I felt sure it was him she went to that night, and I thought about hitting him for not making a faster call, but I felt no heat in my hands, no pull inside me. And I've always hated woman beaters. Part of me thought you got what you deserved. I left Bill Jr. to finish his too-sweet drink.

The following winter I was living in New York City, in a one room studio with my girlfriend. It was late on a Sunday morning and we both sat with our feet up on the couch reading *The New York Times*. Outside our barred window snow fell on parked cars, on the sidewalk and street. I got tired of the movie section and picked up a story about three women in prison, all there for the same reason, for killing the husbands who beat them. And your wife was one of them; they gave her full name, *your* name. They wrote how she chased you outside and stabbed you. They described the town you both lived in as economically depressed, once a thriving textile town but no more. I lowered the paper and started to tell my girlfriend all about you, but she and I weren't doing so well, both past wanting to hear anything extra about each other, so I pulled on my boots and jacket and went walking. I crossed Third Avenue and Second and First. A car alarm went off in front of some Chinese laundry. I stuck my hands in my pockets and wished I'd worn a hat. I passed an empty basketball court, then I waited for the traffic on F.D.R. Drive and walked the last block to the East River. To my right and left were bridges over to Queens though from where I stood I could see only the backs of warehouses, dry weeds five feet tall, then the gray river, swirling by fast.

The snow had stopped and I started walking along the cobblestone walk. One morning I skipped school and cut through back yards to your house. I didn't know your mother was home from

521

Nebraska and I almost stepped back when she answered the door. She'd dyed her brown hair black, she wore sweat pants and a sweater, she had a cold sore on her bottom lip and she'd gained weight, but she smiled and kissed me on the cheek and invited me in. The small kitchen was clean and warm. It smelled like coffee and cinnamon rolls. She put one on a napkin and handed it to me. I thanked her, and while I chewed the sweet buttery bread, she lit up a cigarette and asked about my mother. Then you came downstairs in just your jeans, no shirt, your chest pale and thin, your nipples pink, and your mother rushed over and kissed and hugged you like you'd been gone and just gotten home. And you didn't pull away, you hugged her back, and when your eyes caught mine, you lowered your face into the hair at her shoulder, and kept hugging.

Nominated by DeWitt Henry, Epoch

DAY OF THE TWO BODIES

by JIM DANIELS

from THE MACGUFFIN

Labor Day, lazy flags drooping in the heat.
A cop pulls up in front of the apartments
and pushes his huge weight out of the car,
his belly drooping over his belt
like a lame apology. His radio cuts the air
with its erratic drumbeat and screech,
whiz and howl.

*

Three times the cop had stopped:
a landlord/tenant fight.

This time, the tenant
shoots and kills the landlord,
shoots and kills himself.
Shoots and kills.

This time, a whole tribe of sirens
flashers, slamming doors and shouts.

Chicken scratch guitar. Thumping bass.
Alright funksters, two dead bodies.

*

A boy kicking a ball.
A woman holding her head
like a ball. A kicked ball.
Her husband
            the landlord dead

She ain't gonna find
the fat cop who could've stopped all this.
He's shrinking into a crack in the wall
checking his stomach's heartbeat
listening to the organ pounding
in the cathedral of his gut—
you screwed up, name of that tune.

*

Landlord took the hinges off his door,
tossed his clothes into the hall:
get your black ass outta here.

The shots, the day's record skip- skipping.

*

A handful of gravel, an empty can of paint
a cop waving from the roof: *all clear.*

A kid waves back from the street:
Hey up there.

A door off its hinges. All the doors
off all their hinges. The muted ticking clock
like a handful of green beans: snap, snap.

*

A guy beating off down the hall.

A naked woman pressing herself
against the curtain.

The Big Sound in the hallway, the street:
heavy belts of police, EMS.
Stray cats wary, rats snickering
in the corner by the dumpsters, the crack
dealer sweating silver bullets, silver dollars,
shedding skin after skin, listening
to the pounding up and down stairs.
Paid my rent, he chants.

*

A long time, and no one leaves.
His empty apartment, an efficiency.
Nobody owns this building right now.
Nobody isn't dead. Tom tom drums,
the bass beat—elegy, blues.

The Big Shrug, the Collective Shrug,
a faint ruffle of shoulders in the still air.
Two more bodies tipped over into the ditch.
What's a funkster to do?

We stroke ourselves in the heat, hoping
for a spark. 8 cop cars, 3 ambulances.
The coke plant across the river blowing
its stink this way. Despair,
the threat of a hidden moon.

Efficiency, know what I mean.

*

A hand-painted car bright orange
in the parking lot.

Cops break out of their huddle
put out their cigarettes, light new ones,

the color of the orange car cupped in their hands.
They got a play called the Hang Around.

That orange car ain't goin' nowhere.

*

The neighbor whose husband shot himself
last year grabs a reporter, pulls him
down to her face to talk about her Larry:
Maybe it's the contagion.

The cops drive off at last.
The sun pushes itself against
the cheap wood facade of the apartments,
through cracks and into the bricks underneath.
Neighbors talk about the old bricks.
*This woulda never happened
if he didn't cover up them pretty bricks.*
He being a greedy landlord
who saw a way to subdivide.

The building's almost glowing now,
sun reflecting off sliding glass doors.
As if nothing happened here today.

What usually happens, what doesn't.
The TV was here with their bright lights
and slicked hair, their humpty voices.
Gone now, gone.

A door off its hinges. Rent money.
A fat cop you could almost
feel sorry for.

*

In the street late tonight, two guys dancing
to an old P-Funk tune, the Star-Spangly
Goodbye, the spindly punctuation
to the end of this day.

I want to dance under a streetlight to P-Funk.
I want my voodoo shot against the contagion.

It's too dark to see
our fingerprints over the earth,
all the things of the earth
all the money of the earth
too dark to see our guilt
and our innocence.

We touch ourselves
we protect ourselves
we swing through the air
on the second hand
we gobble up the big fat numbers
of our days.

Someone's left a flag out overnight,
forgotten on the Day of the Two Bodies.
Let's call it that, a new holiday.
Mark your calendars.

We'll have a street dance.
We won't let nothing droop.
We'll start up that old orange car.
We'll wave to each other from balconies
like in the movies. We'll make a list
of things worth dying for.
We'll erase everything on the list
with our funky butts, our shimmering butts.

Nominated by The MacGuffin, Ed Ochester

KICKING THE HABIT

by LAWSON FUSAO INADA

from ERGO!

Late last night, I decided to
stop using English.
I had been using it all day—

    talking all day,
    listening all day,
    thinking all day,
    reading all day,
    remembering all day,
    feeling all day,

    and even driving all day,
    in English—

when finally I decided to
stop.

So I pulled off the main highway
onto a dark country road
and kept on going and going
until I emerged in another nation and
stopped.

    There, the insects
inspected my passport, the frogs
investigated my baggage, and the trees

pointed out lights in the sky,
saying

    "Shhhhlllyyymmm"—

and I, of course, replied.
After all, I was a foreigner,
and had to comply . . .

Now don't get me wrong:
There's nothing "wrong"
with English,
and I'm not complaining
about the language
which is my "native tongue."
I make my living with the lingo;
I was even in England, once.

So you might say I'm actually
addicted to it;
yes, I'm an Angloholic,
and I can't get along without the stuff:
It controls my life.

Until last night, that is.
Yes, I had had it
with the habit.

I was exhausted,
burned out,
by the habit.
And I decided to
kick the habit
cold turkey
right then and there,
on the spot!

And, in so doing, I kicked
open the door of a cage
and stepped out from confinement

into the greater world.

Tentatively, I uttered

      "Chemawa? Chinook?"—

and the pines said

      "Clackamas. Siskiyou."

And before long, everything else
chimed in with their two cents' worth
and we had a fluid and fluent
conversation going,

      communicating, expressing,
      echoing, whatever we needed to
      know, know, know . . .

What was it like?
Well, just listen:

Ah, the exquisite seasonings
of syllables, the consummate consonants, the vigorous
vowels of varied vocabularies

      clicking, ticking, humming,
      growling, throbbing, strumming—

coming from all parts of orifices, surfaces,
in creative combinations, orchestrations,
resonating in rhythm with the atmosphere!

I could have remained there
forever—as I did, and will.
And, when I resumed my way,
my stay could no longer be

      "ordinary"—

as they say,
as *we* say, in English.

For on the road of life,
in the code of life,

there's much more to red than

"stop,"

there's much more to green than

"go,"

and there's much, much more to yellow than

"caution,"

for as the yellow
sun clearly enunciated to me this morning:

"Fusao. Inada."

Nominated by Ergo!, George Keithley, Vern Rutsala

COUNTRYSIDE

by JANE MILLER

from THE KENYON REVIEW

My darling works until she finishes   I resist starting—
        craning out the upper window over the tiled roofs
we each imagine the moon sets in night mist
        she says she sees it I pretend I don't

over our heads someone who makes a lot of money
        does something arty the public likes like pouring color
over red cherries—
        not delicious   wrong language

when she finally finishes I am in the kitchen again
        counting supplies wondering if we can return
neither thinks we've woken from a strange dream
        I'd gotten to the bottom of a sensation

tied up with doing nothing until I felt
        one way or the other   in other words nothing
and then being blown away by relationship never helps
        —did you do that?   no you made me—

it's all I can do to clean up from the night before
        light streaming off the ancient stones
small windows for defensive purposes   the whole village set on
a slope
        the quest was for a form that wouldn't sacrifice presence

the answer Picasso is said to have given the German officer
        who asked   pointing to *Guernica*   did you do that? No you
        did that
it amounts to some ulcerated nights   some tangled hair
        beautiful old bottles   nets

songs before the sun is up
        not proscriptive but love all the same
such that I find I would never talk to anyone
        whose day doesn't last a month or a year

in town shopping we stop for soup
        the canopy's shoved back   there are stars for everyone
& get home drunk
        hoping the bread soaks the burn

mornings I read my tourist book
        ape the population rather than look American
when will I wise up?
        very warm & pleasant   birds despite the heat

we make love waiting to stop the spin by hand
        or the wash charges up again
someone drops by to see the kitchen made from the ruin
        this regular stuff emerges as an image

something scary something to hurt us
        to make us dead
& art—
        she never wakens me so when I'm awake I'm unguarded

could it be relationship & not matter with whom?
        as easily as this sky be a diagram & not an embrace
same sky different death's head behind it
        small jar of anchovies olive oil & salt

Nominated by Sam Hamill, Kristina McGrath

SYBIL

fiction by A. MANETTE ANSAY

from THE NORTH AMERICAN REVIEW

THE TWINS PAT mousse into Sybil's hair, working the tight, carefully-blued curls into stiff barbed wires the color of salmon. She cannot escape without her walker, and they have taken her walker down the front steps and across the lawn to the hickory tree. The mousse stings her scalp. It's strawberry scented, and myriad tiny flies circle blindly overhead, lured into the kitchen through the screen door which is propped open by a brick.

"She's crying," says the first twin.

The second twin peers into Sybil's face, small pink mouth agape. Sybil can see a sliver of white in the child's gum where a new tooth is coming in. The twins have lost their top front teeth this summer. *Angel teeth,* their mother calls them.

"No she's not," says the second twin. "She's just thinking, that's all."

"Maybe she's thirsty."

The second twin considers this and goes over to the refrigerator. She takes out a pitcher and pours Kool-Aid into a glass she finds on the counter. She carefully brushes an ant from the rim of the glass. A smoke-gray cat, panting with heat, is coiled between the dishes in the sink. The twin scratches its head. Everything she touches gets kissed with a faint, pink smear of mousse. She holds the Kool-Aid to Sybil's lips, but Sybil turns her face away.

"See?" says the twin. "She don't want anything."

Her sister kisses Sybil's neck. Both twins are solemn little girls with pale yellow cheeks and yellow ponytails and their voices are pinched and whispery. They make more barbed wires with the mousse. They work until every inch of Sybil's head is spiked and rosy.

"She looks bea-u-tee-ful," says the first twin serenely.

"I don't think she likes it."

"She looks just like a movie star."

The second twin drinks the Kool-Aid. They look at their grandmother with wispy blue eyes, their bright gazes crossing and recrossing her face the way spotlights search a dark sky.

Margie gets home from work at five, and the first thing she sees is Sybil at the table with spiked, rosy hair. The twins are nowhere in sight. Ants cluster on the table where drops of mousse have fallen.

"Oh, God," says Margie. "Where are they? Where'd they go? Oh, Sybil, I'm so sorry! It washes out, though, I've used it on my bangs. It'll rinse away in a jiffy, I swear."

Sybil tries to form words and strange sounds come from her mouth. The stroke has garbled her speech. When she's calm, she can write out words, gripping a pen with her fist. But Sybil is not calm.

"I've got a *date*! Can you believe it?" Margie says, brushing past Sybil and twisting on the cold-water faucet in the sink. The smoke-gray cat hops out onto the counter top. It flicks its paws, one at a time. Margie splashes water on her face. She hasn't had many dates since Victor left four years ago, but she makes the most of what she gets.

"God, this heat, can you believe it? Ninety-five downtown, hotter tomorrow, I bet. Johnny Hecht asked me to dinner at The Gander. They got air conditioning and big-screen TV."

Sybil says, "H-H-Hair!"

"Johnny, he don't mind kids, he got his own two anyway. We got talking on lunch today, and he said, C'mon, let's get outta here, so we went mini-golfing at The Palace. You know, that place off I-94? With the big dinosaurs?"

Margie wipes her face and twists a pen into Sybil's hand.

"Write down where they went to," she says. "I gotta get dressed. And don't worry, I promise that'll wash right out."

She trots down the hall toward her bedroom, unbuttoning her uniform as she goes. Margie is a receptionist at the Lakeside Hotel. Sybil's son, Victor, had been the one to hire her. Sybil scrawls HAIR on the Formica table top. Fingers of mousse seep down her neck.

Victor disappeared when the twins were three years old, and Sybil knew he'd done the smart thing. By that time, they were all living with her. Sybil thinks they brought on her stroke, but Margie says that's ridiculous.

"You're just lucky we're here," she chirps. "If we weren't, you'd be stuck in a home somewhere."

Margie loves Sybil very much. She tells Sybil, *I love you like my own ma!* and she whispers Sybil things she could never say to anyone. She reminds Sybil of Sybil's own mother, Georgia, who died eleven years ago. Georgia was disorganized. Georgia said she loved people all the time, but it never amounted to anything.

Hair, Sybil writes on the Formica. Hair. Hair. Hair.

Margie comes back into the kitchen wearing a red strapless sundress that rides up when she walks. Her body bounces but her hair, stiff with spray, is like a helmet. She yanks down the sundress and leans over to read the Formica.

"I know, your hair, but I gotta get your dinner first. Where'd the twins go?"

Sybil draws a question mark.

Margie sighs. She takes a carton of cottage cheese out of the refrigerator, sniffs it, and brings it over to Sybil.

"It's too hot for anything cooked," she says, "and Johnny'll be here any minute."

She sweeps ants off the table with the flat of her hand and spoons cottage cheese into Sybil's mouth. "Johnny knew Victor and he says Victor was never real responsible. *Johnny's* responsible. He's got two boys, the oldest's just seven. I mean, not to count my chickens, but they'd be good for Trish and Tina, don't you think?"

The smoke-gray cat glides up onto the table and Margie says, "Sybil! Where's your walker?"

Sybil looks out the window.

"Huh? Oh, God, Sybil, I'm sorry. They musta been trying to climb that tree. Here, I'll go get it for you."

She pushes back her chair and trips out the door and down the porch steps. Through the window, Sybil watches her float across the lawn like a large red sun. The smoke-gray cat noses forward. Sybil lifts her arm to wave it away, then lets it drop. The cat's tufted chin sinks into the cottage cheese.

Margie comes in with the walker, and a truck pulls into the drive.

Margie squeals, "It's Johnny!" She yanks at her sundress. A heavy-set man with very red skin and white-yellow hair steps out of the truck. Sybil feels the barbed wire points on her scalp as if they are electrified.

"HAIR!" she chokes.

Margie looks at her, does a double-take.

"Christ, I forgot!"

It's too late: Johnny thumps up the porch steps and swings his head through the doorway.

"Hey," he says to Margie. Then he sees Sybil. His eyes stick to her, caught in a rosy web of mousse.

"Johnny," says Margie in a grand way. "This is my mother-in-law, Mrs. Kelly."

Margie takes Johnny's arm and her face opens up to him like a flower. Sybil has forgotten how Margie acts when she desperately wants to be pretty. Sybil herself never needed to act: at Margie's age, she'd been something to look at. Still, Johnny's eyes slide from Sybil to rest on Margie's thick waist and calves.

"Mama, you are somethin'," he says.

Margie turns to Sybil, winks, and murmurs, "Get the twins to bed at nine." She and Johnny glide down the porch steps, Johnny's hand on her hip, her hip thrust into his hand.

Sybil's throat feels dry and strange. She pulls herself up on her walker and moves out onto the porch to watch the truck bounce down the drive. The floor of the porch boils with ants. The smoke-gray cat twirls around Sybil's ankles, its tail bolt-upright like an exclamation.

Sybil is sixty-eight. When she was forty-one and red-headed and trim, she rode through town shirtless on the back of a Chevy pick-up, eyes tearing, nipples as hard as pits. It was dark, but someone must have recognized her because she got arrested outside of Tiny Joe's.

"Mama, you are somethin'," the officer had said, and drunk as she was then, Sybil still remembers it. Lying in bed, sticky with mousse, she thinks about the coolness of the jail that night where, laughing herself to sleep, she'd had the power to live forever. *Mama, you are somethin'.* It's twelve-fifteen and too hot to sleep. Margie has not come home.

Sybil wears the same housecoat she's worn all day. It smells like onions, sour and hot. Its pattern of pink roses is faded almost white, making the length of her body glow eerily in the darkness. The twins are sleeping on the couch in the living room, nestled together like spoons. They told Sybil it's cooler there than in their bedroom, but Sybil knows they just want to watch adult TV and practice kissing on their hands.

A ragged motor works its way up the drive, idles, coughs, and quits. Margie's giggle floats high in the air; two doors slam, and Sybil hears Johnny say, "SHHH!", extra-quiet, extra-careful, and she realizes they are drunk and that they mean to come inside. They tumble up the porch steps and into the kitchen. Something falls, shatters.

"Shit," Johnny hisses.

"Don' wake th' babies."

Sybil hopes that Margie will come in to check on her so she can get out of her housecoat and sleep in her panties and bra. But Margie moves past Sybil's room toward her own, Johnny plodding behind her. He stops off at the bathroom and releases a stream that makes Sybil think of horses. Then he goes into Margie's bedroom and shuts the door. The smoke-gray cat appears in Sybil's doorway. It pauses, springs like a shadow onto her bed. When the noises start, it stiffens, sniffing the air in the direction of Margie's bedroom wall. Then it curls up against Sybil's leg, its wide eyes green and knowing.

The twins are up; Sybil can hear them. The hall light clicks on and it's not long before they, too, are in Sybil's room.

"She's awake," the first twin says. "Look, her eyes are open."

"She can't sleep cuz of *them*," says the second twin. She picks up the cat, kisses it, and settles into its place with it tucked into her lap. Sybil can feel the heat coming off the child's body. The noises in the next room grow louder, and Sybil wishes the child would move away.

"Aawh," she breathes.

The first twin crawls over her chest and sits cross-legged on her pillow. She looks tenderly into Sybil's face.

"What do you want?" she whispers.

Sybil doesn't know. Johnny's husky cries bead sweat like ice across her forehead.

"She wants them to shut up," says the second twin. The cat's ears rotate, radar style. A breeze lifts the curtains, and Sybil feels her whole body breathe that gasp of air.

The noises stop. The twins settle down next to Sybil, one on either side, their legs draped over her legs. A spiked lock of hair dangles across her eyes, and one of the twins, noticing this, sleepily brushes it back. The cat sleeps at their feet, twitchy with dreams.

In the morning, the twins grab Sybil's arms, pulling her upright. She's still asleep, so they help her swing her feet over the side of the bed. They button up her housecoat, rubbing their faces into her arms, patting her hands.

"You kin use the bathroom now," one of them says. "It's empty."

Sybil gropes for her walker and moves painfully down the hall, stiff with morning. She uses the toilet and tries to wipe some of the mousse off her face with a wet washcloth she finds squashed in the sink. When she comes out of the bathroom, the twins are waiting for her. They're uncertain. They slouch against the walls.

"They're in the kitchen," the first twin says. "They're eating breakfast."

"The *man* is here," says the second twin.

Both girls look to Sybil to see what *she's* going to do. Sybil straightens her shoulders and grips her walker. The twins follow behind her, clutching her housecoat, and the three of them move down the hall and into the kitchen. Johnny's at the table with Margie hanging over his shoulder. Margie's got on a t-shirt that's just long enough. From the table up, Johnny looks naked, but Sybil realizes he has jockeys on, lavender jockeys with a paisley print.

539

Johnny and Margie see Sybil at the same time. The barbed wires on her head have been flattened by sleep, but the color is still true and has spread to her cheeks and neck. Each of the twins has a rosy patina on the side of her head that slept next to Sybil.

"Morning," says Margie, and she and Johnny burst out laughing. They're eating cereal mixed with beer and drinking from a long dark bottle in the center of the table. They go on laughing for a long time. Sybil cannot keep her eyes from the white-yellow hair on Johnny's chest, the hard, rounded mound of his belly. She wants to press her face into his skin.

"Come get your breakfast," Margie says, "and say hello to Johnny. Johnny this is Trish and Tina. And you already met Mrs. Kelly."

Sybil stares at Johnny. Margie tugs her into a chair and fills her mouth with cereal, giving her fresh spoonfuls before she has time to swallow. The twins pick at their Frosty-Pops. Johnny's hands work their way under Margie's shirt; Margie tilts her head back so he can kiss her full on the mouth. Sybil's eyes fix on that kiss. The inside of her mouth fills with water. She wants that kiss to last forever.

"Kiddos, help Gram with her breakfast, okay?"

Margie slides from her chair, and Johnny rises to follow her out of the kitchen. The seat of his jockeys has been worn sheer; Sybil traces the dark flesh-crack with her eyes. She tries to picture the men she has known, but they all disappear into their own laughing mouths and hungry eyes, and she suddenly can't remember if she's ever had a lover at all. The smoke-gray cat skulks into the kitchen, jumps onto the table. It sniffs at a bowl of cereal and beer. When the noises start, its ears fold back like wings.

The twins roll their eyes at each other. They turn to Sybil, but she's reaching for her walker; Sybil can't bear those noises any longer.

"What do you want?" the first twin asks her.

"It's chow time!" says the second twin, and she climbs up onto the counter and reaches into the top cupboard. She pulls down a bag of Choco-Chunk cookies.

Sybil moves out onto the porch; she can tell by the smell of the air it will be another hot day, with more to come. A twin comes out and nudges a cookie into her hand. As Sybil brings it to her lips, it slips, breaking against the wooden floor of the porch.

"Look what you did," the child says, and her voice and inflection are her mother's. She and Sybil stare at the ribbon of ants that already has formed to carry the pieces away.

Nominated by The North American Review

THE ROAD FROM DAMASCUS

fiction by GEORGE WILLIAMS

from GULF COAST

"YOU ARE CARVING A ROASTING CHICKEN. The knife will not—I repeat—not of its own free will stab your lovely wife clean through the back. The chicken is food: it is not a dead bird, a derelict descendant of vanished dinosaurs spilling ammoniac rot and kidney slick onto the carving platter your in-laws from St. Petersburg mailed you two weeks before your wife five years ago was delivered prematurely of a stillborn girl while you were in a topless bar in Fort Lauderdale drunk out of your mind with colleagues.

"You *will* not at your boss's annual summer evening Hawaiian pool party walk up to your associate's wife and pluck the nursing newborn from her disbelieving arms and dash it on the mossy stones of the Japanese rock garden. Nor will you siphon a gallon of gasoline from your car and dousing her dress set her on fire with a luau lantern, payback for making your wife a social pariah by cutting off invitations to dinner parties and ladies' pro-am golf tournament fund-raisers and Woman's Club charity functions because after losing her first child she took an overdose of Placydl and drove her Riviera into a ditch and spent a month recovering in a *wellness center* on company insurance. Nor *will* you contemplate putting a 12-gauge to the back of her head for suggesting your wife is a dysfunctional toxic-parented para-alcoholic co-dependent enabler when after two drinks she has been known to

542

screw anything longer than it is wide and come Sunday still shake her comely butt up to the communion rail at St. Sebastian's for the *body* and *blood* of a God you no longer are afraid to admit you find incredible, the son of the Supreme Being allowing himself to be nailed to planks by half-wit centurions and then possessed of the wherewithal to query his father as to *why* he's been forsaken.

"You will not, out of nowhere, when you are selling a life insurance policy to a black executive, shout, "AVAUNT! DOUBLE INDEMNITY OR CHITLINS!

"You will not walk up to the blond in the secretarial pool and slip the erection you are hiding behind your briefcase between her plum lips, which will, willing, swallow the briny *seed* you have been saving for her since the Christmas party where drunk you passed her in the hall and touched the *nipples* rising through her silk blouse as gingerly as you would a newborn baby's head.

"The fighter pilot in the Phantom jet screaming 70 kilometers to the west over the Gulf of Mexico has not just accidentally fired a heat-seeking missile from its razor wing, which in less than forty seconds will blow the Airbus in which you are riding, a perspiring passenger with drink in hand, clear out of the summer sky, and rain you down on the grey waters of the Gulf in an aluminum-confetti cloudburst of viscera.

"You will not *die*. *If* you rub your face, your skin will not come off. You are *not* going mad. You are not hearing *voices*. It is only the after effects of a poison your system is attempting to purge from said system. Your brain does not feel like a pork rind. You are not an eating breathing defecating worm created to no end and destined to become a maggot-eaten passel of gristly splintered bones turned over in the soil by road crew a hundred years hence. You do not feel like a pelt on the interstate that used to be a dog. You do not have a *skeleton*. You are not an *animal*. Your heart will not stop *right* now.

"You will not wake one morning to discover a cache of firepower in the trunk of your Omega, nor will voices direct you into the crowds of shoppers at the mall, where calm as pond water you will simultaneously open fire with a flamethrower and heavy machine gun, riddling and torching *customers* before you wedge a hand grenade into your mouth and pull the pin for the sales clerk of Radio Shack, who is videotaping the mayhem from behind the safety of a pyramid of Snoopy phones so he can sell the cassette to CNN for 50,000 dollars and take his live-in girlfriend on a skiing vacation in the Alps, where he will recount the story to local reporters and curious tourists over snifters of brandy, boring his companion into having a *menàge a trois* with a German mime and his hermaphrodite lover.

"If you swing your arm in the gym while lifting a weight, the barbell will not fly out of your hand and strike dead an aerobics instructor shouting into a megaphone.

"Your foot does not have a mind of its own. It will not of its own free will lift itself from the brake pedal and stomp the accelerator, thereby running down where they walk two pedestrians crossing at the light.

"Beneath the skin on your face when you look into the mirror is not a *skull*.

"You will never spend another nickel in a strip-bar, nor waste like you did last month 900 dollars on a stunning prostitute, who deliciously feigned and writhed beneath you while you rose to a two-condom climax not even a dozen 50 dollar street walkers allowed you to forget.

"You *will* not have but three drinks before dinner; you *will* not have but two drinks before dinner; you will only have *a* drink before dinner; you will have only ONE drink to steady your nerves; you will not drink a quart of scotch in a 24-hour period; you will not drink ever again; you will drink *only* every third day; you *will* drink today until you pass out; next week you will *go* to AA; you will get *drunk* tonight since you are going to AA next *week*.

"You will not while spending a Marine Reserve weekend at Quantico hi-jack a prototype tank with laser weapons and a 70 millimeter cannon and drive it into the northern Virginia Sunday dawn, blasting split-level houses sky-high and igniting the gastanks of cars with laser light, nor will you mow down with the co-axial machine gun confused *residents* who flee their houses in robes and boxer shorts, or perched out of the hatch roll over the slaughter on the lawns and through flak-blasted gardens and the machine-gunned dog houses and burning picture windows wave an insurance voucher in the air and shout through a bullhorn, "ATTENTION: YOUR HOMEOWNER'S POLICY HAS EXPIRED. HAVE A NICE DAY.

"On a Saturday afternoon in August your self-propelled lawn-mower will not of its own will run you down and cut off your legs at the knees, leaving you an amputee in the hot grass, where your neighbor's dog will drink your intestinal bile and toss your jawbone up and down the yard.

"You love your native America. It is not a rabid behemoth of greed idiotized by advertising and stupefied by cathode rays and narcotized by Twinkies. America is not a land-fill. The interstates are not strip-mines. The federal government is not run by tech-nocratic zombies and National Security Councillors on mood ele-vators. Hidden in the amber waves of grain are not gargantuan warheads poised for global annihilation. You are not responsible for a hole in the ozone because for 24 years you have sprayed Right Guard on your nervous underarms, nor has your car farted hydrocarbons into the atmosphere that rain down acid on the earth like whirlwinds of ammonia in the atmosphere of Jupiter.

"Big Macs are not made of beef steer fed concrete and steroids before auction, nor do the french fries soaked with ketchup re-semble the delighted parasites that will one day dine on your fat-ted carcass.

"Nor will you weep driving in the car over the sadness of life, nor step any closer to the lip of the abyss because your sister and a friend climbed aboard a jet and flew away into the deep blue of a cloudless sky, never to be heard from or seen again.

"Neither is the child in your wife's womb the anti-Christ. It does not look like a frog, nor does it have more than one head. Its limbs, though bowed, are not amphibian. It does not have red eyes, nor fangs, nor claws, nor a tail like a whipsaw. It does not have cloven feet. It is normal. You are normal. Your wife will not die in childbirth. The baby will not be born dead. You will not jump off a building, or a bridge.

"Nor will a rendition of Amazing Grace over the country sta-tion crack you asunder and fill you with the terrifying fire of the Holy Spirit. Also, there is no such place as HELL, where souls are tormented in an eternity of flame for the paltry vanities which sustain your very existence; the vanity of insurance; the vanity of love; the vanity of comfort, peace, friendship, etc.; the vanity of having a family, earning a living, buying a house, and so on; all these illusions and spurious hopes masking a bedrock self-

545

ishness which God in his thunder is readying to avenge right *now*, for the summer thunderhead swept in off the Gulf, it says, and you can hear it say, "BLOWOUT SALE ENDS SATURDAY. PREPARE TO DIE."

Nominated by Gulf Coast, M. D. Elevitch

ROBERT MAPPLETHORPE'S PHOTOGRAPH OF APOLLO (1988)

by MARK IRWIN

from THE PARIS REVIEW

What's missing is the body, its nakedness wrapped
in marble. What's missing is the hair, the floating hair
that falls in chalky tendrils. Only the face, huge
and larval-white, peers into the darkness.
Still, this is perfect youthful manhood, iridescent
against chaos. The eyes, wild and vacant, look
but see nothing. What slaking difference?—
They have known ecstasy, that patina
marble carries everywhere. A suddenness
unwarranted, beautiful. The lips, moistened, part
more to breathe than speak. Such desire,
a poetry. The silk of the moment before him,
the rest becomes salt, memory, history.
There is order here, but passion is its spectacular
disarray. The music turning toward light
shadows. O god of the healing art
where is the beautiful lyre of the body?

Nominated by John Drury

WHICH LETTER ?

by ARTHUR VOGELSANG

from VOLT

Thank you for the booklet with the pictures of where my house
  would be.
Mostly I was interested in the army camels that Sgt. Allen
  brought to my garden.
I mean to where the garden would be in our century.
I can take a short cut through a room with four doors
If I should want to stop writing you and go out
Under the same unique group of imperial palms
Where the camels had been tied. An odd letter
Has arrived from a young sensible woman handsome as water,
No way out of dealing with it or not mentioning it to you.
Perhaps I shall write her at length about the camels and
    that's all,
Their shit sweet at first like horses'
Then a sharp rot,
Their pleasure in pleasing people,
(Despite their meanness—biting each other,
Their rage when bumping people, their repulsive stares.)
But flattering especially the Sgt. with bold careful rides
In the precipitous canyon above my house.
He was given a grant of hills that saw
The sea like a silver roof over half the world.
What had he done?
There was a foreign war then and a Camel Corps
And he must have taken on their vileness, their anger at
    existence.

In a desert, riding wacky tan bodies some with coats on fire,
Some busting like balloons filled with blood,
Balloons with long legs,
Squawks and screams of people and animals one noise only.
Elsewhere you have written
Of the smell of their saddles under the wet, serrated trees.

Nominated by Volt

HEROES, SAINTS, AND NEIGHBORS

by GILLIAN CONOLEY

from THE ANTIOCH REVIEW

X was a common hood.
Taps on his shoes,
what he meant by that, walking Spanish
down the hall, in splendor and in darkness,
car dust all over his jeans.
He wanted love and denial,
frequent and percussive,
the sunburnt evening out of town,
the beginning of a word
an expectation, the maple red ice birch,
Black Cat Fireworks
sign on the side of a barn.
At the grocery, a woman swings her arm out
to get a look at her watch, and an old woman
in hat and gloves, cane at a jaunty angle,
looks out the timed doors, watches the local flag snap.
In the end, nothing a settled thing to have experienced.
Too much government, cold hands portend
a shiver over the grave.
We perform a common language, a harp played
by its errant strands, a harp on fire

on an island no one can remember
one solid thing about.
Gulls sweep the glassy wave before it crashes.
A toddler tumbles into sand.
Downtown buildings all come together
to the hypotenuse,
a myopia stronger than nationalism.
All kinds leave the pool hall,
following the aims of the ruthless.
Rhapsodic minute discriminations
open like snapdragons,
sunlight a bronze armor bound by the season.
We are not a beautiful people.
We are the kind you find dreaming and walking
city streets at dawn, out at the edge
where there is no I or not I,
avoiding the horoscope. No great epigrams
issue forth from us, no thin tigers
prowling, out to earn even more stripes,
no roses on our lapels the way spies
find each other. Consider long the face
of each person next to you: mouth open,
stray sheet mark, and hair
obvious on the skin. Look
for the spirit that hides in the face,
that sinks into deep, marvelous sleeps in the afternoon.
Let others blur the balconies with silk.
A woman, a man lights the desk lamp in the lobby,
then walks into the bar and touches the piano.
High in a hotel a stray hand
surveys the green radio dial,
and down the dim hallway you can never
find out what happens
to most people. Music is expectant,
a lipsticked cigarette, a pink invoice,
a book shorn of its cover.
A broom or a saxophone pierces the highest marrow of sound,
a capture, a release

we believe, we believe all our separate lives,
people framed for an instant by windows,
the colors wet, clear,
common, no dream coming up to the original.

Nominated by Lee Upton

ALMA MAHLER:
A FICTION

fiction by ROLAINE HOCHSTEIN

from KANSAS QUARTERLY

ALMA MAHLER, unbridled, ungirdled. How I admire you! You
of the cocky strut and the blaring blue eyes, eyes as large and
charging as the bowls of twin trumpets. You are my ideal.

Your name wasn't always Mahler, of course, but what's in a
name? Alma Schindler was just as bold. Later there were other
names, not as many names as there were men, but isn't that the
point? Your name on vellum—Mme. Alma Mahler, Mme. Alma
Mahler-Werfel—was engraved without a border, the paper with-
out edging, unbounded as you yourself were uncrimped by mar-
riage or any other intervention. I see you shining out of
photographs. I hear your music.

You were nineteen (twenty-one, really, but nineteen for the
sake of this story) on the night (Vienna, turn-of-the-century)
when you met your first husband-to-be. You were already famous
for your beauty. Also for your independence of mind, which in
those days was often mistaken for brattiness. It wouldn't do to be
bratty before the great conductor. Pert, perhaps. Impertinent,
better not.

Across the broad table, slicing the shimmer of crystal, ringing
of silver, aroma of heavy cooking, your gaze bumped against
Mahler, entered him, became part of his inner mechanics. All
evening long (and a long evening it had been for poor Gustav!) he
had failed to register the presence of Dr. Schindler's tall, dairy-

colored daughter. You were worth a glance but only for the pleasure of looking. Others had stronger claims on his attention.

Frau Westerling, for example. The wife of an important banker. A woman of powerful effect, palatially dressed, a hat like a bush, stone-cut eyes, mouth of fire. She was artfully aware of the weight of her husband's position and the precarious balance of Mahler's. Frau Westerling—older, assuming—thanked the maestro for the experiences he had given her. In regard to his compositions. "No other music penetrates so," Frau Westerling tells Mahler. "Wagner by comparison is distant thunder." Mahler hopes and fears that Frau Westerling will sit beside him at dinner.

Most of the men were familiar to, if not with, him. He had to respect them because pretense is too rough on a man of principle, a man so hot under his choler that his thoughts steam into musical notes, a man who has recently scrapped his fancy that genius could carry him above the scratchings of local politics. Mahler at forty looked both gaunt and paunchy. He floated green-faced among the fragrantly barbered and tailored, over-fed, firmly-planted men.

"Imagine. In a single year." A leather goods merchant playfully punches Mahler on the chest. "In one mere year to become first the chorusmaster of our State Opera, then the director of same, and at last the director of our glorious symphony orchestra."

Our. The rest of the tightly assembled group nodded in unison with plump satisfaction. Their eyes caught the golden light of the chandeliers. What none said and all were thinking: *Baptized also. In that same year. Baptized first. Then promoted.*

Mahler solaced himself by reminding himself that he was no more a Catholic than he had been a Jew. No more observant. No more believing. No more beloved, either. He smiled thinly, removed his pince-nez spectacles and waggled them in dapper green acceptance of the backhanded acclaim. He was damned glad when all the milling about narrowed into a line of entry to the dining room.

His hostess sat him on her right, far up-table from the expressionistic Frau Westerling and closely diagonal to the big, softly-bloused Schindler girl with eyes the color of a prize blue ribbon. A slash of sash (exposed above the table line) matched them to perfection, so that Mahler could not look down without his eyes being drawn up again.

Alma Mahler, outrageous, intractable. I do love you. I envy the quality and quantity of the men you enslaved. Many (including you yourself) suggest that you inspired them. I don't believe it. You were not an inspiration. You were a reward.

Daddy's girl. That's my theory. Doctor Schindler adored you openly, brazenly, purely. You flowered in the sun of his affection. Klimt, I've read, was your first lover. Maybe just a protector. An older man (though he was younger than Mahler). Another Gustav. Klimt was already painting his gilded, subversive, swooning, Byzantium-tainted canvases of luminous, voluminous women, darkling beauties scented with danger, desire and death by sloughing, by swallowing, by snuffing out with hair or breasts. Your mother had misgivings when your father brought Klimt into the house, another of those bohemians to eat her food and keep the doctor up all night with drink and wild talk.

"What does he want with her?" Frau Schindler whispers to her husband. She is afraid to question Alma. The girl seems unaware of the behavior of men, how they parade for her, exhibiting the strong profile, recounting the brave deed. Frau Schindler is afraid to warn Alma lest the girl laugh at her and do for merriment exactly what her mother is warning against. Frau Schindler is afraid lest she plant an idea in her daughter's head.

I know that your father was really a painter himself, but I see him as a respectable, respected physician, in appearance a bit like a jovial Freud, though of nonsemitic background and practicing a specialty more venerated and tangible, more remunerative, than Freud's neurology.

Klimt engages you in conversation about your lessons, your reading, your friends, your ambitions. He finds you refreshing. He enjoys your uncluttered intelligence. "Come, I will take you to Sacher's for tea." Your father has no qualms about letting you go. Klimt, he knows, is principled though radical: courtly, cultivated, complicated, a drop of *weltschmerz* in the droop of his eyelid, the ring of *sprechgesang* in his impassioned talk. The advanced Doctor Schindler encourages the friendship: "You will learn from him," your father tells you. Your father trusts your judgment, your taste. You see in his eyes that you are incapable of wrongdoing, beyond censure, spot-proof. What a dad!

From diagonally across the table Mahler saw that the young woman was looking at him. He looked at her. Hair like butter. Skin like cream. Deep blue eyes gazing without shame or modesty. Mahler responded. His connections with women had always been slippery but perhaps his mother had recently died and there was a slot to be filled. The call that reverberated from this girl's blue eyes was not, however, that of a trumpet (a strumpet? no, not at all!) but of the delicate English horn which the trumpet player keeps at his side to make a finer, more discriminating tone, at once sharp and sweet. The note resonated in the tips of all of Mahler's appendages. It stayed in his mind like the pre-memory of a cymbal clang at measure fifty-four, when he must bring in the percussionist on the crest of a crescendo. She was not a child. An extraordinary woman was looking at him, listening. Everything he said was addressed to her.

The great Mahler! How did you dare? Alma, you schlag-drenched apple strudel! The eminent Doctor Schindler gave you his eyes to see yourself with. Was it all mirrors? Could you have managed it with only an average I.Q.? I ask because I want to know. How much did your quickness count for? How much intensity? How much accomplishment? Little was asked of women so lovely, but you offered more than loveliness. And you wanted more than love. Mahler. You got him, my darling.

After dinner he finds you standing motionless, near the piano. "Do you play?" he asks.

"Quite well. Though I am sure a chimpanzee would play at least as well if he had studied as long as I have."

"Who is your teacher?"

"Please. I have no less than three. For composition. For technique. And a coach for performance."

"You compose?"

I, too, took piano lessons. I played without grace and my father was not enchanted with me. Yet I wanted to please him. I begged him to tell me the name of his favorite music so that I could learn it and play it for him. I was ten years old. It never occurred to me that my father might not have a favorite piece of music.

"*Traumerei*," he said at last. He must have pulled the name out of a hat. *Traumerei*. Robert Schumann. Mahler's forebear in moodswinging introspection. *Traumerei*, from Schumann's *Scenes of Childhood. Dreaming.*

It was a lovely choice, but difficult to play. The stretches were too long for my short fingers. Still, I wanted to please my father and I practiced diligently. I astonished my exacting mother by staying at the piano—practicing, practicing—more than the required thirty minutes a day. Finally, I mastered the piece: notes, timing, expression, pedaling. When practice had made perfect, I memorized it and played it at night, after supper, as a surprise for my father.

"That's a nice piece," my father said when I stood up and bowed.

"It's *Traumerei*," I told him. "I learned it for you."

"Very nice," he said.

Kokoschka. His vision. Not a picture of life but life itself erupts from his canvases. The energy! The passion! Kokoschka was younger than you and in and out of your life forever. I could read all about it in your translated memoirs but I prefer my own reconstructions based on scraps of facts from program notes and histories of turn-of-the-century Vienna. You were not Kokoschka's muse but his companion in outrage. Committing outrage. "Wild brat," he called you, his fighting ally, fence-breaker, icon-toppler, tradition-trampler. You were a denizen of fervent coffee houses, a rally-rousing, banner-bearing enthusiast, valiant in love as well as art wars. Never taken.

"You never cook for me!" Kokoschka howls. He is very young, very tall, very drunk. It's late at night. He has sneaked you into his rooming house. Is the man insane? A matter of definition. Of course you cook. You can do anything. Cook. Sew. Roll up your sleeves, tuck up your skirts, scrub floors, bite your lips and clean war wounds. But under orders? You hurl a plate at him. The fight that follows wakes up his landlady. You slip out through the window. When things have quieted, you climb in again.

But in the end, you leave. You are, in the end, a marrying woman. Everybody knows about the Alma doll that Kokoschka made and carried around with him, his heart on his sleeve, his tongue in his cheek. A feather in your cap. Twenty years later, another admirer, Alban Berg, dedicated to Alma Mahler his masterpiece, the opera *Wozzeck*.

So Mahler was taken at the party that night in Vienna. Taken with you. Taken by you. When you sat at the piano, he stood behind you. You played well and sang (not so well) songs of your own composition, music drawn from the dark forests of German romanticism and dressed in all the latest dissonance and disappearing chords. Mahler heard a leitmotif that wasn't in the notes and it made him feel young for the first time in his life. You raised your hands from the keyboard and turned to him. You looked up for his appraisal but found instead, to your unspeakable joy, his eyes seeing the world in you, the eyes of love. It was a diagnosis you could make as easily as your father identified measles.

So you talk—you and the great composer. Everything about you he finds remarkable. He picks at the hemline of your defiance, the pleats of your arrogance, all the dear dark qualities hastily folded and pinned under the wide skirt of your exuberance.

"With whom are you here?" he asks later in the evening.

"No one. I'm by myself." Dr. Schindler's daughter speaks without affectation (it was never necessary for her to add grace notes) but with a perceptible lift of her strong chin.

"May I see you home?"

"No, you may not. I will see myself home but you can come with me. My papa will be awake and astonished to see you!" She has rather a horsey laugh, quite delightful. "Imagine! Mahler!" She laughs again, more quietly, as if she were commenting to a third party.

Let's pretend I'm Viennese. Call me Schatzi. I have blue eyes. Love me. I have rich, lustrous hair, which I wear in soft curls over my clear, well-proportioned forehead. Love me. My bosom blouses over my narrow waist. I move as if carried by a firm current of air. My hands, from years of piano playing, are shapely and expressive. The tilt of my prominent chin is proud, confident, playful, expectant, promising, trusting, relentless. I stare into the eyes of men, drowning them in my blue sea.

But of course I'm not Viennese, nor young and fair. Never was sure of my charms, Alma. Never had your confidence. It's said that Rilke, too, was on your list. I'm not surprised. Your list went on and on as you went on into middle age and beyond, never doubting yourself, never noticing the signs of change in the eyes of your beholders. In late middle age you were large, white-haired, imperious and impervious. No one forgot the blare of your eyes but some people made fun of you. They found you ridiculous for the very qualities that had made you adorable when young. But you remained Alma Mahler, unrepentant, invincible. Your third husband was the poet Werfel—smaller, younger, deferential. You sailed before him down the aisles of concert halls. You signed your papers Alma Mahler-Werfel and, after his death, Alma Werfel Mahler.

For years I dreamed that no one would marry me. I was waiting, wanting a ring. I cannot describe the depth of my distress. The dream recurred, night after night, long after I was married. You, Alma, would not understand this.

Marriage to Mahler was no picnic but what marriage is? Those married years, fewer than ten, were his most productive: song cycles and symphonies brought him universal acclaim. You produced two daughters, worth more than the world, even Mahler thought so, but they could not release him from the grip of his obsessions. For almost ten years you were appended to a husband oppressed by enemies, yes, but oppressed more killingly by his indigenous furies: music, mother, history, doom. He tried to extinguish your fiery spirit. His emotions filled the house. Your studies, your politics, your tastes, your passions were to be swept aside to make room for genius. The man who had adored you as you were, now wanted you under his baton, so to speak. He wanted to take you in hand. He wanted to strike you with the wand of domesticity. He no longer took pride in your musical accomplishments. One maestro per family.

I'm sure you tried. I see you with your hair pulled back, buttoning up your *decolletage,* pulling down your shades, setting tables, sitting in the audience, sewing on the buttons that were perpetually sprung by the swelling of your husband's chest during the splendid act of conducting the Vienna Philharmonic Or-

chestra. And, of course, you knew how to give a party. Still, to
your credit, you were never a really good wife. You did not sub-
mit gracefully. Nor entirely.

At the wives' table, the much-younger Frau Mahler sits on the
edge of her chair. The archly-corseted Frau Westerling (this time
in a towering yellow turban) asks her: "And you, dear Alma, do
you soak your table linens in vinegar?"

"Vinegar?" You turn to the woman beside you whose red hat is
a tilted tray of poisoned fruit. "Linens?" You stare back at Frau
Westerling. You are in a suit of watered silk with black soutache
around the spread lapels. You rear up in horror.

I am not interested in realism here. I choose to disregard your
domestic calamities just as I overlook your vociferously avowed
contempt for Jews. Antisemitism, for you, was a matter of style.
In substance, only one of your husbands, the architect Gropius,
wasn't Jewish. You always said he was the boring one.

It was Mahler, not you, who finally went to see Freud. The
visit is musical legend, psychoanalytic text. Mahler kept putting
it off until his agony overcame him. (You, Alma, were not the
source of that agony nor could you be expected to be its exorcist).
Freud.

The consultation took place in Leyden, Holland, to meet the
logistical needs of both busy men. Both were so busy that they
had to do the job all in a single afternoon. Freud and Mahler, a
couple of middle-aged Jews, both moody, walked on the shaggy
bank of a striated river. Heads bent. Eyebrows knit. Hands
clasped behind their Viennese waistcoats. Freud was reportedly
impressed by your husband's intelligence, his nimble grasp of the
principles of psychoanalysis. Freud worked with a lightning
touch. He left Mahler stunned and reeling. But when his brain
stopped buzzing, self-doubt, like an iron halo, had been lifted
from the composer's head. He saw himself newly as a man of
weight and consequence, one who need not accuse himself of fri-
volity when humorous or pomposity when sober.

You, Alma, assumed that the riverside session had been all
about you. The maestro, you told the world in your journals,
came home from Leyden and wept. He begged your forgiveness.
He yearned to make retribution. Every piece of music you had

560

composed since you were ten years old, including recent secret works you had been hiding in a blanket chest: all, you drew them all into the gaslight, onto the music stand. Tablets and tablets of onionskin covered with notes like twittering flies. This may all be true. Who can measure the reverberations of such spiritual plumbings as Mahler had just undergone?

The maestro, exalted, personally cancels the evening's dinner engagement (you may have been just a little regretful) and sits down at the piano. "Beautiful, beautiful," he exclaims as he sight-reads your work. Tears flow from under his pince-nez. He plays. You sing (no better than on the night of your first meeting). He makes musical suggestions delicately, tentatively. He is alert to your ambitions and intentions. With your approval, he inks in a few editorial changes. Early the next morning he's ringing his publisher's doorbell.

"I had her," the men tell each other devilishly. They sit spread-legged in parlor chairs, in white duck trousers stretched taut between widely separated thighs. "I've had her," the men remark, but not of Alma Mahler.

This is the way men posed for paintings in turn-of-the-century Vienna and the way they sit now in contemporary theatrical re-productions of plays by Schnitzler and his fellows. Thighs out-spread and sometimes a walking-stick lightly held between them. The love of these men was the passion of possession. But none of them possessed you. What you loved was the weight of a wor-shipper, the acquisition of an admirer of high achievement. Ac-cording to your published count, you wrote a hundred songs and had almost as many men. All the way into old age, you boasted about the men as if recalling an art show, a particularly fine meal or a notable theater piece. Your father could not save you from growing old but he kept you from becoming pleasant.

On an unusually hot day in early September, I was driving home from the supermarket with my car radio tuned as always to the classical music station. I heard the announcer, in his soothing way, introduce a series of works by women composers. Naturally, I thought of you. Your name, your image is always floating near the front of my mind. But, as you do not exactly swim in the mainstream of public consciousness, I did not expect to hear you.

You would never imagine the amazement and delight I felt when that lozenge voice announced two songs—not by Alma Mahler. But by Alma Schindler.

I was carrying bags of frozen food in the back seat of my car and a neighbor was watching my children, but I forgot all that. I pulled over to the curb. Listened. Your songs, sung in German by a mezzo-soprano, sounded like overladen trees, choked forests, gnarled streams, clutching bushes—all struck by spasms of *sturm* and *drang*.

Do not be angry, says one of the songs in its English translation, *if my desire darkly breaks its bounds* . . .

Nominated by Sam Vaughan

FROM *LOOK AHEAD—LOOK SOUTH*

by C. S. GISCOMBE

from OBSIDIAN II

(1962 at the edge of town)

No West Indians that I could see at my grandfather's funeral.

"Long lost relatives always eat a lot," sd my mother (meaning
just as well) on the ride to the graveyard at the furthest Negro
edge of Birmingham proper

—the city got lush in places then gave way
so descriptive shoulders of hills came into view over which
ranged pine trees & on a ridge, through those,

some white people went by on a train
(so near I could see them from where we stood under the
canvas,
their pale arms & faces at the windows, clearly),

the pastoral looming up close as well,

"the mosaic of brightest southern colors"—it was that

for decades my grandfather was doctor too

to people out past the edge of town & took payment for that
in hams, in baskets of greens & fruit:

but all *value* is assigned, is brought in:

still, being the density & mirror both
was what I found confusing—
the fickle layers to endure, the worth standing in

(the 70s—UltraSuede)

In finally

w/ salesmen, facing each other in the bulkhead seats
& one sd Looka here

what's comin
handing a strip on across the table so I could mistake it

for real leather—

arguably it's even possible to assign value to the present

seated among the glib & easy white boys all
of us old enough to recall Jim Crow

crossing the Carolinas low over the trees

into Atlanta then back into the air

(the final being one long stage, up exactly
to the minute

(the distant past—B. W. I.)

Real islands

of English-speaking Negroes, remoteness
w/in the surround of water—

& the shapelessness of relation: unhidden, blood-

direct, but shapeless all the same

Nominated by Clarence Major

OYEZ À BEAUMONT

by VICKI HEARNE

from RARITAN

A STUDENT of mine called two days ago and asked, "What do the experts do when their dogs die?"

He developed a calcium deposit on his upper spine, did my good Airedale Gunner, and it would hurt him to track, so Gunner and I stopped tracking, stopped retrieving and jumping, not because he wouldn't have gone on if it were up to him, and awhile after that he was very ill with cancer, and after a time of that, too much of that, I had him killed. Gallant Gunner, brave Gunner, gay Gunner. Once, late one evening on a beach in Malibu, he took down a man who was attacking me with a knife. The vet had to patch Gunner up some, but he didn't turn tail the way my assailant did. Brave Gunner. Harken to Gunner. Twenty-four hours later, bandaged, he clowned and told jokes for the kids at Juvenile Hall, performing for the annual Orange Empire Dog Club Christmas party. Oh, rare and dauntless Gunner. Even his hip, broken when a prostate tumor grew right through the bone, did not stop the courage of his gaiety, but I did. My friend Dick Koehler said, "He is lucky to have a good friend like you," to encourage me, you see, to get on with it, kill him, and Dick was right, of course, right, because when there is nothing much left of a dog but his wounds you should bury those decently.

Until he died, he was immortal, and the death of an immortal is an event that changes the world. That is all for now about Gunner, because what it does to you when such a dog dies is not fit to print. "Der Tod ist groß," writes Rilke. "Death is huge." But various psychologists deny that it is as huge as all that when it is an animal that is mourned. I have read statistically studded reassurances that mourning for a cat lasts at most one month, for a dog three. I have read that when an animal dies there are no regrets, no rehearsal of the wail, "If only I had," and also that the splendid thing about animals, what is said to make them so convenient to our hearts, like antidepressants, is that when we mourn them, we are only mourning a personal loss and not "the loss of life and potential," according to Professors Beck and Katcher, authorities on all of this at the University of Pennsylvania.

That is the way psychological authorities talk—"Eventually an animal *can* be replaced," they write in their books, but this is not how the experts talk. (I realize that psychologists and such like are generally understood to be experts, but I have met none who were experts in the various ways my good Gunner's work with scent developed, especially when he started scenting out the human heart.) But I am just a dog trainer. My thinking, such as it is, I learned from the animals, for whom happiness is usually a matter of getting the job done. Clear that fence, fetch in those sheep, move those calves, win that race, find that guy, retrieve that bird. The happiness of animals is also ideologically unsound, as often as not, or at least it is frequently wanting in propriety, as when your dog rolls in something awful on his afternoon walk, or your cat turns off your answering machine.

In over a quarter of a century of training I have never met an animal who turned out to be replaceable, and Dick says, "Hell, even trees are irreplaceable, but we don't know that, and *that* is our loss." The loss the dog trainer has in mind is the loss of eternity, for, as Wittgenstein put it: "Denn lebt er ewig, der in der gegenwart lebt." "So he lives forever, who lives in the present," wrote the philosopher, and this is how the animals live, in the present, which is why the expert's difficult and apparently harsh advice, advice they occasionally take themselves, is: "Another dog. Same breed, as soon as possible." Not because another dog of the same breed will be the same, but because that way you can pick up somewhere near where you left off, say that you have it in you.

In a children's book called *Algonquin: The Story of a Great Dog*, there is a quarrel between two brothers, old men they were, grandfather and great-uncle to the boy who tells the story.

Grandsir is angry because Uncle Ovid is going to take on the training of the grand young Pointer named Algonquin; he is angry because he wants no more of the "grief and the rage and the ashes." He shouts at his brother, "Do you know what it does to you? Do you know what it does every time one of them dies?" but Uncle Ovid just says, "Don't tell me. I am an old man and it would not be good for me to know," and he trains that Pointer who turns out to be something else again at the field trials. Mr. Washington says, "I think sometimes that he would pity his bracemates, were he not enough of a gentleman to know that they would rather die than be pitied," and Algonquin wins and wins and wins and then Algonquin starts to get a lung disease and can't work well, is distressed therefore, because he is losing his work, his happiness, and Uncle Ovid sends him out on his last run and shoots him while he is on point, while there is still something more to him than his wounds.

At the end of that story, when Grandsir suggests that it is time for the boy who has been witness to all of this to get another dog, he says to his grandfather, "Irish Setters don't win field trials, do they? I mean, you are not in much danger of getting a great dog?" Grandsir purses his lips and agrees, "Not much." The boy says, "Then an Irish Setter would be nice."

There exist mighty dogs, the dangerous kind who take hold of your heart and do not let go. But avoiding the great ones does not get you out of it. If, like the boy in *Algonquin*, you already know what a great dog is, then the knowledge marks you. If you do not know, then you are still in danger, for if you give her a civilized upbringing, every collie is Lassie *in propria persona*, killing that snake in your heart, driving off the cougar that lurks there, sending for help. This is not because all dogs are great dogs but rather because all dogs are both irreplaceable and immortal and as Rilke says, "Der Tod ist groß."

One day I talked about death with my friend—my teacher and friend, for these are synonyms in the trainer's world—Dick Koehler. I had told him about the results obtained at the University of Pennsylvania. "Dick! The news is out! There are no regrets when a dog dies," and Dick said, "Oh, then my several thousand students who say to me, 'If only I had done what you said, Mr. Koehler,' or 'If only I had worked with her more,'—they're all hallucinating, right?"

"Must be," I reply, "for it says here that dogs are replaceable, and grief for them lasts no more than three months," and right before my eyes Dick Koehler starts looking a little funny; he startles me. He is thinking of Duke, dead several decades now. Hallucinating that Duke had been irreplaceable. Duke was a Great Dane, one of your great dogs, too. Duke was a movie dog; some of you may remember him from *The Swiss Family Robinson.*

"What was so irreplaceable about Duke?" I asked.

"Well, it's not every day you find a Great Dane who thinks a 255-pound tiger is a kitty cat. Not every day you find a Great Dane who will hit a sleeve and go through a second-story window, not just once, not just twice, but seven times and it was as good the last time as the first time."

Soon after Duke died, there was Topper, of *The Ugly Dachshund,* various TV series. "Topper paid the rent for about three years there," said Dick. "I mean, he did all the work on that series." Topper died like this: the great dog and his son were playing, horsing around after a day's work, and his son slammed into him and ruptured his spleen and Dick realized it too late for the vet to fix things up, and so had him put down. That was over two decades ago, Dick's most recent Great Dane.

Dick talks about Duke and Topper and the thing starts to happen to me again, the merging of all of the elegies, all of the great dogs. "There is nothing left but his name . . . but there never was a dog like Algonquin," or, "It's all regrets," or, "After he got in his car and drove away I dug a grave and lined it with the bright fallen leaves and there I buried all that could die of my good Fox," or "He was allus kind to the younguns and he kilt a rattlesnake onct," or one of my favorites, the passage in T. H. White's *The Sword in the Stone.* The great hound named Beaumont is on the ground, his back broken by the boar, and the expert, the Master of Hounds, William Twyti, has been hurt also. Twyti limps over to Beaumont and utters the eternal litany, "Hark to Beaumont. Softly, Beaumont, mon amy. Oyez à Beaumont the valiant. Swef, le douce Beaumont, swef, swef." Then he nods to Robin Wood, and holds the hound's eyes with his own, saying "Good dog, Beaumont the valiant, sleep now, old friend Beaumont, good old dog," while the huntsman kills the dog for him: "Then Robin's falchion let Beaumont out of this world, to run free with Orion and to roll among the stars."

568

What next, though? The narrator of *Algonquin* decides to go for an Irish Setter. But that is not what the experts say to do. They say, "Another dog, same breed, right away." It takes courage, courage that Master Twyti seems to have had, for he rose from beside Beaumont's wounds and "whipped the hounds off the corpse of the boar as he was accustomed to do. He put his horn to his lips and blew the four long notes of the Mort without a quaver." He called the other hounds to him.

Another dog, same breed, right away. Or a pack of them, and not because there were any replacements for Beaumont in that pack. The other hounds were all right, but there were no Beaumonts among them, and there is no point in saying otherwise. I don't mean by that that there are not plenty of great dogs around. "There are a lot of them," says Dick. Yeah. They're a dime a dozen. So are great human hearts; that's not the point. We are by way of being connoisseurs of dogs, some of us, but one falls into that, and a dog is not a collector's item, not for Dick Koehler, anyhow, whom I have seen risk himself in more ways than one, over and over, day in and day out, ever since I met him when I was nineteen and he straightened out Stevie, a German Shepherd cross I had then, who was charging children but was a nice dog after we took care of that, who lived for twelve years after Dick showed me how to train him, who shook the ground just as hard as Beaumont did when he died. My teacher and friend Dick Koehler is a maniac for training dogs instead of killing them. Deaf dogs, three-legged dogs, dogs with chartreuse spots on their heads. He hasn't gotten around to getting another Dane, though there have been other dogs, of course. *Of course.*

But "Master William Twyti startled The Wart, for he seemed to be crying," and this book, *The Sword in the Stone,* is about the education of great hounds and of a great king. King Arthur in fact. Immortal Beaumont, douce, swef, swef. And immortal Arthur—douce, douce, harken to Arthur, they would say in time about: *Regis quondam regisque futuri.* The once and future king. Which is to say, this is all of it about the education of any hound and any boy.

"But won't it hurt?" my student asked me recently when I gave that advice: *another dog, same breed, as soon as possible.* "Won't it hurt my daughter again?" Oh, it hurts, especially when, as is so often the case, you have a part in the dog's death.

Perhaps because you were careless and he got run over, or because, like Master Twyti, you gave the nod to the vet or to the huntsman with his falchion.

There is the falchion, and then sometimes you must speak abruptly into the face of grief, for grief gives bad advice. Grief will tell you to throw your heart into the grave with the dog's corpse, and this is ecologically unsound. The ants will take care of the corpse in a few weeks, but a discarded heart stinks for quite some time. Two days ago that student of mine called, a woman in her late thirties. She had gotten a new pup for her eight-year-old daughter, and at a few months of age the pup had died because left in her crate with her collar on, and the collar got caught on the handle of the crate. "My daughter is so upset, my husband says it would be too bad to get another dog and have something else happen. What do the experts do?"

I said in tones of vibrant command, "Another dog, same breed, right away." Nothing else, for wordiness is not in order when you are discussing, as we so often are, the education of a queen.

A decade went by between the death of Gunner and the purchase of the new Airedale pup. That was as soon as I could get to it, what with one thing and another.

Nominated by Raritan

SPECIAL MENTION

(The editors also wish to mention the following important works published by small presses last year. Listing is in no particular order.)

POETRY

Closed Mill—Maggie Anderson (Pennsylvania Review)
Versification of A Passage from Penthouse—Andrew Hudgins (Western Humanities Review)
The Disfigurement of Shame—Jennifer Atkinson (Delmar 4)
Ohio—Ed Ochester (Ploughshares)
Unseen—Molly Peacock (Northern Sentinel)
The Rookery at Hawthornden—William Matthews (Shenandoah)
Hinglish—Gerald Stern (American Poetry Review)
In The Bamboo Hut—Galway Kinnell (Best of The New England Review)
The Dirty Talker, Boston—C. K. Williams (Best of the New England Review)
My Mouth—Toi Derricotte (New Letters)
Waiting for Kafka—Richard Jackson (Black Warrior Review)
Year's End—Marilyn Hacker (Paris Review)
Big Blue Train—Paul Zimmer (Iowa Review)
We—Karen Swenson (Georgia Review)
In Deliciis—Timothy Russell (Kestrel)
Cannibal Beach—Edward Field (5AM)
Don Giovanni In Hell—Eric Pankey (Kenyon Review)
A Shadow—Elizabeth Spires (American Poetry Review)
Listen Carefully—Philip Levine (Threepenny Review)
Fire—Sherod Santos (The Southern Review)
Elegy for My Brother—Norman Dubie (The Southern Review)
The Book of the Dead Man (#33)—Marvin Bell (Poetry)

ESSAYS

Rings and Crucifixes: A Visit to Eastern Croatia in December, 1992—Josip Novakovich (Chicago Review)

Contingency for Beginners—Adam Phillips (Raritan)

Last Days of Henry Miller—Barbara Kraft (Hudson Review)

From "A Poet's Alphabet of Influences"—Mark Strand (Colorado Review)

Waves—Edwin J. Kenney, Jr. (Epoch)

It's Not Your Father's Youth Movement—Tom Frank (The Baffler)

Lady Be Good—Charles Simic (Boulevard)

FICTION

Other People's Love Letters—Cammie McGovern (Nimrod)

The Gift—Eugene K. Garber (Little Magazine)

The Documentarian—Jaime Manrique (Manoa)

North of Nowhere—Janette Turner Hospital (Nimrod)

Skate Dogs—Kip Kotzen (Open City)

Clown Speaks—Paco (Open City)

Puccini's Last Opera—Jeff Spelman (Byline)

The Shampooing and Resurrection of Vronski—David Comfort (Belletrist Review)

Car Talk—David Phalen (Georgetown Review)

What This Is Between Us—Justin Cronin (Greensboro Review)

Stations—Clark Brown (Writer's Forum)

A Classical Education—Sidney Thompson (Carolina Quarterly)

Do You Know What I Mean—Dan Chaon (Whiskey Island Magazine)

Love in the Present Tense—Abigail Thomas (Santa Monica Review)

Come Visit. Bring Cigarettes—Bonnie Powell (William & Mary Review)

Feet of Clay—W. P. Kinsella (Spitball Magazine)

A Over Middle C—Harriet Doerr (Santa Monica Review)

The Man Who Shot the Maid of Cotton—Candyce Barnes (High Plains Literary Review)

Letter to Mr. Yoshimoto After Time Gone By—Sara Corbett (Indiana Review)

My Father's Pool—David Borofka (West Branch)

Skagway—Ryan Harty (Santa Monica Review)

A Fever of Unknown Origin—Joey Quesada (Culebra!)

Below Marquesas—Jennifer Shull (West Word)

Who I'll Run Away With—Nancy Krusoe (American Writing)

Musical Chairs—Joan Joffe Hall (Whetstone)

Pieces—Michael Wen-ta Chen (Threepenny Review)

When I Was a Child My Daddy Loved Me—Catherine Gammon
(Central Park)

Afterimages—Phillip Garrison (Northwest Review)

I Will Be Walking in the Middle of Your Soul—Steve Heller
(Chariton Review)

The Defector—Ricardo Pau-Llosa (New England Review)

Little White Sister—Melanie Rae Thon (Ploughshares)

Loosestrife—Ellen Akins (Missouri Review)

BlueBoy—Kevin Canty (Missouri Review)

Annunciation—Marjorie Sandor (Shenandoah)

The Waco Wego—Janet Peery (Southwest Review)

The Holocaust Party—Robin Hemley (Prairie Schooner)

Folsom Man—Lex Williford (New Texas)

The Reading—Jonathan Baumbach (Boulevard)

So Far, So Good—Abigail Thomas (Glimmer Train)

March of Dimes—Maxine Rodburg (Boston Review)

Old Mother And the Grouch—Lydia Davis (Partisan Review)

The Rubble—Steve Meixell (The Long Story)

Turk—David Michael Kaplan (TriQuarterly)

Babyman—Brent Spencer (Missouri Review)

Not The Plaster Casters—Janice Eidus (The Baffler)

A Robber In The House—Jessica Treat (Coffee House Press)

A Little Lovely Dream—B. A. Phillips (Goodbye, Friends,
Bridge Works)

Picture Perfect—Leigh Anne Jones (Threepenny Review)

Flight Pattern—Cynthia Shearer (Oxford American)

Benjamin—Naeem Murr (Gettysburg Review)

Self Portrait With A Wooden Leg—Dalia Pagani (Green Moun-
tain Review)

The Recital—Jordan Smith (American Short Fiction)

The Dialogues of Time and Entropy—Aryeh Lev Stollman
(American Short Fiction)

Surati's Revenge—Pramoedya Anata Toer (Grand Street)

La Pourritue Noble—Richard Stern (*Noble Rot*, Another Chicago Press)

Portrait—Stephen Dixon (Bakunin)

The Little Poet—Aryeh Lev Stollman (Story)

Earthmen—Jim Humes (Nimrod)

A Real Durwan—Jhumpa Lahiri (Harvard Review)

Nabakov, Dear—Sandra Christenson (Faultline)

Popular Girls—Beth Nugent (Black Warrior Review)

Walking Tour: Rohnert Park—Molly Giles (Witness)

Never, Ever, Always—Janet Desaulniers (Ploughshares)

The Further Complexities of Intimacy—Mary Caponegro (Conjunction)

Our Underwater Mother—Yannick Murphy (Conjunctions)

Jeremiah's Road—Marlin Barton (Shenandoah)

Blazo—Ron Carlson (Ploughshares)

Sweet Tooth—Pamela Erbe (Antioch Review)

To A Secret Friend—Mikahil Bulgakov (Glas)

Melungeons—Chris Offutt (Story)

A Profound Theory of Complementarity—Jan Emily Ramjerdi (Quarterly West)

After—Lucy Honig (Gettysburg Review)

After Leston—Bret Lott (Chattahoochee Review)

Litmag Chain Letter—Gillian Kendall, Robert Clark Young (ZYZZYVA)

The Tower—Steve Yarbrough (Shenandoah)

The Cross—John Keeble (ZYZZYVA)

A Suitable Good-bye—Christopher Tilghman (Yale Review)

The Other Rs—Dawn Raffel (New Letters)

What She Told Me—Judy Doenges (Georgia Review)

This Is the Story I Told Him—Robie Macauley (Southern Review)

Montenegro's Father—Mark Wisniewski (New Delta Review)

The Spectral University—Tom Whalen (Missouri Review)

Route Coyote—Kurt Hochenauer (Missouri Review)

Who Made You—Wendell Mayo (West Branch)

Miss Eleanore Holm—Richard Elman (Witness)

The Tutor—Gerald Shapiro (Michigan Quarterly Review)

Tizita—Abraham Verghese (Story)

My Other Life—Melanie Sumner (Story)

PRESSES FEATURED IN THE PUSHCART PRIZE EDITIONS SINCE 1976

Acts
Agni Review
Ahsahta Press
Ailanthus Press
Alaska Quarterly Review
Alcheringa/Ethnopoetics
Alice James Books
Ambergris
Amelia
American Literature
American PEN
American Poetry Review
American Scholar
American Short Fiction
The American Voice
Amicus Journal
Amnesty International
Anaesthesia Review
Another Chicago Magazine
Antaeus
Antietam Review
Antioch Review
Apalachee Quarterly
Aphra
Aralia Press
The Ark
Ascensius Press

Ascent
Aspen Leaves
Aspen Poetry Anthology
Assembling
Bamboo Ridge
Barlenmir House
Barnwood Press
The Bellingham Review
Bellowing Ark
Beloit Poetry Journal
Bennington Review
Bilingual Review
Black American Literature Forum
Black Rooster
Black Scholar
Black Sparrow
Black Warrior Review
Blackwells Press
Bloomsbury Review
Blue Cloud Quarterly
Blue Unicorn
Blue Wind Press
Bluefish
BOA Editions
Bomb
Bookslinger Editions
Boulevard

Boxspring
Bridges
Brown Journal of the Arts
Burning Deck Press
Caliban
California Quarterly
Callaloo
Calliope
Calliopea Press
Canto
Capra Press
Carolina Quarterly
Caribbean Writer
Cedar Rock
Center
Chariton Review
Charnel House
Chelsea
Chicago Review
Chouteau Review
Chowder Review
Cimarron Review
Cincinnati Poetry Review
City Lights Books
Clown War
CoEvolution Quarterly
Cold Mountain Press
Colorado Review
Columbia: A Magazine of Poetry
    and Prose
Confluence Press
Confrontation
Conjunctions
Copper Canyon Press
Cosmic Information Agency
Crawl Out Your Window
Crazyhorse
Crescent Review
Cross Cultural Communications
Cross Currents
Cumberland Poetry Review
Curbstone Press
Cutbank

Dacotah Territory
Daedalus
Dalkey Archive Press
Decatur House
December
Denver Quarterly
Domestic Crude
Dragon Gate Inc.
Dreamworks
Dryad Press
Duck Down Press
Durak
East River Anthology
Ellis Press
Empty Bowl
Epoch
Ergo!
Exquisite Corpse
Fiction
Fiction Collective
Fiction International
Field
Firebrand Books
Firelands Art Review
Five Fingers Review
Five Trees Press
The Formalist
Frontiers: A Journal of Women
    Studies
Gallimaufry
Genre
The Georgia Review
Gettysburg Review
Ghost Dance
Goddard Journal
David Godine, Publisher
Graham House Press
Grand Street
Granta
Graywolf Press
Green Mountains Review
Greenfield Review
Greensboro Review

Guardian Press
Gulf Coast
Hard Pressed
Harvard Review
Hayden's Ferry Review
Hermitage Press
Hills
Holmgangers Press
Holy Cow!
Home Planet News
Hudson Review
Hungry Mind Review
Icarus
Iguana Press
Indiana Review
Indiana Writes
Intermedia
Intro
Invisible City
Inwood Press
Iowa Review
Ironwood
Jam To-day
The Kanchenjuga Press
Kansas Quarterly
Kayak
Kelsey Street Press
Kenyon Review
Latitudes Press
Laughing Waters Press
Laurel Review
L'Epervier Press
Liberation
Linquis
The Literary Review
The Little Magazine
Living Hand Press
Living Poets Press
Logbridge-Rhodes
Louisville Review
Lowlands Review
Lucille
Lynx House Press

Magic Circle Press
Malahat Review
Mānoa
Manroot
Massachusetts Review
Mho & Mho Works
Micah Publications
Michigan Quarterly
Milkweed Editions
Milkweed Quarterly
The Minnesota Review
Mississippi Review
Mississippi Valley Review
Missouri Review
Montana Gothic
Montana Review
Montemora
Moon Pony Press
Mr. Cogito Press
MSS
Mulch Press
Nada Press
New America
New American Review
The New Criterion
New Delta Review
New Directions
New England Review
New England Review and Bread
    Loaf Quarterly
New Letters
New Virginia Review
New York Quarterly
New York University Press
Nimrod
North American Review
North Atlantic Books
North Dakota Quarterly
North Point Press
Northern Lights
Northwest Review
O. ARS
O·Blēk

Obsidian
Obsidian II
Oconee Review
October
Ohio Review
Ontario Review
Open Places
Orca Press
Orchises Press
Oxford Press
Oyez Press
Painted Bride Quarterly
Painted Hills Review
Paris Review
Parnassus: Poetry in Review
Partisan Review
Passages North
Penca Books
Pentagram
Penumbra Press
Pequod
Persea: An International Review
Pipedream Press
Pitcairn Press
Ploughshares
Poet and Critic
Poetry
Poetry East
Poetry Northwest
Poetry Now
Prairie Schooner
Prescott Street Press
Promise of Learnings
Provincetown Arts
Puerto Del Sol
Quarry West
The Quarterly
Quarterly West
Raccoon
Rainbow Press
Raritan: A Quarterly Review
Red Cedar Review
Red Clay Books

Red Dust Press
Red Earth Press
Release Press
Review of Contemporary Fiction
Revista Chicano-Riquena
River Styx
Rowan Tree Press
Russian *Samizdat*
Salmagundi
San Marcos Press
Sea Pen Press and Paper Mill
Seal Press
Seamark Press
Seattle Review
Second Coming Press
Semiotext(e)
The Seventies Press
Sewanee Review
Shankpainter
Shantih
Sheep Meadow Press
Shenandoah
A Shout In the Street
Sibyl-Child Press
Side Show
Small Moon
The Smith
Some
The Sonora Review
South Florida Poetry Review
Southern Poetry Review
Southern Review
Southwest Review
Spectrum
The Spirit That Moves Us
St. Andrews Press
Story
Story Quarterly
Streetfare Journal
Stuart Wright, Publisher
Sulfur
The Sun
Sun & Moon Press

Sun Press
Sunstone
Sycamore Review
Tar River Poetry
Teal Press
Telephone Books
Telescope
Temblor
Tendril
Texas Slough
The MacGuffin
13th Moon
THIS
Thorp Springs Press
Three Rivers Press
Threepenny Review
Thunder City Press
Thunder's Mouth Press
Tikkun
Tombouctou Books
Toothpaste Press
Transatlantic Review
TriQuarterly
Truck Press
Undine
Unicorn Press
University of Illinois Press

University of Massachusetts Press
University of Pittsburgh Press
Unmuzzled Ox
Unspeakable Visions of the
    Individual
Vagabond
Virginia Quarterly
Volt
Wampeter Press
Washington Writers Workshop
Water Table
Western Humanities Review
Westigan Review
Wickwire Press
Willow Springs
Wilmore City
Witness
Word Beat Press
Word-Smith
Wormwood Review
Writers Forum
Xanadu
Yale Review
Yardbird Reader
Yarrow
Y'Bird
ZYZZYVA

CONTRIBUTORS' NOTES

RALPH ANGEL's most recent book is *Anxious Latitude* (Wesleyan). Last year he won a Fulbright Scholarship in Yugoslavia. He lives in South Pasadena, California.

A. MANETTE ANSAY teaches at Vanderbilt University. Her first novel, *Vinegar Hill,* is just out from Viking.

JON BARNES grew up on a small farm in the foothills of the Oachita Mountains, Arkansas. He holds an MFA from Penn State University (1991). "Nash" is his first published story.

CHARLES BAXTER's novel *Shadow Play* was recently published by Norton. He is the author of four other books of fiction and a poetry collection.

LUCIA BERLIN was born in Alaska but spent most of her childhood in Chile. Her collections of stories include *Angel's Laundromat* (1981), *Phantom Pain* (1984), *Safe and Sound* (1988) and *Homesick* published by Black Sparrow in 1990 and winner of the American Book Award in 1991.

BLISS BROYARD studies at the University of Virginia's MFA program. "My Father, Dancing" is her first published work.

MARILYN CHIN, born in Hong Kong and raised in Portland, Oregon, is the author of *Dwarf Bamboo* (Greenfield Review Press). Chin is a recipient of a Stegner Fellowship, two National Endowment for the Arts Fellowships, and the Mary Roberts Rinehart Award.

EVAN CONNELL lives in Santa Fe, and is the author of *Mrs. Bridge, Mr. Bridge, Son of the Morning Star* and other works.

GILLIAN CONOLEY's most recent book is *Tall Stranger*, nominated for the National Book Award. She teaches at San Francisco State.

CHARLES D'AMBROSIO's work has appeared in *Paris Review*, *Story* and elsewhere.

JIM DANIELS' books include *M-80* (University of Pittsburgh Press, 1993) and *Niagara Falls* (Adastra Press, 1994). He lives in Pittsburgh.

KIM EDWARDS received a NEA grant for 1994. Her work appeared in *Best American Short Stories* for 1993 and she is currently completing a novel and a short story collection.

EDWIDGE DANTICAT was born in Port-au-Prince, Haiti, but grew up in Brooklyn, New York. She published in many journals and her first novel *Breath, Eyes, Memory* was published by Soho Press this year.

STUART DISCHELL is the author of *Good Hope Road*, a National Poetry Series selection. He teaches at the University of North Carolina, Greensboro.

CHITRA DIVAKARUNI is the author of *Black Candle: Poems About Women from India, Pakistan, and Bangladesh* (Calyx Books). She came to the United States as a girl and now lives in Sunnyvale, California.

RITA DOVE teaches at the University of Virginia, and is Poet Laureate of the United States. Her work previously appeared in *Pushcart Prize VII*.

FRANCES DRISCOLL's most recent book is *Talk to Me* (Black River). She lives in Florida.

ANDRE DUBUS III is the author of *The Cage Keeper and Other Stories* and the novel *Bluesman*. He lives in Newburyport, Massachusetts with his wife and son.

LOUISE ERDRICH is the author of two poetry collections—*Jacklight* and *Baptism of Desire;* and of four novels—*The Beet Queen, Tracks, The Bingo Palace*, and *Crown of Columbus* (with Michael Dorris).

RAYMOND FEDERMAN is the author of seven novels, four volumes of poetry and several critical works. His short stories have appeared in *Chicago Review, North American Review, Paris Review* and elsewhere.

EDWARD FIELD lives in New York City. His books include *New and Selected Poems* (Sheep Meadow, 1987).

MARIA FLOOK's novel *Family Life* (Pantheon) received a Hemingway Foundation citation. Her latest novel is *Open Water* (Pantheon). She teaches at Bennington Writing Seminars.

C. S. GISCOMBE teaches at Cornell. Dalkey Archive will soon publish his poetry collection.

LOUISE GLÜCK's books include *Wild Iris* (1992), winner of a Pulitzer Prize. Her essay herein is part of a collection of her work due from Ecco.

LINDA GREGERSON teaches Renaissance literature at the University of Michigan and is the author of books from Dragon Gate Press and Cambridge University Press.

VICKI HEARNE publishes frequently in *Raritan*. She has become widely recognized for her literature about animals.

ROBIN HEMLEY is the author of *The Last Studebaker* a novel from Graywolf (1992) and the short story collections *All You Can Eat* (Atlantic Monthly Press, 1988), and *Mouse Town* (Word Beat Press, 1987).

ROLAINE HOCHSTEIN is the author of *Table 44* (Doubleday, 1983) and *Stepping Out* (Norton 1977). Her work has appeared in *Antioch Review, Other Voices* and elsewhere.

LINDA HOGAN is a short story writer, poet and novelist. Her several books include *Mean Spirit* and she lives in Idledale, Colorado.

LYNDA HULL died earlier this year. She was the author of two collections, *Ghost Money* (1986) and *Star Ledger* (1991). She was featured in four *Pushcart Prize* editions, and lived in Chicago. She taught in the Vermont College MFA program.

LAWSON FUSAO INADA is a third generation Japanese-American. He is the author of many books and won an American Book Award in 1988 and was named Oregon State Poet for 1991. He teaches at Southern Oregon State College.

MARK IRWIN's collection of elegies, *Against the Meanwhile*, was published by Wesleyan University Press in 1989. He is a NEA Fellow and teaches at the University of Denver.

HA JIN, from mainland China, writes poetry and fiction in English. His book of poems, *Between Silences*, was published by The University of Chicago Press in 1990 and his short story "My Best Soldier" won a Pushcart Prize in 1992.

BRIGIT PEGEEN KELLY teaches at the University of Illinois. Her book, *Song*, will be published soon by BOA Editions.

YUSEF KOMUNYAKAA is the author most recently of *Magic City* and *Neon Venacular* and lives in Bloomington, Indiana.

MARK LEVINE's book *Debt* was a winner of the National Poetry Series in 1992. He teaches at the University of Montana.

LISA LEWIS's first collection of poetry, *The Unbeliever*, won the Brittingham Prize from University of Wisconsin Press. She is writer-in-residence at Rhodes College.

FATIMA LIM-WILSON's first book of poetry, *Wandering Roots/ From The Hothouse*, won the 1992 Philippine National Book Award for poetry and the 1991 Colorado Book Authors award. She teaches at Shoreline Community College, Seattle.

ADRIAN C. LOUIS is a Native American and the author of two poetry collections: *Fire Water World* and *Among the Dog Eaters*.

CAROLE MASO won the 1993 Lannan Award. Her book, *American Woman in A Chinese Hat* was published by Dalkey Archive recently.

SUSAN ONTHANK MATES is a physician in a state tuberculosis clinic in Rhode Island. Her writing has appeared in *Providence Journal*, *Sou'wester* and *Innisfree*. Her story collection, *The Good Doctor*, won the University of Iowa Press 1994 John Simmons Short Fiction Award and is just published.

KHALED MATTAWA, a native of Benghazi, Libya, is working on an MFA in creative writing at Indiana University.

GAIL MAZUR's third book, *The Common*, is forthcoming from University of Chicago Press. Her two previous books were issued by Godine. She is director and founder of the Blacksmith Poetry series.

W. S. MERWIN's numerous volumes of poetry include *The Carrier of Ladders* (1970) for which he was awarded the Pulitzer Prize.

STEVEN MILLHAUSER's most recent book is *Little Kingdoms* (Poseidon), a collection of three novellas. He teaches at Skidmore College.

BRENDA MILLER worked as a massage therapist for four years in Orr Hot Springs, California. She holds degrees from Humbolt State University and the University of Montana.

JANE MILLER's books include the poetry collection *American Odalisque* (Copper Canyon) and *Working Times: Essays on Poetry, Culture and Travel* (University of Michigan Press). She lives in Tucson.

JEWEL MOGAN's stories have appeared in *North American Review, Ascent* and elsewhere. Her first story collection appears from Ontario Review Press in spring, 1995.

JOSIP NOVAKOVICH lived in Yugoslavia and now resides in Cincinnati. His work has appeared in several literary journals and a novel is due from Graywolf Press.

THOMAS RABBITT lives and works on a farm in Elrod, Alabama. His fourth book of poems, *Enemies of the State*, has just been released by David R. Godine.

LISA SANDLIN's story collection, *The Famous Thing About Death*, was published in 1991 by Cinco Puntos Press. She is presently completing her second collection and lives in Santa Fe, New Mexico.

SHEROD SANTOS teaches at The University of Missouri. His poetry appeared in *Pushcart Prize V*, and his books include *The City of Women* (Norton, 1993).

DEAN SCHABNER is a former sports reporter for United Press International. His stories have appeared in *Northwest Review* and elsewhere. He lives in New York City.

DIANN BLAKELY SHOAF has published in *The Louisville Review* and elsewhere.

587

CAROL SNOW lives and works in San Francisco. Her first poetry collection, *Artist and Model*, was published in 1990 by Atlantic Monthly Press.

ROBYN SELMAN's poetry has appeared in *Ploughshares, Kenyon Review,* and *The American Poetry Review.* She works at a photography publishing house in Manhattan.

KIM R. STAFFORD teaches writing at Lewis and Clark College in Portland, Oregon.

EUGENE STEIN has published stories in *The Malahat Review, Confrontation, Gargoyle* and *Satori.* His first novel, *Straitjacket and Tie,* was recently published by Ticknor and Fields.

ROBERT LOVE TAYLOR teaches at Bucknell. His latest book, *Lady of Spain,* was published by Algonquin Books of Chapel Hill.

JEAN THOMPSON has published fiction in *New England Review, Antioch Review, The New Yorker* and *American Short Fiction.* She lives in Urbana, Illinois.

ARTHUR VOGELSANG's books of poetry are *A Planet* (Holt), *Twentieth Century Women* (University of Georgia) and the forthcoming *Cities and Towns.* He lives in Los Angeles.

SUSAN WHEELER lives in New York City. Her poetry has appeared in *Paris Review, Brooklyn Review* and *Best American Poetry.*

GEORGE WILLIAMS is the first recipient of the Michener Fellowship in honor of Donald Barthelme. His stories and essays have appeared in *Gulf Coast, Southern Plains Review* and *New Virginia Review.*

JOY WILLIAMS' first novel, *State of Grace,* was a Paris Review Edition in 1974. She received a Strauss Living Award from the American Academy of Arts and Letters, and she lives in Key West, Florida. Her most recent story collection is *Escapes.*

LOIS-ANN YAMANAKA is a native of Hawaii and she lives in Honolulu. Her work also appeared in *Pushcart Prize XVIII.*

CONTRIBUTING
SMALL PRESSES

(These presses made or received nominations for this edition of *The Pushcart Prize*. See the *International Directory of Little Magazines and Small Presses*, Dustbooks, P.O. Box 100, Paradise, CA 95967, for subscription rates, manuscript requirements and a complete international listing of small presses.)

A

Adastra Press, 101 Strong St, Easthampton, MA 01027

Aegis, 3290 Sixth Ave, IF, San Diego, CA 92103

African American Review, English Dept., Indiana State Univ., Terre Haute, IN 47809

Agni, Boston Univ., 236 Bay State Rd, Boston, MA 02215

Alabama Literary Review, 253 Smith Hall, Troy State Univ., Troy, AL 36082

Alaska Quarterly Review, College of Arts & Sciences, 3211 Providence Dr., Anchorage, AK 99508

Alice James Books, 33 Richdale Ave, Cambridge, MA 02140

Alpha Beat Press, 31A Waterloo St., New Hope, PA 18938

Alyson Publications, Inc., 40 Plympton St., Boston, MA 02118

Ambergris, P.O. Box 29919, Cincinnati, OH 45229

Amelia, 329 "E" St., Bakersfield, CA 93304

American Literary Review, Univ. of No. Texas, Denton, TX 76203

American Poetry Review, 1721 Walnut St., Philadelphia, PA 19103

American Scholar, 1811 Q St., NW, Washington, DC 20009

American Short Fiction, English Dept., Univ. of Texas, Austin, TX 78712

The American Voice, 332 W. Broadway, Ste. 1215, Louisville, KY 40202

American Writing, 4343 Manayunk Ave, Philadelphia, PA 19128

Americas Review, Box 7681, Berkeley, CA 94707

Another Chicago Magazine, 3709 N. Kenmore, Chicago, IL 60613

Antaeus, 100 W. Broad St., Hopewell, NJ 08525

Anterior Fiction Quarterly, 7735 Brand Ave, St. Louis, MO 63135

Anterior Monthly Review, 7735 Brand Ave, St. Louis, MO 63135

Antietam Review, 7 W. Franklin St., Hagerstown, MD 21740

The Antioch Review, P.O. Box 148, Yellow Springs, OH 45387

Apalachee Quarterly, P.O. Box 20106, Tallahassee, FL 32316

Appalachia, 126 Park Rd., Chelmsford, MA 01824

Applezaba Press, P.O. Box 4134, Long Beach, CA 90804

Artful Dodge, English Dept., College of Wooster, Wooster, OH 44691

Ascent, P.O. Box 967, Urbana, IL 61801

Asian Pacific American Journal, 296 Elizabeth St., #2R, New York, NY 10012

Avalon Rising, P.O.Box 1983, Cincinnati, OH 45201

AWP Chronicle, Assoc. Writing Programs, Old Dominion Univ., Norfolk, VA 23529

B

Bakunin, P.O.Box 1853, Simi Valley, CA 93062

Bamberger Books, P.O.Box 1126, Flint, MI 48501

Basement Press, 215 Burlington, Billings, MT 59101

Bastard Review, P.O.Box 422820, San Francisco, CA 94142

Bayousphere, Univ. of Houston-Clear Lake, Box 456, Houston, TX 77058

Bear House Publishing, Rt. 2, Box 94, Eureka Springs, AR 72632

Beggar's Press, 8110 No. 38th St., Omaha, NE 68112

Belletrist Review, 17 Farmington Ave., Ste. 290, Plainville, CT 06062

Bellowing Ark, P.O.Box 45637, Seattle, WA 98145

Beloit Poetry Journal, RFD 2, Box 154, Ellsworth, ME 04605

Bilingual Press, Hispanic Research Ctr., Arizona State Univ., Tempe, AZ 85287

Bilingual Review, see Bilingual Press

Birmingham Poetry Review, English Dept., Univ. of Alabama, Birmingham, AL 35294

BkMk Press, Univ. of Missouri, Kansas City, MO 64110

Black Belt Press, P.O. Box 551, Montgomery, AL 36101

Black Heron Press, P.O. Box 95676, Seattle, WA 98145

Black Sparrow Press, 24 Tenth St., Santa Rosa, CA 95401

Black Warrior Review, P.O. Box 2936, Tuscaloosa, AL 35486

Blue Heron Publishing, Inc., 24450 NW Hansen Rd, Hillsboro, OR 97124

Blue Mountain, 3800 N. Texas, Odessa, TX 79762

BOA Editions, Ltd., 92 Park Avenue, Brockport, NY 14420

Bomb, P.O. Box 2003, Canal Street Station, New York, NY 10013

Bonne Chance Press, 209 River Bluff Rd., Cleveland, SC 29635

Borderlands, P.O. Box 49818, Austin, TX 78765

The Boston Review, 33 Harrison Ave., Boston, MA 02111

Boulevard, P.O. Box 30386, Philadelphia, PA 19103

Brick Books, Box 38, Sta. B, London, Ontario, N6A 4V3, CANADA

The Bridge, 14060 Vernon St., Oak Park, MI 48237

Byline, P.O. Box 130596, Edmond, OK 73013

C

Cadmus Editions, P.O. Box 126, Tiburon-Belvedere, CA 94920

Callaloo, English Dept., Univ. of Virginia, Charlottesville, VA 22903

Camellia, P.O. Box 417, Village Sta., New York, NY 10014

The Caribbean Writer, Research Public. Ctr., Univ. of Virgin Islands, RR02, Box 10,000, Kingshill, St. Croix, U.S. Virgin Islands 00850

Carolina Quarterly, CB #3520-Greenlaw, Univ. of No. Carolina, Chapel Hill, NC 27599

Catbird Press, 16 Windsor Rd., North Haven, CT 06473

Chantry Press, P.O. Box 144, Midland Park, NJ 07432

Chattahoochee Review, DeKalb College, 2101 Womack Rd., Dunwoody, GA 30338

Chelsea, Box 5880, Grand Central Sta., New York, NY 10163

Chicago Review, 5801 S. Kenwood Ave., Chicago, IL 60637

Chicory Blue Press, 795 East St. North, Goshen, CT 06756

Cimarron Review, Oklahoma State Univ., Stillwater, OK 74078

Cincinnati Poetry Review, English Dept., Univ. of Cincinnati, Cincinnati, OH 45221

The Climbing Art, P.O.Box 1378, Laporte, CO 80535

Clockwatch Review, Illinois Wesleyan Univ., P.O.Box 2900, Bloomington, IL 61702

Coffee House Press, 27 N. 4th St., Minneapolis, MN

Colorado Review, English Dept., Colorado State Univ., Ft. Collins, CO 80523

Confrontation, English Dept., C. W. Post of L.I.U., Brookville, NY 11548

Conjunctions, Bard College, Annandale-on-Hudson, NY 12504

The Contemporary Review, 7008 SW 10th, Des Moines, IA 50315

Cooper House Publishing, Inc., P.O.Box 54947, Oklahoma City, OK 73154

Copper Beech Press, Brown Univ., Box 1852, Providence, RI 02912

Corona Publishing Co., 1037 S. Alamo, San Antonio, TX 78210

Crab Creek Review, 4462 Whitman Ave. No., Seattle, WA 98103

Crazyhorse, English Dept., Univ. of Arkansas, Little Rock, AR 72204

Cream City Review, Univ. of Wisconsin, P.O. Box 413, Milwaukee, WI 53201

The Crossing Press, P.O.Box 1048, Freedom, CA 95019

Curbstone Press, 321 Jackson St., Willimantic, CT 06226

CutBank, English Dept., Univ. of Montana, Missoula, MT 59812

D

Dalkey Archive Press, Fairchild Hall, ISU, Normal, IL 61761

John Daniel & Co., P.O.Box 21922, Santa Barbara, CA 93121

Denver Quarterly, English Dept., Univ. of Denver, Denver, CO 80208

A Different Drummer, 84 Bay 28th St., Brooklyn, NY 11214
Dreamstreets, P.O.Box 4593, Newark, DE 19715
Dryad Press, 15 Sherman Ave., Takoma Park, MD 20912

E

the eleventh Muse, P.O.Box 2413, Colorado Springs, CO 80901
ELF: Eclectic Literary Forum, P.O.Box 392, Tonawanda, NY
14150
Emergence, P.O.Box 1615, Bridgeview, IL 60455
Epiphany, see Ogalala Review
Epoch, 251 Goldwin Smith Hall, Cornell Univ., Ithaca, NY 14853
Ergo!, P.O.Box 9750, Seattle, WA 98109
Event Horizon Press, P.O.Box 867, Desert Hot Springs, CA
92240
Evergreen Chronicles, P.O.Box 8939, Minneapolis, MN 55408
Exit 13 Magazine, Box 423, Fanwood, NJ 07023
Expressions, 605 Maple Park Dr., St. Paul, MN 55118
Exquisite Corpse, English Dept., Louisiana State Univ., Baton
Rouge, LA 70803

F

Factor Press, P.O.Box 8888, Mobile, AL 36689
Farmer's Market, P.O.Box 1272, Galesburg, IL 61402
Faultline, P.O.Box 599-4960, Irvine, CA 92714
(Feed.), P.O.Box 1567, Madison Sq. Sta., New York, NY 10159
The Feminist Press at CUNY, 311 East 94th St., New York, NY
10128
Fiction, English Dept., City College of N.Y., Convent Ave. at
138th St., New York, NY 10031
Field, Creative Writing Prog., Rice Hall 17, Oberlin College,
Oberlin, OH 44074
Fine Madness, P.O.Box 31138, Seattle, WA 98103
The Florida Review, English Dept., Univ. of Central Florida,
Orlando, FL 32816
Footfalls Press, 512 Acequia Madre, Santa Fe, NM 87501
Forever Alive, P.O.Box 12305, Scottsdale, AZ

Free Lunch, P.O. Box 7647, Laguna Niguel, CA 92607

G

Gallery, see Montcalm Publishing

Garden Street Press, 126 Garden St., Cambridge, MA 02138

Georgetown Review, 400 E. College St., Box 227, Georgetown, KY 40324

The Georgia Review, Univ. of Georgia, Athens, GA 30602

Gettysburg Review, Gettysburg College, Gettysburg, PA 17325

Ghost Pony Press, 2518 Gregory St., Madison, WI 53711

Glas, see Zephyr Press

Glimmer Train, 812 SW Washington St., Ste. 1205, Portland, OR 97205

Graham House Review, Box 5000, Hamilton, NY 13346

Grand Street, 131 Varick St., #906, New York, NY 10013

Grasslands Review, N.T. Box 13706, Denton, TX 76203

Graywolf Press, 2402 University Ave., Ste. 203, St. Paul, MN 55114

Great River Review, 211 W. 7th, Winona, MN 55987

Great Stream Review, Box 66, Lycoming College, Williamsport, PA 17701

Green Mountain Review, Johnson State College, Johnson, VT 05656

Greenfield Review Press, 2 Middle Grove Rd., Greenfield Center, NY 12833

Greenhouse Review Press, 3965 Bonny Doon Rd., Santa Cruz, CA 95060

Greensboro Review, English Dept., Univ. of North Carolina, Greensboro, NC 27412

Gulf Coast, English Dept., Univ. of Houston, Houston, TX 77204

H

Haight-Ashbury Literary Journal, 558 Joost Ave., San Francisco, CA 94127

Half Tones to Jubilee, English Dept., Pensacola Jr. College, Pensacola, FL 32504

Hanging Loose Press, 231 Wyckoff St., Brooklyn, NY 11217

Harp-Strings, Box 640387, Beverly Hills, FL 34464

Harvard Review, Harvard College Library, Cambridge, MA 02138

Hayden's Ferry Review, Matthews Center, Arizona State Univ., Tempe, AZ 85287

Haypenny Press, 211 New St., West Paterson, NJ 07424

Heartsong Books, P.O. Box 370, Blue Hill, ME 04614

Helicon Nine, Box 22412, Kansas City, MO 64113

High Plains Literary Review, 180 Adams St., Ste. 250, Denver, CO 80206

Home Planet News, P.O. Box 455, High Falls, NY 12440

Hopewell Review, c/o Arts Indiana, 47 S. Pennsylvania St., Ste. 701, Indianapolis, IN 46204

Houston Poetry Fest, P.O. Box 1995, Bellaire, TX 77402

Hubbub, 5344 S.E. 38th, Portland, OR 97202

The Hudson Review, 684 Park Ave., New York, NY 10021

Hungry Mind Review, 1648 Grand Ave., St. Paul, MN 55105

Hyphen, P.O. Box 516, Somonauk, IL 60552

I

The Iconoclast, 1675 Amazon Rd., Mohegan Lake, NY 10547

The Illinois Review, English Dept./4240, Illinois State Univ., Normal, IL 61790

Impatiens, P.O. Box 11897, Philadelphia, PA 19128

Impetus, see Implosion Press

Implosion Press, 4975 Comanche Trail, Stow, OH 44224

Indiana Review, 316 N. Jordan, Indiana Univ., Bloomington, IN 47405

Innisfree, P.O. Box 277, Manhattan Beach, CA 90267

Interim, English Dept., Univ. of Nevada, Las Vegas, NV 89154

International Poetry Review, Dept. of Romance Lang., Univ. of North Carolina, Greensboro, NC 27412

International Quarterly, P.O. Box 10521, Tallahassee, FL 32302

The Iowa Review, 308 EPB, Univ. of Iowa, Iowa City, IA 52242

Iowa Woman, P.O. Box 2938, Waterloo, IA 50704

Ipsissima Verba, see Haypenny Press

Iris, P.O. Box 7263, Atlanta, GA 30357

J

The Journal, English Dept., Ohio State Univ., 164 W. 17th Ave., Columbus, OH 43210

Journal of New Jersey Poets, County College of Morris, 214 Center Grove Rd., Randolph, NJ 07869

K

Kalliope, Florida Community College, 3939 Roosevelt Blvd., Jacksonville, FL 32205

Kansas Quarterly, Kansas State University, Manhattan, KS 66506

Karamu, English Dept., Eastern Illinois Univ., Charleston, IL 61920

Kelsey Review, Mercer Co. Comm. College, P.O.Box B, Trenton, NJ 08690

Kelsey St. Press, P.O.Box 9235, Berkeley, CA 94709

The Kenyon Review, Kenyon College, Gambier, OH 43022

Kestrel, Lang. & Lit., Fairmont State College, 1201 Locust Ave., Fairmont, WV 26554

L

Lactuca Publications, P.O.Box 621, Suffern, NY 10901

Lake Shore Publishing, 373 Ramsay Rd., Deerfield, IL 60015

The Laurel Review, English Dept., Northwest Missouri State Univ., Maryville, MO 64468

The Ledge, 64-65 Cooper Ave., Glendale, NY 11385

Left Bank, see Blue Heron Publishing

Light, Box 7500, Chicago, IL 60680

LILT, Kansas City Art Inst., 4415 Warwick Rd., Kansas City, MO 64111

The Literary Review, Fairleigh Dickinson Univ., 285 Madison Ave., Madison, NJ 07940

The Little Magazine, English Dept., SUNY, 1400 Washington Ave., Albany, NY 12222

Little River Press, 10 Lowell Ave., Westfield, MA 01085

Log Cabin Publishers, P.O.Box 1536, Allentown, PA 18105

The Long Story, 11 Kingston St., No. Andover, MA 01845

Lost & Found Times, c/o Luna Bisonte Prods., 137 Leland Ave., Columbus, OH 43214

The Louisville Review, Bingham Humanities 315, Univ. of Louisville, Louisville, KY 40292

LU Press, Station 22, Livingston Univ., Livingston, AL 35470

Lucidity, see Bear House Publishing

M

The MacGuffin, Schoolcraft College, 18600 Haggerty Rd., Livonia, MI 48152

Maine in Print, MWPA, 12 Pleasant St., Brunswick, ME 04011

The Manhattan Review, 440 Riverside Dr., New York, NY 10027

Hugh Mann, Publisher, P.O.Box 207, Scarsdale, NY 10583

Manoa, English Dept., Univ. of Hawaii, Honolulu, HI 96822

The Massachusetts Review, Univ. of Massachusetts, Amherst, MA 01003

The Match, P.O.Box 3488, Tucson, AZ 85722

The Maverick Press, Rt. 2, Box 4915, Eagle Pass, TX 78852

Mediphors Journal, P.O.Box 327, Bloomsburg, PA 17815

Mellen Poetry Press, P.O.Box 450, Lewiston, NY 14092

Mho & Mho Works, Box 33135, San Diego, CA 92163

Micah Publications, 255 Humphrey St., Marblehead, MA 01945

Michigan Quarterly Review, Univ. of Michigan, 3032 Rackham Bldg., Ann Arbor, MI 48109

Mid-American Review, English Dept., Bowling Green State Univ., Bowling Green, OH 43403

The Midwest Quarterly, Pittsburg State Univ., Pittsburg, KS 66762

Milkweed Editions, 430 First Ave. N, ste. 400, Minneapolis, MN 55401

Mind in Motion, P.O.Box 1118, Apple Valley, CA 92307

Mindscapes, 2252 Beverly Glen Pl., Los Angeles, CA 90077

Minnesota Review, English Dept., East Carolina Univ., Greenville, NC 27858

Mississippi Review, Box 5144, Southern Sta., Hattiesburg, MS 39406

The Missouri Review, 1507 Hillcrest Hall, Univ. of Missouri, Columbia, MO 65211

Momentary Pleasures Press, P.O. Box 700754, Tulsa, OK 74170

Mr. Cogito, Box 627, Pacific Univ., Forest Grove, OR 97116

Mudfish, c/o Box Turtle Press, Inc., 184 Franklin St., New York, NY 10013

My Legacy, see Weems Concepts

N

Nantucket Journal, 7 Sea St., Nantucket, MA 02554

Nebo, English Dept., Arkansas Tech. Univ., Russellville, AR 71801

The Nebraska Review, FA 212, Univ. of Nebraska, Omaha, NE 68182

Negative Capability, 62 Ridgelawn Dr. East, Mobile, AL 36608

New American Writing, 2920 W. Pratt, Chicago, IL 60645

The New Criterion, 850 Seventh Ave., New York, NY 10019

New Delta Review, English Dept., Louisiana State Univ., Baton Rouge, LA 70803

New England Review, Middlebury College, Middlebury, VT 05753

New Letters, UMKC, 5100 Rockhill Rd., Kansas City, MO 64110

New Literati, St. Edwards Univ., New College Writers Group, 3001 S. Congress, Austin, TX 78704

New Native Press, P.O. Box 661, Cullowhee, NC 28723

the new renaissance, 9 Heath Rd., Arlington, MA 02174

New Rivers Press, 420 N. 5th St., Ste. 910, Minneapolis, MN 55401

New Thought Journal, see Momentary Pleasures Press

The New York Quarterly, 232 W. 14th St., New York, NY 10011

Nightshade Press, P.O. Box 76, Troy, ME 04987

Nightsun, Philosophy Dept., Frostburg State College, Frostburg, MD 21532

Nimrod, c/o Arts & Humanities Council of Tulsa, 2210 S. Main, Ste. B, Tulsa, OK 74114

96 inc., P.O. Box 15559, Boston, MA 02215

North American Review, Univ. of Northern Iowa, Cedar Falls, IA 50614

North Carolina Literary Review, English Dept., ECU, Greenville, NC 27858

North Dakota Quarterly, Univ. of North Dakota, P.O. Box 8327, Grand Forks, ND 58202

North Stone Review, D Sta., Box 14098, Minneapols, MN 55414

Northeast, 1310 Shorewood Dr., LaCrosse, WI 54601

Northeast Journal, P.O.Box 2321, Providence, RI 02906

Northwest Review, 369 PLC, Univ. of Oregon, Eugene, OR 97403

Nostoc, Box 162, Newton, MA 02168

O

O.ARS, 21 Rockland Rd., Weare, NH 03281

Oasis, P.O. Box 626, Largo, FL 34649

Oat City Press, 18 Beach Point Dr., East Providence, RI 02915

O.blēk, 68 E. Minning St., Providence, RI 02906

Obsidian II, Dept. of English, NC State Univ., Raleigh, NC 27695

Ogalala Review, Univ. of Arkansas, P.O.Box 2699, Fayetteville, AR 72701

The Ohio Review, Ellis Hall, Ohio Univ., Athens, OH 45701

The Old Red Kimono, Humanities Div., Box 1864, Floyd College, Rome, GA 30162

Olympia Review, 1727 East 4th Ave., Olympia, WA 98506

Ontario Review, 9 Honey Brook Dr., Princeton, NJ 08540

Open-Mic Poetry in Print, 3077 Garner Creek Rd., Dickson, TN 37055

Orchises Press, P.O.Box 20602, Alexandria, VA 22320

Osiris, Box 297, Deerfield, MA 01842

Other Voices, English Dept., Box 4348, Univ. of Illinois, Chicago, IL 60680

Oxalis, P.O.Box 3993, Kingston, NY 12401

Oxford Magazine, Bachelor Hall, Miami Univ., Oxford, OH 45056

P

Pacific International, P.O.Box 250, Davis, CA 95617

The Pacific Review, English Dept., California State Univ., 500 Univ. Pkwy, San Bernardino, CA 92407

Painted Hills Review, 2950 Portage Bay West, #411, Davis, CA 95616

Palo Alto Review, 1400 W. Villaret Blvd., San Antonio, TX 78224

Paper Bag, P.O. Box 268805, Chicago, IL 60626

Papier-Mache Press, 135 Aviation Way, Ste. 14, Watsonville, CA 95076

Parabola, 656 Broadway, New York, NY 10012

Paragraph, see Oat City Press

Paris Press, 22 Bright St., Northampton, MA 01060

The Paris Review, 541 East 72nd St., New York, NY 10021

Parnassus, 41 Union Sq. West, Rm. 804, New York, NY 10003

Parnassus Literary Journal, P.O. Box 1384, Forest Park, GA 30051

Partisan Review, 236 Bay State Rd., Boston, MA 02215

Passages North, Kalamazoo College, 1200 Academy St., Kalamazoo, MI 49007

Paterson Literary Review, 170 College Blvd., Paterson, NJ 07509

Pearl, 3030 E. Second St., Long Beach, CA 90803

Pemmican, P.O. Box 16374, St. Paul, MN 55116

The Pennsylvania Review, English Dept., 526 C.L., Univ. of Pittsburgh, Pittsburgh, PA 15260

Pennywhistle Press, Box 734, Tesuque, NM 87574

Pequod, English Dept., 19 University Pl., New York, NY 10003

Perceptions, 14 Cedar St., Brunswick, ME 04011

Peregrine, P.O. Box 1076, Amherst, MA 01004

Permanent Press, Noyac Rd., Sag Harbor, NY 11963

Piedmont Literary Review, 1017 Spanish Moss Ln., Breaux Bridge, LA 70517

Pineapple Press, P.O. Drawer 16008, Sarasota, FL 34239

Pittenbruach Press, P.O. Box 553, Northampton, MA 01061

Pivot, 250 Riverside Dr., #23, New York, NY 10025

Ploughshares, 100 Beacon St., Boston, MA 02116

The Plum Review, P.O. Box 3557, Washington, DC 20007

Poet, see Cooper House Publishing, Inc.

Poet & Critic, Iowa State Univ., 203 Ross Hall, Ames, IA 50011

Poet Lore, c/o The Writer's Center, 4508 Walsh St., Bethesda, MD 20815

Poetalk, P.O. Box 11435, Berkeley, CA 94701

Poetry, 60 Walton St., Chicago, IL 60610

Poetry East, 802 W. Belden Ave., Chicago, IL 60614

Poetry Flash, 1450 Fourth St., #4, Berkeley, CA 94710

Poetry New York, P.O. Box 3184, Church St. Sta., New York, NY 10008

Poetry Northwest, 4045 Brooklyn N.E., Univ. of Washington, Seattle, WA 98105

Poetry USA, 2569 Maxwell Ave., Oakland, CA 94601

Poet's Fantasy, 227 Hatten Av., Rice Lake, WI 54868

Poets On, 29 Loring Ave., Mill Valley, CA 94941

The Portable Wall, 215 Burlington, Billings, MT 59101

The Portlander, Portland State Univ., Box 751, Portland, OR 97207

Post Fiction, see Little River Press

Potato Eyes, see Nightshade Press

Potpourri, P.O. Box 8278, Prairie Village, KS 66208

Prairie Schooner, 201 Andrews Hall, Univ. of Nebraska, Lincoln, NE 68588

PrePress Publishing, P.O. Box 3396, Kalamazoo, MI 49003

Primavera, Box 37-7547, Chicago, IL 60637

Prism International, Univ. of Brit. Columbia, Buch. E462-1866 Main Mall, Vancouver, B.C. CANADA V6T 1W5

Prophetic Voices, 94 Santa Maria Dr., Novato, CA 94947

The Prose Poem, Providence College, Providence, RI 02918

Provincetown Arts, 650 Commercial St., Provincetown, MA 02657

Puckerbrush Review, 76 Main St., Orono, ME 04473

Pudding House, 60 N. Main St., Johnstown, OH 43031

Puerto del Sol, Box 3E, New Mexico State Univ., Las Cruces, NM 88003

Pulphouse, Box 1227, Eugene, OR 97440

Q

Quarterly Review of Literature, Princeton University, Princeton, NJ 08540

Quarterly West, 317 Alpin Union, Univ. of Utah, Salt Lake City, UT 84112

R

Rajah, Univ. of Michigan, 411 Mason Hall, Ann Arbor, MI 48109

Rant, P.O.Box 6872, Yorkville Sta., New York, NY 10128

Raritan, Rutgers Univ., 31 Mine St., New Brunswick, NJ 08903

Raw Dog Press, 151 S. West St., Doylestown, PA 18901

Red Brick Review, 315 Canal St., #2, Manchester, NH 03101

Red Clay, P.O.Box 65656-566, Lubbock, TX 79464

Red Crane Books, 826 Camino de Monte Rey, Santa Fe, NM 87501

Red Dust, P.O.Box 630, New York, NY 10028

Redneck Press, 1326 W. Sheridan Ct., Milwaukee, WI 53209

Redneck Review of Literature, see Redneck Press

Reed Magazine, English Dept., San Jose State Univ., San Jose, CA 95192

The Review, P.O.Box 3331, Montebello, CA 90690

Review of Contemporary Fiction, see Dalkey Archive Press

rhino, 1808 N. Larrabee St., Chicago, IL 60614

River Oak Review, P.O.Box 3127, Oak Park, IL 60303

River Styx, 14 S. Euclid, St. Louis, MO 63108

Rivercross Publishing, 127 E. 59th St., New York, NY 10022

Rock Falls Review, P.O.Box 104, Stamford, NE 68977

S

San Diego Poets Press, P.O.Box 8638, LaJolla, CA 92038

Santa Monica Review, Santa Monica College, 1900 Pico Blvd., Santa Monica, CA 90405

Scream Press, 509 Enterprise Dr., Rohnert Park, CA 94928

The Seal Press, 3131 Western Ave., #410, Seattle, WA 98121

Seneca Review, Hobart & William Smith Colleges, Geneva, NY 14456

Sewanee Review, Univ. of the South, Sewanee, TN 37375

Shenandoah, Box 722, Lexington, VA 24450

Shockbox, P.O.Box 7226, Nashua, NH 03060

Sidewalks, P.O.Box 321, Champlin, MN 55316

The Silver Web, P.O.Box 38190, Tallahassee, FL 32315

Silver Wings, P.O.Box 1000, Pearblossom, CA 93553

Silverfish Review, P.O.Box 3541, Eugene, OR 97403

Skylark, Purdue Univ.-Calumet, 2200 169th St., Hammond, IN 46323

Slapering Hol Press, P.O.Box 366, Tarrytown, NY 10591

Slipstream, P.O.Box 2071, Niagara Falls, NY 14301

The Snail's Pace Review, RR #2, Box 363, Brownell Rd., Cambridge, NY 12816

Snake Nation Review, 110 #2 West Force St., Valdosta, GA 32601

Snake River Reflections, 1863 Bitterroot Dr., Twin Falls, ID 83301

Snowy Egret, P.O.Box 9, Bowling Green, IN 47833

Somersault Press, 404 Vista Heights Rd., Richmond, CA 94805

South Carolina Review, Strode Tower, Box 341503, Clemson, SC 29634

South Coast Poetry Journal, English Dept., California State Univ., Fullerton, CA 92634

Southern Humanities Review, 9088 Haley Ctr., Auburn Univ., Auburn, AL 36849

Southern Plains Review, P.O.Box 547, Denton, TX 76202

Southern Review, 43 Allen Hall, Louisiana State Univ., Baton Rouge, LA 70803

Southwest Review, 6410 Airline Rd., Southern Methodist Univ., Dallas, TX 75275

Sou'wester Magazine, Box 1438, Southern Illinois Univ., Edwardsville, IL 62026

Sparrow Press, 103 Waldron St., West Lafayette, IN 47906

Spinsters Ink, P.O.Box 300170, Minneapolis, MN 55403

Spitball, 6224 Collegevue Pl., Cincinnati, OH 45224

Spoon River Poetry Review, English Dept., Illinois State Univ., Normal, IL 61790

State Street Press, P.O.Box 278, Brockport, NY 14420

Wallace Stevens Journal, Clarkson Univ., Box 5750, Potsdam, NY 13699

Story, 1507 Dana Ave., Cincinnati, OH 45207

StoryQuarterly, P.O.Box 1416, Northbrook, IL 60062

Sucarnochee Review, see LU Press

The Sun, 107 N. Roberson St., Chapel Hill, NC 27516

Sycamore Review, English Dept., Purdue Univ., West Lafayette, IN 47907

T

Tampa Review, 401 W. Kennedy Blvd., Univ. of Tampa, Tampa, FL 33606

Tar River Poetry, English Dept., East Carolina Univ., Greenville, NC 27834

Thanatos, 25-6 NW 23rd Pl., #261, Portland, OR 97210

Tharpa Publications, 1105 Chinoe Dr., Lexington, KY 40502

Thema, Box 74109, Metairie, LA 70033

Threepenny Review, P.O. Box 9131, Berkeley, CA 94709

Threshold Books, 139 Main St., Rm. 403, Brattleboro, VT 05301

Tikkun, 5100 Lerna St., Oakland, CA 94619

Tilbury House, Publishers, 132 Water St., Gardiner, ME 04345

Tomorrow Magazine, P.O. Box 148486, Chicago, IL 60614

Touchstone, P.O. Box 8308, Spring, TX 77387

TriQuarterly, Northwestern Univ., 2020 Ridge Ave., Evanston, IL 60208

Tucumcari Literary Review, 3108 W. Bellevue Ave., Los Angeles, CA 90026

Turning the Tide, P.O. Box 1990, Burbank, CA 91507

Turnstile, 175 Fifth Ave., Ste. 2348, New York, NY 10010

U

United Artists Books, Box 2616, Peter Stuyvesant Sta., New York, NY 10009

Univ. of Illinois Press, 54 E. Gregory Dr., Champaign, IL 61820

Univ. of Massachusetts Press, P.O. Box 429, Amherst, MA 01004

Univ. of No. Texas Press, P.O. Box 13856, Denton, TX 76203

Univ. of Pittsburgh Press, Pittsburgh, PA 15260

Univ. of Wisconsin Press, 114 N. Murray St., Madison, WI 53715

Urbanus Press, P.O. Box 192561, San Francisco, CA 94119

V

Venom Press, 519 East 5 St., New York, NY 10009

Verve, P.O. Box 3205, Simi Valley, CA 93093

Virginia Quarterly Review, One West Range, Charlottesville, VA 22903

Voices in Italiana Americana, Modern Lang. & Lit., Loyola Univ., 6525 N. Sheridan Rd., Chicago, IL 60626

Voices Israel, Box 5780, 46157 Herzlia, ISRAEL

Volt, 4104 24th St., #355, San Francisco, CA 94114

W

Warm Spring Press, P.O. Box 5199, Harrisburg, PA 17110

Washington Review, Box 50132, Washington, DC 20004

Webster Review, Webster Univ., 470 E. Lockwood, Webster Groves, MO 63119

Weems Concepts, HCR-13, Box 21AA, Artemas, PA 17211

West Branch, English Dept., Bucknell Univ., Lewisburg, PA 17837

Western Humanities Review, Univ. of Utah, Salt Lake City, UT 84112

Whetstone, P.O. Box 1266, Barrington, IL 60011

White Eagle Coffee Store Press, P.O. Box 383, Fox River Grove, IL 60021

White Fields Press, Univ. of Louisville, Louisville, KY 40292

White Wave, P.O. Box 8192, Winslow, ME 04901

Whiskey Island Magazine, Univ. Center 7, Cleveland State Univ., Cleveland, OH 44115

Whisper, see Scream Press

Widener Review, Humanities Dept., Widener Univ., Chester, PA 19013

Willamette River Books, P.O. Box 605, Troutdale, OR 97060

William & Mary Review, P.O. Box 8795, Campus Ctr., Williamsburg, VA 23187

Willow Review, College of Lake County, 19351 W. Washington St., Grayslake, IL 60030

Willow Springs, MS-1, Eastern Washington Univ., Cheney, WA 99004

Wind, P.O. Box 24548, Lexington, KY 40524

Wings Press, 1711 Breckenridge, Austin, TX 78704

Without Halos, P.O. Box 1342, Pt. Pleasant Beach, NJ 08742

Witness, Oakland Community College, Farmington Hills, MI 48334

The Worcester Review, 6 Chatham St., Worcester, MA 01609

Words of Wisdom, 612 Front St. East, Glendora, NJ 08029

The Wormwood Review, P.O. Box 4698, Stockton, CA 95204

Writers Forum, P.O. Box 7150, Univ. of Colorado, Colorado Springs, CO 80933

Writer's World, 204 E. 19th St., Big Stone Gap, VA 24219

The Writing on the Wall, P.O. Box 8, Orono, ME 04473

X

Xizquil, P.O. Box 285, Reserve, NM 87830

Y

The Yale Review, P.O. Box 1902A, Yale Sta., New Haven, CT 06520

Yellow Silk, P.O. Box 6374, Albany, CA 94706

The Yipe, 2127 170th Ave. NE, Bellevue, WA 98008

Z

Zazu's Petals Quarterly, P.O. Box 4476, Allentown, PA 18105

Zephyr Copies, 124 E. Washington St., Iowa City, IA 52240

Zephyr Press, 13 Robinson St., Somerville, MA 02145

ZYZZYVA, 41 Sutter St., San Francisco, CA 94104

INDEX

The following is a listing in alphabetical order by author's last name of works reprinted in the first nineteen *Pushcart Prize* editions.

613

617

618

621

627